BLOODY PALMS

The Deets Shanahan mysteries by Ronald Tierney

THE STONE VEIL
THE STEEL WEB
THE IRON GLOVE
THE CONCRETE PILLOW
NICKEL PLATED SOUL *
PLATINUM CANARY *
GLASS CHAMELEON *
ASPHALT MOON *

* available from Severn House

BLOODY PALMS

A Deets Shanahan Mystery

Ronald Tierney

This first world edition published 2008
in Great Britain and the USA by
SEVERN HOUSE PUBLISHERS LTD of
9–15 High Street, Sutton, Surrey, England, SM1 1DF.

British Library Cataloguing in Publication Data

Tierney, Ronald
  Bloody palms. - (The Deets Shanahan mysteries)
  1. Shanahan, Deets (Fictitious character) - Fiction
  2. Private investigators - Indiana - Indianapolis - Fiction
  3. Detective and mystery stories
  I. Title
  813.5'4[F]

ISBN-13: 978-0-7278-6671-4   (cased)

All Severn House titles are printed on acid-free paper.

Printed and bound in Great Britain by
MPG Books Ltd., Bodmin, Cornwall.

*Thanks to brothers Richard and Ryan; and to friends
David Anderson and Karen Watt*

*He looked around again for the driver. For anyone.
He looked down at the body. In the left palm of the
dead man's hand was the eight ball.*
   'Nice touch,' Shanahan said.

One

It was early Spring. Shanahan was nearly his old self again – 'old' meaning seventy-one and 'nearly' meaning that he had almost fully recovered from the head wound inflicted by a bullet seven months earlier.

Maureen, his younger girlfriend by a couple of decades, was still in bed. Nothing unusual. For her, waking up was a sensual pleasure. She would wake, then drift back, luxuriating in the consciousness between two worlds.

He, on the other hand, was an early riser. If it was light or nearly light and he awoke, he got up. This morning, he had already read the morning paper and had his coffee before setting out to till a new spot in the yard for a bed of lilies.

The sun had barely passed the horizon. The grass was cool and damp from the previous night, a night that he navigated with difficulty, sleep interrupted by dreams and the time between sleep interrupted by haunting thoughts. His brother, Fritz, would not be put aside, could not be dismissed. This whole remembering thing began months ago, when Shanahan uncovered a photograph. In it – and all that was in it of his brother – was part of the young boy's leg as the figure itself ran out of the frame, and was gone from Shanahan forever.

Fritz was a boy when he disappeared. The last time Shanahan saw him was when the young teen was being led to a big, black Hudson late one cold night. Fritz glanced back before he climbed into the back seat. That face wouldn't go away. So long ago, Shanahan had distanced himself from those memories of his brother, as he had others who had brought him regret.

He tried to think of something less depressing. He looked around. The hint of green appeared on the trees. Soon, the dogwoods and redwoods would bloom. The Korean lilac in their yard would follow, then the peonies and iris. There that was better. Winter was gone. It wasn't especially harsh, but winters were something to survive and he had done it. So too the cat and dog, older than he was, in their respective pet years. The bony feline, Einstein, was 124 by that count. And Casey was eighty-four.

With his boot on the edge of the spade, the old detective pushed into the giving ground and upended a tuft of grass and earth. The notion that this was like digging a grave wasn't lost on him. Fortunately, he didn't have to dig that deep. He only had bulbs to bury at the moment.

His single-level home was on the top of a gently sloping hill. The front and side faced a parkway, a narrow stretch of green with a creek that ran for quite some time from the East side toward the center of town. Across the narrow park were another street and more homes on similarly rolling land. Up where Shanahan dug, the lilies would do well, getting good sun and more than adequate drainage.

Shanahan's mood was changing. The heavy residue of the previous night's dreams lifted with advancing daylight.

Maureen came out, preceded by Shanahan's old Catahoula hound, sixty pounds of mottled white, gray, brown, and gold. 'A call,' Maureen said. Her auburn hair caught the light and Shanahan's mood improved still again. In her early fifties, she was beautiful, full of life. He thought what he often thought when he saw her. He didn't deserve her.

Casey sniffed the freshly turned soil, gave Shanahan an inquiring look, and barked.

'Doing Maureen's bidding, are you?' Shanahan asked the dog. The dog barked again.

'You been bribing him with your ice cream?' Shanahan asked Maureen as he passed by her heading toward the wall phone in the kitchen.

'Noooo,' she said. 'You know better than that.'

'What then?'

'I give him a shot of your bourbon every now and then.'

'He would like that,' Shanahan said. He grabbed the phone. 'Yep,' Shanahan said into the receiver.

'I might,' she said. 'You never know. He looks like he could use one sometimes.'

'No, sorry,' Shanahan said to the caller. 'I don't do wayward husbands or wives.' He listened for a moment. 'Because you

never know the whole story. There are plenty of folks . . .'
Shanahan went quiet, waited, brimming with impatience.
'Because I can.'
'Because you can what?' Maureen asked after Shanahan
hung up with a little more force than necessary.
'Decide which cases to take.' The woman had an attitude.
It was clear Shanahan would not only be the hired help, he
would be reminded of that fact constantly.
The kitchen was the house's most used room. Maureen's
laptop was on the kitchen table, a stack of her real estate
flyers were on the counter. Shanahan used the room as his
office as well, using that phone for his work, using the table
for the rare paperwork he needed to do in his semi-retired
private investigator state. It was the room where the cat and
dog ate. It was the room the two of them ate most of the
time. Maureen was folding up her laptop.
'You could have recommended Howie,' she said.
'I didn't like her.'
'He might have,' she said smiling. 'He's not as defiant of
authority as you are.'
'Yes he is,' Shanahan said.
'Unless she was really pretty.'
'You have a point.'
The phone rang again.
'Popular guy,' Maureen said.
'Could be for you,' he said, picking it up. 'You're the one
selling houses.'
'Shanahan?' came the voice.
'Yep.'
'This is Jack.'
'Jack?' Shanahan searched his memory, couldn't find the
voice or the name.
'Jack Wenders.'
Shanahan continued the search. The tone of voice suggested
Shanahan should know him. He felt embarrassed and for a
moment considered pretending to know the guy, talk to him,
until the guy revealed enough clues.
'No, Jack. I'm sorry. I don't know you.'
'Yeah, well, it's been awhile. Seoul. Korea.'
Old memories came easier than recent ones.
'Yes, Jack. I'm sorry. A long time ago.' Vague outlines of

his commanding officer began to sharpen. Younger than
Shanahan. Had a good time when he wasn't working. Wenders
was a major then, Shanahan a master sergeant. Intelligence,
Korea after it was divided. Before Vietnam.

'I didn't know who else to turn to,' Wenders said.

Shanahan waited. He had no idea what to say. His brain
was still wandering around Korea, trying to complete the
picture of his former commanding officer. Wenders filled the
silence.

'I can't do it by myself.'

'Do what?'

Cross stirred. Somehow he'd twisted sheets and blanket so that
they no longer covered the lower half of his body. His feet
were cold. His butt was cold. He must have had a wild night.
He remembered nothing of his dreams, but wondered if he had
enjoyed himself. Had he been wrestling with demons or angels?
Or a beautiful woman? By the time he straightened everything
out to get warm and comfortable, he was wide awake.

'Damn,' he said out loud to no living creature he knew of.
He searched the bed for the TV remote. Then the floor. There
it was, batteries spilled out. He put them all back in and clicked.

Traffic, weather, the basic knowledge the average person needs
to start his or her day. Not Howie Cross. His day began when
he saw fit. On most days, he had absolutely nothing to do. On
others, he might have a couple of hours of work to repossess a
car or find a bail jump. But that kind of work didn't happen
during typical office hours.

On the weekends he drove the hour and a half from
Indianapolis to a small farm in Eaton, where his parents cared
for the five-year-old girl an old flame left on his doorstep last
Halloween. Even this was more responsibility than he was
used to – or desired. But what could he do? The kid, Maya,
might be his. Her mother, Margot, suggested as much before
she disappeared. Again. Could be. Might not be.

On the other hand, did it matter? He felt responsible. He
liked the kid, but he didn't like the feeling that her fate was
in his hands. He didn't even like the idea that his fate was in
his hands. And worse, this little conversation with himself was
going nowhere.

Out of bed. Feet on the cool floor and into the tiny bathroom, where the mirror over the sink revealed a man who looked at least fifty. A shower and a shave could easily shave off five, maybe ten years. In the right light, of course. His chest held firm surprisingly firm for someone who was not kind to his body. He went back into the bedroom, slipped on his jeans and tucked his feet into some COSTCO slippers. Once inside the little room that separated the bedroom from the living room, he found his sweatshirt. He sniffed it. Another day, easy. The little room was his office. The house itself was small yet kept the cool in, a positive quality in the summer, not so good in the winter. The former chauffeur's quarters, it was constructed of one-foot by one-foot clay tiles, six inches in depth. He knew that – even though stucco was applied to the outside and plaster was applied to the inside – because he ripped out part of the wall to turn the attached two-car garage into a living room with a fireplace.

A three-room house with a two-car garage didn't make much sense. It made less sense considering the main house was never built. He loved the place though. It was the odd house on the street – in the neighborhood really – as he was no doubt the odd resident. Steps to his place led up through thick growth – a combination of weeds and bushes – and then a hundred feet back from the road. One went several feet down the path before even seeing there was a house there.

Soon Cross had coffee brewed. He took his first sip looking out of the kitchen window. Then it came back to him.

He hadn't recovered from the mess of a few months ago. Not only had his friend and sometimes partner, Shanahan, nearly died, Cross himself had a nearly fatal brush with reality. It wasn't just his physical being that was challenged, but perhaps a battle for something more important.

Killing those two people as he had – one in self-defense, the other coldly, letting the evil bastard die when maybe he could have saved him hung heavily on his soul. He couldn't come all the way back. After that event, necessary as it was, the way he looked at life was different and he knew it would remain that way.

Even his few years in vice hadn't hardened him enough for the killings to have been casual. His time on the force made him realize that there were crimes with victims and 'crimes' without them. Maybe he was a little too soft then, feeling guilty when he had to arrest someone for prostitution or gambling or a couple of joints. But until now, he never had to shoot anybody. He turned from smart ass, fun-loving cop to smart ass, fun-loving private eye, picking up a bond jumper now and then, repo'ing a car, following a deceitful spouse. It wasn't always fun, but when all was said and done, he didn't feel like this. And he knew he would never be the same again.

He missed his old self.

He noticed the bushes out by the street were gathering leaves and soon his home would be completely hidden again. That would be nice. He liked the idea of no one seeing him. He took another sip of coffee, almost paralyzed by thoughts of the day rolling out before him and his lack of interest in the process.

Shanahan heard enough of the story to know he was the wrong person to help.

'Major . . .'

'Call me Jack,' Wenders said. 'Anyway I made it to Light Colonel before I left.'

'I don't know what I can do. I don't speak Spanish. I don't know the territory, and I'm a couple of hundred years old.'

'A man with experience,' Jack said, possibly with humor. Shanahan couldn't tell. 'Come down, please. You have nothing to lose. I'll pay for the trip. You fly into Puerto Vallarta. I'll get a room for you at a hotel. Enjoy the beach, the food. A couple of days in, I'll send a car for you. We'll meet, talk—'

'What's this about?'

'Not on the phone,' Wenders said.

'Maybe I don't like what you're up to.'

'You probably won't. You won't like what they're up to more.'

'I don't know,' Shanahan said. Curiosity pulled him toward it. Experience suggested he let it go. He looked at Maureen. Listening to one side of the conversation, she still watched him, amused and just as curious as he was.

'That's OK you don't know. That's why you come down,' Wenders said. 'What have you got to lose? A little R & R. Some margaritas. We talk. You say 'no.' Spend a couple more days under the palms, all expenses paid, and go home tall, tan, young and lovely.'

'You sound like a time share salesman,' Shanahan said.

'It really is about time, old pal. Unless I get a little help, I don't have a lot left. I'll call you tonight. I'll need your decision. Oh, and Shanahan. Let's not use my name anymore, OK. It's better that way.'

Shanahan put the phone back on the hook. The 'old pal' line bothered him. He and Wenders weren't close. No bad blood there. Just no there there. The major was competent and fair if he remembered right. Shanahan did his job, the major did his. They got along; but that was it. They didn't go out drinking together or swap stories. Wenders was an avid womanizer, Shanahan a reluctant one.

'What was that about?' Maureen asked.

'I'm not sure.'

'Anything you can talk about?' she asked.

'A guy I knew in the Army wants me to do something, but he won't tell me what it is.'

'And you have to speak Spanish in order to do it?' Her eyebrows rose and her lips widened a bit, the hint of a smile. She sensed a trip. She sensed new places to eat. Now, she was circling her prey.

'He wants me to go down to Mexico.' He withheld his smile.

The hint became a clear statement.

'That's nice,' she said, giving him a fake smile, a smile he knew was fake. This wasn't the end of it.

'I don't know if it's nice or not.'

'Where in Mexico?'

'I think he said, Puerto Vallarta.'

'Oh, that terrible little resort town? The one with too many beaches and too many restaurants?'

Shanahan said nothing.

'Just you?' she asked.

Shanahan shrugged. This wasn't going to be easy.

Cross shook off his bout of depressing introspection by jogging. It was something new. His body, which seemed to hold together pretty well despite how badly he treated it, needed a little help now. The spring morning provided encouragement and the alternative was going back to bed, curling up in the fetal position and . . . what?

He ran along the Broad Ripple Canal, all the way down from where Illinois Street crossed it, beyond the city's modern art museum, then back. In some places neighborhoods butted against the gravel path that ran along the shallow waterway. In other places, small brush led to bigger brush and to a small lake – all somewhat wild. The trees were feathered with budding growth.

Before heading home, he stopped for groceries at the small supermarket on the corner of 56th and Illinois. He picked up a bottle of Tequila from the liquor store on the opposite corner. He walked from there, the air cool on his slightly sweaty flesh, toward his cozy, pleasant neighborhood that bordered Butler University.

Butler-Tarkington was an early integrated area of the city that retained its diverse, liberal, nonjudgmental character. Nice homes, big trees. Cross liked his privacy, and his un-nosy neighbors seemed quite content to let him have it. He was as unseen and anonymous as those who lived in dense urban areas or out in the middle of nowhere.

Inside, after the shower declined earlier, he checked himself again in the mirror. The run hadn't caused any miraculous changes. He dressed, this time in fresh jeans and sweatshirt, and settled in at his desk. He checked for email. None. Nor were there messages on his answering machine. He called both of the bail bond companies he did occasional work for. They were covered, they said. The repo firm had nothing.

Cross had always been good at being lazy. Having nothing to do was a good thing unless he was desperate for cash. He had a little cushion in that department, but he was more than a little antsy because cushions go more easily than they come. Worse, with nothing to concentrate on, his mind wandered indiscriminately. These days, this wasn't a good thing. There were the killings. There was also Margot to think about. Margot, who went from dancer to sex slave operator, who went from mysterious to dangerous. There was Margot's daughter, who might be his own. He wanted work now. Maybe that would take his mind off things he could do nothing about. He called his friend, Shanahan.

But Shanahan had nothing. He mentioned a possible trip to Mexico. But that would be solo. Shanahan apologized for not sending a case his way, but said that he wouldn't have liked the client anyway. Cross reminded him that he was less finicky than Shanahan in that department.

Cross went to the stereo. Too early in the day for the kind of loungy jazz or bluesy reverie he liked. After sifting through several stacks of CDs, he gave up. There wasn't anything he wanted to listen to. He wished it were night already so he could drink without guilt, listen to soulful music, go to bed, and flirt with sleep. However, the sun had its own stubborn cycle, as did the bank that held the mortgage to his home. He hated to face the day without something to do. He picked up his cell, dialed his parents. Moments after he hung up, he was on the road, finding his way out of the city in an old Cadillac Seville, on loan from a used car dealer who owed him money. His parents' small farm was in Eaton, Indiana – a tiny town just beyond Muncie. The whole trip would take him about an hour.

If it were 1983, then Howie would be riding in style. Since it was a few decades later, he was riding in a shiny, gas guzzling, four-door gaudy dinosaur – black with a tan landau roof, power everything and leather seats. It had a long front end like its stable mate, the Eldorado. He felt like he was driving a boat along the interstate. Couldn't complain about the ride, though. It was smooooth.

He and his Cadillac traveled over a flat, near barren country-side. Soybean leaves peaked out from the tilled soil. The trip gave him plenty of time to think. That was a bit ironic, he thought. That's what he was trying to avoid.

Thoughts wrestled for center stage. Were the Pacers going to make it to the finals? Did he care? His income again. He could get by for three months if he played it careful. OK, he told himself, put that problem on hold. The little girl, Maya. Was she his? Is that what Margot meant when she left the child behind when she said, 'She's all yours?'

Howie tried to do the math, but remembering when he was with her and when he wasn't was a problem. It was a calendar that he could not put together with his unfocused mind. She moved from city to city. That was part of her circuit. She was a star dancer. So she'd spend a week or two in Indianapolis, then she'd move on somewhere else. It was a circuit, planned by the owners of the strip clubs, who were also bringing in girls from Asia and South America.

He could be the father. It was possible, though with her experience he didn't know why she would get pregnant or why she would keep the child. Certainly not to remember him. He could do the DNA. Did he really want to know? No. Not right now. Put that problem on hold.

That made him think of his parents, who were watching over the five-year-old. They were getting older and in many ways already failing. Who would take care of them? That fact troubled him. The farm was no longer productive. It had become smaller and smaller over the years, now down to just a dozen chickens, a couple of cows, and a garden no larger than gardens some young couples cultivate the backyards of their suburban homes.

As small as it was, it was becoming a challenge to his aging parents. Soon, someone would have to help them. And he knew who that would be. Add to that their stubborn refusal to accept help. But he didn't have to do anything today or tomorrow.

That put his problems in a brighter perspective. 'I don't need to do anything right now,' he said out loud, as he took the interstate turn-off that would take him past Muncie to Eaton. 'Mission accomplished,' he said, knowingly. But really, and he knew it, it was 'Mission Delayed.'

He had failed to fool himself. Considering everyone else who had fooled him lately, it should have been easy.

All the questions weren't answered and unwelcome thoughts continued to invade his mind. What did he want to do when he grew up? This, whatever it was he was doing, wasn't it. Repossessing cars, following wayward husbands and tracking down bail jumps . . . He wasn't exactly at the top of his profession, was he? And his career path wasn't heading north. Then again, what could he do? What talents did he possess?

Sell cars? Wash dishes? Paint houses? Maybe paint houses. Who was he kidding? What he was doing was what he was cut out to do.

There he was. He was home. The slightly dilapidated farmhouse looked frail, as did his mother who was coming out of the front door to greet him. Oh wait, Cross thought as he pulled into the gravel drive and saw her face. She's not greeting him. She's screaming at him.

Something was wrong. Something was seriously wrong.

Two

O nce he was settled into the hotel, Shanahan went out. The Mexican sun was intense. He thought he was prepared for it. It was only April and he hadn't expected the intensity. Now, he was glad that Maureen had bought him a straw hat. Though he felt a little dandyish, he was comforted by the fact that other than Wenders he wasn't likely to run into anybody he knew.

As it turned out, Maureen couldn't get away anyway. She knew that as she teased him about his 'vacation' without her. If he stayed down there long enough, she said, she'd find a way to join him.

The heat bounced up off the dusty cobblestone streets, narrow and high. At the intersection he could see the clay-roofed buildings as they stair-stepped maybe a mile down the steep hill to Banderas Bay and the tourists below. He bought a cold beer from the little store across from the small hotel Wenders booked for him.

It was all so sudden. Once Shanahan agreed to go, Wenders, or someone, emailed a ticket immediately for a flight the following morning, plus instructions from the airport to the hotel. Shanahan agreed to go with the understanding that it was a no strings visit. If Shanahan didn't like what he heard he would come back. If he stayed down there for a while he'd ask Maureen to join him. Otherwise this was a quick business trip.

Along with the instructions, the message also said that Shanahan shouldn't try to find Wenders. Wenders would find him – maybe not right away. Meanwhile, the note said, 'enjoy your stay.'

The sun was dropping, but there was still plenty of light – a couple of hours. Shanahan found a chaise on the hotel's rooftop garden as he investigated his surroundings. Shanahan relaxed in the chaise. Sipped his beer. Why not try to enjoy it? Give in a bit. Events weren't under his control.

In back of the hotel, the hill rose still more. He could see hundreds of homes, many with terraces or balconies, some with laundry hanging quiet in the still air. Bougainvillea added color to the white walls of some of the buildings. Beyond this hill was another, taller hill, all green. Jungle. A place to hide. Was Wenders up there?

A cat appeared. Looked a lot like Einstein when he was younger. The cat took little notice of the old detective and his beer. Instead the feline was focused on something behind Shanahan, in a wall of bush-like plants. Shanahan could hear a flutter and assumed the cat had found a bird.

The cat was patient, almost casual. He inched closer and his movements became more strategic. At one point the cat stood perfectly still, stared. All was silent. The cat was stone. The bird was quiet. Shanahan too, waited. He looked up at the sky. Pure blue. In the distance a radio was playing. Somewhere, someone was having an animated conversation with someone else. But the three of them – the cat, the bird, and Shanahan – were in their own world. He would be the only witness to a killing.

The only movement during the next fifteen minutes was Shanahan sipping his beer and wiping a light sweat from his brow.

When the bird fluttered again, it was to fly away. The cat closed his eyes in one long blink, then let his body sink to the rooftop. 'Next time,' he seemed to suggest.

Had the bird even known he was in danger? Did he fly away on some whim or was he purposefully evading death? How close had it been?

A church bell rang. Shanahan stood, went to the low wall at the edge of the roof behind where he sat. He could see the church a few blocks to the left, down one block. He looked down. The balcony to his room was one floor below. A car passed through the intersection. Someone came out of the store. A man with a blue baseball cap leaned against a wall. Thin, head down. He was there earlier when Shanahan went for his beer. Where he stood, the man would see who came and went from the hotel.

Bored, Shanahan went down one flight to his room, ran

cold water over his face. He couldn't just sit in the room. He'd go out. No need to wait. Wenders would find him. That was the agreement. Just in case, Shanahan checked with the desk clerk. No messages.

Down another flight of stairs to the lobby and the street. The door locked behind him. The hotel was unmarked. The taxi driver, who brought him in from the airport, had trouble finding it. Outside, Shanahan made sure he noted the cross streets and the look of the place. He headed down toward the town.

The hill was so steep, the sidewalk had steps. And it wasn't until he was nearly at the bottom, seven slanting blocks or so from where he started, did he realize that the real job would be coming back, not going. Once on the flat ground, Banderas Bay stretched out before him. He crossed the street and turned left and walked the *Malecon*. It is a long, palm-lined walkway separated from the bay by a thin strip of beach. After a few yards he saw a life-size, realistic sand sculpture of the 'Last Supper'. Tourists stopped and photographed it, dropped a few pesos into a bucket. A wall separated the fragile, and very temporary work of art from anyone inclined to touch it.

Kind of funny, Shanahan thought. A high tide would dissolve it like sugar in coffee.

Well, there's another omen, he thought. He kept walking, the tourists shopping and dining on the other side of the street. He kept bayside as he walked and eventually came to a wide, new bridge. It crossed a river that fed the bay. Just before the two bodies of water joined, there was a small pool, where Mexican kids swam and played, cooling off in the quiet green water.

Once across the bridge, restaurants and cafes took over the beachfront. They were getting busy. Tables under umbrellas, lazy places to sit, sip a margarita and watch the sunset. Not a bad idea, but he'd walk a little farther, check out all the options.

He came upon a larger beach area. Lots of activity. Volley ball. Wind surfing. Boat rides. Swimmers. Sunbathers. The beach was filled with people. The sky was filled with pelicans.

He stopped for a moment to watch hundreds of pelicans circling the shallows near the beach. Then, quickly one would turn to dive down, turning to get the angle right, it would drop in the water, disappear for a few moments. Up again, it floated

on the water for a few more moments, then take off, low at
first, like a jet taking off.

The fish never knew what hit him.

At the end of the walk, where the beach stopped at the rise
of a mountain, he turned to go back. A less expensive looking
bar on the beach caught his eye earlier. He just needed a chair
facing the ocean and a beer. He went in, ordered a Corona and
a couple of tacos. He looked around to see if the man in the
blue baseball cap was anywhere around. Shanahan didn't see
him. That didn't mean he wasn't there, or that if he wasn't,
someone else that Shanahan couldn't identify was doing the job.

The emotional storm had passed. Cross and his mother sat on
the sofa in the living room. His father, already back from the
hospital, was in his bedroom sleeping. All of them needed
sleep, including Maya, the five-year-old who was or wasn't
Howie's daughter. They had been up all night. They vowed
to stay up until dark to keep their body clocks in keeping with
the central time zone.

It was a mild heart attack. The emergency team was there
quickly, had him off to Muncie's Ball Memorial Hospital. He
was diagnosed, treated, and allowed to return, all the while
protesting 'it was nothing, nothing at all.'

Mrs Cross' neighbor – the next farm over – brought over
something in a covered dish for dinner. Ham with macaroni
and cheese, Cross discovered as the scent of food set off a
sudden hunger.

'There we go,' he said to himself as he pushed a forkful of
macaroni in his mouth, 'we can all check into the hospital.'
A quick recollection of his own eating habits made him an
instant hypocrite. Healthful eating had never been a high
priority.

Mrs Cross seemed to shake off whatever thoughts haunted
her.

'Maya, let me get you something to eat,' she said, giving
her son a glance. Her work-solves-all-problems philosophy
finally kicked in. She was up and moving. He felt appropriately guilty, though the truth was that Maya needed little
nurturing.

Cross looked at Maya, who acted as if she were forty
during the craziness surrounding Mr Cross' attack. She patted

Mrs Cross' arm while they waited for word. She was quiet, but extremely observant – young eyes taking it all in. She inquired after Mr Cross' health. When the doctor explained to them that all was well, that it was not extremely serious, Maya calmly asked whether the elder Cross would be able to do his normal work.

Surprised, the doctor was suddenly quiet. Finally, he smiled, nodded. 'Yes. He needs to take care of himself, but yes, he should be as good as new.'

He said 'good as new' in a way that was just a little too sweet for Maya. It was clear that the girl now regarded him with some suspicion.

While Mrs Cross was in the kitchen, Maya went to the bedroom. He couldn't hear what was being said, but his father and Maya were talking quietly. At one point, he heard his father laugh.

Howie looked around. As he noticed during each prior visit, the house had not changed in the decades that passed since he lived there. The same everything. The same faded floral sofa. The same gray carpet, though more threadbare. The same oak dinner table, now full of fruit, cakes, pies from the neighbors.

Cross was home. And he would be here for at least a few days. He would sleep in his old bedroom. His mother would fix breakfast. And as he did when he was twelve, he'd have chores. It was surreal and sadly sweet – how had things come to this?

'Go tell Howie,' he heard his father say, 'he has to go out and tend to the girls or prop me up so I can do it.'

The girls were the two cows. One Guernsey and one Brown Swiss. When Cross was young, they had two dozen cows. The farm, such as it was, once had 150 acres. Not large, but self-supporting. His parents sold off the land to corporate farmers, little by little as it became too much for them. What was left was no more than a couple of cows, a dozen chickens and a single acre given over to corn and some vegetables. But what was left had to be tended to. The poor cows were probably in pain.

'I'll have dinner ready by the time you're back,' his mother said, coming to the door of the kitchen. Then quietly, 'Thank you Howie.'

She wasn't usually given to praise, or much warmth for that matter.

Howie heard footsteps behind him as he headed toward the barn. It was Maya. He stopped, turned.

'I thought I'd better come along,' she said.

'Show me how to do it?'

She nodded. 'In case you forgot.'

'Mother said that, huh.'

Maya nodded again. Smiled. 'I know how,' she said.

After Cross was seated on the stool, with bucket, two mangy cats came in. They were hesitant.

'They don't know you,' Maya said.

Cross remembered his father, while milking the cows, would periodically aim a teat in the direction of the feral cats and jetted a stream of warm milk their way. In payment for ratting the barns, he told his son. It was all coming back.

'When you get tired, I can take over,' Maya said.

'You make quite a dairy maid,' Cross said.

'You are sooooo silly,' she said.

'OK, I'll do this one,' Cross said.

'Brenda.'

'I'll do Brenda and you do . . .?'

'Helene.'

'OK.' Cross tried to imagine those tiny fingers drawing out the milk.

'Have you heard from her?' Maya asked, referring to her mother.

'I'm afraid not.'

'I hope she's not in trouble.' Her face was serious, but not sad or frightened.

'No, I doubt if she is,' Cross said, though he kind of hoped she was. What kind of woman would do this to a daughter? He guessed the same kind of woman who made him jump through hoops.

Shanahan didn't know how it happened, but he'd been suckered into a trance by the sunset. The sky and ocean were beautiful, especially seen through the palm leaves, and rising above the white sand. The heat retreated and a breeze advanced. He finished his third Corona before he set off back to town and, ultimately, up the steep hill to his lodgings.

The lights were glistening along the *Malecon*. No doubt naps had been taken and the more energetic of tourists were beginning to prepare for an evening of drinking and dancing. He wished them well.

It seemed to take him forever to climb the hill. He stopped several times on the way up. He tried to convince himself that it was to check the view. But he was no fool and had none of it. He hadn't the stamina he once had. And in the heat, he could feel the effects of the third beer.

He checked with the desk clerk and in a combination of mangled English and Spanish, came to the conclusion that he had no messages. There was also no phone.

Across the street, on the outside wall of the store where he bought his beers earlier, was a pay phone. Not the kind Shanahan remembered, however. It didn't take money. It only took phone cards. Luckily the store sold them. After several failed attempts to make his card work, the young lady at the store helped him through the process and he was finally connected to Maureen.

'What's up?' she asked.

'I have no idea,' Shanahan said. 'I just checked with the hotel to see if I had any messages. That was a mess. I don't know what we said to each other. I don't know whether he told me that I have no messages or that I have successfully checked out.'

'Or maybe you asked to have a girl sent to your room,' Maureen said.

'You always were a glass half-full kind of woman,' Shanahan said.

'You feel safe all the way down there in Mexico, I see.'

'What are you doing this evening?' he asked to change the subject.

'A wine tasting.'

'A wine tasting?'

'Yes.'

'Where?'

'Here,' she said.

'Oh, and how many at this tasting?'

'A very select list, I'm told. Maybe only one guest.'

'And that would be you. You are having your very own wine tasting.'

'And I think it will be quite successful. Then again, I could order a boy, you know, to come over.'

'I suppose you could. A boy, though?'

'Well you know. Just a figure of speech.'

'I see. Has the tasting begun?'

'Yes it has.'

'You are just sipping and then spitting it out, right?'

'Oh, I forgot the last part.'

'I'm going to bed, Maureen. That is if I still have a room.'

'I think maybe you should come home,' she said.

Shanahan noticed a man in dark clothing and a dark baseball cap across the street. The man turned quickly, went around the corner.

Shanahan bought another beer from the corner store and went back to his room. The air, in darkness now, was cooler. He turned on the overhead fan and opened the glass doors to the balcony – thinking it would cool off the room. The balcony was large enough for two chairs. He sat in one and put his feet up on the other. He took a swallow of beer and looked out over the lights that glittered down the hill. The lights glittered more down by the bay, where the bars and restaurants were enjoying the infancy of the night.

There was a flash of light, then another. Fireworks. Down on the bay, brilliant, soaring shards of light broke out in the darkness. The sound was muted, but the light was grand. Sunsets and fireworks seem so corny until you are in their seductive presence. He was caught in the moment, perhaps in the importance of the moment, the trip – something he had not really thought about.

Not knowing anything yet, he thought that perhaps this – whatever it was – was bigger than he could imagine, bigger perhaps than he could handle.

Cross woke sometime near morning. His room faced east and he could see a thin stripe of gray on the horizon. He'd heard something. Some thumping sound, then some creaks. Could be from downstairs, one of his aging parents making a trip to the bathroom. Or, getting up. His parents, like most farmers, usually got up before the light, he remembered. He drifted back to sleep uneasily.

Three

The sound of pounding intruded on the darkness.
'Just a moment.' Shanahan opened his eyes and tried to focus. Almost surprised that he wasn't in his own room. 'Wait a minute,' he said, again when the knocking continued. He struggled into his khakis.

When he got to the door, no one was there. There was, however, a folded piece of paper on the floor. He picked it up, went back to the bed stand, retrieved his reading glasses.

Leave by the front door of the hotel. Turn left. Turn left immediately at the next street. Walk straight ahead. You will come to a stairway. Go down.

The note was handwritten, unsigned. He took a deep breath, opened the black-out drapery letting in an avalanche of light. He checked his watch: 6:15 A.M.

Not one to be hurried, he showered, brushed his teeth, dressed. He didn't remember unzipping the leather bag that held his toiletries, but he must have. Outside was about as nice as it was going to be all day. It was warm enough to work up a sweat without trying, but it was not overwhelming. He followed directions. After his second left, he noticed the street went on for several blocks before it appeared to dead-end.

It was quiet. The corner store was closed. No one was on the streets. Air conditioners hummed here and there. A bony dog crossed at an intersection well ahead of the old detective.

He couldn't help but think that all this mystery was unnecessary.

It was easier to walk in the middle of the street than navigate the sidewalks, where there were periodic steps down to the street then again back up. There were detours around building materials and motorcycles blocking the sidewalks as well. There were no cars on the dusty street.

He could get used to the straw hat, he thought. Great for gardening. The buildings, mostly homes or apartments, varied in upkeep. Some looked like small mansions. Some had window boxes, or patios with flowers dripping down the walls. Other buildings were rundown, and still others appeared abandoned.

The sky was clear blue. An occasional glance behind him suggested no one was following him.

At the end of the block was an opening about six feet wide. A set of very steep steps descended at least a block to another street below. He walked down between other homes that opened on to the hillside. Below, at the foot of the steps, was a white sedan. He figured it was waiting for him. Why else would it block the stairway?

Shanahan had to be careful. The steps were steep, rough and uneven. There was no railing. If he tripped, he'd tumble almost an entire block to his death.

When he was a few feet from the bottom, a man got out of the car. He came around the back of the car and opened the rear door.

The man had an old face, a very slender build, and hair matted with so much grease that it looked like leather straps pasted on his skull. His skin was shiny, taut over the skeletal face and arms, also like leather. He was dark, darker than most Mexicans. Perhaps he spent a lot of time in the sun. Shanahan noticed the lines in the man's neck, again the deep set eyes in the death mask of a face, the tattoos on his bare arms too faint on the dark flesh to see clearly. The bony fingers ended with long, sharp fingernails.

Neither spoke. The car took off with Shanahan in the small back seat. The two of them whisked through streets, over the river he'd crossed the day before but on a bridge Shanahan hadn't seen. They drove back through the quiet neighborhoods. The car stopped at a row of storefronts. The driver pointed toward the door directly parallel to the car. Shanahan was eager to get out of the stifling little car.

No sooner than the door was shut, the car zoomed off. Inside was a large pool hall – thirty tables maybe. Shafts of light streamed from high windows into the interior grayness. Dust particles were visible in the stripes of light. There was something oddly geometric in the rectangular tables all in a row and the regular beams of light coming in straight and equal distance from each other.

'Shut the door and lock it,' the voice said.

Was it Wenders standing at the end of one of the tables a couple of rows in? Shanahan hoped so. He was tired of the game. He looked around. No one else there that he could see. He shut the door, flicked the lock.

'Was all this necessary?' he asked the figure standing just in the shadows.

He heard laughter.

Cross fought to stay where he was, but something shook him. Someone was interfering.

'Howie?' The voice was both tentative and urgent and it drew him out of a dream that slipped away the moment he saw the horror on his mother's face. A new dream? He didn't want it.

'We can't find her.'

It wasn't a dream and 'Her' could only mean Maya.

'What do you mean?' he asked, trying to shake all the sleep from him, to kick start the brain. He started to get out of bed, but was momentarily paralyzed as the full meaning of what she said dawned on him.

She turned away in deference to what he might or might not be wearing.

He pulled on his jeans, grabbed his shirt and followed her into the child's bedroom down the hall. There was no sign of a struggle. No sign of anything. The window was open, but it was a two-story drop. The impression in the sheet showed she had slept there. Cross moved to the bed, touched the spot where the girl had slept. It wasn't any warmer than the rest of the bedding. She'd been gone a little while, he guessed.

'Her clothes are gone. The ones she wore yesterday are gone,' his mother said. Perhaps foolishly Cross checked the closets, the crawl space on the sides of the room. Nothing. Barefoot he descended the stairs where his father stood, ashen. His face showed fear. Not a moment during his heart attack did his father reveal this much emotion. Fear seemed to slip into panic.

'It will be all right,' Cross lied. He didn't believe it for a moment. He headed through the kitchen to the back door.

'She probably saw a raccoon or a skunk or something and decided to follow it.'

'She is adventurous,' Cross' father said half-heartedly.

Cross stopped. 'Just rest, Dad.' The old man looked frail and frightened. Frightened was a condition that was foreign to the father and deeply troubling for the son. 'She probably wandered out and lost track of time.'

Outside he called her name several times as he walked, each call louder than the previous one. On three sides of the farm the land was flat. The soybeans had barely poked through the soil. He could see forever. No one was out there for acres. He looked left. A small orchard. Cherry trees. Possible. To the right, lawn leading to a gravel road. Across the road more fields.

His stomach sank. He walked around the house looking for tire tracks or footprints. Not likely. It hadn't rained in awhile. He might find tracks if it was a particularly heavy vehicle or it had abruptly started or stopped. He couldn't see anything. It was doubtful he'd find footprints. At the back, he looked up at the windows to her room. Nothing was out of the ordinary. There were no ladders around.

'Should we call the police?' his mother asked suddenly beside him. His father stood at the door, leaning against it.

'I don't know.' Cross didn't know. Things were strange. Maya wasn't his legally. He had no real claim to her. He didn't know the situation of her disappearance. Could be that she did wander off and would return or be found. Could be . . . 'Damn,' his mind narrowed down a possibility. He thought she'd be safe in Eaton, Indiana. He hadn't counted on someone following him, leading them to her. Right? He asked himself. Yes. Someone patient, just waiting for him to make his move. If that's what happened.

Could be her mother. That wouldn't be all bad. Could be someone who would be hurt by Maya's testimony, about her seeing the body in the trunk of a car, and knowing whose car it was. He thought that was resolved with the deaths and arrests of all the sex traders but Margot. Maybe not.

'We can't wait too long,' his mother said.

'Yes . . . let me think.' What could the police offer? Eaton was a small town. Would Barney Fife show up? Or would there be someone sane and serious? Would cops come up from Muncie? Would that be any better? He had no way of knowing.

FBI? 'I think we need to do some looking first. This could all be . . .'

He walked to the gravel road. He looked both ways. He knew what he would see. Nothing.

'God.' It was more of an exhale than a curse or plea. The other possibility was even worse – could be some perverted stranger. These things happen. And they happen everywhere, including small rural towns early in the morning. Cross stood in the middle of the road for a while without thought before he realized that while his brain shut down his breathing had become shallow and fast. He took a deep breath, held it, let it out.

He felt calmer, but still no answer. No plan.

He called out her name again and again as he walked toward the orchard half afraid he would find her there unable to answer his calls.

'Maya! Maya!'

Beyond the orchard were the woods. It was fenced and posted with a sign that said, 'trespassers will be prosecuted.'

'Forgive those who trespass against us,' slipped through his brain, as it seemed to fire randomly. 'No, no, no,' he said trying to dismiss the images of some hideous man carrying her away. He looked into the woods and its cool, thin foliage. Just a little underbrush and a few pines to create places to obscure the little girl. Wouldn't she be afraid to go in there? No, he answered his own question. She would see the sign and be challenged. She was fearless. 'Oh, God, Maya.'

What was all this God stuff? He could always keep cool. In most circumstances he could either take charge or give in to the inevitable. Here, he seemed to be able to do neither. He didn't know what to do.

'Maya! Maya,' he yelled, before he put his bare foot into the chain-link fence.

'Howie, what are you doing?' his mother yelled, running toward him, stopping once to pull her dress away from a thorny branch. 'What if . . .?' She asked, coming toward him. She was stopped by the fence as he dropped to the other side.

'Go back,' Cross said more harshly than he intended. 'Check on Dad. If I don't find her, we'll call the police, I promise. Please, just go back.'

He saw the pain on her face. She was a good woman who

was suffering too. He promised himself he wouldn't forget that. She relinquished her grip on the fence, but didn't move.

Cross left her at the fence. He looked back to see she was heading back to the house. He moved through the cool morning, between trees and mostly barren bushes hoping that there were no hunters around.

'Maya,' he called not quite as loud as before. Leaves from the previous autumn crunched beneath his feet. Twigs and branches hurt his feet. 'Maya, please!' he said as if he could beg fate.

Four

Wenders, if that was Wenders, stood with the light behind him perhaps to keep the characteristics of his face unclear. With his hands bracing him on the far end of a pool table, he leaned forward. A glass of whiskey sat on the pool table, as did half a bottle.

'Drink?' the man asked.

'Nope,' Shanahan said.

'It's been a long time, what have you learned?'

'How to stay alive . . . so far,' Shanahan said.

'Well, it all comes to a bad end, doesn't it?'

Shanahan thought that a rhetorical question and waited for the man to get down to business. Judging by what he could see, it could be Wenders. Slender. A philosophical bent.

'Of course,' the man continued, 'no matter how resigned we are to the fact that it has to end, that once it's done, it can't be any big deal, we try to stay alive, don't we?'

'What do you want?' Shanahan came around to the other end of the table. It was Wenders. His face showed the passing years. He moved less agilely; but it was the same slender frame, the same eyes.

'A game of eight-ball, maybe.'

'Not my game.'

'I'm behind it, Shanahan.' The man picked up the black

ball and tossed it casually on the table so that it rolled toward
Shanahan. It hit the cushion and moved back toward Wenders.
He grabbed it.

'And?' Shanahan asked. He remembered now Wenders'
sense of theater. This was the same Wenders drama.

'Jesus, Shanahan. You haven't changed at all. You'd think
someone was charging you by the word.'

'I didn't call the meeting.'

'No, no you didn't,' Wenders said. He shook his head and
smiled. A small laugh escaped that indicated he should have
known better. 'This is like sex without foreplay. Look, I have a
story to tell you.'

'That being the foreplay you like so much?'

'Yeah. Let's go in the back. You want to share some Scotch?'

'No. How about coffee?'

'No, don't have any.'

'Coke?'

'Yeah, probably.'

Wenders shrugged and yelled out something in Spanish to
no one Shanahan could see. 'Come on.'

The two of them moved through the tables to the back, behind
a swinging door into a room also lit gray – weak morning light
coming through small dirty windows. The room looked like a
combination office and bare-to-the-bone kitchen. Probably
where the pool hall made something to go along with the beer.

Wenders put his drink and the bottle on a table that would
seat ten and sat down. Shanahan sat as well, a few chairs
away, and in a tentative fashion. He eyed the back door in
case he needed it. The pane of glass by the lock was broken.
Wenders and his strange friend had broken in. Shanahan had
come in through the front. The two of them from the back.
Less likely they'd be seen together.

A bottle of Coca Cola appeared. The driver slipped in and
out almost unnoticed. Shanahan only noticed the long, shiny
dark arm and the long slender fingers.

'Did you ever kill anybody?' Wenders asked.

'A gentleman doesn't tell.'

'You didn't while you were with me. And as far as I know
– and I knew a lot about you back then, the French dancer,
remember?' He smiled, waited to get some sort of response,
but didn't get one. 'Anyway, you were never on the front lines.

Just slinking around in the shadows like me looking for things people didn't want you to find.'

'So the story you want to tell is about me?' Shanahan asked.

'No.'

'I didn't think so.'

'Let me get around to this my own way, would you?'

Shanahan nodded. 'Major . . . Colonel, whatever you are, you're on the clock.'

Wenders smiled. 'Now we understand each other. Like I said, it's been awhile since I was Army. Please call me Jack.'

'Jack, you're on the clock.'

'Shanahan, I need to be somebody else.' Wenders said this solemnly. His eyes bore directly into Shanahan's. This was the heart of it.

Shanahan waited. He took in Wenders. Older obviously, but he had aged gracefully. Had all of his hair, but now it was all silver. If the man was in hiding, as all the elaborate precautions suggested, he wasn't roughing it. The haircut was good. His tan was even. His teeth were white. His fingernails were mani-cured. His khaki shirt and pants were clean and pressed. Wenders wasn't living off the land in the jungles above Vallarta. If he was up there at all, he was probably living in an elegant hacienda.

'Did you hear me?' Wenders asked. 'I need to be someone other than Jack Wenders.'

'I don't have those kinds of connections anymore. I wouldn't know where to begin to get fake passports and all that. I tried to tell you that on the phone before you brought me down here.'

'Now don't get defensive. You told me. I know,' he sighed, poured himself a drink. 'Small town kind of guy.'

'Why in the hell did you pick me? I'm old as salt, out of the business for decades, and a technological idiot. And Jack, we weren't exactly best buddies.'

'Not being best buddies is a plus. But the real reason is that your word is gold. And I think you want to do what's right.'

'One man's right . . .' Shanahan started to say.

'Don't get philosophical,' Wenders grinned. 'It's not you.'

'Thing is,' Shanahan said, 'I do need to know what I'm helping you with. And once I find out, I might not want to help you.'

'I got that. I got that before I tracked you down. I'm counting on it.' Wenders looked at his watch. 'Trust. Everything else I need isn't worth shit if the trust isn't there. Now are you ready for that story? Things will start to pick up here in a few hours and I'm going to need to move on.'

Shanahan glanced back at the door.

'Yeah,' Wenders said, nodding, intentionally confirming Shanahan's suspicion. 'It's important to be places where you aren't expected to be and at a time that is hard to predict.'

Sergeant Mitchell, his police cap covering his red hair, stood on the front lawn, notebook in hand. Cross recognized him from high school – a decent serious kid, smart in a good boy bookish way. He didn't know whether Greg Mitchell remembered him. Just as well if he didn't. Cross was a smart ass, not funny enough to be the class clown, not tough enough to be a bully, but rebellious enough to be a suspect in whatever went wrong. In those days, Cross could be counted on to ride the straight-arrow kids at least verbally. And Mitchell was among the straightest of the arrows.

'Your daughter?' Mitchell asked Cross.

Cross nodded. He thought 'I'm not sure' wasn't the right thing to say just now. 'She's been staying with her grandparents.' Cross knew he had to answer the questions and the sooner he did, the sooner they would be able to do their jobs. But he felt the impatience any parent would feel. Why are they all looking around here? She's gone. Find her. Find her.

'And the mother?'

'She, uh, ooh, uh, ran off.'

Mitchell gave him the same suspicious look his teachers had. No doubt about it. Mitchell remembered Cross.

'I see. What do you think happened?'

OK, Cross thought, this is what good cops do. Get people talking. Get them to incriminate themselves. And in cases of missing or dead children, the first suspects are family. For good reason. The statistics support it.

'I don't know.'

'No idea? That's hard to believe. No thoughts at all. She's gone and you haven't thought what might have happened?'

'Your mind goes through all sorts of things, you know. Could be her mother. Decided to take her back. It's possible.'

'Without letting you know?'

'It would be just like her.'

'I'll need as much information about her as possible. But go on.'

'Could be some pervert.' Cross was already talking too much and he almost started talking about how Maya was the object of a search by some mobsters.

'No registered sex offenders in Eaton,' the officer said.

'You checked?'

'I don't need to check.'

'That doesn't mean one wasn't driving through. Or just didn't register.'

'True. We're ruling nothing and no one out at the moment.' He gave Cross a sly smile, then in a more friendly way he said, 'We've got word out already. The state police and police in surrounding jurisdictions. It doesn't help that you don't have a photograph?'

It was embarrassing. There were no photographs. He knew what the cop was thinking. He would think the same thing. What father, what grandmother and grandfather for that matter, wouldn't have a photograph of the little girl?

'It's a long story,' he said, regretting it immediately.

'I've got time,' Mitchell said.

'No, you don't have the time.'

Cross noticed a uniformed officer coming back out of the orchard. Others were coming in from the woods and the fields. Cross could tell they found nothing. That's when the good news is still bad news.

'Where were you when she came up missing?'

'Asleep.'

'What I want you to do now is describe everything that happened, everything you did from the second your eyes opened until we arrived on the scene.'

Cross filled him in about Margot and about the situation. As he did so, he noticed another cop talking to his father on the front porch, and perhaps another talking to his mother inside. It bothered him some that they were going to compare the stories. Even honest people don't remember things the same way. On the other hand, it gave him some confidence in the profession-alism of the department. This is what they are supposed to do.

When Cross was done and after Mitchell finished his current set of notes, the cop had more questions.

'What was the girl doing up here?'

'She stays up here during the week, while I work.'

'Yet, you were here on a week night,' Mitchell said.

'Work week means different things to me. I am at the mercy of other people's schedules.'

'And what is your work?'

'I'm a private investigator.' That answer caused an eye to twitch. If it was a poker game, Mitchell missed an inside straight. It was a 'tell' in his otherwise cool composure.

'You're living in Indianapolis? Have I got that right?' Mitchell asked.

'Yes.'

'Separated from your wife?'

'We weren't married,' Cross said, thinking he saw a hint of disapproval. This was Indiana, rural Indiana.

'Ever spend any time in jail?'

'Yeah.'

'Where?'

'Marion County, briefly.'

'What for?' Mitchell asked with a flat, seemingly disinterested voice.

'Murder,' Cross said, noticing Mitchell's more pronounced eye twitch. He was sure Mitchell was going to get as much of that story as he could.

'They got the wrong guy, huh?' Mitchell said, recovering.

The constitution not withstanding, most cops believe that if you're arrested you must be guilty of something besides bad luck.

'Yeah,' Cross said ignoring the sarcasm.

'Anything else I might want to know about your past?'

'Criminally speaking, no. I've pissed off a few cops, but no serious arrests.'

'So you travel in some tough circles. Maybe you've made some enemies.'

'I have.' Maybe one more.

'Care to list them?' Mitchell flipped the pages of his notebook, ready to take down the long list.

Cross wasn't sure his brain would cooperate. If he was asked to describe how he felt, he'd have to say 'jumpy'. He didn't want to be standing here going down bad memory lane when the girl was lost somewhere, no doubt scared – really scared – maybe in pain. Maybe worse. Impatience was again turning to anger. But if he wanted to ever move on, he had to eat his anger.

'Can we make this quick?' Cross asked, deliberately calm and friendly. Over the cop's shoulder, he saw his mother bring his father a glass of water. His father tipped his head back, taking some pills, sipping the water.

'That's up to you,' Mitchell said.

Five

Shanahan took a sip of his Coke. It wasn't coffee, but it was caffeine. It would have to do.

'I've done some horrible things,' Wenders said, leaning back, giving Shanahan another once-over, looking for clues so he'd know how to proceed.

The detective remembered now how Wenders weighed words, sometimes advancing an argument, sometimes retreating, but never giving up until he got what he wanted. He would have been as successful a salesman as he was an interrogator. His conversations were choreographed moment by moment. Shanahan gave him nothing.

Wenders smiled. 'Christ, you're like petrified wood.'

'I often feel like petrified wood. That's what happens when you get old.'

'Tell me what you're thinking,' Wenders said.

'I'm thinking you've pissed off someone and someone wants you dead.'

'That's the Cliff Notes version,' Wenders said, grinning. 'I left the Army when it was clear I wasn't going anywhere. The years ran out and I wasn't asked to attend the War College. You know what that means. About that time a couple of guys in Arkansas were putting together a private security force. The idea was that corporations working in dangerous areas of the world need security. Initially, that meant well-trained bodyguards.'

Wenders took a sip of his Scotch.

'It turned out to be a good and profitable idea. Soon,' he continued, 'they needed somebody in intelligence and a guy I know who was already working for them made the introductions. I went to work. This was years ago. The company grew. I was in pretty close to the start up, so the company grew underneath me. I was very near the top of a pyramid that continued to grow – and continues to grow to this day.

'What I overlooked in the beginning, because of need and then because of greed was that the founders were fanatics. I'd call them religious capitalists. Not that religious people are bad or that capitalists are bad, but these guys were creationists when it came to religion and Darwinians when it came to business. Survival of the fittest. Their God was a mean, vengeful son of a bitch and their idea of mission left no prisoners. The ends truly justified the means.

'I could deal with that. Work was work. The rest of the time I had my life, a few good women and a bottle of Scotch. I was earning big bucks. I was meeting important people – some of the most influential people in the world.'

Wenders nodded, agreeing with himself. He looked at Shanahan.

'History books will be filled with their names,' Wenders continued. He called out. The driver appeared. Wenders mimed smoking. The guy nodded, disappeared.

Wenders looked at his watch. An expensive one, Shanahan noticed. Not one you'd wear if you were swinging your machete through thick jungle growth or hiding in dingy basements.

'I'll try to cut to the chase. Iraq came along. Columbia came along. Eastern Europe. Africa. New Orleans. Other places.' Wenders shook his head as if trying to dispel his thoughts. 'You know me well enough to know that I'm willing to cut corners here and there, not too tied to the rule book, right?'

Shanahan nodded. He remembered Wenders' favorite phrase: 'Close enough for government work.' In fact, Wenders and Shanahan's past together came into clearer focus. Wenders was a boozer and womanizer. With an Aston Martin, the right music and special effects, Wenders could be James Bond.

'The company got big, really big,' Wenders continued. 'Every day it gets bigger and more powerful. And they are incredibly connected. With an active intelligence force we became a mirror government. We've got everything – counterfeiters, forgers,

linguists, intelligence gatherers, experts in every field of tech-
nology, snipers, strategists, spies. You name it, we can do it.
We could help our clients frame intelligence and ameliorate
opposition.'
    'Ameliorate?'
    'Great word, isn't it?' Wenders said.
    'What this organization is about is what a certain cadre of
US political leaders are about. Complete privatization of everything, including the military. It was ingenious. It was as if
each new job opened a whole new set of possibilities. Security
for companies, government employees, foreign politicians,
dictators. Anybody and everybody. As a private corporation
we are outside the jurisdiction of the US in many ways and
certainly in some places. In some countries we were also
extra-legal. We are bound by no law. And the way it was set
up, because the company isn't bound, neither are their clients.
Neither are governments. We could do what they couldn't.'
    He looked at Shanahan for a reaction. Still getting none,
he continued.
    'What international law? What constitution? You might ask,'
Wenders said grinning widely.
    'Pretty soon, who needs governments?' Shanahan said.
    'You get it. Boundless, endless free market and fuck every-
thing that got in the way. Before you know it, the courts will
be privatized. Hell, the politicians already are. Under the threat
of terrorism, poof goes the Bill of Rights. But it's more interesting than that. This group and select government officials decide
to blow up bridges and factories. We blow them up and then
we provide the construction companies to rebuild them, and we
provide the security during the construction. We find a cache of
heroin, appropriate an oil field, a warehouse full of guns and
we see that they get to the right people rather than the wrong
people. Somebody interferes, causes trouble, we can fix that.'
    Shanahan nodded. 'And you?'
    'I'm up with the worst of them. Some of the guys working
for us are folks who know little about the operation. They're
in it for God and country, patriots who think they're saving
America from extremists. They don't know what's really going
down. I saw it coming. I watched . . . no . . . helped it evolve
into an extraordinary entrepreneurial enterprise. The money
kept getting better and it went back to the players who were

in on it – all of us – highly placed government officials and their friends, certain corporations, and us.'

Wenders took another sip.

'I've got lots of money, Shanahan.'

The driver came in with a pack of cigarettes, already opened. He placed them on the table in front of Wenders and disappeared. 'My only trusted associate – until now I hope.'

Again he gave Shanahan a serious, but questioning look. Shanahan gave him nothing in return.

Wenders laughed, nodded toward the door where his associate disappeared. 'He can't hear, can't speak. Reads a little. He is a good driver, a decent cook, handy with a knife, and good with animals. And can move without a sound. He's afraid of nothing and no one. And he works cheap.'

'Deal of a lifetime,' Shanahan said.

He lit a cigarette. 'The odds are lower now that this is what will kill me.'

'What else does he do for you?' Wenders eyes shut halfway, like a cat sleeping in the sun. Was he going to answer?

'Whatever I want,' Wenders said, slowly opened his eyes.

'They don't want you to leave the company, is that it?'

'Not to live and tell about it.'

'Because?'

'Because I'm blowing the whistle. Not just what we've done, but why we've done it. Our intent. I know the players. I know the plans. I know everything. I've been feeding information to a reporter in DC. What I have to say will not only take *them* down, it will take down some very important people.'

'What's with the Boy Scout routine?'

'Everybody's got a tipping point, a line he won't cross – however you want to say it.'

'What was that?'

'I'm not saying, Shanahan. Let's just say no matter what happens to me in whatever time I have left, I will never fully pay for what I did.'

'What is it you want from me, exactly? I can't give you absolution.'

Wenders laughed. 'You wouldn't if you could. I know you. I have to live. If not for my own selfish, sorry ass, but to validate the story. And this group, you know, is pretty good at what they do.'

'They're going to ameliorate you. Is that it?' The temperature in the room heated up as the day began in earnest.

'That's it,' Wenders smiled.

'I left my Superman outfit in Indianapolis. You have some
thoughts, I'm guessing.'

'Yeah. I want to be you.'

'Remind me not to look to you for stock recommendations.'

'I'm serious. I want to be Dietrich Shanahan.'

'How much for my soul, Wenders?'

'You can keep your soul, Shanahan. It's not one of those
deals. I've confessed to some evil, but . . .' Wenders shook his
head. 'I just want your identity.'

'Who am I to become? You?'

'That would be nice. But no. That wouldn't be smart. We'd
both be Dietrich Shanahan. You are the Dietrich Shanahan in
Indianapolis. I'll be the Dietrich Shanahan in . . . someplace
else. We coexist. It'll work. I just need some information and
some cover, a birth certificate, passport, a history, build a past
that's convincing until I can create a new one for myself.' Sensing
an objection, he quickly qualified his remarks. 'Just for identity. I don't plan to work. Nothing to screw anything up. Official
copy of a birth certificate. A way to get credit cards billed to
the appropriate Shanahan, an identical passport. I can have it
made. We won't travel at the same time. You won't be burned.
You have me at your mercy. What do you think?'

'You're younger than I am. What happens when I die?'

'Maybe you live on. Maybe I become someone else, another
step removed from the company. C'mon Shanahan, what's
going on in your head?'

'I'm thinking maybe you're crazy. Or maybe you get me
to buy into one story and you're really playing another and
you're just running a game on me.'

'Fair enough. Is the story too far-fetched?'

'I don't know.'

Wenders nodded, sipped his scotch, checked his watch,
buying time while being fully aware that time was running
out at the pool hall.

'I don't know what to tell you. Think about it. It's a lot to
take in. Think about it,' he repeated. He stood. 'You can find
your way back to the hotel. Leave by the back. We'll leave a
few minutes afterward. I'll get in touch with you. Do me a favor.

Don't leave Vallarta until we've talked again. We haven't talked about the deal, you know, the money. You will be rewarded. You will never have to work again.'

He extended his hand.

Shanahan shook it.

'I'm telling you the truth,' Wenders said, 'the whole truth and nothing but the fucking truth so help me. I'm working for people who want to own the rain and sell water back to the peasants. They'd privatize the air if they could and when they figure it out, they will.'

He opened the door, peered out quickly. He looked back at Shanahan. 'It's important that I tell my story. Somebody's got to stop this train.' Wenders reached in his pocket, pulled out the white cue ball. 'Here,' he said tossing it to Shanahan. 'It's all up to you now.'

'What am I supposed to do with this?'

'Keep it until our next meeting. A reminder. You're the kind of guy who would have to return it,' he said.

Cross knew better, but he was doing it anyway. His cop background told him that driving around town was hopeless. He thought it unlikely that the kidnapper was a resident. Who would risk that in such a small town.

If it was Margot taking her daughter back, she wouldn't have had to resort to kidnapping, would she? She was Maya's mother. He had no legal right to her unless it could be proved he was the father. Was she worried about that?

Cross believed this was connected to the body Maya saw in the trunk of a low-level hood's car near her home in Maui, which is why Maya ended up in Cross' lap in the first place. But that story had holes in it as well. The hood was dead too. So were the hood's associates. The head guy was in prison. The only people Maya could hurt with her testimony were her mother and her mother's boyfriend who, despite his lack of a moral compass, was nonetheless incapable of doing any real harm to anyone, let alone pull off something as bold as a kidnapping.

Cross had gone through the streets of Eaton several times looking for something that seemed odd or out of place. As the morning lengthened, he drove out on the back roads. He stopped to check outbuildings. Each time he approached, he'd get that sick feeling in his gut, followed by relief. He knocked on doors, scaring the inhabitants. He talked to farmers in the field and in their barns. He was yelled at, barked at and stared down.

Was it possible that Maya walked away on her own? It seemed preposterous at first, but the five-year-old was independent and precocious. She was unhappy that her mother had been out of her life for months now. Did she think she could just leave and find her? What did he know about a five-year-old brain, especially Maya's strangely precocious one?

Cross was pulled over once by one of Eaton's own and given a stern lecture about letting the police do police business. Cross told the officer that he would do nothing on his own other than see if she were wandering somewhere. He lied to the officer, saying he would not under any conditions take the law into his own hands. The officer, despite the fact he didn't believe him, had nothing to say. Just the stare. The cop stare. He knew the stare. He used to use it himself when he thought it might work.

Before he pulled out on the road again, he let his mind go where he had prohibited it earlier. If the kidnapper – pervert or mobster – wanted to get rid of the body, if there were in fact a body, where would he take it? There were wells on farms all around, ponds, culverts, freshly tilled fields, small patches of woods. But if the perpetrator didn't know the area well, there was always the river. It was obvious.

The Mississinewa River comes in from Ohio, then twists and turns for a 100 miles before it turns into the Wabash. A moment of melody, *Moonlight on the Wabash*, seeped in his brain. He picked up his cell, called the Eaton police.

'You have someone checking the river?' he asked.

They were ahead of him. Again, that was some consolation. He would keep pushing too.

Six

S hanahan figured out which way Banderas Bay was and knew that if he got to the water he could find his way back easily. But what would he do with the day or perhaps days before Wenders got back to him? He was going to say 'no'. Why couldn't he have said it there at the pool hall? He wished he hadn't tacitly agreed to stay and consider the proposal.

He also wished he had encouraged Maureen to come along. She would have enjoyed it and he wouldn't be so lonely.

It was still early. Sidewalks were being washed. Products were being offloaded from trucks and wheeled into store-fronts. Puerto Vallarta's residents began to emerge from their homes to go about their business while the tourists slept off a night of heavy food and drink.

The restaurants on the beach were nearly empty, but would come alive soon, serving margaritas and Coronas. Beach vendors prepared their goods – tee shirts, dresses, carved animals, purses, rugs, jewelry, wooden bowls, and press-on tattoos.

He wound his way back along the beach, over the broad pedestrian bridge and then on the *Malecon*. He was hungry and thought that maybe he'd missed his opportunities since most of the hotels were on the other side of the river. He found a modest place a few streets in from the beach that served eggs and coffee.

If anyone asked, the elder detective would say he liked the idea that he was out and about, away from home. It wasn't entirely true. He missed Maureen immensely, more than he would ever admit to anyone. On the other hand, he had begun to think the bullet that nearly killed him was speeding up the process in the inevitable decline of old age. The trip gave him a bit of confidence. He could still move about, even in un-familiar territory. He wasn't dead yet.

Maybe that wasn't the issue. Maybe the issue was dementia. What person in his right mind would swallow all this foolishness that Wenders espoused? Private armies? The US government as he knew it being dissolved in favor of warring corporations? People trying to kill Wenders because what he knew could unseat powerful politicians who were on the payroll of these corporations? Who was crazier? Wenders for his pretend or imagined martyred heroism? Or Shanahan for thinking, even for a moment, that he could make a difference even if the situation was as Wenders described.

The food in his belly took the edge off his anxiety. The coffee was tolerable. Maybe he should just pack up and go home. Throw tennis balls for his dog, take Maureen out to dinner, grab a drink at Harry's bar and catch up on the very beginning of base-ball season. He could leave a 'not-interested note' at the hotel. He could write: 'May the force be with you.'

He walked up the hill, back to his hotel, stopping frequently to 'admire the scenery behind him'. He pretended to take interest in case anyone noticed. Next time he'd take the longer, but less steep route. Next time? He was cutting it short, wasn't he? At the corner store, he paused, took some deep breaths, looked around for anyone following him.

He used his phone card to call Maureen.

'I'm going to try to get back today or tomorrow,' he told her.

'What's up?'

'If Wenders isn't crazy, then I'm completely out of my league.'

'You're quitting,' she said.

'Looks like it.' He wanted to tell her he missed her, but it was always hard to get those kinds of words started or even keep them together in some rational way.

'I could come down for a few days. Stay on. How's the food?'

'I'm sure there are some nice places down here.'

'The beach?'

'It's a beach,' Shanahan said.

She laughed.

'Did you know that the English language has adjectives? Beautiful. Lovely. Delightful.'

'I don't know if I've ever said delightful.'

'Well there you are. Now, I could come down. We could sip drinks, hold hands, and enjoy the sunsets. Wouldn't it be delightful for us to have a little beachfront vacation?'

'You can get away?' Shanahan asked, suddenly hopeful.

'No,' she said.

'Then, why . . .?'

'Just wanted to know how you felt about it. And you thought it would be delightful and I was delightful and that is all I really need.'

'Did I call *you* "delightful"?'

'Aren't I?'

'Of course you are,' he said, defeated. 'No wonder you sell so many houses.'

He could almost see her on the other end of the phone.

'See you soon,' he said.

'Shanahan? I'm glad you're coming home.'

After he put the phone back, he realized he hadn't picked up anything for her. The neighborhood surrounding the little hotel wasn't exactly full of shops. This was an area for people who lived in Puerto Vallarta, not tourists who wanted to buy a sombrero or a bull carved in wood. He stepped into the street, looked at the long way down.

'Damn,' he said.

Cross had considered himself Maya's guardian and thought of her mother as someone in self-imposed, secret exile, who would return sooner rather than later to collect her daughter. In this 'interim' period he took the word guardian more literally than legally. He was her protector. And he'd failed. He cared for her as much as perhaps anyone.

What he hadn't realized was how much he had come to love Maya. And now that he was beginning to understand that, he couldn't help but think of Maya's mother, Margot – how much pain she brought to him. And this too, as it is playing out, is more pain that came to him because of her.

'OK,' he said to himself. 'Stop it.' This wasn't the time for introspection, let alone self-pity.

He drove back through town until he came to Indiana Avenue. He drove west along the edge of the river. The water wasn't visible but ran parallel to the road. At one point, he pulled over, got out, locked his car, and made his way toward the water. He walked through the barely budding trees down toward the riverbank. It wasn't as wide as he remembered it as a kid, but it was pretty wide – maybe the width of an eight-lane interstate. But at any point along its banks, the viewer could only see a small part of it, unable to see past the many turns, or into the growth that lined it.

He had paddled up and down the Mississinewa many times. It was lined with trees – sycamores and cottonwoods mostly. If you fished, you'd discover sunfish, small-mouth bass and catfish. One could spot the Great Blue Heron as well as mallards and killdeer. He remembered how uninhabited, how isolated so much of it was, how wild it was. What was intriguing to him then, prompting adventures that seemed unimaginably frightening now. So much could be hidden there.

This was hopeless. His cell phone rang.

'Mitchell here. Where are you?'

'By the river.'

'Where by the river?'

'Before you get to the cemetery,' Cross remembered. It was all coming back to him now. The town he'd barely dreamt of since he left home was demanding that he pay attention to it now.

'We've got more than a hundred volunteers,' the officer said. 'We're going to do a search.'

'That's good. Thanks.'

'I need you to stay close.'

'You're still looking at me, aren't you?'

'You know how it goes.'

'I do.'

'I got some people going to gather at your folks' place. You might want to be there.'

Cross understood. He'd become so concerned with Maya – maybe himself – that he forgot the torture his parents were going through and the increased vulnerability brought about by age and poor health. He also knew what Mitchell was telling him. 'Join the search.' The call was a kindness; the officer didn't have to offer. Unfortunately, this kind of search was only 'search for the little girl's body,' not search for the little girl.

When he got back to the farm, he found the crowd had gathered as Mitchell said. Having grown up there, he recognized many of them – the ones his age and older. It was a surreal realization because they weren't as they remained in his mind, frozen in time, a time when he was in his teens, before he ran off to the big city.

No one talked to him. When he came close, they would

move away, discreetly. They seemed to regard him in the same way he regarded them. With suspicion. He understood why this was. It wasn't just that he had always been a bad boy. He had been a pain to his parents. And now here he was again, back like a bad penny, involved in an incident that could come to no good, that brought heartache to his parents.

The county sheriff was there. The state police were there. The fire department. People stood around in small groups chatting, waiting for someone to call them to order, tell them what to do. Sometimes he'd notice someone nod toward him and say something to those near them.

They were there to help. That was the way it was in places like Eaton. He saw his father on the porch, shaking hands solemnly, thanking them. He was one of them.

He had already managed to get away from newspaper reporters from Marion and Muncie. And for the moment there were no television cameras. It was one advantage of being in a market three-times removed from major media. By tomorrow, Indianapolis would be up here, maybe the networks.

Once back down on the *Malecon*, Shanahan found another place for coffee. He had time to kill before the tourist shops opened. He changed his mind about just leaving Wenders a note. It's not the way he did things, sneaking off like that. He felt he had to do this in person even if the answer was 'no'.

He rehashed his thinking about the whole idea. The story his former commanding officer told him might be true, but even if it was, there was little a semi-retired seventy-one-year-old man living in the Midwest could do about it. He had no important contacts, possessed no high-tech skills and, as he thought about it over the last dregs of coffee, he reinforced his decision. He did not want to be drawn into such craziness. And he certainly didn't want to be party to sharing an identity with a madman.

Still, Shanahan couldn't settle things in his mind. Wenders might have already pulled Shanahan into some scheme that was very different from what he described. The spy business was not, by nature, above board. What you think you see isn't what you think you see. A guy could believe he's helping one side only to learn that he'd helped the other.

Shanahan was determined to end the debate with himself.

He wouldn't let this be drawn out. He'd set a time. After a moment's thought, he decided he would give Wenders until tomorrow noon.

Meanwhile, he needed to find Maureen a gift. It was still early in the morning. The nicer shops still hadn't opened. He could climb the hill again and sit in his room. He preferred to stay on flat land and make only one trip up the hill. Instead he wandered about the neighborhoods on the other side of town, away from the tourist district. There were gas stations and car part shops, carpet stores and a supermarket.

The air was heating up and the likelihood that he would find a gift in this part of town was declining as he walked. He headed back, hoping the more fashionable shops – tourist or not – would be open by now so he could take care of this next to the last errand. The last was to inform Wenders of his decision. Beads of perspiration gathered on his neck. His calf muscles protested the earlier climbing.

He sat on the steps of a small church. He retrieved a handkerchief from his back pocket, removed his straw hat, wiped the dampness on his forehead and neck and then the inside of the hat before putting it back on. It was at best midmorning. It was only April.

Rested, Shanahan went back. Soon, there were a few restaurants, next a few shops. He found one that seemed a step up from the beach salesmen, but not too expensive. He found a blue-green scarf that would go with Maureen's auburn hair.

He went back to his room where he could strip down to his shorts, turn on the air conditioning and maybe catch the few hours of sleep he missed this morning.

He angled his way back to the small hotel, taking one block up, then one block across. 'Who said you can't teach an old dog new tricks?' he asked himself. Shops gave way to homes as he moved higher. Pleasant places, he thought. He felt relieved. It was almost over. He was going home.

Yes, he would have a nap. Even with his clever plan to eliminate the steep climb, he was tiring. He felt it most in his legs, but his whole body was wrung out. The store across from his hotel was half a block away. Maybe it was too early for a beer, he thought, but there was no one around to know. A shower, a beer, a nap. Life was good.

He was a few feet from the top of the hill, when the man

appeared directly in front of him. It was the driver. He was wearing a hat now, but the strap-like matted hair on the sides was unmistakable. As the guy turned away, he nodded for Shanahan to follow him.

Seven

This was standard operating procedure. Walking the fields and woods with others only a few feet away created a virtual comb. An article of clothing, drops of blood, an odd turn of the soil, not to mention a body, all would be hard to miss. Even so, if she were in the trunk of a car, she was long gone. If she was dumped in the Mississinewa River, she would be half way to Peru, Indiana. If she were in someone's cellar, this wouldn't help.

He walked on the barely planted soybean field, avoiding the little ridges, an arms length on either side from the closest searcher. There was no point to this. There were no footprints in the soil. Cross wanted to scream, 'Let's look for her in places where she might be alive!' Because if she were dead there was no hurry.

No, he had to play by the rules this time. There wasn't much he could do by himself – except, maybe, track down Margot. There was nothing to point to her. All she needed to do was drop by and take her away, not steal her in the darkness before morning, he kept telling himself. It didn't make sense for it to be Margot. But he wanted it to be her. Otherwise there would be no hope.

'We're doing more than you think.' It was Mitchell. He had come up behind Cross. 'The FBI is out there. The state police are working the highways. The sheriff is working the back roads.'

'Thanks,' Cross said, still impatient, barely able, in fact, to contain the impatience. But Mitchell was being a professional. What more could he ask?

'I need you to come with me.' Mitchell's voice was steady, not unfriendly, but firm.

They wound their way back to the farmhouse. Two men in dark suits were waiting. They went into the kitchen. When Cross' mother offered to get them something, they politely refused and over-politely asked that she and her husband find something else to do.

She viewed them with suspicion, but did as she was told.

'I'm Brant Hanks,' the thinner of the two said. Flecks of silver at the temples. White, even teeth. Eyes that said nothing. 'This is David Chase.' David nodded. Chase's baldness was his only distinguishing characteristic. He seemed bored.

Only Hanks sat. As he did, he motioned for Cross to do the same thing.

'Look, I know this is a rough time. And it's not a pleasant thing for me to ask the kinds of questions I'm going to have to ask you. I'm sorry. But we're gonna go at it, you and I.'

Cross nodded. Chase crossed his arms, stayed by the door.

'This little girl isn't yours, is she?'

'I don't know.'

'Unacceptable answer.'

'The truth is unacceptable?'

Hanks pushed himself away from the table, looked down, as if he was trying to talk himself out of something. Cross couldn't tell whether Hanks was staging this or really had a problem staying calm. Then, without getting up, or raising his head.

'One more time. The little girl is not your daughter?'

'Her mother said I was, but I don't know.'

Hanks looked up, half a grin, one that angled to the right appeared and disappeared.

'Her mother is Margot Hudson?'

'Yes. As far as I know.'

'Margot Hudson was involved in sex slave traffic. Do you know where she is?'

'I don't think Margot was involved . . .'

'We don't care what you think. Do you know where she is?'

'If I did I would tell you. She may have Maya.'

'We know about you,' Hanks said. He scooted back up to the table. 'A cop who was invited to leave the force. A second-rate private investigator, arrested for murder. Never married. Hung around strip clubs.'

'What did my enemies tell you?'

'If you are the kid's dad, she sure didn't hit the lottery when she was born.'

'No she didn't. And her disappearance drew you as the investigators. So it looks like her luck isn't improving any,' Cross said. He thought about countering the slurs, but knew it didn't matter. They would think whatever they wanted to think. And they were only trying to piss him off anyway. 'Are you arresting me?'

Hanks thought awhile. He could, Cross thought, try the material witness idea. He'd be locked up, doing nobody any good.

'We're trying to find the girl. You want to help or not?' Chase said.

'Your questions didn't sound like you were trying to help.'

'I didn't like your answers,' Hanks said.

'Ask different questions.'

Hanks smiled. 'All right. Tell me what you know about Margot.'

'She has a home in Maui. She was a dancer who made the circuit. She got involved with a restaurateur who was a mafia-want-to be and got himself involved with some guys who ran a chain of strip clubs and were apparently bringing girls in from the Far East. Margot wanted a piece of the action. But Maya accidentally saw a body in the trunk of one of the mobster's cars. The guys found out, got worried about having a witness around. Margot afraid that they might do her harm, dropped her daughter off at my place. In effect she was hiding her there. After that Margot disappeared.'

Hanks nodded. 'She came back for her daughter.'

'Yes. Until she thought the police were going to arrest her. She took off again. There was an ambiguous statement about Maya belonging to me, which brings me to my earlier answer about my being the father. I don't know. Margot wasn't known for her honesty.'

'That the end of the story?' Hanks asked.

'Some stories never seem to end. You're not even close to being done here, are you?'

'No.'

'You don't think it's a pervert?'

'No, not a pervert she didn't already know,' Hanks said, a glimmer in his eye as he sensed Cross' blood pressure rise. 'Could be, but no I don't think so. Molestation is usually a crime of opportunity. So climbing up to the second floor of

some remote farmhouse isn't a likely MO. It's possible somebody who saw her, obsessed, and came back for her. It's more
likely, in terms of statistics, that it's a close friend of the family
or a family member.'

Cross was quiet.

'There was no ladder,' Hanks said. 'The guy did this inside
the house. There's no blood, no sign of a struggle. No one hears
anything. No calls for help. The victim knew the perpetrator.
It was someone she trusted, wasn't it?'

Hanks looked at Cross. There was no question about the
meaning of the look. 'Explain yourself,' it said. He might as
well have said, 'I've got you.'

'Circling back to me didn't take long.'

'Maybe you didn't mean to kill her,' Hanks said.

Cross said nothing.

'You did and then decided to use the abduction scenario.
You hid the body somewhere.'

Cross remained quiet. It didn't help to deny it. The questions would keep coming anyway.

'You like young girls?'

Cross knew what he was doing. It was all part of the routine.
Seeing if he would go along with the search party. Now trying
to make him angry. Well. He was. 'I hang out at strip bars,
remember, not playgrounds. Be consistent with your attacks
on my character, please.'

'Would you be willing to take a lie detector test?'

'I'd be willing to call my lawyer.' Cross stood.

'What have you got to hide?'

'You're not being straight with me. You're doing what you're
taught to do. I understand that. But that little girl is missing and
while you think you aren't wasting time, you are. You're wasting
yours and mine. So, I'm asking you to either ask questions that
will help find out who did this, or get the fuck out of here.'

'Relax,' Hanks said. 'You're right, this is what we do. You know
that in most felony cases, it's friends or family. The victim knows
the person. We have to rule you in or rule you out.'

'You still haven't ruled me out?'

'I haven't ruled anybody out. You. Your father. Your mother.'
Again the look.

Cross might have been able to take the questions, the insin-
uations, but not the smug look. Hanks knew he was putting

a knife in the gut intentionally. He intended to make it as hostile as he could. He wanted a reaction. Some sort of anger, some denial that might give away something. Cross wasn't as educated in these techniques as the FBI, but he understood what was happening.

'You're an asshole,' Cross said.

'OK,' Hanks said, relaxing back in his chair. 'What was your relationship with the little girl?'

'She was dropped on my doorstep. I had to take care of her. I told you that already.'

'You didn't call the police? That's pretty routine and you being a former cop and all . . .'

'No. When I found out it was Margot's kid I thought I'd just watch over her until Margot got back. I thought she would.'

'She didn't, did she?'

'Not right way.'

'So'

'So?' Cross countered.

'Cute kid, right? What? Five?'

'Yeah, five going on fifty.'

'So maybe you figured she wasn't all that young?'

Cross wouldn't bite.

'How'd you spend your time?'

'I took her trick or treating. Took her to the movies, fixed dinner and when things got a little scary, I brought her up here so they couldn't find her.'

'Who is this . . . uh . . . 'they' again?'

'Oh, I forgot,' Cross said. 'These are the guys out running lose kidnapping young women around the world and subjecting them to a life of grotesque servitude. The 'they' are the people you can't find either.'

'Mr Cross, there's—'

'You guys have no idea what you're doing, do you?'

'Mr Cross you are a fly on a dog's ass.'

'You're the one who started this.' Cross felt like an eight-year-old. He felt foolish, but he was still pissed. 'Are you guys up to this?'

Cross moved his gaze from Hanks to the bystander, Chase.

'You think you can get off your ass and actually look for her? If not, go take a nap and let me get on with it.'

'And you know what we can do with gnats?'

Cross knew he was just that, a gnat and they could do plenty. 'A little water boarding, maybe?'

The anger and the urgency were undermined by an overwhelming sense of powerlessness. Not just up against an all powerful FBI headed down a road he knew to be the wrong road, but up against all the possibilities. It was a huge world out there that Maya had disappeared into. What could he do, anyway?

He could get them off his back, maybe. Give him a little breathing room to do what they were unwilling to do. Cross plucked his cell phone from his pocket. Chase dropped his arms and moved toward him. Cross put his hand out.

'I'm making a call,' Cross said, noticing that his mother had come into the kitchen.

'Can I get you boys some coffee?' she asked.

'James,' Cross said into the phone. 'I need you.'

'I've been waiting a long time to hear those words,' James Fenimore Kowalski said. 'I hoped it would be over dinner and a little wine in a little cafe, but—'

'I'm in trouble. The FBI—'

'Tell me where you are, I'm on my way out the door.'

Shanahan looked around. No little white car. They would walk wherever it was they were going. He was exhausted and a long walk wasn't something he was looking forward to. Fortunately, the street slanted down. He followed the dark slender man, who wasn't in much of a hurry. Good thing. It was hot. Too hot. A dry heat he told himself, though his sweat glands seemed unable to discern the difference. But all wasn't bad. He thought that seeing Wenders right away was what he wanted, that maybe this was good. He would get this whole affair over with and be on his way.

The skinny little man stopped at a solid blue metal gate at a home at the intersection of two streets. The gate was once secured by a padlock. The lock had been cut, but placed in such a way that looked like it hadn't. The driver opened the gate and Shanahan entered a lush garden. The green was shocking after having just walked the hot, dusty, barren street. The red tile flooring was immaculately clean. The driver slid the gate closed behind them. Another door was several feet in front of them. A small, sun-dappled side garden with a glass-topped table was on the left. Stairs led up to the right where it appeared the garden continued.

The door ahead of them was open. Shanahan followed the man inside. It was cooler. He found himself on a landing of sorts. The hallway continued to the right, to other rooms. Ahead of him was a stairway. They went down, then through an arched doorway, past a dining area and kitchen and into a pleasantly decorated room, half of it walled and roofed, half of it open to the sky.

Wenders was seated ahead of them, his back to them, framed under the arch of a large tree that grew through the floor. Wenders was in the outdoor area – in the light. He had a great view, similar to the view Shanahan had from his hotel balcony, but in a grander setting and with a considerably wider vista. Red-tile roofs stair-stepped down to the Bay. Shanahan waited for the driver to announce their arrival, then remembered the man didn't speak.

'Wenders?' Shanahan said.

There was no response. One arm was down, hand almost touching the floor. Just beyond his grasp was a glass with an ounce or two of gold liquid.

Was he asleep? That would be the normal assumption. But it wasn't what Shanahan thought. He looked back. The driver had disappeared. Shanahan walked cautiously forward and to the side, hoping that he was out of view of what he surmised was a shooter. Wenders' head was back. There were three round holes in his forehead.

He looked around again for the driver. For anyone. He looked down at Wenders. In the left palm of the dead man's hand resting in his lap was the eight ball.

'Nice touch,' Shanahan said.

He pushed the small bag with Maureen's scarf into his pocket. Shanahan moved around to the back of the chair, moved Wenders' head forward. No exit wound. He looked out of the window. He figured he knew where the bullet had to have come from.

Either someone climbed up to shoot him, which was doubtful. Or more likely, the shot came from someone on a balcony straight across and in the same block. This was a small caliber bullet, he was sure. That meant the bullet hadn't gone far. If it was shot at longer range it couldn't have been this accurate. Shanahan removed himself from the line of fire.

He had been foolish already. This was professional. And

quite likely, Shanahan thought, they already knew about him. They may not know that he knew only generalities – that he wasn't a threat to them, whoever they were.

Did the driver not know his boss was dead? Was that why he brought Shanahan here? Or was Wenders shot after the driver left to fetch the detective? Where was he now? Was the driver in on it? Did the driver do it? Why did he bring Shanahan here? He looked out on the landscape.

He looked on the floor, in search of a gun. But it was unlikely that three bullets directly in the middle of the forehead were self-inflicted.

Maybe the driver was going to the police at this very moment. Maybe he was implicating Shanahan. Kill two birds with one stone. Shanahan could clearly understand Wenders' dilemma. He could trust no one.

This was the way these things worked.

'Damn,' Shanahan said.

Eight

There was another door Shanahan discovered when he entered the death scene. It appeared to be the main, formal entrance. He looked around. As far as he could remember, he touched nothing, not even the banister when he came down the stairs. He retrieved his handkerchief from his back pocket and used it to open the door that led outside, directly on the street. He saw no one, not that that meant anything.

He headed back to the hotel until he realized there was nothing of value in his hotel room. Some clothing he could replace in an hour or two at a shopping center back in Indianapolis. He had his passport, credit card, some pesos, and some dollars with him. He could leave Mexico immediately.

The street was steep and he was hot and tired, but he began his descent to the *Malecon*, walking as quickly as he could. He would have his choice of taxis once he made it to the main drag. As he walked, something more than the fact of Wenders' death troubled him. Though he knew few if any facts about what the man was up to, what he did know might shed some, however dim, light on his death. Did that mean he had some responsibility to help sort all of this out? Guilt tugged at him.

No, he told himself. His responsibility was to Maureen, to himself.

Was this pragmatism or cowardice? Yes, he thought. It was both. There was an enemy. Shanahan had no way of identifying them. All he had was Wenders' description of a large private army operating at will and threatening the very existence of the free world – such as it was – but not one specific detail. No names, no places. Just a generic bogeyman. But certainly 'a large private army operating at will' was enough. There was a difference between being brave and foolish.

If Shanahan went to the police, he would be a prime suspect and even if he wasn't a suspect, he would be a prime witness and wouldn't be allowed to leave. He would be lost in the bureaucracy forever or a dead man.

Anyway, how could he investigate something he knew so little about? Hell, he didn't know Wenders well enough to trust him. Who knows what he might have been involved in and who he might have been involved with? Shanahan had no way of knowing that any of what Wenders' said was actually true. Wenders could have been engaged in God knows what. The fact is, Shanahan told himself, he made the final visit to the guy to tell him he wasn't going to get involved. It wasn't his fault the connection went dead. The only thing Shanahan could be blamed for was being such an old fool in the first place.

One block, then the next, looking at each intersection as a place for conflict. He looked up toward the balconies. There was no movement he could detect. He hoped the person who shot Wenders left after the deed was done – that no one had connected Shanahan to him. He would like to believe that. But he didn't.

The airport offered some measure of security for Shanahan. It was unlikely that whoever was doing this would send their goons into a public place. However, the police would have no problem. He stayed alert, scanning the folks in the main lobby as he tried to make arrangements for an immediate flight back. The crowd was a mix of pale, arriving tourists and the more colorful group of those returning home. There were many

Mexican travelers and many more Mexican workers. Among them here were dozens of skinny men who could be the driver.

Getting a flight wasn't easy, but eventually he got on a flight to Chicago on American Airlines that connected him back south to Indianapolis. He'd take it. The good news is that he would be out of Mexico very soon. He felt even better having passed through security. The idea of checking all passengers for dangerous objects had a calming effect.

When he emptied his pockets, he retrieved the cue ball. He thought about leaving it, but kept it as a souvenir. Wenders wanted him to have it. He also still had the scarf. That was good.

There was a time when none of this would bother him. The threat of death meant little. After his wife left him decades ago, taking their young son with her, Shanahan spent most of his free time on a bar stool, patiently and not too unhappily waiting for death to end the boredom. When he met Maureen, things changed. Now he wanted to hang on. After years of estrangement, he met his son. Another reason to hang on. In the last few years he'd developed a taste for living.

But by gaining hope, he sacrificed indifference. By caring, he no longer had the edge when it came to threats and danger. Now, dammit, there was worry to worry about. Of course the bar was still there. His friend Harry ran it. And at the moment, he wouldn't mind sitting there with his beer, looking up at the Cub's losing another game on the TV.

When Cross left the two FBI agents in the kitchen, they didn't go away. As he brought in the feed for the cows, he saw them through the doors to the barn. They stood out in the soybean field, taking to each other. Cross' father had trailed him, noticed his son's long, sour look in their direction.

'They're doing their job,' he said.

'I know,' Cross said, but it didn't make him feel any better about them. Backlit against a bright blue sky, one of them, Hanks, Cross guessed, took a phone call. He was on the line for maybe thirty seconds when he flicked it shut, said something to Chase and headed back down toward the house.

The roar of the cycle invaded the quiet. Kowalski, a hefty, dark-haired man with an unruly head of black and silver hair and a beard to match shut down his Harley, dismounted and went toward the house.

'I can do this,' the senior Cross said. 'I'm not out of the picture yet. Go.' He smiled. 'I can feed the girls. You know more about this investigating business than I do. Go.' He nudged his son.

The three – Hanks, Cross and Kowalski – convened on the front porch as if it were all planned that way.

'Here's the way I see it,' Kowalski said, foregoing all small talk, including introductions, 'Mr Cross will be glad to answer any and all of your questions after dark. Meanwhile, you cut him loose so he can participate in the search for the girl.'

'You're this James Fenimore Kowalski?' Hanks asked, an obvious attempt to trivialize the attorney.

'If you know of another one, you might let me know. And don't get pissy? This is a serious matter. A little girl is missing. And there are many, many people interested in seeing to it that the search is conducted thoroughly and professionally. Do you understand?'

Though it was doubtful he threw any real scare into experienced FBI agents, the lawyer's mammoth, Roman gladiator head was enough of a presence to negate their tendency to bully. As usual the irreverent attorney wore his standard black suit, black boots, and white shirt open at the neck. No tie. He was at once well-dressed establishment and bearded rebel. But it was his voice that backed Hanks off a bit.

'Yeah. Sure.'

'What's your plan?' Kowalski asked as Chase came up to join the group.

'We don't submit these things for your approval,' Hanks said.

'You don't have one?' Kowalski asked.

'You know it's possible to push too hard.'

'I know that you standing around here chewing your gums isn't finding the girl. Now guys, get to work. OK?' He said this with a good old boy attitude, slapping Hanks on the shoulder. Without waiting for a response, or looking at the FBI agent's bitter expression, Kowalski grabbed Cross' arm and pulled him inside.

'OK, fill me in,' Kowalski said, once out of earshot.

'Did that help?' Cross asked him.

'The condescension? It helped me. They are so fucking arrogant. Anyway, it gets them off your back and on to mine. That's where I want them. What do we do?'

* * *

Kowalski was on his cell in the living room calling. He said
he was going to check in on the Karl Herrmann situation.
Herrmann was the last dangerous man standing in the sex
slave business – at least as far as Cross knew. Also, as far as
Cross knew, Herrmann was the one who originally threatened Margot and Maya. The thugs Cross killed belonged to
him. Herrmann was about to go to trial. Cross was under
the impression Herrmann was at the top of that sex slave
trade organization, though he could not be sure. Sometimes
there are people behind the people behind the people. But it
was possible Herrmann was pulling the strings now, could be
the one to abduct Maya – a way to eliminate a witness or, more
likely, use her as a negotiating tool for Margot's testimony.

Kowalski was also calling bail bonders in large cities to see
if they had any business involving Margot Hudson. He would
check city utilities to see if she had settled in somewhere. That
was a particularly daunting task that the Internet made slightly
easier. All this, Cross realized, he should have been doing.

As his mother poured the coffee, Cross called Shanahan to
pick his brain, but got voicemail. His next call was to a cop
in Hawaii, the guy he worked with the last time he searched
for Maya's mother. Margot had a house and a boyfriend on
Maui, he discovered then. Funny how he had an affair with
the woman off and on for years without knowing where she
lived. That was the least of it. The big surprise was that Margot
had a daughter – and further that her daughter might be his.

Cross made contact in Maui.

'Again? You can't go around losing people, especially the
same ones over and over,' Officer Kielinea said.

'This is serious. Right now we don't know whether Margot's
little girl has been taken by her mother, by some child predator,
or somebody involved in that murder in your island paradise.'

'OK, I understand. I'll make some inquiries.'

'Also, Margot's boyfriend.'

'Eddie the restaurant entrepreneur?'

'Yeah, the one with the Maserati.'

'Dead.'

'Dead?'

'Accident. Took his little sports car off road up in Maui
Wowie country, made a wrong turn,' the cop said.

'When?'

'Three weeks ago, maybe. Yes. Almost exactly.'

'Nothing funny about it?'

'No matter how you define funny, nothing funny. What a waste of a Maserati.'

Cross didn't know what to make of the death.

'Let me know about Margot. Maybe she came back for the funeral?' he asked.

'Call me back in a few hours,' Kielinea said.

'Aloha,' Cross said.

'No Hudson needing bail,' Kowalski said, coming into the kitchen with his coffee cup. He poured himself some coffee.

'She's been a good girl,' Cross said.

'Or she changed her name,' Kowalski suggested. 'Got a bite though. A bad one.' He pulled up a chair. 'Karl Herrmann's dead.'

Cross shook his head in disbelief. 'You're kidding. Jesus, what's going on? Fast Eddie's dead in Hawaii. Just found out.'

'Curiouser and curiouser,' Kowalski said, a sly smile on his face.

'Why wasn't Herrmann's death in the papers? It would be local news in Indianapolis.'

'Connections weren't made apparently. He was transferred to a federal prison in Otisville, New York. He was released a month ago, no reason given. A car hit him as he was crossing the street in White Plains. Dying in an accident isn't a criminal offense.'

Kowalski waited for a reaction.

Cross' mind went dead. Kowalski seemed to sense it.

'You've been up awhile. All coffee and no food make Howie a very burnt-out boy. Let's get some food in you.'

The sandwiches Mrs Cross had prepared for that purpose and stacked on a plate on the kitchen counter had gone untouched.

'So, there's two ways of looking at what we know. One is that if all the players are dead who feared the kid's story about the corpse would hurt them, then there's nobody left to kidnap her,' Kowalski continued as he set a sandwich down on the table in front of Cross.

'Two is,' Cross said, still ignoring the food, 'why are all these people connected to the case dying?'

What was worse, Cross thought, was that if the kidnappers were connected with the other deaths, there was no reason to believe they'd keep Maya alive – or Margot for that matter. Margot could already be dead.

Nine

Shanahan called Maureen from the airport. They met at Harry's on 10th Street as the day was slipping away. The area was a little shabby. It used to be for the working class. But industry vanished years ago. The bar was shabby too, but clean enough in the dim light. It was almost as dark inside as it was outside. A light over the bar, the big screen TV above it, and some random beer signs gave it most of the light. Each booth, six of them, lined the wall across from the bar. Each little booth had a small unpretentious fifteen-watt sconce. Just enough light that you could make out the limited choices on the menu, but not so much that you could actually see the food.

Maureen sat in the booth farthest from the door. Shanahan walked past the guys at the bar, regulars who had unofficially reserved stools, which they occupied every night for several hours. They ran tabs, argued politics when they talked at all, and caused very little trouble.

'What's up?' Maureen asked as Shanahan kissed her on the cheek, about as much affection as he was willing to display in public.

'Nothing,' Shanahan said, sliding in beside her, noting her usual choice at Harry's – rum and tonic. She preferred wine, but not the cheap swill Harry offered. 'It was a dead end.' He would tell her about it, but not now. Maybe tomorrow.

'Making the beautiful lady wait, you ought to be ashamed of yourself,' Harry said as he brought Shanahan a shot of J.W. Dant whiskey and a bottle of Guinness. Harry slid in on the other side of the booth. He had the right to intrude, being Shanahan's oldest friend. Oldest in more ways than one. The bar owner had silver hair thinning so much the skull was completely visible beneath the wisps. Thick rimless glasses magnified his eyes. He was a little man closing in on seventy himself, getting smaller and tougher and grumpier as he aged.

'While you were in Mexico taking siestas, Maureen and I decided to elope,' Harry said. 'You should have married her, you know, instead of living in sin.'

'Is that true, Maureen?' Shanahan asked.

'Yes. One more day. That's all I gave you,' Maureen said. 'Harry and I are going to retire in Brazil.'

'Really?'

'Or maybe Belize.'

'Belize,' Shanahan nodded.

'Barbados was a thought,' she continued.

'You didn't get past the Bs, I take it. Beirut?'

'What happened, Deets?' Harry said. He was the only person to call Shanahan 'Deets,' a shortening of his real first name, Dietrich.

'Didn't take the job.'

'Why?' Harry continued.

'Don't you have a bar to run?' Shanahan asked.

'They'll bellow out if they need something. Off on an adventure, you were. So you have to tell us all about it.'

'Hot. Lots of pelicans.'

'That's it?' Harry asked, angry.

'That's it.' Shanahan took the whiskey in a gulp and followed with a sip of beer. It felt good. It would feel good to climb in bed. It was good that this was all over. He didn't want to relive it.

'Where are your bags?' Maureen asked him. 'You leave them in the taxi.'

'Damn, must have.'

Maureen gave him the look, the you're-not-leveling-with-me look. Shanahan returned the look with a smile. That was wrong, he knew immediately. He never smiled. She picked up on it.

'Harry, could you get me another one of these?' she asked.

'What?' Harry said. 'Something's going on here.'

'They lost my baggage,' Shanahan said, wishing he'd thought of that right off.

She gave him another look of disbelief.

'Or I should say, the baggage is lost. Or it probably is.'

Harry shook his head in frustration, went to the bar.

Maureen was waiting.

'I had to leave in a hurry,' Shanahan said. 'I'll tell you about it.'

'They threw you out of Mexico?' she asked, grinning. 'That had to take some doing. You must have been really bad.'

'How were your days as a bachelorette?' Shanahan asked.

'Just a couple of torrid affairs, you know, I didn't have time for everyone who wanted me. I have houses to sell. Oh, Howie called. Left word for you to call him. Sounded important.' She reached for her purse. 'You want to use my cell?'

Shanahan saw Harry coming back. As much as he would trust his friend – with his life – he didn't trust the man with the details of it. Harry was a bit too inquisitive for Shanahan. And Shanahan never liked having telephone conversations when others would be forced to listen.

'I'll use the public phone,' Shanahan said.

'They're coming to take that out,' Harry called out after Shanahan. He handed Maureen her drink. 'Public phones are a thing of the past. Imagine that. Can't get a shoe shine, have an ice cream soda, or go to a drive-in movie, can't buy a DeSoto, or . . .'

Maureen knew better than list cell phones, computers, I-pods, and ATMs as a positive counterbalance to Harry's list of complaints. 'People are living longer,' she said.

'That's supposed to be a good thing?' he asked, then patted her hand. 'It's a good thing, the longer I get to be around you is all to the good.'

She wanted to say, 'all you need is a good woman,' but even if that was true, he'd already had five wives. Apparently he needed something else to make him happy.

The phone in Cross' front pocket buzzed. At this point, any phone call was a potentially earthshaking event. She's been found. She's alive. She's dead. Everyone at the dinner table – Cross, his parents, and Kowalski who stayed on – not only stopped talking, but also stopped eating.

'Yeah?' Cross said. 'Thanks for calling back.' Cross scooted back from the table, shook his head indicating there would be no information on this call and motioned that he'd be right back. He walked out on the front porch. The sun was nearly down. He looked out at the horizon as he explained the circumstances to Shanahan. A thin stripe of flesh-colored light divided day and night.

Cross brought him up to date.

'What can I do?' Shanahan asked.

'I don't know. I may need you.'

'I'm with you. I can talk to the police here.'

'Could you stop by my place to see if anyone left a note or left word on my machine?'

'Sure.'

'You know how to get in?'

'Right, all I have to do is blow on the lock and the tumblers turn.'

Kowalski came out on the porch as Cross signed off.

'I'm getting a little antsy,' he said. 'I'll check back in the morning.'

Cross' father called out. He was on the other side of the screen door.

'You know,' he said, 'you're mother has some Canadian Club. She has it around for hot toddies. Heat up a little whiskey, some honey and lemon and what you have is the cure for the common cold. Interested?'

Kowalski smiled.

'How about one of those toddies, hold the lemon and honey and please don't go to any trouble heating it up,' Kowalski said.

'Son?'

'Me too.'

'Well,' Kowalski said, 'I can stay a few more minutes.' He produced a long, round metal container. From inside he extracted a cigar.

Inside Mrs Cross wondered if anyone wanted any dessert.

'Coming up,' his father said.

'You want a toddy?' he asked her.

'Yes, I feel a little sore throat coming on.'

'Me too, and it's good for my heart.'

Kowalski smiled. He lit the cigar, stepped out away from the front porch. He looked at the sky. He looked back. 'What if they're looking for money?'

Cross didn't consider kidnapping for ransom very high on the list of possibilities. He had no money and it would be clear to anyone with any reasoning ability that people living in this ramshackle old farmhouse wouldn't have enough to make kidnapping worthwhile. Even so, that's why he asked Shanahan to check his house in Indianapolis.

'Try to come up with it, I guess,' Cross said.

'You know that the FBI has everything bugged by now. Your computer, your phones, your house, this place, your car.'

'Pretty much figured that. Maybe a little listening in will get them on a road that will lead somewhere.' Cross stepped out into the yard and more quietly, 'If I need to I can disarm all of them, or selectively.'

Cross' father came out with the glasses, a generous pour of whiskey.

'A couple of thoughts,' Cross senior said. 'May not account for much since I'm not in the business of kidnapping or finding kidnappers. But if I stole a little girl from her bed and I lived in that same town or some small town nearby I'd get her inside as quick as I could and hide her in the cellar or an attic.' He looked at Kowalski and his son and seeing that they were paying attention, he continued. 'If I wasn't from around here, I'd get the hell out of here real quick. I'd do it by car and I'd head to the nearest big town and get lost for awhile. I wouldn't be boarding any planes or taking any real long trips.'

'I think you're right,' Kowalski said.

'And,' the senior Mr Cross added, 'I'd make sure I had plenty of gas before I took her.' He nodded, went back inside.

'Makes a lot of sense,' Cross said. He took a deep breath, took a look at the half moon. The light had just pierced a night of gray clouds.

'You doing OK?' Kowalski took a hit off his cigar. The thick smoke swirled in the dim glow.

'Never felt like this. I thought that whole deal with Margot was the worst I could feel. But it's nothing compared . . .' There was more to say, but his voice escaped him.

Kowalski moved toward his Harley.

'Help the police with factual questions having to do with the event and how to identify the kid. They start getting testy or too personal, tell 'em to see me.'

'The local cop on the case seems like a decent guy,' Cross said.

'You can't rely on that,' Kowalski said. 'Thank your folks for dinner and the special drink. I'll keep checking on your girl Margot. She's got to be somewhere. So does Maya.'

Somewhere, Cross thought. The bottom of Lake Michigan, maybe. But he understood Kowalski's warning. Question authority, don't let them question you. That was Kowalski's approach. And he understood there was nothing personal either. The police – and especially the FBI – weren't really interested in justice; they were interested in closing the case. That was the job description. On the other hand, he had to give them credit. If he were law enforcement, any of them, he'd suspect a guy like him, his age, unmarried, living alone, working on bail skips and repos.

It was Maureen's car, so she drove. Shanahan suggested that they go home, where he'd pick up his car and head on over to Cross' place. Maureen had other ideas. It was dark, but wasn't late, and Maureen was up for a trip – and she wanted a chance to learn more about his trip south of the border.

North on Emerson to Emerson Way, connecting with Kessler Boulevard, which used to be the toniest part of town and was still pricey as it curved through the northern neighborhoods to the canal.

Cross' place, unlike the others, was set back off the street. There was, however, activity in front of the steps that led to his home.

Shanahan had Maureen pull over half a block from where dark vans and sedans were parked.

People were carrying boxes and a computer down the stone steps and into the vans. Before she shut off the lights he could see printing on the back of dark sweatshirts.

'What do the shirts say? Can you read them?' he asked Maureen.

'Something about evidence. It said FBI.'

'Oh. Evidence and Response Team. They're serious about Cross.'

A man started toward them in the dim gray light of the moon and the soft, soft light of the streetlamps. Long coat. He walked slow and purposefully.

'Shall we go?' Maureen asked.

'No.' Shanahan got out of the car, walked toward the figure, both in the center of the street like a confrontation in the old West.

'Your boy's in trouble,' Swann said. 'Again.'

'My boy?' Shanahan shrugged it off. 'You mean Cross. He's his own guy.'

'Putting a little distance between you?'

'Not at all. A good friend. Just letting you know there's no ownership. That was outlawed back in Lincoln's time.'

Shanahan respected Swann. A professional cop in the best sense. Not usually quick to judge. Respectful of the law. He wore a flat top and did so throughout its in- and out-of-favor moments. Though what was once blond hair was now gray and his boyish looks were further tortured with wrinkles making him look more like a wizened youth than a man of fifty-something.

'Last couple of years he's been involved in some pretty questionable goings-on. The murder in Broad Ripple. The two hoods whacked out on a farm having something to do with his old girlfriend. Those were highly suspicious shootings. And the girlfriend herself wasn't exactly in the Junior League.'

'You guys keep trying,' Shanahan said. 'And you always get it wrong.'

'Not my doing anyway.' He nodded his head back toward the commotion. 'FBI. I'm just here as a courtesy.'

'You having a proper upbringing and all.'

Swann smiled. 'It'll all come out in the wash, won't it?'

'They're wasting valuable time,' Shanahan said.

'They're by the book,' Swann said. 'And you can't blame them for looking at Cross. As I said he isn't exactly the most reputable citizen in Indianapolis.'

'It's usually the ones that are who aren't.'

'What?' Swann asked.

'Never mind,' Shanahan said.

'What are you doing here?'

'Cross is up in Eaton trying to find the little girl since everyone else is looking in the wrong direction. I'm going to pick up some things for him.'

'Wait until they're gone.'

'I intend to.'

'You have anything I need to look into down here?'

'Not yet. But thanks for asking.' Shanahan said. He wondered how, after all these years and what Swann must have seen, he could be so uncorrupted.

'Call me when you do.' He waved shyly at Maureen. 'Why

don't you two go park on another street for twenty or thirty minutes.'

Instead they went a few streets over to College and had a drink at the Red Key Tavern – another old bar, except a lot cheerier than Harry's. If you looked around you couldn't tell what year you were in. Could have been 1946. Could have been 1956.

Timeless. He looked at Maureen. She fit right in. She was timeless, he thought. She'd fit in anytime anywhere. But he noticed Maureen wasn't intent on finishing her rum and tonic. But holding the glass gave her comfort.

'A penny for your thoughts,' Shanahan said.

'Is that a pick-up line?'

'Yep.'

'Do you think Maya is OK?' she asked.

'I don't know.'

'What does Howie think?' she asked.

'I don't know. I don't know if he knows what he thinks.'

'Who got her?'

Shanahan shook his head. 'Nothing is nudging in any direction. Except there's been no call for ransom.'

The vehicles were gone. The street was quiet. Maureen followed Shanahan up the uneven stone steps into a main yard, the path leading through a clump of cedars. Shanahan used the flashlight Maureen kept in the glove compartment to navigate the darkness. He aimed the light through the dilapidated metal gate. A possum, with evil-looking red eyes, turned and made its way slowly away from them.

The FBI had locked the door behind them, but Howie's lock was old and was pickable by a five-year-old with a bobby pin in thirty seconds. 'Bobby pin,' he thought to himself. When was the last time he thought of bobby pins? Maybe it was the Red Key.

Inside, Cross' place was dark. The government had been thoughtful. They locked the doors and turned off the lights. Shanahan shined the light on the desk a few feet inside the front door, found the lamp switch and turned it on. The rousting was considerate. The place hadn't been torn up.

But if someone had left a note or a message on the answering machine, it was in the hands of the nosy FBI. The computer was gone. The answering machine was gone. The phone – a landline – was still there, but probably bugged.

He was about to use it to call Cross when it rang. Shanahan looked at Maureen, who shrugged. Might be Cross, Shanahan thought. He picked it up.

'Yeah?'

'Mr X, we need to talk. You got a moment?'

'Mmnnn-hmmnn.' He hoped the sound was good enough.

'Howie?'

He was going to give it away.

'Howie?' she asked again.

'This is a friend . . .'

Shanahan got an earful of dial tone.

Shanahan punched in *69. He didn't expect anyone to answer. No one did. But he was able to count the beeps in the redial. Seven. That told him a lot.

Ten

Cross wasn't surprised to learn the FBI had tossed his house. If they didn't plant anything, little harm was done. They would have seen the poverty of his kitchen cabinets, his refrigerator in need of defrost, his bathroom in need of a higher level of sanitation, and the CD collection that implied he was frozen in roughly 1979. That was their problem.

'They're not only going nowhere, they are in the way,' Cross said, cell phone to his ear. 'Anything?' He was outside again. He could see through the kitchen window. His mother was tidying up, though there was nothing left to clean.

'A woman called while I was there,' Shanahan said. 'She asked for Mr X.'

'Damn,' Cross nodded. 'Margot. She called me Mr X when she wanted to be seductive, which usually meant she wanted something other than . . .'

'The redial was only seven digits,' Shanahan interrupted.

'That means she called from a 317 area code, probably from another landline.'

'She's in Indy,' Cross said.

'Seems so. You want me to bring anything up to you?' Shanahan asked. 'Change of clothes?'

'No, I'm coming down in the morning.'

This was good news, Cross thought. Margot must know something about this. There was no reason for her to be in Indianapolis unless it had to do with her daughter. Maybe she had her after all.

His mother's sister was due in from Kansas City. She was a nurse. Great for his father. Great for his mother. Great for him. He would be leaving them in better care than he could provide.

Maybe this was a turning point, he thought. Couldn't get worse.

But it did. Sleep was ruthless. Howie Cross, in the same bed he slept in while Maya was stolen, wrestled with demons he half knew. Ugly, evil-faced beasts hinted at familiarity and made sounds he knew he was supposed to understand – but didn't. The barely budding orchard where he searched for signs of her presence during the day snarled at his failure, the small gullies that formed the rows of future soybeans were filled with blood rushing toward him.

The open window in her bedroom invited him to jump through it. He went to her bed where the impression of young Maya's body on the sheets only amplified her absence. Margot appeared, naked as he often saw her, sexually inviting as she always was, dared him to make love to her.

'We have to find her,' Cross told her.

'Come to me,' she said.

His eyes were drawn to her neck, the elegant swan-like neck. Her body slowly morphed into a strangely sensuous snake. He was drawn to it. Every synapse – all rational thought – shut down. He was giving in, giving in . . .

Morning was fresh. The air was clear, cool. The light was soft, casting no shadows in his room. For a moment, a split second, Cross thought all was right with the world. But reality intruded, followed by remnants of the nightmares. He didn't remember how they ended or if they did.

He allowed himself a moment of self-pity as he descended

the narrow steps down to the hall on the ground floor. Taking care of Maya was perhaps the only good thing he had tried to do in his otherwise worthless life. And look what happened.

There were sounds of stirring in the kitchen.

'I've got to go back down to the city today,' he said. 'We think Margot might be there.'

His mother, who faced the sink, turned back in surprise. His father looked up from the *Muncie Star Press* spread out on the kitchen table as he did every morning Cross could remember. There was still one television in the house. It was rarely on in the morning or during the day and watched during the evening news and perhaps a few programs before nine. There were no computers. Time was held at bay in the Cross household.

'There's a write-up in the paper,' the senior Cross said. 'The police and the FBI aren't talking about much of anything. Don't go bothering about what the paper's saying about you.'

Cross laughed. He knew he had only two choices. Go crawl in a hole or do something. At the moment, he was trying to convince himself to choose the do-something mode.

'Your sister's coming in today, right?' Cross asked his mother.

'We're going to be fine,' Cross' father said.

'We are.' His mother agreed, though with less certainty.

'Look at me,' the elder Cross said, standing up to prove his point. 'I've got all my color back. I've got some energy. Anything you'd like me to do? I could check out some gas stations, see what kind of folks passed through here. You know, just in case.'

'Sure,' Cross said.

His mother gave him a dirty look.

'The doctors don't want him going to bed, right?' he asked his mother.

Cross believed that part of staying alive was having some-thing to do. He knew how he felt when he didn't.

She shook her head. She walked over to him, kissed him on the cheek. 'Have some breakfast before you go gallivanting off.'

In the end, she tried to make light of difficult situations. 'Gallivanting' was a purposeful choice, as if the world were all OK today and he was off to have a good time.

Indianapolis isn't New York or Chicago. But it isn't Grover's Corners either. More than a million live in the 317 area code. The only blessing Cross had was knowing Margot was somewhere in the vicinity. He now believed that if he found her, he'd find Maya, and the nightmare would end.

It was that glint of silver in the haystack that brought a bit of relief as he drove back to Indianapolis. He was also glad to leave the scene of the abduction where every sight, every sound and smell reminded him of what had happened and how he hadn't prevented it.

The blacktop unrolled ahead of him. The narrow road gave way to a wider highway where the landscape opened up to flatlands and big blue skies. Optimism. He clicked on the radio. Maybe the news would tell him something.

I69 eventually came to 465, which looped the city. He went East, around to the Emerson exit. That would take him to Shanahan's house. No need to go home. His computer was gone, his phone was tapped – probably the whole house was bugged.

For Shanahan it was a day for the long walk. Fortunately, it was on flat ground and in comfortable weather. Casey was good on the leash. Now that he was older, he no longer strained against Shanahan's pace. Perhaps, Shanahan thought, the dog could be off leash now, but a squirrel or raccoon would make him crazy and he'd be off in a second to wherever the creature took him.

It was a pleasant mid-morning walk. A creek meandered on the Eastside providing a green swath through the neighborhoods and eventually passing through a public park with a swimming pool (closed until Memorial Day), tennis courts, a baseball diamond, and a children's playground. All were lifeless now.

Earlier in the morning, he told Maureen about what happened in Mexico, only saying that at the second meeting, it didn't work out. He didn't mention Wenders' death. Maybe he would sometime. He just said that he felt like he had left his old commander in the lurch. Instead, they talked about the missing little Maya. They both knew her, enjoyed her curiosity and her all-too-honest, unfiltered commentary. One minute Maya was a kid, the next a jaded woman of the world.

About Wenders and sensing Shanahan's rare unsettled thoughts on the matter, Maureen said, 'What else could you do?'

'I don't know, but it doesn't feel right just leaving like that.'

'For as long as I've known you, you've always done right – except that evening you hid my Swiss Almond Vanilla. That was seriously wrong.'

'For as long as you've known me?' Shanahan said. 'You've known me probably less than ten percent of my existence.

'But for that ten percent . . . pretty damn good,' she said, with an I've-proved-my-point-so-shut-up look. 'Seriously, what could you have done?'

He didn't know.

The long walks helped him think. Today? Nothing.

Casey sniffed, nose buried in last autumn's uncollected leaves. Like most hounds, Casey lived through his nose. Shanahan wondered what all these scents told him. Did they ignite mental images in his brain? Did some scents make him happy? Others sad? Was it possible for Casey to get a real high this way? Could a sniff give him all the vital information he needed to conclude a really sexy Cocker Spaniel had traveled through here recently? At his age, did he care?

Shanahan pulled the green tennis ball from his jacket, unhooked Casey from his leash. The old hound turned eager puppy, running away from Shanahan and looking back like a receiver looking for the quarterback. Shanahan tossed and Casey's arthritic bones forgot their pain. He raced for the ball. The dog was good. Still good. He brought the soggy ball back and Shanahan, mustering all of his diminishing strength, threw it further, up over a mound. Casey disappeared over the small hill.

Shanahan waited. Seemed as if it was taking too long. Just as Shanahan started up the hill, Casey came back over the top, the ball his mouth. He grabbed Casey's collar, hooked the leash, just as a bicyclist whizzed by.

'C'mon old man, let's head back,' Shanahan said.

He caught movement maybe twenty feet away at the top of the rise. The slim Hispanic man with dark hair plastered to his skull turned back, disappeared.

'This way,' Shanahan said, pulling on the leash. Casey, still obsessed with a scent coming from the area, reluctantly followed. At the top of the small hill were two women with strollers, chatting. There was no slim Hispanic man. Was guilt playing tricks on him? Was it the hallucinations he had after being shot in the head returning? Just old age?

He couldn't discount any of the possibilities. Even so, his senses sharpened. As he always did when faced with danger, he became more keenly aware of his environment.

'Let's go home,' he said to Casey who was generally willing

to go wherever Shanahan wanted, but no doubt wished that on occasion he'd be allowed to dally here and there on the way to wherever they were going next.

Children were in school, adults were at work. At this time of the day, closing in on noon, it was still quiet, but still a little cool to be considered lazy. A car passed now and then on the streets that paralleled each side of the parkway. There were a few inches of water in the creek and one could probably find what some folks further south called crawfish.

That would be down in Louisiana where Catahoula hounds like Casey came from. The little pincher-clawed creatures were called crawdads here. Other than a squirrel or two darting about, families of raccoons sneaking out of their hiding places to check out trash cans across the road, and the glassy-eyed possums waddling about in the night, that was the extent of wildlife on this long narrow stretch of nature.

They walked back to the house with a little more intent than they had left it, Shanahan thinking now about what was going on. There were three things that preyed on his mind – did he see who he thought he saw, the whereabouts of little Maya and, more vaguely, what happened to his brother Fritz some sixty years ago.

Eleven

Shanahan could see the pain in Cross' face, in his body. He understood that what the younger investigator felt was a mix of love, fear, frustration, and guilt. Maya was not only someone he learned to love, but also someone he felt deeply responsible for. She was an innocent. And Cross believed he had betrayed that trust.

'Nothing you could have done,' Shanahan said again. It had no effect.

Cross sat across from Shanahan in a booth at Harry's. He sipped absently at his drink, uncharacteristically non-alcoholic.

'That stuff isn't good for you,' Shanahan said.

'I don't understand why Margot didn't just call me and say she wanted Maya back. What could I have done about it? She knows me. She knows I wouldn't have denied her that. It doesn't make sense.'

Shanahan had thoughts about that, but he kept them to himself.

Something else didn't make sense to Cross. If she did take Maya, why is she still here?

'How can we find her?' Shanahan asked.

'If she's here, it has to be about Maya. Otherwise there are a million other places for her to go. This would be one of the last places she'd be if she wanted to get lost. But find her . . . now that's a problem. The only contact she had with this city was the strip club that I helped close down. The girls have all scattered. And all the players, except her apparently, are dead.'

Cross looked at the ceiling and shook his head.

'Somebody wants all these people dead,' Cross said.

'Maybe she knows that. I know I'm not cheering you up. But she was a player . . .'

' . . . and so was Maya. She's trying to save Maya.'

'You were a player too, weren't you?' Shanahan asked.

Judging by the look on Cross' face, Shanahan was pretty sure he hadn't thought about that.

'Harry,' Cross called out, 'could I get a potassium chloride chaser for this Coke?'

'Comin' right up,' Harry said.

'I could try some of the clubs, see if I can recognize any of the girls who danced at the club when Margot did.'

If this was just a regular case, Shanahan would have kidded him about such rough duty ' . . . a dirty job but . . .' Not this time.

'There has to be a better way,' Cross said, looking at Shanahan.

'Tell me everything you know about her. When she was here, where did she go to eat? She like movies? Read books? What about shopping? Upscale, discount? You know what I need.'

Cross nodded and did his best. The unfortunate thing was that he and Margot didn't really share much information. She came to him in order not to be alone. She didn't need to talk. She just wanted him there. His presence was enough. He didn't have to be a good listener. Hell, he didn't even know she lived in Hawaii, or had a daughter, until he tried to find her the last time. They had sex. So it was sex, sleep, and Margot sitting around drinking coffee and smoking cigarettes.

Shanahan looked around. The usual early afternoon regulars had taken their regular stools. He knew them, was one of them for a long time. They were silent, quiet drinkers. All talked out at the moment. Sometimes though, an argument would break out and these old crows on a wire would get fidgety. Property taxes, Reggie Miller coming out of retirement, Payton Manning.

There would be subtle changes of shifts – early afternoon, late afternoon, early evening. Late night ended eleven. There weren't many pop-ins at this kind of bar in this neck of the woods. So the guy sitting at the end of the bar stood out.

Shanahan turned his attention back to Cross.

'Offstage she was a jeans and sweatshirt kind of girl,' Cross said. 'Nice jeans. Designer casual kind of thing. Even the last times I saw her, when she wasn't dancing, when she was on the run, she made sure the basics were taken care of.' Cross paused. He realized this might go some place. 'This is good. No jewelry. Hair and nails. Very important. She would have them done professionally.'

'Wouldn't she have to work? She's not rich, right?' Shanahan asked. 'Unless someone's keeping her.'

'Yeah. That's how she'd work it. She can't stand to be alone.'

'If she had the resources, she could stay at a girlfriends, couldn't she?'

'She didn't have many of those,' Cross said. 'I don't think she got along with women.' He remembered the conversations he had last time with her co-workers. For someone who didn't like to be alone, she also didn't like being close to anyone. He wasn't even sure how close she was with her daughter.

Shanahan thought that they were beginning to narrow, if you could call it that, her areas of interest. But there was no way two guys could scope out all the fingernail parlors and hair salons in the area code. There were probably seventy towns – besides Indianapolis – in the area code. Even phone calls would be an immense undertaking.

And would she use her real name to make an appointment? Good chance she'd think giving a hair stylist a first name

wasn't a security risk, especially if it wasn't her own. It was
easy to make up a name especially if she used cash. You didn't
have to show a passport to get your nails painted. There would
be no conversation, no intimacy with the folks at the parlor.
She was just passing through. Shanahan hoped she hadn't
already done that.

'She called my landline because she knew my cell had
caller ID. She may not know that I know she's within spitting distance,' Cross said.

The new guy at the bar was in his late forties, early fifties,
white. His clothes were blue collar enough, but looked a little
new. The haircut looked military.

Shanahan motioned Harry to come over.

'You want another Guinness or are you going to come to
your senses and order something American?'

'The guy at the bar in the corner . . . don't look now . . .
you know him?'

'I don't have to look. I know who is at the bar. No. First
time. Now why do you ask? You think that I'm not able to
grow my business?'

'Grow your business? Where did you learn that phrase?
You've been reading *The Wall Street Journal*?'

'I got to be prepared.'

'Prepared for what?'

'Look at this,' Harry made a sweeping gesture encompassing
the bar, 'all you old farts are going to die off. Then where
will my business come from?'

'When we all die off, you can serve us at your little place
in hell,' Shanahan said. 'And I'm sure you will have been in
business awhile before we get there.'

'Why are you asking?' Harry asked now in a soft conspir-
atorial tone.

'Just hadn't seen him before,' Shanahan said.

'FBI,' Cross said.

Harry's eyes got big.

'You don't say.' Harry's excitement died down when he
realized what that meant. 'About Maya? Hey, it's going to
work out. It just has to or there's no justice in the world. Not
one iota.'

Shanahan waited after Cross left. He watched the stranger
at the bar. The guy seemed to notice, but didn't leave. Maybe

paranoia was running a little too high – though there was plenty of justification for it. Or, Shanahan thought, he was just one guy of a two-member team and someone else picked up Cross as he left.

'Harry!' Shanahan called out. 'Another one next time you're around this way.'

Harry came over with a Guinness and a puzzled look. Shanahan never had more than one beer in the afternoon.

'See if you can talk the stranger into another drink,' he told Harry in low tones.

'You buying?'

'No. Please just do as I say. Use your charm to get him to order another drink. Pretend your growing your business.'

Harry smiled, nodded, glad to be in on it even if he didn't exactly know what 'it' was.

Shanahan unfolded a copy of *NUVO*, the city's independent weekly. He reached in his pocket, pulled out some reading glasses, acting as if he was settling in for a few hours. Harry delivered the beer. Shanahan poured half a glass, glanced at Harry who engaged the stranger in a conversation.

It took a few seconds before Harry talked the guy into it. He brought back a bottle. 'On me,' Harry said. 'You being a new customer and all.'

The point was that the customer ordered it. Shanahan looked at his watch, feigned surprise.

'Hey, Harry. I almost forgot. I really have to go. You drink this for me, OK?' He brought the beer to the bar and exited through the front. Out into the sun, which while not so bright, blinded him as he emerged from the movie theater darkness inside. Shanahan waited on the sidewalk.

In seconds the man emerged, suffered a moment of light disorientation, then noticed Shanahan.

'You like older men?' Shanahan asked.

'What are you talking about?' Close up and in the light, the guy didn't have the easy-life smoothness of FBI agents. The guy lived a harder life. Looked like a lifer in the military.

'You have a badge?' Shanahan said. 'You better have something if you're stalking me.'

The idea that there was someone spying on him, a man who supplemented his retirement income by spying on others wasn't lost on him. But still . . .

'I don't know what you're talking about,' the man said. He wasn't nervous or he didn't show it if he was.

'You just got a fresh drink and you leave.'

'I just remembered—'

'That was my story. Be original.'

'You're crazy,' the guy said. He walked away.

It was becoming clear: Cross wasn't the object of this guy's surveillance. Shanahan was. This wasn't FBI or CIA or any of the government's many spy agencies. They would have been smoother, and if caught, more arrogant.

Wenders, Shanahan thought. This guy is from the group Wenders was messing with.

'Damn,' he said.

Shanahan drove the few miles back to the house. His window was down. It was, in terms of the temperature, a nice day. April was generally looked upon favorably by the weather gods. After the nasty chilled wind of March and before summer, the world was promising. But April was also a little fickle. Snow wasn't out of the question. Even a deep freeze. And the promise of warmth that coaxed the little buds out of their branches could easily turn out to be sadistic tease. Just when they thought it was safe to come out, a cold wind would invade and the tender little tendrils would be frozen stiff.

Shanahan hadn't escaped Wenders. It didn't matter that he knew nothing but the vague outlines of some conspiracy. Even if there was this threat to American democracy, there was absolutely nothing an old man on an Army pension and a private investigator's license could do about it.

He spent the rest of the afternoon calling nail parlors, having agreed to take those while Cross did the beauty salons. Shanahan asked about a Margot Hudson, starting first in Indianapolis, then spreading out into the surrounding towns – Carmel, Zionsville, Greenwood, Lawrence. No hits. The luck of actually cashing in on this process was about as good as winning the lottery. But there was nothing else to do.

Cross would do the strip clubs in the evening. If Margot hadn't already split, she would soon. Nothing to keep her here. She'd be better off in some remote area or in a city like New York or LA, where it's easy to get lost.

*   *   *

Over dinner, Shanahan told Maureen everything, not just the bullets in Wenders' forehead, but the possibility that he saw Wenders' man, if he was indeed Wenders' man, at Ellenberger Park that morning and the lurker earlier at Harry's bar.

'You didn't tell me because—'

'No need to worry you. I got out. It was over.'

'It wasn't over in your mind then. And it's certainly not over in your mind now.' Her eyebrows rose. It was the victory look. She grinned. 'You need to tell me everything.'

'Do you tell me everything?' Shanahan asked.

'Do you want me to?'

'Maybe,' he said, the cockiness of her response made him think again.

She raised one eyebrow. This was the I'm-warning-you-look. It suggested that Shanahan was about to enter the scary, unknown world of gossip, cosmetics, and . . . feelings. He thought it likely a bluff. She wasn't all that interested in that either, but it was in his best self-interest not to enter a game he couldn't win.

'Maybe not.'

They sat in a small cafeteria at Arlington and Tenth. The place had been around as long as Shanahan could remember. And, like the Red Key, it showed little respect for change. Most of the customers seemed to be in Shanahan's age group, many no doubt on a modest fixed income with a low-level excitement quotient. None appeared to be a member of a malignant private army bent on destruction of the American way of life.

'What do we do?' Maureen said after Shanahan finished the unabridged account of his trip to Puerto Vallarta.

'I have no idea,' Shanahan said. 'I don't know which reporter Wenders talked to. I don't know any of the players.' He sounded like Cross who voiced similar frustration about Maya and Margot earlier. He had nothing, he said, no place to start. There was no place to start on Wenders' death either.

On the other hand, there was every indication that all he had to do was wait, and someone would come to him.

Twelve

Normally Cross wouldn't have found the task so unpleasant. A single guy with needs and a deep appreciation of the feminine form, he had previously and entirely on his own visited these kinds of places. That's where he met Margot too many years ago and the reason he saw her from time to time. Her tour would bring her through Indianapolis two or three times a year and this little chauffeurs' quarters he inhabited was her home away from home.

The thing is he'd done this search for her before. And when he found her, he was finally, he thought, done with her. Not just done with her but over her. Unfortunately, life refused to conform to his wishes or, he thought in this case, reasonable expectations. She was not only back in his life, but she had brought along an innocent for him to feel responsible for, implied that the child might be his in order to add urgency to his guilt. Then she vanishes only to come back to tease him once again. Maya had simply become a new tease. Allow him to love her, then take her away. To add an especially cold-hearted twist to the scheme, she kidnapped the little girl, leaving him to imagine all sorts of horrors.

That's where he was now, mentally, hoping that it was Margot's game, that she was merely playing another one of her sadistic amusements. Of course, he could not be sure. He had to find her.

With a few phone calls and internet searches, Cross mapped out the dozen or so strip bars, catching those that had earlier shows first and then moving on to those that revved up at night.

Before he got out the front door, Cross cell phone rang. It was his old friend, officer Kielinea, from Maui. Apparently, Margot refinanced her house, took cash for her equity, and skipped out on the new and bigger balance. The bank had the house now. No one had seen her or her kid. Margot, ever the pragmatist, followed the thief's admonition: Take money and run.

She was apparently in a cash-gathering, and hopefully child-gathering mood, getting her nest egg together for what? A small place in Paraguay? She was a survivor, wasn't she? None of this should surprise him – all these people connected to the sex slave trade, getting in trouble, getting killed. She's free and alive. Though, of course, the fear of ending up like the others may have sparked her recent activities.

Kielinea also checked her credit cards. She had significant debt, having taken as much as she could in cash months ago. No records of payment or further use. The Hawaiian cop had been more helpful than the local authorities working the case.

Maybe Cross would enjoy this kind of bar hopping again sometime, but for now it was painful work, drudgery, worse than sitting at home punching in phone numbers of beauty salons.

Cross chatted with bartenders, lounge managers, and dancers as much as he could in various clubs throughout the city. Moving from the shiniest and brightest spot to the darkest hole in the wall, he saw more than he wanted to see. None of this was shocking. He was a former vice cop who saw no harm if the dancers did what they did voluntarily.

Sadly, because the law is what it is, making anything more than a bump and grind illegal, women were set up to be exploited – by pimps and by crime syndicates. And Margot, no doubt realizing that her career as a stripper would end before she could apply for social security and ever the opportunist, jumped on the big business bandwagon in a big way, working with people who made innocent young women slaves. He had no idea she had that much coldness in her. Probably, he didn't want to see.

By midnight, he realized he was striking out at the clubs. Few knew her. A couple of dancers and one bartender remembered her from her work at the now defunct Palace of Gold. None of these folks knew much about her, except that she kept pretty much to herself. Didn't socialize with the other girls. Didn't talk about herself. He knew that. All night long, and he found out precisely nothing.

While he had only sipped drinks on his rounds, by the time he hit the last bar at 1 A.M., he had a little buzz on. Instead of making him feel good, it made him feel worse. For all his belief – and he still believed it – that if girls wanted to make a living by removing their clothes, it was their business, not the law's.

In places like this dreary little backroom with a less than stellar specimen trying hard just to stay on her feet and looking more drunk than sexy, he wasn't sure what he thought anymore.

Maybe, he thought, there was a line. But where do you draw it?

This girl, the only girl, in this squalid little place, had hit the bottom rung and it was a matter of time before she was off the ladder altogether. He had gone to the better places first and moved down as the night moved on. This was because Margot was top of the line, or near it anyway, and less likely to have contacts in places like this. Perhaps, for the sake of his sanity, not to mention his sex drive, he should have done it the other way around.

He would have been disappointed at the results if he actually expected something. Yet, the evening left him feeling even less sure of the goodness of mankind than he was before. He wouldn't have thought that possible when he started out.

Home, he told himself, while he was under .08, or hoped he was. The evening exhausted him. The day exhausted him. He drove carefully and maybe because he was so conscious of getting home without a stop by the police, he was especially alert to his surroundings. Otherwise he might not have noticed the car following him.

Shanahan was pretty sure he had gone through most of his life without dreaming. Maybe as a kid. But as an adult, he didn't recall a lively other world . . . until lately. He'd be the first to admit that he may have dreamed and simply left them behind when he awoke. Now he had them – or remembered them – regularly.

The dreams began when he uncovered a photograph from his childhood, in which his brother Fritz was partially caught by the camera. As far as Shanahan knew, the only likeness of his older brother that existed was this one – a portion of a young boy's leg, the rest of his body escaping from the frame. As far as Shanahan knew, the dreams began then and became more frequent and more vivid after he suffered a bullet to the head. There were times when dreams, hallucinations and reality were indistinguishable. His head was better. No more hallucinations, but the vivid dreams continued.

Awake now, he could hear Maureen's light breathing.

He glanced at the clock radio. The digits said 12:44. He'd had this same dream before – a few times. The young Fritz was in a maze of intersecting hallways and stairways, some leading up, some leading down. Each time Shanahan got close, Fritz would look back for a moment and disappear. But there was something about Fritz's look that urged Shanahan to follow. Was it to find Fritz? Or, Shanahan thought, as he slipped out of bed and headed for the bathroom, was he merely supposed to follow him. Maybe Fritz was leading him somewhere. Maybe he should let him.

Shanahan could find his way in the dark. A small light stayed lit in the bathroom. He didn't bother switching on any others. He was wide awake. The house was chilly. He went to the kitchen, where another little bulb provided enough light to guide him to the bourbon. He filled the glass with a couple of inches of J.W. Dant.

He went into the living room. Casey was asleep in front of the fire place, picking up a little heat from what little was left of the evening fire. He didn't budge as the floors squeaked under his feet. He went to the front window, peeked out through the side of the curtains. There was enough of a moon for him to spot a dark sedan.

Could be a neighbor's car, he thought. But the events of the day prevented him from accepting what otherwise would be obvious. Maybe he should stay up. Casey's hearing had diminished over the years. Maybe they needed to bring a new pup into the household. Shanahan went to the other windows and looked out. Nothing. Grabbing a blanket from the hall closet, he settled on to the sofa. He took a sip, enjoyed the slow burn down his throat and the warmth gathering in his old bones.

'Did you need something from my scarf drawer?' Maureen asked as she came into the kitchen.

'I didn't even know you had a scarf drawer,' he said, sipping his coffee. He had gotten through most of the morning paper, leaving the obituaries until last. 'You are up early.'

'Not as early as you,' she said. 'You slept on the sofa?'

'Had trouble sleeping.' He handed her a glass of orange juice. 'You have time for breakfast?'

'No, early meeting. You didn't go through any of my drawers?'

'No, why?'

Einstein hopped up on the table, seemingly interested in the discussion, but more likely reminding them he was now ready for breakfast.

'Just that things were a bit mixed up.' She shrugged, downed her orange juice.

'Mixed up?'

'Yes, I keep the solids together lighter to dark, the patterns separated by kinds of pattern. Everything was reversed.'

'I didn't realize you were so . . .'

'. . . so what. I am so what?' She smiled. She had him down for the count.

'Orderly. Organized. Fantastically organized.'

'You were going to say something else.'

'More important, you're sure this isn't the way you left your scarves?'

She looked at him. The playfulness was gone.

The two of them investigated the house. Nothing was missing and they couldn't be sure anything else was disturbed. But Maureen reiterated her belief that someone had rearranged her scarves. If Maureen was right, whoever did it must have done it while Shanahan took Casey for a walk.

And if someone had been there, they had done so with a high level of professionalism and near meticulousness. They had bypassed a new alarm system. They got in and out undiscovered except for this weird habit of Maureen's to obsess about her scarf drawer.

Maybe this was the FBI after all. Maybe he didn't see the Mexican guy. Maybe the guy at the bar was somebody who wandered in because he was in the neighborhood. Maybe the FBI connected Shanahan to Cross and was investigating him as a possible suspect. The local police knew that the two PIs were friends, that they worked together, had a beer together from time to time.

Shanahan shook his head. Things were getting muddled. Who was it and what did they want? Who's on first?

What Cross wanted to do was confront the person who was tailing him. There were reasons not to. One of them was he didn't know how dangerous the other person was. The second was that it was probably one of the law enforcement agencies assigned to do so. The third reason was that knowing he was being followed and the follower not knowing he knew meant Cross had a slight advantage. At least that's what he told himself last night when he put a chair up to the front door, the one with the lock so easy to pick. He slept with his gun.

He slept through most of the morning unaware of the world around him, drifting on the edge of consciousness then slipping back into the warm waters of an island lagoon.

It was after ten when he finally agreed to leave paradise. He slept well, very well. He wasn't sure why. Nothing had been resolved and time was running out. But he felt rested, his eyes were wide open, and he felt like he was thinking clearly, which led him directly to the fact that he didn't know what to do. His stomach sank as reality set in again. A little girl. If she wasn't dead, her life and mind were at risk. Unless she was with her mother. And then, who knew.

If it wasn't obvious before – and it should have been, might have been in a fashion – Margot was unknowable. She made herself that way. She didn't talk about what it was like growing up, where she grew up, where she went to school, what she liked to read, or what movies were her favorites. She didn't talk politics. She rarely laughed, and when she did, it was at jokes that only she got.

What Cross knew was that she was afraid to be alone, especially during the gray hours between night and day. He knew she liked sex, coffee, cigarettes and hard liquor. She was a sensuous dancer and she was good in bed. And she was a survivor. That was the inventory. The complete inventory.

The kitchen sink was full of unwashed dishes, the counter littered with containers that once held take out. He made coffee, glancing out of the window at the day. Was his tail still outside? Maybe he should bring them a cup of coffee. Then surreptitiously, insidiously it came to him. Margot's anonymity was her attraction. It was because he didn't know her that he was so obsessed with her. She wasn't a real person. Whatever that said about her, it said more about him.

He shook his head to dismiss the introspection. The only thing that was important at this moment was Maya. He would remind himself of that every chance he could.

When the coffee was ready he took it outside. The morning was still chilly. The sun was up, but fighting to penetrate a thin haze. At a little past ten, the grass was still wet with dew.

He traipsed barefoot and shirtless down the path toward the gate, beyond its creaking decrepitude on to the lawn, skirting the gravel path to walk on the softer grass. He descended the uneven stone steps – awkwardly – to the street.

He saw a few parked cars, but didn't think any of them were occupied. He turned to go back up the steps when his coffee cup exploded, sending hot coffee and shards of ceramic all over his chest and face.

Thirteen

A tall, good-looking black guy, Lieutenant Collins, aka Ace to his friends, stood in Cross' middle room, aka office. The guy wore nice clothes, jacket not off the rack, pants with sharp creases. He stood there, his face showing something between boredom and amusement, with his notebook open, pen in hand.

'Attempted murder?' Collins asked.

'Odds favor it,' Cross said.

'Why is that?' Collins asked, 'other than the fact you and your pal Shanahan seem to attract trouble. You know,' he smiled, 'you're such good customers we should set up an account, maybe arrange an automatic deduction from wherever it is you bank.'

'Who says I have a bank,' Cross said.

'Maybe this was an errant hunter,' Collins said, grinning.

'That was your thought when that crackpot shot Shanahan. You got that wrong, remember?'

'And yet here I am back again?'

'Maybe if you'd done your job the first time—'

'Watch it, Cross. You are a private eye. I'm a cop. You know who wins pissing contests.'

'Figure it out. Everyone involved in the sex-slave thing that Herrmann was running has been killed, including Herrmann.'

'Some suspicious homicides huh? You sure you want me to investigate those?'

'No, investigate this case, OK?'

'Your old girlfriend is still alive, isn't she?'

'I don't know,' Cross said. 'Maybe she's dead. Or maybe she isn't and that's why she's hiding. Maybe that's why she kidnapped her daughter. Oh, and her Hawaiian boyfriend was hit.'

Collins gave Cross a second look. Apparently found something interesting.

'And you?' Collins asked.

'Not yet dead, but shot at, if you'll recall. And if you do happen to remember why you are here, you might bring me hope that at least you're picking up the fuzzy outlines of the situation.' Cross sat at his desk, where his computer used to be.

'And all this is connected to the missing little girl?'

'Could be,' Cross said. 'Probably. I don't know. She saw stuff. You might want to investigate if you remember how.'

Collins let the bullets bounce off his expensive suit.

'Now for a really foolish question. Do you have any other enemies?'

'People keep asking me that and I keep telling them that I do.'

Cross had already told him that he saw no one. Once the cup splintered into a thousand pieces he dove for cover behind the bushes on the hillside. He also told Collins that it was pretty clear that the police had Cross in their sites as a suspect, if not the prime suspect, in Maya's disappearance. Collins already knew that. Cross knew he knew it and understood that's why the lieutenant came out personally. Collins was pretty high up to be taking these kinds of calls. Private investigators weren't high on the list of the city's influential citizens. But missing kids, that could bring in the networks.

'You never know. I've offended enough people in my life for at least one of them to hold a grudge. But the timing . . .'

'The timing,' Collins grinned. 'Yes, the timing. Looks less like you did something with the little girl if someone's shooting at you. You become a victim too. And the cops are out searching for someone else. How does that sound?'

'Glad you have such an open mind,' Cross said, going toward the door, and nodding toward the exit in an effort to lead Collins in that direction. 'Just what a good investigator needs.'

Collins followed but halted just outside. He turned back around.

'I've always been puzzled about people like you,' Collins said. 'Trouble seems to follow you around. Is that just the luck of the draw? I mean sometimes if you throw a nickel in the air it will land on tails half dozen times in a row, beating the odds. Is it just a weird cycle with you? Or are you causing it?'

'I wonder that myself,' Cross said. 'When you figure it out, let me know.'

He swung the door closed with a little more force than was necessary.

The lieutenant's questions hurt, but thirty seconds of self-pity were twenty-nine seconds too long. There was only one priority and that was Maya. And other than searching for the girl's mother, he had no direction at all.

Cross' cell emitted its understated Beatle lyric, 'You say goodbye, I'll say hello.'

He flipped it open. His father was on the other end. A woman, the elder Cross said, about thirty-five, pretty as a picture, filled the tank of her little red, brand new, Toyota at a station near an interstate off-ramp in the middle of the night of Maya's disappearance.

'How'd he know it was brand new?'

'It was this year's model, he said.'

'Thanks, Dad,' Cross said.

'There was a bumper sticker, if that helps.'

'It would. There are a lot of little red Toyotas in this world.'

'Keep Honking, I'm Reloading.'

Cross thanked his father. It would help. The information suggested two things. The car wasn't a rental. People don't put bumper stickers on rental cars. And it was unlikely that Margot bought it. She wouldn't have troubled herself with putting a sticker on her car. And humor wasn't high on her list of priorities. It was likely someone else was involved. Who and how involved were the new questions?

Shanahan finished his phone calls. Only one was even remotely promising. It wasn't a 'Margot,' but an attractive woman in her late thirties, early forties, model quality who had come in less than a week ago. She was a walk-in. The woman at the shop downtown didn't have a name, wasn't sure the woman gave her one. Didn't use a charge card, paid in cash.

When Shanahan got the call from Cross saying that Margot would either be using someone else's credit card or paying cash, Shanahan bumped up the lead rating from promising to likely. He would check it out personally.

'You got a date, handsome?' Maureen asked as Shanahan shaved.

'Mmnnn-hmmnn,' Shanahan said, pulling the safety razor through the lather.

'Pretty?'

'Don't know yet.'

'But definitely a woman?'

'Mmnnn-hmmnn.'

'Young?' Maureen was enjoying herself. That made him happy.

'I'd guess,' Shanahan said. 'Don't you have a house to sell somewhere?' She grinned. 'Could you find a picture of Margot?' he asked her.

'Where would I find one? In one of your old love letter boxes?'

'I don't have a love letter box. Check it out on the machine.'

'Machine?' she giggled.

'The electronic contraption. Go find the Golden Palace or the Palace of Gold, whatever it is. Google it, right? Isn't that what you do? Google – and see if they have a photograph of the dancers. Maybe there's one of Margot. You could print it out for me.'

'I could.'

'Would you?'

'I would.' It looked like she was contemplating carrying on the game awhile longer. She didn't. She would grant him his wish without further harassment.

Shanahan had been forced into ATMs and cell phones, but he couldn't bring himself to become a friend to the computer. Fortunately, Maureen was good at it. Her real estate work demanded it, but once she got the hang of it she used it to search out restaurants, vacations, and all sorts of things. He hoped the fact that the strip club was boarded up didn't mean the image he sought was irretrievable.

She was setting up her laptop in the kitchen while he finished dressing. He was buttoning his shirt as he entered.

'Beautiful shirt,' she said, nibbling on grapes.

'Yes.'

'Did you buy that yourself?'

'No, it was a gift from this woman. We had a torrid affair.'

'Is this her?' Maureen asked, showing a dancer named Margot.

'I did not have sex with that woman,' Shanahan said.

She acknowledged his feeble attempt at humor with an equally feeble smile.

'Yes.' He gave in. 'Could you print that?'

'That was Howie's girlfriend?' she asked, working the keyboard.

'A girl anyway. I think he had sex with that woman.'

'And Maya's mother,' Maureen added.

'Biologically it appears.' Shanahan went to the kitchen door.

Casey took advantage of his owner's proximity to go out. A light breeze with a hint of coolness came through the screen. Outside the sky was blue and the redbud tree was more feathered with blossoms than the last time he looked. He thought about calling Cross, but running this down was something that he could do himself. Nothing else was pressing that he could do anything about.

'You staying?' he asked Maureen.

'Just between appointments,' she said. 'I'm going back out in a few minutes.'

Einstein crossed the kitchen slowly, his fur taut on his bones. He searched for a patch of sun.

'I'll wait with you,' he said. 'Why don't you wait to come home until I get back?'

She looked at him, head crooked, eyes squinting.

'The scarf drawer,' he reminded her.

'You remember . . . we don't do the Tarzan–Jane thing.'

'You mean swing from trees?'

'No, I don't need you to play the role of protector,' she said. It was one of those rare moments of seriousness in their conversations. And he should have known better. They had covered that territory before. 'I can take care of myself. I have a roll of quarters and a revolver in my bag.'

'It's a very dangerous bag, Maureen. I'm sorry I questioned your ability.'

She looked at him hard and long trying to determine if he was being sincere.

He could not laugh. Lord, he thought, don't let me laugh or even grin.

* * *

Her face was fifty. Her hairstyle was twenty-three. Streaks of her hair, her eyelids and her lipstick were magenta. The name 'Vikki' was embroidered on her pink smock. She didn't try to hide her disappointment when she saw that the private eye she talked to on the phone was old enough to be her father, or grandfather depending on whether she was as old as her hair or as old as her face.

'Is this her?' Shanahan asked.

Vikki nodded.

'What do you know about her?'

The place was unpleasant on a number of levels – he wasn't fond of the rose and pinks and lavenders that dominated the room and dominated Vikki herself. He wasn't fond of the traces of ammonia, formaldehyde and alcohol that hung in the air – the near deadly soup made from hair spray, shampoo, conditioners and chemicals for permanents.

He much preferred the inside of Harry's, dark with smells of stale beer, tobacco, and – depending on which booth you sat in – urine.

'I told you, there's not much to tell.' She looked around nervously. Perhaps she had work to do. 'She didn't give her name, paid by cash, and wasn't much of a talker.'

Vikki, uninterested in what she might have perceived as an adventure before he got there, looked like she might shut down and send him away. Shanahan showed her his license. Made things seem a bit more official, a bit more mandatory than they were.

'What did she drive?'

'I didn't pay any attention. She could've taken the bus.'

'Nobody takes the bus. What time was her appointment?'

Vikki went to her book, thumbed through it. 'Three thirty.'

'Afternoon?'

'What do you think?' Vikki asked, rolling her eyes.

'You never know. What did she have done?'

'You mean . . . like her hair?'

'What do you think?' Shanahan rolled his eyes.

'She went from blonde to deep brown.' Again, Vikki looked around, perhaps for a customer to rescue her. A woman under a dryer was the sole customer. Shanahan was surprised this fifties science-fiction looking object was still in use. The customer was reading a magazine, oblivious to what went on around her.

'Was it cut?'

'No, it was long. A little trim, for the split ends, that's all. She had me put it up.'

'Up?'

'Up,' Vikki said. 'On top of her head, a little French roll.'

'She said nothing?'

Vikki shook her head.

'What was she wearing?'

'A sweat suit. Gray.'

'Jewelry?'

'A watch,' she said smiling. 'Cartier.' Her eyebrows rose appropriately. 'No rings or earrings.'

'A purse?'

'No.'

'Where'd she keep her money?'

'In a pocket, I guess. Yes, she pulled the bills from her pocket.'

'She make or receive any calls?'

'No.'

'She's a new customer. Why did she choose you?'

'I don't know. She didn't say.'

'You didn't ask?'

'No. Are we done?' It was a statement rather than a question. 'Wait,' she said, a thought visibly crossing her face. 'Yellow Pages. When I said I wasn't sure we could fit her in, she reminded me that the ad said walk-ins.'

Shanahan looked at her.

She answered his question before he asked it.

'We only advertise in the Yellow Pages.'

It was a worthwhile trip. It was Margot. He got her change in identity. Also, if she wasn't carrying a bag, it's likely she didn't travel far. Maybe she walked. It was likely she looked in the phone book to find a place nearby.

It was speculation, but at this point even having enough information for wild speculation was better than what they had before.

And this is how it's done. Hours of boring phone calls and once in awhile the tedious attention to detail is rewarded.

The shop was on the edge of downtown, near Massachusetts Avenue. He'd bet that Margot was hiding somewhere in the general area, probably less than a mile. He'd start with the idea that she walked there. If she abducted the kid, then it was likely she was living with someone who was taking care of her and the kid, someone who had a day off during the week or someone who worked nights.

Shanahan decided he'd scope out the area. He was under no illusion that he'd find her wandering the streets; but he'd get a sense of where the residences were in the perimeter he would draw later.

It was still a needle in a haystack, but the haystack, he was pretty sure, was smaller now.

A fine rain had come up while Shanahan was inside. The air was fresh, all the more so compared to the polluted atmosphere of the salon. He took a deep breath. He would call Cross when he got back to the house.

Fourteen

Cross pulled his windbreaker up over his head as he made his way out of his house and into the cool rain, moving down the path to the steps and toward his car. All he could see was the gravel and his own feet moving him along. Shanahan's call – and the call from his father – brought him some joy in what had been a series of negative emotions – sorrow, anger, despair. His spirits were higher than they'd been in a long time. He agreed with his older friend's analysis. She was cooped up somewhere in the Massachusetts Avenue neighborhood.

Finding a car on the street was easier than finding a stripper in a house somewhere. Without that he wasn't quite sure how he would conduct a search. What he would do is meet Shanahan at a bar on the Avenue and they would discuss procedure.

The stone steps were not only steep, but now slippery and just as he was ready to lower his jacket and check for anyone out to shoot him, he nearly fell on his butt. Just as he stepped into the street, someone – he couldn't see the person because his jacket blocked his peripheral vision – grabbed him. Cross thought it was someone helping him gain his balance. This turned out to be a false assumption.

His jacket was used as a hood that was pulled down all the way over his head. He could see nothing. His arms, likewise, were rendered useless. Next, in the darkness, he was off the ground and on to a metal floor, where he was completely restrained in very short order. Plastic cuffs on his wrists and ankles. Whoever they were – and there had to be at least two of them – knew what they were doing. They had no doubt done this before.

He heard the metal sound of a door sliding shut. He was pretty sure he was on the floor of a van. The engine was running. He felt the van lurch forward, then smooth out.

The little salon was within walking distance of some of the downtown hotels – though Shanahan thought that Margot wouldn't want the expense or the public exposure of a hotel room. He figured she was here within a mile square of the salon, here in these historic neighborhoods – Chatam Arch and Lockerbie – where old homes had been restored, old factories turned into condos, nice restaurants, galleries. It was a mix of young singles and newly marrieds seeking something safely edgy among the remnants of a grittier, claw-out-a-living population.

Shanahan sat at the meeting place, the Abbey, waiting for Cross. The elder detective felt out of place among the young, mostly alternative types. This coffee shop, in the heart of the Avenue's Arts District, was the spot for students, poets, artists and what few anarchists inhabited this very Midwestern, mainstream city. Shanahan, who found the place refreshing in a town full of chain store everything, nonetheless couldn't help but feel like a dinosaur at a robot convention.

On his second cup of coffee on top of what he had at home, Shanahan was getting jittery. He wasn't sure whether it was the caffeine or the growing impatience. Probably both. He had given Cross enough time to get there. Cross said he was heading out the door as he clicked off his phone. Cross would have had to come all the way from the north side. Still, barring an accident, he should have been there half an hour ago.

Cross stayed quiet. Instinct suggested he ask what this is all about; but he was unlikely to get answers. Instead, he would listen and feel the ride, try to get a sense of where they were going. If the sliding door was on the right side of the van, which it usually was, and he was taken in a straight line to it, then it was likely they were headed north.

Judging by the distance they traveled before stopping and the length of the wait, the turns, one right and one left, the sound of traffic, Cross was pretty sure they were at the intersection of 56th and Illinois. He lost track of specific spots on this little journey, but he sensed they were heading north still and it was likely, based on the next two turns and the gradual change in direction that they just might be on curving Spring Mill Road. He had taken this route many, many times and was sure he was right.

They weren't heading for an interstate. They were either heading for farmland on old highways – that would be a long trip – or they had some residential spot in mind. It turned out to be residential. He felt the van slow down, go over a small curb, then stop. He heard a garage door opening. The van moved forward slowly a short distance, then stopped again. The ignition was turned off. The garage door closed.

They hadn't gone that far. The whole trip was maybe five minutes. Cross surmised he was still in the city. Probably a nice home somewhere. There were several different kinds of homes and different kinds of neighborhoods in the area – sixties' contemporaries fairly close together in some areas, huge mansions on cul-de-sacs in others.

Shanahan found a public phone outside and dialed Cross' cell. It rang four or five times and went to voicemail.

'Call me,' Shanahan said and disconnected.

This was unlike Cross. While many considered him a wild card – and it was true he wasn't conventional in any sense of the word – he did, in fact, keep his word. Shanahan found that when Cross made a commitment, rare as that was, he came through.

Shanahan drove up to Cross' place. Cross' car was there, but Cross wasn't. This wasn't good. He picked the lock and checked the house, hoping he wouldn't find a body. After all, Cross had been shot at. To his relief, there was no body. No sign of disturbance beyond the detective's usual display of bad housekeeping. The next thing that came to Shanahan's mind was that he had been arrested in connection with Maya's disappearance.

He sat at Cross' desk, dialed his friend at IPD, Lieutenant Swann. Swann did some checking but came up empty. His friend, the quiet, by-the-book homicide cop said that Shanahan might check the FBI or the Eaton police. Could be the state police too, apparently.

Shanahan found the phone book, dialed the local office of the FBI. Nothing. They couldn't comment on open cases, period. Shanahan called the Eaton Police. They were more forthcoming. They were holding no one. It was an ongoing investigation, they said. Shanahan didn't tell them Cross was missing. It wouldn't look good.

Shanahan sat at the desk for the moment, thinking. After a few moments he realized that if Cross had been arrested and if he made his one phone call, it would be to his lawyer, who was no doubt, James Fenimore Kowalski.

'This better be good, Shanahan. I have a chicken roasting in the oven, a bottle of Pinot Noir open and I've got *The Godfather* on DVD. Whatever do you have that is more important?'

'Do you ever work?'

'When it's essential to my being able to purchase a nice bottle of Pinot.'

'It's three in the afternoon,' Shanahan pointed out.

'You, my friend, are a captive of time, provincial, pinched by convention.'

'Has Cross called you?'

'No. Perhaps he has better sense than you do.'

Shanahan explained the situation.

'Cold chicken is good,' Kowalski said. 'The wine will keep.'

Cross was in a small sterile room – sterile in the sense that the walls were freshly painted white and the floor was freshly carpeted beige. No furniture except for the metal folding chairs. Three of them. Cross, still handcuffed, sat in one. A man wearing a black hood, with eyeholes and another for the mouth, sat in another. The other guy, who he recognized as the man from the bar, stood by the window. He peered out the edge of the closed Venetian blinds. He seemed nervous.

'Anybody think to bring the cards?' Cross asked.

No response.

To the guy in the hood. 'And for the Klan guy here, black is the new white?'

'Let me know when you're done with the show,' said the man in the hood.

'Anybody out there from Sheboygan?' Cross asked, gesturing broadly to an imaginary audience.

They waited in silence.

Cross knew it was a sign of weakness to be the one to break it; but he had things to do, people to find.

'FBI?'

The two of them looked at each other. The one by the window looked befuddled.

'Then you're not. You the guys who shot at me?'

The two guys looked at each other again.

'Not yet,' said the guy in the hood. 'What are you talking about?'

'OK, do you have the kid?'

'What kid?' said the guy at the window, his face showing complete confusion.

'Well, you see I have the police after me, the FBI too. They think I kidnapped a little girl who may or may not be my daughter. And earlier someone shot at me and destroyed my favorite coffee cup. And if you're not part of all that crap, then who the fuck are you?'

No answer.

'I'm beginning to feel like some big dark hole in space drawing all the crazies in like some cosmic super magnet.'

'What we would like to know, Mr Cross,' the man in the hood said, 'is where is Mr Shanahan keeping the information?'

'I think you want Dan Rather.'

'We're serious.'

'What information?'

'The information Mr Shanahan received from his client.'

It didn't make sense. He didn't wish these two on his old friend, but why weren't they asking *him*? 'If you want to know what *Mister* Shanahan knows, why don't you ask *Mister* Shanahan? Why do you have me here at this particular inquisition? Seems a little inefficient if you ask me. Or stupid.'

'No one asked you,' the man at the window said.

'Oh, I see,' Cross said looking at the man in the hood, 'You ask the questions and he is in charge of witty commentary.'

Cross looked around. There was nothing to give away where he was or what was outside the door.

'This your place?' Cross asked. 'You guys live together?'

'You're scoring points you don't want to score,' the man by the window said.

Cross leaned forward to engage the hooded man.

'You must be Mr Bigshot. Your mask. You must be important.'

'I am,' the man said. There was humor in his voice. 'Glad you can approach these discussions with a sense of mirth.'

Mirth? Cross thought to himself.

'Well, your silly little hood kind of adds to the mirthful mood. It's quite festive.'

'You don't want me to take it off,' the man said. 'I promise you that. Now would you care to help us out so we can help you out?'

'I haven't had any discussion with Shanahan about any information, or any case, for that matter. I have no idea what you are talking about. And I have other problems. Very serious problems. So, as Mr Bigshot, you must be the smart one.' He looked at the guy by the window. 'Sorry.' He returned his gaze to the hooded one. 'So here is the bottom line.' He spoke slowly, clearly. '*I can't help you!*'

'Oh, but you can,' Mr Bigshot said. 'You are going to be a tremendous help. I'm grateful already.'

Fifteen

Shanahan didn't like what he was thinking as he came in the back door of Harry's. Did Cross take a powder? He didn't believe it, but objectively he had to consider it. Did someone drop by and make an offer he couldn't refuse? Lead him to the kid? Maybe the person or people who abducted Maya? Maybe Margot stopped by and they went off to . . . where?

Harry nodded a hello. Shanahan asked him if Kowalski was there yet.

'It's not a big place,' Harry said, 'you see him?'

It was a silly question, Shanahan thought, but he was distracted.

'Get you a beer,' Harry said, his voice a little softer.

Not too long ago, Shanahan remembered, Harry was upset when Shanahan met folks at his bar, thinking that the old detective was taking advantage of his good nature and using the bar as his personal office. Shanahan didn't argue, but continued to meet clients there.

While a good bartender with an unlimited supply of funny stories that Harry told 'as true as your mother's blue eyes,' he was slow on the business side. Shanahan, his friends, and his clients bought drinks and one day, no doubt, Shanahan thought, after years of complaint, Harry figured that out.

Shanahan sat in a booth toward the back, where on the last Friday of the month he, Maureen, Cross and Kowalski played Euchre, or more often a version of it called 'Dirty Clubs.' No games this afternoon. There were missing people to find, more of them, it seemed every time the sun came up.

Kowalski was heard before he was seen. The sound of his Harley cozying up to the curb outside shook the bar. A few minutes after the sound died, daylight came through the door like a gunshot, and the smoke of the wild-haired, silver-streaked bearded homo sapien's cigar preceded him.

'Good Lord,' Harry said, 'you'd think it was the Second Comin'.'

'Watch them swingin' doors,' said one of the old customers who – normally quiet as a church mouse – couldn't resist. The arrival was a little too grand for a small, dingy neighborhood bar on an otherwise quiet afternoon.

'Didn't mean to cause such a stir,' Kowalski said, taking off his wet yellow slicker and sliding in the other side of the booth from Shanahan.

'I think you need to work on your entrances,' Shanahan said.

Kowalski grinned, puffed on his cigar.

'Not big enough?' he asked.

'Maybe you should get more in touch with the inner you,' Shanahan said.

Harry came over with a cup of coffee.

'That's not just coffee, is it?'

'Wouldn't dream of it,' Harry said.

'That's it,' Kowalski said to Harry, 'great minds.' Then to Shanahan. 'Why I rode all the way down here, missed my basil roasted chicken I don't know. I have nothing to add to all of this.'

'I don't either. But we've got three missing people,' Shanahan said. 'Cross, his former girlfriend, and Maya.'

'The kid, right?'

'Yes, Maya's the kid.'

'Maybe Papa Bear, Mama Bear, and Baby Bear are all in the same place.'

'That would be handy,' Shanahan said.

'Well, there you go.' The lawyer acted as if he was going to scoot back out of the booth. 'Glad I could be of help.'

Shanahan downed the shot of J.W. Dant and followed it with a sip of his Guinness.

Kowalski settled back in.

'Haven't finished my coffee,' he said.

'Interesting choice of hideaways,' Cross said. 'I'd have gone for an old meat-packing plant or maybe a dark cellar. You do want me to be afraid, don't you?'

'We won't be here long,' said Mr Bigshot. 'But there's no point in being uncomfortable.'

'If that's the case you should have done something about the furniture. Something a little more comfy. A man with your trendy fashion sense . . . I expected more.'

'We won't be here long,' the man repeated, this time with a sardonic tone.

'Yeah, we probably shouldn't,' Cross said. 'The FBI probably followed me anyway. I thought you were the FBI, but since you're not . . . By the way, what are you? Are you important enough to have initials?'

The guy by the window looked out again. Cross thought he had heightened the guy's natural anxiety.

'I need for you to make a phone call for me,' Mr Bigshot said. 'Your friend, Mr Shanahan. Tell them we have you. Tell them that we are going to kill you if he doesn't turn over the material to us.'

Cross tried to think of something to do or say. He didn't want to do that.

'Give him the phone,' Bigshot said to the other guy.

The other guy pulled a cell phone from his jacket pocket. He punched in the numbers.

'We know enough about Mr Shanahan,' said Bigshot, 'to know that threatening him would do no good.'

'What makes you think that I can do any better?'

'Two things, Mr Cross. I think he just might give it up because he can't allow a friend of his to die. That's the code. And two, if he doesn't respond and we do kill you, then he'll know we mean business, and we have another loved one to work on. So, it's a no lose situation. We get it now or after your dead.'

The guy had keyed in the number and was waiting.

'Clever,' Cross said.

'Got an answering machine,' the guy said, closing the phone.

'You could have left a message,' Cross said. 'That's rude.' He was doing his best to keep it light. However, the idea of his death hovered more than a little unpleasantly and he couldn't describe the feeling he had about Maya, and how all of this was keeping him from finding her. He had this feeling that if he was dead, she was lost.

'Check with Hector,' Bigshot said.

The man punched in some numbers.

Cross' mind darted from one thing to another. How bizarre was this that he was at the center of two unrelated horrors? He knew there were people in the world who had it worse. There were hurricanes and earthquakes. There was Darfur, Bangladesh, New Orleans during and after Katrina, and Iraq during shock and awe. But this? Who were these people? What was Shanahan involved in? Cross knew nothing about it and wondered if, in fact, Shanahan knew anything about it.

'He's at the bar,' the man said.

'Call the bar,' Bigshot said.

The man pulled out a small notebook, squinted, carefully punched in a new set of numbers.

After a moment, the guy said, 'Yeah. I need to talk to Mr Shanahan.' He handed the phone to Cross.

'We got a Shanahan here,' Harry said loud enough for Shanahan to hear. 'I don't know about a Mr Shanahan,' he said to the caller, 'but we got a Shanahan here. Wait a minute.' Harry motioned for the detective to come up to the bar.

'Haven't you heard about cell phones?' Kowalski asked as Shanahan slid out of the booth and headed toward the bar.

'Yeah,' Shanahan said. Harry hovered nearby.

'Cross, what's up? Did you find out anything?'

'Well I found out that you are in possession of some highly desirable information,' Cross said.

'I am?'

'I was afraid of that.'

'What's going on?'

'Well, it's kinda funny, depending on how you look at it. I'm in this nice little sterile room in some empty house some-where dying of paint fumes. I don't know exactly where and the guy at the bar you thought was following you was following me. There's a man pretending to be a low-tech Darth Vader who insists that you have something that he wants. And to top it off, he says he'll kill me if you don't give it to him.'

'Are you pulling my leg?'

'Shanahan, I've got a little girl I'm desperate to find, but at the moment I'm handcuffed at the wrists and ankles and these guys who don't appear to be police or government of any kind think that I'm the way to your heart.'

'Damn,' Shanahan said.

'Do you understand any of this? Cross asked. 'Because I sure as fuck don't.'

'Let me talk to the guy in charge.'

Shanahan heard a muffled, 'He wants to talk with you.' He heard the sound of a reply but not the words.

'He says he doesn't want to talk to you. You know this isn't a spring holiday for me. These guys want what you were given in Mexico. What is this all about? You didn't—'

'Tell the man that he's not in a bargaining position, that he needs to talk with me directly. Now.'

The conversation was muffled.

Shanahan heard the voice of someone else.

'Listen carefully,' Shanahan said. 'I met with Mr Wenders. He had something he wanted me to do. I declined. I told him it was all out of my league. I have nothing. I know nothing.' Shanahan doubted he would be believed, but he had to see if the truth worked.

It didn't.

'You were there when he died,' Mr Bigshot said.

'I was there after he died. I came to tell him that I wasn't going to take his case. He told me nothing at the first meeting other than he wanted to hire me, nothing about what I'd have to do. And the second meeting, as you should know, he didn't have anything to say. Now you let Cross go or I will dig into this. I have friends in high places.'

He wasn't above extreme exaggerations at this point. Though he did know the state attorney general.

'You're in over your head,' the voice said. 'As far as your friends, I doubt they are in the rarified atmosphere they'd have to be in to help you.'

'That's what I was going to tell Wenders, but he wasn't in a listening mood.'

'I'll give you until morning,' the man said, and flipped the phone shut.

'There's an outside chance he doesn't know he has it,' Bigshot told the guy at the window.

'We didn't find it,' the guy said. 'If he had it at home we would have found it. It wasn't in his car or hers.'

'What was that all about?' Kowalski asked.

'You're not going to believe this?'

'I only believe in the unbelievable.'

'What does that mean?'

'I don't know. Carry on.'

'Cross has been kidnapped.'

'Well that explains why he was late for your date. We find him, we find the girl.'

'No.'

'No?'

'This has nothing to do with the girl. This has to do with a little trip I took to Mexico and a dead guy who wanted me to work for him.'

'You were going to work for a dead guy?' Kowalski asked.

'Before he was dead, he had information about a private security force that would, he said, bring down some very powerful national figures. Corruption at the highest level.'

'Dark Wind,' Kowalski said.

'Dark Wind?'

'Private security force connected with some very big and quite shady corporations specializing in unstable parts of the world to stabilize them in ways that would create corporation friendly governments – the next step in public relations work. Corporations as the new feudal lords and these are their private armies.'

'Wenders didn't name them, but yes, you're saying pretty much what he did. Dark Wind?'

'That's the one I know about. There are others. But these guys are on the dark side of the dark side. All sorts of strange connections with strange and scary people. And people you don't even know you should be scared of.'

'I've got until morning to come up with something I don't have. And I don't even know what it is I don't have.'

'Leaves a lot of room for creativity,' Kowalski said. 'You talked to Cross?'

'Yes. He's apparently at an empty house. He called it sterile. It smelled of paint, he said.'

'Anything else?' Kowalski sipped his coffee.

'Maybe. He called the guy a "low-tech Darth Vader." That could be something. He also said he wasn't on a "spring holiday." Weird phrasing.'

'Americans go on vacations, we rarely go on holidays,' Kowalski said. 'Is Cross a secret anglophile?'

'I doubt it. Might mean nothing, but other than paint fumes those were the only words that were unnecessary to the conversation.'

'You think he was trying to give you a location?' Kowalski asked.

'Maybe.'

'Wouldn't his abductors know what he's doing?'

'Not if they're from somewhere else,' Shanahan said.

'So, an artist's studio, a car painting shop, or maybe a new house.'

'Or one that is being fixed up,' Shanahan said.

'Empty.'

'The room's empty, maybe not the house.'

'Probably the house. Empty, but maybe not for long.'

'For sale,' Shanahan said.

'Or rent,' Kowalski said.

'A guy's looking out of the window, he said,' Shanahan looked up at a hovering Harry.

'Means he's not in a basement. You'd think they would put him in a basement. Unless, of course, there is no basement. We're making some huge jumps.'

'Not huge ones.'

'Spring holiday. Holiday spring,' Kowalski said, just to

listen to himself. 'There are some Hot Spring Spas around town.'

'Harry, you have the White Pages?' Shanahan asked.

'What are you looking for?'

'A place somewhere in the city, I hope, that has 'spring' or 'holiday' in its name or relates in some way to those words.

'Holiday Inn,' Harry said. 'Holliday Park.' Harry paused a moment and a slight grin blossomed into a huge smile.

'What are you grinning about?' Shanahan asked. It wasn't a friendly question.

'You always underestimate me, Deets.'

'What?' Shanahan was impatient. He was in no mood for games.

Sixteen

Harry had it. In just those few seconds Harry had figured out that there was a Holliday Park on Spring Mill Road. The group moved their interest from the booth at his place to Shanahan's house, where Maureen would use her real estate knowledge and computer to try to pinpoint a location. Putting Cross in that general area of the city eliminated auto body shops and probably artists' studios.

Maureen was at the kitchen table, huddled over her laptop looking at real estate listings. Harry, who closed his bar early, sat at the table across from her. He stared blankly ahead. Kowalski stood just outside the screen door. He smoked a cigar and sipped on some of Shanahan's sourmash bourbon.

'It's got some rye in it,' Kowalski said, his voice coming back through the door.

Shanahan poured Maureen a glass of chilled white wine.

Only one glass, he thought. She became pleasantly silly on two, and silly, no matter how pleasant, wasn't the goal tonight. Her goal was to look for an empty house somewhere in the general neighborhood of Spring Mill Road and Holliday Park.

She'd been at it for several hours. Kowalski had already buzzed through the park to see if Cross had meant for them to be that literal. Apparently not.

They would do it themselves, Shanahan thought. No police. As much as he respected the work the police have to do, they could be ham fisted when it came to delicate operations.

Maureen had a candidate.

'Maybe,' Maureen said. 'Maybe. Doesn't look like a contemporary home, so the sterile description might disqualify it. Unoccupied though. Just listed. Realtors open house on Tuesday. Regular open house the following weekend.'

'So they are putting the finishing touches on the house, I'd guess. Tomorrow's Sunday. No workers probably. Out before Monday. What else can you find out?'

'I can call the realtor,' Maureen said. 'Find out who owns it or what they know about it. It's a big house. On the market for big bucks. On Somerset. Though not a modern style, there's an add-on in back that looks real basic. Wait.'

She pulled up Google on her screen, clicked on maps, clicked on satellite. As far as Shanahan was concerned, this was pure magic. She keyed in the address and suddenly they had an actual aerial view of the home.

Shanahan looked. The home was big. He didn't know the period, but it was not contemporary and Maureen was right, behind what appeared to be a three-car garage was an add-on. The added room was unremarkable. Flat roof. Functional. The homes in the area were far enough apart that neighbors wouldn't necessarily know what was going on next door. People could come and go. And if he were carted away in a van, then it just looked like workers. Pretty normal for a house undergoing a little construction.

For all Shanahan knew, the people holding Cross and the owners of the house – or the realtors for that matter – could be connected. By it being empty, the owners would have deni-ability if something went wrong. Or, the owners were legit, merely moved on, perhaps to a new city.

'Let's not call anybody.'

'Let me look a little longer,' Maureen said. She took a sip of wine.

They still had time. Some time. The sun was long gone. In

its place was a cool, crisp night, an acknowledgement that they hadn't gotten far beyond winter. Cold was good. Windows in the neighborhoods would be closed. Furnaces would be on.

Maureen found a few other homes for sale in the area, but most were still occupied. The fresh paint comment lent itself to something newly listed and not yet shown; though it could be a house that hadn't sold and needed some sprucing up. She eliminated, perhaps erroneously, colonial and Tudor. It wasn't perfect; but it was the only way to narrow it down to a reasonable search. In addition to diligence they were relying on a bit of luck as well.

Shanahan walked out the back door, stood by Kowalski.

'Do you have an extra piece?' the lawyer asked.

Shanahan nodded.

'Do you think the Over the Hill gang can go against the highly trained pros of Dark Wind?'

'You're not over the hill,' Shanahan said.

'Maybe not as far as you and Harry,' Kowalski said, smiling. 'I mean you guys are over the hill and crossing the River Styx.'

'You don't like the odds?'

'I don't like the whole idea of odds. It means there's a chance we'll fail.'

'You in?'

'Hell yes.'

Kowalski followed Shanahan inside.

'I think we should check this out while we still have a little time to search,' Maureen said. 'Just one of us.'

'I'll go,' Shanahan said.

'With a cell phone,' Maureen said. 'I'll go. I'm a real estate agent, remember.'

'At ten P.M.?' Shanahan asked.

'I'm truly ambitious. I have a potential buyer. I couldn't wait.'

'I don't . . .'

She gave him the look. He couldn't play male chauvinist pig without really pissing her off. And, he argued with himself, she was right.

'I'll drive,' Shanahan said. 'Please.' It was the best he could do. 'It'll be the two of us. Isn't that romantic?'

Maureen gave in. She must have wanted it that way.

'I'll order some pizza,' Kowalski said.

*   *   *

'All right guys,' Cross said. 'Who are you?'

'We're patriots,' the man without the hood said.

'You don't look like football players,' Cross said.

'You see, that's it. I couldn't make the point any better,' he pulled his gaze from the window. The overhead light was on now. Cross saw the challenging stare.

'And what point is that?' Cross asked.

'It doesn't matter,' said the Bigshot.

'Of course it matters,' the guy at the window said. 'He needs to know that this country has gone down the sewer. We need to clean it up. We need to do what the sissy Congress won't do, what the government won't let the FBI do or the military do or the police. We've become a nation of wimps. We're protecting America, protecting a way of life.'

'And that way is?'

'If you have to ask . . .'

'I have to ask,' Cross said. 'Because right now you are acting like a criminal not a patriot.'

'We have to protect—'

'Protect what?' Cross asked.

'Freedom, marriage, unborn children, Christianity, free enterprise, the rule of law.' The man was getting angry and moved closer to Cross then yelled in his face. 'How's that for a list?'

'C'mon Stark,' the hooded man said, 'he's trying to get your goat and you're holding it out for him to take.'

'He should know that his friend is trying to destroy us, trying to destroy America and loyal Americans.'

The hooded man laughed.

The unhooded man went back to the window.

'So, you guys have a name? The Salvation Army? Oh, that's taken.'

'Mr Cross, Stark here is an evangelist. No harm in that. He sells the American dream the way it was first conceived. The world is in a grave situation,' Mr Bigshot said. 'What poor Stark is trying to say is that the United States is in a state of decline, largely because of a decline in values and because we are reluctant to fight for the principles we were founded upon. We are the guardians, a private enterprise incidentally, and our ability to continue to operate in America's best interest was being compromised by a traitor who seems to have engaged your friend, Mr Shanahan. The traitor is dead. But the information he was about to give to the enemy is in Mr Shanahan's hands. Now I don't know if Shanahan knows what he's doing or not. We must have it back.'

'At any price?' Cross asked.

'At any price,' Mr Bigshot said. 'A few to protect the many and the future of a great nation.'

'You running for office?'

'Think about it. Freedom isn't free. If it weren't for soldiers storming the beaches in World War II, Hitler would have won. Mussolini. They were defeated on the backs of patriots willing to die so we could enjoy freedom.'

'Apparently not "we,"' Cross said. 'I don't feel particularly free at the moment.'

'A sacrifice.'

'And you determine who has freedom and who doesn't?'

'We've created a force hired by our government and friendly governments, and corporations to operate behind the scenes because our own government agencies are hamstrung by a bunch of liberals and libertarians.'

'You mean you can do illegal things,' Cross said.

'If our enemies play dirty, what are we supposed to do? Play by the Marquis of Queensbury rules? We have our own intelligence, security, public relations.'

'All bought and paid for by us. But nobody knows about it. Not the Congress, not the American people. It's all decided for them.'

'Yes. There are budgets the Congress knows nothing about, let alone the American people. You know they put up such a ruckus just because the government wants to keep track of who checked which books out of the library or do a random selection of provocative words on emails, can you imagine how upset they'd be if they knew what the FBI and CIA can't do? Well, we can. If you take the right to spy from the government, how do you expect to be protected?'

'Spying. How does that work with freedom?'

'We're only spying on those who hate the idea of freedom. If people don't have anything to hide . . .'

'But you're hiding. You're breaking some serious laws. What about rights?'

'Some rights are more important than others.'

'Who decides which ones are less worthy?'

'People who know what's going on!'

'I'd like to know what's going on,' Cross said.

'You sure you want to worry your pretty little head?'

'Why not?'

Mr Bigshot took off his hood. His head was a smooth as a billiard ball. He seemed ageless.

'That's not a good sign, is it?'

Mr Bigshot sat motionless.

'That means I'm going to die.'

'You were always going to die, Mr Cross,' Bigshot said. 'We keep you breathing in case we need to show Mr Shanahan you're worth saving. Then Mr Shanahan will die. And now you know what's going on. You happy?'

'Positively effervescent, can't you tell.'

'Maybe we won't kill you,' Bigshot said. Was he smiling? 'Maybe we just take you someplace and leave you there.'

'Rendition? Part of that operation?'

'Let me tell you, the world is at war. As trite as it may seem to you, we are in a battle, likely the final one, between good and evil. We must defeat evil. Everything is at stake. I have to admit, not even all of our soldiers believe that, or know that. But they do the job. And eventually they will understand.'

'Maybe I can understand,' Cross said. 'I could give it a chance.'

'What world do you live in? The one in the US history books? Democracy, constitution, bill of rights? That's for kindergarten. We are threatened by people who want to kill us. They have no rules. There's no Geneva convention for them. They don't care about the UN or the world court or the Red Cross. They want to destroy us. When it really comes down to it, it's good or evil. In your heart, you understand that. We don't have time for everybody to have elections. We don't have time for endless legislation. They want to kill us now. If we want a free world, we have to keep it free.'

'For who? God and the corporation, that it?'

Cross couldn't tell if Mr Bigshot was smiling or smirking. Death might be like that.

'In the end, the point is: you don't have to get it. Just watch TV, go to the movies, you don't have to do anything. We're taking care of it.'

'Just like you're taking care of me.'

'And there you go. As they say, you are either with us, against us or in the way. You're in the way.'

Cross had nothing to say. It was quiet. The two of them got ready to go, but first the guy at the window made sure Cross wouldn't move an inch when they left.

'Mr Cross, if its any consolation to you, once the evil has been dealt with, the country can go back to the way it was . . . fat, lazy, thinking about baseball games and TV shows.'

'Unless the rapture comes,' Cross said, just before cloth was stuffed into his mouth.

'Precisely,' Mr Bigshot said.

It was dark. Cross had been blindfolded and gagged. His hands were also now bound to his feet in an uncomfortable way not only intended to keep him from standing but also from moving. Because it was dark and he was unsure of the comings and goings of his captors, he wasn't sure if he was alone in the room. He suspected he was.

Besides the usual objections to dying, he had one more. Maya. He missed her more than he had ever missed anyone, more than he could have ever imagined he'd miss anyone. He wanted to live to find her, to protect her, to do as much as he could to lessen the amount of pain she would suffer in her life.

He remembered that, chilly autumn day Margot left her on his doorstep. She wore a thin dress and clasped her mother's pendant, which is how he knew who she was. They had an uneasy relationship the first few days, while they waited for Margot to come or at least to call. She didn't. What was he supposed to do with her? While he didn't stop worrying about her mother, in days he stopped worrying about the little girl's ability to adapt to the strange situation. The two of them got along. She loved her morning cereal with cartoons as much as she liked to dress up and go out to dinner, where she ordered a gin and tonic with lemon.

'Hold the gin,' she told the waiter.

Darkness. Quiet. Without sight to distract him or sound for that matter, his mind would drift not always pleasantly. He'd bring it back. He couldn't be passive. Wherever he was, he wasn't on a busy street. No sounds of voices or car doors or dogs. He squirmed, trying his best to figure out if there was a weakness in the hard plastic cords that bound him. None. The more he tried to wrangle free, the more they cut into him.

Shanahan carried the canvas bag. It contained a crowbar, flashlight, heavy-duty bolt cutter, lock pick, and glasscutter. In his jacket, he had a Smith & Wesson 637 airweight – a lightweight .38. Maureen had her own 9 mm, which she carried regularly in spite of the fact she wasn't sure the average citizen should be walking around with concealed weapons. But a couple of incidents suggested that Shanahan's part-time job sometimes got her in trouble too. And for a woman real estate agent, there were those one-on-one, late-night meetings in empty homes.

The house was dark, and there was no reason to believe that this was the one where Cross was being held except that they eliminated most of the others. This was the best candidate of those that remained. If it wasn't the house, the idea of finding Cross was nil. The two of them didn't crouch or slink as they crossed the street in near darkness. They approached it as if they were visiting friends.

Shanahan shined the flashlight on the door.

Maureen pointed at the realtor's lock. It was a small box a little larger than a padlock and had buttons to enter a combination. He flashed the light on her face. She grinned and punched in some numbers. Was this all too easy?

Shanahan held up his hand, suggesting she wait, and slipped around the side of the huge home. At the side of the home he flashed the light through a window into the garage. Empty. Nothing. There were no cars on the street, and none in the garage. He had the feeling that that's exactly what they'd find – nothing – but he went around back, went around the house. No lights. No sign of activity. He completed the circle and came up beside Maureen.

He shrugged.

She shrugged. She unlocked the odd looking lock and entered. Some quick sweeps of the flashlight and it was clear the home was empty, recently painted. They were walking on plastic. It was a nice home, worth a fortune. Stairs led up from the large entry. He stood for a moment to get his bearings. The living room was two-story and had a balcony.

'This way,' Maureen said in a whisper.

He shined the light in front of her stride. She was convinced that Cross would be in the new addition, which was, according to the description she read on the computer, located behind the garage. The door was locked. But, unlike the rest of the house, this was a cheap door. A hollow door that even he could kick in. Fortunately it was also a cheap lock. A quick pick.

There was a body on the floor, not moving. Shanahan flashed the light on its face. It was Cross, bound, gagged and blindfolded in the center of the room. He moved as the light hit his eyes. Shanahan handed Maureen the cutter, and stayed by the door. He held his .38 in his right hand. Though he expected whoever grabbed Cross was sleeping in a hotel room somewhere, one couldn't be sure. It was a house with a lot of rooms, and he hadn't checked them out.

She undid the blindfold first, then the gag.

'How in the hell . . .' Cross said in a hoarse whisper.

'Shhhh,' Maureen said to the surprised private eye, as she easily cut through the plastic.

Shanahan set the flashlight on the floor so the light bounced off the ceiling providing just enough light for people to move around, but probably not all that noticeable outside.

'Why did they take you if they wanted what I have?'

'They thought you were this great unselfish tough guy who wouldn't give it up to save your own skin, but would to save a friend?'

'They chose you?' Maureen asked. 'What about me?'

'You're not chopped liver,' Cross said. 'They were working their way up to you. I was the low-hanging fruit . . . so to speak.'

'Let's not leave anything,' Maureen said.

'I'm sure the maid will clean up in the morning,' Cross said.

'No,' she said, 'let them wonder if you were even here.'

'Screw with their heads.' Cross smiled. 'These aren't guys you want to piss off.'

'That's already happened,' Shanahan said. 'Let's have some fun.'

'Let's have some fun?' Cross said, incredulous. He looked at Maureen. 'What have you done with Shanahan?'

Maureen grinned. 'He's screwing with your head.'

Cross gathered up the gag, the blindfold, and the remnants of the plastic cuffs.

'Let's take the chairs,' Cross said, getting into the game.

Maureen was on her knees smoothing out the squashed nap in the carpet that Cross' body had made.

The three of them made their way through the carpeted house, checking each empty room.

Seventeen

'So now what happens?' Cross asked from the backseat of the silver Infiniti – 'baby Infiniti' Maureen called it because it was G20, not the big luxury model. The car headed away from the expensive neighborhood, over to Spring Mill and back down to Kessler. 'They still want what you have.'

'And if I have it, I don't know I have it,' Shanahan said from the driver's seat, Maureen riding shotgun.

'And now I have to deal with them as well as search for Maya,' Cross said.

'I had no idea they'd involve anyone but me,' Shanahan said. 'I didn't even know I was involved. I turned down the job.'

'We'll pitch in,' Maureen said to Howie.

'What did I bring back from Puerto Vallarta?' Shanahan asked out loud but to himself.

'The clothes on your back,' Maureen said.

'So my wallet, notebook, keys . . . what? Oh, the cue ball.' There was a long quiet, the barely audible sound of the engine the only sound. 'Damn.'

'What?' Maureen said.

'Wenders had the eight ball in his hand when he died. I have the cue ball. I didn't mean to take it, in fact I was going to return it to him when I told him I wasn't going to help.'

'You must have had one hell of a past life,' Kowalski said to Cross, chewing on cold pizza. 'Seems as if the whole world is dumping on you.'

The seven of them, Shanahan, Maureen, Kowalski, Cross, Harry, Casey and Einstein were in the kitchen. Casey stared at Kowalski's pizza. Einstein worked his way through some cheese Harry had given him. Cross was pouring tequila into a glass. Maureen was uncorking the wine. And Shanahan was trying to unscrew the unscrewable – a cue ball.

'Or,' Cross said, taking a sip and enjoying it, 'I'm paying up front and eternity will be a party.'

Everyone understood not only the danger, horror and sadness of the current situations, but also the incomprehensible silliness of it all. How could all this be happening at the same time and for the most part, to the same guy?

The little girl Cross wanted to protect was kidnapped. He is the suspected kidnapper. He was shot at. He doesn't know why or who was gunning for him. And there is a private security force who abducted him and who planned to kill him; but they weren't the ones who shot at him. And there was Shanahan, normally sane, trying to unscrew a cue ball.

Cross went out the back door.

'Where's he going?' Harry asked.

'Off to howl at the moon, I suspect,' Kowalski said. 'I don't blame him.'

'What do we do?' Beneath Harry's anxiety was more anxiety.

Shanahan tossed the cue ball to Kowalski.

'Tomorrow we're going to comb the Massachusetts Avenue area. Margot doesn't know Maureen or Harry. We can pretend to be looking for a lost dog or taking an opinion survey. We can all do something. Tomorrow morning, early I suspect, the goons from Dark Wind will discover Cross is gone and they're going to come looking for him.'

'Now this may be a dumb question, guys,' Maureen said, 'but have you thought of calling the police?'

The men looked at each other, shrugged in unison.

'It would take the fun out of it,' Kowalski said. He gave in, plucking a slice of cold pepperoni off the last slice of pizza and giving to Casey. 'Besides, take a look at this group. Who's going to mess with us?'

He grinned big and took another gulp of whiskey. He tapped the cue ball on the table.

'It's not an egg, for Christ's sake,' Harry said.

'It's not a cue ball either,' Kowalski said. He used his thumbnail to cut into the surface and peel back a layer of plastic or wax. He then twisted the ball much in the same way Shanahan had. 'Voila.'

The air, with a distant hint of the arctic, gave Cross a chill. He looked up at the moon, and thought about what was beyond it. More. Merely more. If he could only get his mind in a place so that none of it mattered to him. If only he could convince himself that compared to the known universe he was smaller than a speck of dust on a mite. Hell the earth was a speck of dust on a mite. And shouldn't that mean that there was little consequence to actions taken on this little piece of real estate? Maybe he could live with the knowledge that life was meaningless – if it were someone other than a largely innocent little girl.

Clouds drifted across the moon and in seconds the light was gone, and the little piece of earth that Cross stood on was shrouded.

There were shouts inside. He looked back through the screen, saw them in the gold light celebrating, it seemed.

He took a deep breath.

'Tomorrow will be a busy day.'

He went inside. They had found something. They didn't know what it was, but they had found what the goons were looking for.

'Are you going to give it to them?' Harry asked.

'Nope,' Shanahan said.

'What'll you do with it?'

'Harry, I have no idea,' Shanahan said.

The night was not kind to Shanahan. Sleep was interrupted again and again by his brother Fritz who continued to lead the pursuing Shanahan through dusty hallways, damp catacombs and dark paths.

The bunch of them had stayed up later, plugging the little thumb drive into Maureen's computer and reading a document that was just a list of names – some of them recognizable as being part of the president's administration and pretty high up at that. These were names they had seen on the news and at press conferences, and heard blabbering incessantly on Sunday mornings.

The names had numbers after them. That's all. Just names and numbers. By itself, the list meant nothing, unless of course the intended recipient had something that correlated with it. But who was the intended recipient? Someone at the *Washington Post.* Shanahan thought he remembered Wenders saying that. But who?

When the party broke up at midnight, that little mystery remained unsolved. Kowalski, with the loan of a .45 from Shanahan, would stay at Cross' in the event someone dropped by.

Shanahan, who wasn't sure he actually slept, was fully awake at 5:30 A.M. and in the kitchen fixing coffee when the call came. It was raining again. Casey had spent less than thirty seconds outside and was shaking his coat, flinging water off his fur like he was an automatic sprinkler.

'What's your decision on Mr Cross?' the voice asked.

Shanahan could hear windshield wipers. The caller was in a car, probably headed back to pick up Cross. He might not know he no longer had the power of life and death, at least any time real soon. Maureen came into the room, unhappily awake, worried and just in time to hear Shanahan utter the harsh words.

'Kill him.'

'What?' The caller was caught off guard.

'Kill him. What do I care?'

Shanahan put the phone back on the hook.

'I've always wanted to say that,' he said.

'Kill Howie?'

'No. Just say the words "kill him."' Shanahan repressed what would have been a rare smile. 'Or her. "Kill her" would work too. I don't want to be sexist.'

'You're a strange man, Mr Shanahan. You know they might. And after they are done with him and me, you're next.'

She was right. It wasn't just him anymore. His attitude affected others. There was Maureen . . . and Maya. The police may not be a bad idea now that Cross was free.

There was much to do.

'Not a bad place,' Kowalski said. He was up before Cross, had taken it upon himself to make coffee. 'Strange though.'

'Used to be a chauffeur's quarters. The living room was a two-car garage. The middle room and the kitchen are original,' Cross said. 'The bedroom was added on later.'

'Nice. Tiled roof. Mediterranean.'

'Yeah, we're so close to the sea here in Indianapolis,' Cross said.

'Well, you know we have Tudors all over the Northside. When did the Tudors come through here? So why not Mediterranean? Anyway couple of more earthquakes out west, you could be on the Ocean.' He took a sip of coffee, felt his pockets looking for something, probably a cigar that he discovered he didn't have. 'You ready for them?'

Cross shook his head. 'I don't want to have to think about them. I want to find Maya. And that's what I'm going to do.'

'They could get in the way.'

Unless they climbed fences from other people's yards, there was only one way on to Cross' property – straight up the front steps, across the lawn to the gate and then they had the choice of front or back. Kowalski had been glancing out of the kitchen window, which provided the full view. Nothing. It was still early. It was possible no one had yet discovered Cross' absence from the little room.

Cross called Shanahan, asked him if he heard anything about anything.

Maureen sat in the kitchen with a laptop, cup of coffee, grapefruit juice and a scone, with butter and jam. Shanahan picked up the phone, watched as she typed and clicked, searching for the listing agent of the home they visited last night. After that she would look for the owner. There had to be a connection.

'I got a call telling me that it was the information or you,' Shanahan said after the introduction.

'And you said?'

'I told them to kill you.'

'OK, I'm taking you out of the will.'

'He either didn't know you got away or thought I might not know you got away.'

'What's next?'

'Good question.'

'You help with Maya?'

'Yep. We could spend some time in the neighborhoods, looking around, asking questions. Why don't you and Kowalski drop by here. I'll call Harry. We'll divide up the area. Get copies of pictures of the girls to show. Check out restaurants, drug stores, home owners, everybody.'

The odds weren't on their side with an approach like this. But there was no other approach available to them.

'I don't have a picture of Maya,' Cross said.

'We have one of Margot, right?'

'Yes.'

Shanahan used the intersection where three streets meet – Massachusetts Avenue, where the beauty shop was located, and East and North Streets. He assigned Cross, Kowalski, Harry, and Maureen to each of the sections off the intersection. Since there were six sections, Kowalski and Cross each had two. Shanahan, himself, would go where he was needed most – Chatham Arch, the struggling historic neighborhood where he'd assigned Harry, and Lockerbie a neighborhood of polished restorations where he'd assigned Maureen. These were the most populated areas.

Shanahan was connected with the others, except Harry, by cell phone. Harry was convinced the phones would give him ear cancer. Shanahan, who wasn't convinced there was anything called 'ear cancer,' had been a reluctant convert himself, agreeing to carry a cell only after almost losing Maureen to a vengeful man.

While the others focused on residences, Shanahan would check out the stores that Margot might have to visit to buy cigarettes, liquor, toothpaste, necessities of life. Laundromats, drycleaners – anyplace that she might have to visit. Then he'd play back up to Harry and Maureen. This was the long, boring work that cops and private eyes have to endure. Even though they were starting early, they might not finish in one day. There were no promises that all of this work would mean anything no matter how long they took or how thorough they were.

After all, this was just a theory. Margot could be staying anywhere in this spread-out city if, in fact, she was still there. And it wasn't clear that she had the child with her. But Shanahan believed that if nothing else, the search gave Cross something constructive to do with his time. He was no longer powerless. It gave Shanahan something to do as well while he waited for the private army boys to make their next move. He had no idea how to contact them.

It wouldn't do them any good. Maureen sent the list of names and numbers to the editor of *The Washington Post*, to both Indiana senators, to the crazy congressman who loved conspiracy theories, and to her cousin in Lexington, Kentucky.

'If anything happens to me . . .' was the message to her cousin.

Why would anyone want to kill them now? Shanahan asked himself. If the message was delivered, if the deed they seemed to want to prevent was done, what good would it do for this group to keep pressing?

Those were his thoughts as he asked questions at O'Malia's Lockerbie Marketplace on New Jersey. He checked with cashiers, the guys behind the meat counter, the person in produce and two of the pharmacists.

He got nothing. Of course, Margot could have come in, shopped, and left without anyone taking special note. Lots of folks passed through checkout, and the checkers weren't paid to remember faces.

Before noon a call came in. Shanahan thought it felt like there was a fish in his pants. It was the cell phone, set on vibrate. Cross was on the other end.

'Good news and strange news,' Cross said.

'Go ahead.'

'I'm pretty sure I found Margot's car. Red Toyota, and the bumper sticker.'

'Good,' Shanahan said.

'It's in an alley, so it might be behind the place she's staying.'

'And the strange news.'

'I'm being shadowed.'

'You sure?'

'Ninety percent,' Cross said. 'I feel it.'

'FBI, police . . .'

'Dark Wind maybe. Who knows?'

'You're a popular guy.'

'Stalked by the very best,' Cross said.

'Tell me where you want us to meet. We'll come over that way.'

Shanahan and Maureen walked down to the others. They had gathered and huddled in a narrow alley that was lined with ramshackle garages, carriage houses. Some of the buildings were victimized by all-too creative minds before the rules of historic preservation were set up. Others were preserved by historic purists.

The morning chill was gone as was the drizzle. Warm sun, cool breeze, new leaves, young blooms. The scene was set. One could easily believe by what lay before them that there was no evil in the world, only curly-headed little girls, puppies and family-rated happy endings. Kowalski, smoking a stogie and looking like the executive director of the Hell's Angels, was there to counter the near Disney look.

Shanahan asked Kowalski and Maureen to take the front. Maureen would knock and see who answered, and if not Margot, then what intelligence she could gather from whoever did. Cross and Shanahan would watch the back to catch a possibly fleeing Margot.

What Shanahan saw, standing back from the house and able to see over the garage and what Cross didn't see, was the face of little Maya in an upstairs window. The little girl smiled and waved and disappeared.

He would wait to tell Cross. Shanahan, as much as he could, wanted to keep emotion out of whatever happened next. He saw something out of the corner of his eye. He looked. Two men dressed in suits were at one end of the alley. Another two were at the other. They were moving in.

Cross saw them too.

'Shit,' Cross said.

'We could shoot them, but they might be government.' Shanahan looked back up at the window. No one was there. But in the open window next to it Shanahan first saw smoke creep out in the daylight, then flames lapped at the top of the window. 'We have to go in.'

'What?'

'The place is on fire. The kid's inside.'

They both ran to the back door. A steel gate prevented them from getting in. They ran to the front. Same thing. The windows were gated as well. Maureen and Kowalski sensed the urgency, but didn't yet know why. All four raced around to the back. A red Toyota lurched from the garage and nearly ran over the two, gun-toting suits in the alley.

Cross used Kowalski's body to grab hold of the guttering on the garage. The gutters detached at the weight and Cross fell. Up again, with Shanahan on one side helping him on to Kowalski's shoulders Cross managed to get on the roof and run toward the open window.

Fire leapt out.

'Maya!' he hoped she was with Margot, but he couldn't take a chance that she wasn't. 'Maya!'

'It's hotter than hell in here.' He heard her voice from a distance.

'Can you get downstairs?'

'No. It's on fire.' Her yell was to be heard. It didn't contain the panic they knew she must feel.

'Are you near a window?'

'Yes.'

'Can you get to it?'

'Yes.'

'Go to it, but don't open it yet, please. Don't open it. Just go to it.'

'All right.'

She appeared at the window, the window Shanahan had seen her in. It was a two-story drop and unreachable from Cross' perch on top of the garage.

'Get over there!' Cross shouted to Kowalski, Maureen, Shanahan and the four suits. 'Get ready to catch her.'

'Hurry up!' came Maya's tiny but firm voice.

'Don't open the window until I tell you to. Can you hear me?'

'Yes.'

'Do you understand?'

'Yes, stop talking and do something.'

'When I tell you to, open the window and then jump immediately.' There was a moment of silence. Her face disappeared from the window. 'Do you understand?'

'Yes,' she said reappearing. 'You know I can't fly, don't you?'

'When I tell you, don't think about it, don't look down, just jump. Not now. You have to do this just the way I'm telling you to do it. Don't think about it. Are you ready?'

'Yes, yes, yes.' She said impatiently, then coughed.

The men in suits had come. One was on the phone.

Cross looked at the guys who had gathered beneath the window. The men had tied their suit jackets together.

'DO IT!' Cross yelled.

She opened the window, drawing the flames immediately. Fire gushed from behind, igniting her. She seemed almost to flutter, an angel on fire, down. Cross' heart leapt and sank. Maureen gasped. Maya landed and smothered in the blanket of coats.

Eighteen

The flight of young Maya seemed an eternity in hell. Shanahan saw the pain on Cross' face and understood that emotion affects time. And for all of the strangeness of his brain after the bullet altered it months ago, he could now grasp that time did not pass in ticks and tocks of equal duration. It seemed as if Maya's descent lasted ten excruciating years, an angel with flames for wings.

And so it was, he suspected for Cross. He saw the man's anguish, hope and fear riding the blade of a razor.

But she was fine. The coats had smothered the flames instantly. Her hair was singed, her clothing charred and falling from her. Her flesh was pinker in some places than in others, but she said she felt no pain and seemed oblivious to both the danger she had been in and the apparent abandonment – again – by her mother. If nothing else Margot had created an independent child and one with less than high expectations of her mother.

The sounds of sirens were in the air before she could be draped in Cross' jacket. The home crackled and the fire sent heat in visible waves toward them. They stepped back. The men, obviously FBI, the other guys didn't dress that well, slipped back into their suit coats and talked among themselves.

Maureen took charge of Maya, who, wide-eyed, seemed more exhilarated than shocked or frightened.

No one else was in the house, Maya said. The man who lived there was at work. And her mother? The girl told Maureen that Margot was going downstairs to fix lunch.

Cross eventually spoke with the FBI and Shanahan wondered what he was saying. If they were keeping such close tabs on Cross, why didn't they know he was abducted?

Kowalski relit his cigar, looking bored.

Shanahan wanted a jigger of bourbon, but settled for the end of the drama, or at least of this dramatic moment.

He wondered what kind of person would put her own daughter
in mortal danger to create a diversion for her escape. He also
posed a question for himself. Now that Maya was safe, was
there any reason why anyone, other than the police – who
would want her for arson and child endangerment or worse
– would want to find her?

Yes they would. He would. It was simple. People shouldn't
be allowed to do things to other people, play with people's
lives. Not Margot. Not Dark Wind.

Cross had his own answer to that question. At Harry's place,
he sat with Shanahan and Maureen who seemed lost in their
thoughts. Only Maya was animated, questioning Kowalski
about his beard and admonishing the attorney for his 'stinky
cigar.' Cross' answer was that Margot had to be caught, had
to be put away. He thought that Margot, as long as she lived,
remained a threat not just to him, but also to Maya. He had
thought that before. He knew it now. What he didn't want to
go into was the real question he had for himself. How had he
not seen who she really was? He realized, as Harry brought
over the bottles and glasses for a low-key celebration, that he
hadn't wanted to know.

Cross used Margot as much as she used him. She was good
sex, someone he could miss when she was elsewhere, but who
made no real demands except during those brief interludes
when they were together. She didn't prescribe or proscribe a
future. He was off the hook even if he didn't want to be. For
her, he was the guard at the door, the person who could get
her from nightfall to morning. The sex? Maybe she enjoyed
it. Maybe it was work.

Whatever the reality was for her, he didn't realize who she
was because he didn't want to.

What he knew now was that he was committed to someone.
Maya. Maya was his no matter what the DNA would say.

A toast. To Maya's return. And the little girl joined in with
a ginger ale. And another toast to Cross' new status with the
police. He would take Maya up to Eaton later in the afternoon.
They would go to bring peace to his parents, tie up loose ends.

He'd like to take her on a long walk down Harris Street,
make sure the town knew he wasn't the disgusting criminal
some must have thought he was.

* * *

Cross checked his rear-view mirror many times on the trip back up to Eaton. He made some illogical turns before righting the course just to see if he had been followed. Of course Margot knew about the place now. He didn't know what to do about that. There were only so many places they could go, and he was trying to convince himself she wouldn't pull the exact same trick again.

With that last act, maybe she was gone and gone for good.

The drive was familiar now. Once out of the metropolitan area, the land slipped by on secondary highways. Vast plots had been tilled but showed only tiny explosions of green. He reminded himself that spring held only promise of better things to come. It wasn't a sure thing.

He spent part of the trip explaining the idea of farming to Maya and talking about how wonderful it was to eat fresh tomatoes, corn, and melon in the summer and how, a couple of farms over from his parents' place, they grew pumpkins. He thought that would interest her.

'Why don't they just go to the store?' she asked. 'That's what we did.'

'Fresh food is better,' Cross countered.

'I like frozen peas better.'

'Yeah, well, there's an exception to every rule . . . So what did you and your mom do together when you left the farm?'

Maya looked frustrated. She shrugged a no comment.

'What about the man who owned the house?'

'He wasn't home much.'

'But when he was?'

'He did things for her.'

'Like what?' Cross asked, hungry for any information that might help him find her, get her put away.

'Made her dinner.'

'Didn't he make your dinner?'

'Yes,' she hissed her 's's. 'But he made what she wanted,' Maya said. There was bitterness in her voice.

Cross sensed that Margot was in some way competition for Maya and, as he thought about it, visa versa. Some mother, Cross thought. A dark moment passed before he realized that now, on a very different level, he was probably being taken in by Margot's offspring. Would he ever learn?

Cross would get the homeowner's name from the police.

In fact he decided he would talk to the police, let them in on Margot's involvement in the sex slave trade. In the end, with all the players being executed, she might be high on the list herself. That's why she was hiding. But he didn't mind putting her away. She would never get Maya back. And if Shanahan wouldn't do it, he'd talk to the police about the people who kidnapped him. He couldn't let it happen again and dealing with it was too much to handle alone.

Cross' parents were happy to see Maya, happy to have Cross off the suspect list, happy that senior Cross was getting his color and his energy back. Maya was happy as well. Mrs Cross fixed her meatloaf, macaroni and cheese and Waldorf salad with apples, grapes, nuts and raisins.

That night Cross slept in the same room with Maya. At one point when he came back in from a middle of the night trip to the bathroom, she called out to him.

'Tell me that everything's going to be OK,' she said in a sleep-filled voice.

He must have paused a moment too long because she continued.

'It doesn't have to be the truth.'

The morning light was brighter in the kitchen than the rest of the house. It seemed to have caught Maureen by surprise. She grimaced and shielded her eyes as if she were witnessing an atomic blast.

Shanahan, who had quieted Einstein with a breakfast from a can that had the words 'chicken, sauce, and feast' on its label and shuffled Casey out for his morning constitutional, sipped his morning coffee. The *Indianapolis Star* was spread out on the table before him. He read most every word, usually before she arrived to grab all his attention. As much as he loved her, he loved this time in the morning when all was quiet and he was alone.

'Thanks for doing the laundry,' Maureen said, lifting up the lid of the washer and nodding approvingly.

'I think I forgot to put in the soap,' Shanahan said.

She was quiet for a moment, pensive.

'Pretend you don't remember you forgot,' she said. 'Then everything will be fine.'

She was fine with his forgetting. He wasn't. It was also the

increasing slowness of his mind that bothered him. Details he
shouldn't even have to think about were hard to retrieve from
the recesses of his brain. Sometimes something he was
searching for would pop up the next day. Often it was too
late or he had forgotten why he wanted it.

Worse, he believed that last night as he moved from bedroom
to living room, he had just suddenly appeared in the living
room, that he had not walked there, had not passed through
the hall. He could admit the laundry incident, but not the other.
No point in both of them worrying about this new accidental,
uncontrollable magic of his.

However, to Maureen's wonderfully compassionate logic,
he could only say, 'I see.'

'And get some sleep.'

'What? Why?'

'Because you didn't sleep last night. You were busy
protecting the castle,' she said.

She poured herself some grapefruit juice. She held the belief
that juice of the unsweetened grapefruit devoured fat calories
– a negative calorie content, that was indeed magic. So after
a late night binge on Häagan Dazs Swiss Almond Vanilla, the
next morning she would drink two glasses of grapefruit juice
before she settled in for her coffee and scone.

'You know we're not out of the woods,' Shanahan said.
'Dark Wind is still out there. Margot is still out there.'

'I know.'

Casey barked at the door. The temperature outside wasn't
yet within his increasingly narrow comfort range. He wanted
in so he could lay his bony body down on a carpet. They were
all growing old together, he and the animals, in the winter of
their lives, except for Maureen, who seemed to have her own
beautiful season.

'That stupid security force had a window of opportunity,'
Maureen said. 'Maybe they know the window is closed. The
information is gone. It wouldn't do them any good to torture
anybody for it or kill them for that matter.'

'Could be.' She could put a positive twist on just about
anything.

'On the other hand,' she continued, 'we can't risk it. Let's
get the authorities involved.'

'Which authorities?' Shanahan asked. 'Whose side is the

CIA on? The FBI? We don't know. This security force is employed by the US. They work with government agencies. As Wenders told me, they can do things because they are connected in the highest places and because they don't have to follow the rules, merely the orders of the folks on that list.'

It caught her off guard for a moment.

'OK, you see you've made my point.'

'What point?'

'Don't you mean, what is the point? I'm asking you what the point is.'

'That's the point?'

She nodded, eyes closed, her expression oozing feigned patience, barely suppressing a grin.

'You're right,' she said, admitting but not exactly withering under Shanahan's intense stare. 'I hate it when it turns out that way.' She nibbled at her scone. 'What this sounds like is that we are in way over our heads.'

'Wouldn't be the first time.' He meant to reassure her and he hoped he had; but she was right too. He needed some sort of official help. He didn't know where to put his trust. He had no idea what was coming after him or how. They still had the advantage and they might still feel that those who knew shouldn't be able to talk about it.

'What about that guy you know at the police department? Bird?'

'Swann?'

It was a thought.

When Cross woke up, there were a few seconds of anxiety. Relief came when he saw Maya still there, hidden in the sheets. She hadn't been stolen in the night. The sunlight streamed in, its rays fractured by the old, irregular glass of the window.

It was at this odd moment that the abduction made sense. Margot wasn't hiding because she believed the person who killed all of the others involved in the murder and sex trafficking was going to kill her. She was the killer. Margot hadn't gambled with her daughter's life when she set the house on fire and escaped. She meant to kill her. And it was a bullet from her gun that shattered the coffee cup in Cross' hand that day. The bullet wasn't meant to scare him. It was meant to kill him.

It all made sense. Margot wanted everyone involved in her past, anyone who could identify her, who could witness against her – including her daughter – eliminated. The corpse that Maya accidentally saw that day in Maui, was quite likely a victim of momma Margot, not the thugs she ran around with. She was trying to take over the operation, not the thugs who pursued her after she made her move. Margot dropped Maya at Cross' that first time not for her daughter's protection as Cross assumed, but to travel lighter.

It was as shocking as it was obvious. How had he missed it?

Cross got up, crossed the room and put his hand on Maya's forehead. She was warm, meaning she was alive. Even so, he waited until he saw her small chest rise and fall before he could fully relax.

Margot wasn't going far. She still had work to do. So did he. In the meantime, where could the girl be safe?

Shanahan met Lieutenant Swann at City Market, across from the high-rise box that housed the mayor, the city council, courtrooms, police, and various other metropolitan agencies.

Shanahan knew other cops at IMPD and like the populace at large, they had their good points and their bad ones. Swann may have some personal problems somewhere in his life, but he didn't bring them to work. He was by the book, looked for all of the evidence, not just the evidence that would support the prosecution.

His view of the world was just as constant as his haircut. There were laws governing our existence in the US, the state of Indiana, and the city of Indianapolis. The laws came from the democratic process. His job was to see that they were followed. Don't like the laws, change them. Until then abide by them.

While Shanahan saw more shades of gray than Swann and bent the law at times to meet his own interpretation of right and wrong, the cop's philosophy was exactly what the old detective thought he was looking for, 'thought' being the operative word.

Inside the large, high-ceilinged building, most booths were empty. In the summer, Shanahan and Maureen would stop in for fresh produce on Wednesdays, but farmers wouldn't start bringing in their bounty until May. A few of the hot food vendors were there to provide lunch for the office workers. Shanahan and Swann grabbed hot dogs and coffee and found a place to sit.

'How do you do it?' Swann said, after listening to a detailed story about Dark Wind. Listening while Shanahan talked, Swann had consumed his dog before Shanahan took his first bite. The cop wiped Ketchup from the corner of his mouth with a napkin that seemed to be disintegrating. 'You have to go out of your way to find things like this.'

'Sometimes it just comes to me,' Shanahan said. 'This one did.'

Swann shook his head in what Shanahan assumed was both wonderment and disbelief.

'Sounds like an FBI problem to me. I don't know, maybe CIA, Homeland Security, or maybe the loony bin.'

'Were you listening?'

'You turning into a crackpot?' Swann asked matter-of-factly.

'These guys work *for* the government, I don't know who to go to.'

'Things don't work that way,' Swann said.

'I saw the bullet in Wenders' head.'

'That was in Mexico, you said.'

'Yes.'

Swann threw up his hands.

Shanahan got up.

'They're operating here, Swann. Everywhere, without license, without oversight.'

Swann had become sullenly quiet.

'All right. I reported it,' Shanahan said.

Swann had a sour look on his face.

'I'm done,' Shanahan said. 'I wanted it on the record. Consider this an official complaint.'

Swann looked even less comfortable.

'You don't want to do that,' he said. The cop got up, put his paper cup and napkin in the proper receptacle, and walked away. With his back to Shanahan he waved a hand dismissively. 'I have no idea what you're talking about. I don't want to know.'

Shanahan had misjudged Swann. No doubt Swann knew there was such a thing as bad cops and corrupt judges and while the lieutenant's honesty and courage were never in question, he had no capacity to understand that his government could do evil. When someone has such rigid views and something comes along that simply doesn't fit those views, Swann simply denied its existence. It doesn't exist because it can't exist. And in a democracy, organizations like Dark Wind with all those official connections couldn't possibly operate outside the law while in such plain sight of it.

Swann wasn't naive. He had seen enough in his life to know that evil exists, and he willingly took it on. He just refused to acknowledge the many shapes it could take – like this one dressed up in the cloak of entrepreneurial patriotism and supported by those who wore flag pins in the lapels of their suits. Shanahan would have preferred the world to be the way Swann saw it, but he knew it to be otherwise.

Nineteen

C ross didn't like the idea he was afraid of a woman. He knew that was foolish. Over the years, a number of women have killed people. But the male-coded remnants of a twelve-year-old mind haunted him more than he'd like. But there it was. Margot had killed at least three others and was out to kill him and Maya. It was one thing to be hunted. He'd almost – almost – welcome the challenge at this point. It was quite another to try and protect the little girl and take care of her deranged mother at the same time.

He thought about checking into a cheap motel somewhere on the outskirts of Indianapolis until he could figure something out, but he realized what that would look like. Rightly or wrongly the world was suspicious of someone like him checking into a cheap motel with a little girl.

Shanahan and Maureen were having troubles of their own. Their place wasn't a safe place for them, let alone a child. In the midst of his ruminating, the call came. It was Kowalski. Anything he could do?

'How much do you charge to baby sit?' Cross asked.

'Depends on the baby,' Kowalski said, his voice amplified over the cell phone.

'I need a place for Maya . . . and me, I guess. For a little while. Crazy Margot is still on the loose and Shanahan's friends are probably still a little pissed.'

'You're welcome here. Quiet little place by the river,' Kowalski said.

'You're an angel and a psychic.'

'I know many people who would have you committed.' Kowalski laughed.

Cross had never been to Kowalski's place. He knew the Harley riding attorney lived in Ravenswood, a river community inside the city limits and known for its insular nature and its suspicion of strangers.

Kowalski lived in a well-kept white frame home that backed up to the river. On the outside it was surprisingly charming with a huge weeping willow that leaned slightly over the water.

The attorney met them at the door. He wore a sweatshirt and jeans and by his side was a big, white, bow-legged bulldog with bloodshot eyes, breathing heavily. The dog, having inspected Cross and the little girl and found no threat and nothing else of interest, left them.

'Can I get you a beer?' Kowalski asked, as they followed him in.

'No thank you,' Maya said. 'Maybe a Coke or a ginger ale.'

'Too early in the day?' Kowalski asked her and looked at Cross. Cross nodded. He wanted one.

The large open living room radiated warmth. Wood everywhere. Leather chairs and a gray corduroy sofa that all but devoured Maya when she sat on it. The walls were filled with either books or art. He could be convinced he was in the home of a professor of literature rather than a tough, streetwise criminal lawyer.

'I appreciate this,' Cross said, settling into one of the big leather chairs.

'I've got a housekeeper coming in tomorrow,' Kowalski said, bringing in the beer and Coke. 'I can get her to watch Maya – she'll love it – and we can set out on a little Margot hunting.'

Cross took a sip of beer.

'Don't you have regular work to do?' he asked Kowalski.

'It's under control, I promise. And this is my idea of fun. I talked with Shanahan. He has his hands full too and I'd love to get my teeth into these private armies. So, let's just see how all of this plays out.'

Maya, with an extremely bored expression on her face was thumbing rapidly through a copy of *The Atlantic* magazine.

'You like salmon?' Kowalski asked.

Cross nodded. Maya looked up with hope on her face.

'Tonight. Frozen now. But straight from Alaska.' Kowalski went over to Maya. 'And you. Are your hands clean?'

'I haven't done anything,' Maya said, eyes wide.

'No, I mean are your hands clean? Go up the stairs first door on your right and wash your hands. I'll show you some very interesting books to read.'

She looked puzzled, but did as she was told. As she climbed the stairs, looking every bit like the five-year-old she was, Kowalski went to the bookshelves.

'I'm not a clean freak,' Kowalski said to Cross. 'I have some first editions. Some of them with great illustrations.' He went to one of the bookshelves. 'A joy, of course, but an investment as well. They might be my retirement later.'

'A book collector, attorney, Harley rider, cigar smoker, and gourmet. What else do you do?'

'No, I got started on Indiana authors several years ago. So I've got a few first editions of people like Booth Tarkington, Theodore Dreiser, Dan Wakefield, Kurt Vonnegut.'

Cross recognized the names. After all, he lived in the Butler-Tarkington neighborhood, had certainly heard of Dan Wakefield, but he'd only read Vonnegut.

'I'll have to read more.'

'You should. General Lew Wallace wrote *Ben Hur*, did you know that? And a Hoosier named Joseph Hayes wrote *Desperate Hours* . . . you might remember the movie with Humphrey Bogart?'

Cross remembered it. He'd gone through a Bogart DVD rental phase not long ago. Kowalski pulled down various books, looked through them, and either set them on the table or returned them to the shelf.

'Now would you tell me why I had to go to all this trouble?' Maya asked, waving the slightly damp palms of her hands at Kowalski.

'Pity any future kidnapper,' Kowalski said, going back into the kitchen for a beer.

'Because the books are very valuable and they must be kept in proper shape. No peanut and jelly stains.'

She looked at him, shook her head.

In the evening, the three had a nice dinner, polite conversation about politics and literature and philosophy. Cross mostly nodded, and wondered what he'd done all his life. Shouldn't he know more about these things? He spent half his time just trying to stay afloat and the other half trying to forget what a struggle it was.

Maya was polite and very, very quiet. There was a sadness about her he hadn't noticed before. Periodically, both he and Kowalski tried to engage her in conversation, but two childless, not quite middle-aged guys could not find the key to unlock her introspection. Instead, she'd smile and remain quiet.

Kowalski stoked up a fire. The bulldog, who had been content to sleep in a corner, slowly got to his feet and moved in a slow and seemingly painful way to his place in front of the fire. Kowalski read Maya poems by James Whitcomb Riley. After three or four from the homespun Hoosier poet, including the all too appropriate *Little Orphan Annie*, she asked a question. 'How much more of this is there?'

'I think she'd prefer *Lady Chatterley's Lover*,' Cross said.

Kowalski pushed a button on the stereo and some bluesy notes escaped.

Cross looked around the room. Warm and cozy. Everything should be all right, shouldn't it? But he had trouble being in the here and now – at least at this particular here and now. He felt it somehow silly that they would sit around conversing and enjoying the evening in such a civilized manner. It was as if there wasn't a mad woman out to kill them and what might amount to a mirror government trying to do them in as well.

'Not a lot we can do at the moment,' Kowalski said, reading Cross' mind or perhaps just his body language. 'Relax tonight. Port?'

'No, thanks.'

'You're a tequila guy, right?

Cross nodded.

'Eat, drink and be merry,' Kowalski said.

'For tomorrow . . .' Cross thought.

Shanahan generally preferred beer over wine, except when they were eating Italian. And that was a recent thing. Except for his stint in Paris and the affair with the dancer, Shanahan drank no wine until he met Maureen. At Amici's, the little Italian restaurant that occupied a small 200-year-old house near Lockerbie, the two dined on pasta and Cabernet in a pleasantly funky converted living room, while upstairs a party roared.

The place was appropriately dimly lit. The wine was good.

At home now, Shanahan and Maureen danced in the flickering light of the fire and to Sinatra's version of *Bewitched, Bothered, and Bewildered.*

'I don't know what's gotten into you Shanahan,' Maureen said, 'but let's find out what it is and get some more of it.'

It was true. He would never have done this with Elaine. Never. He would never have had a candlelit dinner or a half bottle of wine. Looking back, which he did increasingly, yet still reluctantly, he hadn't been a good husband or father. It had taken him a lifetime to understand things. Regrets, he had more than a few, he thought. He would do his best not to regret the years he had left.

'The answer is you,' Shanahan said. 'Can I get more of that?'

'Sweet,' came a voice that wasn't Maureen's. It was the sound of wind over dried leaves.

The two of them stopped dancing turned in the direction of the voice. A form could be seen beneath the arch that divided living room and dining room. There was little detail in the image though it stood straight and still – just the suggestion of a form of a man.

'I came in the front, while you let your dog out back,' the voice said.

Shanahan went to the stereo receiver, clicked it off, turned on a table lamp. The room was still barely lit, dark shadows mingled with the weak gold light from the incandescent bulb. It was as if the light was being swallowed by a greater darkness.

The man was tall, very thin – angular in every way – shoulders broader than his waist, cheekbones broader than his chin. Thick horn-rimmed glasses widened his face further, making him look like a praying mantis. The man wore a charcoal gray suit with a vest, a narrow tie. He seemed oddly timeless and – perhaps more oddly, considering his illegal entry – unarmed.

'Strange apparition,' Maureen said.

Shanahan said nothing.

'I am sorry to intrude, but I thought it best to address the situation personally.'

'This situation? You have something against dancing?' Maureen asked.

'Mr Shanahan, you've made us look foolish.' He laughed a raspy laugh. 'That's a compliment to you. You were underestimated. We've been unwise and unprofessional. This worked to your advantage. Just so you know, the people involved with you and your friend, Mr Cross, are no longer involved. They have been reassigned in a fashion. I'm taking over myself.'

He paused as if waiting for a question or suggestion. Not getting any, he continued. 'With all of that being said and with all due respect, you are in over your head. Considerably so.'

'I've heard him say the same thing,' Maureen said, 'but he won't listen.'

'You need to listen to your better nature, Mr Shanahan.' The man smiled. His thin lips formed two perfectly parallel lines. 'I understand that you have received and transmitted information to people who might wish to do our organization and consequently our country harm.'

Shanahan said nothing.

'Perhaps you do not approve of who we are or what we're doing. I cannot know all of what Mr Wenders told you, but in the end it doesn't matter. The world has changed. The world order has changed. Our concern with you is that you will merely muck up the works, make what is inevitable difficult. You won't change anything, you will simply embarrass people we would like to see avoid embarrassment. The program will go on in any event, and you will be ground up in it. You and your lovely friend.'

'I'm afraid I can't help you,' Shanahan said. 'Call ahead next time you want to visit.'

The man didn't move. He seemed calm, an unrepentant intruder, a self-assured intimidator.

'What has gotten you in trouble, however, can also save you. There is a second part to the information you provided.

It is quite like a map that is ripped in half. What's done is done, but I must make sure that I recover this new half or at least make sure that no one else does.'

'I don't like repeating myself, but one more time. "I can't help you."'

'Not convinced.' The man smiled again. 'We do the same kind of work, you and I. You have already passed along information that didn't belong to you. I understand that. But remember your client is dead.'

'Then what are you worried about? What's done is done. I have no client. I never had a client. I passed along what I had because you people were messing with my life. So, it's simple, get out of my life and leave my friends alone. And I'll stop messing with yours. You have that?'

'If you have or receive additional information, you are required to turn it over to us. If you do, you both can live out what remains of your natural lives. We'll be in touch. Do you understand?'

'Yes, we are very grateful,' Maureen said. She didn't mean it. Shanahan was sure the man picked up on it.

Shanahan said nothing.

'I'll bet you were good in your day,' the man said. He turned, went toward the door, stopped. 'Oh, I understand you were there with Mr Wenders at the end. Remember that image, Mr Shanahan. And remember this too. That information? We can pay you for it or kill you for it.'

He left.

'I'll check Casey,' Maureen said.

Shanahan stood in the middle of the room, seething. The sheer arrogance of the man bothered him as much as being threatened. But the truth was easier. It wasn't over. This group couldn't afford to take Shanahan's word, even if he was willing to give it.

If it was the beginning of an effort for private enterprise to finally take over the government – completely – Shanahan didn't and couldn't know, but it certainly felt like it. Wenders said corporations had begun to take over the schools, the prisons, and the hospitals. The corporations own most of the water and electricity. The common man's health is in their hands and they are working on state and federal highways. Privatizing social security is on the horizon. And this is how the new economy would work. 'They will charge you for the air you breathe,' Wenders had said. If they can't bribe, they'll threaten. If the threats don't work, they ameliorate the opposition, one way or another, with their private police.

What could an old man like him do to stop it?

Twenty

A s a rule, Cross didn't engage in drinking contests, didn't measure his manhood by the quantity of hard liquor consumed. If he had, he would have come up short compared to James Fenimore Kowalski who seemed to gain both energy and clarity with each glass of Scotch.

That was all fine last night; but this morning Cross endured a rare hangover, and an atomic bomb of a headache. He couldn't go back to sleep. Having slept, or more likely slipped into unconsciousness, on the sofa, he could move to the kitchen without waking the others. He searched for something that would reduce the pain.

Thin morning light seemed to cast the room in a mist. For that Cross was grateful. No harsh light. No harsh sounds. He found tomato juice in the refrigerator. More good fortune, he thought. He poured himself a glass.

He clicked on the television, with the sound muted.

After a few moments of cuts from wars, an arrested celebrity or two, and the morning traffic report, the news switched to an early morning crash followed by the passport photos of the two men who grabbed him. Cross searched for the remote again, brought up the sound, but caught only the words 'fiery crash.'

He took a deep breath, looked around for his shoes. He went upstairs. Maya was asleep in the guest room where he left her. He remembered that and a few hours into the evening before his mind went blank.

Coming down to the other end of the hall, he heard singing. There, standing at the bathroom sink shaving, was Kowalski.

'I thought the whole point in having a beard is that you didn't have to shave,' Cross said.

'Oh, it's a lot more work. Shaving for you is like mowing the lawn. Keeping up my appearance requires the work of a talented gardener, trimming this, cutting that, shaping something else.' He went back to his task. 'You're up early.'

'I just thought I'd cram as much as I could into my short life.' He told Kowalski what he saw and what he believed was happening about the two men in the 'fiery crash,' and that he concluded Margot was killing everyone who could connect her to the sex slave trade and to the dead man that Maya saw in the trunk.

'Hence leaving her daughter to die,' Kowalski said.

'Yes. It was a no lose situation for her. She used her. While everyone was trying to rescue Maya, she could escape. If Maya didn't make it, one more witness down.'

'That leaves you.'

A strange mechanical sound, a low-pitched buzz pulled Shanahan from a light sleep. Judging by the sun, the day had begun without him. Maureen lay in her usual coma-like slumber beside him. He would normally linger a little, feel her warmth beside him, take in the scent of her hair, but his bleary eyes searched for what his ears heard.

He found it. Maureen's cell phone gyrated on the top of the bureau. He got to it before it vibrated off the edge. At this time of morning and without his reading glasses he couldn't identify the caller, but chanced it anyway.

'Hello,' he said softly, slipping out of the bedroom.

'Can't talk long,' Cross said.

'Why are you calling Maureen?'

'I'm calling you. Didn't want to use your regular phone . . . your landline. You might be bugged and I don't want them to find me. Just wanted you to know that the guys who abducted me are dead. Their car wrapped around a tree somewhere out near Geist Reservoir.'

'Well I got a little visit from what I suspect is a higher up,' Shanahan said. 'He said they were reassigned.'

'That's quite a transfer,' Cross said.

'He's promised me a little shock and awe if I don't give him what I don't have.'

'OK, gotta go. Call me from a cell, Shanahan, if you need to reach me.'

That was it. Wenders' former employers obviously played for keeps. It occurred to him that the only reason Shanahan wasn't similarly disposed might be that they believe Shanahan doesn't have the other half of the map and they not only want that, they also want to see who delivered the information to him.

'What are you smiling at?' Maureen asked. 'You never smile.'

'Was I smiling?'

'Yes, you most certainly were smiling. A big wide smile. Now I know why you don't smile.'

'Why is that?'

'You look foolish.'

'You know more than you think you know about your girl-friend,' Kowalski said. He had a mug of coffee. 'So stop being pissed, stop feeling guilty, stop feeling anything and think. What is it she has to do?'

'Besides kill a couple of more people who are very dear to me?' Cross said.

'And you,' Kowalski reminded him.

'I am dear to me too.'

Hester Ledford, Kowalski's once-a-week housekeeper, was in the kitchen with Maya, who was directing the preparation of scrambled eggs. Hester was in her seventies, at least. She was tall, thin, bony, but moved quickly.

'Good thing she wasn't twins,' Hester said when she came out to refill the coffee. 'Lord gave her enough energy to light up a city and enough confidence to . . .' Her voice trailed off.

The way Maya adapted yet again to new surroundings was a tribute to her mother, Cross thought. Maya learned to survive. It wasn't necessarily a good thought. Look what this skill or need did to her mother.

Kowalski leaned forward and said quietly but with great passion, 'Stop feeling sorry for the God awful condition of the universe. You didn't make it.'

'I know,' Cross said. 'But I should have known more about her.'

'You *do* know her. How and where is she living now that

she's burned down her lodging?' Not getting anything, he continued. 'All right, what is it in life that she holds most important?'

'Money,' Cross said, eyes widening.

'You're having an epiphany?'

'I hope not. I didn't bring my medication.'

'You're on to something, Cross.'

'Maybe the only thing she wants more than seeing us dead is not losing all the money she squeezed out of her home, her charge cards, and who knows what or who else. We find out where she keeps it and . . .'

'An account in Switzerland?'

'No, the opposite. She'd keep it close.'

'With her? In her car?' Kowalski asked.

'Oh no. She is cautious. What if the car was stolen? What if she was stopped? She wouldn't give it to anybody because she wouldn't trust them. She wouldn't bury it because there was a chance someone would find it. But she wouldn't put it in a bank because it could be tracked. She would need to identify herself. But she could put it into a safety deposit box. Even a bank safety deposit. No one would know what was inside. No one has access to it.'

'Banks report large deposits, but they don't report who opened a lock box and they don't know what's inside,' Kowalski said. 'Fascinating. See, you are thinking like she does. Only you can do that.'

'And she would keep it close,' Cross said, now sure of his theory. 'It would be here in the city so that her money went with her.'

'What about one of those mail drop places? They have boxes, besides the ones the clerk stuff mail into.'

'Not likely. Banks would be more secure. She can't afford to lose this. This is her survival money and we know what survival means to her,' Cross said, standing. He was impatient, though he wasn't sure what to do about his new theory.

'Once she's finished here she's off to Brazil or Paraguay or some other place without extradition,' Kowalski said, getting up and going into the kitchen.

It all seemed logical to Cross. She had enough money to hang out in a less expensive country until she met a man who had money and was willing to support her. All this, he reminded

himself, was more easily accomplished without a kid tagging
along. Having the kid would make her easier to identify. It
would make her less desirable. The kind of guy she'd be
looking for probably didn't want a family.

The man came out to the lobby to greet Shanahan. They shook
hands.

'Brant Hanks,' the man said, showing a smile that could be
used in a toothpaste commercial. He had to be pushing fifty,
but he was in shape as Shanahan suspected FBI agents were
required to be. 'Let's go for a walk.'

Shanahan was surprised that he actually got to see someone.
Government agencies weren't usually accessible so quickly.
Having no luck calling the various fed agencies, the elder
detective decided he'd try just dropping in at the Indianapolis
office. And well, it worked.

The building itself was a little forbidding. Shanahan knew
it as the Capehart Building, but somewhere along the line
someone added 'Minton' and a hyphen. Capehart was a long-
time Indiana senator a long time ago. Shanahan didn't know
who in the hell Minton was and how Minton came to share
the honor of the edifice that held the branch or regional offices
of various federal agencies.

'And we're walking because?' Shanahan asked in the elevator.

'Because I need a smoke,' Hanks said. 'And fresh air is
always good, don't you think.'

'I was just out there in the fresh air so it doesn't matter to
me one way or other.'

They didn't speak again until they crossed Pennsylvania
and on to the green lawn between the American Legion
National Headquarters and the Legion's Women's Auxiliary
Building. The area was quiet and very monumental. Lots of
flags blowing in the wind. South was Veteran's Memorial Park
with a DC looking obelisk at its center. It used to have either
a canon or a tank on each corner. And beyond that was the
World War Memorial – a huge building with stairway walls
that had lists of those who had died in wars. In the center of
the building was a large room of granite and marble and a
huge tomb.

Once they settled in the middle of a field of grass, Hanks
lit a cigarette.

'The famous Shanahan,' he said.

'I don't have a cape or a rabbit in a hat. I hope I haven't disappointed you.'

'No, you are famous in some circles,' Hanks said. 'You've heard the phrase "that dog won't hunt?"'

Shanahan nodded.

'You're known around our office as "the dog that won't stop hunting."'

Shanahan didn't respond.

'How's your friend, Cross?'

'You know him?'

'I went up to Eaton to help out the guys in the Muncie office. I was a little hard on the guy. I'm glad the kid turned up.'

'Me too.'

'I like happy endings.'

'I do too except that the crazy woman trying to kill him and the kid is still on the loose.'

Hanks bowed his head, shook it in a world-weary way, 'It's no longer in our jurisdiction. Anyway she took her own daughter. No crime in that. And the attempted murder? Local.' He let his sentence drift off. 'When we ran a list of Cross' known associates, there you were. Somehow you're involved in all sorts of things. What would the city do if you stopped making people mad?'

'I hadn't realized I was so much a part of your life, Mr Hanks.'

'That's the only reason I decided to see you. From our files you've not only ticked off some local muckety mucks, you also managed to convict one senator and raise the ire of another, not to mention a publisher, religious icon and, well, the list goes on, doesn't it?'

'I do what I can.'

'So what are you up to these days?' Hanks looked north in the direction of the tomb of the unknown solider. Across from the tomb, the Central Library, an elegant old building, was an end cap to the four-block run of conspicuous patriotism.

'It's a fitting space to be having this discussion,' Shanahan said. 'What do you know about Dark Wind?'

It was Hanks' turn to be quiet. He stubbed out his cigarette on the bottom of his shoe, and put the dead butt in his suit coat pocket. He looked Shanahan straight in the eye, then turned away from him. It was obvious that tension had tightened the agent's shoulders and when he turned back, he had a sour look on his face. Again, he looked at Shanahan and looked away. He shook his head in disbelief.

The old detective surmised the man was having a great debate with himself. The contortions and ticks headed toward comedy.

'You know something, don't you?' Shanahan asked. 'About two guys and a tree maybe? What else?'

Shanahan had the guy's attention, but he wasn't answering.

'I came upon a dead man in Mexico,' Shanahan said. 'He had information. Somehow I ended up with it.'

Hanks looked toward the ground. 'I had to talk to you, didn't I? What a fucking idiot I can be sometimes. Nothing good ever comes with meeting with people you don't have to meet with.'

'I was visited last night,' Shanahan continued. 'A man popped out of the shadows, threatened me in my own home. The local police say I'm just a crackpot.'

'How . . . what . . . Christ!' He blew the air out of his lungs. 'Why didn't you go to the CIA? This is international shit.'

'Can't find them. Tried to call. Got involved with the voice of a female robot that had me pushing buttons that led me in circles. Didn't figure the Secret Service would tell me anything either. Their name says it all. You, the FBI on the other hand, have a convenient branch office, just like a bank or a post office.'

'Look, when we're done talking, all we've talked about is the kid and the kidnapping. You agree with that? And I didn't tell you anything about that either, right? Just being a nice guy, right?'

'OK.'

'I swear Shanahan I didn't tell you any of this.' He didn't look around. In fact, he looked more relaxed. Shanahan thought he was just acting more relaxed. 'First, you get involved with this you are going to have the entire office of Homeland Security come down hard on you and the horse you rode in on.'

'I'm already involved and that wasn't my idea, believe me.'

'You seek out trouble.'

'Not this time,' Shanahan said. 'I was roped in against my will.'

'By who?'

'A whistle blower.'

'Crap!' Hanks was blowing his cool. If he were in the lenses of FBI binoculars or Dark Wind's for that matter, they would see by the agent's body language that he was upset, that he was hearing something he didn't want to hear.

'I refused the job he offered. But before he died I received half a message. Dark Wind is convinced that I either have the other half or it's on its way to me.'

'Listen,' Hanks said, forcing a calm. 'We like to think we're in charge of things. The FBI I'm talking about. We like to believe that even the President listens to us. We like to believe that. But it's fucking untrue. He's only interested if we're telling him what he likes to hear. Now, I know I'm only a lowly peon even in the FBI, but what I do know is that at the moment Homeland Security, for all of its bad rep in New Orleans, is under the thumb of someone who has a very vested interest in seeing that Dark Wind, a pet project of someone who calls most of the shots, is successful – very successful.'

Shanahan waited for something that related directly to him.

'Then there's the State Department, the CIA's National Clandestine Service and God knows who else. They can rain down on you from all directions. And if that's not enough, be advised fortunes will be won and lost over the success or failure of Dark Wind in various places around the globe. Long after this administration goes and that writing is on the wall, Dark Wind and various other conflict-related corporations will retain their power and they will continue to make trouble for anyone making trouble for them.'

'That means?'

'You're screwed!' Hanks almost lost it. 'Nobody can help you. Not the FBI, not the police, not your favorite politician. Not God. Nobody.'

'So,' Shanahan said.

'Give them what they want. I don't want to know what it is. Give it to them and they might let you live. If they don't kill you and you make a scene they will turn on their PR machine and make you look like a raving loony – and if you continue with this, I'm convinced you are.'

'You sure you have no interest in this?' Shanahan said.

'I'm sure,' he said. He looked at Shanahan for an uncomfortably long time. Then, embarrassed, he turned away. Hanks had given up. Fate was in charge.

Hanks walked across the field, back toward the Federal Building. Shanahan glanced around. He was alone on the long green, ceremonial lawn between the two grand Legion buildings.

Twenty-One

Cross, though he'd been a cop, spent little time with the Indianapolis Metropolitan Police Department's Homicide and Robbery Branch. He knew a few of the homicide detectives mostly from them investigating him. Kowalski had more to do with them. He'd worked with several cops there in his role as criminal defense attorney, but like Shanahan tended toward Swann when he had a choice in the matter.

Swann, who was interviewing someone, waved Kowalski and Cross away. He apparently wanted nothing to do with any of Shanahan's friends.

Lieutenant Maurice 'Ace' Collins was leaning against a doorway on the other side of the big room. He smiled.

'Even Swann doesn't want anything to do with you.'

'Not just Swann, I'm feeling particularly unloved at the moment,' Cross said.

'Where's the third musketeer?' Collins asked the tall, well-built black guy, handsome in his conservative but clearly expensive suit. Cross thought him to be smart, but arrogant. In the end though, with a little pushing and shoving, maybe Collins would come down on the right side.

As the story went, Collins shipped into Indianapolis from Detroit to make a name for himself. He knew that if he wanted to head a division one day, perhaps make chief, he had to make a dent in crime. That part was good. Solving murder cases would help with that. That he tended to think he was the only star in the show didn't make him easy to be around.

Cross resisted calling him 'Maurice,' which was his name. While it would be great fun, it would be counter-productive.

He and Kowalski wanted someone to help them out with crazy, deadly Margot. They hoped someone in the police department would help. At the moment, they couldn't be picky.

'Lieutenant? You have a moment for us?' Cross asked, in his best cheery, hopeful voice.

'This can't be good,' Collins said, but said it smiling. He seemed willing to entertain a few minutes of diversion from whatever tasks were at hand if only to break up the day with something amusing.

They followed him into the small, efficiently appointed seventies' office.

'This about Shanahan and his alien adventures?' Collins asked.

'No,' Cross said. He wanted to say more about the lack of police interest in such things, but this too would work to his disadvantage. But it reminded him that the bureaucracies reacted slowly to things that didn't fit the rulebook. One thing at a time, he told himself. At the moment Margot was the bigger threat, if only because she was a threat to Maya.

Kowalski found a wall to lean against and remained surprisingly quiet.

'You got the kid, right?' Collins asked.

'Yes. But not the mother.'

'We've got an APB out on her. Arson. Attempted murder.'

'Good,' Cross said. 'We've got an idea.'

'You see,' Collins said, sitting now behind his desk and putting his feet up. 'This is where things get funky.'

'An idea. You can't listen to an idea?'

'Go ahead.'

Cross explained his theory about Margot and the money and safety deposit boxes.

'Look,' Collins said when Cross came to the end of it. 'It's possible. But it's just one scenario out of thousands. She could have it in a Swiss Bank or wired it to Sao Paulo. She could have put it under a rock in Zionsville or any other place near here or far away. She could already be gone. What's left for her here? You?'

'For one.'

'Don't be such an egotist.'

'Not to kiss me, Ace, to kill me. And her daughter.'

'Tell me again why she'd bother.'

'The pattern is that everyone involved in her slave trade operation and a related murder in Maui is dead, except for Maya and me. And she's tried to kill us both.'

Collins put his feet down, scratched the back of his neck.

'All right. This isn't official, but follow up on your hunch and let me know what you find. I haven't got the people to go off searching for what might be anywhere on the planet.'

'I could have done that without you.'

Collins smiled. 'I'm surprised you didn't. You usually do.'

'We thought you might be interested in solving a kidnapping, arson, and attempted murder, and several successful ones,' Kowalski said, 'silly us.'

'Silly you. Let me know if you see anything shiny.'

Cross and Kowalski left. Collins followed.

'Hey!' When the two stopped. 'I promise. We are looking for her,' Collins said. 'But we're doing it our way.'

'Thanks, I understand,' Cross said. And he did.

'One more thing,' Collins said, coming up to them and speaking softly, 'we found the Toyota.'

'Where?' Cross asked.

'Downtown. Near Union Station,' Collins said.

'Hotels?' Kowalski asked.

'We checked. Nothing. We think maybe she took a train outta here.'

'Trains?' Cross shook his head. 'I didn't even think about trains, but it makes sense. Less security, ID problems. Takes everything with her.'

'It also means that she could buy a ticket to New York and get off in DC or in some small town in between,' Kowalski said.

Collins nodded. 'This was smart. She could have headed for Chicago and changed trains for all points west. We have no idea. She can pay cash for a train ticket, unlike renting a car where she would need a charge card and ID.'

'Or she's still here and just dumped the car because it was hot,' Cross said.

'Or that.' Collins looked over to Kowalski. 'I doubt if you'll listen, but I feel like I have to tell you anyway. If you find her – and I hope somebody does soon – let us know. Don't try to take her.'

Cross took a deep breath. 'I appreciate what you've done.'

Outside, Cross seemed lost.

'What's up?' Kowalski asked.

'One step ahead. She's always one step ahead. Trains. Didn't even think of that.'

'The city used to be a real hub for trains. Two hundred a day. Huge. Now, maybe a train a day comes in and out.'

It was true. The grand old railroad station was just another historic landmark. It now housed a hotel – tourists can sleep on old Pullman cars – the Mexican Consulate and a couple of museums. It was easy to forget about the trains.

'She could still be here. She's still screwing with my head.'

'She's that good?'

'I had no idea who I was dealing with.'

'We have a guest,' Maureen said, meeting Shanahan at the door.

'What kind of guest? A possum?'

She shook her head. 'No.'

'The man from last night?'

'You're getting warmer. Come see.'

He followed her into the living room, where a large man in a gray suit, but one size too small, stood. The suit jacket had wrinkles fully pressed in. As he turned toward Shanahan, he nodded. His rimless glasses hugged his not quite hairless skull.

'Good afternoon, Mr Shanahan. I'm Frank Singella.' He almost fell forward as he reached for Shanahan's hand. 'I'm an attorney for DWE and I've . . .'

'What is DWE?' Shanahan asked.

'Dark Wind Enterprises,' Maureen said, wearing her intentionally fake smile.

'Dark Wind seems to have quite a few employees, Mr Singella,' Shanahan said.

'And most of them paying attention to us.' Maureen continued her smile.

'You could run for public office with that smile,' Shanahan told her.

'Well, you are in the spotlight, it appears,' Singella said. He turned back to his briefcase, open on the cocktail table. He pulled out some papers and arranged them, so that there was something in each hand. He turned back to Shanahan.

'In my left hand, I have a check made out to you in the amount of $200,000 dollars.'

The man's eyebrows raised, inviting it seemed, a sound of approval from his audience of two. Both were quiet. The man's eyebrows dropped.

'In the other,' he said. 'I have a restraining order from the 7th District Federal Court. You may read it.' He handed the sheath of stapled papers to Shanahan who handed it to Maureen.

'What it says,' Singella continued, 'is, essentially, that you must turn over all information you have in your possession and any that you might yet receive relating to or about or referencing in any way Dark Wind Enterprises to me. I'll give you my card. In addition, you are not to mention to anyone at any time anything at all about said information, or your dealings with DWE.'

Maureen continued to read the restraining order.

'It mentions a Sedition Act and an Espionage Act,' Maureen said, 'and gag order is mentioned a dozen times, blah, blah, blah, national security, special wartime blah, blah, blah, Homeland Security Act, domestic terrorism, and the riot act.'

'The riot act?' Shanahan asked.

'Just wanted to make sure you were listening. But they do mention Patriot Act. I think it means you really have to shut up about all this. You really can't say anything about anything. If you tell the truth at any time during the rest of your life, you are unpatriotic.'

'If you'll notice, it applies to you too, ma'am, and to anyone with whom you may have discussed this.'

'With that, what about the $200,000? Why offer it?'

'Ooooh,' Maureen said with pain in her voice.

'You've been inconvenienced, Mr Shanahan. We don't believe that you intentionally set out to harm the interests of DWE or the United States.'

'Oh that's nice of you,' Shanahan said.

'We want to show our good faith,' Singella said, a modest smile, no doubt intended to show sincerity.

'Oh good faith. Then why the restraining order?'

'We want to be sure our good faith is appreciated.'

'They want to make sure their appreciation is appreciated,' Maureen said. 'I can appreciate that.'

Shanahan said nothing. The attorney became uncomfortable.

'You're not required to keep the $200,000, Mr Shanahan, but you are required to keep the restraining order, and for some free legal advice, I suggest you take this a little more seriously than you are.'

'Keep your money,' Shanahan said.

'I knew you'd do that,' Maureen said.

'And you guys have a habit of just dropping in,' Shanahan said. 'That's rude. Call ahead.'

The attorney smirked, found his briefcase and nodded before turning toward the door.

Kowalski, Cross, Shanahan and Maureen met at Harry's just as day was turning to night. Inside the bar, it didn't matter. It was always night of some indeterminate time. Soccer was on television, but the sound had been muted and no one watched.

Kowalski was reading the restraining order from Dark Wind that contained, coincidentally and oddly enough, endorsement by the FBI – the local office. Only Kowalski and Shanahan drank. Kowalski sipped on a Scotch and Shanahan had a shot of J.W. Dant whiskey and a bottle of Guinness. Cross was on coffee and Maureen on grapefruit juice.

'Maureen,' Cross said, 'could you call around the various banks to see if Margot has a safety deposit box?'

'I'm the girl, so I get the phone,' she said.

'We need a woman's voice and some gimmick to get them to say whether she has a box there or not. Kowalski would have a hard time explaining he was Margot Hudson.'

'That's a helluva job,' Harry said, interrupting them to refill the lone coffee cup. 'All the banks have them, all their branches.'

'Maybe,' Maureen said, 'just maybe we contact the main office of each bank and I can say something like 'I know it's silly, but it's been awhile since I've gotten into my safety deposit box and I can't remember which branch it's in.' What do you think?'

'That might do it,' Cross said. 'You're a genius.'

'By the way and speaking of phones, I talked to the owner of the house that Margot burnt down.'

All eyes but Kowalski's – he remained transfixed on the restraining order – were on her.

'But he didn't live there. He rented the place to some guy named . . . Chester Thurman.'

'We can appeal,' Kowalski said, putting down the papers and changing the subject. 'I've not seen one like this. It's a gag order and a restraining order.'

'Sounds like bondage to me,' Cross said.

'What's the basis for an appeal?' Shanahan asked.

'Prior restraint, maybe. They are telling you what you can't do with something you haven't even received. I'm not sure that will hold up. We can also do the freedom of speech, whistleblower thing. We could do Cross' abduction, but you guys made sure there was no trace left, no evidence.'

'How long will this take?' Maureen asked.

'Forever,' Kowalski said. 'If all we're after is to kill the restraining order then it doesn't make much sense. But the fact that we're going to court over it will make them nervous, I'm sure. Is that good or bad? That's for you to decide. We can get the Indiana Civil Liberties Union involved, maybe. They might like a shot at the government's private and apparently secret army.'

'Shove a stick in the hornet's nest.' Cross said. He said it with warning in his voice, not enthusiasm.

'It's an approach,' Kowalski said, 'and I like the idea.'

'Rebel with a cause,' Maureen said.

'Who'd you say the guy was?' Kowalski asked her. 'The guy who rented the house.'

'Chester Thurman. You know him?'

'Slurpy,' Kowalski said.

'How do you know him?' Cross asked.

'Defended him a dozen times at least. Big guy, dumb as a box of rocks. Worked as a bouncer, bodyguard. But his steady job was driver. He'd drive the girls to their johns, wait outside in the car, with a cell phone in his hand. Any trouble? Let's say the john doesn't pay, or gets rough with the girls. He's on it.'

'Why Slurpy? Or should I ask?' Maureen waited for the worst.

'He always had one of those Big Slurpies in his hand, the

kind you get from a 7–11. He was like a Hummer. He had to just keep filling up.'

'That's how she met him,' Cross said. 'Probably made him fall for her.'

'I'd bet on it. And if your girl is as smart as you make her out to be, she could wrap that pile of . . . that big ole guy around her little finger.'

'I take it you don't like him,' Shanahan said.

'Oh, I should be more charitable. He's just as entitled to life as anyone else. But people like him are completely unaware of how much harm they do. God forbid he should reproduce.'

'Can't be,' Cross said only to himself. This Thurman guy couldn't be the father.

'We have work to do,' Shanahan said, feeling like things were about to get more interesting.

Twenty-Two

What the news about Slurpy did for Cross was provide something to grab on to. Unlike Margot, Slurpy probably had friends, favorite haunts, a car, maybe a job. If she was with him, the trick was to forget about her for the moment. She was good at covering her tracks. He might not be so good. You get him, the theory goes, you get her.

Cross convened a meeting with Kowalski after the others left. He bought Kowalski a Scotch and himself a margarita in exchange for everything Kowalski knew about Thurman. Known hangouts. Known associates. Work. Habits.

'You want a bucket of sand and a heat lamp with this?' Harry said, when he set the margarita down in front of Cross. 'Damn, Howie, it ain't even summer.'

Cross knew Harry had an intense dislike for any mixed drink. Somehow, like wine, it wasn't an honest drink.

For Cross, life was good again. 'God bless Slurpy,' Cross said as he got into the Cadillac and drove to the car lot from which it was borrowed. He'd switch off before driving back to Ravenswood. He wouldn't make it easy for Margot to follow him let alone kill him.

Armed with some names, some places, Cross could get more names, family, for example, and more places – not just places he frequently visited but maybe faraway places where he could hole up.

The Cadillac was gone. He now drove a used, or abused, four-year-old VW bug. Lime green. But the color was the least of its problems. It felt like he had traded a seventy-five-foot yacht for a rowboat. On the other hand, with all that driving, he'd save on gas.

Kowalski didn't have a photograph. If he was nice to the cops, maybe he could get a mug shot. Thurman had been booked many times on charges that ranged from drunk and disorderly to assault and battery. Lots of violence in his files, but not burglary, kidnapping or murder. Kowalski told Cross that he would have no trouble identifying the guy without a photo. The top third of his left ear was missing. Bit off in a bar fight.

His sudden good feelings began to drift when his gypsy mind began to question the night before. What happened in those missing minutes? Missing hours? He knew some time was missing because one minute he was drinking and talking and the next he was waking up.

Kowalski was at his place about an hour and a half before Cross got there. In addition to switching cars, Cross picked up some clothes and picked up some food. He couldn't expect the attorney to do everything. A few steaks, a bottle of good red wine – he had help from the storekeeper on the latter account – and that should keep the debt from rising too much.

Approving of the wine, Kowalski was a happy man. Maya enjoyed switching the channels on the large screen TV in the back room, the one that overlooked the river. There was no cable at the Cross Eaton household. She was in heaven.

'Wine with dinner,' Kowalski said. 'How about a little something before?'

'Maybe not,' Cross said.

'Suit yourself,' the attorney, now in sweatshirt and jeans, poured himself some Scotch.

'Kowalski?' Cross called to him.

'Yeah.'

'Last night . . . when we had a few drinks?'

'Yeah.' Kowalski smiled.

'Did I behave like an ass or anything?'

'What? You don't remember?'

'Not the whole night.'

'You didn't do anything to be ashamed of,' Kowalski said. 'If that's what you're asking.'

'No, no, no. I know that. Did I get stupid? You know what I mean?'

'We talked.'

'What about?'

'Women, something about reincarnation, eternity through our children . . .'

'Really?' Cross sat on the sofa.

'Good and evil.'

'I talked about good and evil?'

'Your other personality, Mr Hyde, is very interesting, more than . . . well let's just say it was a stimulating evening. You sure I can't get you a tequila?'

'Maybe not. There's still a lot to do.'

'How often do you have these blackouts?'

'Not often. Maybe three times in twenty-five years.'

'That you know of.'

'That I know of.' Did he reveal a secret? Did he even have one? Maybe he did and maybe he didn't.

'I'll fix the steaks,' Kowalski said. 'How do you like it?'

'Medium.'

'I could have guessed.'

'And the lovely Miss Maya?'

'Rare,' Cross said. 'I know, you could've guessed.'

Kowalski laughed and headed toward the kitchen.

'Come talk to me,' Kowalski said. 'We can talk about the weather if that will make you more comfortable.

Shanahan felt less threatened having just received the restraining order. Surely they wouldn't try to kill him after going to all that trouble to shut him up. Then again? The restraining order was perfect cover for just that reason. He decided to sleep on the sofa just in case.

He awakened with something on his forehead. He jerked forward.

'It's OK,' Maureen said.

'I don't want you away from me,' she said. 'Come to bed.' They spoke in near complete darkness.

'You were asleep,' Shanahan said.

'It doesn't matter. I know. It's hard enough when you go away.'

'We'll get through this,' he said.

The digital clock said 3:44 as he climbed into bed, soon feeling the warmth of her body pressed against him. The last thing he remembered, until light woke him, was the familiar scent of her hair.

'Mr Kowalski had to be in court early,' Hester said. 'He asked me to tell you that he'd be back at eleven.' She handed him a cup of coffee. Cross could hear the television in the back room, glanced that way.

'She's had her breakfast,' Hester said, referring to Maya. 'What would you like?'

'Thank you, coffee is fine for now,' Cross said. He wasn't used to being waited on and felt odd asking anyone to fix his breakfast.

'Mr Kowalski asked me to come back in today to watch over Maya.'

'That was nice of you, thank you.' He'd have to reimburse Kowalski. 'I know she's a challenge.'

'Like I said yesterday, there's a lot of life in that girl,' Hester said. 'She could be president some day.'

'Or head the mafia,' Cross said under his breath. He had this creeping fear that she was going to be like her mother.

He'd check in with Shanahan. He'd try looking up some of the folks Kowalski gave him. He could make some calls. Did Slurpy have a day job? He could get some things done by phone and then talk to Kowalski when he got back.

'Maya,' Cross said coming into the room. 'How are you holding up?'

'I'm not holding up anything, silly.'

'No, I meant are you OK? You know, happy?'

She shrugged.

'I'm fine, but I'd like to go back to Jack and Margaret's.'

Jack and Margaret were his parents. She said it so casually, so familiarly. He could never bring himself to call them Jack and Margaret. It struck him odd that a five-year-old would do that. Her old friends, Jack and Margaret. Jesus.

'Better TV here,' Cross said.

'Yes, but Brenda and Helene need me.'

'Yes. That's true. Well, soon. I'm going to do a little work. Are you OK?'

She looked at him like he was crazy to ask the question.

The telephone book had become virtually obsolete, especially in this case. The names he tried looking up belonged to a group of folks – those operating on the fringes of society – who had no use for landlines. They had cell phones. Often disposable. There was no real directory for that.

He found only one name among those Kowalski had given. One of Slurpy's known associates was Dixie Swift. She was listed. He didn't know what she was to Slurpy, but she had posted bail a couple of times.

The odds of there being two Dixie Swifts were relatively long. Dixie was home. And after he did some cajoling and promised to bring a bottle of Wild Turkey she agreed to meet with him. He could get there, talk to Dixie, and be back by noon.

Maureen had an early morning meeting with the other realtors at the office. When she returned she would make calls to banks. Shanahan spent the morning getting the main numbers and listing them so she could call.

Even if they could find a bank where Margot had a safety deposit box, it didn't mean she and her money were still around. And if she was, what would they do, camp out day and night just to see if she showed up? Ah, she could only show up when the bank was open. That helped.

A call to one of the major banks indicated that banks were basically nine to five during the week and open Saturday mornings. They could divide up the stakeout. While it still didn't seem an efficient method, it was a method. He felt better after talking with Cross, who had a line on a close Margot associate.

Maureen called to say that the meeting was dragging on more than expected. Back in an hour. Shanahan took Casey for his day's walk, but this time he shortened the trip and he brought his .38 with him. Carrying the weapon was based on

Maureen's philosophy that if you bring an umbrella it wouldn't rain. He hoped that was the case.

Cross came down Rural, past 10th, near Harry's place, to Michigan Street. When people were asked to describe the area, they would struggle for words. Tough, maybe. Dicey. Back in the fifties, it was the neighborhood of blue collar factory workers. When manufacturing dispersed to the less expensive rural areas, then overseas, the area was low-rent rednecks. Now it was the convergence of gang-bangers of different cultures. Tough Blacks and Hispanics joined their white brethren for all sorts of mischief.

Dixie Swift lived in a two-story frame house. The paint was largely missing from the wood and the filmy glass in the windows looked as though they could be blown out by a stiff breeze. The small front yard was bare earth and dandelion.

She was a white lady, fifty, give or take ten years, short but hefty. She wore a cotton dress, cut square across the bosom to show off what must have been one of her best assets when she was in the running. The lipstick, applied by an unsteady hand, was fresh. Her eyes sparkled. That was surprising. The eyes of most alcoholics seemed passive, quiet, dying. Perhaps he had misjudged her based on the bribe she desired.

'Miss Swift, I'm Howie Cross.' He handed her the paper bag that contained the liquor.

'Mrs Swift,' she corrected him. 'Come in.'

They were immediately in the living room. There were matching, worn sofa and chairs covered in faded coral. Two lamps – one with a half-naked Hawaiian girl and the other a half-naked Hawaiian boy holding up the lamp shades – flanked the sofa. They were on, providing the only light in the rooms. The curtains were drawn. The house smelled mildly of mildew and tobacco.

'Would you like some?' she asked.

'No. No thank you.'

She looked relieved.

'It's flu season,' she said. 'I'll just go pour myself a little. I'll be right back.'

Another hot toddy, he thought, without the heat.

The ashtray on the coffee table was filled with butts. Looked to be two brands. One had a white filter and was put out while there was an inch of cigarette left. The other was a tan filter. The smoker got every ounce of nicotine out of his or her cigarette. One looked to be a Benson & Hedges Menthol. That was Margot's brand.

The coffee table also held frayed copies of *People* and *Us*. A worn paperback, *Five Days in Paris*, by Danielle Steele, was open, but face down. A television was in the corner. Off. He could hear her fussing in the kitchen. He could hear her refrigerator running before the heat clicked on. She could pay her electric and heating bills.

She came back in the room carrying a glass – the kind that jelly comes in – with a couple inches of undiluted Wild Turkey. She seemed happy.

'Oh please sit down,' she said nodding toward one of the upholstered chairs. She sat on one end of the sofa, taking a sip, and putting the glass down on one of the magazines. 'You wanted to talk about Chester, you said?'

He was glad she remembered and glad that she mentioned 'Chester.' He might have asked about 'Slurpy.'

'Yes, Mrs Swift, here's my dilemma. I'm trying to find a little girl's mother and the only thing I know is that Chester knows the mother and has seen her lately. I need to find Chester to find the mother.'

'How funny,' she said.

'What?'

'Well you are asking a mother to help you find her son so he can help you find the daughter's mother.'

'Very good. I don't think I could have put that sentence together.'

'I won't be able to very much longer.' She winked and reached for her glass.

'He's your son?'

'Yes. My one and only. From my first husband,' she said. She looked at Cross with a very serious look on her face. 'You must promise me you mean him no harm.'

'I promise I mean him no harm. Finding the little girl's mother is my only interest. Do you know where he is?'

'In general, yes.' She smiled, then coyly, 'He's around. He drops in from time to time.'

'You have any idea where I might find him?'

'I don't know if he's working.'

Remembering his rented home was incinerated, maybe Slurpy bedded at home these days.

'Maybe he crashes here.'

'No. Not since he was thirty-five or so. We don't get along.'

'Where does he hang out?'

'He plays in the neighborhood sometimes.'

'You know where he's staying these days?'

'Last time I heard he was living somewhere near the Murat Temple.'

She apparently didn't know his place was burned to the ground, or she was playing him. He couldn't be sure.

As she took another sip, he looked around for any traces of a male living in the house. Nothing in the living room suggested it. But he remembered there were *two* brands of cigarettes in the ashtray. Did Mrs Swift smoke?

'Could I use your restroom?'

'Sure, down that hall. And I'll just freshen this up.'

Cross went toward the bathroom, which was at the end of the hall. He passed by two bedrooms. One looked completely unlived in. Bed was made, blinds drawn. Some impersonal bric-a-brac on the bureau. No sign that anyone was staying there.

The other bedroom was obviously hers. A little frilly. A stack of paperbacks. Another television. Her bed had half a dozen pillows. A robe was draped across a chair.

In the bathroom, the medicine cabinet revealed an abundance of plastic prescription drug containers. Blood pressure. Cholesterol. Acid reflux. Other prescriptions that he knew nothing about. But the key was that they were all hers. None for Chester Thurman. Still, she could have put things away before his arrival. Why not the cigarettes?

Cross flushed the toilet, turned on the water for a few seconds. As he came back he noticed some loose mail on the dining room table. He noticed she was already back in her seat and sipping and therefore could get nothing but a quick glimpse. He saw a blue envelope he was sure contained coupons and a ripped brown envelope that looked to be one that contained a check from the federal government. So far, nothing suggested Slurpy spent any significant time here.

'I wonder if I could beg another favor. Could I get a cigarette off you?' Cross asked. 'I left mine in the car.'

'I don't smoke,' she said.

'Well, that's all right, I shouldn't smoke anyway. You live alone in this old big house.'

'It's my world, Howie, and doesn't seem so big to me.'

Howie stood. 'I should go, I suppose.'

'You don't have to. Mr Swift is dead you know.' She grinned. Cross was sure she didn't mean it. She just liked saying it.

'How do you get around?'

'I drive, Mr Cross. I'm not in the grave yet.'

'It will be a long time before that happens,' Cross said. 'I'm sorry, I've taken up your time. You have things to do and people to see.'

'You are wrong again,' she smiled. 'You are my first guest in a very long time. Thank you for your gift. Did you get everything you needed?'

'Yes. Thank you for your time,' Cross said.

He walked to his car, called Lieutenant Collins.

'I can't promise it,' Cross said, 'but our little arsonist may be at Slurpy's mom's house.'

'How'd we end up in junior high?'

Cross explained. He also asked Collins to check the Department of Motor Vehicles – to get the make, model and year of the car Dixie Swift drove.

At least two people were in Dixie's house recently. Judging by the mingling of cigarette butts, they were there at roughly the same time. If Slurpy and Margot weren't staying there, they may have dropped by having run out of options. They could have easily had a long talk with Dixie. Maybe about Dixie's car.

Twenty-Three

Casey's short walk turned out to be uneventful. They walked on the street. The strip of green between was muddy and even if Shanahan were willing, Casey wouldn't be. When he was young, neither hell nor high water could keep him from exploring every inch of the landscape. He'd once wallowed ecstatically in the smelly remains of a wild animal. No more. The hound, regularly dosed with buffered aspirin to ease the pain in his old bones, had become fussy about such things.

In the kitchen, Shanahan reached down to undo the leash from Casey's collar and found something foreign dangling below. He rolled the collar so that the object was at the top. It was clear. This was the same kind of device that had been sealed inside the fake cue ball.

How did this happen? He was with Casey every second. During the night? That was scary. No, now that he had a moment to think about it, he knew when it happened. The afternoon he took the walk to the park and let Casey off leash. It was when Shanahan tossed the ball up over the hill and Casey took longer than usual to return. That was the same time Shanahan thought he saw Wenders' driver. He did see him. The guy was loyal to Wenders, even in death.

Shanahan carefully removed what Maureen called a thumb drive. Casey lapped at his water bowl and ambled off to find a comfortable place to nap. Nothing he could do with it now. He would wait for Maureen. He started to put it in his pants pocket, decided not to.

Where would he put it? He looked around the kitchen, wandered through the rooms. He had several ideas – inside a videocassette, somewhere in the basement maybe in a box of books. He could even hollow out a small section of a book. Bury it in the garden. Tie it to a tree limb.

Instead, he reattached it to Casey's collar, this time putting it on the under side of the collar. Wenders' man had a good idea.

Shanahan fixed himself some lunch, and thought about what he could fix for dinner. It was his turn. He had some chicken sausage, pasta, some fresh basil growing in a clay pot – Maureen's idea. That would work. One of his one-pan wonders.

When Maureen returned she found she had two jobs in addition to the one that helped pay the bills. She had to call the banks. She had to get into the information on the small portable drive.

She slipped the drive into her computer, brought the document up and gave Shanahan instructions on how to scroll down. That kept him busy while she started making the phone calls.

'Hi, this is Margot Hudson,' Maureen said. 'This is so embarrassing, but I opened a safety deposit box at one of your branches and I can't remember which one. It's so foolish. But you know, from time to time I use several of your branches.' There was a pause. 'Oh, thank you.'

She waited.

'Verify my address?' Maureen looked at Shanahan.

She gave the banker the address in Lockerbie.

Maureen had it from her search for the owner. But she didn't know whether the address worked or not because the bank had no record of a Margot Hudson having any kind of account. One down.

As Maureen repeated the script again and again, Shanahan scrolled down the documents. It was broken into sections. Each section had a number, presumably one that connected with the individuals listed in the other document.

What Shanahan saw were corporations, governments, dictators, royalties involved in what appeared to be a good old boy network. This wasn't new. It was like the good old boys in just about any good sized town in America. Developers, construction companies, city planners, and politicians pooled their resources in some huge project that the public knew nothing about until it was too late to object or invest. The rich and powerful would get richer and more powerful.

It appeared to be the same here except this was on a global scale replete with wars based on something other than protecting the homeland. Greedy international corporations hungry for oil rights as well as construction, supply and security contracts determined national policy. With no great leap of the imagination these were linked with other politicians and bureaucrats who could trouble shoot and stall investigations and reward political muckety-mucks who could guide lucrative contracts to the favored few.

No doubt, Shanahan thought, these good old boys would be rewarded by promotion and a successful career with those corporations once they left office. There might also be funds deposited in overseas bank accounts making eventual retirement significantly more than comfortable. If true, it was corruption on such a scale that ENRON would look like petty larceny.

The information wasn't as specific as it might be, but it

would provide industrious investigative reporters the names of the players and how they related to each other.

This was much, much bigger than Dark Wind. They were merely one of the players, fairly new on the scene at that.

Shanahan couldn't read it all in one sitting. The document went on for more than 300 pages. It wasn't necessary for him to do so. Shanahan and the illusive Mexican were just messengers. The next step would be to somehow get this to someone who could do something with it. The same folks the others went to. But he realized sending it out on the home computer would make it easy to convict him of disobeying the restraining order.

'Oh yes, thank you. Now I remember,' Maureen said into the phone. She smiled as she penciled some notes on a piece of paper.

Cross stopped at his place to pick up his mail and get some fresh clothes. Down to a pair of jeans and a sweatshirt, he gathered socks and underwear for two more days. That was it. As for the mail, nothing but advertising. The country was insane with advertising. He bought what he needed. Buying wasn't a way of life. What a waste of trees, he thought, as he disposed of the flyers in the kitchen trash. When he came out, there was a man, as big as a small building, standing in his way. The man had a piece of one ear missing.

'Slurpy!' Cross said with as much cheer as he could muster. 'I've been looking for you.'

'I know.' He looked pretty serious for a guy with that nickname. Pretty dangerous too.

'So . . . so good to see you,' Cross said, trying to keep it light while he tried to figure out how to get out of there with his bones in tact. At the moment, he was trapped in the kitchen. Slurpy was between Cross and both exits. No way out.

'Where's the kid?' Slurpy asked.

'Let's go in the room there,' Cross said, motioning toward the middle room, where he'd at least have a chance to run for it. 'We'll talk about it.'

'Don't take a conversation,' Slurpy said.

'Oh, but it does,' Cross said, as he ordered himself to think. THINK. Why does it take conversation? 'You see I don't know exactly where she is, but between us, I bet we could figure it out.'

'I ain't no fool.' He stood his ground.

'Yeah, well maybe you are,' Cross said, changing tactics.

'What do you mean?' he asked. His eyes nearly closed and his body seemed to anchor itself in place.

'I bet you don't know Margot tried to kill her daughter,' Cross said.

'That's ain't how it went down. She said you were slippery.'

'I was there. She set fire to the house.'

'You set fire to the house. She couldn't get upstairs to save her daughter.'

This wasn't working either. Cross doubted he could bridge the credibility gap. He'd bet anything Slurpy was in love. Margot was a master.

'That's not how it happened,' Cross said. 'By the way, I met your mother.'

'I know.'

'Nice lady.'

'You don't know her.'

'Well . . .' Cross was happy that Slurpy seemed in no hurry to beat the crap out of him. But he was also aware that Slurpy's body was a lethal weapon. For it, he needed no permit. He couldn't forget to bring it with him. And it was always loaded and ready.

Cross had no such weapon. It would be Fay Wray beating on King Kong's chest all over again, but with a happy ending for Mr Kong. There were a couple of big knives in the drawer by the sink – if he needed them, if he could get to them.

'Where's the little girl?' Slurpy asked. He wasn't going to be diverted from his simple task.

'Safe,' Cross said.

'That's not an answer.'

'It's true though.' Cross was thinking as fast as he could, while trying not to trigger anything rash. 'And isn't that important?' He wished Slurpy was either smarter or dumber. As it was he was just smart enough not to be convinced. If he were just a little smarter, Cross could explain Margot to the guy, how she was using him like she had used Cross.

'Margot told me that Maya was my daughter,' Cross said. 'She dropped her off last year for her safety when she was pursued by some really nasty guys.'

'So?'

'So, she did the same again, this time saying that Maya was mine and that I had to take care of her. Then, she kidnapped her. You know what if feels like to love someone. I learned to love Maya, wanted to protect her. I didn't set that fire. Margot did to create a diversion to keep from being caught.'

'For what? You're the only one after her.'

'I'm after her now. She has killed all her associates from her sex slave days.'

'Cut it out,' Slurpy said, readying himself for something.

'I'm telling you the truth. She shot at me. She left Maya to burn.'

Slurpy's face telegraphed his intent. He lurched forward. Cross flung the refrigerator door in his face, dazing Slurpy and nudging him away from the center of the room. Cross swung into the hole, but Slurpy caught his foot. Cross hit the floor face first. Twisting his body as far as he could so he could see, he kicked Slurpy in the face. Cross scooted away and got to his feet. The only advantage he had was speed and he used it to get to the front door, then to the front gate.

Cross was sure he felt the earth move under Slurpy's heavy feet. Not fast off the start, the big guy had real cruising speed, but like a locomotive not a lot of ability to stop. Cross had no time to open the gate and he didn't have confidence that he could jump it easily. Slurpy bore down. Cross quickly stepped aside. Slurpy crashed into the wooden gate, unhinging it and sending it crashing to the ground. He followed.

Cross got the cell phone from his jacket pocket, dialed 911. Gave the operator the address.

'They're coming for you Slurpy,' Cross said. It was a game of not being 'it' as Slurpy lunged and Cross dodged. 'They're coming to take you away.'

The whoops of a siren were faint at first, but gained strength.

'I have no reason to lie to you,' Cross said. 'She's playing you for a fool. And you will pay. She never does. She doesn't pay for anything.'

There was something frantic, almost desperate in Slurpy's face. Cross felt sorry for him. Slurpy knew, maybe he'd known for a long time. That's how these things worked with guys. And he was pissed. Somebody had to pay. Cross was there to receive his uncontrollable anger.

'You bought her a car.'

He shook his head. 'I lent it to her.'

'No big straight guy like you buys a little red car,' Cross said. 'Wrong size, wrong color.'

Slurpy didn't say anything.

'She told you she was broke, right?'

He stopped moving, looked at Cross.'

'She's not broke. She sold her house in Hawaii, drained all the cash out of her credit cards. She's got a wad of cash that would choke a whale and once she's taken care of Maya and me she will take her cash and go.'

He shook his head 'no.'

'You're not going with her.'

The sirens were on the street in front of them.

'You're up to your kneecaps in debt just to please her, aren't you?'

He looked like he might cry. Cross definitely did not want to see that.

'It's OK, Slurpy,' Cross said. 'She did it to me too.'

Slurpy stopped. He sat down on the ground.

The police came. Cross explained things. Slurpy went quietly.

Shanahan called Kowalski on one of Harry's customer's cell phones. The elder detective sat at the end of the bar. Harry futzed around, swiping his damp towel on surfaces already swiped clean.

'Your phone clear?'

'Yeah,' Kowalski said.

'What do I do?' he asked the attorney after filling him in on the new information.

'Get it to me,' Kowalski said. 'I'll drive down to Louisville, send it out from a coffee shop.'

'You go all the way to Louisville?'

'Two hours. I have things to do there, anyway. Get me the email addresses you want me to send this to. All right?'

'You're willing to do this?' Shanahan asked.

'It's my pleasure. Remember, we're not sending this to North Korea. We're sending this to senators and reporters. Against the law? I call it civil disobedience.'

Shanahan sipped his Guinness.

'How do I get this to you?'

'Where are you now?'

'Harry's.'

'Leave it there. It's on the way.'

'When are you going?'

'Tonight. Right after I stop at the downtown and free a guy who was trying to kill our friend Howie.'

'You operate in strange ways.'

'God and I have much in common,' Kowalski said. 'Slurpy's a client. What can I say? And speaking of Cross, the man himself is at my door.'

'Dixie Swift drives a gray Ford Taurus,' Collins said.

'Thank you,' Cross said, cell phone to his ear, coming into Kowalski's living room.

'You might be interested. Dixie has a record,' Collins said.

'Really.'

'You visited her over there on Rural?'

'I did.'

'She used to live a little further west. Lots of big brick buildings. Big fence.'

'Women's prison. What did she do?' Cross asked.

'Manslaughter. Mr Swift. You say she's Slurpy's mother?'

Slurpy was no stranger to tough women, Cross thought. 'Nature is cruel.'

'That's why I have a job.'

'Slurpy's going downtown, courtesy of your peers, but I'm not going to press charges.'

'He came after you?' Collins asked.

'Yeah. Poor boy is in love.'

'That'll do it.'

'He wants to find Margot's little girl, save Margot from all evil . . .'

'And drive off into the sunset in Mommy's Taurus. We'll watch the house. Seems likely the two of them will hook up soon.'

'He probably can't stay away.'

The conversation with Collins was over. Kowalski was slipping on his black suit jacket as Cross folded up his phone.

'Glad you made it,' Kowalski said to Cross. 'I've got to go. I'll be back tonight, before ten, I'm guessing. Hester will be back in the morning. We'll go full bore tomorrow. Food in the fridge.'

He was out the door. But this time, Kowalski took his car, not his bike. A long trip, probably.

'Just like old times,' Cross said to Maya, after Kowalski left. 'Just you and me.'

As always, her face gave her away. She was clearly weighing the implication of that statement. How would that affect her life?

'I'll make some pasta and we'll watch a movie, or something,' Cross said.

'Let's go to a movie,' she said, smiling as if this was such a good idea Cross couldn't possibly object.

'I wish we could. Maybe in a few days.'

'That's because you're hiding me again?'

'Not much longer, I promise. Then things will be back to normal.'

Maya shook her head, frustrated but not fighting it.

For Maya it had never been normal. Even when she was in Maui, her mother was gone most of the time. In Indianapolis, she'd been shifted from Margot to Cross, from Cross to his parents, back to Margot and now she's in hiding at Kowalski's place. Was the future going to be any better? If mom's in prison . . . what?

Twenty-Four

Shanahan and Maureen had no trouble returning to Harry's before Kowalski. And there was no one in the bar but the regulars. He gave Harry the envelope that contained the thumb drive and the email list.

Harry convinced them to have a drink. Shanahan and Maureen sat at the bar, where not all that long ago Indiana's blue laws prohibited a woman to sit. Shanahan told Harry to hold the whiskey back. Just a Guinness. Maureen had a rum and tonic, light on the rum. They planned to have dinner at Sakura's, a Japanese restaurant on the north side. A beer was an essential ingredient with his Teriyaki fish and whatever her more adventurous choice would be.

Shanahan was a little more relaxed. He didn't know if the powers that be would come down on him after the transfer of information was completed. Maybe. But this was a window, both in terms of Dark Wind and at least for the evening it was the quiet before the storm with Margot. Margot, if she hadn't already, couldn't get to her money tonight. Cross was babysitting. The evening should be quiet for everyone.

But as Shanahan stared at the cash register where Harry had placed the information, a thought slowly burned its way to his consciousness. Something wasn't right about this. What Shanahan was doing, essentially emailing the information or having it emailed should have been redundant. Why couldn't Wenders have emailed it himself? From some out of the way coffee shop in Puerto Vallarta or Mexico City?

He didn't need Shanahan to do that. In fact, that's not what Wenders had asked him to do. He wanted to share Shanahan's identity. Think about it, he told himself.

'No,' Shanahan said out loud and forcefully.

'No?' Maureen asked. 'Who are you saying "no" to?'

Shanahan just shook his head. What was going on?

'Since no one else asked you a question,' Maureen said, 'then I assume you told yourself "no," which wasn't a very smart thing to do because it will just make you want to do it more.'

'What?' Shanahan asked, coming back to the moment at hand.

'What's wrong?' she asked.

He explained.

'The information was passed on to you when it was clear your friend could no longer deliver it himself,' she said. 'Maybe that's why you were brought back. To see that he was dead. To carry out his wishes.'

The explanation was helpful, calmed him, but it didn't erase the uneasy feeling in his belly. Had he been played?

Dinner at Sakura's was good as always, the place lively and a little loud. Maureen had sushi. They shared a big bottle of Asahi beer. Cold and dry, it hit the spot.

At home, he felt antsy. The boys from Dark Wind or possibly CIA seemed to be able to come and go at will. At eight

Shanahan got the one-ring phone call he'd expected. It was Kowalski's way of letting Shanahan know that the information had gone out. If there were problems, there would be a ring, then a few minutes later, another one.

In theory, Shanahan told himself, this bit with Wenders and the mirror government should be over for him. There was no reason for anyone to complicate matters any further. Getting back at Shanahan would gain them nothing, only one more way they could make costly mistakes. They were too smart for that, he thought. He hoped.

Maureen went to bed early with a thick book. Shanahan let Casey out in the back. The dog wasn't eager, but it was the routine. And routines were important to him. Time for dinner. Time for a walk. Time for the last outing of the evening.

Inside, Shanahan sat in the upholstered chair in the living room. The only light came from the hallway. It made a sharp pattern on the dark floors, an angle that ended at Shanahan's feet.

He wasn't going to sleep tonight unless he sorted some things out. He goes over it. Out of the blue, he's called down to Mexico by someone who was a very small part of his past. The man who called him waits a while before actually meeting with him. The man wants to trade identities. There is another wait while Shanahan presumably decides if he'll go along with the idea. He's brought back to meet him again. But now he's dead, apparently killed by the organization he'd worked for and the one he'd chosen to betray.

And why would he want Shanahan's identity if Shanahan was implicated in the process? He looked at it again. He leaves Mexico, but finds that he is inadvertently a messenger delivering the man's last whistle-blowing correspondence. What, if anything, is wrong with this picture?

The answer wasn't forthcoming.

Shanahan checked the locks on the doors, not that it would prevent these guys. He climbed in beside Maureen who was deeply involved in another story. He slipped his revolver under his pillow. He would sleep, but it wouldn't be the sleep of a man at peace – with anything.

'What are you thinking?' Maureen asked, collapsing her book and reaching for the light.

He tried to think of what he was thinking.

'You think this isn't over with the Dark Wind guys?'
'They may be done,' he said.
'But you're not?'
'I don't think so.'
'Why am I not surprised?' She kissed him on the cheek.

Kowalski was back right at ten. Maya was in bed. Cross had allowed himself a finger of pure Tequila. Nothing more. While it was normal for him to take it all in one big, satisfying gulp, Cross sipped it. Kowalski bought the best, not the kind you'd mix in a margarita or a Tequila sunrise.
'You mind?' Cross nodded toward the stairway.
'No. You looking for trouble?' He smiled.
'Yeah. I am. I hope I find her.'
'Where are you going to look?'
'Momma Swift says her son Slurpy plays in the neighborhood. I figure these places are going to come to life in the next hour. I'm going to check out the neighborhood.'
'Where's that?'
'Rural, Michigan, Tenth. That area.'
'You shouldn't go down there alone.'
'Who says I'll be alone? There will be plenty of people there.'
'Not the kind of people you want to invite home for dinner.'
'I won't invite them to dinner.'
'Well,' Kowalski said.
'Well what?'
'I don't know. I thought I had something say. I guess I didn't.'
'I really need for you to stay with Maya.'
'You know what I make an hour?' Kowalski said, smiling.
'Just tonight, for a couple of hours.'
He nodded. 'I know. Not a problem.'

Cross didn't have to look far. The place he entered had a check cashing center, a liquor store, and a bar. Now if only there was a section to buy meth, crack, and oxycotin. Oh, there was. The parking lot. This was the place to be if you wanted to be in places like this.
Slurpy was there. He was at the bar, listening intensely to a man with tattoos, beard, and a shaved head. The place wasn't

crowded, but people were coming in. The sound system blasted ZZ Top. *Rough boy*. So far, this was the only plus. It was also fitting.

Cross scanned the place. No Margot. She wouldn't like it here. On the other hand, he was sure she could handle it. And where else could she be? She couldn't afford to be running around town. If she was in town.

Cross had dressed for the occasion. He picked the most worn jeans from his small wardrobe and a black leather jacket, a faded tee shirt with a beer logo, and a pair of work boots. He also had two-day's growth of beard. It must have worked. Nobody noticed him.

He moved to the bar, but stayed at Slurpy's back. He ordered a tequila. The bartender waited. 'Straight,' Cross said. The bartender nodded. Cross thought he saw approval on the man's otherwise belligerent face. A good face to have in a place like this.

So far, so good, Cross thought. He wasn't sticking out in the crowd. There was a problem though. He had come without a specific plan. A confrontation with Slurpy wouldn't be productive. Maybe he could just dissolve into the crowd until Slurpy went somewhere or Margot showed up. Cross sipped slowly.

He looked around again. He noted the layout of the place – restrooms to the rear. Also, because the law would demand it, a back door, no doubt somewhere back by the restrooms. He looked at each new arrival. This wasn't quite the bar scene from the first *Star Wars*, but close.

An hour passed. Slurpy moved around the bar, stopping here and there to talk. Cross, who remained at the bar, turned his body accordingly to keep from being recognized. He still hadn't a plan. The bartender stopped to check on Cross' drink and saw that little of it was gone.

'You pregnant?' the bartender asked, offended. He didn't wait for a reply.

He thought the bartender's disdain was his way of increasing revenue. Sales through intimidation. Cross paid no mind until he saw the bartender talking with some others at the bar. Each one he talked to would turn and look back toward Cross. In a place like this, a good bartender knows more than how to fix a drink and make change. He knows his customers. Cross had been made, thought to be a cop or a bounty hunter, both likely objects of scorn.

Slurpy, fortunately, was in the middle of the room, talking with a guy who could have been his twin, except that Slurpy wasn't Hispanic.

She came in from the back. She wore a black wig and a long, dark raincoat. He might not have recognized her, but no one else had a neck like that. She looked around. Cross turned away from her, glad she was at the opposite end of the room. She caught Slurpy's eye. He nodded. She retreated.

Cross worked his way toward the back, but not without being discovered. Slurpy moved through the bodies like a bull in a cornfield, his Hispanic friend behind him. Margot disappeared in the back.

Cross moved as quick as he could toward her but he didn't have the girth of a Slurpy to move obstacles aside.

Just as Slurpy intersected Cross' path and a fat hand wrapped around Cross' throat, a .38 was shoved between them. It was Collins. Cross would never have recognized him in his thug-like attire. The gun was placed at Slurpy's forehead.

'Go,' Collins said to Cross.

'Behave yourself, Slurp,' Cross heard Collins say. 'I can call you Slurp, right?'

Cross checked the bathrooms, then moved out the back door. He saw a slender figure racing through the parking lot, then back to an alley. Cross pursued. He was gaining though intermittently in the darkness, he would lose sight of her. He saw her again before she ducked in the space between the houses.

He followed, but she was nowhere to be seen. He stopped, took some deep breaths, to regain his strength and to clear his head. He knew where he was. Mama Slurpy's house was within a block. She had run in that direction.

He heard footsteps behind him. He wasn't sure who it was, but it wasn't Slurpy. Cross ran to Dixie Swift's house. He didn't knock, just kicked in the front door, startling Dixie, who was sipping on her whiskey and watching television.

Cross knew the house well enough. No one in the bedrooms or bathroom.

'She here?' Cross asked Dixie.

'Haven't seen her.'

'You know who I mean, then?' Cross asked.

'Yes,' she said with obvious distaste. She was still coherent, but at least two sheets to the wind.

'Basement?'

'I wouldn't let her in the house,' Dixie said. 'Not after what she's done.

Cross didn't have time for conversation. He went out through the back door. A single car garage stood like a huge gravestone in the darkness.

Twenty-Five

The doors weren't locked. He slowly opened them. Though he couldn't exactly see it, he could make out the shape of an automobile. He felt the metal, a tail pipe. He ran his hand along the side as he started to move in. Was she inside? He walked slowly in the darkness to the driver's side of the car, opened the door. The light inside switched on. Other than a few empty potato chip bags and giant paper cups no doubt once holding Slurpy's legendary namesake, the car was empty.

If he left the car interior light on, he was essentially blinded to everything else. If he shut it, he would be in nearly pure darkness. He reached in, switched on the headlights and shut the car door. He saw nothing. He had to believe she wasn't up in the rafters because he couldn't see anything above him. He moved around toward the front of the car where the headlights illuminated the back wall.

There, huddled in the opposite corner, her face ashen, her eyes frightened and dangerous, was Margot. She put her arm up to shield her face from the harsh beam of the headlight. She stared at him. Pure hatred.

'She's not yours,' Margot said, hatefully.

'I thought you said she was.' He could ask her, but he couldn't believe her. No matter what she said.

'She's not.' She spoke through her teeth.

'Margot, you're going to jail. Who is going to take care of her?'

She didn't answer, but her hateful, willful eyes continued to stare at him. She couldn't let herself believe him. She had beaten them all. How could what she wanted not happen?

He wanted to hate her for what she had done to her daughter, what she had tried to do to him. He wanted to hate her for the way she worked him, twisted him emotionally over the years. But he couldn't. There was – not quite buried – an urge to hold her, protect her, despite her willingness to betray anything and anyone.

He moved toward her, to help her up.

'It's been a long, tough ride, but it's over,' he said.

She sprang up so quickly it shocked him and he caught only a flash of the blade that was now sweeping toward him. He thought he could grab her wrist before the blade struck him, but he misjudged. The blade went into the palm of his hand. The action had hardly registered when his arm caught the second slash and he backed away. She moved toward him, her arm raised, again. His back was now against the wall and she came at him like a shark.

Cross was completely surprised, confused, but he heard the sound, a somewhat muffled explosion. Margot dropped limply on to the hood of the car, and rolled off.

'The crazy bitch,' came the voice of a woman. A flashlight appeared. It blinded Cross.

'Are you all right?'

Cross didn't know what to say. Who were these people?

Someone flicked on the garage light. Collins took the handgun from Dixie Swift.

'She was going to kill him,' Dixie said defensively. 'She tried to kill my granddaughter. She was going to take my boy away. She'd have done the same thing to him. She is evil.'

'You OK?' Collins asked Cross.

'Not altogether.' He looked down, saw Margot crumpled on the garage floor. The bullet went through her ear. And whoever Margot was, she no longer inhabited her body. Her final escape.

'Call an ambulance?'

Cross went toward the door. 'If you want, but she's gone.'

Slurpy was there. He was quiet, still as a stone.

'Better call anyway,' Collins said. He used his cell.

'She's dead, honey,' Dixie said to Slurpy. 'I had to shoot her.' Slurpy said nothing. She put a hand on his shoulder. 'But you're going to be all right.' As an afterthought, it seemed to Cross, she said, 'She'd have killed you too, you know. It's the way she was.'

Collins' flashlight caught Cross' wound. There was blood.

Cross took off his jacket, thankful he'd worn the leather. It blunted the force of Margot's second thrust. He took off his tee shirt, ripped it, tied a section around the puncture in his palm, then another around the lesser wound in his forearm. He put his jacket back on, feeling a little silly, not to mention cold, with no shirt. Lights in the driveway, headlights, police lights. Car doors slammed. Shadowy figures moved toward them.

'What were you doing here?' Cross asked Collins.

'Kowalski called me. He was worried about you.'

'What about Dixie?'

'Not my favorite place,' Collins said.

'You know what I mean. What's going to happen?'

'Don't know yet.'

'She might have saved my life,' Cross said, nodding toward Dixie, who was coaxing her son inside the house.

'Not sure what we would have her on. Maybe saving your life. How many years will she get for that?'

'Thanks,' Cross said to Collins.

'Thank her.'

'No, I mean for showing up.'

'You guys need to be put on a leash.' He smiled, walked toward the approaching uniforms.

Cross saw a fire rescue truck pull up, behind the police car. Other cop cars arrived.

'Oh, Collins!' Cross called out.

'What?'

'Looking good, my man.'

'Fuck you,' Collins said, quickening his gait.

Cross' moment of humor dissolved quickly as the ramifications of the evening extended to Maya. Was she Slurpy's daughter? Would this petty criminal get custody? If he did, Dixie would probably raise her. 'And Dixie did such a good job with Slurpy,' Cross said out loud as he headed back toward the bar to pick up his car.

He didn't want to think about it. Not tonight.

Shanahan was up very early in the morning. There could be lively debate whether it was, in fact, morning. Light was at least an hour away. But he could not sleep. He let Casey out in the back. Apparently even Einstein didn't get up this early – even knowing that when Shanahan fiddled in the kitchen, he could expect breakfast.

Shanahan went to the front door, opened it. The newspaper hadn't arrived. Outside was dark, deadly quiet and cool. The fresh air seemed to add to the clarity of thought he felt. He went back to the kitchen and let Casey back in.

Shanahan sipped his coffee and fumbled with Maureen's computer. He found himself online. He also found, by roaming about the desktop, the Google bookmark. He clicked. He had watched her do her searches. In the little box, he typed, using one finger, a few words.

A series of choices came up. A couple of them looked promising.

'This isn't so hard,' Shanahan told Casey.

Before sleep, Kowalski cleaned Cross' wound and bound it. The leather coat had spared him a deep gash.

He told Kowalski about the Slurpy claim on Maya.

'Get a DNA test on you, Slurpy and little Maya before you panic,' Kowalski said. He grinned. 'I'd be surprised if there's a Thurman gene anywhere in that girl.'

When he went up to bed, Cross worried about the Margot gene. Already smart and tough, had she had a moment to be a little girl?

Cross woke up, if he slept at all, before morning light. Kowalski's sofa was surprisingly comfortable, but Cross was still torn by the events of the last several days and last night. The moment of Margot's death was a vivid image whenever he closed his eyes. Though he had imagined it, probably wanted it, there was no relief in her death.

He climbed up the stairs to the bathroom. Kowalski's door was closed and so was Maya's, so he turned on the hall light. He slowly turned the doorknob to the room Maya slept in. The sliver of light from the hall cut across her sleeping face.

Cross looked for signs of similarity, first to Slurpy and Dixie. To his relief, he saw none. He looked for a nose, a mouth, an ear that was like his own, and was disappointed that he could find nothing but Margot. He stifled his laugh. Margot would never go away. Not completely.

Shanahan couldn't wait to tell Maureen. Because of his impatience the morning was painfully long. Once the sun entered the kitchen, Einstein wandered in looking for breakfast. The newspaper arrived. Shanahan, on his third cup, went through it all and still the woman slept. He clattered a few pans, perhaps with a little too much enthusiasm, in his preparation for a hot breakfast – a break from routine.

Finally, she arrived. 'What's all the noise?'

'Oh, just fixing breakfast.'

'And what is this all about?' She was suspicious already.

He handed her a cup of coffee.

'How would you like a tropical vacation?'

She looked at him, somehow combining a look of genuine interest with one that said 'Have you gone mad?'

'When?'

'Today. We could be in Puerto Vallarta by nightfall.'

She was beyond surprise.

'Have you gone all silly again?'

This was a reference to some of his strange utterances after being shot in the head.

'I'm thinking four days. Some sun, some swimming—'

'What—'

'Some really great food. Do you think you could sneak away?'

'What about our dependents?' she asked, referring to Casey and Einstein.

'Harry. Howie. Tag-team babysitters.'

'What is this all about?' she asked.

'Relaxation. It's been stressful lately. Now that it's over . . .'

'No,' she said. 'It's because it's not over. Isn't it?' She smiled.

'I have a minor piece of business, maybe. Maybe not. Then, it's fun, fun, fun.' He knew his uncharacteristic rah-rah enthusiasm just made him look foolish.

'What are you not telling me?'

'Did I tell you about the food? Sitting on the beach at sunset . . .'

'Are we going to die?'

'What a way to go, don't you think?'

There was no Hester at the Kowalski home. And Kowalski, himself, had things to do. He grabbed coffee in a portable mug and was out the door.

Cross decided to pack the two of them up and head back to his house. He and Maya straightened the house, did the few dishes that were in the sink, and said goodbye to the Bulldog who – Cross would swear – gave a sigh of relief.

On the way, they found a Denny's and had breakfast. Maya was quiet. So was Cross. He was thinking about how he would tell Maya about her mother. He had no idea how to say it. He had no idea how she would take it.

While Maya was in the restroom, Cross called Shanahan and was happy to learn the Dark Wind affair was over. He also agreed to take Einstein and Casey for the four days Shanahan would be in Mexico. They deserved a vacation. Well so did he, but that would have to wait. Taking the animals was a good idea. Company for Maya.

It was good to be home, even though her presence meant Cross was about to spend more nights on a sofa. It gave him a further sense of impermanence in a world that had become more tentative every day. As Maya settled her things in the bedroom, he thought about taking her back up to Eaton. It might be a good idea because he expected now that the law was involved and Slurpy's mom was conceivably laying claim, Maya might be taken from him.

There was that chance anyway.

The animals arrived after lunch, dropped off as Shanahan and Maureen headed for the airport. Neither the dog nor the cat found the location problematical. They both had spent time there before and knew the layout. A quick inspection and they were fine.

'I need to talk to you for a few minutes,' Cross said to Maya, who was engaged in television.

She looked up. Curious. She muted the sound on the set. Waited.

'Maya, some bad news.'

She gave no change in expression.

'Your mother is gone. You won't be seeing her again.'

'Why?'

'She died, Maya.'

Cross expected sadness or anger or panic. None. She seemed to go away for a few seconds. Her eyes registered nothing. It was as if, for a moment, her soul skipped out on her. It came back.

'You understand what I'm saying?'

'Yes,' she said, impatiently. 'She's dead like that man in the trunk of the car.'

'Yes.'

'Can we eat out tonight?' she asked.

'Yeah.' He waited to see if she might yet react. She didn't. 'What are you in the mood for?'

Twenty-Six

An eight-hour flight with a connection in Sky Harbor in Phoenix meant an evening arrival in Puerto Vallarta. Cabbies vied for passengers, holding signs. Outside, it was mostly small white sedans, the kind Wenders' guy drove. Many of the drivers resembled Wenders' guy – thin, black hair, white clothes.

The carry-ons were stowed in the trunk. Shanahan and Maureen filled the tiny backseat. Fortunately, she had found a place near the beach in old town in her computer search. It wasn't top of the line; but that was fine with Shanahan as he wanted to avoid the more modern resort hotels closer to the airport. Too far from town. This way the two of them could walk most places.

And just as importantly, this trip was on his own dime.

They took a few moments to organize their belongings in bureaus and in the bathroom. Shanahan took note of the air conditioner and the overhead fan. Maureen freshened up in the bathroom and came out ready to take on the town.

The night was warm, a slight breeze. They headed toward La Palapa, a restaurant on the sand. They had missed sunset, but the lights illuminated the palms and the light reflected in the water. A ship, rigged with sparkling lights, was returning from its sunset cruise. The restaurant was pricey, but the mood was right. The music was live. Latin. She had the sea bass with a macadamia crust, he a chile rubbed beef tenderloin. She was in heaven. He loved seeing her in heaven. He was delivering on his promise.

Unlike his previous trip, Shanahan was bedding down in the tourist area. He didn't mind. When he'd leave Maureen in the morning, he wanted to be sure she was in safe territory. He knew the Puerto Vallarta police wanted nothing more than to protect visitors, to make sure they told their friends how warm, how friendly, and especially how safe this little resort town was.

With the bedside lamp on, Maureen looked through some pamphlets, looking for things to do for the next few days.

'Want to go parasailing?' she asked.

'I'll hold the line for you.'

'I would you know?'

'I believe it.'

'OK.'

Shanahan was relaxed. Belly full. A very light and pleasant buzz in his brain. The hum of the overhead fan was comforting. He could feel himself drift.

In the morning, the roles were reversed. She slept deeply. His mind was alert, clear. He showered as quietly as he could, dressed, wrote a short note.

'Need to go out for walk. Be back before noon. Go for a swim. Have breakfast.'

He thought about signing his name, maybe 'love, Shanahan,' but that was uncharacteristic and might increase her concern. Maybe she would just think he couldn't sleep and went out for breakfast or to get a paper. Best not to say anything rather than lie.

Shanahan made sure he had nothing on him that identified their hotel. He doubted they would be expecting him. But he was pretty sure he wouldn't be a welcomed sight. He didn't want them coming back to Maureen. And he couldn't afford to have her be someone who saw too much.

The light was what he remembered from his earlier visit. Even in the morning, it was sharper, harder than any summer day in the Midwest. He moved along the narrow boardwalk on the beach. Only a few swimmers this early in the morning. But the pelicans were fishing. Venders were getting their day's wares – scarves, purses, tee shirts, carved wooden trinkets – loaded up for their treks back and forth along the beach. It was a day-long job, slow going earlier in the day but later catching sentimental tourists on their second margaritas. He headed north across the pedestrian bridge and on to the *Malecon*.

Shanahan found a place that served breakfast two streets off the main drag. He didn't want too much solid food until this was over. He sat for a few moments and nibbled at a dry pastry with his coffee. He was in no hurry, but he wasn't delaying it either. When he left, he knew where to go and how to get there. He took the less steep route up the hill, walking on the dusty, uneven stone street. He was still out of breath.

He waited outside the house for a few moments to get his breath.

The lock on the garden gate was replaced with a functioning one. Shanahan went to the front door. He looked down the street that went down and down eventually to the Bay. The street was empty. He looked up. A truck rolled by two streets up.

The door was locked.

He knocked.

The Mexican answered the door. If he was surprised, his eyes didn't show it. Some people are never surprised. Maybe it's because they expect nothing, certainly not something good and regard danger and death with indifference. The man nodded, stepped aside in a modest welcoming gesture.

Shanahan walked into the middle room. Off to the left was where he found Wenders' body, in a chair facing out over the tiled roofs. A man was there. Just as Wenders' had been, the man's back was to the visitor.

'To use a current phrase, I misunderestimated you.'

It was Wenders' voice. Shanahan walked around to confront him.

'If I can find you, so can they,' he said.

Wenders' head and face were bandaged. Only his eyes, lips, and ears were uncovered.

'Are you sure it's me?'

'Even if your voice didn't, your hands give you away. You made death mighty realistic.'

'The art of make-up has come a long way since you dabbled in intrigue. A drink?'

'Just a little early.'

'Though not by much, right? Coffee?'

'Yes to both.'

The Mexican disappeared.

'You're risking a lot just to show me you figured this out.'

'You don't want me dying down here. Or even disappearing.'

Shanahan thought he saw a smile.

'You're right.'

'Why?'

'I needed to die so I could move on.'

'Yet you're right here where I found you.'

'There was a man assigned to shoot me. He told his superiors he did.'

'Another whistleblower?'

'Sort of. Let's just say that you did what you were supposed to do, that is confirm to them what the shooter said he did. And my death certificate, after an extensive medical examination, is a dutifully filed public record. That's three sources. That's what it takes to make it true.'

'I thought the government supported Dark Wind,' Shanahan said, taking the cup of coffee. He must have looked a little odd.

'You want me to taste it first?' Wenders said.

'No,' Shanahan took a sip. It was better than the one at the café.

'You use the word 'government' as if it were this monolithic force. Sometimes leaders misuse their power. Sometimes, there are those willing to make an adjustment of one kind or another to ratchet down that power.'

'Why are you staying here?' Shanahan asked.

'Because I like it here. Why would they look here? And when they do? Who will they find?'

'Who will they find?' Shanahan asked.

Wenders' laughed.

'Me?' Shanahan smiled. 'Your friend, while I was asleep the first night I was here, took my passport, license, everything and got it back before I woke up. That's why I had to wait to see you.'

'One can't have too many identities. I'm not using yours right away.'

'You'll wait until I'm dead?'

'If I need it.'

'Don't kill me for it. I'm just now enjoying life,' Shanahan said.

'I don't kill friends – however distant. But I am younger than you. And the odds are, you know.'

'Why stay here?'

'This is a nice place. You should understand I'm getting too old to go running around the world. I speak Spanish. I like the heat. Don't spoil it for me.'

'You have a woman here.'

'A fool for love,' Wenders said.

'It'll do that to you. From what you know, are they done with us? Whoever *they* are.'

'Yeah. They are in damage control mode. People are talking to people.'

'And so you played me?'

'Shanahan, everybody gets played. Look at the world. Are you an exception?

'What made you think I was still alive?' Wenders asked.

'You didn't need me to send emails. I guessed that was what you wanted everyone to think. So there had to be something else. My identity. And a dead man doesn't need a passport.'

Wenders nodded. 'I won't look exactly like you. Just enough. Just in case.'

'I'm flattered.'

'I could have done worse,' Wenders said. 'For what it's worth, thanks for your help.'

'Will anything change? Was all this worth it?'

'Don't know. Depends on whether any of our politicians or reporters have the courage to make the needed changes. Is anyone willing to challenge the power of the international corporations? I don't know. I played my part for the good guys. So did you, whether you knew it or not.'

'And I can believe all you're saying now?'

'It's a tough fucking world. Knowing who to trust is the hardest part, isn't it?'

Shanahan turned to leave.

'Hey, one final thing,' Wenders said, 'you've got a reservation for two at eight tonight at Trio. Great restaurant on Guerrero, just down the hill.' He nodded in the direction that Shanahan had come. 'On me.'

'Two you say?'

'You have a woman here, right?' He seemed to smile.

Cross plucked a couple of hairs from the front gate. Slurpy left them there involuntarily when he went at Cross and got the gate instead. A saliva swab would be better, but he had to work with what he had. He had Slurpy's hair samples and Maya's swab. Kowalski gave him the name of a local company that could test DNA for a surprisingly reasonable fee. It would take five working days – could be longer to process the DNA from hair.

Five working days and maybe he'd know. In the interim, Cross would try to keep Maya out of Slurpy's and his mother's hands and away from the government agency likely to claim her until her legal guardians were found. Things could get messed up and Maya didn't need to spend anytime in still other places. She'd been through enough. Too much, Cross thought.

The two of them took in a movie the previous night. Collins called in the morning. Cross had given him the bank branch where Margot stuffed a safety deposit box with money. Apparently they warned the bank. Dixie was arrested trying to counterfeit Margot's name to gain entry.

'She's a treat,' Cross said.

'You're worried,' Collins said.

'For Maya to go from a murderous mother to a murderous grandmother seems like overkill, doesn't it?'

'What's your attraction?' Collins asked.

'What?'

'All these strange people involved in your life.'

'It's a gift.'

'About the money in the box,' Collins said, 'it'll likely pay off any debt. If there's anything left it will go to Maya in some sort of trust, I suspect.'

'Thanks for everything,' Cross said.

'Why don't you go work in a factory or something?' Collins said.

Cross, with Maya in tow, dropped the hair samples at the lab and took Casey for a walk down by the canal in the afternoon. A drizzling rain fell before they could make it back. Maya took a warm bath and seemed content to stay in the rest of the day and evening. She helped him in the kitchen as he made a pot of chili. She liked it hot, she said.

Maureen called Trio 'lovely.' Shanahan thought it probably was. The food, she told him was French and Middle Eastern. Whatever it was, it was good. The atmosphere was comfortable, but formal enough that the clientele were fully dressed. No shorts and halter-tops. For Shanahan that was a good and bad thing. It depended. Overall, he was pleased that Maureen was pleased. He had promised her good food. Things were going well, and he was relaxing.

'So where were you this morning?' she asked after dinner was served and the two of them had at least half a glass of wine.

'Went for a walk. Talked to an old friend.'

'Is everything all right?'

'Probably. But things are often not what they seem.'

'What about me?'

'What about you?'

'Am I what I seem?'

'You seem to be.'

'What?'

'Maureen, you are so much more than anyone can think you seem to be.'

'What does that mean?' she asked, raising her critical eyebrow.

'I have no idea.'

'You're slipping,' she said, taking a generous sip of her wine. She grinned.

'I am,' he said. He was, he thought. Slipping. He just hoped he had a long way to go before it ended.

Twenty-Seven

C ross sat on the front porch of his parents' home in Eaton. Occasionally, a car went by. Rarely were the drivers in a hurry. Cross wasn't either. He sipped on a beer, noticed how the fields had turned from earth to leaf. The trees in the orchard were filling out.

Maya was in the barn entertaining the young goat Cross' father got for her. A goat served no purpose for his parents, but the elder Cross believed she needed a pet who would give as good as he would get. The old man's humor always had a bit of the dark side. And this little bit of devilish humor was a sign he was pushing back against his own death.

Cross saw her coming toward him, dirty knuckles wiping the tears from her eyes.

'He won't behave,' she shouted to Cross. 'He won't do a thing I say.'

'Wait 'til he grows up,' Cross said.

'He booted me,' she said. It was a child's whiny voice. He was glad to hear the child inside her. She hadn't shown this much lately.

'He butted you.'

'Yes.'

'What did you do?'

'I butted him.'

Cross took a sip of his beer, more to stifle his smile than to quench his thirst.

'Then what did he do?'

'He waited until I was ready to leave and he butted me in the butt.'

'You fell down.'

She nodded.

'Are you hurt?'

'No,' she said, but she started crying. He held her as she gave it a pretty big go.

Cross was never so happy to see someone cry. He doubted all this was the goat's fault.

In the afternoon, the lab called. The results were in. They would mail him the information, but for now they wanted him to know there were no matches.

Cross knew what it was like to be butted.

A few days after they returned from Mexico, Shanahan woke up in the middle of the night. His body was drenched in sweat. He remembered his dream as if it were real. Another one about his brother. But there were none of the usual chases through dim hallways. It wasn't the dream where the two of them by the pond talked about protecting each other. Somehow it didn't seem like something from the past. Fritz faced him. He nodded knowingly. And Shanahan did know. Now was the time to find him.

Shanahan got up, slipped out of bed. The sheet, where he had slept was damp and cold. He stripped down, put on fresh underwear, grabbed a blanket. He would sleep on the sofa. He went into the living room.

He didn't need a light. He was at home in the dark.

It wasn't quite dawn when Shanahan awoke again. The table lamp by the upholstered chair was on. Sitting in the chair was the skinny man with big spectacles – the man who looked like a praying mantis.

A raspy voice said, 'You have gotten your message through, and you might even cause a stir. A ripple in a pond. In the end, no one will see it. No one will hear it. That's how it's been, that's how it will be.'

'I see,' Shanahan said. 'You going to drop by from time to time?' Shanahan asked, wrapping the blanket around his coldness.

'Next time I'll bring a scythe.' He laughed his raspy laugh and flicked off the lamp.

'Oh good,' Shanahan said, thinking this was another ghost to haunt him. He still had his long-lost brother inhabiting his dreams.

The hall light switched on. Maureen appeared, much too coincidentally, as an apparition might, in a flowing white gown, light behind her.

'What's going on? I heard voices.'

'Talking to myself,' Shanahan said. As he always did, he would eventually tell her everything. Tonight they just needed to sleep.

'What were you saying?' she asked.

'I was saying what a lucky fellow I was to have someone like you.'

'You're learning. Now, in the morning, I want you to tell me the truth.'

THE NAVARRE BIBLE

The Acts of the Apostles

THE NAVARRE BIBLE
The Acts of the Apostles

in the Revised Standard Version and New Vulgate
with a commentary by members of the
Faculty of Theology of the University of Navarre

FOUR COURTS PRESS

Original title: *Sagrada Biblia: V. Hechos de los Apóstoles*.
Quotations from Vatican II documents
are based on the translation in *Vatican Council II:
The Conciliar and Post Conciliar Documents*,
ed. A. Flannery, OP (Dublin 1981).

Nihil obstat: Stephen J. Greene, *censor deputatus*.
Imprimi potest: Desmond,
Archbishop of Dublin, 9 January 1989.

The typesetting of this book was produced by Gilbert Gough Typesetting.
The book, designed by Jarlath Hayes, is published by
Four Courts Press, Kill Lane, Blackrock, Co. Dublin, Ireland.

© Text of Acts of the Apostles in English: The translation used in this book is
the Revised Standard Version, Catholic Edition [RSVCE], copyrighted
1965 and 1966 by the Division of Christian Education of the National
Council of the Churches of Christ in the U.S.A. and used by permission.

© Other material (origination and selection):
Ediciones Universidad de Navarra, SA 1984

© Translation and typography: Michael Adams 1989, 1992

A catalogue record for this book
is available from the British Library.

ISBN 1-85182-045-0
ISBN 1-85182-044-2 pbk

First impression 1989
Second impression, with corrections 1992

Printed in Ireland
by Colour Books Ltd, Dublin

Contents

Preface

In providing both undergraduate and postgraduate education, and in the research it carries out, a university is ultimately an institution at the service of society. It was with this service in mind that the theology faculty of the University of Navarre embarked on the project of preparing a translation and commentary of the Bible accessible to a wide readership—a project entrusted to it by the apostolic zeal of the University's founder and first chancellor, Monsignor Josemaría Escrivá de Balaguer.

Monsignor Escrivá did not live to see the publication of the first volume, the Gospel according to St Matthew; but he must, from heaven, continue to bless and promote our work, for the volumes, the first of which appeared in 1976, have been well received and widely read.

This edition of the Bible avoids many scholarly questions, discussion of which would over-extend the text and would be of no assistance to the immense majority of readers; these questions are avoided, but they have been taken into account.

The Spanish edition contains a new Spanish translation made from the original texts, always taking note of the Church's official Latin text, which is now that of the New Vulgate, a revision of the venerable Latin Vulgate of St Jerome: on 25 April 1979 Pope John Paul II, by the Apostolic Constitution *Scripturarum thesaurus*, promulgated the *editio typica prior* of the New Vulgate as the new official text; the *editio typica altera*, issued in 1986, is the Latin version used in this edition. For the English edition of this book we consider ourselves fortunate in having the Revised Standard Version as the translation of Scripture and wish to record our appreciation for permission to use that text, an integral part of which are the RSV notes, which are indicated by superior letters.

The introductions and notes have been prepared on the basis of the same criteria. In the notes (which are the most characteristic feature of this Bible, at least in its English version), along with scriptural and ascetical explanations we have sought to offer a general exposition of Christian doctrine—not of course a systematic exposition, for we follow the thread of the scriptural text. We have also tried to explain and connect certain biblical passages by reference to others, conscious that Sacred Scripture is ultimately one single entity; but, to avoid tiring the reader, most of the cross-references are given in the form of marginal notes (the marginal notes in this edition are, then, those of the Navarre Bible, not the RSV). The commentaries contained in the notes are the result of looking up thousands of sources (sometimes reflected in explicit references given in our text)—documents of the Magisterium, exegesis by Fathers and Doctors of the Church, works by important spiritual writers (usually saints, of every period) and writings of the founder of our University. It would have been impertinent of us to comment on the Holy Bible using our own expertise alone. Besides, a basic principle of exegesis is that Scripture should be interpreted in the context of Sacred Tradition and under the guidance of the Magisterium.

From the very beginning of our work our system has been to entrust each volume to a committee which then works as a team. However, the general editor of this edition takes ultimate responsibility for what it contains.

It is our pleasant duty to express our gratitude to the present chancellor of the University of Navarre, Bishop Alvaro del Portillo y Diez de Sollano, for his continued support and encouragement, and for reminding us of the good our work can do for the Church and for souls.

"Since Sacred Scripture must be read and interpreted with its divine authorship in mind,"[1] we pray to the Holy Spirit to help us in our work and to help our readers derive spiritual benefit from it. We also pray Mary, our Mother, Seat of Wisdom, and St Joseph, our Father and Lord, to intercede that this sowing of the Word of God may produce holiness of life in the souls of many Christians.

---

1   Vatican Council II, Dogm. Const. *Dei Verbum*, 12.

Abbreviations and Sources

1. BOOKS OF SACRED SCRIPTURE

Acts	Acts of the Apostles	2 Kings	2 Kings
Amos	Amos	Lam	Lamentations
Bar	Baruch	Lev	Leviticus
1 Chron	1 Chronicles	Lk	Luke
2 Chron	2 Chronicles	1 Mac	1 Maccabees
Col	Colossians	2 Mac	2 Maccabees
1 Cor	1 Corinthians	Mal	Malachi
2 Cor	2 Corinthians	Mic	Micah
Dan	Daniel	Mk	Mark
Deut	Deuteronomy	Mt	Matthew
Eccles	Ecclesiastes (Qohelet)	Nah	Nahum
Esther	Esther	Neh	Nehemiah
Eph	Ephesians	Num	Numbers
Ex	Exodus	Obad	Obadiah
Ezek	Ezekiel	1 Pet	1 Peter
Ezra	Ezra	2 Pet	2 Peter
Gal	Galatians	Phil	Philippians
Gen	Genesis	Philem	Philemon
Hab	Habakkuk	Ps	Psalms
Hag	Haggai	Prov	Proverbs
Heb	Hebrews	Rev	Revelation (Apocalypse)
Hos	Hosea	Rom	Romans
Is	Isaiah	Ruth	Ruth
Jas	James	1 Sam	1 Samuel
Jer	Jeremiah	2 Sam	2 Samuel
Jn	John	Sir	Sirach (Ecclesiasticus)
1 Jn	1 John	Song	Song of Solomon
2 Jn	2 John	1 Thess	1 Thessalonians
3 Jn	3 John	2 Thess	2 Thessalonians
Job	Job	1 Tim	1 Timothy
Joel	Joel	2 Tim	2 Timothy
Jon	Jonah	Tit	Titus
Josh	Joshua	Tob	Tobit
Jud	Judith	Wis	Wisdom
Jude	Jude	Zech	Zechariah
Judg	Judges	Zeph	Zephaniah
1 Kings	1 Kings		

2. OTHER SOURCES REFERRED TO

Ambrose, St
Expositio in Ps 118

Anon.
Didache (c. 100 A.D.)
Letter to Diognetus

Athanasius, St
De decretis nicaenae synodi
Historia arianorum
Oratio I contra arianos

Augustine, St
Confessions
De correptione et gratia
De praedestinatione sanctorum

Basil, St
On the Holy Spirit

Bede, St
Super Acta Apostolorum expositio

Catherine of Siena, St
Dialogue

Clement of Alexandria
Stromata

Cano, Melchor
De locis

Code of Canon Law, 1983

Cyprian, St
De bono patientiae
De opere et eleemosynis
Quod idola dii non sint

Ephraem, St
Armenian Commentary on Acts

Escrivá de Balaguer, J.
Christ is passing by (section no.)
Conversations (do.)
Friends of God (do.)
The Way (do.)
Holy Rosary

Eusebius of Caesarea
Ecclesiastical History

Flavius Josephus
Jewish Antiquities
The Jewish War

Francis of Sales, St
Introduction to the Devout Life
Lenten Sermons

Gregory of Nyssa
De instituto christiano
De perfecta christiana forma
On the Life of Moses

Jerome, St
Dialogue adversus pelagianos
Epistles

John of Avila, St
Audi, filia

John Chrysostom, St
Baptismal catechesis
Homilies on the Acts of the Apostles

John of the Cross, St
Ascent of Mount Carmel
Spiritual Canticle

John Paul II
Address (on date given)
Apos. Exhort. *Reconciliatio et paenitentia*,
2 December 1984

John Paul II
Apos. Exhort. *Catechesi tradendae*,
16 October 1979
Apos. Exhort. *Familiaris consortio*,
22 November 1981
Enc. *Laborem exercens*, 14 September 1981
Homilies and addresses
Letter to all priests, 8 April 1979

Justin, St
Dialogue with Trypho
First and Second Apologies

Leo the Great, St
Homilies

Liturgy of the Hours

Newman, J.H.
Biglietto Speech
Discourses to Mixed Congregations
Historical Sketches

Origen
Against Celsius
De Principiis
*Dialogue with Heraclides*In Exodum
homiliae

Paul VI
Apos. Exhort, *Evangelii nuntiandi*,
8 December 1975
Creed of the People of God, 30 June 1968
Homilies and addresses

Pius V, St
*Catechism of the Council of Trent for Parish
Priests*

Sacred Congregation for the Doctrine of the Faith
Instruction on Infant Baptism,
20 October 1980

Teresa of Avila, St
Interior Castle
Life
Way of Perfection

Tertullian
To Scapula

Thomas Aquinas, St
  Commentary on Hebrews
  Summa theologiae
Trent, Council of
  De iustificatione
Vincent Ferrer, St
  Treatise on the Spiritiual Life
Vatican I
  Dogm. Const. *Dei Filius*

Vatican II
  Const. *Sacrosanctum concilium*
  Decl. *Dignitatis humanae*
  Decl. *Nostra aetate*
  Decree Ad gentes
  Decree *Apostolicum actuositatem*
  Decree *Presbyterorum ordinis*
  Decree *Unitatis redintegratio*
  Dogm. Const. *Dei Verbum*
  Dogm. Const. *Lumen gentium*
  Past. Const. *Gaudium et spes*

3. OTHER ABBREVIATIONS

ad loc.	*ad locum*, commentary on this passage	f	and following (*pl.* ff)
Exhort.	Exhortation	*ibid.*	*ibidem*, in the same place
Apost.	apostolic	*in loc.*	*in locum*, commentary on this passage
can.	canon		
chap.	chapter	*loc.*	*locum*, place or passage
cf.	*confer*, compare	n.	number (*pl.* nn.)
Const.	Constitution	p.	page (*pl.* pp.)
Decl.	Declaration	*pl.*	plural
Dz-Sch	Denzinger-Schönmetzer, *Enchiridion Symbolorum*	par.	and parallel passages
		Past.	Pastoral
Dogm.	Dogmatic	SCDF	Sacred Congregation for the Doctrine of the Faith
EB	*Enchiridion Biblicum* (4th edition, Naples-Rome, 1961)	sess.	session
		v.	verse (*pl.* vv.)
Enc.	Encyclical		

The Navarre Bible (New Testament)

St Matthew's Gospel
St Mark's Gospel
St Luke's Gospel
St John's Gospel
Acts of the Apostles
Romans and Galatians
Corinthians
Captivity Epistles
Thessalonians and Pastoral Epistles
Hebrews
Catholic Epistles
Revelation

ESSAYS ON BIBLICAL SUBJECTS

In addition to special introduction(s) in each volume, the following essays etc. are published in the series:

St Mark — General Introduction to the Bible; Introduction to the Books of the New Testament; Introduction to the Holy Gospels; and The Dates in the Life of our Lord Jesus Christ

St Luke — Index to the Four Gospels

Acts — The History of the New Testament Text

Romans & Galatians — Introduction to the Epistles of St Paul

Corinthians — Divine Inspiration of the Bible

Captivity Epistles — The Canon of the Bible

Thessalonians — The Truth of Sacred Scripture

Hebrews — Interpretation of Sacred Scripture and the Senses of the Bible; Divine Worship in the Old Testament

Catholic Epistles — Rules for Biblical Interpretation

Revelation — Index to the New Testament

The History of the New Testament Text*

The sacred books inspired by God which contain supernatural revelation are listed in the "canon" of Scripture fixed by the Church. These books were written in Hebrew, Aramaic and Greek, the languages of their various human authors. The text of the Bible which has come down to us is substantially the same as that written by these inspired writers (prophets, evangelists etc.), as can be demonstrated by the normal procedures used by scholars.

Biblical scholarship has also contributed and is still contributing to improving that text, that is to say, eradicating errors and defective corrections which found their way into the text in the course of time due to manuscripts having to be constantly copied and recopied by hand prior to the invention of printing.

All the books of the New Testament were written in Greek, which was the lingua franca of the Mediterranean countries from the time of Alexander the Great onwards (fourth to third centuries B.C.). The only non-Greek original—an Aramaic or Hebrew text of St Matthew's Gospel—has not survived. The original manuscripts of the New Testament were lost quite early on, the reason being that the papyrus on which they were written normally had a life-span of not more than 200 years. We know that as early as the middle of the second century none of these manuscripts was still extant. They were not used, for example, in the controversy against the heretic Marcion: this controversy hinged on which texts were authentic and which not, indicating that the original text had already disappeared. The original text was conserved in the form of copies, and very early on more and more copies came to be made. In addition to papyrus, leather was also used as a writing material, but a real breakthrough came with the development of *parchment* or vellum. In the second century parchment began to be made or at least sold commercially in the city of Pergamon, from which it took its name. Initially texts were copied on to rolls of parchment; later they began to be produced in book form, as "codexes"; this book form meant that the text was easier to access and it also had the advantage of saving parchment. Parchments dating from the fourth century are still in existence.

*This essay is one of introductory essays in different volumes of the Navarre Bible (see p. 12); taken together these essays (which do not necessarily refer to the particular volumes in which they appear) form a short general introduction to Sacred Scripture.

13

The oldest papyrus New Testament text still extant contains some verses of St John's Gospel (18:31-33, 37-38) and has been dated *c*. A.D. 125.

The documentary sources of the New Testament fall into three groups:

a) *Greek copies* According to a 1976 survey there are over 5,000 texts extant:

88	papyrus fragments;
274	manuscripts written in capitals (that is, each letter is separate and there are no accents);
2795	manuscripts written in lower case letters (that is, the letters in each word are linked); and
2209	lectionaries for public liturgical use.

New copies are continually being discovered. The catalogue published by K. Aland in 1963 listed 4869, whereas the 1976 count was 5366. This means that no other document of antiquity compares with the New Testament as far as historico-critical verification of the text is concerned. In no other instance does the number of extant manuscripts exceed the thousand mark.

b) *Early translations* These comprise some 4,000 documents containing partial or complete translations of the New Testament. They were made for liturgical, catechetical, theological and other purposes, keeping pace with the spread of the Gospel among new peoples. The most important translations are those made into Latin (from the second century onwards, described generically as the *Vetus Latina* version; these were translations made prior to St Jerome's Vulgate); Syriac (second to third centuries, the most important Syriac version being that called the *Peshitta*, which is fifth century); Coptic (third century); Armenian (fourth century), Ethiopian, Slav, Gothic (fourth century) and Arabic.

In ancient times translations were made in a very literal way—almost word for word; for this very reason these early translations have special importance as far as establishing the history of the text is concerned: they maintain the "shape", as it were, as well as the content of the originals from which they were made; originals were located in regions which each had its own distinct culture and therefore a translation made in one region can often be used as a check on the completeness of a version made in another; the range of translations can also help in the choice of a better reading in cases of doubt.

c) *Quotations from the New Testament in the works of ecclesiastical writers* These quotations are, as it were, indirect witnesses to the correct text and are of very considerable value where they corroborate the direct witness of the Greek manuscripts. On the basis of these quotations, which are scattered over a wide range of theological texts and biblical commentaries, it is possible to reconstruct virtually the entire New Testament text, Greek and Latin. The text used by these authors is usually older than that in most of the manuscripts that have come down to us, thereby allowing us to check which biblical text was in use in any particular period or region. In the case of fragments quoted in sermons, it has to be remembered that the writers were usually quoting from memory. In all other cases the quotations usually follow an available text word for word. The Fathers of the Church who most extensively cite the New Testament in Greek or Latin are Origen, St John Chrysostom, St Cyril, St Jerome, St Cyprian, St Hilary and St Augustine.

PAPYRI AND CODEXES

Almost one hundred New Testament papyri have so far come to light; all of them are Egyptian, preserved by the extremely dry climate of that country. They began to be discovered in the nineteenth century and—due to their antiquity—they are of tremendous value for establishing the authentic text. The most remarkable of these papyri are:

a) three papyri in the Chester Beatty collection (housed in Dublin) known as p^{45}, p^{46} and p^{47}. These are portions of second-century documents which originally contained the Gospels, the epistles of St Paul and Revelation, respectively. The first shows that very early on the four Gospels had already been brought together into one single collection. The second papyrus is one hundred and fifty years older than any other source of the Pauline text.

b) The Roberts or Rylands Papyrus (p^{52}). Dating from $c.$ 125, and containing some verses of chapter 18 of St John's Gospel, this was decisive in disproving rationalist theses arguing for a later date for this Gospel.

c) The Bodmer Papyrus II (p^{66}). This contains most of St John's Gospel (1:1-14:26) and was written around the year 200.

The extant papyri fill the gap in sources between the original text and later manuscripts. They constitute, therefore, a quite unique source of documentation for establishing the career of the New Testament text. Thus, historico-literary scholarship combines with faith to show that we do possess the original revealed text of the New Testament in a form which is unanimously accepted to be much more than merely "substantial".

The most important Greek codexes of the New Testament are:

a) the Codex Vaticanus (B, or 03). This is the most valuable of all because of its antiquity. It is a copy made in Egypt in the fourth century, containing all the Old Testament (in the Septuagint version) and all the New Testament except for some chapters of Hebrews; the Epistles to Timothy, Titus and Philemon; and Revelation. It is housed in the Vatican Library.

b) the Codex Sinaiticus (S, or 01). Written in the fourth century from an Egyptian MS, this contains the Old and New Testaments, except for some pages. It was discovered in 1844 in the monastery of St Catherine on Mount Sinai. It is housed in the British Library.

c) the Codex Alexandrinus (A, or 02). Written in the fifth century, this contains virtually the entire Old and New Testaments. It is in the British Library.

d) Codex Ephraemi (C, or 04). Egyptian in origin, this was written in the fifth century. In the middle ages it was salvaged from a "palimpsest" (a recycled parchment from which text has been erased and which is then reused: by means of chemicals the older text can be recovered). It contains the entire New Testament and fragments of the Old Testament. It is housed in the Bibliothèque Nationale in Paris.

e) the Codex Bezae or Cambridge Codex (D, or 05). Written in the West in the sixth century, this contains the Gospels and the Acts of the Apostles in Greek and Latin. It is in the Cambridge University Library.

f) the Codex Claromontanus (Dᵖ, or 06). Written in the sixth century, this contains the epistles of St Paul in Greek and Latin and is kept in the Bibliothèque Nationale in Paris.

TEXTUAL VARIATIONS AND RULES OF TEXTUAL CRITICISM

Two kinds of variations frequently found in biblical texts are:

a) Involuntary variations introduced by copyists. These are material errors arising from misreading or mishearing on the part of the copyist. Mistakes of this type occur in all ages and consist of omissions (of letters, syllables, words and phrases), additions and changes, or are due to the copyist mixing up similar sounds when taking down dictation.

b) Variations consciously made by educated copyists. These occur when copyists "correct" the text from which they are working, thinking that it contains an error, or else introduce a variant reading which in their opinion is more correct. These variations are "linguistic", where the copyist replaces one word with another; or "doctrinal" where he changes the text to adapt it to the mentality of the reader—for example, by eliminating in Luke 2:33-48 the reference to Joseph being the father of Jesus (the heretic Marcion suppressed in St Luke's Gospel and in the epistles of St Paul everything which he regarded as Judaizing falsification of the text). Almost all these "corrections" were made in the second century and early third century.

Another common source of variations is the introduction into the text of words, phrases or short paragraphs, which were only marginal notes on the parent text: the new copyist, in doubt, would incorporate these notes into his text.

In the case of the New Testament, most of these variant readings have been identified, thanks to the large number of manuscripts which have come down, thus allowing the correct text to be established. This work of textual criticism has been carried out by scholars— evidencing the veneration which Christians in all ages have shown the sacred texts. The Fathers of the Church led the way in this work of textual criticism aimed at eliminating errors introduced by copyists and translators. St Irenaeus (A.D. 140-202), for example, was very familiar with the age and quality of the texts available to him and was able to identify the source of the textual corruptions he encountered. Allowing for the technical limitations of the time, some Fathers of the Church—particularly Origen and St Jerome—were as competent at textual criticism as modern scholars.

16

No one extant codex reproduces the original text of the New Testament with total fidelity. Therefore, every existing document—papyrus, codex etc.—has importance for scholars engaged in textual criticism because examination of the entire range of documents allows a text to be reconstructed which is an improvement on any one manuscript on its own. This reconstruction of the text is a particularly laborious aspect of the work of textual criticism, which is therefore both a science and an art because it aims at building up objective knowledge of the text and yet is very dependent on the alertness of the individual scholar. In other words, there is a limit to the absolute, invariable rules that can be devised for work in this field, a limit which has to be overcome by the experience and expertise of the scholars involved.

Despite all these difficulties, certain *basic principles of textual criticism* have been established which act as general criteria when it comes to clearing up doubts raised by the variants which are discovered. These principles are *external* and *internal*. The external principles are derived from the various aspects of documentary evidence and the weight assigned to each. The internal principles derive from experience and are used to complement the external ones.

The *external* principles are these:

a) That reading is to be preferred which is supported by better codexes and by more diverse codexes. However, mere quantitative support is insufficient.

b) The influence of parallel texts should be taken into account, as also the influence of the Septuagint in the case of quotations from the Old Testament, and preference is to be given to that reading which least coincides with those sources, on the grounds that attempts may have been made to harmonize the codex with those sources.

c) Where there are a number of different readings, their relationship one to another should be studied, because once a "correction" is made to a text, the copyist may have omitted to make further changes necessitated by the initial change (for example, agreement between subject and verb).

The *internal* principles are these:

a) The more difficult reading is the more reliable, because copyists tend to clarify and simplify ideas.

b) The shorter reading is to be preferred, given the tendency for marginal notes to be imported into the text, thereby lengthening it.

c) That reading is authentic which best explains the presence of other readings when the latter seem likely to be a correction, clarification or obvious error with respect to the former.

d) Only in extreme cases is "conjecture" permissible—that is, any correction of the text which is unsupported by documentary proof. A sound conjecture should be clear itself and helpful in clarifying a false reading or false readings of the text.

Between 1456, when the first book (an edition of the Vulgate) was produced from movable type at Mainz, and 1500, the Latin Bible was printed more than one hundred times. The first Greek editions appeared during the Renaissance, the main ones being those of the University of Alcala (the Complutense Polyglot Bible, 1514), Erasmus (1516), Estienne (1546ff) and Theodore Beza (1565ff).

Of the modern editions the following are particularly important:

a) The edition of C. von Tischendorf, the discoverer of the Codex Sinaiticus. This edition, published in 1869-1872, was reprinted in 1965. Its critical apparatus is of great value.

b) The edition made by two English scholars, B.F. Westcott and F.J.A. Hort, published in 1881-1883. This edition, the outcome of thirty years' research, includes an outline of the basic principles of textual criticism.

c) The massive work of H. von Soden, *Die Schriften das Neuen Testaments* . . . , vol. II (text, with commentary) (1913).

d) *Novum Testamentum Graece et Latine*, edited by H.J. Vogels (1922; 4th ed. 1955).

e) *Novum Testamentum*, edited by A. Merk, Professor at the Biblical Institute, Rome (1933; 9th ed. 1964).

f) *The Greek New Testament*, edited by K. Aland, M. Black, B. Metzger, A. Wikgren and C. Martini (1966, 3rd ed. 1975). In this edition, an initiative of the United Bible Societies, the authors make extensive use of manuscripts, early versions and quotations from the Fathers.

g) J. M. Bover's edition (Madrid 1943; 5th ed. 1968) which is included in the *Nuevo Testamento Trilingue*, ed. J. O'Callaghan (1977). This latter edition includes the text of the New Vulgate and a Spanish translation.

h) *Novum Testamentum Graece*, edited by E. Nestle (1898-1941), developed in 1952 by K. Aland in its 21st edition. In 1979 the 26th edition was published, which incorporates the improvements in the 3rd edition of the *Greek New Testament* cited above: this edition has a much better critical apparatus but the text itself is virtually unchanged, with only minor alterations in spelling, paragraphization and punctuation. This edition has been reprinted many times. In 1984 was published the *Novum Testamentum Graece et Latine* (Stuttgart, with the text of the 26th edition and the Latin of the New Vulgate).

Introduction to the Book of the Acts of the Apostles

The usual English title—"The Acts of the Apostles"—corresponds to the Latin "Actus" or "Acta Apostolorum" and the Greek "Práxeis Apostolicón". This is the title invariably given the book from the middle of the second century onwards in all Greek manuscripts, in early translations and in references in the works of the Fathers and ecclesiastical writers. It seems likely, however, that the author did not give it this title but that it received some time after it was written. It is not really an account of the activity of the Apostles but rather a description of the early years of Christianity linked to the missionary work of the two most prominent Apostles, Peter and Paul.

The Acts of the Apostles seeks to give an account of how the Church was originally established and of the first stage of the spread of the Gospel, after our Lord's ascension. It is a type of history book, the first history of Christianity. However, it does not belong only or primarily to the category of history; it is not a mere chronicle of events; it cannot and should not be separated from the Third Gospel, with which it is in total continuity as history and as theology. It is a book dominated by a religious purpose— to report events which, under the impulse of the Holy Spirit, reveal God's saving plan for mankind.

The sacred author has managed to combine history and theology remarkably well. He does not limit himself to producing a narrative similar in style to profane history; yet neither has he written a sacred book which totally detached from the cultural environment in which he is living. He is well aware that any proclamation of the Gospel must also be to some degree an account of historical events which truly happened.

The Acts of the Apostles, in relating the beginnings of the Church, aims primarily at strengthening the faith of Christians, assuring them as to the origin and basis of that faith. Secondarily, it discreetly anticipates the kind of writing typical of the apologists of the second and third centuries, by arguing that Christ's disciples had a right to the same freedom and the same respect as the Empire gave to what were called "lawful religions" (particularly Judaism).

Acts portrays Christianity as an outstanding faith, trusting in God and self-assured, which has no time for obscurantism or the kind of secrecy typical of sects, and which is not afraid to debate its principles and convictions with all comers.

The entire narrative is imbued with an extraordinary spiritual joy—a joy which comes from the Holy Spirit, from certainty about the supernatural origin of the Church, from contemplation of the prodigies which God works in support of the preachers of his Gospel, from—essentially—the protection God gives his disciples despite the persecution they undergo.

THEME AND STRUCTURE

The book describes the way Jesus' prediction to his disciples prior to his Ascension was fulfilled: "You shall be my witnesses in Jerusalem and in all Judea and Samaria and to the end of the earth" (1:8). Following a fairly precise and detailed chronological order, it covers events over a period of about thirty years—from the death, resurrection and ascension of our Lord until the end of St Paul's imprisonment in Rome about the year 63.

Commentators have suggested different ways of dividing the book up as a guide to understanding it better. From the point of view of God's plans of salvation, which the book reflects, it divides into two sections—before and after the Council of Jerusalem (15:6-29). This assembly at Jerusalem is certainly the theological centre of the book, due to the unique role it played in explaining God's will about the catholic nature of the Church and the primacy of grace over the Mosaic Law, and the impetus it gave to the universal spread of the Gospel.

If we look at the book in terms of the episodes it contains—stages as it were in the history of the preaching of the Gospel—the Acts of the Apostles can be divided into four parts:

I. *Chapters 1-7* These tell of the life of the early community in Jerusalem. They begin with our Lord's ascension, the sending of the Holy Spirit on Pentecost and the revealing of the supernatural character of the Church that followed on from that. Then comes the account of the growth of the first community around the Apostle Peter. Miracles and prodigies accompany the spread of the Gospel. This is followed by persecution by the Jewish establishment, culminating in the martyrdom of Stephen.

II. *Chapters 8-12* These report the dispersion of the Christians: with the exception of the Twelve, this scattering is the result of persecution and it in turn leads to the Gospel being preached in Judea, Samaria and Syria. The Church begins to open its doors to the Gentiles. We are told of the conversion of the Ethiopian, an official of the court of the queen of that country, and learn that many Samaritans received Baptism. The conversion of Cornelius, a Gentile—an event of extraordinary significance, with the Gospel breaking down ethnic barriers—is described in great detail. This section ends with the death of James, the brother of John, and the arrest and miraculous release of St Peter.

III. *Chapters 13-20* This section focusses on the missionary endeavours of Paul, who on his first journey with Barnabas prior to the Council of Jerusalem, and on two other subsequent journeys, brings the Gospel to the pagan world, in keeping with his special vocation as Apostle of the Gentiles.

IV. *Chapters 21-28* This begins in Jerusalem with the imprisonment of Paul, who from this point onwards will, in chains, bear witness to the Gospel up to the time of his stay in Rome. From that city of cities the way lies open for the Gospel to be spread all over the world.

AUTHOR AND DATE OF COMPOSITION

Christian tradition and almost all commentators assert that the book of the Acts of the Apostles was written by the author of the Third Gospel and that that author was St Luke, the companion of St Paul on his second journey and his loyal aide (cf. Acts 16:10ff; Col 4:14; Philem 24). St Luke was also with the Apostle from Troas to Jerusalem (cf. Acts 20:5ff) and, later on, from Caesarea to Rome (cf. 27:1ff). He was probably not Jewish by birth. An early tradition, attested by Eusebius of Caesarea, the historian,[1] and by St Jerome,[2] gave Antioch as his birthplace.

There are a number of good reasons for identifying St Luke as the author of Acts.[3] The best internal evidence is found in the passages of the book written in the first person plural (cf. Acts 16:10-17; 20:5-15; 21:1-18; 27:1 - 28:16). The most obvious interpretation is that these passages were written by a companion of Paul and incorporated into the book without any change in style for the simple reason that the author of this source—which is possibly a travel diary—and the author of the rest of the book were one and the same person. By eliminating everyone mentioned in Acts by name, we are left with St Luke as the only one who could have been Paul's companion in Caesarea and Rome.

The external arguments are mainly the testimony of Christian writers, especially St Irenaeus of Lyons (*d.* 180), who refers to St Luke as author of the Third Gospel and of the Acts of the Apostles. This is also stated in the Muratorian Canon (end of the second century).

The date of the book can be established by reference to certain factors which place it within a period and help to pin it down more specifically. The main factors in question are Paul's Roman imprisonment and the destruction of Jerusalem. Clearly St Luke could not have written his work earlier than the year 62 or 63, the date of the Apostle's confinement in Rome. Whether it was written before or after Paul's martyrdom is disputed, but that does not affect the choice of the earlier limit. On the other hand, it is virtually certain that Acts was written before the destruction of Jerusalem, that is, before the year 70. It is difficult to conceive how Luke could have been written after that date and yet made no reference of any kind to such a tremendous event and one so relevant to the relationship between the nascent Church and Judaism and the

1 *Ecclesiastical History*, III, 4, 6.
2 Cf. *Comm. in Matth*, preface.
3 Cf. *Eleventh Reply* of the Pontifical Biblical Communion, 12 June 1913.

Temple. The reader of the book has the impression all along that the Holy City is still standing and that the Temple is still the centre of Jewish worship. Some authors reach the same conclusion by arguing from the book's silence on the martyrdom of James, the brother of the Lord, and of Peter, who fell victim to Nero's persecution.[4]

We can conclude, then, that the Third Gospel and the Acts of the Apostles, which are two parts of a single work, could have been written over quite a short period of time and were completed prior to the year 70.

The book's dedication to Theophilus tells us—as does every such dedication in ancient writings—that the author has completed his work and made it available to the Christian readership for which he intended it, and indeed to Jewish readership also.

HISTORICAL ACCURACY

The Church has always maintained that the Acts of the Apostles is a true history of events. Luke's evangelizing and theological purpose did not prevent him from collecting, evaluating and interpreting facts with a skill that demonstrates he was an excellent historian. We have to put down to theological prejudice that scepticism expressed by some non-Catholic scholars about the historical value of Acts. These exegetes quite arbitrarily claim that the supernatural events reported in the book are later additions included into the text by an anonymous imaginative writer interested in projecting a particular image of Paul. Nowadays, there is a growing acceptance of the historicity of Acts: many non-Catholic scholars have come to this view through detailed study of the text, and their conviction has led others to tend in the same direction.

Few ancient texts provide such scope for checking their accuracy as Acts does. It is full of references to contemporary Jewish, Greek and Roman history, culture and topography. Everything it recounts is carefully set into an historical framework. Details of time and place are invariably found to be accurate, and the atmosphere of the period imbues the entire book. The writer leads his reader on a tour of the streets, markets, theatres and assemblies of the Ephesus, Thessalonica, Corinth and Philippi of the first century of the Christian era.

The events narrated in Acts invite and permit the scholar to check them for historical accuracy against the letters of St Paul, which deal with the same material, to some degree.

Like all writers of antiquity, the author of Acts focuses his attention on his principal characters and builds the narrative around them. He presents Paul as a fully mature Christian personality from the day of his conversion forward. This understandable simplification does not prevent us, however, from recognizing the Paul of Acts and the Paul of the Letters as being the same person. The Paul of Acts is the real Paul as seen retrospectively by a disciple who is also a friend.

4 The *Eleventh Reply* cited above, par. 4, is inclined towards the view that Acts was written towards the close of Paul's first imprisonment in Rome. Cf. *The Navarre Bible: St Mark*, p. 30.

The connexions between Acts and the Letters point to one and the same Paul. His activity as persecutor of the Church is recorded in similar language in Acts (8:3; 9:1) as in Galatians 1:13 and 1 Corinthian 15:9. Galatians 1:17 confirms what Acts says (9:3) about his conversion taking place in Damascus. In Acts 9:23-27 and Galatians 1:18 we are told that Paul made his first journey after his conversion from Damascus to Jerusalem. In Acts 9:30 and Galatians 1:21 we are told about Paul being sent to Tarsus after his stay in Jerusalem. His missionary companions after the split with Barnabas—that is, Silas and Timothy (cf. Acts 15:22, 40; 16:1)—are to be found in the letters written during this period. The itinerary in Acts 16-19—Philippi - Thessalonica - Athens - Corinth - Ephesus - Macedonia - Achaia—is confirmed by 1 Thess 2:2; 3:1; 1 Cor 2:1; 16:5-9; 2 Cor 12:14ff, Rom 16:1, 23). Only the Letters tell us that Paul was of the tribe of Benjamin (cf. Rom 11:1; Phil 3:5). Acts merely says that his Jewish name was Saul (cf. Acts 7:58; 9:1; 13:9): this ties in, because it would be quite reasonable for parents from that tribe to call a child after the first king of Israel, its most outstanding member (cf. 1 Sam 9:1ff). Many more examples could be given in support of the historical accuracy of the book.

Another source which throws a great deal of light on Luke's narrative is Flavius Josephus' *Jewish Antiquities*, written some twenty years after Acts. Josephus helps us establish the dates of Herod Agrippa I's reign (from the year 41 to 10 March 44), and we can see the agreement between Acts 12 and *Antiquities*, XIX, 274-363 on the circumstances of the king's death. Josephus' account also helps explain Luke's references (cf. Acts 5:36-37; *Jewish Antiquities*, XX, 169-172) to the Jewish rebels Judas of Galilee and Theudas. Luke's profile of the two governors Felix and Festus and of King Herod Agrippa II is confirmed and developed by Josephus. Another instance of corroboration is that Acts 18:12 describes Gallio as being proconsul of Achaia and this has been confirmed by an inscription found at Delphi, near Corinth.

This historical reliability of Acts only serves to reinforce its validity as a testimony to the faith of that early Church governed by the Apostles and guided at every step by the invisible and often visible power of the Holy Spirit: Acts sets an example of faith and doctrine for the Church in every era.

The speeches which the book contains, especially the more important ones of Peter (cf. 2:14ff; 3:12ff; 10:34ff; 11:5ff), Stephen (cf. 7:1ff) and Paul (cf. 13:16ff; 17:22ff; 20:18ff; 22:1ff; 24:10ff; 26:2ff) have been the subject of many detailed studies. Naturally, the actual address in each case would have been longer than the version given in the book, and Luke would have had more to draw on for some than for others. However, the accounts which Luke gives are to be taken as accurate. The addresses can be seen to reflect traditional Jewish styles of quoting and interpreting Sacred Scripture and, although similar in structure, there is also quite a variety in them. They obviously reflect the different speakers, locations and audiences, and they give a good idea of the Church's earliest form of preaching.

In line with the style of Jewish and Hellenist writers, St Luke made use of written sources to produce his book. He had not been an eyewitness of everything he reported and he would not have settled for simply word-of-mouth information: he would have used documents of different kinds, such as short narrative accounts, summaries of speeches, notes, travel diaries etc. It is quite likely that for the earlier part of the book he used material collected from the various churches or from the main people involved.

However, the book is so all-of-a-piece that it is difficult to reconstruct, with any accuracy, the sources he would have used. Some commentators suggest that Acts is based on two main groups of documents—a) an Antiochene source, containing information about Stephen, Philip, Barnabas and the early years of St Paul; and b) a collection of accounts of St Peter's activity. But this only a hypothesis.

Nor is it possible to say whether Luke included all the material available to him or instead operated selectively. He certainly seems to have used his own judgment as to what material to incorporate and what not to, and when to edit, re-use, combine or divide up material made available to him. Whatever his method, he did manage to impose remarkable unity on his work, every page of which evidences the supernatural action of the Spirit of God.

DOCTRINAL CONTENT

Acts is a sort of compendium of the Christian faith in action. St Luke's purpose, which is one of instruction, leads him to put forward all the main truths of the Christian religion and to show the main outlines of the liturgical and sacramental life of the infant Church. His book also gives us accurate insights into the way the Church was structured and managed, and into the attitudes of Christians towards political and social questions of their time.

Its teachings on Christ, the Holy Spirit and the Church merit special attention.

Christology Teaching on Christ in Acts is based on the Synoptic Gospels, on Jesus' life on earth and his glorification, which are the core of the Gospel message. All aspects of the paschal mystery—Passion, Death, Resurrection and Ascension—are given prominence, and that mystery is shown to fulfil the plans revealed by God in the Old Testament prophecies. Various Christological titles are applied to Jesus which show his divinity and his redemptive mission— titles such as Lord (2:36), Saviour (5:31), Servant of Yahweh (3:13, 16), the Righteous One (7:52), the Holy One (3:14) and especially Christ—the Messiah —which becomes his proper name.

Theology of the Holy Spirit St Luke stresses the key role of the Holy Spirit in all aspects of the life of the Church. At one and the same time the Spirit of God and the Spirit of Jesus Christ, at Pentecost the Holy Spirit causes the

Church to be made manifest to all the people and enables it to begin its salvific activity. The Spirit is the personal possession and the common inheritance of Christians, and also the source of their joy and spiritual vitality. He endows and supports in a special way those Christians who are ordained to carry out the various sacred ministries; and it is he who guides the Church in its choice of rulers and missionaries and encourages it and protects it in its work of evangelization. This second book by St Luke has rightly been called "the Gospel of the Holy Spirit".

Ecclesiology   Acts is an indispensable source of documentation on the life of the Church in its very earliest period. In it we are shown the Church as the instrument of God uses to fulfil the Old Testament promises. The Church is, then, the true Israel, a new people, a world-wide community of people joined by spiritual links, a people which is essentially missionary.

The Church is the outcome of the invisible but real presence of the risen Christ, who is the focus of Christian worship and the only Name by which men can be saved. Jesus' presence is really and truly affected in the "breaking of the bread", that is, in the eucharistic sacrifice, which his disciples already celebrate on Sunday, the first day of the week.

Acts describes the lifestyle of the early Christians in a very direct and moving way. Their life centres on prayer, the Eucharist and the Apostles' teaching, and it expresses itself in attitudes and actions of detachment, concord and love. St Luke offers this lifestyle as a kind of model and heritage for future generations of Christians.

Two aspects of Christianity are combined extemely well in this book—expectation of our Lord's second coming (which runs right through the New Testament) and the need to commit oneself, through prayer, work and cheerful sacrifice, to the building up of the Kingdom of God on earth.

Acts also tells us a good deal about the structure of the Church in earliest times and provides us with a most valuable account of the first council of the Church (cf. 15:6ff).

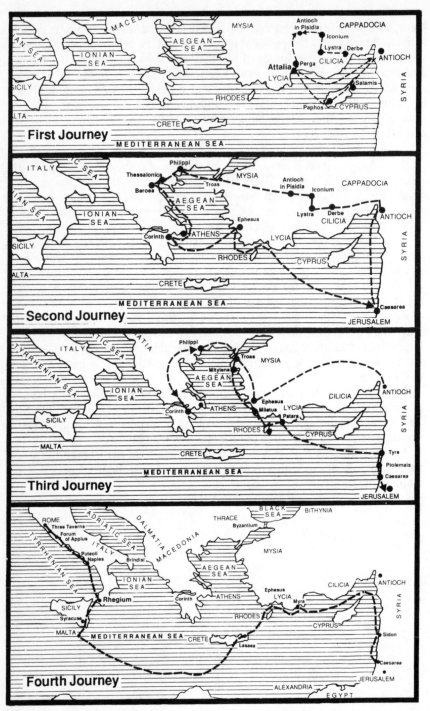

MISSIONARY JOURNEYS OF SAINT PAUL

The Acts of the Apostles

ENGLISH AND LATIN VERSIONS, WITH NOTES

1

¹In the first book, O Theophilus, I have dealt with all that Jesus began to do and teach, ²until the day when he was taken up, after he had given commandment through the Holy Spirit to the apostles whom he had chosen. ³To them he presented

Lk 1:3
Mt 28:20
Lk 6:13
Jn 20:22
1 Tim 3:16
Acts 13:31

---

¹Primum quidem sermonem feci de omnibus, o Theophile, quae coepit Iesus facere et docere, ²usque in diem, qua, cum praecepisset apostolis per Spiritum Sanctum, quos elegit, assumptus est; ³quibus et praebuit seipsum vivum post

---

1-5. St Luke is the only New Testament author to begin his book with a prologue, in the style of secular historians. The main aim of this preface is to convey to the reader the profoundly religious character of the book which he is holding in his hands. It is a work which will give an account of events marking the fulfilment of the promises made by the God of Israel, the Creator and Saviour of the world. Under the inspiration of the Holy Spirit, into his book St Luke weaves quotations from the Psalms, Isaiah, Amos and Joel; it both reflects the Old Testament and interprets it in the light of its fulfilment in Jesus Christ.

The prologue refers to St Luke's Gospel as a "first book". It mentions the last events of our Lord's life on earth—the appearances of the risen Christ and his ascension into heaven—and links them up with the account which is now beginning.

St Luke's aim is to describe the origins and the early growth of this Christianity, of which the main protagonist of this book, the Holy Spirit, has been the cause. Yet this is not simply an historical record: the Acts of the Apostles, St Jerome explains, "seems to be a straightforward historical account of the early years of the nascent Church. But if we bear in mind it is written by Luke the physician, who is praised in the Gospel (cf. 2 Cor 8:18), we will realize that everything he says is medicine for the ailing soul" (*Epistle* 53, 9).

The spiritual dimension of this book, which is one of a piece with the Third Gospel, nourished the soul of the first generations of Christians, providing them with a chronicle of God's faithful and loving support of the new Israel.

"This book", St John Chrysostom writes at the start of his great commentary, "will profit us no less than the Gospels, so replete is it with Christian wisdom and sound doctrine. It offers an account of the numerous miracles worked by the Holy Spirit. It contains the fulfilment of the prophecies of Jesus Christ recorded in the Gospel; we can observe in the very facts the bright evidence of Truth which shines in them, and the mighty change which is taking place in the Apostles: they become perfect men, extraordinary men, now that the Holy Spirit has come upon them. All Christ's promises and predictions—He who believes in me will do these and even greater works, you will be dragged before tribunals

29

Lk 24:49
Acts 10:41

himself alive after his passion by many proofs, appearing to them during forty days, and speaking of the kingdom of God. [4]And while staying[a] with them he charged them not to depart from Jerusalem, but to wait for the promise of the Father,

---

passionem suam in multis argumentis, per dies quadraginta apparens eis et loquens ea, quae sunt de regno Dei. [4]Et convescens praecepit eis ab

---

and kings and beaten in the synagogues, and will suffer grievous things, and yet you will overcome your persecutors and executioners and will bring the Gospel to the ends of the earth—all this, how it came to pass, may be seen in this admirable book. Here you will see the Apostles speeding their way over land and sea as if on wings. These Galileans, once so timorous and obtuse, we find suddenly changed into new men, despising wealth and honour, raised above passion and concupiscence" (*Hom. on Acts*, 1).

St Luke dedicates this book to Theophilus—as he did his Gospel. The dedication suggests that Theophilus was an educated Christian, of an upper-class background, but he may be a fictitious person symbolizing "the beloved of God", which is what the name means. It also may imply that Acts was written quite soon after the third Gospel.

1. "To do and teach": these words very concisely sum up the work of Jesus Christ, reported in the Gospels. They describe the way in which God's saving Revelation operates: God lovingly announces and reveals himself in the course of human history through his actions and through his words. "The economy of Revelation is realized by deeds and words, which are intrinsically bound up with each other", Vatican II teaches. "As a result, the works performed by God in the history of salvation show forth and bear out the doctrine and realities signified by the words; the words, for their part, proclaim the works, and bring to light the mystery they contain. The most intimate truth which this revelation gives us about God and the salvation of man shines forth in Christ, who is himself both the mediator and the sum total of Revelation" (*Dei Verbum*, 2).

The Lord "proclaimed the kingdom of the Father both by the testimony of his life and by the power of his word" (Vatican II, *Lumen gentium*, 35). He did not limit himself to speech, to being simply the Teacher whose words opened man's minds to the truth. He was, above all, the Redeemer, able to save fallen man through the divine efficacy of each and every moment of his life on earth.

"Our Lord took on all our weaknesses, which proceed from sin—with the exception of sin itself. He experienced hunger and thirst, sleep and fatigue, sadness and tears. He suffered in every possible way, even the supreme suffering of death. No one could be freed from the bonds of sinfulness had He who alone was totally innocent not been ready to die at the hands of impious

[a]Or *eating*.

30

which, he said, "you heard from me, ⁵for John baptized with water, but before many days you shall be baptized with the Holy Spirit."

Mt 3:11
Lk 3:16
Acts 11:16

Hierosolymis ne discederent, sed exspectarent promissionem Patris: "Quam audistis a me, ⁵quia Ioannes quidem baptizavit aqua, vos autem baptizabimini

---

men. Therefore, our Saviour, the Son of God, has left all those who believe in him an effective source of aid, and also an example. The first they obtain by being reborn through grace, the second by imitating his life" (St Leo the Great, *Twelfth homily on the Passion*).

Jesus' redemptive action—his miracles, his life of work, and the mystery of his death, resurrection and ascension, whose depth and meaning only faith can plumb—also constitute a simple and powerful stimulus for our everyday conduct. Faith should always be accompanied by words, by deeds, that is, our humble and necessary cooperation with God's saving plans.

"Don't forget that doing must come before teaching. '*Coepit facere et docere*', the holy Scripture says of Jesus Christ: 'He began to do and to teach.'

"First deeds: so that you and I might learn" (J. Escrivá, *The Way*, 342).

3. This verse recalls the account in Luke 24:13-43 of the appearances of the risen Jesus to the disciples of Emmaus and to the Apostles in the Cenacle.

It stresses the figure of *forty* days. This number may have a literal meaning and also a deeper meaning. In Sacred Scripture periods of forty days or forty years have a clearly salvific meaning: they are periods during which God prepares or effects important stages in his plans. The great flood lasted forty days (Gen 7:17); the Israelites journeyed in the wilderness for forty years on their way to the promised land (Ps 95:10); Moses spent forty days on Mount Sinai to receive God's revelation of the Covenant (Ex 24:18); on the strength of the bread sent by God Elisha walked forty days and forty nights to reach his destination (1 Kings 19:8); and our Lord fasted in the wilderness for forty days in preparation for his public life (Mt 4:2).

5. "You shall be baptized with the Holy Spirit": this book has been well described as the "Gospel of the Holy Spirit". "There is hardly a page in the Acts of the Apostles where we fail to read about the Spirit and the action by which he guides, directs and enlivens the life and work of the early Christian community. It is he who inspires the preaching of St Peter (cf. Acts 4:8), who strengthens the faith of the disciples (cf. Acts 4:31), who confirms with his presence the calling of the Gentiles (cf. Acts 10:44-47), who sends Saul and Barnabas to distant lands, where they will open new paths for the teaching of Jesus (cf. Acts 13:2-4). In a word, his presence and doctrine are everywhere" (J. Escrivá, *Christ is passing by*, 127).

31

Lk 19:11
Dan 2:21
Mt 24:36
1 Thess 5:1-2
Mt 28:19
Lk 24:47-48
Acts 2:32;
10:39

The Ascension

⁶So when they had come together, they asked him, "Lord, will you at this time restore the kingdom of Israel?" ⁷He said to them, "It is not for you to know times or seasons which the Father has fixed by his own authority. ⁸But you shall

---

in Spiritu Sancto non post multos hos dies." ⁶Igitur qui convenerant, interrogabant eum dicentes: "Domine, si in tempore hoc restitues regnum Israeli?" ⁷Dixit autem eis: "Non est vestrum nosse tempora vel momenta, quae Pater posuit in sua potestate, ⁸sed accipietis virtutem superveniente Sancto Spiritu in vos et eritis mihi testes et in Ierusalem et in omni Iudaea et Samaria et usque

---

6-8. The Apostles' question shows that they are still thinking in terms of earthly restoration of the Davidic dynasty. It would seem that for them—as for many Jews of their time— eschatological hope in the Kingdom extended no further than expectation of world-embracing Jewish hegemony.

"It seems to me", St John Chrysostom comments, "that they had not any clear notion of the nature of the Kingdom, for the Spirit had not yet instructed them. Notice that they do not ask when it shall come but 'Will you at this time restore the Kingdom to Israel?', as if the Kingdom were something that lay in the past. This question shows that they were still attracted by earthly things, though less than they had been" (*Hom. on Acts*, 2).

Our Lord gives an excellent and encouraging reply, patiently telling them that the Kingdom is mysterious in character, that it comes when one least expects, and that they need the help of the Holy Spirit to be able to grasp the teaching they have received. Jesus does not complain about their obtuseness; he simply corrects their ideas and instructs them.

8. The outline of Acts is given here: the author plans to tell the story of the growth of the Church, beginning in Jerusalem and spreading through Judea and Samaria to the ends of the earth. This is the geographical structure of St Luke's account. In the Third Gospel Jerusalem was the destination point of Jesus' public life (which began in Galilee); here it is the departure point.

The Apostles' mission extends to the whole world. Underlying this verse we can see not so much a "geographical" dimension as the universalist aspirations of the Old Testament, articulated by Isaiah: "It shall come to pass in the latter days that the mountain of the house of the Lord shall be established as the highest of the mountains, and shall be raised above the hills; and all the nations shall flow to it, and many peoples shall come, and say: 'Come, let us go up to the mountain of the Lord, to the house of the God of Jacob; that he may teach us his ways and that we may walk in his paths. For out of Zion shall go forth the law, and the word of the Lord from Jerusalem" (Is 2:2-3).

receive power when the Holy Spirit has come upon you; and
you shall be my witnesses in Jerusalem and in all Judea and
Samaria and to the end of the earth." ⁹And when he had said
this, as they were looking on, he was lifted up, and a cloud
took him out of their sight. ¹⁰And while they were gazing
into heaven as he went, behold, two men stood by them in

Mk 16:19
Lk 24:50-51
Jn 6:62
Eph 4:8-10
1 Pet 3:22
Lk 24:4

---

ad ultimum terrae." ⁹Et cum haec dixisset, videntibus illis, elevatus est, et nubes
suscepit eum ab oculis eorum. ¹⁰Cumque intuerentur in caelum eunte illo, ecce

---

9. Jesus' life on earth did not end with his death on the Cross but with his
ascension into heaven. The ascension, reported here, is the last event, the last
mystery of our Lord's life on earth (cf. also 24:50-53)—and also it concerns
the origins of the Church. The ascension scene takes place, so to speak, between
heaven and earth. "Why did a cloud take him out of the Apostles' sight?", St
John Chrysostom asks. "The cloud was a sure sign that Jesus had already
entered heaven; it was not a whirlwind or a chariot of fire, as in the case of the
prophet Elijah (cf. 2 Kings 2:11), but a cloud, which was a symbol of heaven
itself" (*Hom. on Acts*, 2). A cloud features in theophanies— manifestations of
God—in both the Old Testament (cf. Ex 13:22) and the New (cf. Lk 9:34f).

Our Lord's ascension is one of the actions by which Jesus redeems us from
sin and gives us the new life of grace. It is a redemptive mystery. "What we
have already taught of the mystery of his death and resurrection the faithful
should deem not less true of his ascension. For although we owe our redemption
and salvation to the passion of Christ, whose merits opened heaven to the just,
yet his ascension is not only proposed to us as a model, which teaches us to
look on high and ascend in spirit into heaven, but it also imparts to us a divine
virtue which enables us to accomplish what it teaches" (*St Pius V Catechism*,
I, 7, 9).

Our Lord's going up into heaven is not simply something which stirs us to
lift up our hearts—as we are invited to do at the preface of the Mass, to seek
and love the "things that are above" (cf. Col 3:1-2); along with the other
mysteries of his life, death and resurrection, Christ's ascension *saves* us. "Today
we are not only made possessors of paradise", St Leo says, "but we have
ascended with Christ, mystically but really, into the highest heaven, and through
Christ we have obtained a more ineffable grace than that which we lost through
the devil's envy" (*First homily on the ascension*).

The ascension is the climax of Christ's exaltation, which was achieved in the
first instance by his resurrection and which— along with his passion and
death—constitutes the paschal mystery. The Second Vatican Council expresses
this as follows: "Christ our Lord redeemed mankind and gave perfect glory to
God [. . .] principally by the paschal mystery of his blessed passion, resurrection

white robes, [11]and said, "Men of Galilee, why do you stand looking into heaven? This Jesus, who was taken up from you into heaven, will come in the same way as you saw him go into heaven."

---

duo viri astiterunt iuxta illos in vestibus albis, [11]qui et dixerunt: "Viri Galilaei, quid statis aspicientes in caelum? Hic Iesus, qui assumptus est a vobis in caelum, sic veniet quemadmodum vidistis eum euntem in caelum." [12]Tunc

---

from the dead, and glorious ascension" (*Sacrosanctum Concilium*, 5; cf. *Dei Verbum*, 19).

Theology has suggested reasons why it was very appropriate for the glorified Lord to go up into heaven to be "seated at the right hand of the Father." "First of all, he ascended because the glorious kingdom of the highest heavens, not the obscure abode of this earth, presented a suitable dwelling place for him whose body, rising from the tomb, was clothed with the glory of immortality. He ascended, however, not only to possess the throne of glory and the kingdom which he had merited by his blood, but also to attend to whatever regards our salvation. Again, he ascended to prove thereby that his kingdom is not of this world" (*St Pius V Catechism*, I, 7, 5; cf. *Summa theologiae*, III, q. 57, a. 6).

The ascension marks the point when the celestial world celebrates the victory and glorification of Christ: "It is fitting that the sacred humanity of Christ should receive the homage, praise and adoration of all the hierarchies of the Angels and of all the legions of the blessed in heaven" (J. Escrivá, *Holy Rosary*, second glorious mystery).

11. The angels are referring to the Parousia—our Lord's second coming, when he will judge the living and the dead. "They said to them, What are you doing here, looking into heaven? These words are full of solicitude, but they do not proclaim the second coming of the Saviour as imminent. The angels simply assert what is most important, that is, that Jesus Christ will come again and the confidence with which we should await his return" (St John Chrysostom, *Hom. on Acts*, 2).

We know for a certainty that Christ will come again at the end of time. We confess this in the Creed as part of our faith. However, we know "neither the day nor the hour" (Mt 25:13) of his coming. We do not need to know it. Christ is always imminent. We must always be on the watch, that is, we should busy ourselves in the service of God and of others, which is where our sanctification lies.

PART ONE
THE CHURCH IN JERUSALEM

The apostolic college

¹²Then they returned to Jerusalem from the mount called Olivet, which is near Jerusalem, a sabbath day's journey away; ¹³and when they had entered, they went up to the upper room, where they were staying, Peter and John and James and Andrew, Philip and Thomas, Bartholomew and Matthew, James the son of Alphaeus and Simon the Zealot and Judas the son of James. ¹⁴All these with one accord

Mt 10:2-4
Lk 6:14-16

Mt 13:55
Lk 8:2-3
24:10
Acts 12:12

---

reversi sunt in Ierusalem a monte, qui vocatur Oliveti, qui est iuxta Ierusalem sabbati habens iter. ¹³Et cum introissent, in cenaculum ascenderunt, ubi manebant et Petrus et Ioannes et Iacobus et Andreas, Philippus et Thomas,

---

13-14. St Luke mentions the twelve Apostles by name, with the exception of Judas Iscariot.

This is the first passage which tells of the spiritual life and devout practices of the disciples. Significantly it places the emphasis on prayer, in keeping with our Lord's own practice and with his constant recommendation to his followers (cf. Mt 6:5; 14:23; etc).

"Prayer is the foundation of the spiritual edifice. Prayer is all-powerful" (J. Escrivá, *The Way*, 83). It can truly be said that prayer is the bedrock of the Church, which will be made manifest with the coming of the Holy Spirit. The prayer of the disciples, including the women, in the company of Mary would have been a supplication of entreaty and praise and thanksgiving to God. This union of hearts and feelings produced by prayer is a kind of anticipation of the gifts the Holy Spirit will bring.

"We are told this time and again in the passage narrating the lives of the first followers of Christ. 'All these with one accord devoted themselves to prayer' (Acts 1:14). [. . .] Prayer was then, as it is today, the only weapon, the most powerful means, for winning the battles of our interior struggle" (J. Escrivá, *Friends of God*, 242).

Here we see Mary as the spiritual centre round which Jesus' intimate friends gather: tradition has meditated on this "tableau", and found it to depict our Lady's motherhood over the whole Church, both at its beginning and over the course of the centuries.

On 21 November 1964, at the closing of the third session of Vatican II, Paul VI solemnly proclaimed Mary Mother of the Church: "Our vision of the Church must include loving contemplation of the marvels which God worked in his holy Mother. And knowledge of the true Catholic doctrine about Mary will

35

devoted themselves to prayer, together with the women and Mary the mother of Jesus, and with his brethren.

Bartholomaeus et Matthaeus, Iacobus Alphaei et Simon Zelotes et Iudas Iacobi. [14]Hi omnes erant perseverantes unanimiter in oratione cum mulieribus et Maria matre Iesu et fratribus eius. [15]Et in diebus illis exsurgens Petrus in medio fratrum

---

always be the key to correct understanding of the mystery of Christ and of the Church.

"Reflection on the close ties linking Mary and the Church, so clearly indicated by the present constitution [*Lumen gentium*], allows us to think this is the most appropriate moment to satisfy a desire which, as we pointed out at the end of the last session, many council Fathers have made their own, calling insistently for an explicit declaration during this council of the maternal role which the Blessed Virgin exercises towards the Christian people. To this end we have considered it opportune to dedicate a title in honour of the Virgin which has been proposed in different parts of the Catholic world and which we find particularly touching, for it sums up in a wonderfully succinct way the privileged position which this council has recognized the Blessed Virgin to have in the Church.

"And so, for the glory of the Virgin and for our consolation, we proclaim Mary Most Holy to be the Mother of the Church, that is, Mother of the entire people of God, faithful as well as pastors, who call her loving Mother, and we desire that from now on she be honoured and invoked by the entire people of God under this most pleasing title."

The text makes reference to Jesus' "brethren", an expression which also appears in the Gospels. Given that the Christian faith teaches us that the Virgin Mary had no children other than Jesus, whom she conceived by the action of the Holy Spirit and without intervention of man, this expression cannot mean that Jesus had blood brothers or sisters.

The explanation lies in the peculiarities of Semitic languages. The word used in the New Testament translates a Hebrew term which applied to all the members of a family group and was used for even distant cousins (cf. Lev 10:4) and for nephews (Gen 13:8). See note on Mt 12:46-47. In the New Testament then, the word "brethren" has a very wide meaning—as happens, also, for example, with the word "apostle."

At one point Jesus describes those who hear and keep his word as his "brethren" (Lk 8:21), which seems to imply that, in addition to meaning belonging to the same family group, the word "brother" in the New Testament may be a designation for certain disciples who were particularly loyal to our Lord.

St Paul, for his part, uses this term for all Christians (cf., for example, 1 Cor 1:10; etc), as does St Peter, according to Acts 12:17.

The election of Matthias

¹⁵In those days Peter stood up among the brethren (the company of persons was in all about a hundred and twenty), and said, ¹⁶"Brethren, the scripture had to be fulfilled, which the Holy Spirit spoke beforehand by the mouth of David, concerning Judas who was guide to those who arrested Jesus. ¹⁷For he was numbered among us, and was allotted his share in this ministry. ¹⁸(Now this man bought a field with the reward of his wickedness; and falling headlong^b he burst open in the middle and all his bowels gushed out. ¹⁹And it became known to all the inhabitants of Jerusalem, so that the

Ps 41:10
Lk 22:47
Jn 13:18
Acts 1:20

Mt 27:3-10

---

dixit—erat autem turba hominum simul fere centum viginti—: ¹⁶"Viri fratres, oportebat impleri Scripturam, quam praedixit Spiritus Sanctus per os David de Iuda, qui fuit dux eorum, qui comprehenderunt Iesum, ¹⁷quia connumeratus erat in nobis et sortitus est sortem ministerii huius. ¹⁸Hic quidem possedit agrum de mercede iniquitatis et pronus factus crepuit medius, et diffusa sunt omnia viscera eius. ¹⁹Et notum factum est omnibus habitantibus Ierusalem, ita ut appellaretur ager ille lingua eorum Aceldamach, hoc est ager Sanguinis.

15-23. "Peter is the ardent and impetuous apostle to whom Christ entrusted the care of his flock; and since he is first in dignity, he is the first to speak" (Chrysostom, *Hom. on Acts*, 3).

Here we see Peter performing his ministry. Events will make for the gradual manifestation of the supreme role of government which Christ entrusted to him. His is a ministry of service— he is the *servus servorum Dei*, the servant of the servants of God—a ministry given to none other, different from all other ministries in the Church. Peter will carry it out in solidarity with his brothers in the Apostolate and in close contact with the whole Church represented here in the one hundred and twenty brethren around him.

This account of Peter with the other Apostles and disciples all brought together is described by St John Chrysostom in these words: "Observe the admirable prudence of St Peter. He begins by quoting the authority of a prophet and does not say, 'My own word suffices,' so far is he from any thought of pride. But he seeks nothing less than the election of a twelfth apostle and he presses for this. His entire behaviour shows the degree of his authority and that he understood the apostolic office of government not as a position of honour but as a commitment to watch over the spiritual health of those under him.

"The disciples were one hundred and twenty, and Peter asks for one of these. But he it is who proposes the election and exercises the principal authority because he has been entrusted with the care of all" (*Hom. on Acts*, 3).

^bOr *swelling up*.

field was called in their language Akeldama, that is, Field of Blood.) ²⁰For it is written in the Book of Psalms,

'Let his habitation become desolate,
and let there be no one to live in it';

and

'His office let another take.'

²¹So one of the men who have accompanied us during all the time that the Lord Jesus went in and out among us,

²²beginning from the baptism of John until the day when he was taken up from us — one of these men must become with us a witness to his resurrection."

²³And they put forward two, Joseph called Barsabbas, who was surnamed Justus, and Matthias. ²⁴And they prayed and said, "Lord, who knowest the hearts of all men, show which

---

²⁰Scriptum est enim in libro Psalmorum: 'Fiat commoratio eius deserta, et non sit qui inhabitet in ea' et: 'Episcopatum eius accipiat alius'. ²¹Oportet ergo ex his viris, qui nobiscum congregati erant in omni tempore, quo intravit et exivit inter nos Dominus Iesus, ²²incipiens a baptismate Ioannis usque in diem, qua assumptus est a nobis, testem resurrectionis eius nobiscum fieri unum ex istis." ²³Et statuerunt duos, Ioseph, qui vocabatur Barsabbas, qui cognominatus est Iustus, et Matthiam. ²⁴Et orantes dixerunt: "Tu, Domine, qui corda nosti

---

21-22. The Apostles are the witnesses *par excellence* of Jesus' public life. The Church is "apostolic" because it relies on the solid testimony of people specially chosen to live with our Lord, witnessing his works and listening to his words. The twelve Apostles certify that Jesus of Nazareth and the risen Lord are one and the same person and that the words and actions of Jesus preserved and passed on by the Church are indeed truly reported.

Everyone who maintains unity with the Pope and the bishops in communion with him maintains unity with the Apostles and, through them, with Jesus Christ himself. "Orthodox teaching has been conserved by being passed on successively since the time of the Apostles and so it has remained up to the present in all the churches. Therefore, only that teaching can be considered true which offers no discord with ecclesiastical and apostolic tradition" (Origen, *De principiis*, Preface, 2). See the note on Acts 1:26.

24-26. Vv. 24-25 record the first prayer of the Church, which is linked with what we were told in v. 14—"all these with one accord devoted themselves to prayer"—and shows the disciples' firm belief that God rules over all things and all events and looks after the Church in a very special way.

The Christian community leaves in God's hands the choice as to who will fill the empty place in the Twelve. It does this by using the traditional Hebrew

one of these two thou hast chosen ²⁵to take the place in this ministry and apostleship from which Judas turned aside, to go to his own place." ²⁶And they had cast lots for them, and the lot fell on Matthias; and he was enrolled with the eleven apostles.

1 Sam 14:41
Prov 16:33

---

omnium, ostende quem elegeris ex his duobus unum ²⁵accipere locum ministerii huius et apostolatus, de quo praevaricatus est Iudas, ut abiret in locum suum." ²⁶Et dederunt sortes eis, et cecidit sors super Matthiam, et annumeratus est cum undecim apostolis.

---

method of casting lots, the outcome of which will reveal God's Will. This method of divining God's will is to be found quite a number of times in the Old Testament (cf. 1 Sam 14:41f); its use was restricted to Levites, to prevent it degenerating into a superstitious practice. In casting lots the Jews used dice, sticks, pieces of paper etc. each bearing the name of a candidate for an office, or of people suspected of having committed some crime etc. Lots were cast as often as necessary to fill the number of places to be filled or the suspected number of criminals.

In this instance they decide to cast lots because they consider that God has already made his choice and all that remains is for him to make his will known: his decision can be ascertained unerringly by using this simple human device. This method of appointing people, borrowed from Judaism, did not continue to be used in the Church for very long.

Now that Matthias has been appointed the Twelve is complete again. The Apostolic College is now ready to receive the Holy Spirit whom Jesus promised to send, and to go on to bear universal witness to the Good News.

26. St Luke usually applies the term "apostles" only to the Twelve (cf., for example, Acts 6:6), or the Eleven plus Peter, who appears as head of the Apostolic College (cf.2:14). Except in Acts 14:14, Luke never describes St Paul as an apostle—not because he minimizes Paul's role (indeed, half the chapters of Acts deal with Paul) but because he reserves to the Twelve the specific function of being witnesses to our Lord's life on earth.

This apostolic character or apostolicity is one of the marks of the true Church of Christ—a Church built, by the express wish of its Founder, on the solid basis of the Twelve.

The *St Pius V Catechism* (I, 10, 17) teaches that "the true Church is also to be recognized from her origin, which can be traced back under the law of grace to the Apostles; for her doctrine is the truth not recently given, nor now first heard of, but delivered of old by the Apostles, and disseminated throughout the entire world. [. . .] That all, therefore, might know which was the Catholic Church, the Fathers, guided by the Spirit of God, added to the Creed the word 'apostolic'. For the Holy Spirit, who presides over the Church, governs her by no other ministers than those of apostolic succession. This Spirit, first imparted to the Apostles, has by the infinite goodness of God always continued in the Church."

The principal role of the Apostles is to be witnesses to the resurrection of Jesus (cf. 1:22). They perform it through the ministry of the word (6:4), which takes various forms, such as preaching to the people (cf. 2:14-40; 3:12-26; 4:2, 33; 5:20-21), teaching the disciples within the Christian community itself (2:42), and declarations uttered fearlessly against the enemies and persecutors of the Gospel of Jesus (4:5-31; 5:27-41). Like the word of the Lord, that of the Apostles is supported by signs and wonders, which render visible the salvation which they proclaim (2:14-21, 43; 3:1-11, 16; 4:8-12, 30; 5:12, 15-16; 9:31-43).

The Twelve also perform a role of government in the Church. When the members of the community at Jerusalem give up their property to help their brothers in need, they lay the money "at the apostles' feet" (4:35). When the Hellenist Christians need to be reassured, the Twelve summon the assembly to establish the ministry of the diaconate (6:2). When Saul goes up to Jerusalem after his conversion, he is introduced to the Apostles by Barnabas (9:26-28). The Apostles quite evidently exercise an authority given them by our Lord who invested them with untransferable responsibilities and duties connected with service to the entire Church.

The Apostles also intervene outside Jerusalem as guarantors of internal and external unity, which also is an essential distinguishing mark of the Church. After Philip baptizes some Samaritans, the Apostles Peter and John travel from Jerusalem to give them the Holy Spirit by the laying on of hands (8:14-17).

After the baptism of the pagan Cornelius, the Apostles study the situation with Peter, to ascertain more exactly the designs of God and the details of the new economy of salvation (11:1-18). Apropos of the debate in Antioch about the circumcision of baptized pagans, the community decides to consult the Apostles (15:2) to obtain a final decision on this delicate matter.

Most of St Luke's attention is concentrated on the figure of Peter, whom he mentions 56 times in Acts. Peter is always the centre of those scenes or episodes in which he appears with other apostles or disciples. In matters to do with the community at Jerusalem Peter acts as the spokesman of the Twelve (2:14, 37; 5:29) and plays a key role in the opening up of the Gospel to pagans.

The College of the twelve Apostles, whose head is Peter, endures in the Episcopacy of the Church, whose head is the Pope, the bishop of Rome, successor of Peter and vicar of Jesus Christ. The Second Vatican Council proposes this once again when it teaches that the "Lord Jesus, having prayed at length to the Father, called to himself those whom he willed and appointed twelve to be with him, whom he might send to preach the Kingdom of God (cf. Mk 3:13-19; Mt 10:1-42). These Apostles (cf. Lk 6:13) he constituted in the form of a college or permanent assembly, at the head of which he placed Peter, chosen from among them (cf. Jn 21:15-17)" (*Lumen gentium*, 19).

"Just as, in accordance with the Lord's decree, St Peter and the rest of the Apostles constitute a unique apostolic college, so in like fashion the Roman

40

2

PENTECOST

The coming of the Holy Spirit

Lev 23:15-21
Jn 3:8
Acts 4:31
Ps 104:30
Mt 3:11
Acts 10:44-46;
19:6

¹When the day of Pentecost had come, they were all together in one place. ²And suddenly a sound came from heaven like the rush of a mighty wind, and it filled all the house where they were sitting. ³And there appeared to them tongues as of

---

¹Et cum compleretur dies Pentecostes, erant omnes pariter in eodem loco. ²Et factus est repente de caelo sonus tamquam advenientis spiritus vehementis et replevit totam domum, ubi erant sedentes. ³Et apparuerunt illis dispertitae

---

Pontiff, Peter's successor, and the bishops, the successors of the Apostles, are related and united to one another. [. . .]

"In it the bishops, whilst loyally respecting the primacy and pre-eminence of their head, exercise their own proper authority for the good of their faithful, indeed even for the good of the whole Church, the organic structure and harmony of which are strengthened by the continued influence of the Holy Spirit. The supreme authority over the whole Church, which this college possesses, is exercised in a solemn way in an ecumenical council. [. . .] And it is the prerogative of the Roman Pontiff to convoke such councils, to preside over them and to confirm them" (*ibid.*, 22).

1-13. This account of the Holy Spirit visibly coming down on the disciples who, in keeping with Jesus' instructions, had stayed together in Jerusalem, gives limited information as to the time and place of the event, yet it is full of content. Pentecost was one of the three great Jewish feasts for which many Israelites went on pilgrimage to the Holy City to worship God in the temple. It originated as a harvest thanksgiving, with an offering of first-fruits. Later it was given the additional dimension of commemorating the promulgation of the Law given by God to Moses on Sinai. The Pentecost celebration was held fifty days after the Passover, that is, after seven weeks had passed. The material harvest which the Jews celebrated so joyously became, through God's providence, the symbol of the spiritual harvest which the Apostles began to reap on this day.

2-3. Wind and fire were elements which typically accompanied manifestations of God in the Old Testament (cf. Ex 3:2; 13:21-22; 2 Kings 5:24; Ps 104:3). In this instance, as Chrysostom explains, it would seem that separate tongues of fire came down on each of them: they were "separated, which means they came from one and the same source, to show that the Power all comes from the

41

Mk 16:17   fire, distributed and resting on each one of them. ⁴And they
were all filled with the Holy Spirit and began to speak in
other tongues, as the Spirit gave them utterance.

---

linguae tamquam ignis, seditque supra singulos eorum; ⁴et repleti sunt omnes
Spiritu Sancto et coeperunt loqui aliis linguis, prout Spiritus dabat eloqui illis.

Paraclete" (*Hom. on Acts*, 4). The wind and the noise must have been so intense
that they caused people to flock to the place. The fire symbolizes the action of
the Holy Spirit who, by enlightening the minds of the disciples, enables them
to understand Jesus' teachings—as Jesus promised at the Last Supper (cf. Jn
16:4-14); by inflaming their hearts with love he dispels their fear and moves
them to preach boldly. Fire also has a purifying effect, God's action cleansing
the soul of all trace of sin.

4. Pentecost was not an isolated event in the life of the Church, something
over and done with. "We have the right, the duty and the joy to tell you that
Pentecost is still happening. We can legitimately speak of the 'lasting value'
of Pentecost. We know that fifty days after Easter, the Apostles, gathered
together in the same Cenacle as had been used for the first Eucharist and from
which they had gone out to meet the Risen One for the first time, *discover* in
themselves the power of the Holy Spirit who descended upon them, the strength
of Him whom the Lord had promised so often as the outcome of his suffering
on the Cross; and strengthened in this way, they began to act, that is, to perform
their role. [. . .] Thus is born the *apostolic Church*. But even today—and herein
the continuity lies—the Basilica of St Peter in Rome and every Temple, every
Oratory, every place where the disciples of the Lord gather, is an extension of
that original Cenacle" (John Paul II, *Homily*, 25 May 1980).

Vatican II (cf. *Ad gentes*, 4) quotes St Augustine's description of the Holy
Spirit as the soul, the source of life, of the Church, which was born on the Cross
on Good Friday and whose birth was announced publicly on the day of
Pentecost: "Today, as you know, the Church was fully born, through the breath
of Christ, the Holy Spirit; and in the Church was born the Word, the witness to
and promulgation of salvation in the risen Jesus; and in him who listens to this
promulgation is born faith, and with faith a new life, an awareness of the
Christian vocation and the ability to hear that calling and to follow it by living
a genuinely human life, indeed a life which is not only human but holy. And to
make this divine intervention effective, today was born the apostolate, the
priesthood, the ministry of the Spirit, the calling to unity, fraternity and peace"
(Paul VI, *Address*, 25 May 1969).

"Mary, who conceived Christ by the work of the Holy Spirit, the Love of the
living God, presides over the birth of the Church, on the day of Pentecost, when
the same Holy Spirit comes down on the disciples and gives life to the mystical
body of Christians in unity and charity" (Paul VI, *Address*, 25 October 1969).

⁵Now there were dwelling in Jerusalem Jews, devout men from every nation under heaven. ⁶And at this sound the multitude came together, and they were bewildered, because each one heard them speaking in his own language. ⁷And they were amazed and wondered, saying, "Are not all these who are speaking Galileans? ⁸And how is it that we hear, each of us in his own native language? ⁹Parthians and Medes and Elamites and residents of Mesopotamia, Judea and Cappadocia, Pontus and Asia, ¹⁰Phrygia and Pamphylia, Egypt and the parts of Libya belonging to Cyrene, and visitors from Rome, both Jews and proselytes, ¹¹Cretans and Arabians, we hear them telling in our own tongues the

Gen 11:1-9

---

⁵Erant autem in Ierusalem habitantes Iudaei, viri religiosi ex omni natione, quae sub caelo est; ⁶facta autem hac voce, convenit multitudo et confusa est, quoniam audiebat unusquisque lingua sua illos loquentes. ⁷Stupebant autem et mirabantur dicentes: "Nonne ecce omnes isti, qui loquuntur, Galilaei sunt? ⁸Et quomodo nos audimus unusquisque propria lingua nostra, in qua nati sumus? ⁹Parthi et Medi et Elamitae, et qui habitant Mesopotamiam, Iudaeam quoque et Cappadociam, Pontum et Asiam, ¹⁰Phrygiam quoque et Pamphyliam, Aegyptum et partes Libyae, quae est circa Cyrenem, et advenae Romani, ¹¹Iudaei quoque et proselyti, Cretes et Arabes, audimus loquentes eos nostris

---

5-11. In his account of the events of Pentecost St Luke distinguishes "devout men" (v. 5), Jews and proselytes (v. 11). The first-mentioned were people who were residing in Jerusalem for reasons of study or piety, to be near the only temple the Jews had. They were Jews—not to be confused with "God-fearing men", that is, pagans sympathetic to Judaism, who worshipped the God of the Bible and who, if they became converts and members of the Jewish religion by being circumcised and by observing the Mosaic Law, were what were called "proselytes", whom Luke distinguishes from the "Jews", that is, those of Jewish race.

People of different races and tongues understand Peter, each in his or her own language. They can do so thanks to a special grace from the Holy Spirit given them for the occasion; this is not the same as the gift of "speaking with tongues" which some of the early Christians had (cf. 1 Cor 14), which allowed them to praise God and speak to him in a language which they themselves did not understand.

11. When the Fathers of the Church comment on this passage they frequently point to the contrast between the confusion of languages that came about at Babel (cf. Gen 11:1-9)—God's punishment for man's pride and infidelity—and the reversal of this confusion on the day of Pentecost, thanks

1 Cor 14:22-25 mighty works of God." [12]And all were amazed and perplexed, saying to one another, "What does this mean?" [13]But others mocking said, "They are filled with new wine."

---

linguis magnalia Dei." [12]Stupebant autem omnes et haesitabant ad invicem dicentes: "Quidnam hoc vult esse?"; [13]alii autem irridentes dicebant: "Musto

---

to the grace of the Holy Spirit. The Second Vatican Council stresses the same idea: "With- out doubt, the Holy Spirit was at work in the world before Christ was glorified. On the day of Pentecost, however, he came down on the disciples that he might remain with them forever (cf. Jn 14;16); on that day the Church was openly displayed to the crowds and the spread of the Gospel among the nations, through preaching, was begun. Finally, on that day was foreshadowed the union of all peoples in the catholicity of the faith by means of the Church of the New Alliance, a Church which speaks every language, understands and embraces all tongues in charity, and thus overcomes the dispersion of Babel" (*Ad gentes*, 4).

Christians need this gift for their apostolic activity and should ask the Holy Spirit to give it to them to help them express themselves in such a way that others can understand their message; to be able so to adapt what they say to suit the outlook and capacity of their hearers, that they pass Christ's truth on: "Every generation of Christians needs to redeem, to sanctify, its own time. To do this, it must understand and share the desires of other men—their equals—in order to make known to them, with a 'gift of tongues', how they are to respond to the action of the Holy Spirit, to that permanent outflow of rich treasures that comes from our Lord's heart. We Christians are called upon to announce, in our own time, to this world to which we belong and in which we live, the message — old and at the same time new—of the Gospel" (J. Escrivá, *Christ is passing by*, 132).

12. The action of the Holy Spirit must have caused such amazement, in both the disciples and those who heard them, that everyone was "beside himself". "The Apostles were so filled with the Holy Spirit that they seemed to be drunk (Acts 2:13).

"Then Peter stood up with the Eleven and addressed the people in a loud voice. We, people from a hundred nations, hear him. Each of us hears him in his own language—you and I in ours. He speaks to us of Christ Jesus and of the Holy Spirit and of the Father.

"He is not stoned nor thrown into prison; of those who have heard him, three thousand are converted and baptized.

"You and I, after helping the Apostles administer baptism, bless God the Father, for his Son Jesus, and we too feel drunk with the Holy Spirit" (J. Escrivá, *Holy Rosary*, third glorious mystery).

13. These devout Jews, from different countries, who happened to be in

Peter's address

¹⁴But Peter, standing with the eleven, lifted up his voice and addressed them, "Men of Judea and all who dwell in Jerusalem, let this be known to you, and give ear to my words. ¹⁵For these men are not drunk, as you suppose, since

Acts 1:15; 15:7

---

pleni sunt isti." ¹⁴Stans autem Petrus cum Undecim levavit vocem suam et locutus est eis: "Viri Iudaei et, qui habitatis Ierusalem universi, hoc vobis notum sit, et auribus percipite verba mea. ¹⁵Non enim, sicut vos aestimatis, hi ebrii

---

Jerusalem on the day of Pentecost—many of them living there, for reasons of study or piety, and others who had come up on pilgrimage for these days—listen to the Apostles' preaching because they are impressed by the amazing things they can see actually happening. The same Holy Spirit who acted in our Lord's disciples also moved their listeners' hearts and led them to believe. There were others, however, who resisted the action of grace and looked for an excuse to justify their behaviour.

14-36. Even as the Church takes its first steps St Peter can be seen to occupy the position of main spokesman. In his address we can distinguish an introduction and two parts: in the first part (vv. 16-21) he is explaining that the messianic times foretold by Joel have now arrived; in the second (vv. 22-36) he proclaims that Jesus of Nazareth, whom the Jews crucified, is the Messiah promised by God and eagerly awaited by the righteous of the Old Testament; it is he who has effected God's saving plan for mankind.

14. In his commentaries St John Chrysostom draws attention to the change worked in Peter by the Holy Spirit: "Listen to him preach and argue so boldly, who shortly before had trembled at the word of a servant girl! This boldness is a significant proof of the resurrection of his Master: Peter preaches to men who mock and laugh at his enthusiasm. [. . .] Calumny ('they are filled with new wine') does not deter the Apostles; sarcasm does not undermine their courage, for the coming of the Holy Spirit has made new men of them, men who can put up with every kind of human test. When the Holy Spirit enters into hearts he does so to elevate their affections and to change earthly souls, souls of clay, into chosen souls, people of real courage [. . .]. Look at the harmony that exists among the Apostles. See how they allow Peter to speak on behalf of them all. Peter raises his voice and speaks to the people with full assurance. That is the kind of courage a man has when he is the instrument of the Holy Spirit . [. . .] Just as a burning coal does not lose its heat when it falls on a haystack but instead is enabled to release its heat, so Peter, now that he is in contact with the life-giving Spirit, spreads his inner fire to those around him" (*Hom. on Acts*, 4).

45

it is only the third hour of the day; [16]but this is what was spoken by the prophet Joel:

Joel 3:1-5

[17]'And in the last days it shall be, God declares,
that I will pour out my Spirit upon all flesh,
and your sons and your daughters shall prophesy,
and your young men shall see visions,
and your old men shall dream dreams;

Rom 5:5

[18]yea, and on my manservants and my maidservants in those days
I will pour out my Spirit; and they shall prophesy.

Acts 5:12

[19]And I will show wonders in the heaven above
and signs on the earth beneath,
blood, and fire, and vapour of smoke;

Rev 6:12

[20]the sun shall be turned into darkness
and the moon into blood,
before the day of the Lord comes,
the great and manifest day.

Rom 10:9-13

[21]And it shall be that whoever calls on the name of the Lord shall be saved.'

Mt 2:23
Jn 3:2; 5:36

[22]"Men of Israel, hear these words: Jesus of Nazareth with mighty works and wonders and signs which God did through

---

sunt, est enim hora diei tertia, [16]sed hoc est, quod dictum est per prophetam Ioel: [17]'Et erit: in novissimis diebus, dicit Deus, effundam de Spiritu meo super omnem carnem, et prophetabunt filii vestri et filiae vestrae, et iuvenes vestri visiones videbunt, et seniores vestri somnia somniabunt; [18]et quidem super servos meos et super ancillas meas in diebus illis effundam de Spiritu meo, et prophetabunt. [19]Et dabo prodigia in caelo sursum et signa in terra deorsum, sanguinem et ignem et vaporem fumi; [20]sol convertetur in tenebras et luna in sanguinem, antequam veniat dies Domini magnus et manifestus. [21]Et erit: omnis quicumque invocaverit nomen Domini, salvus erit.' [22]Viri Israelitae, audite verba haec: Iesum Nazarenum, virum approbatum a Deo apud vos

---

17. "In the last days": a reference to the coming of Christ and the era of salvation which follows; and also to the fact that the Holy Spirit, whom God would pour out on men of every nation and era when the Kingdom of the Messiah arrived, would continue to aid his Church until the day of the Last Judgment, which will be heralded by amazing events.

22-36. To demonstrate that Jesus of Nazareth is the Messiah foretold by the

him in your midst, as you yourselves know — ²³this Jesus, Jn 19:6-11
Acts 3:15
delivered up according to the definite plan and fore-
knowledge of God, you crucified and killed by the hands of
lawless men. ²⁴But God raised him up, having loosed the Ps 18:6
Acts 13:34-37
pangs of death, because it was not possible for him to be held
by it. ²⁵For David says concerning him, Ps 16:8-11
'I saw the Lord always before me,
for he is at my right hand that I may not be shaken;
²⁶therefore my heart was glad, and my tongue rejoiced;
moreover my flesh will dwell in hope.
²⁷For thou wilt not abandon my soul to Hades,
nor let thy Holy One see corruption.
²⁸Thou hast made known to me the ways of life;
thou wilt make me full of gladness with thy presence.'
²⁹"Brethren, I may say to you confidently of the patriarch 1 Kings 2:10
David that he both died and was buried, and his tomb is with
us to this day. ³⁰Being therefore a prophet, and knowing that 2 Sam 7:12
Ps 132:11
God had sworn with an oath to him that he would set one of
his descendants upon his throne, ³¹he foresaw and spoke of Ps 16:10
the resurrection of the Christ, that he was not abandoned to

---

virtutibus et prodigiis et signis, quae fecit per illum Deus in medio vestri, sicut
ipsi scitis, ²³hunc definito consilio et praescientia Dei traditum per manum
iniquorum affligentes interemistis, ²⁴quem Deus suscitavit solutis doloribus
mortis, iuxta quod impossibile erat teneri illum ab ea. ²⁵David enim dicit circa
eum: 'Providebam Dominum coram me semper, quoniam a dextris meis est,
ne commovear. ²⁶Propter hoc laetatum est cor meum, et exsultavit lingua mea,
insuper et caro mea requiescet in spe. ²⁷Quoniam non derelinques animam
meam in inferno, neque dabis Sanctum tuum videre corruptionem. ²⁸Notas
fecisti mihi vias vitae, replebis me iucunditate cum facie tua.' ²⁹Viri fratres,
liceat audenter dicere ad vos de patriarcha David quoniam et defunctus est et
sepultus est et sepulcrum eius est apud nos usque in hodiernum diem; ³⁰propheta
igitur cum esset et sciret quia iure iurando iurasset illi Deus de fructu lumbi
eius sedere super sedem eius, ³¹providens locutus est de resurrectione Christi

---

prophets, St Peter reminds his listeners of our Lord's miracles (v. 22), as well
as of his death (v. 23), resurrection (v. 24-32) and glorious ascension (vv.
33-35). His address ends with a brief summing-up (v. 36).

Acts 5:31
Phil 2:9

Ps 110:1
Mt 22:44

Hades, nor did his flesh see corruption. [32]This Jesus God raised up, and of that we all are witnesses. [33]Being therefore exalted at the right hand of God, and having received from the Father the promise of the Holy Spirit, he has poured out this which you see and hear. [34]For David did not ascend into the heavens; but he himself says,

'The Lord said to my Lord, Sit at my right hand,
[35]till I make thy enemies a stool for thy feet.'

[36]Let all the house of Israel therefore know assuredly that God has made him both Lord and Christ, this Jesus whom you crucified.''

The baptisms

[37]Now when they heard this they were cut to the heart, and

---

quia neque derelictus est in inferno, neque caro eius vidit corruptionem. [32]Hunc Iesum resuscitavit Deus, cuius omnes nos testes sumus. [33]Dextera igitur Dei exaltatus et, promissione Spiritus Sancti accepta a Patre, effudit hunc, quem vos videtis et auditis. [34]Non enim David ascendit in caelos; dicit autem ipse: 'Dixit Dominus Domino meo: Sede a dextris meis, [35]donec ponam inimicos tuos scabellum pedum tuorum.' [36]Certissime ergo sciat omnis domus Israel quia et Dominum eum et Christum Deus fecit, hunc Iesum, quem vos crucifixistis.'' [37]His auditis, compuncti sunt corde et dixerunt ad Petrum et reliquos apostolos:

---

32. To proofs from prophecy, very important to the Jews, St Peter adds his own testimony on the resurrection of Jesus, and that of his brothers in the Apostolate.

36. During his life on earth Jesus had often presented himself as the Messiah and Son of God. His resurrection and ascension into heaven reveal him as such to the people at large.

In Peter's address we can see an outline of the content of the apostolic proclamation (*kerygma*), the content of Christian preaching, the object of faith. This proclamation bears witness to Christ's death and resurrection and subsequent exaltation; it recalls the main points of Jesus' mission, announced by John the Baptist, confirmed by miracles and brought to fulfilment by the appearances of the risen Lord and the outpouring of the Holy Spirit; it declares that the messianic time predicted by the prophets have arrived, and calls all men to conversion, in preparation for the Parousia or second coming of Christ in glory.

37. St Peter's words were the instrument used by God's grace to move the hearts of his listeners: they are so impressed that they ask in all simplicity what

said to Peter and the rest of the apostles, "Brethren, what shall we do?" ³⁸And Peter said to them, "Repent, and be baptized every one of you in the name of Jesus Christ for the forgiveness of your sins; and you shall receive the gift of the

Mt 3:2
Lk 13:3
Acts 3:19;
8:16

"Quid faciemus, viri fratres?" ³⁸Petrus vero ad illos: 'Paenitentiam, inquit, agite, et baptizetur unusquisque vestrum in nomine Iesu Christi in remissionem

---

they should do. Peter exhorts them to be converted, to repent (cf. note on 3:19). The *St Pius V Catechism* explains that in order to receive Baptism adults "need to repent the sins they have committed and their evil past life and to be resolved not to commit sin henceforth [. . .], for nothing is more opposed to the grace and power of Baptism than the outlook and disposition of those who never decide to abjure sin" (II, 2, 4).

38. "Be baptized in the name of Jesus Christ": this does not necessarily mean that this was the form of words the Apostles normally used in the liturgy, rather than the Trinitarian formula prescribed by Jesus. In the *Didache* (written around the year 100) it is stated that Baptism should be given in the name of the Father and of the Son and of the Holy Spirit, but this does not prevent it, in other passages, from referring to "those baptized in the name of the Lord." The expression "baptized in the name of Christ" means, therefore, becoming a member of Christ, becoming a Christian (cf. *Didache*, VII, 1; IX, 5).

"Like the men and women who came up to Peter on Pentecost, we too have been baptized. In baptism, our Father God has taken possession of our lives, has made us share in the life of Christ, and has given us the Holy Spirit" (J. Escrivá, *Christ is passing by*, 128). From this point onwards, the Trinity begins to act in the soul of the baptized person. "In the same way as transparent bodies, when light shines on them, become resplendent and bright, souls elevated and enlightened by the Holy Spirit become spiritual too and lead others to the light of grace. From the Holy Spirit comes knowledge of future events, understanding of mysteries and of hidden truths, an outpouring of gifts, heavenly citizenship, conversation with angels. From him comes never-ending joy, perseverance in good, likeness to God and—the most sublime thing imaginable—becoming God" (St Basil, *On the Holy Spirit*, IX, 23).

This divinization which occurs in the baptized person shows how important it is for Christians to cultivate the Holy Spirit who has been infused into their souls, where he dwells as long as he is not driven out by sin. "Love the third person of the Blessed Trinity. Listen in the intimacy of your being to the divine motions of encouragement or reproach you receive from him. Walk through the earth in the light that is poured out in your soul. [. . .] We can apply to ourselves the question asked by the Apostle: 'Do you not know that you are God's temple and that God's Spirit dwells in you?' (1 Cor 3:16). And we can understand it as an invitation to deal with God in a more personal and direct

Is 57:19
Acts 3:26;
13:46
Eph 2:13-17

Deut 32:5
Mt 17:17
Lk 9:41
Acts 5:14; 6:7

Holy Spirit. ³⁹For the promise is to you and to your children and to all that are far off, every one whom the Lord our God calls to him." ⁴⁰And he testified with many other words and exhorted them, saying, "Save yourselves from this crooked generation." ⁴¹So those who received his word were baptized, and there were added that day about three thousand

---

peccatorum vestrorum, et accipietis donum Sancti Spiritus; ³⁹vobis enim est repromissio et filiis vestris et omnibus, qui longe sunt, quoscumque advocaverit Dominus Deus noster." ⁴⁰Aliis etiam verbis pluribus testifactus est et exhortabatur eos dicens: "Salvamini a generatione ista prava." ⁴¹Qui ergo, recepto sermone eius, baptizati sunt; et appositae sunt in illa die animae circiter

---

manner. For some, unfortunately, the Paraclete is the Great Stranger. He is merely a name that is mentioned, but not Someone—not one of the three Persons in the one God—with whom we can talk and with whose life we can live. No: we have to deal with him simply and trustingly, as we are taught by the Church in its liturgy. Then we will come to know our Lord better, and at the same time, we will realize more fully the great favour that was granted us when we became Christians. We will see all the greatness and truth of this divinization, which is a sharing in God's own life" (J. Escrivá, *Christ is passing by*, 133-134).

39. The "promise" of the Holy Spirit applies to both Jews and Gentiles, but in the first instance it concerns the Jews: it is they to whom God entrusted his oracles; theirs was the privilege to receive the Old Testament and to be preached to directly by Jesus himself. St Peter makes it clear that this promise is also made "to all that are far off"— a reference to the Gentiles, as St Paul explains (cf. Eph 2:13-17) and in line with Isaiah's announcement, "Peace, peace to the far and to the near" (Is 57:19). Cf. Acts 22:21.

40. "This crooked generation" is not only that part of the Jewish people who rejected Christ and his teaching, but everyone who is estranged from God (cf. Deut 32:5; Phil 2:5).

41. St Luke here concludes his account of the events of the day of Pentecost and prepares to move on to a new topic. Before he does so he adds a note, as it were, to say that "about three thousand souls" became Christians as a result of Peter's address.

St Luke often makes reference to the numerical growth of the Church (2:47; 4:4; 5:14; 6:1, 7; 9:31; 11:21, 24; 16:5). Interesting in itself, this growth clearly shows the effectiveness of the Gospel message boldly proclaimed by the Apostles. It proves that if the Gospel is preached with constancy and clarity it

souls. [42]And they devoted themselves to the apostles' teaching and fellowship, to the breaking of bread and the prayers.

---

tria milia. [42]Erant autem perseverantes in doctrina apostolorum et communi-

---

can take root in any setting and will always find men and women ready to receive it and put it into practice.

"It is not true that everyone today—in general—is closed or indifferent to what our Christian faith teaches about man's being and destiny. It is not true that men in our time are turned only toward the things of this earth and have forgotten to look up to heaven. There is no lack of narrow ideologies, it is true, or of persons who maintain them. But in our time we find both great desires and base attitudes, heroism and cowardice, zeal and disenchantment—people who dream of a new world, more just and more human, and others who, discouraged perhaps by the failure of their youthful idealism, take refuge in the selfishness of seeking only their own security or remaining immersed in their errors.

"To all those men and women, wherever they may be, in their more exalted moments or in their crises and defeats, we have to bring the solemn and unequivocal message of St Peter in the days that followed Pentecost: Jesus is the cornerstone, the Redeemer, the hope of our lives. 'For there is no other name under heaven given among men by which we must be saved' (Acts 4:12)" (J. Escrivá, *Christ is passing by*, 132).

42-47. This is the first of the three summaries contained in the early chapters of Acts (cf. 4:32-35 and 5:12- 16). In simple words it describes the key elements in the ascetical and liturgical-sacramental life of the first Christians. It gives a vivid spiritual profile of the community which now—after Pentecost—extends beyond the Cenacle, a contemplative community, more and more involved in the world around it.

42. "The sacred writer", St John Chrysostom observes, "draws attention to two virtues in particular—perseverance and fellowship and tells us that the Apostles spent a long period instructing the disciples" (*Hom. on Acts*, 7).

"The apostles' teaching": the instruction normally given new converts. This is not the proclamation of the Gospel to non-Christians but a type of *catechesis* (which became more structured and systematic as time went on) aimed at explaining to the disciples the Christian meaning of Sacred Scripture and the basic truths of faith (out of this grew the credal statements of the Church) which they had to believe and practise in order to attain salvation.

Catechesis—an ongoing preaching and explanation of the Gospel *within* the Church—is a phenomenon to be found even in the very early days of Christianity. "An evangelizer, the Church begins by evangelizing itself. A community of believers, a community of hope practised and transmitted, a community of fraternal love, it has a need to listen unceasingly to what it must believe, to the reasons for its hope, to the new commandment of love" (Paul VI, *Evangelii nuntiandi*, 15).

If catechesis is something which converts and in general all Christians *need*, obviously pastors have a grave duty to provide it. "The whole of the book of the Acts of the Apostles is a witness that they were faithful to their vocation and to the mission they had received. The members of the first Christian community are seen in it as 'devoted to the apostles' teaching and fellowship, to the breaking of bread and the prayers'. Without any doubt we find in that a lasting image of the Church being born of and continually nourished by the word of the Lord, thanks to the teaching of the Apostles, celebrating that word in the eucharistic Sacrifice and bearing witness to it before the world in the sign of charity" (John Paul II, *Catechesi tradendae*, 10).

The "fellowship" referred to in this verse is that union of hearts brought about by the Holy Spirit. This profound solidarity among the disciples resulted from their practice of the faith and their appreciation of it as a peerless treasure which they all shared, a gift to them from God the Father through Jesus Christ. Their mutual affection enabled them to be detached from material things and to give up their possessions to help those in need.

The "breaking of bread" refers to the Blessed Eucharist and not just to an ordinary meal. This was a special way the early Christians had of referring to the making and distribution of the sacrament containing the Lord's body. This expression, connected with the idea of a banquet, was soon replaced by that of "Eucharist", which emphasizes the idea of thanksgiving (cf. *Didache*, IX, 1). From Pentecost onwards the Mass and eucharistic communion form the centre of Christian worship. 'From that time onwards the Church has never failed to come together to celebrate the paschal mystery, reading those things 'which were in all the scriptures concerning him' (Lk 24:27), celebrating the Eucharist in which 'the victory and triumph of his death are again made present' (Council of Trent, *De SS. Eucharistia*, chap. 5), and at the same time giving thanks to God" (Vatican II, *Sacrosanctum Concilium*, 6).

By receiving the Eucharist with a pure heart and clear conscience the disciples obtain the nourishment needed to follow the new life of the Gospel and to be in the world without being worldly. This connexion between the Eucharist and Christian living was something Pope John Paul II vigorously reminded Catholics about when he said in Dublin, "It is from the Eucharist that all of us receive the grace and strength for daily living—to live real Christian lives, in the joy of knowing that God loves us, that Christ died for us, and that the Holy Spirit lives in us.

"Our full participation in the Eucharist is the real source of the Christian spirit that we wish to see in our personal lives and in all aspects of society. Whether we serve in politics, in the economic, cultural, social or scientific fields—no matter what our occupation is—the Eucharist is a challenge to our daily lives.

The early Christians

⁴³And fear came upon every soul; and many wonders and
signs were done through the apostles. ⁴⁴And all who

Acts 5:11-12
Acts 4:32,
34-35

---

catione, in fractione panis et orationibus. ⁴³Fiebat autem omni animae timor;
multa quoque prodigia et signa per apostolos fiebant. ⁴⁴Omnes autem, qui

---

"Our union with Christ in the Eucharist must be expressed in the truth of our lives today—in our actions, in our behaviour, in our lifestyle, and in our relationships with others. For each one of us the Eucharist is a call to ever greater effort, so that we may live as true followers of Jesus: truthful in our speech, generous in our deeds, concerned, respectful of the dignity and rights of all persons, whatever their rank or income, self-sacrificing, fair and just, kind, considerate, compassionate and self-controlled. [. . .] The truth of our union with Jesus Christ in the Eucharist is tested by whether or not we really love our fellow men and women; it is tested by how we treat others, especially our families. [. . .] It is tested by whether or not we try to be reconciled with our enemies, on whether or not we forgive those who hurt us or offend us" (*Homily in Phoenix Park*, 29 September 1979).

43. The fear referred to here is the religious awe the disciples felt when they saw the miracles and other supernatural signs which the Lord worked through his Apostles. A healthy type of fear, denoting respect and reverence for holy things, it can cause a great change of attitude and behaviour in those who experience it.

An outstanding example of this sense of awe is St Peter's reaction at the miraculous catch of fish: "Depart from me, for I am a sinful man, O Lord": as St Luke explains, "he was astonished, and all that were with him, at the catch of fish they had taken" (Lk 5:9).

44. Charity and union of hearts lead the disciples to sacrifice their own interest to meet the material needs of their poorer brothers and sisters. The sharing of possessions referred to here was not a permanent, "communistic" kind of system. The more well-to-do Christians freely provided for those in need. Each of the disciples retained ownership of such property as he or she had: by handing it over to the community they showed their charity.

"This voluntary poverty and detachment", Chrysostom comments, "cut at the selfish root of many evils, and the new disciples showed that they had understood the Gospel teaching.

"This was not recklessness of the kind shown by certain philosophers, of whom some gave up their inheritance and others cast their gold into the sea: that was no contempt of riches, but folly and madness. For the devil has always made it his endeavour to disparage the things God has created, as if it were impossible to make good use of riches" (*Hom. on Acts*, 7).

Acts 6:1 believed were together and had all things in common; ⁴⁵and they sold their possessions and goods and distributed them Lk 24:53
Acts 8:8; 16:34 to all, as any had need. ⁴⁶And day by day, attending the temple together and breaking bread in their homes, they Acts 2:21;
13:48 partook of food with glad and generous hearts, ⁴⁷praising God and having favour with all the people. And the Lord added to their number day by day those who were being saved.

---

crediderant erant pariter et habebant omnia communia ⁴⁵et possessiones et substantias vendebant et dividebant illas omnibus, prout cuique opus erat; ⁴⁶cotidie quoque perdurantes unanimiter in templo et frangentes circa domos panem, sumebant cibum cum exsultatione et simplicitate cordis, ⁴⁷collaudantes Deum et habentes gratiam ad omnem plebem. Dominus autem augebat, qui salvi fierent cotidie in idipsum.

A spendthrift who wastes his resources does not have the virtue of detachment; nor can someone be called selfish becaue he retains his property, provided that he uses it generously when the need arises. "Rather than in not having, true poverty consists in being detached, in voluntarily renouncing one's dominion over things.

"That is why there are poor who are really rich. And vice-versa" (J. Escrivá, *The Way*, 632).

46. In the early days of the Church the temple was a centre of Christian prayer and liturgy. The first Christians regarded it as God's house, the House of the Father of Jesus Christ. Although Christianity involved obvious differences from Judaism, they also realized that Christ's message was an extension of Judaism; for a while, it was quite natural for them to maintain certain external aspects of the religion of their forefathers.

In addition to this legitimate religious instinct to venerate the one, true, loving God, whom Jews and Christians adore, St Jerome suggests that prudence may have dictated this practice: "Because the early Church was made up of Jews," he says, "the Apostles were very careful not to introduce any innovations, in order to avoid any possible scandal to believers" (*Epistle* 26, 2).

However, the temple was not the only place in the holy city where Christians met for prayer and worship. The reference to "breaking bread in their homes" reminds us that the Christian community in Jerusalem, as also the communities later founded by St Paul, did not yet have a building specially reserved for liturgical functions. They met in private houses—presumably in suitable rooms specially prepared. For financial as well as policy reasons (persecutions etc.), it was not until the third century that buildings designed solely for liturgical purposes began to be erected.

Cure of a man lame from birth

¹Now Peter and John were going up to the temple at the hour of prayer, the ninth hour. ²And a man lame from birth was being carried, whom they laid daily at the gate of the temple which is called Beautiful to ask alms of those who entered the temple. ³Seeing Peter and John about to go into the

Acts 10:3-30
Jn 9:1
Acts 14:8-10

---

¹Petrus autem et Ioannes ascendebant in templum ad horam orationis nonam. ²Et quidam vir, qui erat claudus ex utero matris suae, baiulabatur, quem ponebant cotidie ad portam templi, quae dicitur Speciosa ut peteret eleemosynam ab introeuntibus in templum; ³is cum vidisset Petrum et Ioannem

---

1. This was the hour of the evening sacrifice, which began around three o'clock and was attended by a large number of devout Jews. The ritual, which went on until dusk, was the second sacrifice of the day. The earlier one, on similar lines, began at dawn and lasted until nine in the morning.

2. None of the documents that have come down to us which describe the Temple mentions a gate of this name. It was probably the Gate of Nicanor (or Corinthian Gate), which linked the court of the Gentiles with the court of the women which led on to the court of the Israelites. It was architecturally a very fine structure and because of its location it was a very busy place, which would have made it a very good place for begging.

3-8. The cure of this cripple was the first miracle worked by the Apostles. "This cure", says St John Chrysostom, "testifies to the resurrection of Christ, of which it is an image. [. . .] Observe that they do not go up to the temple with the intention of performing a miracle, so clear were they of ambition, so closely did they imitate their Master" (*Hom. on Acts*, 8).

However, the Apostles decide that the time has come to use the supernatural power given them by God. What Christ did in the Gospel using his own divine power, the Apostles now do in his name, using his power. "The blind receive their sight, the lame walk, lepers are cleansed, and the deaf hear, the dead are raised up" (Lk 7:22). Our Lord now keeps his promise to empower his disciples to work miracles—visible signs of the coming of the Kingdom of God. These miracles are not extraordinary actions done casually or suddenly, without his disciples' involvement: they occur because our Lord is moved to perform them by the Apostles' faith (faith is an essential pre- condition). The disciples are conscious of having received a gift and they act on foot of it.

These miracles in the New Testament obviously occur in situations where

temple, he asked for alms. [4]And Peter directed his gaze at him, with John, and said, "Look at us." [5]And he fixed his attention upon them, expecting to receive something from them. [6]But Peter said, "I have no silver and gold, but I give you what I have; in the name of Jesus Christ of Nazareth, walk." [7]And he took him by the right hand and raised him up; and immediately his feet and ankles were made strong. [8]And leaping up he stood and walked and entered the temple with them, walking and leaping and praising God. [9]And all the people saw him walking and praising God, [10]and

Acts 3:16

Is 35:6
Lk 7:22

---

incipientes introire in templum, rogabat, ut eleemosynam acciperet. [4]Intuens autem in eum Petrus cum Ioanne dixit: "Respice in nos." [5]At ille intendebat in eos, sperens se aliquid accepturum ab eis. [6]Petrus autem dixit: "Argentum et aurum non est mihi; quod autem habeo, hoc tibi do: In nomine Iesu Christi Nazareni surge et ambula!" [7]Et apprehensa ei manu dextera, allevavit eum; et protinus consolidatae sunt bases eius et tali, [8]et exsiliens stetit et ambulabat et intravit cum illis in templum, ambulans et exsiliens et laudans Deum. [9]Et vidit omnis populus eum ambulantem laudantem Deum, [10]cognoscebant autem illum quoniam ipse erat, qui ad eleemosynam sedebat ad Speciosam portam templi,

---

grace is intensely concentrated. However, that is not to say that miracles do not continue to occur in the Christian economy of salvation—miracles of different kinds, performed because God is attracted to men and women of faith. "The same is true of us. If we struggle daily to become saints, each of us in his own situation in the world and through his own job or profession, in our ordinary lives, then I assure you that God will make us into instruments that can work miracles and, if necessary, miracles of the most extraordinary kind. We will give sight to the blind. Who could not relate thousands of cases of people, blind almost from the day they were born, recovering their sight and receiving all the splendour of Christ's light? And others who were deaf, or dumb, who could not hear or pronounce words fitting to God's children. . . . Their senses have been purified and now they hear and speak as men, not animals. *In nomine Iesu!* In the name of Jesus his Apostles enable the cripple to move and walk, when previously he had been incapable of doing anything useful; and that other lazy character, who knew his duties but didn't fulfil them. [. . .] In the Lord's name, *surge et ambula!*, rise up and walk.

"Another man was dead, rotting, smelling like a corpse: he hears God's voice, as in the miracle of the son of the widow at Naim: 'Young man, I say to you, rise up'. We will work miracles like Christ did, like the first Apostles did" (J. Escrivá, *Friends of God*, 262).

Miracles call for cooperation—faith—on the part of those who wish to be cured. The lame man does his bit, even if it is only the simple gesture of obeying Peter and looking at the Apostles.

56

recognized him as the one who sat for alms at the Beautiful Gate of the temple; and they were filled with wonder and amazement at what had happened to him.

Peter's address in the temple

[11]While he clung to Peter and John, all the people ran together to them in the portico called Solomon's, astounded. [12]And when Peter saw it he addressed the people, "Men of Israel, why do you wonder at this, or why do you stare at us, as though by our own power or piety we had made him walk? [13]The God of Abraham and of Isaac and of Jacob, the God of our fathers, glorified his servant[c] Jesus, whom you delivered up and denied in the presence of Pilate, when he

Jn 10:23
Acts 5:12
Ex 3:6, 15
Is 52:13
Lk 23:22
Jn 18:38; 19:4
Rom 4:25
Eph 5:2
Mk 1:24
Lk 1:35; 23:25
Jn 6:69; 18:40
Acts 7:52
Rev 3:7

---

et impleti sunt stupore et exstasi in eo, quod contigerat illi. [11]Cum teneret autem Petrum et Ioannem, concurrit omnis populus ad eos ad porticum, qui appellatur Salomonis, stupentes. [12]Videns autem Petrus respondit ad populum: "Viri Israelitae, quid miramini in hoc aut nos quid intuemini, quasi nostra virtute aut pietate facerimus hunc ambulare? [13]Deus Abraham et Deus Isaac et Deus Iacob, Deus patrum nostrorum glorificavit Puerum suum Iesum, quem vos quidem

---

11-26. This second address by St Peter contains two parts: in the first (vv. 12-16) the Apostle explains that the miracle has been worked in the name of Jesus and through faith in his name; in the second (vv. 17-26) he moves his listeners to repentance—people who were responsible in some degree for Jesus' death.

This discourse has the same purpose as that of Pentecost—to show the power of God made manifest in Jesus Christ and to make the Jews see the seriousness of their crime and have them repent. In both discourses there is reference to the second coming of the Lord and we can clearly see the special importance of testifying to the resurrection of Jesus; the Apostolic College is presented as a witness to that unique event.

13. "Servant": the original Greek word (*pais*) is the equivalent of the Latin *puer* (slave, servant) and *filius* (son). By using this word St Peter must have in mind Isaiah's prophecy about the Servant of Yahweh: "Behold, my servant shall prosper, he shall be exalted and lifted up, and shall be very high. As many were astonished at him—his appearance was so marred, beyond human semblance, and his form beyond that of the sons of men—so shall he startle many nations" (52:13-15).

Peter identifies Jesus with the Servant of Yahweh, who, because he was a man of suffering and sorrow, the Jews did not identify with the future Messiah. That Messiah, Jesus Christ, combines in his person suffering and victory.

[c]Or *child*.

Acts 1:8; 13:31
Heb 2:10

Acts 4:10;
16:18;
19:13-17

Lk 23:34
Acts 13:27
1 Cor 2:8

had decided to release him. ¹⁴But you denied the Holy and Righteous One, and asked for a murderer to be granted to you, ¹⁵and killed the Author of life, whom God raised from the dead. To this we are witnesses. ¹⁶And his name, by faith in his name, has made this man strong whom you see and know; and the faith which is through Jesus^d has given the man this perfect health in the presence of you all.

¹⁷"And now, brethren, I know that you acted in ignorance,

---

tradidistis et negastis ante faciem Pilati, iudicante illo dimitti; ¹⁴vos autem Sanctum et Iustum negastis et petistis virum homicidam donari vobis, ¹⁵auctorem vero vitae interfecistis, quem Deus suscitavit a mortuis, cuius nos testes sumus. ¹⁶Et in fide nominis eius hunc, quem videtis et nostis, confirmavit nomen eius, et fides, quae per eum est, dedit huic integritatem istam in conspectu omnium vestrum. ¹⁷Et nunc, fratres, scio quia per ignorantiam

---

14. St Peter, referring to Jesus, uses terms which Jews can readily understand in a messianic sense. The expression "the Holy One of God" was already used by Jesus as referring to the Messiah in Mk 1:24 and Lk 4:34. It is reminiscent of Old Testament language (cf. Ps 16:10).

The "Righteous One" also refers to the Messiah, whom the prophets described as a model and achiever of righteousness (cf. Acts 7:52). "Holy", "righteous" and "just" all have similar meaning.

15. When St Peter reminds his listeners about their choice of a murderer (Barabbas) in place of Jesus, the Author of Life, we might usefully consider that he was referring not only to physical life but also to spiritual life, the life of grace. Every time a person sins—sin means the death of the soul—this same choice is being made again. "It was he who created man in the beginning, and he left him in the power of his own inclination. If you will you can keep the commandments, and to act faithfully is a matter of your own choice. He has placed before you fire and water: stretch out your hand for whichever you wish. Before a man are life and death, and whichever he chooses will be given to him" (Sir 15:14-18).

16. The original text, structured in a very Jewish way, is difficult to understand. One reason for this is the use of the word "name" instead of simply identifying who the person is. In this passage "name" means the same as "Jesus". Thus the verse can be interpreted in this way: through faith in Jesus, the man lame from birth, whom they know and have seen, has been cured; it is Jesus himself who has worked this complete and instantaneous cure.

17-18. The Jewish people acted in ignorance, St Peter says. Indeed, when he was on the cross Jesus had prayed, "Father, forgive them, for they know not

^d Greek *him*.

as did also your rulers. ¹⁸But what God foretold by the mouth
of all the prophets, that his Christ should suffer, he thus
fulfilled. ¹⁹Repent therefore, and turn again, that your sins

fecistis, sicut et principes vestri; ¹⁸Deus autem, quae praenuntiavit per os
omnium prophetarum pati Christum suum, implevit sic. ¹⁹Paenitemini igitur et

what they do" (Lk 23:34). The people did not know that Jesus was the Christ,
the Son of God. They let themselves be influenced by their priests. These, who
were familiar with the Scriptures, should have recognized him.

God's pardon is offered to one and all. St Peter "tells them that Christ's death
was a consequence of God's will and decree. [. . .] You can see how incomprehensible and profound God's design is. It was not just one but all the prophets
who foretold this mystery. Yet although the Jews had been, without knowing
it, the cause of Jesus' death, that death had been determined by the wisdom and
will of God, who used the malice of the Jews to fulfil his designs. The Apostle
does not say, Although the prophets foretold this death and you acted out of
ignorance, do not think you are entirely free from blame; Peter speaks to them
gently: 'Repent and turn again.' To what end? 'That your sins may be blotted
out'. Not only your murder but all the stains on your souls" (Chrysostom, *Hom.
on Acts*, 9).

The Second Vatican Council tells us how Christians should treat Jewish
people and those who follow other non-Christian religions—with respect and
also a prudent zeal to attract them to the faith. "Even though the Jewish
authorities and those who followed their lead pressed for the death of Christ
(cf. Jn 19:6), neither all Jews indiscriminately at that time, nor Jews today, can
be charged with the crimes committed during his passion. It is true that the
Church is the new people of God, yet the Jews should not be spoken of as
rejected or accursed. [. . .] Jews for the most part did not accept the Gospel; on
the contrary, many opposed the spreading of it (cf. Rom 11:28-29). Even so,
the apostle Paul maintains that the Jews remain very dear to God, for the sake
of the patriarchs, since God does not take back the gifts he bestowed or the
choice he made" (Vatican II, *Nostra aetate*, 4). We must not forget this special
position of the Jewish people (cf. Rom 9:4-5) and the fact that from them came
Jesus as far as his human lineage was concerned, and his Mother, the Blessed
Virgin Mary, and the Apostles—the foundation, the pillars of the Church—and
many of the first disciples who proclaimed Christ's Gospel to the world.

Moved by charity, the Church prays to our Lord for the spiritual conversion
of the Jewish people: "Christ, God and man, who is the Lord of David and his
children, we beseech you that in keeping with the prophecies and promises,
Israel recognize you as Messiah" (*Liturgy of the Hours*, Morning Prayer, 31
December).

19. One result of sorrow for sin is a desire to make up for the damage done.
On the day of Pentecost many Jews were moved by grace to ask the Apostles

may be blotted out, that times of refreshing may come from
the presence of the Lord, [20]and that he may send the Christ
appointed for you, Jesus, [21]whom heaven must receive until
the time for establishing all that God spoke by the mouth of
his holy prophets from of old. [22]Moses said, 'The Lord God
will raise up for you a prophet from your brethren as he raised
me up. You shall listen to him in whatever he tells you. [23]And
it shall be that every soul that does not listen to that prophet
shall be destroyed from the people.' [24]And all the prophets

2 Pet 3:11-13
Acts 1:11
Rev 1:7

Deut 18:15, 19
Acts 7:37

Lev 23:29

---

convertimini, ut deleantur vestra peccata, [20]ut veniant tempora refrigerii a
conspectu Domini, et mittat eum, qui praedestinatus est vobis Christus, Iesum,
[21]quem oportet caelum quidem suscipere usque in tempora restitutionis
omnium, quae locutus est Deus per os sanctorum a saeculo suorum
prophetarum. [22]Moyses quidem dixit: 'Prophetam vobis suscitabit Dominus
Deus vester de fratribus vestris tamquam me; ipsum audietis iuxta omnia,
quaecumque locutus fuerit vobis. [23]Erit autem: omnis anima, quae non audierit
prophetam illum, exterminabitur de plebe.' [24]Et omnes prophetae a Samuel et

---

what they should do to make atonement. Here also St Peter encourages them
to change their lives and turn to God. This repentance or conversion which Peter
preaches is the same message as marked the initial proclamation of the
Kingdom (cf. Mk 1:15; 13:1-4). "This means a change of outlook, and it applies
to the state of sinful man, who needs to change his ways and turn to God,
desirous of breaking away from his sins and repenting and calling on God's
mercy" (Paul VI, *Homily*, 24 February 1971).

On another occasion Paul VI explained that the word "conversion" can be
translated normally as "change of heart". "We are called to this change and it
will make us see many things. The first has to do with interior analysis of our
soul [. . .]: we should examine ourselves as to what is the main direction our
life is taking, what attitude is usually to the fore in the way we think and act,
what is our reason of being. [. . .] Is our rudder fixed so as to bring us exactly
to our goal or does its direction need perhaps to be changed? [. . .] By examining
ourselves in this way [. . .] we will discover sins, or at least weaknesses, which
call for penance and profound reform" (Paul VI, *General Audience*, 21 March
1973).

20. A reference to the Parousia or second coming of Christ as Judge of the
living and the dead (cf. note on 1:11).

22-24. St Peter wants to show that the Old Testament prophecies are fulfilled
in Jesus: he is descended from David (2:30), a prophet (cf. Deut 18:15), who
suffered (2:23), who is the cornerstone (4:11) and who rose from the dead and
sits in glory at the right hand of the Father (2:25-34).

who have spoken, from Samuel and those who came afterwards, also proclaimed these days. [25]You are the sons of the
prophets and of the covenant which God gave to your fathers,
saying to Abraham, 'And in your posterity shall all the
families of the earth be blessed.' [26]God having raised up his
servant,[c] sent him to you first, to bless you in turning every
one of you from your wickedness."

Gen 12:3;
22:18
Acts 13:32-34;
26:6-8

Gal 3:8

4

Peter and John are arrested

[1]And as they were speaking to the people, the priests and the
captain of the temple and the Sadducees came upon them,
[2]annoyed because they were teaching the people and proclaiming in Jesus the resurrection from the dead. [3]And they
arrested them and put them in custody until the morrow, for
it was already evening. [4]But many of those who heard the
word believed; and the number of men came to about five
thousand.

Lk 22:4-52
Acts 5:24

Acts 23:6-8
1 Cor
15:20-23

Acts 2:47

---

deinceps quotquot locuti sunt, etiam annuntiaverunt dies istos. [25]Vos estis filii
prophetarum et testamenti, quod disposuit Deus ad patres vestros dicens ad
Abraham: 'Et in semine tuo benedicentur omnes familiae terrae.' [26]Vobis
primum Deus suscitans Puerum suum, misit eum benedicentem vobis in
avertendo unumquemque a nequitiis vestris."
[1]Loquentibus autem illis ad populum, supervenerunt eis sacerdotes et
magistratus templi et sadducaei, [2]dolentes quod docerent populum et
annuntiarent in Iesu resurrectionem ex mortuis, [3]et iniecerunt in eos manus et
posuerunt in custodiam in crastinum, erat enim iam vespera. [4]Multi autem

---

1-4. On the Sadducee sect see the note on Mt 3:7.

In this chapter St Luke reports on the first conflict between the Apostles and
the Jerusalem authorities. Despite the incident at the end of Peter's address, his
words are still an instrument of grace, stirring his listeners to believe and
moving them to love.

A large crowd has gathered round Peter after the curing of the cripple, which
brings on the scene the "captain of the temple", a priest second in line to the
high priest whose function it was to maintain order. The priests St Luke refers
to here would have been those who were on for this particular week and were
responsible for the day-to-day affairs of the temple.

[c]Or *child*.

Address to the Sanhedrin

Acts 5:21
Lk 3:2
Mt 21:23
Lk 20:2
Mt 10:19-20

⁵On the morrow their rulers and elders and scribes were gathered together in Jerusalem, ⁶with Annas the high priest and Caiaphas and John and Alexander, and all who were of the high-priestly family. ⁷And when they had set them in the midst, they inquired, "By what power or by what name did you do this?" ⁸Then Peter, filled with the Holy Spirit, said to

---

eorum, qui audierunt verbum, crediderunt; et factus est numerus virorum quinque milia. ⁵Factum est autem in crastinum; ut congregarentur principes eorum et seniores et scribae in Ierusalem, ⁶et Annas princeps sacerdotum et Caiaphas et Ioannes et Alexander et quotquot erant de genere pontificali, ⁷et statuentes eos in medio interrogabant: "In qua virtute aut in quo nomine fecistis hoc vos?" ⁸Tunc Petrus repletus Spiritu Sancto dixit ad eos "Principes populi

---

5-7. These three groups—rulers, elders, scribes—made up the Sanhedrin, the same tribunal as had recently judged and condemned our Lord (cf. note on Mt 2:4). Jesus' words are already being fulfilled: "A servant is not greater than his master. If they persecuted me, they will persecute you" (Jn 15:20).

Annas was not in fact the high priest at this time, but the title was applied to him along with Caiaphas because of the authority he still wielded: he had been high priest and five of his sons succeeded him in the office, as well as Caiaphas, his son-in-law (cf. Josephus, *Jewish Antiquities*, XX, 198f).

8-12. The Apostles' confidence and joy is quite remarkable, as is their outspokenness in asserting that "we cannot but speak of what we have seen and heard" (v. 20). "This is the glorious freedom of the children of God. Christians who let themselves be browbeaten or become inhibited or envious in the face of the licentious behaviour of those who do not accept the Word of God, show that they have a very poor idea of the faith. If we truly fulfil the law of Christ—that is, if we make the effort to do so, for we will not always fully succeed—we will find ourselves endowed with a wonderful gallantry of spirit" (J. Escrivá, *Friends of God*, 38).

Christians have a duty to confess their faith where silence would mean its implicit denial, disrespect for religion, an offence against God or scandal to their neighbour. Thus Vatican II: "Christians should approach those who are outside wisely, 'in the Holy Spirit, genuine love, truthful speech' (2 Cor 6:6-7), and should strive, even to the shedding of their blood, to spread the light of life with all confidence (Acts 4:29) and apostolic courage. The disciple has a grave obligation to Christ, his Master, to grow daily in his knowledge of the truth he has received from him, to be faithful in announcing it and vigorous in defending it" (*Dignitatis humanae*, 14).

Pope Paul VI asked Catholics to check on any weak points in their faith, including ignorance and human respect, "that is, shame or timidity in pro-them, "Rulers of the people and elders, [9]if we are being examined today concerning a good deed done to a cripple, by what means this man has been healed, [10]be it known to you all, and to all the people of Israel, that by the name of Jesus Christ of Nazareth, whom you crucified, whom God raised from the dead, by him this man is standing before you

Acts 3:16

---

et seniores, [9]si nos hodie diiudicamur in benefacto hominis infirmi, in quo iste salvus factus est, [10]notum sit omnibus vobis et omni plebi Israel quia in nomine Iesus Christi Nazareni, quem vos crucifixistis, quem Deus suscitavit a mortuis,

---

fessing their faith. We are not speaking of that discretion or reserve which in a pluralist and profane society like ours avoids certain signs of religion when with others. We are referring to weakness, to failure to profess one's own religious ideas for fear of ridicule, criticism or others' reactions [. . .] and which is a cause—perhaps the main cause—of the abandonment of faith by people who simply conform to whatever new environment they find themselves in" (Paul VI, *General Audience*, 19 June 1968).

8. Even in the very early days of Christianity Jesus' prediction is borne out: "Beware of men; for they will deliver you up to councils. . . . When they deliver you up, do not be anxious how you are to speak or what you are to say; for what you are to say will be given you in that hour, for it is not you who speak, but the Spirit of your Father speaking through you" (Mt 10:17-20).

10. "Whom God raised from the dead": St Peter once again bears witness to the resurrection of Jesus, the central truth of apostolic preaching; he uses here the same words as he did at Pentecost. These are compatible with our holding that Jesus "rose by his own power on the third day" (Paul VI, *Creed of the People of God*, 12). The power by which Christ rose was that of his divine person, to which both his soul and his body remained joined even after death separated them. "The divine power and operation of the Father and of the Son is one and the same; hence it follows that Christ rose by the power of the Father and by his own power" (St Thomas Aquinas, *Summa theologiae*, III, q. 53, a. 4).

"By the word 'Resurrection'," the *St Pius V Catechism* explains, "we are not merely to understand that Christ was raised from the dead, which happened to many others, but that he rose by his own power and virtue, a singular prerogative peculiar to him alone. For it is incompatible with nature and was never given to man to raise himself by his own power, from death to life. This was reserved for the almighty power of God. [. . .] We sometimes, it is true, read in Scripture that he was raised by the Father; but this refers to him as man, just as those passages on the other hand, which say that he rose by his own power, relate to him as God" (I, 6, 8).

Ps 118:22
Mt 21:42
1 Pet 2:4-7
Joel 3:5
Mt 1:21
Jn 1:12
Acts 2:21
Lk 21:12-15
Jn 7:15

well. ¹¹This is the stone which was rejected by you builders, but which has become the head of the corner. ¹²And there is salvation in no one else, for there is no other name under heaven given among men by which we must be saved."

¹³Now when they saw the boldness of Peter and John, and perceived that they were uneducated, common men, they wondered; and they recognized that they had been with Jesus. ¹⁴But seeing the man that had been healed standing beside them, they had nothing to say in opposition. ¹⁵But when they had commanded them to go aside out of the

---

in hoc iste astat coram vobis sanus. ¹¹Hic est lapis qui reprobatus est a vobis aedificatoribus, qui factus est in caput anguli. ¹²Et non est in alio aliquo salus, nec enim nomen aliud est sub caelo datum in hominibus, in quo oportet nos salvos fieri." ¹³Videntes autem Petri fiduciam et Ioannis, et comperto quod homines essent sine litteris et idiotae, admirabantur et cognoscebant eos quoniam cum Iesu fuerant; ¹⁴hominem quoque videntes stantem cum eis, qui curatus fuerat, nihil poterant contradicere. ¹⁵Iubentes autem eos foras extra

---

11. St Peter applies the words of Psalm 118:22 to Jesus, conscious no doubt that our Lord had referred to himself as the stone rejected by the builders which had become the cornerstone, the stone which keeps the whole structure together (cf. Mt 21:42 and par.).

12. Invocation of the name of Jesus is all-powerful because this is our Saviour's own name (cf. note on Mt 1:21). Our Lord himself told his Apostles this: "If you ask anything of the Father, he will give it to you in my name" (Jn 16:23), and they, trusting in this promise, work miracles and obtain conversions "in the name of Jesus". Today—as ever—the power of this name will work wonders in the souls of those who call upon him. Monsignor Escrivá gives this advice: "Don't be afraid to call our Lord by his name—Jesus—and to tell him that you love him" (*The Way*, 303); and the Liturgy of the Hours invites us to pray: "God our Father, you are calling us to prayer, at the same hour as the Apostles went up to the temple. Grant that the prayer we offer with sincere hearts in the name of Jesus may bring salvation to all who call upon that holy name" (Week 1, Monday afternoon).

13. The members of the Sanhedrin are surprised by Peter's confidence and by the way these men, who are not well versed in the Law, are able to use Sacred Scripture. "Did not the Apostles," Chrysostom asks in admiration, "poor and without earthly weapons, enter into battle against enemies who were fully armed [. . .]? Without experience, without skill of the tongue, they fought against experts in rhetoric and the language of the academies" (*Hom. on Acts*, 4).

council, they conferred with one another, ¹⁶saying, "What Jn 11:47
shall we do with these men? For that a notable sign has been
performed through them is manifest to all the inhabitants of
Jerusalem, and we cannot deny it. ¹⁷But in order that it may
spread no further among the people, let us warn them to
speak no more to any one in this name." ¹⁸So they called them
and charged them not to speak or teach at all in the name of
Jesus. ¹⁹But Peter and John answered them, "Whether it is Acts 5:29
right in the sight of God to listen to you rather than to God,
you must judge; ²⁰for we cannot but speak of what we have 1 Cor 9:16
2 Tim 1:7-8

concilium secedere, conferebant ad invicem ¹⁶dicentes: "Quid faciemus
hominibus istis? Quoniam quidem notum signum factum est per eos omnibus
habitantibus in Ierusalem manifestum, et non possumus negare; ¹⁷sed ne
amplius divulgetur in populum, comminemur eis, ne ultra loquantur in nomine
hoc ulli hominum." ¹⁸Et vocantes eos denuntiaverunt, ne omnino loquerentur
neque docerent in nomine Iesu. ¹⁹Petrus vero et Ioannes respondentes dixerunt
ad eos: "Si iustum est in conspectu Dei vos potius audire quam Deum, iudicate;
²⁰non enim possumus nos, quae vidimus et audivimus, non loqui." ²¹At illi ultra

18-20. In one of his homilies John Paul II gives us a practical commentary
on this passage, which helps us see the right order of priorities and give pride
of place to the things of God: "Whereas the elders of Israel charge the Apostles
not to speak about Christ, God, on the other hand, does not allow them to remain
silent. [. . .] In Peter's few sentences we find a full testimony to the Resurrection
of the Lord. [. . .] The word of the living God addressed to men obliges us more
than any other human commandment or purpose. This word carries with it the
supreme eloquence of truth, it carries the authority of God himself. [. . .]

"Peter and the Apostles are before the Sanhedrin. They are completely and
absolutely certain that God himself has spoken in Christ, and has spoken
definitively through his Cross and Resurrection. Peter and the Apostles to
whom this truth was directly given— as also those who in their time received
the Holy Spirit—must bear witness *to it*.

"*Believing* means accepting with complete conviction the truth that comes
from God, drawing support from the grace of the Holy Spirit 'whom God has
given to those who obey him' (Acts 5:32) to accept what God has revealed and
what comes to us through the Church in its living transmission, that is, in
tradition. The organ of this tradition is the teaching of Peter and of the Apostles
and of their successors.

"Believing means accepting their testimony in the Church, who guards this
deposit from generation to generation, and then—basing oneself upon it—
expounding this same truth, with identical certainty and interior conviction.

"Over the centuries the sanhedrins change which seek to impose silence,
abandonment or distortion of this truth. The *sanhedrins of the contemporary*

seen and heard." ²¹And when they had further threatened them, they let them go, finding no way to punish them, because of the people; for all men praised God for what had happened. ²²For the man on whom this sign of healing was performed was more than forty years old.

The Church's thanksgiving prayer

Ex 20:11
Ps 146:6
Is 37:16
Jer 32:17
Rev 10:6

²³When they were released they went to their friends and reported what the chief priests and the elders had said to them. ²⁴And when they heard it, they lifted their voices

---

comminantes dimiserunt eos, nequaquam invenientes, quomodo punirent eos, propter populum, quia omnes glorificabant Deum in eo, quod acciderat; ²²annorum enim erat amplius quadraginta homo, in quo factum erat signum istud sanitatis. ²³Dimissi autem venerunt ad suos et annuntiaverunt, quanta ad eos principes sacerdotum et seniores dixissent. ²⁴Qui cum audissent unanimiter

---

world are many and of all types. These sanhedrins are each and every person who rejects divine truth; they are systems of human thought, of human knowledge; they are the various *conceptions of the world* and also the various programmes of human behaviour; they are also the different *forms of pressure* used by so-called public opinion, mass civilization, media of social communication, which are materialist or secular agnostic or anti-religious; they are, finally, certain contemporary *systems of government* which—if they do not totally deprive citizens of scope to profess the faith—at least limit that scope in different ways, marginalize believers and turn them into second-class citizens . . . and against all these modern types of the Sanhedrin of that time, the response of faith is always the same: 'We must obey God rather than men' (Acts 5:29)" (*Homily*, 20 April 1980).

24-30. This prayer of the Apostles and the community provides Christians with a model of reliance on God's help. They ask God to give them the strength they need to continue to proclaim the Word boldly and not be intimidated by persecution, and they also entreat him to accredit their preaching by enabling them to work signs and wonders.

The prayer includes some prophetic verses of Psalm 2 which find their fulfilment in Jesus Christ. The psalm begins by referring to earthly rulers plotting against God and his Anointed. Jesus himself experienced this opposition, as the Apostles do now and as the Church does throughout history. When we hear the clamour of the forces of evil, still striving to "burst their bonds asunder, and cast their cords from us" (v. 3), we should put our trust in the Lord, who "holds them in derision. [. . .] He will speak to them in his wrath, and terrify them in his fury" (vv. 4-5); in this way we make it possible for God's message to be heard by everyone: "Now, therefore, O kings, be wise; be warned,

together to God and said, "Sovereign Lord, who didst make
the heaven and the earth and the sea and everything in them,
^{25}who by the mouth of our father David, thy servant,^{c} didst
say by the Holy Spirit,

Ps 2:1-2

   'Why did the Gentiles rage,
   and the peoples imagine vain things?
   ^{26}The kings of the earth set themselves in array,
   and the rulers were gathered together,
   against the Lord and against his Anointed' —^{e}

^{27}for truly in this city there were gathered together against
thy holy servant^c Jesus, whom thou didst anoint, both Herod
and Pontius Pilate, with the Gentiles, and the peoples of
Israel, ^{28}to do whatever thy hand and thy plan had pre-
destined to take place. ^{29}And now, Lord, look upon their
threats, and grant to thy servants^f to speak thy word with all
boldness, ^{30}while thou stretchest out thy hand to heal, and
signs and wonders are performed through the name of thy
holy servant^c Jesus." ^{31}And when they had prayed, the place

Lk 23:12
Mt 3:16
Acts 10:38

Acts 2:23

Eph 6:19

---

levaverunt vocem ad Deum et dixerunt: "Domine, tu, qui fecisti caelum et
terram et mare et omnia, quae in eis sunt, ^{25}qui Spiritu Sancto per os patris nostri
David pueri tui dixisti: 'Quare fremuerunt gentes, et populi meditati sunt
inania? ^{26}Astiterunt reges terrae, et principes convenerunt in unum adversus
Dominum et adversus christum eius.' ^{27}Convenerunt enim vere in civitate ista
adversus sanctum puerum tuum Iesum, quem unxisti, Herodes et Pontius
Pilatus cum gentibus et populis Israel ^{28}facere, quaecumque manus tua et
consilium praedestinavit fieri. ^{29}Et nunc, Domine, respice in minas eorum et da
servis tuis cum omni fiducia loqui verbum tuum, ^{30}in eo quod manum tuam
extendas, sanitatem et signa et prodigia fieri per nomen sancti Pueri tui Iesu."
^{31}Et cum orassent, motus est locus, in quo erant congregati, et repleti sunt omnes

---

O rulers of the earth. Serve the Lord with fear, with trembling kiss his
feet. [. . .] Blessed are all who take refuge in him" (vv. 10-12).

   Meditation on this psalm has comforted Christians in all ages, filling them
with confidence in the Lord's help: "Ask of me, and I will make the nations
your heritage, and the ends of the earth your possession" (v. 8).

   31. The Holy Spirit chose to demonstrate his presence visibly in order to
encourage the nascent Church. The shaking that happens here was, St John
Chrysostom comments, "a sign of approval. It is an action of God to instil a
holy fear in the souls of the Apostles, to strengthen them against the threats of
senators and priests, and to inspire them with boldness to preach the Gospel.

^{c}Or *child.* ^{e}Or *Christ.* ^{f}Or *slaves*

in which they were gathered together was shaken; and they were all filled with the Holy Spirit and spoke the word of God with boldness.

The way of life of the early Christians

Jn 17:11-21
Phil 1:27
Acts 2:44

Acts 1:8, 22

32Now the company of those who believed were of one heart and soul, and no one said that any of the things which he possessed was his own, but they had everything in common. 33And with great power the apostles gave their

---

Sancto Spiritu et loquebantur verbum Dei cum fiducia. 32Multitudinis autem credentium erat cor et anima una, nec quisquam eorum, quae possidebant, aliquid suum esse dicebat, sed erant illis omnia communia. 33Et virtute magna

---

The Church was just beginning and it was necessary to support preaching with wonders, in order the better to win men over. It was needed at this time but not later on. [. . .] When the earth is shaken, this sometimes is a sign of heaven's wrath, sometimes of favour and providence. At the death of our Saviour the earth shook in protest against the death of its author. . . . But the shaking where the Apostles were gathered together was a sign of God's goodness, for the result was that they were filled with the Holy Spirit" (*Hom. on Acts*, 11).

32-37. Here we are given a second summary of the life of the first Christian community—which, presided over by Peter and the other Apostles, was *the Church*, the entire Church of Jesus Christ.

The Church of God on earth was only beginning, all contained within the Jerusalem foundation. Now every Christian community— no matter how small it be—which is in communion of faith and obedience with the Church of Rome is the Church.

"The Church of Christ", Vatican II teaches, "is really present in all legitimately organized local groups of the faithful, which, in so far as they are united to their pastors, are also quite appropriately called churches in the New Testament. [. . .] In them the faithful are gathered together through the preaching of the Gospel of Christ, and the mystery of the Lord's Supper is celebrated. [. . .] In each altar community, under the sacred ministry of the bishop, a manifest symbol is to be seen of that charity and 'unity of the mystical body, without which there can be no salvation' (*Summa theologiae*, III, q. 73, a. 3). In these communities, though they may often be small and poor, or existing in the diaspora, Christ is present through whose power and influence the one, holy, catholic and apostolic Church is constituted" (*Lumen gentium*, 26).

32. The text stresses the importance of "being one": solidarity, unity, is a virtue of good Christians and one of the marks of the Church: "The Apostles

testimony to the resurrection of the Lord Jesus, and great
grace was upon them all. ³⁴There was not a needy person
among them, for as many as were possessors of lands or
houses sold them, and brought the proceeds of what was sold
³⁵and laid it at the apostles' feet; and distribution was made

Deut 15:7-8
Lk 12:33
Acts 8:27;
11:22-30;
12:25;
13:1-15:39
1 Cor 9:6

---

reddebant apostoli testimonium resurrectionis Domini Iesu, et gratia magna erat
super omnibus illis. ³⁴Neque enim quisquam egens erat inter illos; quotquot
enim possessores agrorum aut domorum erant, vendentes afferebant pretia
eorum, quae vendebant, ³⁵et ponebant ante pedes apostolorum; dividebatur

---

bore witness to the Resurrection not only by word but also by their virtues"
(Chrysostom, *Hom. on Acts*, 11). The disciples obviously were joyful and
self-sacrificed. This disposition, which results from charity, strives to promote
forgiveness and harmony along the brethren, all sons and daughters of the same
Father. The Church realizes that this harmony is often threatened by rancour,
envy, misunderstanding and self-assertion. By asking, in prayers and hymns
like *Ubi caritas*, for evil disputes and conflicts to cease, "so that Christ our God
may dwell among us", it is drawing its inspiration from the example of unity
and charity left it by the first Christian community in Jerusalem.

Harmony and mutual understanding among the disciples both reflects the
internal and external unity of the Church itself and helps its practical imple-
mentation.

There is only one Church of Jesus Christ because it has only "one Lord, one
faith, one baptism" (Eph 4:5), and only one visible head—the Pope—who
represents Christ on earth. The model and ultimate source of this unity is the
Trinity of divine persons, that is, "the unity of one God, the Father and the Son
in the Holy Spirit" (Vatican II, *Unitatis redintegratio*, 2). This characteristic
work of the Church is visibly expressed: in confession of one and the same
faith, in one system of government, in the celebration of the same form of divine
worship, and in fraternal concord among all God's family (cf. *ibid.*).

The Church derives its life from the Holy Spirit; a main factor in nourishing
this life and thereby reinforcing the Church's unity is the Blessed Eucharist: it
acts in a mysterious but real way, incessantly, to build up the mystical body of
the Lord.

God desires all Christians separated from the Church (they have Baptism,
and the Gospel truths in varying degrees) to find their way to the flock of
Christ—which they can do by spiritual renewal, and prayer, dialogue and study.

34-35. St Luke comes back again to the subject of renunciation of possessions, repeating what he says in 2:44 and going on to give two different kinds
of example—that of Barnabas (4:36f) and that of Ananias and Sapphira (5:1f).

The disciples' detachment from material things does not only mean that they
have a caring attitude to those in need. It also shows their simplicity of heart,

to each as any had need. [36]Thus Joseph who was surnamed
by the apostles Barnabas (which means, Son of encouragement), a Levite, a native of Cyprus, [37]sold a field which
belonged to him, and brought the money and laid it at the
apostles' feet.

5

Deception by Ananias and Sapphira

Acts 4:35, 37   [1]But a man named Ananias with his wife Sapphira sold a
piece of property, [2]and with his wife's knowledge he kept

---

autem singulis, prout cuique opus erat. [36]Ioseph autem, qui cognominatus est
Barnabas ab apostoli, quod est interpretatum filius Consolationis, Levites,
Cyprius genere, [37]cum haberet agrum, vendidit et attulit pecuniam et posuit ante
pedes apostolorum.
[1]Vir autem quidam nomine Ananias cum Sapphira uxore sua vendidit agrum

---

their desire to pass unnoticed and the full confidence they place in the Twelve.
"They gave up their possessions and in doing so demonstrated their respect for
the Apostles. For they did not presume to give it into their hands, that is, they
did not present it ostentatiously, but left it at their feet and made the Apostles
its owners and dispensers" (Chrysostom, *Hom. on Acts*, 11).

The text suggests that the Christians in Jerusalem had an organized system
for the relief of the poor in the community. Judaism had social welfare
institutions and probably the early Church used one of these as a model.
However, the Christian system of helping each according to his need would
have had characteristics of its own, deriving from the charity from which it
sprang and as a result of gradual differentiation from the Jewish way of doing
things.

36-37. Barnabas is mentioned because of his generosity and also in view of
his important future role in the spreading of the Gospel. It will be he who
introduces the new convert Saul to the Apostles (9:27). Later, the Apostles will
send him to Antioch when the Christian church begins to develop there (11:22).
He will be Paul's companion on his first journey (13:2) and will go up to
Jerusalem with him in connexion with the controversy about circumcising
Gentile converts (15:2). St Paul praises Barnabas' zeal and disinterest in the

1-11. Ananias hypocritically pretended that he had given all the money from
the sale of the land to the community welfare fund, whereas in fact he kept part
of it, and his wife went along with him on that. No one was obliged to sell his
property or give it to the Apostles: people who did so acted with complete
freedom. Ananias was free to sell the land or not, and to give all or part of the

back some of the proceeds, and brought only a part and laid
it at the apostles' feet. ³But Peter said, "Ananias, why has   Lk 22:3
Satan filled your heart to lie to the Holy Spirit and to keep
back part of the proceeds of the land? ⁴While it remained
unsold, did it not remain your own? And after it was sold,
was it not at your disposal? How is it that you have contrived
this deed in your heart? You have not lied to men but to God."
⁵When Ananias heard these words, he fell down and died.   Acts 5:11; 19:17
And great fear came upon all who heart of it. ⁶The young
men rose and wrapped him up and carried him out and buried
him.

   ⁷After an interval of about three hours his wife came in,
not knowing what had happened. ⁸And Peter said to her,
"Tell me whether you sold the land for so much." And she
said, "Yes, for so much." ⁹But Peter said to her, "How is it   1 Cor 10:9; 11:30-32
that you have agreed together to tempt the Spirit of the Lord?
Hark, the feet of those that have buried your husband are at
the door, and they will carry you out." ¹⁰Immediately she fell

---

²et subtraxit de pretio, conscia quoque uxore, et afferens partem quamdam ad
pedes apostolorum posuit. ³Dixit autem Petrus: "Anania, cur implevit Satanas
cor tuum mentiri te Spiritui Sancto et subtrahere de pretio agri? ⁴Nonne manens
tibi manebat et venundatum in tua erat potestate? Quare posuisti in corde tuo
hanc rem? Non es mentitus hominibus sed Deo!" ⁵Audiens autem Ananias haec
verba cecidit et exspiravit; et factus est timor magnus in omnes audientes.
⁶Surgentes autem iuvenes involverunt eum et efferentes sepelierunt. ⁷Factum
est autem quasi horarum trium spatium, et uxor ipsius nesciens, quod factum
fuerat, introivit. ⁸Respondit autem ei Petrus: "Dic mihi si tanti agrum
vendidistis?" At illa dixit: "Etiam, tanti." ⁹Petrus autem ad eam. "Quid est quod
convenit vobis tentare Spiritum Domini? Ecce pedes eorum, qui sepelierunt
virum tuum, ad ostium et efferent te." ¹⁰Confestim cecidit ante pedes eius et
exspiravit; intrantes autem iuvenes invenerunt illam mortuam et efferentes

---

proceeds to help needy brethren. But he had no right to disguise his greed as
charity and try to deceive God and the Church.

   God punished Ananias and Sapphira, St Ephraem says, "not only because
they stole something and concealed it, but because they did not fear and sought
to deceive those in whom dwelt the Holy Spirit who knows everything"
(*Armenian Commentary on Acts, ad loc.*). By their hypocritical attitude Ananias
and Sapphira show their greed and particularly their vainglory. The severe
punishment they receive befits the circumstances: the Church was in a
foundational period, when people had a special responsibility to be faithful and
God was specially supportive.

down at his feet and died. When the young men came in they found her dead, and they carried her out and buried her beside her husband. ¹¹And great fear came upon the whole church, and upon all who heard of these things.

The growth of the Church

¹²Now many signs and wonders were done among the people by the hands of the apostles. And they were all together in Solomon's Portico. ¹³None of the rest dared join them, but the people held them in high honour. ¹⁴And more than ever believers were added to the Lord, multitudes both

---

sepelierunt ad virum suum. ¹¹Et factus est timor magnus super universam ecclesiam et in omnes, qui audierunt haec. ¹²Per manus autem apostolorum fiebant signa et prodigia multa in plebe; et erant unanimiter omnes in porticu Salomonis. ¹³Ceterorum autem nemo audebat coniungere se illis; sed magnificabat eos populus; ¹⁴magis autem addebantur credentes Domino, multitudines virorum ac mulierum, ¹⁵ita ut in plateas efferrent infirmos et

---

"This fault could not have been treated lightly", St John Chrysostom explains; "like a gangrene it had to be cut out, before it infected the rest of the body. As it is, both the man himself benefits in that he is not left to advance further in wickedness, and the rest of the disciples, in that they were made more vigilant" (*Hom. on Acts*, 12). Some Fathers (cf. St Augustine, *Sermon 148*, 1) think that God's punishment was that of physical death, not eternal reprobation.

This episode shows once again how much God detests hypocrisy; and from it we can appreciate the virtue of truthfulness. Veracity inclines people to bring what they say and what they do into line with their knowledge and convictions and to be people of their word. It is closely connected to the virtue of fidelity, which helps one to stay true to promises made (cf. *Summa theologiae*, II-II, q. 80, a. 1). Only the truthful person, the faithful person, can keep the Lord's commandment: "Let what you say be simply 'Yes' or 'No'" (Mt 5:37).

12-16. In this third summary (cf. 2:42-47 and 4:32-37) of the lifestyle of the first community St Luke refers particularly to the Apostles' power to work miracles. These miracles confirm to the people that the Kingdom of God has in fact come among them. Grace abounds and it shows its presence by spiritual conversions and physical cures. These "signs and wonders" are not done to amaze people or provoke curiosity but to awaken faith.

Miracles always accompany God's Revelation to men; they are part of that Revelation. They are not simply a bending of the laws of nature: they are a kind of advance sign of the glorious transformation which the world will undergo at the end of time. Thus, just as a sinner, when he repents, obeys God without

of men and women, [15]so that they even carried out the sick into the streets, and laid them on beds and pallets, that as Peter came by at least his shadow might fall on some of them. [16]The people also gathered from the towns around Jerusalem, bringing the sick and those afflicted with unclean spirits, and they were all healed.

Mk 6:56
Acts 19:11-12

Acts 8:6-7

The Apostles are arrested and miraculously freed

[17]But the high priest rose up and all who were with him, that is, the party of the Sadducees, and filled with jealousy [18]they arrested the apostles and put them in the common

Acts 4:1-6;
13:45

---

ponerent in lectulis et grabatis, ut, veniente Petro, saltem umbra illius obumbraret quemquam eorum. [16]Concurrebat autem et multitudo vicinarum civitatum Jerusalem, afferentem aegros et vexatos ab spiritibus immundis, qui curabantur omnes. [17]Exsurgens autem princeps sacerdotum et omnes, qui cum illo erant, quae est haeresis sadducaeorum, repleti sunt zelo [18]et iniecerunt

---

ceasing to be free, so matter can be changed if its Creator so ordains, without undermining or destroying its own laws.

Miracles are a form of accreditation God gives to the Gospel message: they are actions of God in support of the truth of his messengers' preaching. "If they had not worked miracles and wonders," Origen says, "Jesus' disciples could not have moved their hearers to give up their traditional religion for new teachings and truths, and to embrace, at the risk of their lives, the teachings which were being proclaimed to them" (*Against Celsus*, I, 46). And St Ephraem comments: "The Apostles' miracles made the resurrection and ascension of the Lord credible" (*Armenian Commentary, ad loc.*).

Through miracles God speaks to the minds and hearts of those who witness them, inviting them to believe but not forcing their freedom or lessening the merit of their faith. The Apostles follow in the footsteps of our Lord, who "supported and confirmed his preaching by miracles to arouse the faith of his hearers and give them assurance, not to coerce them" (Vatican II, *Dignitatis humanae*, 11). If people have the right dispositions they will generally have no difficulty in recognizing and accepting miracles. Common sense and religious instinct tell them that miracles are possible, because all things are subject to God; however, prejudice and resistance to conversion and its implications can blind a person and make him deny something which is quite obvious to a man of good will.

"Since the Apostles were all together, the people brought them their sick on beds and pallets. From every quarter fresh tribute of wonder accrued to them—from them that believed, from them that were healed, such was the Apostles' boldness of speech and the virtuous behaviour of the believers.

Acts 12:7

Acts 7:38;
13:26
Phil 2:16
1 Jn 1:1
Acts 4:5

prison. ¹⁹But at night an angel of the Lord opened the prison doors and brought them out and said, ²⁰"Go and stand in the temple and speak to the people all the words of this Life." ²¹And when they heard this, they entered the temple at daybreak and taught.

Now the high priest came and those who were with him and called together the council and all the senate of Israel, and sent to the prison to have them brought. ²²But when the officers came, they did not find them in the prison and they returned and reported, ²³"We found the prison securely locked and the sentries standing at the doors, but when we opened it we found no one inside." ³⁴Now when the captain of the temple and the chief priests heard these words, they were much perplexed about them, wondering what this would come to. ²⁵And some one came and told them, "The

---

manus in apostolos et posuerunt illos in custodia publica. ¹⁹Angelus autem Domini per noctem aperuit ianuas carceris et educens eos dixit: ²⁰"Ite et stantes loquimini in templo plebi omnia verba vitae huius." ²¹Qui cum audissent, intraverunt diluculo in templum et docebant. Adveniens autem princeps sacerdotum et, qui cum eo erant, convocaverunt concilium et omnes seniores filiorum Israel et miserunt in carcerem, ut adducerentur illi. ²²Cum venissent autem ministri, non invenerunt illos in carcere; reversi autem nuntiaverunt ²³dicentes: "Carcerem invenimus clausum cum omni diligentia et custodes stantes ad ianuas, aperientes autem intus neminem invenimus!" ²⁴Ut audierunt autem hos sermones, magistratus templi et principes sacerdotum ambigebant de illis quidnam fieret illud. ²⁵Adveniens autem quidam nuntiavit eis: "Ecce viri, quos posuistis in carcere, sunt in templo stantes et docentes populum."

Although the Apostles modestly ascribe these things to Christ, in whose name they acted, their own life and noble conduct also helped to produce this effect" (*Hom. on Acts*, 12).

19. In Sacred Scripture we meet angels as messengers of God and also as mediators, guardians and ministers of divine justice. Abraham sent his servant on a mission to his kindred and told him, "The Lord will send his angel before you and prosper your way" (Gen 24:7, 40). Tobit, Lot and his family, Daniel and his companions, Judith etc. also experienced the help of angels. The Psalms refer to trust in the angels (cf. Ps 34:8; 91:11-13) and the continuous help they render men in obedience to God's command.

This episode of the freeing of the Apostles is one of the examples the *St Pius V Catechism* gives to illustrate "the countless benefits which the Lord

man whom you put in prison are standing in the temple and teaching the people."

The Apostles before the Sanhedrin

²⁶Then the captain with the officers went and brought them, but without violence, for they were afraid of being stoned by the people.

²⁷And when they had brought them, they set them before the council. And the high priest questioned them, ²⁸saying, "We strictly charged you not to teach in this name, yet here you have filled Jerusalem with your teaching and you intend to bring this man's blood upon us." ²⁹But Peter and the

Lk 20:19; 22:2

Mt 27:25
Acts 4:18

Acts 4:19

---

²⁶Tunc abiens magistratus cum ministris adducebat illos, non per vim, timebant enim populum, ne lapidarentur. ²⁷Et cum adduxissent illos, statuerunt in concilio. Et interrogavt eos princeps sacerdotum ²⁸dicens: "Nonne praecipiendo praecepimus vobis, ne doceretis in nomine isto? Et ecce replevistis Ierusalem doctrina vestra et vultis inducere super nos sanguinem hominis istius." ²⁹Respondens autem Petrus et apostoli dixerunt: "Oboedire oportet, Deo magis

---

distributes among men through angels, his interpreters and ministers, sent not only in isolated cases but appointed from our birth to watch over us, and constituted for the salvation of every individual person" (IV, 9, 6).

This means, therefore, that the angels should have a place in a Christian's personal piety: "I ask our Lord that, during our stay on this earth of ours, we may never be parted from our divine travelling companion. To ensure this, let us also become firmer friends of the Holy Guardian Angels. We all need a lot of company, company from heaven and company on earth. Have great devotion to the Holy Angels" (J. Escrivá, *Friends of God*, 315).

29. The Apostles' failure to obey the Sanhedrin is obviously not due to pride or to their not knowing their place (as citizens they are subject to the Sanhedrin's authority); the Sanhedrin is imposing a ruling which would have them go against God's law and their own conscience.

The Apostles humbly and boldly remind their judges that obedience to God comes first. They know that many members of the Sanhedrin are religious men, good Jews who can understand their message; they try not so much to justify themselves as to get the Sanhedrin to react: they are more concerned about their judges' spiritual health than about their own safety. St John Chrysostom comments: "God allowed the Apostles to be brought to trial so that their adversaries might be instructed, if they so desired. [. . .] The Apostles are not irritated by the judges; they plead with them compassionately, with tears in their eyes, and their only aim is to free them from error and from divine wrath"

(*Hom. on Acts*, 13). They are convinced that "those who fear God are in no danger, only those who do not fear him" (*ibid.*) and that it is worse to commit injustice than to suffer it. We can see from the Apostles' behaviour how deep their convictions run; grace and faith in Jesus Christ have given them high regard for the honour of God. They have begun at last to love and serve God without counting the cost. This is true Christian maturity. "In that cry *serviam!* [I will serve!] you express your determination to 'serve' the Church of God most faithfully, even at the cost of fortune, of reputation and of life" (J. Escrivá, *The Way*, 519).

The Church often prays to God to give its children this resilience: they need it because there is always the danger of growing indifferent and of abandoning the faith to some extent. "Lord, fill us with that spirit of courage which gave your martyr Sebastian," his feast's liturgy says, "strength to offer his life in faithful witness. Help us to learn from him to cherish your law and to obey you rather than men" (*Roman Missal*).

A Christian should conform his behaviour to God's law: that law should be his very life. He should obey and love God's commandments as taught by the Church, if he wishes to live a truly human life. The law of God is not something burdensome: it is a way of freedom, as Sacred Scripture is at pains to point out: "The Lord is my portion, I promise to keep thy words. I entreat thy favour with all my heart; be gracious to me according to thy promise. When I think of thy ways, I turn my feet to thy testimonies; I hasten and do not delay to keep thy commandments. Though the cord of the wicked ensnare me, I do not forget thy law. At midnight I rise to praise thee, because of thy righteous ordinances. I am a companion of all who fear thee, of those who keep thy precepts. The earth, O Lord, is full of thy steadfast love; teach me thy statutes" (Ps 119:57-64).

Conscience, which teaches man in the depths of his heart, gradually shows him what the law of God involves: "Man has in his heart a law inscribed by God. His dignity lies in observing this law, and by it he will be judged (cf. Rom 2:15-16). His conscience is man's most secret core, and his sanctuary. There he is alone with God, whose voice echoes in his depths. By conscience, in a wonderful way, that law is made known. [. . .] The more a correct conscience prevails, the more do persons and groups turn aside from blind choice and try to be guided by the objective standards of moral conduct" (Vatican II, *Gaudium et spes*, 16).

Good and evil are facts of life. A person can identify them. There are such things as good actions—and there are evil actions, which should always be avoided. The goodness or badness of human actions is not essentially dependent on the circumstances, although sometimes these can affect it to some extent.

Like the eye, conscience is designed to enable a person to see, but it needs light from outside (God's law and the Church's guidance) to discover religious and moral truths and properly appreciate them. Without that help man simply tires himself out in his search; he seeks only himself and forgets about good and evil, and his conscience becomes darkened by sin and moral opportunism.

"With respect to conscience," Paul VI teaches, "an objection can arise: Is

apostles answered. "We must obey God rather than men. Acts 2:23
³⁰The God of our fathers raised Jesus whom you killed by Gal 3:13
hanging him on tree. ³¹God exalted him at his right hand as Acts 2:33;
Leader and Saviour, to give repentance to Israel and 10:43; 13:38

---

quam hominibus. ³⁰Deus patrum nostrorum suscitavit Iesum, quem vos interemistis suspendentes in ligno; ³¹hunc Deus Principem et Salvatorum exaltavit dextera sua ad dandam paenitentiam Israel et remissionem peccatorum. ³²Et nos sumus testes horum verborum, et Spiritus Sanctus, quem

---

conscience not enough on its own as the norm of our conduct? Do the decalogues, the codes, imposed on us from outside, not undermine conscience [. . .]? This is a delicate and very current problem. Here all we will say is that subjective conscience is the first and immediate norm of our conduct, but it needs light, it needs to see which standard it should follow, especially when the action in question does not evidence its own moral exigencies. Conscience needs to be instructed and trained about what is the best choice to make, by the authority of a law" (*General Audience*, 28 March 1973).

A right conscience, which always goes hand in hand with moral prudence, will help a Christian to obey the law like a good citizen and also to take a stand, personally or in association with others, against any unjust laws which may be proposed or enacted. The State is not almighty in the sphere of law. It may not order or permit anything it likes; therefore not everything legal is morally lawful or just. Respect due to civil authority—which is part of the Gospel message and has always been taught by the Church— should not prevent Christians and people of good will from opposing legislators and rulers when they legislate and govern in a way that is contrary of the law of God and therefore to the common good. Obviously, this legitimate kind of resistance to authority should always involve the use of lawful methods.

It is not enough for good Christians to profess *privately* the teaching of the Gospel and the Church regarding human life, the family, education, freedom etc. They should realize that these are subjects of crucial importance for the welfare of their country, and they should strive, using all the usual means at their disposal, to see that the laws of the State are supportive of the common good. Passivity towards ideologies and stances that run counter to Christian values is quite deplorable.

30. "Hanging him on a tree": this is reminiscent of Deuteronomy 21:23: if a criminal is put to death "and you hang him on a tree, his body shall not remain all night upon the tree, but you shall bury him the same day, for a hanged man is accursed by God." This is a reference to crucifixion, a form of capital punishment which originated in Persia; it was common throughout the East and was later adopted by the Romans.

Lk 24:48
Jn 7:39;
15:26-27

forgiveness of sins. ³²And we are witnesses to these things, and so is the Holy Spirit whom God has given to those who obey him."

³³When they heard this they were enraged and wanted to kill them.

Gamaliel's intervention

Acts 22:3

³⁴But a Pharisee in the council named Gamaliel, a teacher of the law, held in honour by all the people, stood up and ordered the men to be put outside for a while. ³⁵And he said to them, "Men of Israel, take care what you do with these

---

dedit Deus oboedientibus sibi." ³³Haec cum audissent, dissecabantur et volebant interficere illos. ³⁴Surgens autem quidam in concilio pharisaeus nomine Gamaliel, legis doctor honorabilis universae plebi, iussit foras ad breve homines fieri ³⁵dixitque ad illos: "Viri Israelite, attendite vobis super hominibus

---

32. God sends the Holy Spirit to those who obey him, and, in turn, the Apostles obey the indications of the Spirit with complete docility.

If we are to obey the Holy Spirit and do what he asks us, we need to cultivate him and listen to what he says. "'Get to know the Holy Spirit, the Great Stranger, on whom depends your sanctification.

"Don't forget that you are God's temple. The Advocate is in the centre of your soul: listen to him and be docile to his inspirations" (J. Escriv", *The Way*, 57).

34-39. Gamaliel had been St Paul's teacher (cf. 22:3). He belonged to a moderate grouping among the Pharisees. He was a prudent man, impartial and religiously minded. The Fathers of the Church often propose him as an example of an upright man who is awaiting the Kingdom of God and dares to defend the Apostles.

"Gamaliel does not say that the undertaking is of man or of God; he recommends that they let time decide. [. . .] By speaking in the absence of the Apostles he was better able to win over the judges. The gentleness of his word and arguments, based on justice, convinced them. He was almost preaching the Gospel. Indeed, his language is so correct that he seemed to be saying: Be convinced of it: you cannot destroy this undertaking. How is it that you do not believe? The Christian message is so impressive that even its adversaries bear witness to it" (St John Chrysostom, *Hom. on Acts*, 14).

This commentary seems to be recalling our Lord's words, "He that is not against us is for us" (Mk 9:40). Certainly, Gamaliel's intervention shows that a person with good will can discern God's action in events or at least investigate objectively without prejudging the issue.

men. ³⁶For before these days Theudas arose, giving himself out to be somebody, and a number of men, about four hundred, joined him; but he was slain and all who followed him were dispersed and came to nothing. ³⁷After him Judas the Galilean arose in the days of the census and drew away some of the people after him; he also perished, and all who followed him were scattered. ³⁸So in the present case I tell you, keep away from these men and let them alone; for if this plan or this undertaking is of men, it will fail; ³⁹but if it is of God, you will not be able to overthrow them. You might even be found opposing God!"

Lk 2:2

2 Mac 7:19
Mt 15:13

The Apostles are flogged

⁴⁰So they took his advice, and when they had called in the apostles, they beat them and charged them not to speak in the name of Jesus, and let them go. ⁴¹Then they left the presence of the council, rejoicing that they were counted

Mt 10:17
Acts 22:19

Mt 5:10-12
1 Pet 4:13-14

---

istis quid acturi sitis. ³⁶Ante hos enim dies exstitit Theudas dicens esse se aliquem, cui consensit virorum numerus circiter quadringentorum; quo occisus est, et omnes, quicumque credebant ei, dissipati sunt et redacti sunt ad nihilum. ³⁷Post hunc exstitit Iudas Galilaeus in diebus census et avertit populum post se; et ipse periit, et omnes, quotquot consentiebant ei, dispersi sunt. ³⁸Et nunc dico vobis: Discedite ab hominibus istis et sinite illos. Quoniam si est ex hominibus consilium hoc aut opus hoc, dissolvetur; ³⁹si vero ex Deo est, non poteritis dissolvere eos, ne forte et adversus Deum pugnantes inveniamini!" Consenserunt autem illi ⁴⁰et convocantes apostolos, caesis denuntiaverunt, ne loquerentur in nomine Iesu, et dimiserunt eos. ⁴¹Et illi quidem ibant gaudentes a conspectu concilii quoniam digni habiti sunt pro nomine contumeliam pati;

The revolts of Theudas and Judas are referred to by Flavius Josephus (cf. *Jewish Antiquities*, XVIII, 4-10; XX, 169-172), but the dates he gives are vague; apparently these events occurred around the time of Jesus' birth. Both Theudas and Judas had considerable following; they revolted against the chosen people having to pay tribute to foreigners such as Herod and Imperial Rome.

40-41. Most members of the Sanhedrin are unimpressed by Gamaliel's arguments; they simply decide to go as far as they safely can: they do not dare to condemn the Apostles to death; but, in their stubborn opposition to the Gospel message, they decree that they be put under the lash in the hope that this will keep them quiet. However, it has just the opposite effect.

"It is true that Jeremiah was scourged for the word of God, and that Elijah

worthy to suffer dishonour for the name. [42]And every day in the temple and at home they did not cease teaching and preaching Jesus as the Christ.

6

The appointment of the seven deacons

[1]Now in these days when the disciples were increasing in

---

[42]et omni die in templo et circa domos non cessabant docentes et evangelizantes Christum, Iesum.

[1]In diebus autem illis, crescente numero discipulorum, factus est murmur

---

and other prophets were also threatened, but in this case the Apostles, as they did earlier by their miracles, showed forth the power of God. He does not say that they did not suffer, but that they rejoiced over having to suffer. This we can see from their boldness afterwards: immediately after being beaten they went back to preaching" (Chrysostom, *Hom. on Acts*, 14).

The Apostles must have remembered our Lord's words, "Blessed are you when men revile you and persecute you and utter all kinds of evil against you falsely on my account. Rejoice and be glad, for so men persecuted the prophets who were before you" (Mt 5:11-12).

42. The Apostles and the first disciples of Jesus were forever preaching, with the result that very soon all Jerusalem was filled with their teaching (cf. v. 28). These early brethren are an example to Christians in every age: zeal to attract others to the faith is a characteristic of every true disciple of Jesus and a consequence of love of God and love for others: "You have but little love if you are not zealous for the salvation of all souls. You have but poor love if you are not eager to inspire other apostles with your craziness" (J. Escrivá, *The Way*, 796).

1-6. A new section of the book begins at this point. It is introduced by reference to two groups in the early community, identified by their background prior to their conversion—the Hellenists and the Hebrews. From this chapter onwards, Christians are referred to as "disciples"; in other words this term is no longer applied only to the Apostles and to those who were adherents of Jesus during his life on earth: all the baptized are "disciples". Jesus is the Lord of his Church and the Teacher of all: after his ascension into heaven he teaches, sanctifies and governs Christians through the ministry of the Apostles, initially, and after the Apostles' death, through the ministry of their successors, the Pope and the bishops, who are aided by priests.

Hellenists were Jews who had been born and lived for a time outside Palestine. They spoke Greek and had synagogues of their own where the Greek translation of Scripture was used. They had a certain amount of Greek culture; the Hebrews would have also had some, but not as much. The Hebrews were Jews born in Palestine; they spoke Aramaic and used the Hebrew Bible in their synagogues. This difference of backgrounds naturally carried over into the Christian community during its early years. but it would be wrong to see it as divisive or to imagine that there were two opposed factions in early Christianity. Before the Church was founded there existed in Jerusalem a well-established Hellenist-Jewish community—an influential and sizeable grouping.

This chapter relates the establishment by the Apostles of "the seven": this is the second, identifiable group of disciples entrusted with a ministry in the Church, the first being "the twelve".

Although St Luke does not clearly present this group as constituting a holy "order", it is quite clear that the seven have been given a public role in the community, a role which extends beyond distribution of relief. We shall now see Philip and Stephen preaching and baptizing—sharing in some ways in ministry of the Apostles, involved in "care of souls".

St Luke uses the term *diakonia* (service), but he does not call the seven "deacons". Nor do later ancient writers imply that these seven were deacons (in the later technical sense of the word)—constituting with priests and Bishops the hierarchy of the Church. Therefore, we do not know for certain whether the diaconate as we know it derives directly from "the seven". St John Chrysostom, for example, has doubts about this (cf. *Hom. on Acts*, 14). However, it is at least possible that the ministry described here played a part in the instituting of the diaconate proper.

In any event, the diaconate is a form of sacred office of apostolic origin. At ordination deacons take on an obligation to perform—under the direction of the diocesan bishop—certain duties to do with evangelization, catechesis, organization of liturgical ceremonies, Christian initiation of catechumens and neophytes, and Church charitable and social welfare work.

The Second Vatican Council teaches that "at a lower level of the hierarchy are to be found deacons, who receive the imposition of hands 'not unto the priesthood, but unto the ministry'. For, strengthened by sacramental grace they are dedicated to the people of God, in conjunction with the bishop and his body of priests, in the service of the liturgy, of the Gospel and of works of charity. It pertains to the office of a deacon, in so far as it may be assigned to him by the competent authority, to administer Baptism solemnly, to be custodian and distributor of the Eucharist, in the name of the Church to assist at and to bless marriages, to bring Viaticum to the dying, to read the Sacred Scripture to the faithful, to instruct and exhort the people, to preside over the worship and the prayer of the faithful, to administer sacramentals, and to officiate at funeral and burial services" (*Lumen gentium*, 29).

numbers, the Hellenists murmured against the Hebrews because their widows were neglected in the daily distribution.
Ex 18:17-23 ²And the twelve summoned the body of the disciples and
said, "It is not right that we should give up preaching the
1 Tim 3:8-10 word of God to serve tables. ³Therefore, brethren, pick out
from among you seven men of good repute, full of the Spirit
and of wisdom, whom we may appoint to this duty. ⁴But we
will devote ourselves to prayer and to the ministry of the

Hellenistarum adversus Hebraeos, eo quod neglegerentur in ministerio
cotidiano viduae eorum. ²Convocantes autem Duodecim multitudinem
discipulorum, dixerunt: "Non est aequum nos derelinquentes verbum Dei
ministrare mensis; ³considerate vero, fratres, viros ex vobis boni testimonii
septem plenos Spiritu et sapientia, quos constituemus super hoc opus; ⁴nos vero

---

2-4. The Twelve establish a principle which they consider basic: their
apostolic ministry is so absorbing that they have no time to do other things. In
this particular case an honorable and useful function—distribution of
food—cannot be allowed get in the way of another even more important task
essential to the life of the Church and of each of its members. "They speak of
it 'not being right' in order to show that the two duties cannot in this case be
made compatible" (Chrysostom, *Hom. on Acts*, 14).

The main responsibility of the pastors of the Church is the preaching of the
word of God, the administration of the sacraments and the government of the
people of God. Any other commitment they take on should be compatible with
their pastoral work and supportive of it, in keeping with the example given by
Christ: he cured people's physical ailments in order to reach their souls, and he
preached justice and peace as signs of the Kingdom of God.

"A mark of our identity which no doubt ought to encroach upon and no
objection eclipse is this: as pastors, we have been chosen by the mercy of the
Supreme Pastor (cf. 1 Pet 5:4), in spite of our inadequacy, to proclaim with
authority the Word of God, to assemble the scattered people of God, to nourish
this people on the road to salvation, to maintain it in that unity of which we are,
at different levels, active and living instruments, and increasingly to keep this
community gathered around Christ faithful to its deepest vocation" (Paul VI,
Evangelii nuntiandi, 68).

A priest should be avid for the word of God, John Paul II emphasizes; he
should embrace it in its entirety, meditate on it, study it assiduously and spread
it through his example and preaching (cf. e.g., *Addresses* in Ireland and the
United States, 1 October and 3 October 1979 respectively). His whole life
should be a generous proclamation of Christ. Therefore, he should avoid the
temptation to "temporal leadership: that can easily be a source of division,
whereas he should be a sign and promoter of unity and fraternity" (*To the priests
of Mexico*, 27 January 1979).

word." [5]And what they said pleased the whole multitude, and Acts 8:5; 21:8
they chose Stephen, a man full of faith of the Holy Spirit,
and Philip, and Prochorus, and Nicanor, and Timon, and
Parmenas, and Nicolaus, a proselyte of Antioch. [6]These they Acts 13:3
1 Tim 4:14
set before the apostles, and they prayed and laid their hands 2 Tim 1:6
upon them.

---

orationi et ministerio verbi instantes erimus." [5]Et placuit sermo coram omni
multitudine, et elegerunt Stephanum, virum plenum fide et Spiritu Sancto, et
Philippum et Prochorum et Nicanorem et Timonem et Parmenam et Nicolaum
proselytum Antiochenum, [6]quos statuerunt ante conspectum apostolorum, et

---

This passage allows us to see the difference between election and appointment to a ministry in the Church. A person can be elected or designated by the faithful; but power to carry out that ministry (which implies a calling from God) is something he must receive through ordination, which the Apostles confer. "The Apostles leave it to the body of the disciples to select the [seven], in order that it should not seem that they favour some in preference to others" (Chrysostom, *Hom. on Acts*, 14). However, those designated for ordination are not representatives or delegates of the Christian community; they are ministers of God. They have received a calling and, by the imposition of hands, God—not men—gives them a spiritual power which equips them to govern the Christian community, make and administer the sacraments and preach the Word.

Christian pastoral office, that is, the priesthood of the New Testament in its various degrees, does not derive from family relationship, as was the case with the Levitical priesthood in the New Testament; nor is it a type of commissioning by the community. The initiative lies with the grace of God, who calls whom he chooses.

5. All the people chosen have Greek names. One of them is a "proselyte", that is, a pagan who became a Jew through circumcision and observance of the Law of Moses.

6. The Apostles establish the seven in their office or ministry through prayer and the laying on of hands. This latter gesture is found sometimes in the Old Testament, principally as a rite of ordination of Levites (cf. Num 8:10) and as a way of conferring power and wisdom on Joshua, Moses' successor as leader of Israel (Num 27:20; Deut 13:9).

Christians have retained this rite, as can be seen quite often in Acts. Sometimes it symbolizes curing (9:12, 17; 28:8), in line with the example given by our Lord in Luke 4:40. It is also a rite of blessing, as when Paul and Barnabas are sent out on their first apostolic journey (13:3); and it is used as a post-baptismal rite for bringing down the Holy Spirit (8:17; 19:5).

⁷And the word of God increased; and the number of the disciples multiplied greatly in Jerusalem, and a great many of the priests were obedient to the faith.

ST STEPHEN

Stephen's arrest

⁸And Stephen, full of grace and power, did great wonders and signs among the people. ⁹Then some of those who belonged to the synagogue of the Freedmen (as it was called), and of the Cyrenians, and of the Alexandrians, and of those from Cilicia and Asia, arose and disputed with Stephen. ¹⁰But they could not withstand the wisdom and the Spirit with

---

orantes imposuerunt eis manus. ⁷Et verbum Dei crescebat, et multiplicabatur numerus discipulorum in Ierusalem valde; multa etiam turba sacerdotum oboediebat fidei. ⁸Stephanus autem plenus gratia et virtute faciebat prodigia et signa magna in populo. ⁹Surrexerunt autem quidam de synagoga quae appellatur Libertinorum et Cyrenensium et Alexandrinorum et eorum, qui erant a Cilicia et Asia, disputantes cum Stephano, ¹⁰et non poterant resistere

---

In this case it is a rite for the ordination of ministers of the Church—the first instance of sacred ordination reported by Acts (cf. 1 Tim 4:14; 5:22; 2 Tim 5:22). "St Luke is brief. He does not say how they were ordained, but simply that it was done with prayer, because it was an ordination. The hand of a man is laid [upon the person], but the whole work is of God and it is his hand which touches the head of the one ordained" (Chrysostom, *Hom. on Acts*, 14).

The essential part of the rite of ordination of deacons is the laying on of hands; this is done in silence, on the candidate's head, and then a prayer is said to God asking him to send the Holy Spirit to the person being ordained.

7. As in earlier chapters, St Luke here refers to the spread of the Church—this time reporting the conversion of "a great many of the priests." Many scholars think that these would have come from the lower ranks of the priesthood (like Zechariah: cf. Lk 1:5) and not from the great priestly families, which were Sadducees and enemies of the new-born Church (cf. 4:1; 5;17). Some have suggested that these priests may have included members of the Qumran sect. However, the only evidence we have to go on is what St Luke says here.

8-14. From the text it would appear that Stephen preached mainly among Hellenist Jews; this was his own background. Reference is made to synagogues of Jews of the Dispersion (Diaspora). These synagogues were used for worship

which he spoke. [11]Then they secretly instigated men, who said, "We have heard him speak blasphemous words against Moses and God." [12]And they stirred up the people and the elders and the scribes, and they came upon him and seized him, and brought him before the council, [13]and set up false witnesses who said, "This man never ceases to speak words against this holy place and the law; [14]for we have heard him say that this Jesus of Nazareth will destroy this place, and will change the customs which Moses delivered to us." [15]And gazing at him, all who sat in the council saw that his face was like the face of an angel.

Mt 26:59-66
Mt 10:17
Jer 26:11
Acts 21:28
Mk 14:58

---

sapientiae et Spiritui, quo loquebatur. [11]Tunc submiserunt viros, qui dicerent: "Audivimus eum dicentem verba blasphema in Moysen et Deum;" [12]et commoverunt plebem et seniores et scribas, et concurrentes rapuerunt eum et adduxerunt in concilium [13]et statuerunt testes falsos dicentes: "Homo ist non cessat loqui verba adversus locum sanctum et legem; [14]audivimus enim eum dicentem quoniam Iesus Nazarenus hic destruet locum istum et mutabit consuetudines, quas tradidit nobis Moyses." [15]Et intuentes eum omnes, qui sedebant in concilio, viderunt faciem eius tamquam faciem angeli.

---

and as meeting places. The very fact that these Hellenist Jews were living in the Holy City shows what devotion they had to the Law of their forebears.

No longer is it only the Sanhedrin who are opposed to the Gospel; other Jews have been affected by misunderstanding and by misrepresentation of the Christian message.

The charge of blasphemy—also made against our Lord—was the most serious that could be made against a Jew. As happened in Jesus' case, the accusers here resort to producing false witnesses, who twist Stephen's words and accuse him of a crime the penalty for which is death.

15. St John Chrysostom, commenting on this verse, recalls that the face of Moses, when he comes down from Sinai (cf. Ex 34:29-35), reflected the glory of God and likewise made the people afraid: "It was grace, it was the glory of Moses. I think that God clothed him in this splendour because perhaps he had something to say, and in order that his very appearance would strike terror into them. For it is possible, very possible, for figures full of heavenly grace to be attractive to friendly eyes and terrifying to the eyes of enemies" (*Hom. on Acts*, 15).

7

Stephen's address to the Sanhedrin

Acts 24:9
Ps 29:3

Gen 12:1

Gen 11:32;
12:5

Gen 12:7;
13:15; 17:8;
Gal 3:16

Gen 15:13-14
Ex 12:40

[1]And the high priest said, "Is this so?" [2]And Stephen said:

"Brethren and fathers, hear me. The God of glory appeared to our father Abraham, when he was in Mesopotamia, before he lived in Haran, [3]and said to him, 'Depart from your land and from your kindred and go into the land which I will show you.' [4]Then he departed from the land of the Chaldeans, and lived in Haran. And after his father died, God removed him from there into this land in which you are now living; [5]yet he gave him no inheritance in it, not even a foot's length, but promised to give it to him in possession and to his posterity after him, though he had no child. [6]And God

---

[1]Dixit autem princeps sacerdotum: "Si haec ita se habent?" [2]Qui ait: "Viri fratres et patres, audite. Deus gloriae apparuit patri nostro Abraham, cum esset in Mesopotamia, priusquam moraretur in Charran, [3]et dixit ad illum: 'Exi de terra tua et de cognatione tua, et veni in terram, quam tibi monstravero.' [4]Tunc egressus de terra Chaldaeorum habitavit in Charran. Et inde postquam mortuus est pater eius, transtulit illum in terram istam, in qua nunc vos habitatis, [5]et non dedit illi hereditatem in ea nec passum pedis et repromisit dare illi eam in possessionem et semini eius post ipsum, cum non haberet filium. [6]Locutus est

---

1-53. Stephen's discourse is the longest one given in Acts. It is a summary of the history of Israel, divided into three periods—of the Patriarchs (1-16), of Moses (17-43) and of the building of the temple (44-50). It ends with a short section (51-53) where he brings his argument together.

One thing that stands out is that Stephen does not defend himself directly. He answers his accusers with a Christian vision of salvation history, in which the temple and the Law have already fulfilled their purpose. He tells them that he continues to respect the Mosaic Law and the temple, but that as a Christian his idea of God's law is more universal and more profound, his concept of the temple more spiritual (for God can be worshipped anywhere in the world). This approach, which respects and perfects the religious values of Judaism (because it probes their true meaning and brings them to fulfilment), is reinforced by the way he presents the figure of Moses. Stephen shows Moses as a "type" of Christ: Christ is the new Moses. Small elucidations of the Greek text of the Old Testament help in this direction: expressions like "they refused" or "deliverer" (v. 35) are not applied to Moses in the books of the Old Testament, but they are used here to suggest Christ. The Israelites' rebellious and aggressive treatment of Moses, who had a mission from God, is being repeated—much more seriously—in their rejection of the Gospel.

spoke to this effect, that his posterity would be aliens in a land belonging to others, who would enslave them and ill-treat them four hundred years. [7]'But I will judge the nation which they serve,' said God, 'and after that they shall come out and worship me in this place.' [8]And he gave him the covenant of circumcision. And so Abraham became the father of Isaac, and circumcised him on the eighth day; and Isaac became the father of Jacob, and Jacob of the twelve patriarchs.

[9]"And the patriarchs, jealous of Joseph, sold him into Egypt; but God was with him, [10]and rescued him out of all his afflictions, and gave him favour and wisdom before Pharaoh, king of Egypt, who made him governor over Egypt and over all his household. [11]Now there came a famine throughout all Egypt and Canaan, and great affliction, and our fathers could find no food. [12]But when Jacob heard that there was grain in Egypt, he sent forth our fathers the first time. [13]And at the second visit Joseph made himself known to his brothers, and Joseph's family became known to Pharaoh. [14]And Joseph sent and called to him Jacob his father and all his kindred, seventy-five souls; [15]and Jacob went

Ex 3:12

Gen 17:10; 21:4

Gen 37:11, 28
Wis 10:13
Gen 39:21; 41:40-41

Gen 41:54

Gen 42:2

Gen 45:3-16

Gen 46:27
Gen 46:6; 49:33

---

autem sic Deus: 'Erit semen eius accola in terra aliena, et servituti eos subicient et male tractabunt annis quadringentis; [7]et gentem, cui servierint, iudicabo ego, dixit Deus, et post haec exibunt et deservient mihi in loco isto'. [8]Et dedit illi testamentum circumcisionis; et sic genuit Isaac et circumcidit eum die octava, et Isaac Iacob, et Iacob duodecim patriarchas. [9]Et patriarchae aemulantes Ioseph vendiderunt in Aegyptum; et erat Deus cum eo, [10]et eripuit eum ex omnibus tribulationibus eius, et dedit ei gratiam et sapientiam in conspectu pharaonis regis Aegypti, et constituit eum praepositum super Aegyptum et super omnem domum suam. [11]Venit autem fames in universam Aegyptum et Chanaan et tribulatio magna, et non inveniebant cibos patres nostri. [12]Cum audisset autem Iacob esse frumentum in Aegypto, misit patres nostros primum; [13]et in secundo cognitus est Ioseph a fratribus suis, et manifestatum est pharaoni genus Ioseph. [14]Mittens autem Ioseph accersivit Iacob patrem suum et omnem cognationem in animabus septuaginta quinque, [15]et descendit Iacob in

---

St John Chrysostom expands on the last words of the discourse in this way: "Is it to be wondered that you do not know Christ, seeing that you did not know Moses, and God himself, who was manifested by such wonders? [. . .] 'You always resist the Holy Spirit'. [. . .] When you received commandments, you neglected them; when the temple already stood, you worshipped idols" (*Hom. on Acts*, 17). Despite the vigour of his reproaches, Chrysostom has to point out

87

Gen 50:13 down into Egypt. And he died, himself and our fathers, [16]and
they were carried back to Shechem and laid in the tomb that
Abraham had bought for a sum of silver from the sons of
Hamor in Shechem.

Ex 1:7 [17]"But as the time of the promise drew near, which God
had granted to Abraham, the people grew and multiplied in
Egypt [18]till there arose over Egypt another king who had not
Ex 1:10-22 known Joseph. [19]He dealt craftily with our race and forced
our fathers to expose their infants, that they might not be kept
Ex 2:2
Heb 11:23 alive. [20]At this time Moses was born, and was beautiful
before God. And he was brought up for three months in his
Ex 2:5, 10 father's house; [21]and when he was exposed, Pharaoh's
daughter adopted him and brought him up as her own son.
Lk 24:19 [22]And Moses was instructed in all the wisdom of the
Egyptians, and he was mighty in his words and deeds.

Ex 2:11 [23]"When he was forty years old, it came into his heart to
Ex 2:12 visit his brethren, the sons of Israel. [24]And seeing one of them

---

Aegyptum. Et defúnctus est ipse et patres nostri, [16]et translati sunt in Sichem
et positi sunt in sepulcro, quod emit Abraham pretio argenti a filiis Hemmor in
Sichem. [17]Cum appropinquaret autem tempus repromissionis, quam confessus
erat Deus Abrahae, crevit populus et multiplicatus est in Aegypto,
[18]quoadusque surrexit rex alius super Aegypto, qui non sciebat Ioseph. [19]Hic
circumveniens genus nostrum, afflixit patres, ut exponerent infantes suos, ne
vivi servarentur. [20]Eodem tempore natus est Moyses et erat formosus coram
Deo; qui nutritus est tribus mensibus in domo patris. [21]Expositio autem illo,
sustulit eum filia pharaonis et enutrivit eum sibi in filium; [22]et eruditus est
Moyses in omnia sapientia Aegyptiorum et erat potens in verbis et in operibus
suis. [23]Cum autem impleretur ei quadraginta annorum tempus, ascendit in cor
eius, ut visitaret fratres suos filios Israel. [24]Et cum vidisset quendam iniuriam

---

Stephen's meekness: "he did not abuse them; all he did was remind them of the
words of the Prophets" (*ibid.*).

St Ephraem, however, stresses other aspects of Stephen's prayer: "Since he
knew that the Jews were not going to take his words to heart and were only
interested in killing him, full of joy in his soul . . . he censured their hardness
of heart. [. . .] He discussed circumcision of the flesh, to exalt instead
circumcision of the heart which sincerely seeks God, against whom they were
in rebellion. In this way he added his own accusations to those of the prophet"
(*Armenian Commentary, ad loc.*).

16. According to Genesis 50:13, Abraham bought the burial ground from
Ephron the Hittite. The Old Testament tells us that the field in Shechem was

being wronged, he defended the oppressed man and avenged him by striking the Egyptian. [25]He supposed that his brethren understood that God was giving them deliverance by his hand, but they did not understand. [26]And on the following day he appeared to them as they were quarrelling and would have reconciled them, saying, 'Men, you are brethren, why do you wrong each other?' [27]But the man who was wronging his neighbour thrust him aside, saying, 'Who made you a ruler and a judge over us? [28]Do you want to kill me as you killed the Egyptian yesterday?' [29]At this retort Moses fled, and became an exile in the land of Midian, where he became the father of two sons.

[30]'Now when forty years had passed, an angel appeared to him in the wilderness of Mount Sinai, in a flame of fire in a bush. [31]When Moses saw it he wondered at the sight; and as he drew near to look, the voice of the Lord came, [32]'I am the God of your fathers, the God of Abraham and of Isaac and of Jacob.' And Moses trembled and did not dare to look. [33]And the Lord said to him, 'Take off the shoes from your feet, for the place where you are standing is holy ground. [34]I have surely seen the ill-treatment of my people that are in Egypt and heard their groaning, and I have come down to

Ex 2:13

Ex 2:14
Lk 12:14

Ex 2:15, 22;
8:3

Ex 3:1-2
Deut 33:16

Ex 3:4

Ex 3:6
Mt 22:32

Ex 3:5

Ex 3:7-10

---

patientem, vindicavit et fecit ultionem ei, qui opprimebatur, percusso Aegyptio. [25]Existimabat autem intellegere fratres quoniam Deus per manum ipsius daret salutem illis, at illi non intellexerunt. [26]Atque sequenti die apparuit illis litigantibus et reconciliabat eos in pacem dicens: 'Viri, fratres estis; ut quid nocetis alterutrum?' [27]Qui autem iniuriam faciebat proximo, reppulit eum dicens: 'Quis te constituit principem et iudicem super nos? [28]Numquid interficere me tu vis, quemadmodum interfecisti heri Aegyptium?' [29]Fugit autem Moyses propter verbum istud et factus est advena in terra Madian, ubi generavit filios duos. [30]Et expletis annis quadraginta, apparuit illi in deserto montis Sinai angelus in ignis flamma rubi. [31]Moyses autem videns admirabatur visum; accedente autem illo, ut consideraret, facta est vox Domini: [32]'Ego Deus patrum tuorum, Deus Abraham et Isaac et Iacob.' Tremefactus autem Moyses non audebat considerare. [33]Dixit autem illi Dominus: 'Solve calceamentum pedum tuorum; locus enim, in quo stas, terra sancta est. [34]Videns vidi afflictionem populi mei, qui est in Aegypto, et gemitum eorum audivi et

---

bought by Jacob (Gen 33:19) and that the patriarch buried there was Joseph (Josh 24:32). Stephen seems to be following a Jewish tradition which varies somewhat from the Hebrew text of the Old Testament.

deliver them. And now come, I will send you to Egypt.'

Ex 2:14
35"This Moses whom they refused, saying, 'Who made you a ruler and a judge?' God sent as both ruler and deliverer by the hand of the angel that appeared to him in the bush.

Ex 7:3; 14:21
Num 14:33
36He led them out, having performed wonders and signs in Egypt and at the Red Sea, and in the wilderness for forty years. 37This is the Moses who said to the Israelites, 'God

Deut 18:15
Acts 3:22
Ex 19:3
Deut 4:10;
9:10
Gal 3:19
Heb 2:2
Num 14:3
will raise up for you a prophet from your brethren as he raised me up.' 38This is he who was in the congregation in the wilderness with the angel who spoke to him at Mount Sinai, and with our fathers; and he received living oracles to give to us. 39Our fathers refused to obey him, but thrust him aside,

Ex 32:1, 23
and in their hearts they turned to Egypt, 40saying to Aaron, 'Make for us gods to go before us; as for this Moses who led us out from the land of Egypt, we do not know what has

Ex 32:4-6
Jer 19:13
Amos 5:25-27
become of him.' 41And they made a calf in those days and offered a sacrifice to the idol and rejoiced in the works of their hands. 42But God turned and gave them over to worship the host of heaven, as it is written in the book of the prophets:

'Did you offer to me slain beasts and sacrifices,

forty years in the wilderness, O house of Israel?

43And you took up the tent of Moloch,

---

descendi liberare eos; et nunc veni, mittam te in Aegyptum.' 35Hunc Moysen, quem negaverunt dicentes: 'Quis te constituit principem et iudicem?', hunc Deus et principem et redemptorem misit cum manu angeli, qui apparuit illi in rubo. 36Hic eduxit illos faciens prodigia et signa in terra Aegypti et in Rubro mari et in deserto annis quadraginta. 37Hic est Moyses, qui dixit filiis Israel: 'Prophetam vobis suscitabit Deus de fratribus vestris tamquam me.' 38Hic est qui fuit in ecclesia in solitudine cum angelo, qui loquebatur ei in monte Sinai et cum patribus nostris, qui accepit verba viva dare nobis, 39cui noluerunt oboedire patres nostri, sed reppulerunt et aversi sunt in cordibus suis in Aegyptum 40dicentes ad Aaron: 'Fac nobis deos, qui praecedant nos; Moyses enim hic, qui eduxit nos de terra Aegypti, nescimus quid factum sit ei.' 41Et vitulum fecerunt in illis diebus et obtulerunt hostiam simulacro et laetabantur in operibus manuum suarum. 42Convertit autem Deus et tradidit eos servire militiae caeli, sicut scriptum est in libro Prophetarum: 'Numquid victimas et hostias obtulistis mihi annis quadraginta in deserto, domus Israel? 43Et

---

42-43. "The host of heaven": Scripture normally uses this expression to refer to the stars, which were worshipped in some ancient religions. God sometimes allowed the Israelites to forget him and worship false gods.

and the star of the god Rephan,
the figures which you made to worship;
and I will remove you beyond Babylon.'
    ⁴⁴"Our fathers had the tent of witness in the wilderness,
even as he who spoke to Moses directed him to make it,
according to the pattern that he had seen. ⁴⁵Our fathers in turn
brought it in with Joshua when they dispossessed the nations
which God thrust out before our fathers. So it was until the
days of David, ⁴⁶who found favour in the sight of God and
asked leave to find a habitation for the God of Jacob. ⁴⁷But
it was Solomon who built a house for him. ⁴⁸Yet the Most
High does not dwell in houses made with hands; as the
prophet says,
    ⁴⁹'Heaven is my throne,
and earth my footstool.
What house will you build for me, says the Lord,
or what is the place of my rest?
    ⁵⁰Did not my hand make all these things?'
    ⁵¹"You stiff-necked people, uncircumcised in heart and
ears, you always resist the Holy Spirit. As your fathers did,
so do you. ⁵²Which of the prophets did not your fathers

Ex 25:40
Heb 8:5

Josh 3:14; 18:1

2 Sam 7:2
Ps 132:5
1 Kings 6:1
Is 66:1
Acts 17:24
Heb 9:11, 24

Ex 33:3
Is 63:10
Jer 4:4; 6:10;
9:26
Mt 23:31
Acts 3:14

suscepistis tabernaculum Moloch et sidus dei vestri Rhaephan, figuras, quas
fecistis ad adorandum eas. Et transferam vos trans Babylonem.' ⁴⁴Taber-
naculum testimonii erat patribus nostris in deserto, sicut disposuit, qui loquebatur ad Moysen, ut faceret illud secundum formam, quam viderat; ⁴⁵quod et
induxerunt suscipientes patres nostri cum Iesu, in possessionem gentium, quas
expulit Deus a facie patrum nostrorum usque in diebus David, ⁴⁶qui invenit
gratiam ante Deum et petiit, ut inveniret tabernaculum domui Iacob. ⁴⁷Salomon
autem aedificavit illi domum. ⁴⁸Sed non Altissimus in manufactis habitat, sicut
propheta dicit: ⁴⁹'Caelum mihi thronus est, terra autem scabellum pedum
meorum. Quam domum aedificabitis mihi, dicit Dominus, aut quis locus
requietionis meae? ⁵⁰Nonne manus mea fecit haec omnia?' Duri cervice et
incircumcisi cordibus et auribus, vos semper Spiritui Sancto resistitis, sicut
patres vestri et vos. ⁵²Quem prophetarum non sunt persecuti patres vestri? Et

The quotation from "the book of the prophets" to which Stephen refers is
from Amos 5:25-27 (which in Acts is taken from the Septuagint Greek). It is
not easy to work out what Amos means. We know from the Pentateuch that the
Israelites a number of times offered sacrifices to Yahweh when they were in
Sinai during the Exodus (cf. Ex 24:4-5; chap. 29; Lev: chaps. 8-9; Num: chap.

persecute? And they killed those who announced beforehand the coming of the Righteous One, whom you have now betrayed and murdered, ⁵³you who received the law as delivered by angels and did not keep it."

The martyrdom of St Stephen

⁵⁴Now when they heard these things they were enraged, and they ground their teeth against him. ⁵⁵But he, full of the Holy Spirit, gazed into heaven and saw the glory of God, and Jesus standing at the right hand of God; ⁵⁶and he said, "Behold, I see the heavens opened, and the Son of man standing at the right hand of God." ⁵⁷But they cried out with

---

occiderunt eos, qui praenuntiabant de adventu Iusti, cuius vos nunc proditores et homicidae fuistis, ⁵³qui accepistis legem in dispositionibus angelorum et non custodistis." ⁵⁴Audientes autem haec, dissecabantur cordibus suis et stridebant dentibus in eum. ⁵⁵Cum autem esset plenus Spiritu Sancto, intendens in caelum vidit gloriam Dei et Iesum stantem a dextris Dei, et ait: "Ecce video caelos apertos et Filium hominis a dextris stantem Dei." ⁵⁷Exclamantes autem voce

---

7), but all these sacrifices were offered at the foot of Mount Sinai, before they started out on their long pilgrimage through the wilderness, before they reached the promised land. Perhaps St Stephen is referring to those long years (about forty years) during which nothing is said in the Old Testament about their offering sacrifice to Yahweh. Even during the Exodus—a period when God frequently showed his special favour—the Israelites strayed from Yahweh.

55-56. "It is clear", St Ephraem comments, "that those who suffer for Christ enjoy the glory of the whole Trinity. Stephen saw the Father and Jesus at his side, because Jesus appears only to his own, as was the case with the Apostles after the Resurrection. While the champion of the faith stood there helpless in the midst of those who had killed the Lord, just at the point when the first martyr was to be crowned, he saw the Lord, holding a crown in his right hand, as if to encourage him to conquer death and to show that he inwardly helps those who are about to die on his account. He therefore reveals what he sees, that is, the heavens opened, which were closed to Adam and only opened to Christ at the Jordan, but open now after the Cross to all those who share Christ's sufferings, and in the first instance open to this man. See how Stephen reveals why his face was lit up: it was because he was on the point of contemplating this wondrous mission. That is why he took on the appearance of an angel—so that his testimony might be more reliable" (*Armenian Commentary, ad loc.*).

57-59. The cursory trial of Stephen ends without any formal sentence of

a loud voice and stopped their ears and rushed together upon
him. [58]Then they cast him out of the city and stoned him; and Acts 22:20
the witnesses laid down their garments at the feet of a young
man named Saul. [59]And as they were stoning Stephen, he Ps 31:6
Lk 23:46

---

magna continuerunt aures suas et impetum fecerunt unanimiter in eum [58]et
eicientes extra civitatem lapidabant. Et testes deposuerunt vestimenta sua secus
pedes adulescentis, qui vocabatur Saulus. [59]Et lapidabant Stephanum invo-

---

death: this Jewish tribunal was unable to pass such sentences because the
Romans restricted its competence. In any event no sentence proves necessary:
the crowd becomes a lynching party: it takes over and proceeds to stone
Stephen, with the tacit approval of the Sanhedrin.

Tradition regards Stephen as the first Christian martyr, an example of
fortitude and suffering for love of Christ. "Could you keep all God's commandments," St Cyprian asks, "were it not for the strength of patience? That
was what enabled Stephen to hold out: in spite of being stoned he did not call
down vengeance on his executioners, but rather forgiveness. . . . How fitting it
was for him to be Christ's first martyr, so that by being, through his glorious
death, the model of all the martyrs that would come after him, he should not
only be a preacher of the Lord's Passion, but should also imitate it in his
meekness and immense patience" (*De bono patientiae*, 16).

Martyrdom is a supreme act of bravery and of true prudence, but to the world
it makes no sense. It is also an expression of humility, because a martyr does
not act out of bravado or overweening self-confidence; he is a weak man like
anyone else, but God's grace gives him the strength he needs. Although
martyrdom is something which happens rarely, it does show Christians what
human nature can rise to if God gives it strength, and it establishes a standard,
both real and symbolic, for the behaviour of every disciple of Christ.

"Since all the virtues and the perfection of all righteousness are born of love
of God and one's neighbour," St Leo says, "in no one is this love more worthily
found than in the blessed martyrs, who are nearest to our Lord in terms of
imitation of both his charity and his Passion.

"The martyrs have been of great help to others, because the Lord has availed
of the very strength as he granted them to ensure that the pain of death and the
cruelty of the Cross do not frighten any of his own, but are seen as things in
which man can imitate him . . . .

"No example is more useful for the instruction of the people of God than that
of the martyrs. Eloquence is effective for entreating, argument for convincing;
but examples are worth more than words, and it is better to teach by deeds than
by speech" (*Hom. on the feast of St Laurence*).

The Second Vatican Council has reminded us of the excellence of martyrdom
as a form of witness to the faith. Although there are heroic ways of imitating

prayed, "Lord Jesus, receive my spirit." [60]And he knelt down and cried with a loud voice, "Lord, do not hold this sin against them." And when he had said this, he fell asleep.

---

cantem et dicentem: "Domine Iesu, suscipe spiritum meum." [60]Positis autem genibus clamavit voce magna: "Domine, ne statuas illis hoc peccatum"; et cum hoc dixisset, obdormivit.

---

and following our Lord which do not involve the drama of bloodshed and death, all Christians should realize that confession of the faith in this way is not a thing of the past and is sometimes necessary.

"Since Jesus, the Son of God, showed his love by laying down his life for us, no one has greater love than he who lays down his life for him and for his brothers (cf. 1 Jn 3:16; Jn 15:13). Some Christians have been called from the beginning, and will always be called, to give this greatest testimony of love to all, especially to persecutors. Martyrdom makes the disciple like his Master. [. . .] Therefore, the Church considers it the highest gift and supreme test of love. And although it is given to few, all must be prepared to confess Christ before men and to follow him along the way of the Cross amidst the persecutions which the Church never lacks.

"Likewise the Church's holiness is fostered [. . .] by the manifold counsels which the Lord proposes to his disciples in the Gospel" (Vatican II, *Lumen gentium*, 42).

The Liturgy of the Church sums up the asceticism and theology of martyrdom in the preface for Christian martyrs: "Your holy martyr followed the example of Christ, and gave his life for the glory of your name. His death reveals your power shining through our human weakness. You choose the weak and make them strong in bearing witness to you."

Like Jesus, Stephen dies commending his soul to God and praying for his persecutors. At this point St Luke brings in Saul, who cooperates in the proceedings by watching the executioners' clothes; Saul will soon experience the benefit of Stephen's intercession. "If Stephen had not prayed to God, the Church would not have had Paul" (St Augustine, *Sermons*, 315, 7).

Stephen has died, but his example and teaching continue to speak across the world.

PART TWO
THE CHURCH SPREADS BEYOND JERUSALEM

Persecution of the Church

¹And Saul was consenting to his death.

And on that day a great persecution arose against the church in Jerusalem; and they were all scattered throughout the region of Judea and Samaria, except the apostles. ²Devout men buried Stephen, and made great lamentation over him. ³But Saul laid waste the church, and entering house after house, he dragged off men and women and committed them to prison.

Jn 16:2
Acts 7:58;
11:19; 26:10

Acts 9:1; 22:4
Gal 1:13
1 Cor 15:9
1 Tim 1:13

---

¹Saulus autem erat consentiens neci eius. Facta est autem in illa die persecutio magna in ecclesiam quae erat Hierosolymis; et omnes dispersi sunt per regiones Iudeae et Samariae praeter apostolos. ²Sepelierunt autem Stephanum viri timorati et fecerunt planctum magnum super illum. ³Saulus vero devastabat ecclesiam per domos intrans et trahens viros ac mulieres tradebat in custodiam.

---

1. Stephen's death signals the start of a violent persecution of the Christian community and Hellenist members in particular.

A new situation has been created. "Far from diminishing the boldness of the disciples, Stephen's death increased it. Christians were scattered precisely in order to spread the word further afield" (Chrysostom, *Hom. on Acts*, 18). This scattering of the disciples is not simply flight from danger. It originates in danger, but they avail of it to serve God and the Gospel. "Flight, so far from implying cowardice, requires often greater courage than not to flee. It is a great trial of heart. Death is an end of all trouble; he who flees is ever expecting death, and dies daily. [. . .] Exile is full of miseries. The after- conduct of the saints showed they had not fled for fear. [. . .] How would the Gospel ever have been preached throughout the world, if the Apostles had not fled? And, since their time, those, too, who have become martyrs, at first fled; or, if they advanced to meet their persecutors, it was by some secret suggestion of the Divine Spirit. But, above all, while these instances abundantly illustrate the rule of duty in persecution, and the temper of mind necessary in those who observe it, we have that duty itself declared in a plain precept by no other than our Lord: 'When they shall persecute you in this city,' He says, 'flee into another'" (John Henry Newman, *Historical Sketches*, II, 7).

Philip's preaching in Samaria

⁴Now those who were scattered went about preaching the word. ⁵Philip went down to a city of Samaria, and proclaimed

---

⁴Igitur qui dispersi erant, pertransierunt evangelizantes verbum. ⁵Philippus autem descendens in civitatem Samariae praedicabat illis Christum.

---

4. "Observe how, in the middle of misfortune, the Christians keep up their preaching instead of neglecting it" (Chrysostom, *Hom. on Acts*, 18) Misfortune plays its part in the spread of the Gospel. God's plans always exceed man's calculations and expectations. An apparently mortal blow for the Gospel in fact plays a decisive role in its spread. What comes from God cannot be destroyed; its adversaries in fact contribute to its consolidation and progress. "The religion founded by the mystery of the cross of Christ cannot be destroyed by any form of cruelty. The Church is not diminished by persecutions; on the contrary, they make for its increase. The field of the Lord is clothed in a richer harvest. When the grain which falls dies, it is reborn and multiplied" (St Leo the Great, *Hom. on the feast of St Peter and St Paul*).

The disciples are disconcerted to begin with, but then they begin to have a better understanding of God's providence. They may well have been reminded of Isaiah's words: "My thoughts are not your thoughts, neither are your ways my ways" (55:8), and of the promises of a heavenly Father, who arranges all events to the benefit of his elect.

The different periods of Church history show certain similarities, and difficulties caused by hidden or overt enemies never create totally new situations. Christians always have good reason to be optimistic—with an optimism based on faith, self-sacrifice and prayer. "Christianity has been too often in what seemed deadly peril that we should fear for it any new trial now. So far is certain; on the other hand, what is uncertain [. . .] is the particular mode by which, in the event, Providence rescues and saves His elect inheritance. Sometimes our enemy is turned into a friend; sometimes he is despoiled of that special virulence of evil which was so threatening; sometimes he falls to pieces himself; sometimes he does just so much as is beneficial, and then is removed. Commonly the Church has nothing more to do than to go on in her own proper duties, in confidence and peace; to stand still and to see the salvation of God" (J. H. Newman, *Biglietto Speech*, 1879).

Those who do not know Christ may resist the Gospel, but that resistance makes good Christians spiritually stronger and helps to purify the Church. "The storm of persecution is good. What is the loss? What is already lost cannot be lost. When the tree is not torn up by the roots—and there is no wind or hurricane that can uproot the tree of the Church—only the dry branches fall. And they ... are well fallen" (J. Escrivá, *The Way*, 685).

5. This is not Philip the Apostle (1:13) but one of the seven deacons

to them the Christ. ⁶And the multitudes with one accord gave heed to what was said by Philip, when they heard him and saw the signs which he did. ⁷For unclean spirits came out of many who were possessed, crying with a loud voice; and many who were paralyzed or lame were healed. ⁸So there was much joy in that city.

Mt 8:29
Mk 16:17

Jn 4:38-41

Simon the magician

⁹But there was a man named Simon who had previously practised magic in the city and amazed the nation of Samaria,

---

⁶Intendebant autem turbae his, quae a Philippo dicebantur, unanimiter, audientes et videntes signa, quae faciebat: ⁷ex multis enim eorum, qui habebant spiritus immundos clamantes voce magna exibant; multi autem paralytici et claudi curati sunt. ⁸Factum est autem magnum gaudium in illa civitate. ⁹Vir autem quidem nomine Simon iampridem erat in civitate magias faciens et

---

appointed to look after Christians in need (6:5). The Gospel is proclaimed to the Samaritans—who also were awaiting the Messiah. This means that it now spreads beyond the borders of Judea once and for all, and our Lord's promise (Acts 1:8) is fulfilled: "you shall be my witnesses in Jerusalem and in all Judea and Samaria."

The despised Samaritans became the first to benefit from the Gospel's determination to spread all over the world. We can sense St Luke's pleasure in reporting its proclamation to the Samaritans; earlier he already showed them in a favourable light: he is the only evangelist to recount the parable of the Good Samaritan (cf. Lk 10:30-37) and to mention that the leper who came back to thank Jesus after being cured was a Samaritan (cf. Lk 17:16). On the Samaritans in general, see the note on Jn 4:20.

6-13. Simon the magician is an imposter who pretends to have spiritual powers and who trades on the credulity and superstition of his audience.

St Luke uses this episode to show the difference between the genuine miracles performed by the Apostles in the name of Jesus and using Jesus' authority, and the real or apparent wonders worked by a charlatan: "As in the time of Moses, so now the distinction is made between different kinds of prodigies. Magic was practised, but it was easy to see the difference between it and genuine miracles. [. . .] Unclean spirits, in great numbers, went out of possessed people, protesting as they went. This showed that they were being expelled. Those who practised magic did just the opposite: they reinforced the bonds that bound the possessed" (Chrysostom, *Hom. on Acts*, 18).

The power which Peter and John have is different from Simon Magus'. Further on (vv. 15-17), St Luke contrasts the magician and his desire to make

saying that he himself was somebody great. ¹⁰They all gave heed to him, from the least to the greatest, saying, "This man is that power of God which is called Great." ¹¹And they gave heed to him, because for a long time he had amazed them

Mt 28:19

with his magic. ¹²But when they believed Philip as he preached good news of the kingdom of God and the name of Jesus Christ, they were baptized, both men and women. ¹³Even Simon himself believed, and after being baptized he continued with Philip. And seeing signs and great miracles performed, he was amazed.

---

dementans gentem Samariae, dicens esse se aliquem magnum, ¹⁰cui attendebant omnes a minimo usque ad maximum dicentes: "Hic est virtus Dei, quae vocatur Magna". ¹¹Attendebant autem eum propter quod multo tempore magiis dementasset eos. ¹²Cum vero credidissent Philippo evangelizanti de regno Dei et nomine Iesu Christi, baptizabantur viri ac mulieres. ¹³Tunc Simon et ipse credidit, et cum baptizatus esset, adhaerebat Philippo; videns etiam signa et virtutes magnas fieri stupens admirabatur. ¹⁴Cum autem audissent apostoli, qui erant Hierosolymis, quia recepit Samaria verbum Dei, miserunt ad illos Petrum

---

money, and the Apostles who are themselves poor but who enrich others with the Spirit. The Apostles do not perform miracles through powers which they have in their personal control; they always perform them by virtue of God's power, which they obtain by means of prayer. The miracles which Christians work are accompanied by prayer and never involve conjuring or spells. Luke makes the same point when recounting the episodes of Elymas (13:6ff), the diviner in Philippi (16:16ff) and the sons of Sceva (19:13ff).

Magic (occultism) and superstition (attempting to obtain supernatural effects using methods which cannot produce them) are a symptom of debased religion. Man has a natural obligation to be religious—to seek God, worship him and atone to him for sin. However, natural religion needs to be corrected, purified and filled out by supernatural revelation, whereby God seeks man out, raises him up and guides him on his way. Left to its own devices, natural religion can easily deviate and become useless or even harmful.

10. "That power of God which is called Great": it is not very clear what this means. It may mean that the Samaritans called that divine power "the Great" which they regarded as being the strongest. Another interpretation is that the Greek adjective *megálê*, great, is not a Greek word, but a transcription of an Aramaic word meaning "Revealing". Whichever interpretation is correct, Simon Magus claimed to have this divine power.

Peter and John in Samaria

¹⁴Now when the apostles at Jerusalem heard that Samaria Acts 11:1-22
had received the word of God, they sent to them Peter and
John, ¹⁵who came down and prayed for them that they might Acts 2:38
receive the Holy Spirit; ¹⁶for it had not yet fallen on any of Acts 19:2-6
them, but they had only been baptized in the name of the
Lord Jesus. ¹⁷Then they laid their hands on them and they 1 Tim 4:14
received the Holy Spirit.

---

et Ioannem, ¹⁵qui cum descendissent, oraverunt pro ipsis, ut acciperent Spiritum
Sanctum; ¹⁶nondum enim super quemquam illorum venerat, sed baptizati
tantum erant in nomine Domini Iesu. ¹⁷Tunc imposuerunt manus super illos, et
accipiebant Spiritum Sanctum. ¹⁸Cum vidisset autem Simon quia per

---

14-17. Here we see the Apostles exercising through Peter and John the
authority they have over the entire Church. The two Apostles proceed to
confirm the disciples recently baptized by Philip: we may presume that in
addition to laying their hands on them to communicate the Holy Spirit, the
Apostles made sure that they had a correct grasp of the central points of the
Gospel message. At this time the Apostles constituted the spiritual centre of the
Church and took an active interest in ensuring that the new communities were
conscious of the links—doctrinal and affective—that united them to the mother
community in Jerusalem.

This passage bears witness to the existence of Baptism and the gift of the
Holy Spirit (or Confirmation) as two distinct sacramental rites. The most
important effects Christian Baptism has are the infusion of initial grace and the
remission of original sin and any personal sin; it is the first sacrament a person
receives, which is why it is called the "door of the Church".

There is a close connexion between Baptism and Confirmation, so much so
that in the early centuries of Christianity, Confirmation was administered
immediately after Baptism. There is a clear distinction between these two
sacraments of Christian initiation, which helps us understand the different
effects they have. A useful comparison is the difference, in natural life, between
conception and later growth (cf. *St Pius V Catechism*, II, 3, 5). "As nature
intends that all her children should grow up and attain full maturity [. . .], so
the Catholic Church, the common mother of all, earnestly wishes that, in those
whom she has regenerated by Baptism, the perfection of Christian manhood be
completed" (*ibid.*, II, 3, 17).

"The nature of the sacrament of Confirmation," John Paul II explains, "grows
out of this endowment of strength which the Holy Spirit communicates to each
baptized person, to make him or her—as the well-known language of the
Catechism puts it—a perfect Christian and soldier of Christ, ready to witness
boldly to his resurrection and its redemptive power: 'You shall be my

The sin of Simon

Mt 10:8

Heb 12:15

Deut 29:17

[18]Now when Simon saw that the Spirit was given through the laying on of the apostles' hands, he offered them money, [19]saying, "Give me also this power, that any one on whom I lay my hands may receive the Holy Spirit." [20]But Peter said to him, "Your silver perish with you, because you thought you could obtain the gift of God with money! [21]You have neither part nor lot in this matter, for your heart is not right before God. [22]Repent therefore of this wickedness of yours, and pray to the Lord that, if possible, the intent of your heart may be forgiven you. [23]For I see that you are in the gall of bitterness and in the bond of iniquity." [24]And Simon answered, "Pray for me to the Lord, that nothing of what you have said may come upon me."

impositionem manum apostolorum daretur Spiritus, obtulit eis pecuniam [19]dicens: "Date et mihi hanc potestatem, ut cuicumque imposuero manum, accipiat Spiritum Sanctum." [20]Petrus autem dixit ad eum: "Argentum tuum tecum sit in perditionem, quoniam domum Dei existimasti pecunia possideri! [21]Non est tibi pars neque sors in verbo isto, cor enim tuum non est rectum coram Deo. [22]Paenitentiam itaque age ab hac nequitia tua et roga Dominum, si forte remittatur tibi haec cogitatio cordis tui; [23]in felle enim amaritudinis et obligatione iniquitatis video te esse." [24] Respondens autem Simon dixit:

witnesses'" (Acts 1:8)" (*Homily*, 25 May 1980). "All Christians, incorporated into Christ and his Church by Baptism, are consecrated to God. They are called to profess the faith which they have received. By the sacrament of Confirmation they are further endowed by the Holy Spirit with special strength to be witnesses of Christ and sharers in his mission of salvation" (*Homily in Limerick*, 1 October 1979). "This is a sacrament which in a special way associates us with the mission of the Apostles, in that it inserts each baptized person into the apostolate of the Church" (*Homily in Cracow*, 10 June 1979). In the sacrament of Confirmation divine grace anticipates the aggressive and demoralizing temptations a young Christian man or woman is likely to experience, and reminds them of the fact that they have a vocation to holiness; it makes them feel more identified with the Church, their Mother, and helps them live in accordance with their Catholic beliefs and convictions. From their formative years Christ makes them defenders of the faith.

18-24. Simon's disgraceful proposition—offering the Apostles money in exchange for the power to transmit the Holy Spirit—gave rise to the term "simony", that is, trading in sacred things. Simony is the sin of buying or selling, in exchange for money or some other temporal thing, something spiritual—a

²⁵Now when they had testified and spoken the word of the
Lord, they returned to Jerusalem, preaching the gospel to
many villages of the Samaritans.

Philip baptizes a eunuch

²⁶But an angel of the Lord said to Philip, "Rise and go
toward the south^g to the road that goes down from Jerusalem

"Precamini vos pro me ad Domimum, ut nihil veniat super me horum, quae
dixistis." ²⁵Et illi quidem testificati et locuti verbum Domini, redibant
Hierosolymam, et multis vicis Samaritanorum evangelizabant. ²⁶Angelus
autem Domini locutus est ad Philippum dicens: "Surge et vade contra

---

sacrament, an indulgence, a ecclesiastical office, etc. It is sinful because it
degrades something supernatural, which is essentially a free gift, by using it
unlawfully to obtain material benefit.

However, there is no simony involved in ministers of sacred worship
accepting reasonable alms, in cash or kind, for their maintenance. Jesus teaches
that the Apostle deserves to receive wages (cf. Lk 10:7), and St Paul says that
those who proclaim the Gospel should get their living from it (cf. 1 Cor 9:14).
An example of valid earnings is the alms or stipend given to a minister to say
Mass for one's intention: it is not given as payment for spiritual benefit, but as
a contribution to the priest's keep.

The Church has striven and warned against its ministers falling into the sin
of simony (cf. 1 Pet 5:2; 2 Pet 2:3), often recalling what our Lord said to his
disciples in this connexion: "Heal the sick, raise the dead, cleanse lepers, cast
out demons. You have received without pay, give without pay" (Mt 10:8), and
particularly setting before them the wonderful example Jesus himself gave, in
the way he lived and in the manner of his death.

Our Lord has left us a supreme example of disinterest and uprightness of
intention in the service of men—by living and dying on our behalf, asking
nothing in exchange except the just response his love merits.

A pastor of souls would be guilty of a serious sin if through his ministry he
sought financial gain, social prestige, esteem, honours or political leadership.
Instead of being a pastor he would be a mercenary, a hireling, who in time of
real danger would only think of himself, leaving the faithful to fend for
themselves (cf. Jn 10:12).

26-40. The baptism of the Ethiopian official marks an important step in the
spread of Christianity. St Luke's account underlines the importance of Sacred
Scripture, and its correct interpretation, in the work of evangelization. This
episode encapsulates the various stages in apostolate: Christ's disciple is moved

^gOr at noon

101

to Gaza." This is a desert road. [27]And he rose and went. And behold, an Ethiopian, a eunuch, a minister of Candace the queen of the Ethiopians, in charge of all her treasure, had come to Jerusalem to worship [28]and was returning; seated in his chariot, he was reading the prophet Isaiah. [29]And the Spirit said to Philip, "Go up and join this chariot." [30]So Philip

---

meridianum ad viam, quae descendit ab Ierusalem in Gazam; haec est deserta." [27]Et surgens abiit; et ecce vir Aethiops eunuchus potens Candacis reginae Aethiopum, qui erat super omnem gazam eius, qui venerat adorare in Ierusalem [28]et revertebatur sedens super currum suum et legebat prophetam Isaiam. [29]Dixit autem Spiritus Philippo: "Accede et adiunge te ad currum istum". [30]Accurrens autem Phillipus audivit illum legentem Isaiam prophetam et dixit:

---

by the Spirit (v.29) and readily obeys his instruction; he bases his preaching on Sacred Scripture—as Jesus did in the case of the disciples of Emmaus—and then administers Baptism.

27. Ethiopia: the kingdom of Nubia, whose capital was Meroe, to the south of Egypt, below Aswan, the first cataract on the Nile (part of modern Sudan). Candace, or Kandake, is not the name of an individual; it was the dynastic name of the queens of that country, a country at that time ruled by women (cf. Eusebius, *Ecclesiastical History*, II, 1, 13).

The term "eunuch", like its equivalent in Hebrew, was often used independently of its original physiological meaning and could refer to any court official (cf. for example, Gen 39:1; 2 Kings 25:19). This particular man was an important official, the equivalent of a minister of finance. We do not know if he was a member of the Jewish race, a proselyte (a Jew not by race but by religion) or—perhaps—a God-fearer (cf. note on Acts 2:5-11).

28. "Consider," St John Chrysostom says, "what a good thing it is not to neglect reading Scripture even when one is on a journey. . . . Let those reflect on this who do not even read the Scriptures at home, and, because they are with their wife, or are fighting in the army, or are very involved in family or other affairs, think that there is no particular need for them to make the effort to read the divine Scriptures. [. . .] This Ethiopian has something to teach us all—those who have a family life, members of the army, officials, in a word, all men, and women too (particularly those women who are always at home), and all those who have chosen the monastic way of life. Let all learn that no situation is an obstacle to reading the word of God: this is something one can do not only when one is alone at home but also in the public square, on a journey, in the company of others, or when engaged in one's occupation. Let us not, I implore you, neglect to read the Scriptures" (St John Chrysostom, *Hom. on Acts*, 35).

29-30. The fact that they are alone, that the road is empty, makes it easier

ran to him, and heard him reading Isaiah the prophet, and
asked, "Do you understand what you are reading?" ³¹And he
said, "How can I, unless some one guides me?" And he
invited Philip to come up and sit with him. ³²Now the passage
of the scripture which he was reading was this:

"As a sheep led to the slaughter
or a lamb before its shearer is dumb,
so he opens not his mouth.
³³In his humiliation justice was denied him.

Rom 10:14

Is 53:7-8
Lk 18:31

"Putasne intellegis, quae legis?" ³¹Qui ait: "Et quomodo possum, si non aliquis
ostenderit mihi?" Rogavitque Philippum, ut ascenderet et sederet secum.
³²Locus autem Scripturae, quem legebat, erat hic: "Tamquam ovis ad
occisionem ductus est et sicut agnus coram tondente se sine voce, sic non aperit
os suum. ³³In humilitate eius iudicium eius sublatum est. Generationem illius

---

for them to have a deep conversation and easier for Philip to explain Christian
teaching. "I think so highly of your devotion to the early Christians that I will
do all I can to encourage it, so that you—like them—will put more enthusiasm
each day into that effective Apostolate of discretion and friendship" (J. Escrivá,
The Way, 971). This was in fact one of the characteristic features of the kind
of apostolate carried out by our first brothers and sisters in the faith as they
spread gradually all over the Roman empire. They brought the Christian
message to the people around them—the sailor to the rest of the crew, the slave
to his fellow slaves, soldiers, traders, housewives. . . . This eager desire of theirs
to spread the Gospel showed their genuine conviction and was an additional
proof of the truth of the Christian message.

31. "How can I understand it, unless some one guides me?": to a Jew of this
period the very idea of a Messiah who suffers and dies at the hands of his
enemies was quite repugnant. This explains why the Ethiopian has difficulty
in understanding this passage—and, indeed, the entire song of the Servant of
Yahweh, from which it comes (cf. Is 53).
Sometimes it is difficult to understand a passage of Scripture; as St Jerome
comments: "I am not," to speak in passing of himself, "more learned or more
holy than that eunuch who travelled to the temple from Ethiopia, that is, from
the end of the earth: he left the royal palace and such was his desire for divine
knowledge that he was even reading the sacred words in his chariot. And yet
. . . he did not realize whom he was venerating in that book without knowing
it. Philip comes along, he reveals to him Jesus hidden and as it were imprisoned
in the text [. . .], and in that very moment he believes, is baptized, is faithful
and holy. [. . .] I tell you this to show you that, unless you have a guide who
goes ahead of you to show you the way, you cannot enter the holy Scriptures"
(*Letter 53*, 5-6).

Who can describe his generation?
For his life is taken up from the earth."
³⁴And the eunuch said to Philip, "About whom, pray, does
the prophet say this, about himself or about some one else?"

Lk 24:27
Acts 10:47;
11:17

³⁵Then Philip opened his mouth, and beginning with this
scripture he told him the good news of Jesus. ³⁶And as they

---

quis enarrabit? Quoniam tollitur de terra vita eius." ³⁴Respondens autem
eunuchus Philippo dixit: "Obsecro te, de quo propheta dicit hoc? De se an de
alio aliquo?" ³⁵Aperiens autem Philippus os suum et incipiens a Scriptura ista,
evangelizavit illi Iesum. ³⁶Et dum irent per viam, venerunt ad quandam aquam,

---

This guide is the Church; God, who inspired the sacred books, has entrusted
their interpretation to the Church. Therefore, the Second Vatican Council
teaches that "If we are to derive their true meaning from the sacred texts,"
attention must be devoted "not only to their content but to the unity of the whole
of Scripture, the living tradition of the entire Church, and the analogy of faith.
[. . .] Everything to do with the interpretation of Scripture is ultimately subject
to the judgment of the Church, which exercises the divinely conferred
communion and ministry of watching over and interpreting the Word of God"
(Vatican II, *Dei Verbum*, 12).

35. "The eunuch deserves our admiration for his readiness to believe," St
John Chrysostom comments. "He has not seen Jesus Christ nor has he witnessed
any miracle; what then is the reason for his change? It is because, being
observant in matters of religion, he applies himself to the study of the sacred
books and makes them his book of meditation and reading" (*Hom. on Acts*, 19).

36. "What is to prevent my being baptized?": the Ethiopian's question
reminds us of the conditions necessary for receiving Baptism. Adults should
be instructed in the faith before receiving this sacrament; however, a period of
"Christian initiation" is not required if there is a good reason, such as danger
of death.

The Church's Magisterium stresses the obligation to baptize children without
delay. "The fact that children are incapable of making a personal profession of
faith does not deter the Church from conferring this sacrament on them; what
it does is baptize them in its own faith. This teaching was already clearly
expressed by St Augustine: 'Children are presented for the reception of spiritual
grace, not so much by those who carry them in their arms—although also by
them, if they are good members of the Church—as by the universal society of
saints and faithful. [. . .] It is Mother Church herself who acts in her saints,
because the whole Church begets each and all' (*Letter 98*, 5; cf. *Sermon 176*,
2). St Thomas Aquinas, and after him most theologians, take up the same
teaching: the child who is baptized does not believe for itself, by a personal act
of faith, but rather through others 'by the faith of the Church which is

went along the road they came to some water, and the eunuch said, "See, here is water! What is to prevent my being baptized?"ʰ ³⁸And he commanded the chariot to stop, and they both went down into the water, Philip, and the eunuch, and he baptized him. ³⁹And when they came up out of the

1 Kings 18:12
Lk 24:31-32

et ait eunuchus: "Ecce aqua; quid prohiber me baptizari?" ⁽³⁷⁾ ³⁸Et iussit stare currum, et descenderunt uterque in aquam Philippus et eunuchus, et baptizavit eum. ³⁹Cum autem ascendissent de aqua, Spiritus Domini rapuit Philippum, et

communicated to the child' (*Summa theologiae*, III, q.69, a.6, ad 3; cf. q. 68, a. 9, ad 3). This same teaching is expressed in the new rite of Baptism, when the celebrant asks the parents and godparents to profess the faith of the Church 'in which the children are being baptized'" (*Instruction on Infant Baptism*, 20 October 1980).

The Instruction goes on to say that "it is true that apostolic preaching is normally addressed to adults, and that the first to be baptized were adults who had been converted to the Christian faith. From what we read in the New Testament we might be led to think that it deals only with adults' faith. However, the practice of Baptism of infants is based on an ancient tradition of apostolic origin, whose value must not be underestimated; furthermore, Baptism has never been administered without faith: in the case of infants the faith that intervenes is the Church's own faith. Besides, according to the Council of Trent's teaching on the sacraments, Baptism is not only a sign of faith: it is also the cause of faith" (*ibid.*).

Christian parents have a duty to see that their children are baptized quickly. The *Code of Canon Law* specifies that "parents are obliged to see that their infants are baptized within the first few weeks. As soon as possible after the birth, indeed often before it, they are to approach the parish priest to ask for the sacrament for their child, and to be themselves duly prepared for it" (can. 867).

37. This verse, not to be found in some Greek codexes or in the better translations, was probably a gloss which later found its way into the text. In the Vulgate it is given in this way: "Dixit autem Philippus: Si credis ex toto corde, licet. Et respondens ait: Credo, Filium Dei esse Jesum Christum", which translated would be: "Philip said, If you believe with all your heart, you may. And he replied, I believe that Jesus Christ is the Son of God." This very ancient gloss, inspired by baptismal liturgy, helps to demonstrate that faith in Christ's divine worship was the nucleus of the creed a person had to subscribe to in order to be baptized. On this occasion Philip, guided by the Holy Spirit, lays down no further condition and he immediately proceeds to baptize the Ethiopian.

39. St John Chrysostom pauses to note that the Spirit takes Philip away

ʰOther ancient authorities add all or most of verse 37, And Philip said, *"If you believe with all your heart, you may."* And he replied, *"I believe that Jesus Christ is the Son of God."*

water, the Spirit of the Lord caught up Philip; and the eunuch saw him no more, and went on his way rejoicing. [40]But Philip was found at Azotus, and passing on he preached the gospel to all the towns till he came to Caesarea.

9

THE CONVERSION OF ST PAUL

Acts 22:5-16;
26:10-18
Gal 1:12-17

Saul on his way to Damascus

[1]But Saul, still breathing threats and murder against the

---

amplius non vidit eum eunuchus; ibat autem per viam suam gaudens.
[40]Philippus autem inventus est in Azoto et pentransiens evangelizabat civitatibus cunctis, donec venirer Caesaream.
[1]Saulus autem, adhuc spirans minarum et caedis in discipulos Domini, accessit

---

without giving him time to rejoice with the man he has just baptized: "Why did the Spirit of the Lord bear him away? Because he had to go on to preach in other cities. We should not be surprised that this happened in a divine rather than a human way" (*Hom. on Acts*, 19).

The official "went on his way rejoicing" that God had made him his son through Baptism. He had received the gift of faith, and with the help of divine grace he was ready to live up to all the demands of that faith, even in adverse circumstances: quite probably he would be the only Christian in all Ethiopia.

Faith is a gift of God and is received as such at Baptism; but man's response is necessary if this gift is not to prove fruitless.

Baptism is one of the sacraments which imprints an indelible mark on the soul and which can be received only once. However, a baptized person needs to be continually renewing his commitment; this is not something to be done only during the Easter liturgy: in his everyday activity he should be striving to act like a son of God.

It is natural and logical for the Ethiopian to be so happy, for Baptism brings with it many graces. These St John Chrysostom lists, using quotations from the Gospels and from the letters of St Paul: "The newly baptized are free, holy, righteous, sons of God, heirs of heaven, brothers and co-heirs of Christ, members of his body, temples of God, instruments of the Holy Spirit. . . . Those who yesterday were captives are today free men and citizens of the Church. Those who yesterday were in the shame of sin are now safe in righteousness; not alone are they free, they are holy" (*Baptismal Catechesis*, III, 5).

1-3. The Roman authorities recognized the moral authority of the Sanhedrin

disciples of the Lord, went to the high priest ²and asked him for letters to the synagogues at Damascus, so that if he found any belonging to the Way, men or women, he might bring them bound to Jerusalem. ³Now as he journeyed he

---

ad principem sacerdotum ²et petiit ab eo epistulas in Damascum ad synagogas, ut si quos invenisset huius viae, viros ac mulieres, vinctos perduceret in Ierusalem. ³Et cum iter faceret, contigit ut appropinquaret Damasco, et subito

---

and even permitted it to exercise a certain jurisdiction over members of Jewish communities outside Palestine—as was the case with Damascus. The Sanhedrin even had the right to extradite Jews to Palestine (cf. 1 Mac 15:21).

Damascus was about 230-250 kilometres (150 miles) from Jerusalem, depending on which route one took. Saul and his associates, who would probably have been mounted, would have had no difficulty in doing the journey in under a week. This apparition took place towards the end of the journey, when they were near Damascus.

2. "The Way": the corresponding word in Hebrew also means religious behaviour. Here it refers to both Christian lifestyle and the Gospel itself; indirectly it means all the early followers of Jesus (cf. Acts 18:25f; 19:9, 23; 22:4) and all those who come after them and are on the way to heaven; it reminds us of Jesus' words, "The gate is narrow and the way is hard, that leads to life, and those who find it are few" (Mt 7:14).

3-19. This is the first of the three accounts of the calling of Saul—occurring probably between the years 34 and 36—that are given in the Acts of the Apostles (cf. Acts 22:5-16; 26:10-18); where important events are concerned, St Luke does not mind repeating himself. Once again the Light shines in the darkness (cf. Jn 1:5). It does so here in a spectacular way and, as in every conversion, it makes the convert see God, himself and others in a new way.

However, the episode on the road to Damascus is not only a conversion. It marks the beginning of St Paul's vocation: "What amazes you seems natural to me: that God has sought you out in the practice of your profession!

"This is how he sought the first, Peter and Andrew, James and John, beside their nets, and Matthew, sitting in the custom-house.

"And—wonder of wonders!—Paul, in his eagerness to destroy the seed of the Christians" (J. Escrivá, *The Way*, 799).

The background to St Luke's concise account is easy to fill in. There would have been no Hellenist Christians left in Jerusalem: they had fled the city, some going as far afield as Phoenicia, Cyprus and Antioch. Many had sought refuge in Damascus, and Saul must have realized that their evangelizing zeal would win many converts among faithful Jews in that city. Saul genuinely wanted to serve God, which explains his readiness to respond to grace. Like most Jews of his time, he saw the Messiah as a political liberator, a warrior-king, a

1 Cor 15:8

approached Damascus, and suddenly a light from heaven flashed about him. [4]And he fell to the ground and heard a voice saying to him, "Saul, Saul, why do you persecute me?" [5]And he said, "Who are you, Lord?" And he said, "I am Jesus,

---

circumfulsit eum lux de caelo, [4]et cadens in terram audivit vocem dicentem sibi: "Saul Saul, quid me persequeris?" [5]Qui dixit: "Quis es, Domine?" Et ille:

---

half-heavenly, half-earthly figure such as described in the apocryphal *Book of Enoch*, 46: "It is impossible to imagine how even his glance terrifies his enemies. Wherever he turns, everything trembles; wherever his voice reaches everything is overwhelmed and those who hear it are dissolved as wax in fire." A hero of this type does not fall into the power of his enemies, much less let them crucify him; on the contrary, he is a victor, he annihilates his enemies and establishes an everlasting kingdom of peace and justice. For Saul, Jesus' death on a cross was clear proof that he was a false messiah; and the whole notion of a brotherhood of Jews and Gentiles was inconceivable.

He has almost reached Damascus when a light flashes; he is thrown onto the ground and hears a voice from heaven calling his name twice, in a tone of sad complaint.

Saul surrenders unconditionally and places himself at the Lord's service. He does not bemoan his past life; he is ready to start anew. No longer is the Cross a "scandal": it has become for him a sign of salvation, the "power of God", a throne of victory, whose praises he will sing in his epistles. Soon St Paul will learn more about this Way and about all that Jesus did and taught, but from this moment onwards, the moment of his calling, he realizes that Jesus is the risen Messiah, in whom the prophecies find fulfilment; he believes in the divinity of Christ: he sees how different his idea of the Messiah was from the glorified, pre-existing and eternal Son of God; he understands Christ's mystical presence in his followers: "Why do you persecute *me*?" In other words, he realizes that he has been chosen by God, called by God, and he immediately places himself at his service.

4. This identification of Christ and Christians is something which the Apostle will later elaborate on when he speaks of the mystical body of Christ (cf. Col 1:18; Eph 1:22f).

St Bede comments as follows: "Jesus does not say, 'Why do you persecute my members?', but, 'Why do you persecute me?', because he himself still suffers affronts in his body, which is the Church. Similarly Christ will take account of the good actions done to his members, for he said, 'I was hungry and you gave me food . . .' (Mt 25:35), and explaining these words he added, 'As you did it to one of the least of these my brethren, you did it to me' (Mt 25:40)" (*Super Act. expositio, ad loc.*).

5-6. In the Vulgate and in many other translations these words are added

whom you are persecuting; ⁶but rise and enter the city, and
you will be told what you are to do." ⁷The men who were   Dan 10:7

"Ego sum Iesus, quem tu persequeris! ⁶Sed surge et ingredere civitatem, et
dicetur tibi quid te oporteat facere." ⁷Viri autem illi, qui comitabantur cum eo,

between the end of v. 5 and the start of v. 6: "It is hard for thee to kick against
the goad. And he, trembling and astonished, said: Lord, what wilt thou have
me to do? And the Lord said to him". These words do not seem to be part of
the original sacred text but rather a later explanatory gloss; for this reason the
New Vulgate omits them. (The first part of the addition comes from Paul's
address in Acts 26:14.)

6. The calling of Saul was exceptional as regards the manner in which God
called him; but the effect it had on him was the same as what happens when
God gives a specific calling to the apostolate to certain individual Christians,
inviting them to follow him more closely. Paul's immediate response is a model
of how those who receive these specific callings should act (all Christians, of
course, have a common calling to holiness and apostolate that comes with
Baptism).

Paul VI describes in this way the effects of this specific kind of vocation in
a person's soul: "The apostolate is [. . .] an inner voice, which makes one both
restless and serene, a voice that is both gentle and imperious, troublesome and
affectionate, a voice which comes unexpectedly and with great events and then,
at a particular point, exercises a strong attraction, as it were revealing to us our
life and our destiny. It speaks prophetically and almost in a tone of victory,
which eventually dispels all uncertainty, all timidity and all fear, and which
facilitates—making it easy, desirable and pleasant—the response of our whole
personality, when we pronounce that word which reveals the supreme secret of
love: Yes; Yes, Lord, tell me what I must do and I will try to do it, I will do it.
Like St Paul, thrown to the ground at the gates of Damascus: What would you
have me do?

"The roots of the apostolate run deep: the apostolate is vocation, election,
interior encounter with Christ, abandonment of one's personal autonomy to his
will, to his invisible presence; it is a kind of substitution of our poor, restless
heart, inconstant and at times unfaithful yet hungry for love, for his heart, the
heart of Christ which is beginning to pulsate in the one who has been chosen.
And then comes the second act in the psychological drama of the apostolate:
the need to spread, to do, to give, to speak, to pass on to others one's own
treasure, one's own fire. [. . .]

"The apostolate becomes a continuous expansion of one's soul, the
exuberance of a personality taken over by Christ and animated by his Spirit; it
becomes a need to hasten, to work, to do everything one can to spread the
Kingdom of God, to save other souls, to save all souls" (*Homily*, 14 October
1968).

travelling with him stood speechless, hearing the voice but seeing no one. ⁸Saul arose from the ground; and when his eyes were opened, he could see nothing; so they led him by the hand and brought him into Damascus. ⁹And for three days he was without sight, and neither ate nor drank.

Ananias baptizes Saul

1 Sam 3:4 ¹⁰Now there was a disciple at Damascus called Ananias. The Lord said to him in a vision, "Ananias." And he said, "Here I am, Lord." ¹¹And the Lord said to him, "Rise and go to the street called Straight, and inquire in the house of Judas for a man of Tarsus named Saul; for behold, he is praying, ¹²and he has seen a man named Ananias come in and lay his hands on him so that he might regain his sight." ¹³But Ananias answered, "Lord, I have heard from many about this man, how much evil he has done to thy saints at Jerusalem; 1 Cor 1:2 ¹⁴and here he has authority from the chief priests to bind all

---

stabant stupefacti, audientes quidem vocem, neminem autem videntes. ⁸Surrexit autem Saulus de terra apertisque occulis nihil videbat; ad manus autem illum trahentes introduxerunt Damascum. ⁹Et erat tribus diebus non videns et non manducavit, neque bibit. ¹⁰Erat autem quidam discipulus Damasci nomine Ananias, et dixit ad illum in visu Dominus: "Anania!" At ille ait: "Ecce ego, Domine!" ¹¹Et Dominus ad illum: "Surgens vade in vicum, qui vocatur Rectus, et quaere in domo Iudae Saulum nomine Tarsensem; ecce enim orat ¹²et vidit virum Ananiam nomine introeuntem et imponentem sibi manus, ut visum recipiat." ¹³Respondit autem Ananias: "Domine, audivi a multis de viro hoc, quanta mala sanctis tuis fecerit in Ierusalem; ¹⁴et hic habet potestatem a principibus sacerdotum alligandi omnes, qui invocant nomen tuum." ¹⁵Dixit

---

8-11. Straight Street runs through Damascus from east to west and can still be identified today.

13. Ananias refers to Christ's followers as "saints"; this was the word normally used to describe the disciples, first in Palestine and then in the world at large. God is *the* Holy One (cf. Is 6:3); as the Old Testament repeatedly says, those who approach God and keep his commandments share in this holiness: "The Lord said to Moses, 'Say to all the congregation of the people of Israel, You shall be holy; for I the Lord your God am holy'" (Lev 19:1-2).

The use of this term is an example of the spiritual sensitivity of our first brothers and sisters in the faith: "What a moving name—saints!—the early Christians used to address each other! . . .

"Learn to be a brother to your brothers" (J. Escrivá, *The Way*, 469).

who call upon thy name." [15]But the Lord said to him, "Go, for he is a chosen instrument of mine to carry my name before the Gentiles and kings and the sons of Israel; [16]for I will show him how much he must suffer for the sake of my name." [17]So Ananias departed and entered the house. And laying his hands on him he said, "Brother Saul, the Lord Jesus who appeared to you on the road by which you came, has sent me that you may regain your sight and be filled with the Holy Spirit." [18]And immediately something like scales fell from his eyes and he regained his sight. Then he rose and was baptized, [19]and took food and was strengthened.

For several days he was with the disciples at Damascus.

1 Cor 4:9-13
2 Cor 11:23-28
2 Tim 3:11-12
Acts 15:8;
22:14-16

Tob 11:10-15

---

autem ad eum Dominus: "Vade, quoniam vas electionis est mihi iste, ut portet nomen meum coram gentibus et regibus et filiis Israel; [16]ego enim ostendam illi quanta oporteat eum pro nomine meo pati." [17]Et abiit Ananias et introivit in domum et imponens ei manus dixit: "Saul frater, Dominus misit me, Iesus qui apparuit tibi in via, qua veniebas, ut videas et implearis Spritu Sancto." [18]Et confestim ceciderunt ab oculis eius tamquam squamae, et visum recepit. Et surgens baptizatus est [19]et, cum accepisset cibum, confortatus est. Fuit autem

---

15-16. Our Lord calls St Paul his "vessel of election", which is a Hebraicism equivalent to "chosen instrument", and he tells Ananias how much the Apostle will have to suffer on his account. A Christian called to the apostolate is also, by virtue of this divine vocation, an instrument in the hands of God; to be effective he must be docile: he must let God use him and must do what God tells him.

The task God has given him is far beyond Paul's ability—"to carry my name before the Gentiles and kings and the sons of Israel". In Acts we will see how Paul fulfils his mission, with the help of God's grace and suffering a great deal on account of his name. Down through the centuries, in diverse circumstances, those whom the Lord elects to carry out specific missions will also be able to perform them if they are good instruments who allow grace to act in them and who are ready to suffer for their ideals.

19. In spite of the exceptional manner in which God called St Paul, he desired him to mature in the normal way— to be instructed by others and learn God's will through them. In this case he chose Ananias to confer Baptism on Paul and teach him the basics of the Christian faith.

In Ananias we can see a trace of the role of the spiritual director or guide in Christian asceticism. There is a principle which states that "no one can be a good judge in his own case, because everyone judges according to his own

Paul begins his apostolate

Gal 1:16 | 20And in the synagogues immediately he proclaimed Jesus, saying, "He is the Son of God." 21And all who heard him were amazed, and said, "Is not this the man who made havoc in Jerusalem of those who called on this name? And he has come here for this purpose to bring them bound before Acts 15:5, 28 | the chief priests." 22But Saul increased all the more in strength, and confounded the Jews who lived in Damascus by proving that Jesus was the Christ.

Paul flees from Damascus

23When many days had passed, the Jews plotted to kill

---

cum discipulis, qui erant Damasci, per dies aliquot 20et continuo in synagogis praedicabat Iesum, quoniam hic est Filius Dei. 21Stupebant autem omnes, qui audiebant et dicebant: "Nonne hic est, qui expugnabat in Ierusalem eos, qui invocabant nomen istud, et huc ad hoc venerat, ut vinctos illos duceret ad principes sacerdotum?" 22Saulus autem magis convalescebat et confundebat Iudaeos, qui habitabant Damasci, affirmans quoniam hic est Christus. 23Cum

---

inclinations" (cf. Cassian, *Collationes*, XVI, 11). A person guiding a soul has a special "grace of state" to make God's will known to him; and even if the guide makes a mistake, the person who is being guided will—if obedient—always do the right thing, always do God's will. In this connexion St Vincent Ferrer says: "Our Lord Jesus Christ, without whom we can do nothing, will not give his grace to him who, though he has access to an expert guide, rejects this precious means of sanctification, thinking that he can look after on his own everything that touches on his salvation. He who has a director, whom he obeys in everything, will reach his goal more easily and more quickly than if he acted as his own guide, even if he be very intelligent and have the very best of spiritual books" (*Treatise on the Spiritual Life*, 2, 1).

On the spiritual guidance of ordinary Christians, who seek holiness and carry out apostolate in the context of everyday life, Monsignor Escrivá, writes: "A Director. You need one. So that you can give yourself to God, and give yourself fully ... by obedience. A director who understands your apostolate, who knows what God wants: that way he will second the work of the Holy Spirit in your soul, without taking you from your place, filling you with peace, and teaching you how to make your work fruitful" (*The Way*, 62).

20-23. In his letter to the Galatians (cf. Gal 1:16f) St Paul tells of how he went into Arabia after his conversion and then returned to Damascus. He spent almost three years away, and it was on his return that he preached the divinity of Jesus, using all his energy and learning, now placed at the service of Christ.

him, ²⁴but their plot became known to Saul. They were 2 Cor 11:32-33 watching the gates day and night, to kill him; ²⁵but his disciples took him by night and let him down over the wall, lowering him in a basket.

Barnabas and Paul in Jerusalem

²⁶And when he had come to Jerusalem he attempted to join Gal 1:18f the disciples; and they were all afraid of him, for they did not believe that he was a disciple. ²⁷But Barnabas took him, and brought him to the apostles, and declared to them how on the road he had seen the Lord, who spoke to him, and how at Damascus he had preached boldly in the name of Jesus. ²⁸So he went in and out among them at Jerusalem, ²⁹preaching boldly in the name of the Lord. And he spoke and disputed against the Hellenists; but they were seeking to kill him.

---

implerentur autem dies multi, consilium fecerunt Iudaei, ut eum interficerent; ²⁴notae autem factae sunt Saulo insidiae eorum. Custodiebant autem et portas die ac nocte, ut eum interficerent; ²⁵accipientes autem discipuli eius nocte per murum dimiserunt eum submittentes in sporta. ²⁶Cum autem venisset in Ierusalem, tentabat iungere se discipulis; et omnes timebant eum, non credentes quia esset discipulus. ²⁷Barnabas autem apprehensum illum duxit ad apostolos, et narravit illis quomodo in via vidisset Dominum et quia locutus est ei, et quomodo in Damasco fiducialiter egerit in nomine Iesu. ²⁸Et erat cum illis intrans et exiens in Ierusalem, fiducialiter agens in nomine Domini. ²⁹Loquebatur quoque et disputabat cum Hellenistis; illi autem quarebant

---

This surprised and confounded the Jews, who immediately began to take action against him.

25. In 2 Corinthians 11:32f St Paul tells of how he fled, after King Aretas tried to seize him at the instigation of the Jews of Damascus.

26. This is the first time Paul presents himself in Jerusalem after his conversion. He went up to see Peter, with whom he spent fifteen days (cf. Gal 1:18), and put himself at Peter's disposal; and to check that his teaching was in line with that of the Apostles.

Barnabas (see note on 4:36) dispelled the Jerusalem community's initial understandable suspicion of their one-time persecutor. They had been only too well aware of his determination to suppress the Church and had not yet heard about his preaching in Damascus.

During his short stay in Jerusalem Paul preached boldly his faith in the divinity of Jesus and met the same kind of opposition as he did in Damascus.

Acts 11:25
Gal 1:21
³⁰And when the brethren knew it, they brought him down to Caesarea, and sent him off to Tarsus.

The growth of the Church

Acts 2:46
³¹So the church throughout all Judea and Galilee and Samaria had peace and was built up; and walking in the fear of the Lord and in the comfort of the Holy Spirit it was multiplied.

---

occidere eum. ³⁰Quod cum cognovissent, fratres deduxerunt eum Caesaream et dimiserunt Tarsum. ³¹Ecclesia quidem per totam Iudaeam et Galilaeam et Samariam habebat pacem, aedificabatur et ambulabat in timore Domini et

---

30. For the second time St Paul has to flee for his life. Commenting on this episode, St John Chrysostom explains that, in addition to grace, human resourcefulness has a part to play in apostolic activity. "The disciples were afraid that the Jews would do to Saul what they had done to St Stephen. This may be why they sent him to preach the Gospel in his homeland, where he would be safer. In this action of the Apostles you can see that God does not do everything directly, by means of his grace, and that he frequently lets his disciples act in line with the rule of prudence" (*Hom. on Acts*, 20).

Chrysostom also sees in Paul's earlier flight from Damascus an example of prudent conduct: "Despite his great desire to be with God, he first had to carry out his mission for the salvation of souls. [. . .] Jesus Christ does not preserve his Apostles from dangers: he lets them confront them, because he wants men to use the resources of prudence to escape from them. Why does he arrange things in this way? In order to have us understand that the Apostles are also men and that grace does not do everything in its servants. Otherwise, would people not have seen them as inert and lifeless things? That is why the Apostles did many things by following the dictates of prudence. Let us follow their example and use all our natural abilities to work with grace for the salvation of our brethren" (*ibid.*).

31. St Luke breaks his narrative to give an over-view of the steady progress of the Church as a whole and of the various communities that have grown up as a result of the Christians' flight from Jerusalem (cf. Acts 2:40, 47; 4:4; 5:14; 6:1, 7; 11:21, 24; 16:5). He emphasizes the peace and consolation the Holy Spirit has brought them. This note of justified optimism and trust in God confirms that God is with his Church and that no human force can destroy it (cf. 5:39).

ST PETER'S ACTIVITY

Peter cures a paralytic at Lydda

³²Now as Peter went here and there among them all, he Acts 8:4 came down also to the saints that lived at Lydda. ³³There he found a man named Aeneas, who had been bedridden for eight years and was paralyzed. ³⁴And Peter said to him, Acts 3:7 "Aeneas, Jesus Christ heals you; rise and make your bed." And immediately he rose. ³⁵And all the residents of Lydda and Sharon saw him, and they turned to the Lord.

---

consolatione Sancti Spiritus crescebat. ³²Factum est autem Petrum, dum pertransiret universos, devenire et ad sanctos, qui habitabant Lyddae. ³³Invenit autem ibi hominem quendam nomine Aeneam ab annis octo iacentem in grabato, qui erat paralyticus. ³⁴Et ait illi Petrus: "Aenea, sanat te Iesus Christus; surge et sterne tibi." Et continuo surrexit. ³⁵Et viderunt illum omnes, qui

---

32. Acts now turns to recount St Peter's apostolic activity in Palestine. Lydda (cf. 9:32-35), Joppa (cf. 9:36-43) and Maritime Caesarea (cf. 10:24-28; 12:19) were some of the cities in which the head of the Apostles preached the Good News.

"St Luke goes on to speak about Peter and his visits to the faithful. He does not want to give the impression that fear is the reason for Peter's leaving Jerusalem, and so he first gives an account of the situation of the Church, after indicating, previously, that Peter had stayed in Jerusalem during the persecution. [. . .] Peter acts like a general reviewing his troops to see that they are properly trained and in good order, and to discover where his presence is most needed. We see him going in all directions and we find him in all parts. If he makes this present journey it is because he thinks that the faithful are in need of his teaching and encouragement" (Chrysostom, *Hom. on Acts*, 21).

The last report Acts gives of St Peter deals with his intervention at the Council of Jerusalem (chap. 15).

33-35. St Peter takes the initiative; he does not wait for the paralyzed man to seek his help. We are told about the man being sick for eight years, to show how difficult he was to cure—and yet through the power of Jesus Christ he is cured "immediately". "Why did Peter not wait for the man to show his faith? Why did he not first ask him if he wanted to be cured? Surely because it was necessary to impress the people by means of this miracle" (Chrysostom, *Hom. on Acts*, 21). However, the conversion of the people of Lydda and Sharon was also the result of Peter's work: miracles are not designed to make life easier for the Apostles; their tireless preaching is by no means secondary or superfluous.

Peter raises Tabitha to life

Lk 12:33

³⁶Now there was at Joppa a disciple named Tabitha, which means Dorcas or Gazelle. She was full of good works and acts of charity. ³⁷In those days she fell sick and died; and when they had washed her, they laid her in an upper room. ³⁸Since Lydda was near Joppa, the disciples, hearing that Peter was there, sent two men to him entreating him, "Please come to us without delay." ³⁹So Peter rose and went with them. And when he had come, they took him to the upper room. All the widows stood beside him weeping, and showing coats and garments which Dorcas made while she was with them. ⁴⁰But Peter put them all outside and knelt down and prayed; then turning to the body he said, "Tabitha, rise." And she opened her eyes, and when she saw Peter she

Mk 5:40

---

inhabitabant Lyddam et Saron, qui conversi sunt ad Dominum. ³⁶In Ioppe autem erat quaedam discipula nomine Tabitha, quae interpretata dicitur Dorcas; haec erat plena operibus bonis et eleemosynis, quas faciebat. ³⁷Factum est autem in diebus illis ut infirmata moreretur; quam cum lavissent posuerunt in cenaculo. ³⁸Cum autem prope esset Lydda ab Ioppe, discipuli audientes quia Petrus esset in ea, miserunt duos viros ad eum rogantes: "Ne pigriteris venire usque ad nos!" ³⁹Exsurgens autem Petrus venit cum illis; et cum advenisset, duxerunt illum in cenaculum et circumsteterunt illum omnes viduae flentes et ostendentes tunicas et vestes, quas faciebat Dorcas, cum esset cum illis. ⁴⁰Eiectis autem omnibus

---

36-43. Joppa (Jaffa, today virtually part of Tel Aviv) is mentioned in the writings of Tell-el-Amarna where it is called Iapu. Its people were converted to Judaism in the time of Simon Maccabeus (*c.* 140 B.C.).

The miracle of the raising of Tabitha by Peter is the first one of its kind reported in Acts. Here, as in the Gospel, miracles are performed to awaken faith in those who witness them with good dispositions and a readiness to believe. In this case the miracle is a kindness God shows Tabitha to reward her virtues, and an encouragement to the Christians of Joppa.

"In the Acts of the Apostles," St Cyprian writes, "it is clear that alms not only free us from spiritual death, but also from temporal death. Tabitha, a woman who did many 'good works and acts of charity,' had taken ill and died: and Peter was sent for. No sooner had he arrived, with all the diligence of his apostolic charity, than he was surrounded by widows in tears . . . , praying for the dead woman more by gestures than by words. Peter believed that he could obtain what they were asking for so insistently and that Christ's help would be available in answer to the prayers of the poor in whose persons He himself had been clothed. [. . .] And so it was: he did come to Peter's aid, to whom he had

sat up. ⁴¹And he gave her his hand and lifted her up. Then calling the saints and widows he presented her alive. ⁴²And it became known throughout all Joppa, and many believed in the Lord. ⁴³And he stayed in Joppa for many days with one Simon, a tanner.

Lk 7:15
Acts 3:7

Acts 10:6

10

The vision of the centurion Cornelius

¹At Caesarea there was a man named Cornelius, a centurion of what was known as the Italian Cohort, ²a devout man who

Lk 7:5

---

foras Petrus, et ponens genua oravit et conversus ad corpus dixit: "Tabitha, surge!" At illa aperuit oculos suos et, viso Petro, resedit. ⁴¹Dans autem illi manum erexit eam, et cum vocasset sanctos et viduas exhibuit eam vivam. ⁴²Notum autem factum est per universam Ioppen, et crediderunt multi in Domino. ⁴³Factum est autem ut dies multos moraretur in Ioppe apud quemdam Simonem coriarium.

¹Vir autem quidam in Caesarea nomine Cornelius, centurio cohortis, quae dicitur Italica, ²religiosus et timens Deum cum omni domo sua, faciens

---

said in the Gospel that he would grant everything asked for in his name. For this reason he stops the course of death and the woman returns to life, and to the amazement of all she revives, restoring her risen body to the light of day. Such was the power of works of mercy, of good deeds" (*De opere et eleemosynis*, 6).

43. Tanning was a permitted trade, but observant Jews regarded it as unclean because it involved contact with dead animals (cf. Lev 11:39: "If any animal of which you may eat dies, he who touches its carcass shall be unclean until the evening").

By staying with Simon the tanner, St Peter shows that these Jewish prohibitions and standards no longer oblige in conscience. The freedom of the Gospel takes over and the only reason why one might sometimes observe them would be out of charity, to avoid giving scandal.

1-48. The conversion of the pagan Cornelius is one of the high points of Acts. It is an extremely important event because it demonstrates the fact that the Gospel is addressed to all men and shows that the power of the Holy Spirit knows no limits.

Up to this point the Gospel has been preached only to Jews. Its extension to the Samaritans was seen as an announcement of salvation to people who had at one time formed part of the chosen people. By preaching only to Jews, the disciples were having regard to the fact that the people of Israel was the only people chosen by God to be bearers of the divine promises: as such, they had a right to be the first to receive the definitive message of salvation. Our Lord himself had acted on this principle, and he had told his disciples to preach only "to the lost sheep of the house of Israel" (Mt 10:6; cf. 15:24).

The Apostles had not yet asked themselves whether this preferential right of the Jewish people to receive the Gospel proclamation implied a certain exclusive right. Now God steps in to make Peter realize that the Good News is meant for all: it is his desire that all men be saved and therefore the Christians need to shed the narrow ideas of Judaism as regards the scope of salvation.

Peter is surprised to learn this, but he is completely docile to the voice of God and now begins to play an active part in the fulfilment of the divine promises. "God had previously foretold", St Cyprian writes, "that in the fulness of time much more faithful worshippers would adhere to him, people from every nation, race and city; that they would receive mercy through the divine gifts which the Jews had lost through not appreciating their own religion" (*Quod idola dii non sint*, 11).

St Luke describes the conversion of Cornelius at great length and in great detail, deliberately repeating parts of the story to make sure that its key features are fully grasped. His whole account shows how important it is that pagans can and in fact do enter the Church without first being Jews.

Cornelius is regarded as the first pagan convert to Christianity. We do not know if the baptism of the Ethiopian, narrated in chapter 8, occurred after that of Cornelius or if the Ethiopian was in fact a pagan (cf. note on Acts 8.27); but in any case that was an isolated, marginal event which does not affect the solemn character of the Roman centurion's conversion, which affects the core of the economy of salvation.

1. Maritime Caesarea, where Cornelius was living, should not be confused with Caesarea Philippi, where our Lord promised the primacy to Peter (cf. Mt 16:13-20). Maritime Caesarea was the seat of the Roman governor and was situated on the coast, about 100 kilometres (60 miles) from Jerusalem. It had a Roman garrison made up of auxiliaries, that is, not of legionaries.

2. Cornelius was a religious man, one who "feared God". "God-fearing men" or "God-fearers" was a special expression used to describe people who worshipped the God of the Bible and practised the Law of Israel without being formally converts to Judaism (cf. note on Acts 2:5-11).

He was not a proselyte and therefore had not been circumcised (cf. Acts 11:3). "Do not imagine that grace was given them [Cornelius and the Ethiopian] because of their high rank: God forbid! It was because of their piety. Scripture mentions their distinguished stations to show the greatness of their piety; for it is more remarkable when a person in a position of wealth and power is such as these were" (Chrysostom, *Hom. on Acts*, 22).

feared God with all his household, gave alms liberally to the people, and prayed constantly to God. ³About the ninth hour of the day he saw clearly in a vision an angel of God coming in and saying to him, "Cornelius." ⁴And he stared at him in terror, and said, "What is it, Lord?" And he said to him, "Your prayers and your alms have ascended as a memorial before God. ⁵And now send men to Joppa, and bring one Simon which is called Peter; ⁶he is lodging with Simon, a tanner, whose house is by the seaside." ⁷When the angel who spoke to him had departed, he called two of his servants and

Acts 9:10

Tob 12:12
Lk 1:12
Rev 8:3-4

---

eleemosynas multas plebi et deprecans Deum semper, ³vidit in visu manifeste quasi hora nona diei angelum Dei introeuntem ad se et dicentem sibi: "Corneli!" ⁴At ille intuens eum et timore correptus dixit: "Quid est, domine?" Dixit autem illi: "Orationes tuae et eleemosynae tuae ascenderunt in memoriam in conspectu Dei. ⁵Et nunc mitte viros in Ioppen et accersi Simonem quendam, qui cognominatur Petrus; ⁶hic hospitatur apud Simonem quendam coriarium, cui est domus iuxta mare." ⁷Ut autem discessit angelus, qui loquebatur illi, cum vocasset duos domesticos suos et militem religiosum ex his, qui illi parebant,

---

In religious terms Cornelius was rather like the centurion in Capernaum, whose faith Jesus praises in St Luke's Gospel (7:1f). Some authors think that Cornelius was a member of the Roman *gens* of that name and that St Luke who, in writing Acts, had Roman readers in mind, takes special pleasure in recounting the story of Cornelius.

4. "Prayers and alms" were regarded by Jews and Christians as works pleasing to God and an expression of genuine piety. Cornelius' true devotion brings God's grace and mercy upon himself and his household. "Do you see how the work of the Gospel begins among the Gentiles? Through a devout man, whose deeds have made him worthy of this favour" (*ibid.*).

The habitual practice of almsgiving—the epitome of many virtues—is highly praised in the Old Testament. "Give alms from your possessions," says the Book of Tobit, ". . . so you will be laying up a good treasure for yourself against the day of necessity. For charity delivers from death and keeps you from entering the darkness; and for all who practise it charity is an excellent offering in the presence of the Most High" (4:7, 9-11; cf. 12:9). Almsgiving is an excellent work of mercy which sanctifies the giver and denotes God's preferential love for him.

"Give, and it will be given to you" (Lk 6:38): these words of Christ, which his disciples should keep before their minds, are echoed in Christian writings down the ages. "Give to everyone what he asks you for, and do not claim it back, for it is the Father's wish that you give to all from the gifts you yourself

a devout soldier from among those that waited on him, [8]and having related everything to them, he sent them to Joppa.

Peter's vision

[9]The next day, as they were on their journey and coming near the city, Peter went up on the housetop to pray, about the sixth hour. [10]And he became hungry and desired something to eat; but while they were preparing it, he fell into a trance [11]and saw the heaven opened, and something descending, like a great sheet, let down by four corners upon the earth. [12]In it were all kinds of animals and reptiles and birds of the air. [13]And there came a voice to him, "Rise, Peter;

---

[8]et narrasset illis omnia, misit illos in Ioppen. [9]Postera autem die iter illis facientibus et appropinquantibus civitati, ascendit Petrus super tectum, ut oraret circa horam sextam. [10]Et cum esuriret, voluit gustare; parantibus autem eis, cecidit super eum mentis excessus, [11]et videt caelum apertum et descendens vas quoddam velut linteum magnum quattuor initiis submitti in terram, [12]in quo erant omnia quadrupedia et serpentia terrae et volatilia caeli. [13]Et facta est vox ad eum: "Surge, Petre, occide et manduca!" [14]Ait autem Petrus: "Nequaquam,

---

have received. Blessed is he who, in accord with God's command, gives alms to the needy" (*Didache*, I, 5)

Generous alms to help those in need, and contributions to the upkeep of the Church, its ministers and its works of zeal, are the responsibility of all Christians. It is not a matter of giving whatever one has left over. Obviously, people to whom God has given wealth and resources in plenty have to give more alms. The fact that they are well-to-do is a sign of the will of God, and he expects them to be ready to meet the reasonable needs of their neighbours.

A Christian who does not understand this obligation or is reluctant to meet it runs the risk of becoming like that rich man (cf. Lk 16:19ff) who was so selfish and so attached to his wealth that he failed to realize that the Lord had placed Lazarus at his gate for him to help him.

" '*Divitiae, si affluant, nolite cor apponere*. Though riches may increase keep your heart detached.' Strive to use them generously. And, if necessary, heroically. Be poor of spirit" (J. Escrivá, *The Way*, 636).

"True detachment leads us to be very generous with God and with our fellow men. It makes us actively resourceful and ready to spend ourselves in helping the needy. A Christian cannot be content with a job that only allows him to earn enough for himself and his family. He will be big-hearted enough to give others a helping hand both out of charity and as a matter of justice" (J. Escrivá, *Friends of God*, 126).

"As a memorial": in the Old Testament certain sacrifices are described as

kill and eat." [14]But Peter said, "No, Lord; for I have never eaten anything that is common or unclean." [15]And the voice came to him again a second time, "What God has cleansed, you must not call common." [16]This happened three times, and the thing was taken up at once to heaven.

Ezek 4:14

Mt 15:11
Rom 14:14
1 Tim 4:4

[17]Now while Peter was inwardly perplexed as to what the vision which he had seen might mean, behold, the men that were sent by Cornelius, having made inquiry for Simon's house, stood before the gate [18]and called out to ask whether Simon who was called Peter was lodging there. [19]And while

Acts 13:2

Domine, quia numquam manducavi omne commune et immundum." [15]Et vox iterum secundo ad eum: "Quae Deus purificavit, ne tu commune dixeris." [16]Hoc autem factum est per ter, et statim receptum est vas in caelum. [17]Et dum intra se haesitaret Petrus quidnam esset visio, quam vidisset, ecce viri, qui missi erant a Cornelio, inquirentes domum Simonis astiterunt ad ianuam [18]et, cum vocassent, interrogabant si Simon, qui cognominatur Petrus, illic haberet hospitium. [19]Petro autem cogitante de visione, dixit Spiritus ei: "Ecce viri tres quaerunt te; [20]surge itaque et descende et vade cum eis nihil dubitans, quia ego

---

"memorial"—that is, offered to remind God, to have him be considerate towards the offerer (cf. Lev 2:1- 3; Tob 12:12).

14. This imperious commandment to eat unclean food is something the Apostle initially cannot understand. He reacts like a good Jew who loves and observes the divine law he has learned from his youth, including the regulations referring to food and the distinction between clean and unclean. But now he is invited to rise above so-called legal uncleanness.

Peter's humble attitude to what he is told during the vision enables him to take in God's will and realize that Jewish ritual precepts are not necessary for Christians. He does not arrive at this insight by a process of reasoning: rather, he obeys the voice of God; virtuous obedience, not simple human logic, causes him to change his attitude.

Peter's docility to the Holy Spirit gradually leads him to realize, first, that the regulations forbidding Jews to eat certain kinds of meat do not apply to Christians.

This simple and very important discovery, which he could not have made without special divine intervention, leads him to another even more important one: he now sees the full significance of all Jesus' teaching and realizes that in God's salvific plans Jews and pagans are equals.

Restrictions concerning food had led observant Jews to avoid sitting down to table with pagans. Food regulations and contact with Gentiles were very closely connected with one another and were subject to rigorous prohibition.

Peter was pondering the vision, the Spirit said to him, "Behold, three men are looking for you. ²⁰Rise and go down, and accompany them without hesitation; for I have sent them." ²¹And Peter went down to the men and said, "I am the one you are looking for; what is the reason for your coming?" ²²And they said, "Cornelius, a centurion, an upright and God-fearing man, who is well spoken of by the whole Jewish nation, was directed by a holy angel to send for you to come to his house, and to hear what you have to say." ²³So he called them in to be his guests.

Peter in the house of Cornelius

The next day he rose and went off with them, and some of the brethren from Joppa accompanied him. ²⁴And on the

---

misi illos." ²¹Descendens autem Petrus ad viros dixit: "Ecce ego sum, quem quaeritis; quae causa est, propter quam venistis?" ²²Qui dixerunt: "Cornelius centurio, vir iustus et timens Deum et testimonium habens ab universa gente Iudaeorum, responsum accepit ab angelo sancto accersire te in domum suam et audire verba abs te." ²³Invitans igitur eos recepit hospitio. Sequenti autem die surgens profectus est cum eis, et quidam ex fratribus ab Ioppe comitati sunt eum. ²⁴Altera autem die introivit Caesaream; Cornelius vero exspectabat illos,

---

Once the distinction between clean and unclean food was done away with, there would be no obstacle to communication with pagans: it would become quite clear what it meant in practice to say that the Lord "is not partial" (Deut 10:17), is no respecter of persons, and that having a clean heart is what really matters.

20. "Notice that the Holy Spirit does not say, 'Here is the explanation of the vision you have received' but 'I have sent them', to show thereby that obedience is called for and that it is not a matter of asking questions. This sufficed for Peter to realize he had to listen to the Holy Spirit" (Chrysostom, *Hom. on Acts*, 22).

24. Cornelius, in his zeal, calls in his family and friends to listen to the saving word of God. The group he assembles represents the pagan world which has for centuries been waiting for Christ without knowing it. "I was ready to be sought by those who did not ask for me; I was ready to be found by those who did not seek me" (Is 65:1).

This episode, in which Cornelius the Roman officer plays the leading role, has a much wider significance. His conversion means that the Jews are not the only heirs of the promises: it shows that the Gospel brings a universal remedy to solve a universal need. "Cornelius was such a servant of God that an angel

following day they entered Caesarea. Cornelius was
expecting them and had called together his kinsmen and
close friends. [25]When Peter entered, Cornelius met him and
fell down at his feet and worshipped him. [26]But Peter lifted
him up, saying, "Stand up; I too am a man." [27]And as he
talked with him, he went in and found many persons

Mt 8:8
Acts 14:15
Rev 19:10

---

convocatis cognatis suis et necessariis amicis. [25]Et factum est cum introisset
Petrus obvius ei Cornelius procidens ad pedes adoravit. [26]Petrus vero levavit
eum dicens: "Surge, et ego ipse homo sum." [27]Et loquens cum illo intravit et

---

was sent to him, and to his merits must be attributed the mysterious event
through which Peter was to rise above the restrictions of circumcision. . . . Once
the Apostle baptized him, the salvation of the Gentiles had begun" (St Jerome,
Epistle 79, 2).

25-26. It is difficult at first for pagans to realize what is happening when
God manifests himself to them, makes his will known and confers his gifts upon
them through the medium of other men: their first reaction is to think that these
must be celestial beings or gods in human form (cf. 14:11), until it is quite clear
that they are men of flesh and blood. That is how it is: men and women are the
defective but essential instruments whom God normally uses to make known
his plans of salvation. God in his providence acts in this way, first in the Old
Testament and particularly in the New Testament; a prime example is to be
seen in the Christian priesthood.

"Every high priest [is] chosen from among men" (Heb 5:1) to be sent back
to his brethren as a minister of intercession and forgiveness. "He must therefore
be a member of the human race, for it is God's desire that man have one of his
like to come to his aid" (St Thomas Aquinas, *Commentary on Heb*, 5, 1).

It has been said that everything about the Gospel of Jesus Christ is quite
excellent, except the persons of his ministers— because these priests, who have
been consecrated by a special sacrament, are also sons of Adam, and they still
have the weak nature of sons of Adam even after being ordained.

"Most strange is this in itself [. . .] but not strange, when you consider it is
the appointment of an all- merciful God; not strange in him. [. . .] The priests
of the New Law are men, in order that they may 'condole with those who are
in ignorance and error, because they too are encompassed with infirmity' (Heb
5:2)" (J. H. Newman, *Discourses addressed to Mixed Congregations*).

If priests were not men of flesh and blood, they would not feel for others,
who are made of the same stuff; they would not understand their weakness. But
in fact they do share the human condition and do experience the same
temptations.

Gal 2:12

gathered; ²⁸and he said to them, "You yourselves know how unlawful it is for a Jew to associate with or to visit any one of another nation; but God has shown me that I should not call any man common or unclean. ²⁹So when I was sent for, I came without objection. I ask then why you sent for me."

³⁰And Cornelius said, "Four days ago, about this hour, I was keeping the ninth hour of prayer in my house; and behold a man stood before me in bright apparel, ³¹saying, 'Cornelius, your prayer has been heard and your alms have been remembered before God. ³²Send therefore to Joppa and ask for Simon who is called Peter; he is lodging in the house of Simon, a tanner, by the seaside.' ³³So I sent for you at

---

invenit multos, qui convenerant, ²⁸dixitque ad illos: "Vos scitis quomodo illicitum sit viro Iudaeo coniungi aut accedere ad alienigenam. Et mihi ostendit Deus neminem communem aut immundum dicere hominem; ²⁹propter quod sine dubitatione veni accersitus. Interrogo ergo quam ob causum accersistis me." ³⁰Et Cornelius ait: "A nudius quarta die usque in hanc horam orans eram hora nona in domo mea, et ecce vir stetit ante me in veste candida ³¹et ait: 'Corneli, exaudita est oratio tua, et eleemosynae tuae commemoratae sunt in conspectu Dei. ³²Mitte ergo in Ioppen et accersi Simonem, qui cognominatur Petrus; hic hospitatur in domo Simonis coriarii iuxta mare'. ³³Confestim igitur misi ad te, et tu bene fecisti veniendo. Nunc ergo omnes nos in conspectu Dei

---

28. "The Apostle did not wish it to appear that he was doing something prohibited out of consideration for Cornelius. Peter desires to make it plain that the Lord is the only reason for his action. That is why he reminds them that contact with pagans and even entering their houses is forbidden" (Chrysostom, *Hom. on Acts*, 23).

Peter justifies his actions, which are not in line with the way a strict Jew would act, by saying that he is obeying God's will, made known to him only a short while before. The Gospel no longer recognizes any distinction between clean and unclean people. All are equal in the sight of God if they listen to his word with a pure heart and repent their sins.

33. Grace disposes Cornelius to accept Peter's words as coming from God. The centurion was a man of good will and upright conscience, who worshipped God according to his lights. Prior to meeting Peter, he is an example of the religious person who sincerely seeks the truth and is therefore on the way to ensuring his eternal destiny. The Second Vatican Council teaches that "those who, through no fault of their own, do not know the Gospel of Christ or his Church, but who nevertheless seek God with a sincere heart, and, moved by grace, try in their actions to do his will as they know it through the dictates of

once, and you have been kind enough to come. Now therefore we are all here present in the sight of God, to hear all that you have been commanded by the Lord."

Peter's address

³⁴And Peter opened his mouth and said: "Truly I perceive that God shows no partiality, ³⁵but in every nation any one who fears him and does what is right is acceptable to him. ³⁶You know the word which he sent to Israel, preaching good

Deut 10:17
Rom 2:11
Gal 2:6
1 Pet 1:17
Is 56:7
Rom 15:16

---

adsumus audire omnia, quaecumque tibi praecepta sunt a Domino." ³⁴Aperiens autem Petrus os dixit: "In veritate comperior quoniam non est personarum acceptor Deus, ³⁵sed in omni gente, qui timet eum et operatur iustitiam, acceptus est illi. ³⁶Verbum misit filiis Israel evangelizans pacem per Iesum Christum;

---

their conscience—those too may achieve eternal salvation" (*Lumen gentium*, 16).

However, the spiritual blessings given to Cornelius and those with him go further than this: they actually prepare them to enter the Church. When God gives initial graces to people who are not yet Christians, he wishes them to attain the fullness of grace, which they will find in the Catholic Church. "This is God's intention, this is what he does. If he did not despise the Magi, the Ethiopian, the thief or the courtesan, how much less will he despise those who practise righteousness and desire it" (Chrysostom, *Hom. on Acts*, 23).

34-43. Peter's short address is his first to non-Jews. It begins with the central idea that God is impartial: he wants all men to be saved through the proclamation of the Gospel (vv. 34-36). This is followed by a summary of Jesus' public life (vv. 37-41) and, finally, the statement (the first time it appears in Acts) that Jesus Christ has been made Judge of the living and the dead (v. 42). As in all Christian preaching to Gentiles, proofs from Scripture take a secondary place (v. 43).

34. This verse refers to 1 Samuel 16:7, where the Lord, in connexion with the anointing of David as king of Israel, tells the prophet, "Do not look on his appearance or on the height of his stature, because I have rejected him; for the Lord sees not as man sees; man looks on the outward appearance, but the Lord looks on the heart." When God calls and offers salvation to his elect, he does not judge as men do. With him distinctions regarding social class, race, sex or education do not count.

Here St Peter proclaims that the Old Testament prophecies about the Jews and the Gentiles forming one single nation (Is 2:2-4; Joel 2:28; Amos 9:12; Mich 4:1) and Jesus' words calling everyone to enter his Kingdom (cf. Mt 8:11; Mk 16:15-16; Jn 10:16) should be interpreted literally.

Is 52:7
Nahum 2:1

Is 61:1
Mt 3:16
Acts 4:27

Acts 1:8

1 Cor 15:4
Lk 24:43
Jn 14:22

Acts 17:31
2 Tim 4:1
1 Pet 4:5

news of peace by Jesus Christ (he is Lord of all), [37]the word which was proclaimed throughout all Judea, beginning from Galilee after the baptism which John preached: [38]how God anointed Jesus of Nazareth with the Holy Spirit and with power; how he went about doing good and healing all that were oppressed by the devil, for God was with him. [39]And we are witnesses to all that he did both in the country of the Jews and in Jerusalem. They put him to death by hanging him on a tree; [40]but God raised him on the third day and made him manifest; [41]not to all the people but to us who were chosen by God as witnesses, who ate and drank with him after he rose from the dead.[42]And he commanded us to

---

hic est omnium Dominus. [37] Vos scitis quod factum est verbum per universam Iudaeam incipiens a Galilaea post baptismum, quod praedicavit Ioannes: [38]Iesum a Nazareth, quomodo unxit eum Deus Spiritu Sancto et virtute, qui pertransivit benefaciendo et sanando omnes oppressos a Diabolo, quoniam Deus erat cum illo. [39]Et nos testes sumus omnium, quae fecit in regione Iudaeorum et Ierusalem; quem et occiderunt suspendentes in ligno. [40]Hunc Deus suscitavit tertia die et dedit eum manifestum fieri, [41]non omni populo sed testibus praeordinatis a Deo, nobis, qui manducavimus et bibimus cum illo postquam resurrexit a mortuis; [42]et praecepit nobis praedicare populo et

---

40. Peter's summary of the Gospel of Jesus (vv. 37-41) reaches its climax with his statement that "God raised him on the third day." This had become the usual way of referring to our Lord's resurrection (cf. 1 Cor 15:4); see note on Acts 4:10.

42. This verse refers to Christ's role as Judge: he has been made supreme Judge over all mankind and will deliver his judgment at his second coming (Parousia). "The Sacred Scriptures inform us that there are two comings of the Son of God: the one when he assumed human flesh for our salvation in the womb of a virgin; the other when he shall come at the end of the world to judge all mankind" (*St Pius V Catechism*, I, 8, 2).

Christ's coming as Judge means that men will appear before him twice, to render an account of their lives—of their thoughts, words, deeds and omissions. The first judgment will take place "when each of us departs this life; for then he is instantly placed before the judgment-seat of God, where all that he has ever done or spoken or thought during his life shall be subjected to the most rigid scrutiny. This is called the particular judgment. The second occurs when on the same day and in the same place all men shall stand together before the tribunal of their Judge [. . .] , and this is called the general judgment" (*ibid.*, I, 8, 3).

preach to the people, and to testify that he is the one ordained by God to be judge of the living and the dead. [43]To him all the prophets bear witness that every one who believes in him receives forgiveness of sins through his name."

Is 33:24
Jer 31:34

The baptism of Cornelius and his family

[44]While Peter was still saying this, the Holy Spirit fell on all who heard the word. [45]And the believers from among the circumcised who came with Peter were amazed, because the gift of the Holy Spirit had been poured out even on the Gentiles. [46]For they heard them speaking in tongues and extolling God. Then Peter declared, [47]"Can any one forbid water for baptizing these people who have received the Holy Spirit just as we have?" [48]And he commanded them to be baptized in the name of Jesus Christ. Then they asked him to remain for some days.

Acts 11:15;
15:8

Acts 2:4-11;
19:6
Acts 8:36;
11:17

---

testificari quia ipse est, qui constitutus est a Deo iudex vivorum et mortuorum. [43]Huic omnes prophetae testimonium perhibent remissionem peccatorum accipere per nomen eius omnes, qui credunt in eum." [44]Adhuc loquente Petro verba haec, cecidit Spiritus Sanctus super omnes, qui audiebant verbum. [45]Et obstupuerunt, qui ex circumcisione fideles, qui venerant cum Petro, quia et in nationes gratia Spiritus Sancti effusa est; [46]audiebant enim illos loquentes linguis et magnificantes Deum. Tunc respondit Petrus: [47]"Numquid aquam quis prohibere potest, ut non baptizentur hi, qui Spiritum Sanctum acceperunt sicut et nos?" [48]Et iussit eos in nomine Iesu Christi baptizari. Tunc rogaverunt eum, ut maneret aliquot diebus.

44-48. This scene is reminiscent of Pentecost. There the Holy Spirit came down on the first disciples, Jews all of them. Now he is given to Gentiles, unexpectedly and irresistibly. It is as if the Lord wanted to confirm to Peter everything he had so far revealed to him about the admission of Cornelius to the Church. The centurion and his family are baptized on Peter's instructions, without first becoming Jews through circumcision.

In Jerusalem Peter justifies his conduct

Acts 10:28, 48
Eph 2:11

Acts 10:9-48

¹Now the apostles and the brethren who were in Judea heard that the Gentiles also had received the word of God. ²So when Peter went up to Jerusalem, the circumcision party criticized him, ³saying, "Why did you go to uncircumcised men and eat with them?" ⁴But Peter began and explained to them in order: ⁵"I was in the city of Joppa praying; and in a trance I saw a vision, something descending, like a great sheet, let down from heaven by four corners; and it came down to me. ⁶Looking at it closely I observed animals and beasts of prey and reptiles and birds of the air. ⁷And I heard a voice saying to me, 'Rise, Peter; kill and eat.' ⁸But I said, 'No, Lord; for nothing common or unclean has ever entered my mouth.' ⁹But the voice answered a second time from heaven, 'What God has cleansed you must not call common.'

---

¹Audierunt autem apostoli et fratres, qui erant in Iudaea, quoniam et gentes receperunt verbum Dei. ²Cum ascendisset autem Petrus in Ierusalem, disceptabant adversus illum, qui erant ex circumcisione, ³dicentes: "Introisti ad viros praeputium habentes et manducasti cum illis!" ⁴Incipiens autem Petrus exponebat illis ex ordine dicens: ⁵"Ego eram in civitate Ioppe orans et vidi in excessu mentis visionem, descendens vas quoddam velut linteum magnum quattuor initiis submitti de caelo, et venit usque ad me; ⁶in quod intuens considerabam et vidi quadrupedia terrae et bestias et reptilia et volatilia caeli. ⁷Audivi autem et vocem dicentem mihi: 'Surgens, Petre, occide et manduca!' ⁸Dixi autem: Nequaquam, Domine, quia commune aut immundum numquam introivit in os meum. ⁹Respondit autem vox secundo de caelo: 'Quae Deus mundavit, tu ne commune dixeris.' ¹⁰Hoc autem factum est per ter, et retracta

---

1-18. Some members of the Jerusalem community are shocked to learn that Peter has eaten with people who are legally unclean and has allowed them to be baptized without first being circumcised.

"The circumcision party" refers, therefore, to those Christians who are scandalized by the Gospel's attitude to the ritual prohibitions and ethnic exclusiveness of the Mosaic Law.

The Apostle's address has a positive effect and sets their minds at ease. This attitude of the disciples, who are interested only in the will of God and the spread of the Gospel, shows how ready they are to accept instruction: their initial reserve was quite conscientious. Peter once again describes the vision he received (10:9-23), to show that if he had not baptized Cornelius he would have been disobeying God.

¹⁰This happened three times, and all was drawn up again into heaven. ¹¹And that very moment three men arrived at the house in which we were, sent to me from Caesarea. ¹²And the Spirit told me to go with them, making no distinction. These six brethren also accompanied me, and we entered the man's house. ¹³And he told us how he had seen the angel standing in this house and saying, 'Send to Joppa and bring Simon called Peter; ¹⁴he will declare to you a message by which you will be saved, you and all your household.' ¹⁵As I began to speak, the Holy Spirit fell on them just as on us at the beginning. ¹⁶And I remembered the word of the Lord, how he said, 'John baptized with water, but you shall be baptized with the Holy Spirit.' ¹⁷If then God gave the same gift to them as he gave to us when we believed in the Lord Jesus Christ, who was I that I could withstand God?" ¹⁸When they heard this they were silenced. And they glorified God, saying, "Then to the Gentiles also God has granted repentance unto life."

Acts 1:5

Acts 15:8-9; 10:47

Acts 14:27

---

sunt rursum omnia in caelum. ¹¹Et ecce confestim tres viri astiterunt in domo, in qua eramus, missi a Caesarea ad me. ¹²Dixit autem Spiritus mihi, ut irem cum illis nihil haesitans. Venerunt autem mecum et sex fratres isti, et ingressi sumus in domum viri. ¹³Narravit autem nobis quomodo vidisset angelum ad domum suam stantem et dicentem: 'Mitte in Ioppen et accersi Simonem, qui cognominatur Petrus, ¹⁴qui loquetur tibi verba, in quibus salvus eris tu et universa domus tua.' ¹⁵Cum autem coepissem loqui, decidit Spiritus Sanctus super eos sicut et super nos in initio. ¹⁶Recordatus sum autem verbi Domini sicut dicebat: 'Ioannes quidem baptizavit aqua, vos autem baptizabimini in Spiritu Sancto.' ¹⁷Si ergo aequale donum dedit illis Deus sicut et nobis, qui credidimus in Dominum Iesum Christum, ego quis eram qui possem prohibere Deum?" ¹⁸His autem auditis acquieverunt et glorificaverunt Deum dicentes:

This account of the vision differs slightly from his earlier one, the main addition being in vv. 15-16, which connect the coming of the Holy Spirit at Pentecost (2:1ff) with his descent on the Gentile converts in Caesarea (10:44).

Unfortunately the stubborn Judaizing tendencies exhibited by some members of the infant Church took a long time to disappear, as is dramatically borne out in some of St Paul's letters: he refers to "false brethren secretly brought in, who slipped in to spy on our freedom which we have in Jesus Christ, that they might bring us into bondage" (Gal 2:4) and warns Christians to be on their guard against fanatics of the Law of Moses who are self-serving and "want to pervert the Gospel of Christ" (Gal 1:7).

The beginning of the Church in Antioch

Acts 8:1-4 ¹⁹Now those who were scattered because of the persecution that arose over Stephen travelled as far as Phoenicia and Cyprus and Antioch, speaking the word to none except Jews. ²⁰But there were some of them, men of Cyprus and Cyrene, who on coming to Antioch spoke to the Greeks[i] also, preach-

---

"Ergo et gentibus Deus paenitentiam ad vitam dedit." ¹⁹Et illi quidem, qui dispersi fuerant a tribulatione, quae facta fuerat sub Stephano, perambulaverunt usque Phoenicen et Cyprum et Antiochiam, nemini loquentes verbum nisi solis Iudaeis. ²⁰Erant autem quidam ex eis viri Cyprii et Cyrenaei, qui cum introissent Antiochiam, loquebantur et ad Hellenistas evangelizantes Dominum Iesum. ²¹Et erat manus Domini cum eis; multusque numerus credentium conversus est

---

19-30. This account links up with Acts 8:1-4, which describes the flight of Christians from Jerusalem due to the first persecution following on the martyrdom of St Stephen. We are now told about the spread of the Gospel to Antioch on the Orontes, the capital of the Roman province of Syria. Antioch was the first major city of the ancient world where the word of Jesus Christ was preached. It was the third city of the empire, after Rome and Alexandria, with a population of about half a million and a sizeable Jewish colony, and was a very important cultural, economic and religious centre.

In Antioch the Gospel is proclaimed not only to Jews and proselytes. These Hellenist Jews from Jerusalem preach the Gospel to all and sundry as part of their ordinary everyday activity. St Luke does not give us any names: the preachers are ordinary Christians. "Notice", says Chrysostom, "that it is grace which does everything. And also reflect on the fact that this work is begun by unknown workers and only when it begins to prosper do the Apostles send Barnabas" (*Hom. on Acts*, 25).

The Christian mission at Antioch played a key part in the spread of Christianity. Evangelization of non-Jews becomes the norm; it is not just something which happens in a few isolated cases. Nor is it limited to "God-fearers"; it extends to all the Gentiles. The centre of gravity of the Christian Church begins to move from Jerusalem to Antioch, which will become the springboard for the evangelization of the pagan world.

20. The title "Lord", often applied to Jesus in the New Testament and in the early Church, is a confession of faith in his divinity. To say "Jesus is Lord" (1 Cor 12:3; Rom 10:9) is the same as saying that Jesus Christ is God. It means that he is worshipped as the only Son of the Father and as sovereign of the Church, and receives the cult of *latria* which is rendered to God alone.

This acclamation of Jesus as Lord shows that from the very beginning the young Christian communities knew that he had dominion over all mankind and was not just the Messiah of one nation.

[i]Other ancient authorities read *Hellenists*.

ing the Lord Jesus. ²¹And the hand of the Lord was with them,
and a great number that believed turned to the Lord. ²²News
of this came to the ears of the church in Jerusalem, and they
sent Barnabas to Antioch. ²³When he came and saw the grace
of God, he was glad; and he exhorted them all to remain
faithful to the Lord with steadfast purpose; ²⁴for he was a
good man, full of the Holy Spirit and of faith. And a large
company was added to the Lord. ²⁵So Barnabas went to
Tarsus to look for Saul; ²⁶and when he had found him, he
brought him to Antioch. For a whole year they met with^j the

---

ad Dominum. ²²Auditus est autem sermo in auribus ecclesiae, quae erat in
Ierusalem, super istis, et miserunt Barnabam usque Antiochiam; ²³qui cum
pervenisset et vidisset gratiam Dei, gavisus est et hortabatur omnes proposito
cordis permanere in Domino, ²⁴quia erat vir bonus et plenus Spiritu Sancto et
fide. Et apposita est turba multa Domino. ²⁵Profectus est autem Tarsum, ut
quaereret Saulum, ²⁶quem cum invenisset, perduxit Antiochiam. Factum est

22-26. The community at Jerusalem, where the Apostles were based, felt
responsible for everything that happened in the Christian mission-field. This
was why they sent Barnabas to oversee developments in Antioch. Barnabas
was a man whom the Apostles trusted, noted for his virtue (he was mentioned
in Acts 4:36).

No doubt it was because of all the work opening before the preachers of the
Gospel that Barnabas sought out Paul, who had returned to Tarsus after his
conversion and his visit to Jerusalem (9:30). Barnabas probably knew that the
future Apostle was the very man he needed to join him in the work of
evangelization about to be undertaken by the Antiochene church. Barnabas'
sense of responsibility and his zeal to find labourers for the Lord's harvest (cf.
Mt 9:38) lead to the first of the great missionary journeys, in which Paul's
vocation finds full scope.

26. We do not exactly know who first began to describe the disciples as
"Christians". In any event the fact that they were given a name shows that
everyone recognized them as an identifiable group. The name also suggests that
the term *Christos* —Messiah, Anointed—is no longer regarded simply as a
messianic title but also as a proper name.

Some Fathers of the Church see this name as further indication that people
do not become disciples of the Lord through human causes. "Although the holy
Apostles were our teachers and have given us the Gospel of the Saviour, it is
not from them that we have taken our name: we are *Christians* through Christ
and it is for him that we are called in this way" (St Athanasius, *Oratio I contra
arianos*, 2).

^jOr *were guests of.*

church, and taught a large company of people and in Antioch the disciples were for the first time called Christians.

Antioch helps the Church in Judea

27Now in these days prophets came down from Jerusalem

---

autem eis ut annum totum conversarentur in ecclesia et docerent turbam multam, et cognominarentur primum Antiochiae discipuli Christiani. 27In his

27. This is the first reference to prophets in the first Christian communities (cf. 13:1). As was the case with the Old Testament prophets, these prophets of the early Church receive special illumination from God—charisms—to speak in his name under the inspiration of the Holy Spirit. Their function is not only to predict future events (cf. 11:28; 21:11) but to show the way the divine promises and plans contained in Sacred Scripture have been fulfilled.

Acts refers to prophets a number of times. In addition to Agabus, it describes as prophets Judas and Silas (15:32) and the daughters of Philip the deacon (21:9). We also know that Paul had the gift of prophecy (cf. 1 Cor 12-14). In the infant Church the prophetic office was subordinate to the apostolic ministry and was exercised under the control of the Apostles in the service and building up of the Christian community. "And God has appointed in the church first apostles, second prophets, third teachers" (1 Cor 12:28).

The gift of prophecy in the sense of a special charism as found in the early years of the Church is not to be found in later times. But the gifts of the Holy Spirit are still to be found in all the members of the mystical body of Christ, varying with the ecclesial role which each person has.

The hierarchy of the Church, with the Pope as its head, has the prophetic mission of unerringly proclaiming true teaching within and without the Church.

"The holy People of God", Vatican II teaches, "shares also in Christ's prophetic office: it spreads abroad a living witness to him, especially by a life of faith and love. [. . .] The whole body of the faithful, who have an anointing that comes from the holy one (cf. 1 Jn 2:20, 27) cannot err in matters of belief. This characteristic is shown in the supernatural appreciation of the faith [*sensus fidei*] of the whole people, when, 'from the bishops to the last of the faithful' (St Augustine, *De praed. sanct.*, XIV, 27) they manifest a universal consent in matters of faith and morals. By this appreciation of the faith, aroused and sustained by the Spirit of truth, the People of God, guided by the sacred teaching authority [*magisterium*], and obeying it, receives not the mere word of men, but truly the word of God (cf. 1 Thess 2:13), the faith once for all delivered to the saints (cf. Jud 3). The People unfailingly adheres to this faith, penetrates it more deeply with right judgment, and applies it more fully in daily life.

It is not only through the sacraments and the ministrations of the Church that the Holy Spirit makes holy the People, leads them and enriches them with his virtues. Allotting his gifts according as he wills (cf. 1 Cor 12:11), he also

to Antioch. [28]And one of them named Agabus stood up and Acts 21:10
foretold by the Spirit that there would be a great famine over
all the world; and this took place in the days of Claudius.
[29]And the disciples determined, every one according to his Gal 2:10
ability, to send relief to the brethren who lived in Judea; [30]and Acts 12:25
they did so, sending it to the elders by the hand of Barnabas
and Saul.

---

autem diebus supervenerunt ab Hierosolymis prophetae Antiochiam; [28]et
surgens unus ex eis nomine Agabus, significavit per Spiritum famem magnam
futuram in universo orbe terrarum; quae facta est sub Claudio. [29]Discipuli
autem, prout quis habebat, proposuerunt singuli eorum in ministerium mittere
habitantibus in Iudaea fratribus; [30]quod et fecerunt, mittentes ad presbyteros
per manum Barnabae et Sauli.

---

distributes special graces among the faithful of every rank. By these gifts he
makes them fit and ready to undertake various tasks and offices for the renewing
and building up of the Church" (Vatican II, *Lumen gentium*, 12).

28-29. During the reign of Claudius (41-54), the empire suffered a severe
food crisis. This famine, which afflicted Greece, Syria and Palestine as well as
Rome during the years 47-49 A.D., would have been the one which Agabus
foretold.

This imminent food shortage is what leads the prosperous Antiochene
community to send aid to the mother community in Jerusalem. Like their first
brothers in the faith (cf. 4:34), the disciples in Antioch show their charity and
concern for their fellow-Christians and prove that they have the true Christian
spirit.

30. This journey may be the same one as mentioned in 15:2 (cf. Gal 2:1-10).
The money which Paul and Barnabas bring to Jerusalem on this occasion should
not be confused with the results of the big collection organized later (cf. 24:17).

It is the elders of the community who receive and organize the distribution
of the collection. These "elders" or presbyters—the traditional Jewish name for
those in charge of the community—seem to have been aides of the Apostles.
We are not told about how they were instituted, but they appear a number of
times in Acts (15:2—16:4; 21:18), they perform functions which are somewhat
different from those of the Twelve, and they take part in the Council of
Jerusalem.

Paul and Barnabas appoint elders and put them in charge of the churches
they found during their first great missionary journey (cf. 14:33), and in the
epistles to Timothy (5:17-19) and Titus (1:5) those entrusted with an established
ministry in each community are described as elders.

12

Persecution by Herod. Peter's arrest and deliverance
¹About that time Herod the king laid violent hands upon

---

¹Illo autem tempore misit Herodes rex manus, ut affligeret quosdam de ecclesia.

Apparently, at the start the terms "bishop" and "elder" (cf. 10:17, 28; 1 Tim 3:2; Tit 1:7) were used interchangeably and then later on came to refer to the two highest levels of the hierarchy. By the second century the meaning of each term was clearly fixed. The difference consists in this: bishops have the fullness of the sacrament of Order (cf. Vatican II, *Lumen gentium*, 11), and presbyters, "true priests of the New Testament [. . .] after the image of Christ" (*ibid.*, 28), carry out pastoral ministry as co-workers of their bishops and in communion with them.

The New Testament texts use the term "priest" only to refer to the ministers of the Old Law (cf. Mt 8:4; 20:18; Heb 7:23) and as a title belonging to Jesus Christ, the only true Priest (cf. Heb 4:15; 5:5; 8:1; 9:11), from whom all lawful priesthood derives. In general, the early Church avoids, where possible, the use of terminology which might imply that it was simply one more among the many religions in the Greco-Roman world.

1-19. This is an account of persecution of the Church by Herod Agrippa (37-44), which took place before the visit of Paul and Barnabas to the Holy City (cf. 11:30).

The information given in this chapter about the latest persecution of the Jerusalem community—more severe and more general than the earlier crises (cf. 5:17; 8:1)—gives an accurate picture of the situation in Palestine and describes events in chronological sequence. Prior to this the Roman governors more or less protected the rights of the Jerusalem Christians. Now Agrippa, in his desire to ingratiate himself with the Pharisees, abandons the Christians to the growing resentment and hatred the Jewish authorities and people feel towards them.

This chapter brings to an end, so to speak, the story of the first Christian community in Jerusalem. From now on, attention is concentrated on the church of Antioch. The last stage of the Palestinian Judeo-Christian church, under the direction of James "the brother of the Lord", will not experience the expansion enjoyed by other churches, due to the grave turn which events take in the Holy Land.

1. This Herod is the third prince of that name to appear in the New Testament. He was a grandson of Herod the Great, who built the new temple of Jerusalem and was responsible for the massacre of the Holy Innocents (cf. Mt 2:16); he was also a nephew of Herod Antipas, the tetrarch of Galilee at the

some who belonged to the church. ²He killed James the Mt 20:22-23
brother of John with the sword; ³and when he saw that it
pleased the Jews, he proceeded to arrest Peter also. This was
during the days of Unleavened Bread. ⁴And when he had
seized him, he put him in prison, and delivered him to four
squads of soldiers to guard him, intending after the Passover
to bring him out to the people. ⁵So Peter was kept in prison; Jas 5:16

---

²Occidit autem Iacobum fratrem Ioannis gladio. ³Videns autem quia placeret
Iudaeis, apposuit apprehendere et Petrum—erant autem dies Azymorum—
⁴quem cum apprehendisset, misit in carcerem tradens quattuor quaternionibus
militum custodire eum, volens post Pascha producere eum populo. ⁵Et Petrus
quidem servabatur in carcere; oratio autem fiebat sine intermissione ab ecclesia

---

time of our Lord's death. Herod Agrippa I was a favourite of the emperor
Caligula, who gradually gave him him more territory and allowed him to use
the title of king. Agrippa I managed to extend his authority over all the territory
his grandfather had ruled: Roman governors had ruled Judea up to the year 41,
but in that year it was given over to Herod. He was a sophisticated type of
person, a diplomat, so bent on consolidating his power that he had became a
master of intrigue and a total opportunist. For largely political motives he
practised Judaism with a certain rigour.

2. James the Greater would have been martyred in the year 42 or 43. He was
the first Apostle to die for the faith and the only one whose death is mentioned
in the New Testament. The Liturgy of the Hours says of him: "The son of
Zebedee and the brother of John, he was born in Bethsaida. He witnessed the
principal miracles performed by our Lord and was put to death by Herod around
the year 42. He is held in special veneration in the city of Compostela, where
a famous church is dedicated to his name."

"The Lord permits this death," Chrysostom observes, "to show his murderers
that these events do not cause the Christians to retreat or desist" (*Hom. on Acts*,
26).

5. "Notice the feelings of the faithful towards their pastors. They do not riot
or rebel; they have recourse to prayer, which can solve all problems. They do
not say to themselves: We do not count, there is no point in our praying for him.
Their love led them to pray and they did not think along those lines. Have you
noticed what these persecutors did without intending to? They made (their
victims) more determined to stand the test, and (the faithful) more zealous and
loving" (*Hom. on Acts*, 26).

St Luke, whose Gospel reports our Lord's words on perseverance in prayer
(cf. 11:11-13; 18:1-8), here stresses that God listens to the whole community's
prayer for Peter. He plans in his providence to save the Apostle for the benefit

Acts 5:18-23;
16:25-40

1 Kings 19:5

Acts 10:17

but earnest prayer for him was made to God by the church. ⁶The very night when Herod was about to bring him out, Peter was sleeping between two soldiers, bound with two chains, and sentries before the door were guarding the prison; ⁷and behold, an angel of the Lord appeared, and a light shone in the cell; and he struck Peter on the side and woke him, saying, "Get up quickly." And the chains fell off his hands. ⁸And the angel said to him, "Dress yourself and put on your sandals." And he did so. And he said to him, "Wrap your mantle around you and follow me." ⁹And he went out and followed him; he did not know that what was done by the angel was real, but thought he was seeing a vision. ¹⁰When they had passed the first and the second guard, they came to the iron gate leading into the city. It opened to them of its own accord, and they went out and passed on through one street; and immediately the angel left him. ¹¹And Peter came to himself, and said, "Now I am sure that the Lord has sent

ad Deum pro eo. ⁶Cum autem producturus eum esset Herodes, in ipsa nocte erat Petrus dormiens inter duos milites vinctus catenis duabus, et custodes ante ostium custodiebant carcerem. ⁷Et ecce angelus Domini astitit, et lumen refulsit in habitaculo; percusso autem latere Petri, suscitavit eum dicens: "Surge velociter!" Et ceciderunt catenae de manibus eius. ⁸Dixit autem angelus ad eum: "Praecingere et calcea te sandalia tua!" Et fecit sic. Et dicit illi: "Circumda tibi vestimentum tuum et sequere me!" ⁹Et exiens sequebatur et nesciebat quia verum est, quod fiebat per angelum; aestimabat autem se visum videre. ¹⁰Transeuntes autem primam custodiam et secundam venerunt ad portam ferream, quae ducit ad civitatem, quae ultro aperta est eis, et exeuntes processerunt vicum unum, et continuo discessit angelus ab eo. ¹¹Et Petrus ad se reversus dixit: "Nunc scio vere quia misit Dominus angelum suum et eripuit me de manu Herodis et de omni exspectatione plebis Iudaeorum." ¹²Con-

of the Church, but he wants the outcome to be seen as an answer to the Church's fervent prayer.

7-10. The Lord comes to Peter's help by sending an angel, who opens the prison and leads him out. This miraculous freeing of the Apostle is similar to what happened at the time of Peter and John's detention (5:19f) and when Paul and Silas are imprisoned in Philippi (16:19ff).

This extraordinary event, which must be understood exactly as it is described, shows the loving care God takes of those whom he entrusts with a mission. They must strive to fulfil it, but they will "see" for themselves that he guides their steps and watches over them.

his angel and rescued me from the hand of Herod and from all that the Jewish people were expecting."

¹²When he realized this, he went to the house of Mary, the mother of John whose other name was Mark, where many were gathered together and were praying. ¹³And when he knocked at the door of the gateway, a maid named Rhoda came to answer. ¹⁴Recognizing Peter's voice, in her joy she did not open the gate but ran in and told that Peter was standing at the gate. ¹⁵They said to her, "You are mad." But

Acts 12:25
13:5, 13; 15:37
Col 4:10
Philem 24
2 Tim 4:11
1 Pet 5:13

---

sideransque venit ad domum Mariae matris Ioannis, qui cognominatur Marcus, ubi erant multi congregati et orantes. ¹³Pulsante autem eo ostium ianuae, processit puella ad audiendum, nomine Rhode; ¹⁴et ut cognovit vocem Petri prae gaudio non aperuit ianuam, sed intro currens nuntiavit stare Petrum ante ianuam. ¹⁵At illi dixerunt ad eam: "Insanis!" Illa autem affirmabat sic se habere.

---

12. John Mark was Barnabas' cousin (cf. Col 4:10). He will accompany Barnabas and Paul on the first missionary journey (cf. 13:5) up to the point when they enter the province of Asia (cf. 13:13). Despite Paul's not wanting to have him on the second journey (cf. 15:37-39), we find him later again as a co-worker of the Apostle (cf. Col 4:10; 2 Tim 4:11) and also as a disciple and helper of Simon Peter (1 Pet 5:13). The tradition of the Church credits him with the authorship of the second Gospel.

"The house of Mary": this may have been the same house as the Cenacle, where Jesus celebrated his Last Supper with his disciples. Cf. *The Navarre Bible: St Mark*, pp. 57f.

15. The first Christians had a very lively faith in the guardian angels and their God-given role of assisting men. In the Old Testament God reveals the existence of angels; on various occasions we see them playing an active part (cf., for example, Gen 48:16; Tob 5:22; etc). In the apocryphal books of the Old Testament and in writings composed between the two Testaments (which flourished around the time of Christ's life on earth) there are many references to angels. Our Lord spoke about them often, as we can see from the Gospels.

"In many parts of Sacred Scripture it is said that each of us has an angel. Our Lord affirms this when he speaks about children: 'in heaven their angels always behold the face of my Father' (Mt 18:10). And Jacob refers to the angel 'who freed him from all evil'. On this occasion the disciples thought that the angel of the apostle Peter was approaching" (St Bede, *Super Act. expositio, ad loc.*).

The first Christians' behaviour in adversity and their trust in God's help are an enduring example. "Drink at the clear fountain of the Acts of the Apostles. In the twelfth chapter, Peter, freed from prison by the ministry of Angels, comes to the house of the mother of Mark. Those inside will not believe the girl, who says that Peter is at the door. '*Angelus ejus est!* It must be his Angel!' they said.

137

Acts 15:13;
21:18
Gal 1:19

she insisted that it was so. They said, "It is his angel!" [16]But Peter continued knocking; and when they opened, they saw him and were amazed. [17]But motioning to them with his hand to be silent, he described to them how the Lord had brought him out of the prison. And he said, "Tell this to James and to the brethren." Then he departed and went to another place.

[18]Now when day came, there was no small stir among the soldiers over what had become of Peter. [19]And when Herod had sought for him and could not find him, he examined the sentries and ordered that they should be put to death. Then he went down from Judea to Caesarea, and remained there.

The death of Herod

[20]Now Herod was angry with the people of Tyre and

Illi autem dicebant: "Angelus eius est." [16]Petrus autem perseverabat pulsans; cum autem aperuissent, viderunt eum et obstupuerunt. [17]Annuens autem eis manu, ut tacerent, enarravit quomodo Dominus eduxisset eum de carcere dixitque: "Nuntiate Iacobo et fratribus haec." Et egressus abiit in alium locum. [18]Facta autem die erat non parva turbatio inter milites, quidnam de Petro factum esset. [19]Herodes autem cum requisisset eum et non invenisset, interrogatis custodibus iussit eos abduci; descendensque a Iudaea in Caesaream ibi commorabatur. [20]Erat autem iratus Tyriis et Sidoniis; at illi unanimes venerunt ad eum et persuaso Blasto, qui erat super cubiculum regis, postulabant pacem, eo

---

"See on what intimate terms the early Christians were with their guardian Angels.

"And you?" (J. Escrivá, *The Way*, 570).

17. After Peter and the other Apostles leave Jerusalem, the community in that city is governed by James the Less, the "brother" of the Lord; even before that he was a prominent figure in the Jerusalem church. According to Flavius Josephus, this James was stoned to death by order of the Sanhedrin (cf. *Jewish Antiquities*, XX, 200).

We do not know where Peter went after leaving Jerusalem—probably to Antioch or Rome. He was certainly in Antioch at one stage (cf. Gal 2:11), but it may not have been at this point. Tradition does state that Peter had his see in Antioch for a period. We do know that he was present at the Council of Jerusalem. In any event he ultimately settled in Rome.

According to St Jerome, Peter arrived in Rome in the second year of Claudius' reign (43 A.D.) and had his see there for twenty-five years, up to the fourteenth year of Nero's reign, that is, 68 A.D. (cf. St Jerome, *De viris illustribus*, I).

20-23. Herod Agrippa I must have died in Caesarea in the year 44 during

Sidon; and they came to him in a body, and having persuaded Blastus, the king's chamberlain, they asked for peace, because their country depended on the king's country for food. ²¹On an appointed day Herod put on his royal robes, took his seat upon the throne, and made an oration to them. ²²And the people shouted, "The voice of a god, and not of man!" ²³Immediately an angel of the Lord smote him,

Ezek 28:2
Dan 5:20
2 Mac 9:5, 28

---

quod aleretur regio eorum ab annona regis. ²¹Statuto autem die, Herodes, vestitus veste regia, sedens pro tribunali, contionabatur ad eos; ²²populus autem acclamabat: "Dei vox et non hominis!" ²³Confestim autem percussit eum angelus Domini, eo quod non dedisset gloriam Deo, et consumptus a vermibus exspiravit. ²⁴Verbum autem Dei crescebat et multiplicabatur. ²⁵Barnabas autem

---

the games in honour of Claudius. St Luke's brief account agrees with that of Josephus. "When at daybreak of the second day he made his way to the theatre", the Jewish historian writes, "and the rays of the sun made his garments look like silver and made him look splendid, his sycophants acclaimed him as a god and said, 'Up to this we regarded you as a man, but from now on we shall revere you as one who is more than mortal.' The king accepted this blasphemous flattery: he made no comment. But immediately he began to feel terrible stomach pains and he was dead within five days" (*Jewish Antiquities*, XIX, 344- 346).

The painful and unexpected death of this king who had persecuted the Church recalls the death of King Antiochus Epiphanes (cf. 2 Mac 9:5ff), another declared enemy of God's elect and of divine Law: "The all-seeing God of Israel struck him with an incurable and unseen blow."

Not content with persecuting the Church, Agrippa attributes to himself glory which belongs only to God; his evil life eventually provokes God to judge him in this way. "The hour of judgment has not yet come, but God wounds the most blameworthy of all, as an object lesson for others" (Chrysostom, *Hom. on Acts*, 27).

Agrippa's persecution of the Church and of Christians was the logical result of his failure to acknowledge God as lord of all: Agrippa sees him as a kind of rival. In his pride, he refuses to admit his human limitations and dependence on God; and he goes further and attacks God's work and God's servants. Human dignity is only possible if God's majesty is positively asserted and adored: in that recognition and service man's true wisdom lies.

" '*Deo omnis gloria*. All glory to God.' It is an emphatic confession of our nothingness. He, Jesus, is everything. We, without him, are worth nothing: nothing.

"Our vainglory would be just that: vain glory; it would be sacrilegious robbery. There should be no room for that 'I' anywhere" (J. Escrivá, *The Way*, 780).

because he did not give God the glory; and he was eaten by worms and died.

Barnabas and Saul return to Antioch

²⁵And Barnabas and Saul returned from^k Jerusalem when they had fulfilled their mission, bringing with them John whose other name was Mark.

PART THREE

THE SPREAD OF THE CHURCH AMONG THE GENTILES. MISSIONARY JOURNEYS OF ST PAUL

ST PAUL'S FIRST APOSTOLIC JOURNEY

13

The mission of Barnabas and Paul

¹Now in the church at Antioch there were prophets and

---

et Saulus reversi sunt in Ierusalem expleto ministerio, assumpto Ioanne, qui cognominatus est Marcus.
¹Erant autem in ecclesia, quae erat Antiochiae, prophetae et doctores: Barnabas

---

24. St Luke contrasts the failure and downfall of the Church's persecutors with the irresistible progress of the Word of God.

25. They "returned from Jerusalem": following the best Greek manuscripts, the reading accepted by the New Vulgate is "returned to Jerusalem" (cf. RSV note). However, it does not seem to fit in with the end of chapter 11 and the beginning of chapter 13. Therefore, from very early on many Greek manuscripts and translations (including the Sixto-Clementine edition of the Vulgate) read "returned from Jerusalem". It is not clear which is correct; the Navarre Spanish follows the New Vulgate.

1. From this point onwards Luke's account centres on the church of Antioch. This was a flourishing community, with members drawn from all sectors of society. In some respects its organization structure was like that of the

^kOther ancient authorities read *to*.

140

teachers, Barnabas, Symeon who was called Niger, Lucius of Cyrene, Manaen a member of the court of Herod the tetrarch, and Saul. ²While they were worshipping the Lord and fasting, the Holy Spirit said, "Set apart for me Barnabas and Saul for the work to which I have called them." ³Then after fasting and praying they laid their hands on them and sent them off.

Gal 1:15

Acts 6:6

---

et Simeon, qui vocabatur Niger, et Lucius Cyrenensis, et Manaen, qui erat Herodis tetrarchae collactaneus, et Saulus. ²Ministrantibus autem illis Domino et ieiunantibus, dixit Spiritus Sanctus: "Separate mihi Barnabam et Saulum in opus, ad quod vocavi eos." ³Tunc ieiunantes et orantes imponentesque eis

---

Jerusalem church; in others, not. It clearly had ordained ministers who were responsible for its government, who preached and administered the sacraments; alongside these we find prophets (cf. 11:28) and teachers, specially trained members of the community.

In the early Church "teachers" were disciples well versed in Sacred Scripture who were given charge of catechesis. They instructed the catechumens and other Christians in the basic teaching of the Gospel as passed on by the Apostles, and some of them had a capacity for acquiring and communicating to others an extensive and profound knowledge of the faith.

Teachers do not necessarily have to be priests or preachers. Preaching was usually reserved to ordained ministers; teachers had an important position in the Church: they were responsible for on-going doctrinal and moral education and were expected faithfully to hand on the same teaching as they themselves had received. A virtuous life and due learning would have protected them against any temptation to invent new teachings or go in for mere speculation not based on the Gospel (cf. 1 Tim 4:7; 6:20; Tit 2:1).

The *Letter to Diognetus* describes the ideal Christian teacher: "I do not speak of passing things nor do I go in search of new things, but, like the disciple of the Apostles that I am, I become a teacher of peoples. I do nothing but hand on what was given me by those who made themselves worthy disciples of the truth" (XI, 1).

2-3. "Worship" of the Lord includes prayer, but it refers primarily to the celebration of the Blessed Eucharist, which is at the centre of all Christian ritual. This text indirectly establishes a parallel between the Mass and the sacrificial rite of the Mosaic Law. The Eucharist provides a Christian with the nourishment he needs, and its celebration "causes the Church of God to be built up and grow in stature" (Vatican II, *Unitatis redintegratio*, 15). Significantly, the Eucharist is associated with the start of this new stage in the expansion of the Church.

Paul and Barnabas receive a missionary task directly from the Holy Spirit, and by an external sign—the laying on of hands—the Antiochene community prays God to go with them and bless them. In his promotion of the spread of the Church the Holy Spirit does not act at a distance, so to speak. Every step in the progress of the Church in the world is rightly attributed to the initiative of the Paraclete. It is as if God were repeatedly ratifying his salvific plans to make it perfectly plain that he is ever-faithful to his promises. "The mission of the Church is carried out by means of that activity through which, in obedience to Christ's command and moved by the grace and love of the Holy Spirit, the Church makes itself fully present to all men and people" (Vatican II, *Ad gentes*, 5).

The dispatch of Paul and Barnabas is inspired by the Holy Spirit, but it is also an ecclesial act: the Church gives them this charge, specifying God's plans and activating the personal vocation of the two envoys.

The Lord, "who had set me apart before I was born, and had called me by his grace [sent me] in order that I might preach him among the Gentiles" (Gal 1:15-16), now arranges, through the Church, for this mission to begin.

Fasting and prayer are the best preparation for the spiritual enterprise on which Paul and Barnabas are about to embark. "First, prayer; then, atonement; in the third place, very much 'in the third place', action" (J. Escrivá, *The Way*, 82). They know very well that their mission is not man-made and that it will produce results only with God's help. The prayer and penance which accompany apostolate are not just aimed at obtaining graces from God for others: the purpose of this prayer and fasting is to purify hearts and lips, so that the Lord will be at their side and ensure that none of their words "fall to the ground" (1 Sam 3:19).

13:4 - 14:28. This first missionary journey took Paul, accompanied by Barnabas, to Cyprus and central Galatia, in Asia Minor. He left Antioch in the spring of 45 and returned almost four years later, after preaching Christ to both Jews and Gentiles wherever he went.

St Luke's account, which covers chapters 13 and 14, is sketchy but accurate. At Seleucia (the port of Antioch, about 35 kilometres or 22 miles from the city) they embarked for Cyprus, the largest island in the eastern Mediterranean, where Barnabas came from. They disembarked at Salamis, the island's main city and port. There they went to the Jewish synagogues on a series of sabbaths.

In v. 6 it says that they crossed the island to Paphos, which is on the extreme west. This would have taken them several months because, although it is only 150 kilometres as the crow flies, there were many towns with Jewish communities, and since they had to stay in each for a number of sabbaths their progress would have been slow. We are told nothing about the result of this work of evangelizing en route from Salamis to Paphos, but the indications are that it was fruitful, because Barnabas will later go back to Cyprus, accompanied by Mark (cf. 15:39), to consolidate the work done on this first mission. New Paphos was where the proconsul resided.

From there they went on board ship again and travelled north, probably disembarking, after a short crossing, at Attalia. After a few miles they reached

They arrive in Cyprus

⁴So, being sent out by the Holy Spirit, they went down to Seleucia; and from there they sailed to Cyprus. ⁵When they Acts 12:12 arrived at Salamis, they proclaimed the word of God in the synagogues of the Jews. And they had John to assist them.

---

manus dimiserunt illos. ⁴Et ipsi quidem missi ab Spiritu Sancto devenerunt Seleuciam et inde navigaverunt Cyprum ⁵et, cum venissent Salamina, praedicabant verbum Dei in synagogis Iudaeorum; habebant autem et Ioannem

---

Perga in Pamphylia, a barren, inhospitable region at the base of the Taurus mountains, where Mark took leave of his companions.

Going from Perga to Pisidian Antioch (v. 14) meant a difficult journey of about 160 kilometres over mountain roads. This other Antioch was 1,200 metres above sea level and would have had a sizeable Jewish community, connected with the trade in hides. The busy commercial life of the region helped the spread of the Christian message (v. 49). Paul addressed his preaching to the Gentiles because of the hostility of many Jews.

The Apostles were expelled and they headed for Iconium, about 130 kilometres south east, where they stayed some months and then left because of disturbances created by both Gentiles and Jews: they had to flee to the region of Lycaonia, to two minor cities, Lystra and Derbe. There were very few Jews in Lystra, and no synagogue, and therefore Paul preached to the local people, in the open air; but some Jews, who had arrived from Antioch and Iconium, stoned him and left him for dead. Possibly with the help of Timothy (cf. 16:1) they managed to reach Derbe, where they made many disciples, and then set out on the journey home, retracing their steps through Lystra, Iconium and Pisidian Antioch. Things had quietened down, the local magistrates were new, and with a little prudence everything worked out quite well. The new disciples were confirmed in the faith, and priests, elders, were appointed to each local church. Paul and Barnabas then went back to Pamphylia and Attalia, where they took ship for Antioch, arriving probably well into the year 49.

5. In each city he visits, Paul usually begins his preaching of the Gospel in the local synagogue. This is not simply a tactic: it is in line with what he knows is God's plan of salvation. Like Jesus, he feels obliged to proclaim the Kingdom first to "Israelites [for] to them belong the sonship, the glory, the covenants, the giving of the Law, the worship, and the promises; to them belong the patriarchs, and of their race, according to the flesh, is the Christ" (Rom 9:4-5). The Jews have a right to be the first to have the Gospel preached to them, for they were the first to receive the divine promises (cf. 13:46).

Although many Jews choose not to listen to or understand the Word of God, there are many who do accept the Gospel for what it is—the fulness of the Old Testament. All over the Diaspora thousands of men and women like Simeon

143

⁶When they had gone through the whole island as far as Paphos, they came upon a certain magician, a Jewish false prophet, named Bar-Jesus. ⁷He was with the proconsul, Sergius Paulus, a man of intelligence, who summoned Barnabas and Saul and sought to hear the word of God. ⁸But Elymas the magician (for that is the meaning of his name) withstood them, seeking to turn away the proconsul from the faith. ⁹But Saul, who is also called Paul, filled with the Holy Spirit, looked intently at him ¹⁰and said, "You son of the devil, you enemy of all righteousness, full of all deceit and villainy, will you not stop making crooked the straight paths

2 Tim 3:8

Hos 14:10
Jn 8:44

---

ministrum. ⁶Et cum perambulassent universam insulam usque Paphum, invenerunt quendam virum magum pseudoprophetam Iudaeum, cui nomen Bariesu, ⁷qui erat cum proconsule Sergio Paulo, viro prudente. Hic accitis Barnaba et Saulo, quaesivit audire verbum Dei; ⁸resistebat autem illis Elymas, magus, sic enim interpretatur nomen eius, quaerens avertere proconsulem a fide. ⁹Saulus autem, qui et Paulus, repletus Spiritu Sancto, intuens in eum ¹⁰dixit: "O plene omni dolo et omni fallacia, fili Diaboli, inimice omnis iustitiae, non desines subvertere vias Domini rectas? ¹¹Et nunc ecce manus Domini super te: et eris caecus, non videns solem usque ad tempus." Et confestim cecidit in

---

and Anna, who were awaiting the Kingdom and serving the God of their forefathers with fasting and prayer (cf. Lk 2:25, 37), will receive the light of the Holy Spirit enabling them to recognize and accept Paul's preaching as coming from God.

It is true that the many Jewish communities established in the main cities of the Roman empire often hindered the spread of the Gospel; yet their very existence played a providential part in its progress.

6-7. Since the year 22 Cyprus had been a senatorial province and, as such, was governed by a proconsul. Sergius Paulus was the brother of the philosopher Seneca, Nero's tutor. He is described here as "a man of intelligence", in other words, he was a man of upright conscience and with the right disposition to listen to the Word of God. The proconsul's discernment helps him resist and reject the evil influence of the false prophet Bar-Jesus.

9. Here we learn, in an aside, that Saul has changed his name and now calls himself Paul. He did not do this at God's bidding, as in the case of Abraham (cf. Gen 17:5) or that of Peter (cf. Mt 16:18), to show that God had given him a new charge or mission. He was simply following the eastern custom of using a Roman name when it suited. Paul is the Roman name for Saul, and from now on he uses it instead of Saul.

of the Lord? [11]And now, behold, the hand of the Lord is upon Jn 9:39
you, and you shall be blind and unable to see the sun for a
time." Immediately mist and darkness fell upon him and he
went about seeking people to lead him by the hand. [12]Then Lk 4:32
the proconsul believed, when he saw what had occurred, for
he was astonished at the teaching of the Lord.

They cross into Asia Minor

[13]Now Paul and his company set sail from Paphos, and Acts 15:38
came to Perga in Pamphylia. And John left them and returned
to Jerusalem; [14]but they passed on from Perga and came to
Antioch of Pisidia.

Preaching in the synagogue of Antioch of Pisidia

And on the sabbath day they went into the synagogue and
sat down. [15]After the reading of the law and the prophets, the Acts 15:21
rulers of the synagogue sent to them, saying, "Brethren, if

---

eum caligo et tenebrae, et circumiens quaerebat, qui eum manum darent. [12]Tunc
proconsul, cum vidisset factum, credidit admirans super doctrinam Domini.
[13]Et cum a Papho navigassent, qui erant cum Paulo, venerunt Pergen
Pamphyliae; Ioannes autem discedens ab eis reversus est Hierosolymam. [14]Illi
vero pertranseuntes, a Perge venerunt Antiochiam Pisidiae, et ingressi
synagogam die sabbatorum sederunt. [15]Post lectionem autem Legis et
Prophetarum, miserunt principes synagogae ad eos dicentes: "Viri fratres, si
quis est in vobis sermo exhortationis ad plebem, dicite!" [16]Surgens autem

---

11. Paul's punishment of Bar-Jesus, Elymas, is one of the few punitive
miracles in the New Testament; in fact his purpose is not so much to punish the
false prophet as to convert him. "Paul chooses to convert him by means of a
miracle similar to that by which he himself was converted. The words 'for a
time' is not the word of one who punishes but of one who converts. If it had
been the word of one who punishes it would have left him blind for ever. He
punishes him only for a time, and also to win over the proconsul" (St John
Chrysostom, *Hom. on Acts*, 28).

"From his own experience," St Bede says, "the Apostle knew that the mind
can raise itself to the light from the darkness of the eyes" (*Super Act expositio,
ad loc.*).

The punishment of Elymas does influence Sergius Paulus' conversion, but
it is not crucial to it. What convinces the proconsul is the consistency and
sublimity of Christian teaching, which speaks for itself to people of good will.

15. Sabbath services in synagogues went right back to the post-exilic period

you have any word of exhortation for the people, say it." ¹⁶So Paul stood up, and motioning with his hand said:

Ex 3-15
Is 1:2

"Men of Israel, and you that fear God, listen. ¹⁷The God of this people Israel chose our fathers and made the people great during their stay in the land of Egypt, and with uplifted

Deut 1:31

arm he led them out of it. ¹⁸And for about forty years he bore

Deut 7:1
Josh 14:2

with^m them in the wilderness. ¹⁹And when he had destroyed seven nations in the land of Canaan, he gave them their land as an inheritance, for about four hundred and fifty years.

Gen 15:13
Ex 12:40
Judg 2:16
1 Sam 3:20
1 Sam 8-10
Ps 89:21
Is 44:28

²⁰And after that he gave them judges until Samuel the prophet. ²¹Then they asked for a king; and God gave them Saul the son of Kish, a man of the tribe of Benjamin, for forty years. ²²And when he had removed him, he raised up David to be their king; of whom he testified and said, 'I have found in David the son of Jesse a man after my heart, who will do

2 Sam 7:12

all my will.' ²³Of this man's posterity God has brought to

Paulus et manu silentium indicens ait: "Viri Israelitae et qui timetis Deum, audite. ¹⁷Deus plebis huius Israel elegit patres nostros et plebem exaltavit, cum essent incolae in terra Aegypti, et in brachio excelso eduxit eos ex ea ¹⁸et per quadraginta fere annorum tempus mores eorum sustinuit in deserto ¹⁹et destruens gentes septem in terra Chanaan sorte distribuit terram eorum, ²⁰quasi quadringentos et quinquaginta annos. Et post haec dedit iudices usque ad Samuel prophetam. ²¹Et exinde postulaverunt regem, et dedit illis Deus Saul filium Cis, virum de tribu Beniamin, annis quadraginta. ²²Et amoto illo, suscitavit illis David in regem, cui et testimonium perhibens dixit: 'Inveni David filium Iesse, virum secundum cor meum, qui faciet omnes voluntates meas.' ²³Huius Deus ex semine secundum promissionem eduxit Israel

---

(after the Babylonian captivity, which lasted from 586 to 539 B.C.), and by now they had a very settled form. They consisted of readings from Sacred Scripture, preaching and public prayers. No one was especially appointed to preside over these services; the president or ruler of the synagogue could ask any member of the community to take the ceremony (cf. 18:8); he supervised the preparations and made sure that everything was done properly.

16-41. Paul's address here is an excellent example of the way he used to present the Gospel to a mixed congregation of Jews and proselytes. He lists the benefits conferred by God on the chosen people from Abraham down to John the Baptist (vv. 16-25); he then shows how all the messianic prophecies were fulfilled in Jesus (vv. 26-37), and, by way of conclusion, states that justification

^mOther ancient authorities read *cared for* (Deut 1:31)

Israel a Saviour, Jesus, as he promised. ²⁴Before his coming
John had preached a baptism of repentance to all the people
of Israel. ²⁵And as John was finishing his course, he said,
'What do you suppose that I am? I am not he. No, but after
me one is coming, the sandals of whose feet I am not worthy
to untie.'

²⁶"Brethren, sons of the family of Abraham, and those
among you that fear God, to us has been sent the message of
this salvation. ²⁷For those who live in Jerusalem and their
rulers, because they did not recognize him nor understand
the utterances of the prophets which are read every sabbath,
fulfilled these by condemning him. ²⁸Though they could

Lk 3:3

Mt 3:11
Jn 1:20-27

Acts 3:17

Mt 27:22-23

salvatorem Iesum, ²⁴praedicante Ioanne ante adventum eius baptismum
paenitentiae omni populo Israel. ²⁵Cum impleret autem Ioannes cursum suum,
dicebat: 'Quid me abritramini esse? Non sum ego; sed ecce venit post me, cuius
non sum dignus calceamenta pedum solvere.' ²⁶Viri fratres, filii generis
Abraham et qui in vobis timent Deum, nobis verbum salutis huius missum est.
²⁷Qui enim habitabant Ierusalem et principes eorum, hunc ignorantes et voces
Prophetarum, quae per omne sabbatum leguntur, iudicantes impleverunt, ²⁸et

comes about through faith in Jesus, who died and then rose from the dead (vv.
38-41).

This address contains all the main themes of apostolic preaching, that is,
God's saving initiative in the history of Israel (vv. 17-22); reference to the
Precursor (vv. 24-25); the proclamation of the Gospel or *kerygma* in the proper
sense (vv. 26b-31a); mention of Jerusalem (v. 31b); arguments from Sacred
Scripture (vv. 33-37), complementing apostolic teaching and tradition (vv.
38-39); and a final exhortation, eschatological in character, announcing the
future (vv. 40-41). In many respects this address is like those of St Peter (cf.
2:14ff; 3:12ff), especially where it proclaims Jesus as Messiah and in its many
quotations from Sacred Scripture, chosen to show that the decisive event of the
Resurrection confirms Christ's divinity.

Paul gives a general outline of salvation history and then locates Jesus in it
as the expected Messiah, the point at which all the various strands in that history
meet and all God's promises are fulfilled. He shows that all the steps which
lead up to Jesus Christ, even the stage of John the Baptist, are just points on a
route. Earlier, provisional, elements must now, in Christ, give way to a new,
definitive situation.

"You that fear God" (v. 26): see the notes on Acts 2:5-11 and 10:2.

28. Paul does not back off from telling his Jewish listeners about the cross,
the painful death freely undergone by the innocent Jesus. They naturally find
it shocking and hurtful, but it is true and it is what brings salvation. "When I

charge him with nothing deserving death, yet they asked Pilate to have him killed. ²⁹And when they had fulfilled all that was written of him, they took him down from the tree, and laid him in a tomb. ³⁰But God raised him from the dead; ³¹and for many days he appeared to those who came up with him from Galilee to Jerusalem, who are now his witnesses

---

nullam causam mortis invenientes petierunt a Pilato, ut interficeretur; ²⁹cumque consummassent omnia, quae de eo scripta erant, deponentes eum de ligno posuerunt in monumento. ³⁰Deus vero suscitavit eum a mortuis; ³¹qui visus est per dies multos his, qui simul ascenderant cum eo de Galilaea in Ierusalem, qui

---

came to you, brethren," he says on another occasion, "I did not come proclaiming to you the testimony of God in lofty words or wisdom. For I decided to know nothing among you except Jesus Christ and him crucified" (1 Cor 2:1f).

Sometimes human logic cannot understand how Jesus could have died in this way. But the very fact that he did is evidence of the divine character of the Gospel and supports belief in the Christian faith. With the help of grace man can in some way understand the Lord making himself "obedient unto death, even death on a cross" (Phil 2:8). He can discover some of the reasons why God decided on this superabundant way of redeeming man. "It was very fitting," St Thomas Aquinas writes, "that Christ should die on a cross. First, to give an example of virtue. [. . .] Also, because this kind of death was the one most suited to atoning for the sin of the first man. . . . It was fitting for Christ, in order to make up for that fault, to allow himself be nailed to the wood, as if to restore what Adam had snatched away. [. . .] Also, because by dying on the cross Jesus prepares us for our ascent into heaven. [. . .] And because it also was fitting for the universal salvation of the entire world" (*Summa theologiae*, III, q. 46, a. 4).

Through Jesus' death on the cross we can see how much God loved us and consequently we can feel moved to love him with our whole heart and with all our strength. Only the cross of our Lord, an inexhaustible source of grace, can make us holy.

29-31. The empty tomb and the appearances of the risen Jesus to his disciples are the basis of the Church's testimony to the resurrection of the Lord, and they demonstrate that he did truly rise. Jesus predicted that he would rise on the third day after his death (cf. Mt 12:40; 16:21; 17:22; Jn 2:19). Faith in the Resurrection is supported by the fact of the empty tomb (because it was impossible for our Lord's body to have been stolen) and by his many appearances, during which he conversed with his disciples, allowed them to touch him, and ate with them (cf. Mt 28; Mk 16; Lk 24; Jn 20-21). In his First Letter to the Corinthians (15:3-6) Paul says that "[what I preached was] that

to the people. [32]And we bring you the good news that what God promised to the fathers, [33]this he has fulfilled to us their children by raising Jesus; as also it is written in the second psalm,

> 'Thou art my Son,
>
> today I have begotten thee.'

[34]And as for the fact that he raised him from the dead, no more to return to corruption, he spoke in this way,

> 'I will give you the holy and sure blessings of David.'

[35]Therefore he says also in another psalm,

> 'Thou wilt not let thy Holy One see corruption.'

[36]For David, after he had served the counsel of God in his own generation, fell asleep, and was laid with his fathers, and saw corruption; [37]but he whom God raised up saw no corruption. [38]Let it be known to you therefore, brethren, that

Acts 13:23
Ps 2:7
Is 55:3
Ps 16:10
I Kings 2:10
Acts 2:29
Rom 3:20

---

nunc sunt testes eius ad plebem. [32]Et nos vobis evangelizamus eam, quae ad patres promissio facta est, [33]quoniam hanc Deus adimplevit filiis eorum, nobis resuscitans Iesum, sicut et in Psalmo secundo scriptum est: 'Filius meus es tu; ego hodie genui te.' [34]Quod autem sucitaverit eum a mortuis, amplius iam non reversurum in corruptionem, ita dixit: 'Dabo vobis sancta David fidelia.' [35]Ideoque et in alio dicit: 'Non dabis sanctum tuum videre corruptionem.' [36]David enim sua generatione cum administrasset voluntati Dei, dormivit et appositus est ad patres suos et vidit corruptionem; [37]quem vero Deus suscitavit, non vidit corruptionem. [38]Notum igitur sit vobis, viri fratres, quia per hunc vobis

---

Christ died for our sins in accordance with the scriptures, that he was buried, that he was raised on the third day in accordance with the scriptures, and that he appeared to Cephas, then to the twelve. Then he appeared to more than five hundred brethren."

32-37. Paul gives three pertinent quotations from Scripture—Ps 2:7 ("Thou art my Son"), Is 55:3 ("I will give you the holy and sure blessings of David") and Ps 16:10 ("thy Holy One"). All refer to aspects of the Lord's Resurrection. Taken together, they help support and interpret one another, and to someone familiar with the Bible and with ways of interpreting it then current they reveal the full meaning of the main texts concerning the promises made to David. Paul's interpretation of Psalms 2 and 16 gets beneath the surface meaning of the texts and shows them to refer to the messianic king who, since he is born of God, will never experience the corruption of the grave.

38-39. This passage is reminiscent of Paul's teaching on justification as given in his Letter to the Romans. There we read that God "justifies him who

Acts 15:11
Rom 10:4
Heb 10:1-4

Heb 1:5

Acts 11:23

through this man forgiveness of sins is proclaimed to you, [39]and by him every one that believes is freed from everything from which you could not be freed by the law of Moses. [40]Beware, therefore, lest there come upon you that is said in the prophets:

[41]'Behold, you scoffers, and wonder, and perish;
for I do a deed in your days,
a deed you will never believe, if one declares it to you.'"

[42]As they went out, the people begged that these things might be told them the next sabbath. [43]And when the meeting of the synagogue broke up, many Jews and devout converts to Judaism followed Paul and Barnabas, who spoke to them and urged them to continue in the grace of God.

Paul and Barnabas preach to the pagans

[44]The next sabbath almost the whole city gathered together to hear the word of God. [45]But when the Jews saw

---

remissio peccatorum annuntiatur; ab omnibus, quibus non potuistis in lege Moysi iustificari, [39]in hoc omnis, qui credit, iustificatur. [40]Videte ergo, ne superveniat, quod dictum est in Prophetis: [41]'Videte, contemptores, et admiramini et disperdimini, quia opus operor ego in diebus vestris, opus, quod non credetis, si quis enarraverit vobis!'" [42]Exeuntibus autem illis, rogabant, ut sequenti sabbato loquerentur sibi verba haec. [43]Cumque dimissa esset synagoga, secuti sunt multi Iudaeorum et colentium proselytorum Paulum et Barnabam, qui loquentes suadebant eis, ut permanerent in gratia Dei. [44]Sequenti vero sabbato paene universa civitas convenit audire verbum Domini. [45]Videntes

---

has faith in Jesus" (3:26). The Council of Trent explains that "when the Apostle says that man is justified by faith . . . , these words must be taken in the sense that [. . .] 'faith is the beginning of salvation' (St Fulgentius, *De fide ad Petrum*, 1), the basis and root of all justification, without which 'it is impossible to please God' (Heb 11:6)" (*De iustificatione*, chap. 8).

Once he has received faith, man with the help of grace can address God freely, can accept as true everything that God has revealed, can recognize that he is a sinner, can trust in God's mercy and—ready at last to receive Baptism—can decide to keep the commandments and begin to live a new life (cf. *ibid.*, chap. 6).

However, what brings about justification—by eliminating sin and sancti-fying the person—is sanctifying grace, with the virtues and gifts that come in its train.

45. The opposition of these Jews, who in their jealousy contradict what Paul

the multitudes, they were filled with jealousy, and contradicted what was spoken by Paul, and reviled him. [46]And Paul and Barnabas spoke out boldly, saying, "It was necessary that the word of God should be spoken first to you. Since you thrust it from you, and judge yourselves unworthy of eternal life, behold, we turn to the Gentiles. [47]For so the Lord has commanded us, saying,

'I have set you to be a light for the Gentiles,
that you may bring salvation to the uttermost parts of the earth.'"

[48]And when the Gentiles heard this, they were glad and glorified the word of God; and as many as were ordained to

Mt 10:6

Is 49:6

Rom 8:28-30

---

autem turba Iudaei repleti sunt zelo et contradicebant his, quae a Paulo dicebantur, blasphemantes. [46]Tunc audenter Paulus et Barnabas dixerunt: "Vobis oportebat primum loqui verbum Dei; sed quoniam repellitis illud et indignos vos iudicatis aeternae vitae, ecce convertimur ad gentes. [47]Sic enim praecepit nobis Dominus: 'Posui te in lumen gentium, ut sis in salutem usque ad extremum terrae'." [48]Audientes autem gentes gaudebant et glorificabant verbum Domini, et crediderunt, quotquot erant praeordinati ad vitam aeternam;

---

says, will from now be the typical attitude of the synagogue to the Gospel. It emerges everywhere the Apostle goes, with the exception of Beroea (cf. 17:10-12).

46. Paul may have been hoping that Christianity would flourish on the soil of Judaism, that the Jews would peacefully and religiously accept the Gospel as the natural development of God's plans. His experience proved otherwise: he encountered the terrible mystery of the infidelity of most of the chosen people, his own people.

Even if Israel had been faithful to God's promises, it would still have been necessary to preach the Gospel to the Gentiles. The evangelization of the pagan world is not a consequence of Jewish rejection of the Word; it is required by the universal character of Christianity. To all men Christianity is the only channel of saving grace; it perfects the Law of Moses and reaches out beyond the ethnic and geographical frontiers of Judaism.

47. Paul and Barnabas quote Isaiah 49:6 in support of their decision to preach to the Gentiles. The Isaiah text referred to Christ, as Luke 2:32 confirms. But now Paul and Barnabas apply it to themselves because the Messiah is "light for the Gentiles" through the preaching of the Apostles, for they are conscious of speaking in Christ's name and on his authority. Therefore, probably here "the Lord" refers not to God the Father but to Christ.

eternal life believed. ⁴⁹And the word of the Lord spread throughout all the region. ⁵⁰But the Jews incited the devout women of high standing and the leading men of the city, and stirred up persecution against Paul and Barnabas, and drove

Mt 10:14
Acts 18:6

them out of their district. ⁵¹But they shook off the dust from their feet against them, and went to Iconium. ⁵²And the disciples were filled with joy and with the Holy Spirit.

14

Iconium evangelized. Persecution

Acts 13:14, 44

¹Now at Iconium they entered together into the Jewish synagogue, and so spoke that a great company believed, both

1 Thess 2:14

of Jews and of Greeks. ²But the unbelieving Jews stirred up the Gentiles and poisoned their minds against the brethren.

Mk 16:17-20
Heb 2:4

³So they remained for a long time, speaking boldly for the Lord, who bore witness to the word of his grace, granting signs and wonders to be done by their hands. ⁴But the people

---

⁴⁹ferebatur autem verbum Domini per universam regionem. ⁵⁰Iudaei autem concitaverunt honestas inter colentes mulieres et primos civitatis et excitaverunt persecutionem in Paulum et Barnabam et eiecerunt eos de finibus suis. ⁵¹At illi, excusso pulvere pedum in eos, venerunt Iconium; ⁵²discipuli quoque replebantur gaudio et Spiritu Sancto.
¹Factum est autem Iconii, ut eodem modo introirent synagogam Iudaeorum et ita loquerentur, ut crederet Iudaeorum et Graecorum copiosa multitudo. ²Qui vero increduli fuerunt Iudaei, suscitaverunt et exacerbaverunt animas gentium adversus fratres. ³Multo igitur tempore demorati sunt, fiducialiter agentes in Domino, testimonium perhibente verbo gratiae suae, dante signa et prodigia fieri per manus eorum. ⁴Divisa est autem multitudo civitatis: et quidam quidem

---

51. "They shook the dust from their feet": a traditional expression; the Jews regarded as unclean the dust of anywhere other than the holy land of Palestine. Our Lord extended the meaning of the phrase when he told the disciples he was sending them out to preach, "If any one will not receive you or listen to your words, shake off the dust from your feet" (Mt 10:14; cf. Lk 9:5). This gesture of Paul and Barnabas echoes what Jesus said and amounted to "closing the case" or putting on record the unbelief of the Jews.

4. "He who is not with me is against me," our Lord says in the Gospel (Mt 12:30). The Word of God is a direct, personal call to which man cannot adopt an indifferent or passive attitude. He has to take sides, whether he likes it or not; and in fact he does take sides. Many people who persecute or criticize the

of the city were divided; some sided with the Jews, and some
with the apostles. [5]When an attempt was made by both
Gentiles and Jews, with their rulers, to molest them and to
stone them, [6]they learned of it and fled to Lystra and Derbe,
cities of Lycaonia, and to the surrounding country; [7]and there
they preached the gospel.

2 Tim 3:11

Mt 10:23
Acts 11:19-20

Cure of a cripple at Lystra

[8]Now at Lystra there was a man sitting, who could not use
his feet; he was a cripple from birth, who had never walked.
[9]He listened to Paul speaking; and Paul, looking intently at
him and seeing that he had faith to be made well, [10]said in a
loud voice, "Stand upright on your feet." And he sprang up

Acts 3:2; 9:33

Mt 9:28

---

erant cum Iudaeis, quidam vero cum apostolis. [5]Cum autem factus esset impetus
gentilium et Iudaeorum cum principibus suis, ut contumeliis afficerent et
lapidarent eos, [6]intelligentes confugerunt ad civitates Lycaoniae, Lystram et
Derben et ad regionem in circuitu, [7]et ibi evengelizantes erant. [8]Et quidam vir
in Lystris infirmus pedibus sedebat, claudus ex utero matris suae, qui numquam
ambulaverat. [9]Hic audivit Paulum loquentem; qui intuitus eum et videns quia
haberet fidem, ut salvus fieret, [10]dixit magna voce: "Surge super pedes tuos

---

Church and Christians are often trying to justify their own personal infidelity
and resistance to God's grace.

St Luke here describes Paul and Barnabas as "apostles" (cf. 14:14). Even
though Paul is not one of the group of "the Twelve", for whom Luke usually
reserves the name of Apostles, he is regarded as and regarded himself as an
Apostle by virtue of his unique vocation (cf. 1 Cor 15:9; 2 Cor 11:5) and was
tireless in preaching to the Gentiles. When the writings of the Fathers mention
"the Apostle" without being any more specific than that, they mean St Paul,
because he is the Apostle most quoted and commented on, due to his many
letters.

6. Lystra was a Roman colony; Timothy was born and grew up there (cf.
16:1-2).

8-10. "Just as the lame man whom Peter and John cured at the gate of the
temple prefigured the salvation of the Jews, so too this cripple represents the
Gentile peoples distanced from the religion of the Law and the temple, but now
brought in through the preaching of the Apostle Paul" (St Bede, *Super Act
expositio, ad loc.*).

We are told that Paul realized the man "had faith to be made well". The man
is sure that he is going to be cured of his infirmity and he seems to be hoping
also that Paul will cure his soul. Paul responds to the man's faith and, as our

Acts 28:6 and walked. ¹¹And when the crowds saw what Paul had done, they lifted up their voices, saying in Lycaonian, "The gods have come down to us in the likeness of men!" ¹²Barnabas they called Zeus, and Paul, because he was the chief speaker, they called Hermes. ¹³And the priest of Zeus, whose temple was in front of the city, brought oxen and garlands to the gates and wanted to offer sacrifice with the people. ¹⁴But when the apostles Barnabas and Paul heard of it, they tore their garments and rushed out among the multitude, crying, Acts 10:26;
17:22-30 ¹⁵"Men, why are you doing this? We also are men, of like

rectus!" Et exsilivit et ambulabat. ¹¹Turbae autem cum vidissent, quod fecerat Paulus, levaverunt vocem suam Lycaonice dicentes: "Dii similes facti hominibus descenderunt ad nos!"; ¹²et vocabant Barnabam Iovem, Paulum vero Mercurium, quoniam ipse erat dux verbi. ¹³Sacerdos quoque templi Iovis, quod erat ante civitatem, tauros et coronas ad ianuas afferens cum populis, volebat sacrificare. ¹⁴Quod ubi audierunt apostoli Barnabas et Paulus, conscissis tunicis suis, exsilierunt in turbam clamantes ¹⁵et dicentes: "Viri, quid haec facitis? Et

Lord did in the case of the paralytic in Capernaum (cf. Mk 2:1ff), he enables him to walk and cleanses his soul of sin.

11-13. Astonished by the miracle, the pagans of Lystra are reminded of an ancient Phrygian legend according to which Zeus and Hermes (Mercury) once visited the area in the guise of travellers and worked wonders for those who gave them hospitality. They think this is a repeat and therefore prepare to give Paul and Barnabas honours, thinking they are gods in human form (cf. 10:26).

14. Jews rent their garments to symbolize their feelings of shock at something they heard and to reject it out of hand. However, sometimes they did it only as a matter of form and not for genuine religious reasons (cf. Mt 26:65). By rending their garments Paul and Barnabas dramatically display their deepest convictions and religious feelings against the slightest sign of idolatry.

15-18. Paul and Barnabas not only prevent any idolatry being offered them: they try to explain why they act in this way; they tell the Lystrans about the living God, the Creator of all things, who in his providence watches over mankind.

"Throughout history even to the present day, there is found among peoples a certain awareness of a hidden power, which lies behind the course of nature and the events of human life. At times there is even a recognition of a supreme being, or even a Father. This awareness and recognition results in a way of life that is imbued with a deep religious sense" (Vatican II, *Nostra aetate*, 2).

In this short exhortation (which anticipates some of the themes of Paul's

nature with you, and bring you good news, that you should turn from these vain things to a living God who made the heaven and the earth and the sea and all that is in them. ¹⁶In past generations he allowed all the nations to walk in their own ways; ¹⁷yet he did not leave himself without witness, for he did good and gave you from heaven rains and fruitful seasons, satisfying your hearts with food and gladness." ¹⁸With these words they scarcely restrained people from offering sacrifice to them.

Jer 5:24
Ps 147:8

Paul is stoned

¹⁹But Jews came there from Antioch and Iconium; and

2 Cor 11:25

---

nos mortales sumus similes vobis homines, evangelizantes vobis ab his vanis converti ad Deum vivum, qui fecit caelum et terram et mare et omnia, quae in eis sunt. ¹⁶Qui in praeteritis generationibus permisit omnes gentes ambulare in viis suis; ¹⁷et quidem non sine testimonio semetipsum reliquit benefaciens, de caelo dans vobis pluvias et tempora fructifera, implens cibo et laetitia corda vestra." ¹⁸Et haec dicentes vix sedaverunt turbas, ne sibi immolarent. ¹⁹Supervenerunt autem ab Antiochia et Iconio Iudaei et persuasis turbis lapidantesque Paulum trahebant extra civitatem aestimantes eum mortuum esse. ²⁰Circum-

---

address in Athens: cf. 17:22-31), the apostles use religious concepts accepted by pagans, trying to bring out their full meaning. They invite their listeners to give up idolatry and turn to the living God, of whom they have a vague knowledge. They speak to them, therefore, about a true God, who transcends man but is ever concerned about him. Everyday experience—the course of history, the changing seasons, and the fulfilment of noble human yearnings—demonstrates the providence of a God who invites people to find him in his works.

This first "natural" encounter with God, presaging future and greater revelations, stirs their consciences to interior conversion, that is, to change their lives and turn away from any action which deprives them of spiritual peace and prevents them from knowing God.

Acknowledging that God exists involves all kinds of practical consequences and is the foundation of the new type of life which the Gospel proposes and makes possible. When a person truly and sincerely recognizes his Creator as speaking to him through external things and in the intimacy of his conscience, he has taken a huge step in his spiritual life: he has controlled his tendency to assert moral autonomy and false independence and has taken the path of obedience and humility. It becomes easier for him to recognize and accept supernatural Revelation under the inspiration of grace.

19. Paul mentions this stoning in his Second Letter to the Corinthians. "Five

155

having persuaded the people, they stoned Paul and dragged him out of the city, supposing that he was dead. ²⁰But when the disciples gathered about him, he rose up and entered the city; and on the next day he went on with Barnabas to Derbe.

The return journey to Antioch

Mt 28:19   ²¹When they had preached the gospel to that city and had made many disciples, they returned to Lystra and to Iconium
Mt 10:22
Acts 11:23   and to Antioch, ²²strengthening the souls of the disciples,
1 Thess 3:3   exhorting them to continue in the faith, and saying that
Heb 10:36   through many tribulations we must enter the kingdom of

---

dantibus autem eum discipulis, surgens intravit civitatem. Et postera die profectus est cum Barnaba in Derben. ²¹Cumque evangelizassent civitati illi et docuissent multos, reversi sunt Lystram et Iconium et Antiochiam ²²confirmantes animas discipulorum, exhortantes, ut permanerent in fide, et quoniam per multas tribulationes oportet nos intrare in regnum Dei. ²³Et cum ordinassent

---

times I have received at the hands of the Jews the forty lashes less one. Three times I have been beaten with rods; once I was stoned" (11:24f).

20-22. "If you accept difficulties with a faint heart you lose joy and your peace, and you run the risk of not deriving spiritual profit from the trial" (J. Escrivá, *The Way*, 696).

St Paul is not cowed by persecution and physical suffering. He knows that this crisis is the prelude to abundant spiritual fruit, and in fact many people in this region do embrace the Gospel.

Even though St Luke records the progress and success of the Word of God, he also shows that its preachers certainly encounter the cross (cf. 13:14, 50). The Gospel meets with acceptance everywhere—and also with opposition. "Where there are many laurels", St Ambrose says, "there is fierce combat. It is good for you to have persecutors: that way you attain more rapid success in your enterprises" (*Expositio in Ps 118*, 20, 43).

The apostles have no difficulty in pointing to events to show the disciples that suffering and difficulties form part of Christian living.

"Cross, toil, anguish: such will be your lot as long as you live. That was the way Christ went, and the disciple is not above his master" (J. Escrivá, *The Way*, 699). "Each one of us has at some time or other experienced that serving Christ our Lord involves suffering and hardship; to deny this would imply that we had not yet found God [. . .]. Far from discouraging us, the difficulties we meet have to spur us on to mature as Christians. This fight sanctifies us and gives effectiveness to our apostolic endeavours" (J. Escrivá, *Friends of God*, 28 and 216).

God. [23]And when they had appointed elders for them in every Acts 13:3
church, with prayer and fasting, they committed them to the
Lord in whom they believed.

---

illis per singulas ecclesias presbyteros et orassent cum ieiunationibus, com-
mendaverunt eos Domino, in quem crediderant. [24]Transeuntesque Pisidiam

---

23. The appointment of elders in each church means that certain Christians
were invested with a ministry of government and religious worship, by a
liturgical rite of ordination. These have a share in the hierarchical and priestly
ministry of the Apostles, from whom their own ministry derives.

"The ministry of priests [. . .]", Vatican II teaches, "shares in the authority
by which Christ himself builds up and sanctifies and rules his Body" (*Presbyterorum ordinis*, 2). The ministerial office of priests is essential to the life of
every Christian community, which draws its strength from the Word of God
and the sacraments. Their priesthoood, derived from our Lord, is essentially
different from what is called the "priesthood common to all the faithful".

A man becomes a priest of the New Testament through a special calling from
God. "Our vocation," John Paul II told a huge gathering of priests in
Philadelphia, "is a gift from the Lord Jesus himself. It is a personal, individual
calling: we have been called by our name, just as Jeremiah was" (*Homily at the
Civic Center*, 4 October 1979).

The priestly life is a sublime vocation which cannot be delegated or
transferred to anyone else. It is a lifelong vocation and means that one has to
give himself entirely to God—and this he can do, with the help of grace, because
"we do not claim back our gift once given. It cannot be that God, who gave us
the impulse to say Yes, should now desire to hear us say No. . . .

"It should not surprise the world that God's calling through the Church
should continue, offering us a celibate ministry of love and service according
to our Lord Jesus Christ's example. This calling from God touched the very
depths of our being. And after centuries of experience the Church knows how
appropriate it is that priests should respond in this specific way in their lives,
to demonstrate the totality of the Yes they have said to our Lord" (*ibid.*).

"Since he wishes that no one be saved who has not first believed (cf. Mk
16:16), priests, like the co-workers of the bishops that they are, have as their
first duty to proclaim to all men the Gospel of God" (Vatican II, *Presbyterorum
ordinis*, 4). To carry out his mission well, a priest needs to be in contact with
our Lord all the time—"a personal, living encounter—with eyes wide open and
a heart beating fast—with the risen Christ" (John Paul II, *Homily in Santo
Domingo Cathedral*, 26 January 1979).

Reminding priests of their special duty to be witnesses to God in the modern
world, John Paul II invites them not only to bear in mind the Christian people,
from whom they come and whom they must serve, but also people at large;
they should not hide the fact that they are priests: "Do not help the trends

Acts 13:1

Acts 14:3; 15:4

²⁴Then they passed through Pisidia, and came to Pamphylia. ²⁵And when they had spoken the word in Perga, they went down to Attalia; ²⁶and from there they sailed to Antioch, where they had been commended to the grace of God for the work which they had fulfilled. ²⁷And when they arrived, they gathered the church together and declared all that God had done with them, and how he had opened a door of faith to the Gentiles. ²⁸And they remained no little time with the disciples.

---

venerunt Pamphyliam, ²⁵et loquentes in Perge verbum descenderunt in Attaliam. ²⁶Et inde navigaverunt Antiochiam, unde erant traditi gratiae Dei in opus, quod compleverunt. ²⁷Cum autem venissent et congregassent ecclesiam, rettulerunt quanta fecisset Deus cum illis et quia aperuisset gentibus ostium fidei. ²⁸Morati sunt autem tempus non modicum cum discipulis.

---

towards 'taking God off the streets' by yourselves adopting secular modes of dress and behaviour" (*Address at Maynooth University*, 1 October 1979).

24-26. Paul and Barnabas return to Syrian Antioch, taking in the cities they have visited—in reverse order: Derbe, Lystra, Icononium, Pisidian Antioch and Perga. At the port of Attalia they take ship for Syria and arrive shortly afterwards in Antioch. Their journey, which began around the year 45, has taken four years.

Despite the animosity and persecution they experienced in these cities, the two missionaries do not avoid returning. They want to complete arrangements for the government of the new churches and to consolidate the faith of the disciples. The possible risks involved do not cause them any concern.

"Whosoever would save his life will lose it; and whoever loses his life for my sake and the gospel's will save it" (Mk 8:35). "These are mysterious and paradoxical words," John Paul II writes. "But they cease to be mysterious if we strive to put them into practice. Then the paradox disappears and we can plainly see the deep simplicity of their meaning. To all of us this grace is granted in our priestly life and in our zealous service" (*Letter to all priests*, 8 April 1979, 5).

15

THE COUNCIL OF JERUSALEM

Dissension at Antioch; Judaizers

¹But some men came down from Judea and were teaching the brethren, "Unless you are circumcised according to the custom of Moses, you cannot be saved." ²And when Paul and Barnabas had no small dissension and debate with them, Paul and Barnabas and some of the others were appointed to go up to Jerusalem to the apostles and the elders about this question.

Gen 17:10
Gal 2:12

Gal 2:1-2

---

¹Et quidem descendentes de Iudaea docebant fratres: "Nisi circumcidamini secundum morem Moysis, non potestis salvi fieri." ²Facta autem seditione et conquisitione non minima Paulo et Barnabae adversum illos, statuerunt, ut ascenderent Paulus et Barnabas et quidam alii ex illis ad apostolos et

---

1-35. This chapter is the centre of Acts, not just because it comes right in the middle of the book but also because it covers the key event as far as concerns the universality of the Gospel and its unrestricted spread among the Gentiles. It is directly linked to the conversion of the pagan Cornelius; here, with the help of the Holy Spirit, all the consequences of that event are drawn out.

Christians with a Pharisee background—"certain men [who] came from James" (Gal 2:12)—arriving in Antioch, assert categorically that salvation is impossible unless a person is circumcised and practises the Law of Moses. They accept (cf. 11:18) that Gentile converts can be baptized and become part of the Church; but they do not properly understand the economy of the Gospel, that it is the *new* way; they think that the Mosaic rites and precepts are all still necessary for attaining salvation. The need arises, therefore, for the whole question to be brought to the Apostles and elders in Jerusalem, who form the government of the Church.

2. Paul and Barnabas are once again commissioned by the Antiochene community to go to Jerusalem (cf.11:30). Paul says in Galatians 2:2 that this journey to the Holy City was due to a special revelation. Possibly the Holy Spirit inspired him to volunteer for it. "Paul," St Ephraem writes, "so as not to change without the Apostles' accord anything which they would allow to be done perhaps because of the weakness of the Jews, make his way to Jerusalem to see to the setting aside of the Law and of circumcision in the presence of the disciples: without the Apostles' support they [Paul and Barnabas] do not want to set them aside" (*Armenian Commentary, ad loc.*).

Paul and Barnabas go to Jerusalem

Acts 14:27

³So, being sent on their way by the church, they passed through both Phoenicia and Samaria, reporting the conversion of the Gentiles, and they gave great joy to all the brethren. ⁴When they came to Jerusalem, they were welcomed by the church and the apostles and the elders, and they declared all that God had done with them. ⁵But some believers who belonged to the party of the Pharisees rose up, and said, "It is necessary to circumcise them, and to charge them to keep the law of Moses."

Peter's address to the elders

⁶The apostles and the elders were gathered together to

---

presbyteros in Ierusalem super hac quaestione. ³Illi igitur deducti ab ecclesia pertransiebant Phoenicem et Samariam narrantes conversionem gentium et faciebant gaudium magnum omnibus fratribus. ⁴Cum autem venissent Ierusalem, suscepti sunt ab ecclesia et apostolis et presbyteris et annuntiaverunt quanta Deus fecisset cum illis. ⁵Surrexerunt autem quidam de haeresi pharisaeorum, qui crediderunt, dicentes: "Oportet circumcidere eos, praecipere quoque servare legem Moysis!" ⁶Conveneruntque apostoli et presbyteri videre

---

4. This does not mean that all the members of the Church were present to receive Paul: the whole Church was morally present in those brethren who attended the gathering and particularly in the Apostles and elders.

5. "Party": the Greek and the New Vulgate both literally say "heresy". However, in this context the word is not pejorative. It is a correct use of language in view of the religious exclusivity and separateness practised by the Pharisees: they saw themselves as, and in fact were, the rightful representatives of post-exilic Judaism (cf. note on Acts 13:15). The Pharisees mentioned here were Christians who in practice still lived like Jews.

6-21. The hierarchical Church, consisting of the Apostles and elders or priests, now meets to study and decide whether baptized Gentiles are obliged or not to be circumcised and to keep the Old Law. This is a question of the utmost importance to the young Christian Church and the answer to it has to be absolutely correct. Under the leadership of St Peter, the meeting deliberates at length, but it is not going to devise a new truth or new principles: all it does is, with the aid of the Holy Spirit, to provide a correct interpretation of God's promises and commandments regarding the salvation of men and the way in which Gentiles can enter the New Israel.

This meeting is seen as the first general council of the Church, that is, the prototype of the series of councils of which the Second Vatican Council is the

consider this matter. [7]And after there had been much debate, Acts 2:14
Peter rose and said to them, "Brethren, you know that in the
early days God made choice among you, that by my mouth
the Gentiles should hear the word of the gospel and
believe.[8]And God who knows the heart bore witness to them, Acts 10:44; 11:15
giving them the Holy Spirit just as he did to us; [9]and he made
no distinction between us and them, but cleansed their hearts
by faith. [10]Now therefore why do you make trial of God by Mt 11:30; 23:4 Gal 5:1
putting a yoke upon the neck of the disciples which neither

---

de verbo hoc. [7]Cum autem magna conquisitio fieret, surgens Petrus dixit ad
eos: "Viri fratres, vos scitis quoniam ab antiquis diebus in vobis elegit Deus
per os meum audire gentes verbum evangelii et credere; [8]et qui novit corda,
Deus testimonium perhibuit illis dans Spiritum Sanctum sicut et nobis [9]et nihil
discrevit inter nos et illos fide purificans corda eorum. [10]Nunc ergo quid tentatis
Deum imponere iugum super cervicem discipulorum, quod neque patres nostri

---

most recent. Thus, the Council of Jerusalem displays the same features as the
later ecumenical councils in the history of the Church: a) it is a meeting of the
rulers of the entire Church, not of ministers of one particular place; b) it
promulgates rules which have binding force for all Christians; c) the content of
its decrees deals with faith and morals; d) its decisions are recorded in a written
document—a formal proclamation to the whole Church; e) Peter presides over
the assembly.

According to the *Code of Canon Law* (can. 338-341) ecumenical councils
are assemblies—summoned and presided over by the Pope—of bishops and
some others endowed with jurisdiction; decisions of these councils do not
oblige unless they are confirmed and promulgated by the Pope. This assembly
at Jerusalem probably took place in the year 49 or 50.

7-11. Peter's brief but decisive contribution follows on a lengthy discussion
which would have covered the arguments for and against the need for
circumcision to apply to Gentile Christians. St Luke does not give the
arguments used by the Judaizing Christians (these undoubtedly were based on
a literal interpretation of the compact God made with Abraham—cf. Gen
17—and on the notion that the Law was perennial).

Once again, Peter is a decisive factor in Church unity. Not only does he draw
together all the various legitimate views of those trying to reach the truth on
this occasion: he points out where the truth lies. Relying on his personal
experience (what God directed him to do in connexion with the baptism of
Cornelius: cf. chap. 10), Peter sums up the discussion and offers a solution
which coincides with St Paul's view of the matter: it is grace and not the Law
that saves, and therefore circumcision and the Law itself have been superseded
by faith in Jesus Christ. Peter's argument is not based on the severity of the Old

Gal 2:15-21;
3:22-26
Eph 2:1-10
our fathers nor we have been able to bear? ¹¹But we believe
that we shall be saved through the grace of the Lord Jesus,
just as they will."

James' speech

Acts 12:17
Gal 2:9
¹²And all the assembly kept silence; and they listened to
Barnabas and Paul as they related what signs and wonders
God had done through them among the Gentiles. ¹³After they
finished speaking, James replied, "Brethren, listen to me.

---

neque nos portare potuimus? ¹¹Sed per gratiam Domini Iesu credimus salvari
quemadmodum et illi." ¹²Tacuit autem omnis multitudo, et audiebant Barnabam
et Paulum narrantes quanta fecisset Deus signa et prodigia in gentibus per eos.
¹³Et postquam tacuerunt, respondit Iacobus dicens: "Viri fratres, audite me.

Law or the practical difficulties Jews experience in keeping it; his key point is
that the Law of Moses has become irrelevant; now that the Gospel has been
proclaimed the Law is not necessary for salvation: he does not accept that it is
necessary to obey the Law in order to be saved. Whether one can or should
keep the Law for other reasons is a different and secondary matter.

As a gloss on what Peter says, St Ephraem writes that "everything which
God has given us through faith and the Law has been given by Christ to the
Gentiles through faith and without observance of the Law" (*Armenian
Commentary, ad loc.*).

11. St Paul makes the same point in his letter to the Galatians: "We
ourselves, who are Jews by birth and not Gentile sinners, yet who know that a
man is not justified by works of the law but through faith in Jesus Christ, even
we have believed by faith in Christ, and not by works of the law, because by
works of the law shall no one be justified" (2:15f).

"No one can be sanctified after sin," St Thomas Aquinas, says, "unless it be
through Christ. [. . .] Just as the ancient fathers were saved by faith in the Christ
to come, so we are saved by faith in the Christ who was born and suffered"
(*Summa theologiae*, III, q. 61, a. 3 and 4).

"That thing is absolutely necessary without which no one can attain
salvation: this is the case with the grace of Christ and with the sacrament of
Baptism, by which a person is reborn in Christ" (*ibid.*, q. 84, a. 5).

13-21. James the Less, to whose authority the Judaizers had appealed,
follows what Peter says. He refers to the Apostle by his Semitic
name—Symeon—and accepts that he has given a correct interpretation of what
God announced through the prophets. In saying that God had "visited the
Gentiles to take out of them a people for his name" he seems to be giving up
the Jewish practice of using "people" to refer to the Israelites (Ex 19:9; Deut

[14]Symeon has related how God first visited the Gentiles, to take out of them a people for his name. [15]And with this the words of the prophets agree, as it is written,
[16]'After this I will return,   Amos 9:11-12
And I will rebuild the dwelling of David, which has fallen;
I will rebuild its ruins,
and I will set it up,
[17]that the rest of men may seek the Lord,
and all the Gentiles who are called by my name,
[18]says the Lord, who has made these things known from of old.'
[19]Therefore my judgment is that we should not trouble those

---

[14]Simeon narravit quemadmodum primum Deus visitavit sumere ex gentibus populum nomini suo, [15]et huic concordant verba Prophetarum, sicut scriptum est: [16]'Post haec revertar et reaedificabo tabernaculum David, quod decidit, et diruta eius reaedificabo et erigam illud, [17]ut requirant reliqui hominum Dominum et omnes gentes, super quas invocatum est nomen meum, dicit Dominus faciens haec [18]nota a saeculo'. [19]Propter quod ego iudico non inquietari eos, qui ex gentibus convertuntur ad Deum, [20]sed scribere ad eos, ut

---

7:6; 14:2) as distinct from the Gentiles—again the central message of Paul, that baptized pagans also belong to the people of the promise: "You are no longer strangers and sojourners, but you are fellow citizens with the saints and members of the household of God" (Eph 2:19).

James' concurrence with what Peter says and the fact that both are in agreement with the basic principles of Paul's preaching indicate that the Holy Spirit is at work, giving light to all to understand the true meaning of the promises contained in Scripture. "As I see it, the richness of these great events cannot be explained unless it be with help from the same Holy Spirit who was their author" (Origen, *In Ex hom.*, IV, 5).

James immediately goes on to propose that the meeting issue a solemn, formal statement which proclaims the secondary character of the Law and at the same time makes allowance for the religious sensitivity of Jewish Christians by prohibiting four things— 1) the eating of meat from animals used in sacrifices to idols; 2) avoidance of fornication, which goes against the natural moral order; 3) eating meat which has blood in it; and 4) eating food made with the blood of animals.

These prohibitions are laid down in Leviticus and to be understood properly they must be read in the light of Leviticus. The Jews considered that if they ate meat offered to idols this implied in some way taking part in sacrilegious

Gen 9:4
Lev 17:11
1 Cor 8-10

Acts 13:27

of the Gentiles who turn to God, [20]but should write to them to abstain from the pollutions of idols and from unchastity and from what is strangled[n] and from blood. [21]For from early generations Moses has had in every city those who preach him, for he is read every sabbath in the synagogues."

The council's decision

[22]Then it seemed good to the apostles and the elders, with the whole church, to choose men from among them and send them to Antioch with Paul and Barnabas. They sent Judas called Barsabbas, and Silas, leading men among the brethren, [23]with the following letter: "The brethren, both the apostles and the elders, to the brethren who are of the

---

abstineant se a contaminationibus simulacrorum et fornicatione et suffocato et sanguine. [21]Moyses enim a generationibus antiquis habet in singulis civitatibus, qui eum praedicant in synagogis, ubi per omne sabbatum legitur." [22]Tunc placuit apostolis et presbyteris cum omni ecclesia electos viros ex eis mittere Antiochiam cum Paulo et Barnaba: Iudam, qui cognominatur Barsabbas, et Silam, viros primos in fratribus, [23]scribentes per manum eorum: "Apostoli et presbyteri fratres his, qui sunt Antiochiae et Syriae et Ciliciae fratribus,

---

worship (Lev 17:7-9). Although St Paul makes it clear that Christians were free to act as they pleased in this regard (cf. 1 Cor 8-10), he will also ask them not to scandalize "the weak".

Irregular unions and transgressions in the area of sexual morality are mentioned in Leviticus 18:6ff; some of the impediments will later be included in Church law on marriage.

Abstention from blood and from the meat of strangled animals (cf. Lev 17:10ff) was based on the idea that blood was the container of life and as such belonged to God alone. A Jew would find it almost impossible to overcome his religious and cultural repugnance at the consumption of blood.

22-29. The decree containing the decisions of the Council of Jerusalem incorporating St James' suggestions makes it clear that the participants at the Council are conscious of being guided in their conclusions by the Holy Spirit and that in the last analysis it is God who has decided the matter.

"We should take," Melchor Cano writes in the sixteenth century, "the same road as the apostle Paul considered to be the one best suited to solving all matters to do with the doctrine of the faith. [. . .] The Gentiles might have sought satisfaction from the Council because it seemed to take from the freedom granted them by Jesus Christ, and because it imposed on the disciples certain ceremonies as necessary, when in fact they were not, since faith is the key to

[n]Other early authorities omit *and from what is strangled*

Gentiles in Antioch and Syria and Cilicia, greeting. [24]Since we have heard that some persons from us have troubled you with words, unsettling your minds, although we gave them no instructions, [25]it has seemed good to us in assembly to choose men and send them to you with our beloved Barnabas and Paul, [26]men who have risked their lives for the sake of our Lord Jesus Christ. [27]We have therefore sent Judas and Silas, who themselves will tell you the same things by word of mouth. [28]For it has seemed good to the Holy Spirit and to us to lay upon you no greater burden than these necessary things: [29]that you abstain from what has been sacrificed to

---

salutem! [24]Quoniam audivimus quia quidam ex nobis exeuntes turbaverunt vos verbis evertentes animas vestras, quibus non mandavimus, [25]placuit nobis collectis in unum eligere viros et mittere ad vos cum carissimis nobis Barnaba et Paulo, [26]hominibus, qui tradiderunt animas suas pro nomine Domini nostri Iesu Christi. [27]Misimus ergo Iudam et Silam, qui et ipsi verbis referent eadem. [28]Visum est enim Spiritu Sancto et nobis nihil ultra imponere vobis oneris quam haec necessario: [29]abstinere ab idolothytis et sanguine et suffocatis et

---

salvation. Nor did the Jews object by invoking Sacred Scripture against the Council's decision on the grounds that Scripture seems to support their view that circumcision is necessary for salvation. So, by respecting the Council they gave us all the criterion which should be observed in all later times; that is, to place full faith in the authority of synods confirmed by Peter and his legitimate successors. They say, It has seemed good to the Holy Spirit and to us; thus, the Council's decision is the decision of the Holy Spirit himself" (*De locis*, V, 4).

It is the Apostles and the elders, with the whole Church, who designate the people who are to publish the Council's decree, but it is the Hierarchy which formulates and promulgates it. The text contains two parts—one dogmatic and moral (v. 28) and the other disciplinary (v. 29). The dogmatic part speaks of imposing no burden other than what is essential and therefore declares that pagan converts are free of the obligation of circumcision and of the Mosaic Law but are subject to the Gospel's perennial moral teaching on matters to do with chastity. This part is permanent: because it has to do with a necessary part of God's salvific will it cannot change.

The disciplinary part of the decree lays down rules of prudence which can change, which are temporary. It asks Christians of Gentile background to abstain—out of charity towards Jewish Christians—from what has been sacrificed to idols, from blood and from meat of animals killed by strangulation.

The effect of the decree means that the disciplinary rules contained in it, although they derive from the Mosaic Law, no longer oblige by virtue of that Law but rather by virtue of the authority of the Church, which has decided to apply them for the time being. What matters is not what Moses says but what

idols and from blood and from what is strangled[n] and from
unchastity. If you keep yourselves from these, you will do
well. Farewell."

The reception of the council's decree

[30]So when they were sent off, they went down to Antioch;
and having gathered the congregation together, they
delivered the letter. [31]And when they read it, they rejoiced at

Acts 11:27

the exhortation. [32]And Judas and Silas, who were themselves
prophets, exhorted the brethren with many words and
strengthened them. [33]And after they had spent some time,
they were sent off in peace by the brethren to those who had

Acts 14:28

sent them.[o] [35]But Paul and Barnabas remained in Antioch,
teaching and preaching the word of the Lord, with many
others also.

---

fornicatione; a quibus custodientes vos bene agetis. Valete." [30]Illi igitur dimissi
descenderunt Antiochiam et congregata multitudine, tradiderunt epistulam;
[31]quam cum legissent, gavisi sunt super consolatione. [32]Iudas quoque et Silas,
cum et ipsi essent prophetae, verbo plurimo consolati sunt fratres et
confirmaverunt. [33]Facto autem tempore, dimissi sunt cum pace a fratribus ad
eos, qui miserant illos.[(34)] [35]Paulus autem et Barnabas demorabantur Antiohciae
docentes et evangelizantes cum aliis pluribus verbum Domini. [36]Post aliquot
autem dies dixit ad Barnabam Paulus: "Revertentes visitemus fratres per

---

Christ says through the Church. The Council "seems to maintain the Law in
force", writes St John Chrysostom, "because it selects various prescriptions
from it, but in fact it suppresses it, because it does not accept *all* its prescriptions.
It had often spoken about these points, it sought to respect the Law and yet
establish these regulations as coming not from Moses but from the Apostles"
(*Hom. on Acts*, 33).

34. This verse is not to be found in the more important manuscripts and is
not in the New Vulgate. It did appear in the Sixto-Clementine edition of the
Vulgate. It was probably a gloss added for clarification and not a part of the
authentic text of Acts.

35. It was probably during this period that the incident took place in Antioch
when St Paul publicly taxed St Peter with drawing back and separating himself
from Gentile Christians "fearing the circumcision party" (cf. Gal 2:11-14).

---

[n]Other early authorities omit *and from what is strangled*
[o]Other ancient authorities insert verse 34, *But it seemed good to Silas to remain there*

ST PAUL'S SECOND APOSTOLIC JOURNEY

Silas, Paul's new companion

³⁶And after some days Paul said to Barnabas, "Come, let us return and visit the brethren in every city where we proclaimed the word of the Lord, and see how they are." ³⁷And Barnabas wanted to take with them John called Mark. ³⁸But Paul thought best not to take with them one who had withdrawn from them in Pamphylia, and had not gone with them to the work. ³⁹And there arose a sharp contention, so that they separated from each other; Barnabas took Mark with him and sailed away to Cyprus, ⁴⁰but Paul chose Silas

Acts 12:12

Act 13:13
Col 4:10
2 Tim 4:11

---

universas civitates, in quibus praedicavimus verbum Domini, quomodo se habeant." ³⁷Barnabas autem volebat secum assumere et Ioannem, qui cognominatur Marcus; ³⁸Paulus autem iudicabat eum, qui discessisset ab eis a Pamphylia et non esset cum eis in opus, non debere recipi eum. ³⁹Facta est autem exacerbatio, ita ut discederent ab invicem, et Barnabas assumpto Marco navigaret Cyprum. ⁴⁰Paulus vero, electo Sila, profectus est traditus gratiae

---

36-39. Paul and Barnabas part company because of a disagreement over Mark. "Paul sterner, Barnabas kinder, each holds on to his point of view. The argument shows human weakness at work" (St Jerome, *Dialogus adversus pelagianos*, II, 17). At any event, both apostles are acting in good conscience and God amply blesses their new missionary journeys. "The gifts of the two men differ," Chrysostom comments, "and clearly this difference is itself a gift. [. . .] Now and then one hears an argument, but even that is part of God's providence, and all that happens is that each is put in the place which suits him best. . . .

"Observe that there is nothing wrong in their separating if this means that they can evangelize all the Gentiles. If they go different ways, in order to teach and convert people, there is nothing wrong about that. What should be emphasized is not their difficulties but what unites them. [. . .] If only all our divisions were motivated by zeal for preaching!" (*Hom. on Acts*, 34).

This disagreement does not mean that the two disciples have become estranged. Paul always praised Barnabas and Mark for their zeal (cf. 1 Cor 9:6; Gal 2:9) and later on he was happy to have Mark work with him (cf. Col 4:10).

15:40 - 18:23. The original purpose of this second apostolic journey is to re-visit the brethren in the cities evangelized during the first journey and to confirm them in the faith. Once again the journey begins at Antioch and it will end there in the spring of 53.

and departed, being commended by the brethren to the grace of the Lord. [41]And he went through Syria and Cilicia, strengthening the churches.

Domini a fratribus; [41]perambulabat autem Syriam et Ciliciam confirmans ecclesias.

St Paul is now acting on his own initiative: he has not been commissioned by any community to undertake this journey. He takes with him Silas, a Christian from Jerusalem and a Roman citizen, who like Paul has two names—Silas and Silvanus. This is the same Silvanus as mentioned in 2 Cor 1:19; 1 Thess 1:1; 2 Thess 1:1; and 1 Pet 5:12.

The account takes up almost three chapters of Acts, up to 18:23, at which point St Luke moves directly into his account of the Apostle's third journey.

Paul sets out early in the year 50, with no fixed itinerary, heading for the as yet unevangelized cities which he aims to visit. The two apostles go to Derbe from Cilicia, Paul's native region, following the line of the Taurus mountains and the plain of Lycaonia. They then go on to Lystra, where Timothy lives, and he joins them as they make their way to Iconium and Pisidian Antioch. The Holy Spirit then instructs them to go north into Phrygia and Galatia, where Paul is taken ill: this illness must have held them up for some months; after evangelizing the Galatians the Spirit directs them to Macedonia and they make for Troas to take ship. St Luke, whom the Apostle will later call "the beloved physician" (Col 4:13), must have joined them at this point.

The sea journey from Troas to Neapolis is 230 kilometres (150 miles) and half-way across lay the island of Samothrace, where they briefly stopped. About 15 kilometres north of Neapolis lay Philippi, a Roman colony where the events described in chapter 16 take place. From there they went to Thessalonica, the seat of government of the Roman province of Macedonia. Due to disturbances they had to leave there and go to Beroea, and some of the disciples brought the Apostle as far as Athens. The last part of chapter 17 describes what happened in Athens.

The next city to be evangelized was Corinth, where St Paul stayed over a year and a half; at the end of his stay he decided to go to Jerusalem before returning to Antioch. On his way there he made a short stop at Ephesus, where he left Priscilla and Aquila, who had travelled with him from Corinth.

The whole journey lasted three years, in the course of which St Paul suffered illnesses, the lash, imprisonment and persecution, and won for Christ disciples in more than ten cities of Asia Minor and Europe and numerous other places on his route.

Timothy joins Paul

¹And he came also to Derbe and to Lystra. A disciple was there, named Timothy, the son of a Jewish woman who was a believer; but his father was a Greek. ²He was well spoken of by the brethren at Lystra and Iconium. ³Paul wanted Timothy to accompany him; and he took him and circumcised him because of the Jews that were in those places, for they all knew that his father was a Greek.

Phil 2:19-22
2 Tim 1:5

---

¹Pervenit autem in Derben et Lystram. Et ecce discipulus quidam erat ibi nomine Timotheus, filius mulieris Iudaeae fidelis, patre autem Graeco; ²huic testimonium reddebant, qui in Lystris erant et Inconii fratres. ³Hunc voluit Paulus secum proficisci et assumens circumcidit eum propter Iudaeos, qui erant

---

1-3. At Lystra, a city which he evangelized during his first journey (cf. 14:6), Paul meets a young Christian, Timothy, of whom he had received good reports. His Jewish mother Eunice and his grandmother Lois were Christians, and Timothy had received the faith from them.

Paul's apostolic plans for Timothy, and the fact that, despite being Jewish through his mother, he had not been circumcised, lead him to circumcise him: everyone in the city knew he was a Jew and those who practised the Mosaic Law might easily have regarded him as an apostate from Judaism, in which case he would be unlikely to be an effective preacher of the Gospel to Jews.

"He took Timothy," St Ephraem comments, "and circumcised him. Paul did not do this without deliberation: he always acted prudently; but given that Timothy was being trained to preach the Gospel to Jews everywhere, and to avoid their not giving him a good hearing because he was not circumcised, he decided to circumcise him. In doing this he was not aiming to show that circumcision was necessary—he had been the one most instrumental in eliminating it—but to avoid putting the Gospel at risk" (*Armenian Commentary, ad loc.*).

In the case of Titus, St Paul did not have him circumcised (cf. Gal 2:3-5); which showed that he did not consider circumcision to be a matter of principle; it is simply for reasons of pastoral prudence and common sense that he has Timothy circumcised. Titus was the son of Gentile parents; to have circumcised him—at a point when Paul was fighting against Judaizers—would have meant Paul giving up his principles. However, the circumcision of Timothy, which takes place later, is in itself something that has no relevance from the Christian point of view (cf. Gal 5:6, 15).

Timothy became one of Paul's most faithful disciples, a most valuable associate in his missionary work (cf. 17:14ff; 18:5; 19:22; 20:4; 1 Thess 3:2; Rom 16:21) and the recipient of two of the Apostle's letters.

A tour of the churches of Asia Minor

Acts 15:23-29 ⁴As they went on their way through the cities, they delivered to them for observance the decisions which had been reached by the apostles and elders who were at Acts 2:41 Jerusalem. ⁵So the churches were strengthened in the faith, and they increased in numbers daily.

Acts 18:23 ⁶And they went through the region of Phrygia and Galatia, Gal 4:13-15 having been forbidden by the Holy Spirit to speak the word in Asia. ⁷And when they had come opposite Mysia, they

---

in illis locis; sciebant enim omnes quod pater eius Graecus esset. ⁴Cum autem pertransirent civitates, tradebant eis cusodire dogmata, quae erant decreta ab apostolis et presbyteris, qui essent Hierosolymis. ⁵Ecclesiae quidem confirmabantur fide et abundabant numero cotidie. ⁶Transierunt autem Phrygiam et Galatiae regionem, vetati a Sancto Spiritu loqui verbum in Asia; ⁷cum venissent autem circa Mysiam, tentabant ire Bithyniam, et non permisit eos

---

4. The text suggests that all Christians accepted the decisions of the Council of Jerusalem in a spirit of obedience and joy. They saw them as being handed down by the Church through the Apostles and as providing a satisfactory solution to a delicate problem. The disciples accept these commandments with internal and external assent: by putting them into practice they showed their docility. Everything which a lawful council lays down merits and demands acceptance by Christians, because it reflects, as the Council of Trent teaches, "the true and saving doctrine which Christ taught, the Apostles then handed on, and the Catholic Church, under the inspiration of the Holy Spirit, ever maintains; therefore, no one should subsequently dare to believe, preach or teach anything different"(*De iustificatione*, preface).

John Paul II called on Christians to adhere sincerely to conciliar directives when he exhorted them in Mexico City to keep to the letter and the spirit of Vatican II: "Take in your hands the documents of the Council. Study them with loving attention, in a spirit of prayer, to discover what the Spirit wished to say about the Church" (*Homily in Mexico Cathedral*, 26 January 1979).

6. In Galatia Paul had the illness which he refers to in Galatians 4:13: "You know it was because of a bodily ailment that I preached the gospel to you at first . . .": his apostolic zeal makes him turn his illness, which prevented him from moving on, to good purpose.

7. We are not told how the Holy Spirit prevented Paul from going to Bithynia. It would have been through an interior voice or through some person sent by God.

Some Greek codexes and a few translations say simply "Spirit" instead of "Spirit of Jesus", but really the two mean the same: cf. Phil 1:19; Rom 8:9; 1 Pet 1:11.

attempted to go into Bithynia, but the Spirit of Jesus did not allow them; [8]so, passing by Mysia, they went down to Troas. [9]And a vision appeared to Paul in the night: a man of Macedonia was standing beseeching him and saying, "Come over to Macedonia and help us." [10]And when he had seen the vision, immediately we sought to go on into Macedonia, concluding that God had called us to preach the gospel to them.

Spiritus Iesu; [8]cum autem praeterissent Mysiam, descenderunt Troadem. [9]Et visio per noctem Paulo ostensa est: vir Macedo quidam erat stans et deprecans eum et dicens: "Transiens in Macedoniam, adiuva nos!" [10]Ut autem visum vidit, statim quaesivimus proficisci in Macedoniam, certi facti quia vocasset nos Deus

---

9. This vision probably took place in a dream: Acts tells us of a number of instances where God made his will known in that way (cf. 9:10,12; 10:3, 17; 18:9; 22:17). Paul and his companions were convinced he had received a message from God.

The vision is quite right to describe the preaching of the Gospel as help for Macedonia: it is the greatest help, the greatest benefit, a person or a country could be given, an immense grace from God and a great act of charity on the part of the preacher, preparing his listeners, as he does, for the wonderful gift of faith.

10. The conviction that Paul and his companions have about what they must do is the way every Christian, called as he is at Baptism, should feel about his vocation to imitate Christ and therefore be apostolic.

"All Christians", John Paul II teaches, "incorporated into Christ and his Church by baptism, are consecrated to God. They are called to profess the faith which they have received. By the sacrament of confirmation, they are further endowed by the Holy Spirit with special strength to be witnesses of Christ and sharers in his mission of salvation. Every lay Christian is therefore an extraordinary work of God's grace and is called to the heights of holiness. Sometimes, lay men and women do not seem to appreciate to the full the dignity and the vocation that is theirs as lay people. No, there is no such thing as an 'ordinary layman', for all of you have been called to conversion through the death and resurrection of Jesus Christ. As God's holy people you are called to fulfil your role in the evangelization of the world. Yes, the laity are 'a chosen race, a holy priesthood', also called to be 'the salt of the earth' and 'the light of the world'. It is their specific vocation and mission to express the Gospel in their lives and thereby to insert the Gospel as a leaven into the reality of the world in which they live and work" (*Homily in Limerick*, 1 October 1979).

Now the narrative moves into the first person plural (16:10-17; 20:5 - 8:13-15; 21:1-18; 27:1-28, 16). The author includes himself among St Paul's

They go over into Macedonia

¹¹Setting sail therefore from Troas we made a direct voyage to Samothrace, and the following day to Neapolis, ¹²and from there to Philippi, which is the leading city of the district^x of Macedonia, and a Roman colony.

The conversion of Lydia

Acts 13:5-14

We remained in this city some days; ¹³and on the sabbath day we went outside the gate to the riverside, where we supposed there was a place of prayer; and we sat down and spoke to the women who had come together. ¹⁴One who

---

evangelizare eis. ¹¹Navigantes autem a Troade recto cursu venimus Samothraciam et sequenti die Neapolim ¹²et inde Philippos, quae est prima partis Macedoniae civitas, colonia. Eramus autem in hac urbe diebus aliquot commorantes. ¹³Die autem sabbatorum egressi sumus foras portam iuxta flumen, ubi putabamus orationem esse, et sedentes loquebamur mulieribus, quae convenerant. ¹⁴Et quaedam mulier nomine Lydia, purpuraria civitatis

---

companions, as an eyewitness of what he reports. Luke must have joined the missionaries at Troas and then stayed behind in Philippi.

12. Philippi was a prosperous city, founded by the father of Alexander the Great (in the fourth century B.C.). Nearby, in 42 B.C., there took place the battle in which those who assassinated Julius Caesar were defeated. Octavius raised Philippi to the status of a *colonia* and endowed it with many privileges.

Very few Jews lived in the city, as can be seen from the fact that it had no synagogue (for there to be a synagogue there had to be at least ten Jewish men living in a place). The text refers only to a group of women who met on the riverside to pray—a location probably chosen for the purpose of ritual purification.

14. Lydia was probably a surname taken from the region this woman came from. She was not a Jew by birth but a "God-fearer" (cf. note on Acts 2:5-11). God chose her from this group of women to enlighten her with the light of faith, opening her heart to understand the words of the Apostle. Origen explains that "God opens our mouth, our ears and our eyes to make us say, hear and see divine things" (*In Ex hom.*, III, 2). This shows that we can and ought to address God using the words of the Church's liturgy: "Open my lips, Lord, to bless your holy name; clean my heart of all evil thoughts; enlighten my understanding and inflame my will . . . so that I merit to be admitted to your presence" (*Liturgy of the Hours*, introductory prayer).

When Christians address God, they ask him for the grace to pray well—not only at times of prayer but also in the course of everyday activities: "Lord, be the beginning and end of all that we do and say. Prompt our actions with your

^xThe Greek text is uncertain

heard us was a woman named Lydia, from the city of
Thyatira, a seller of purple goods, who was a worshipper of
God. The Lord opened her heart to give heed to what was
said by Paul. [15]And when she was baptized, with her Acts 10:44-48
household, she besought us, saying, "If you have judged me
to be faithful to the Lord, come to my house and stay." And
she prevailed upon us.

Cure of a possessed girl. Imprisonment of Paul and Silas

[16]As we were going to the place of prayer, we were met Acts 19:15-24

Thyatirenorum colens Deum, audiebat, cuius Dominus aperuit cor intendere
his, quae dicebantur a Paulo. [15]Cum autem baptizata esset et domus eius,
deprecata est dicens: "Si iudicastis me fidelem Domino esse, introite in domum
meam et manete"; et coegit nos. [16]Factum est autem euntibus nobis ad

---

grace, and complete them with your all-powerful help" (*ibid.*, morning prayer,
Monday, first week).

This episode shows faith to be a gift from God, stemming from his Goodness
and Wisdom: for "no one can give his assent to the Gospel message in a truly
salvific way except it be by the light and inspiration of the Holy Spirit: he it is
who gives to all the power necessary for affirming and believing the truth"
(Vatican I, *Dei Filius*, chap. 3).

15. St Luke's succinct account shows that Lydia's good dispositions allow
St Paul's preaching to bear fruit very quickly. Her whole family receives
Baptism and she insists on the apostles' staying in her house. "Look at her
wisdom, how full of humility her words are: 'If you have judged me to be
faithful to the Lord.' Nothing could be more persuasive. Who would not have
been softened by these words. She did not simply request or entreat: she left
them free to decide and yet by her insistence obliged them to stay at her house.
See how she straightaway bears fruit and accounts her calling a great gain" (St
John Chrysostom, *Hom. on Acts*, 35).

It is worth reflecting on the fact that Christianity began in Europe through a
housewife's response to God's calling. Lydia set about her mission to
Christianize the whole world from within, starting with her own family.
Commenting on the role of women in the spread of Christianity, Monsignor
Escrivá says: "The main thing is that like Mary, who was a woman, a virgin
and a mother, they live with their eyes on God repeating her words '*fiat mihi
secundum verbum tuum*' (Lk 1:38) 'let it be to me according to your word'. On
these words depends the faithfulness to one's personal vocation—which is
always unique and non-transferable—which will make us all cooperators in the
work of salvation which God carries out in us and in the entire world"
(*Conversations*, 112).

Mt 8:29

Mk 16:17

by a slave girl who had a spirit of divination and brought her owners much gain by soothsaying. [17]She followed Paul and us, crying, "These men are servants of the Most High God, who proclaim to you the way of salvation." [18]And this she did for many days. But Paul was annoyed, and turned and said to the spirit, "I charge you in the name of Jesus Christ to come out of her." And it came out that very hour.

[19]But when her owners saw that their hope of gain was gone, they seized Paul and Silas and dragged them into the

---

orationem, puellam quandam habentem spiritum pythonem obviare nobis, quae quaestum magnum praestabat dominis suis divinando. [17]Haec subsecuta Paulum et nos clamabat dicens: "Isti homines servi Dei Altissimi sunt, qui annuntiant vobis salutis." [18]Hoc autem faciebat multis diebus. Dolens autem Paulus et conversus spiritui dixit: "Praecipio tibi in nomine Iesu Christi exire ab ea", et exiit eadem hora. [19]Videntes autem domini eius quia exivit spes

---

16-18. This slave girl must have been possessed by the devil; the devil knows the present and the past and he is so intelligent that he is good at divining the future (cf. St Thomas, *Summa theologiae*, I, q. 57, a. 3). In Greek mythology Python was a serpent which uttered the Delphic oracles (hence *spiritus pythonis*, "a spirit of divination").

St Paul did not believe in Python but he did believe in the devil. "An unclean spirit is unworthy to proclaim the word of the Gospel; that is why (Paul) commands him to desist and to come out of the girl, for demons ought to confess God in fear and trembling, and not praise him with joy" (St Bede, *Super Act expositio, ad loc.*).

Jesus addressed demons in the same kind of way (cf. Mk 1:24-27). St Ephraem comments: "The apostles were displeased to be honoured and praised by the evil spirit, just as our Lord rejected the devil who proclaimed him to the Jews. In like manner St Paul upbraids him, because he was motivated by deception and malice" (*Armenian Commentary, ad loc.*).

19-40. This is the first time St Paul comes into conflict with Gentiles. As might be expected, the incident does not take the form of a riot, as happened in cities of Asia Minor (13:50; 14:5, 19), but of a civil suit before local magistrates. The people who bring the charge say nothing about their real reason—loss of profit. They accuse Paul of two things. Their first charge is disturbance of the peace. The second seems to be based on regulations forbidding Roman citizens to practise alien cults, especially where these conflict with Roman custom. They see Paul's exorcism and his preaching as an attempt to propagate what they see as an unacceptable religion. It may well be that the charge also had to do with specific prohibitions on the propagation of Judaism to non-Jews. However, there is no hard evidence that any such prohibition existed; therefore, the charge

market place before the rulers; [20]and when they had brought them to the magistrates they said, "These men are Jews and they are disturbing our city. [21]They advocate customs which it is not lawful for us Romans to accept or practise." [22]The crowd joined in attacking them; and the magistrates tore the garments off them and gave orders to beat them with rods.[23]And when they had inflicted many blows upon them, they threw them into prison, charging the jailer to keep them safely. [24]Having received this charge, he put them into the inner prison and fastened their feet in the stocks.

2 Cor 11:25
Phil 1:30
1 Thess 2:2

---

quaestus eorum, apprehendentes Paulum et Silam traxerunt in forum ad principes [20]et producentes eos magistratibus dixerunt: "Hi homines conturbant civitatem nostram, cum sint Iudaei, [21]et annuntiant mores, quos non licet nobis suscipere neque facere cum simus Romani." [22]Et concurrit plebs adversus eos, et magistratus scissis tunicis eorum iusserunt virgis caedi [23]et, cum multas plagas eis imposuissent, miserunt eos in carcerem, praecipientes custodi, ut caute custodiret eos; [24]qui cum tale praeceptum accepisset, misit eos in interiorem carcerem et pedes eorum strinxit in ligno. [25]Media autem nocte

---

against Paul must have been based on regulations in the colony separating Roman from alien religious practices.

21. For St Luke "Roman" means the same as "Roman citizen" (cf. 16:37-38; 22:25-29; 23:27-28): he is using legal terminology of the time.

23. St Paul refers specifically to this punishment in 1 Thess 2:2. It was one of the three beatings mentioned in 2 Cor 11:25.

24. St John Chrysostom, reflecting on the punishment Paul and Silas underwent, sees them as sitting or lying on the ground, covered with wounds caused by the beating. He contrasts this suffering with the way many people avoid anything which involves effort, discomfort or suffering: "How we should weep over the disorders of our time! The apostles were subjected to the worst kinds of tribulation, and here we are, spending our time in search of pleasure and diversion. This pursuit of leisure and pleasure is the cause of our ruin. We do not see the value of suffering even the least injury or insult for love of Jesus Christ.

"Let us remember the tribulations the saints experienced; nothing alarmed them or scared them. Severe humiliations made them tough, enabled them to do God's work. They did not say, If we are preaching Jesus Christ, why does he not come to our rescue?" (*Hom. on Acts*, 35).

The baptism of the jailer

Col 3:16

Acts 12:6-11

Acts 12:19

²⁵But about midnight Paul and Silas were praying and singing hymns to God, and the prisoners were listening to them, ²⁶and suddenly there was a great earthquake, so that the foundations of the prison were shaken; and immediately all the doors were opened and every one's fetters were unfastened. ²⁷When the jailer woke and saw that the prison doors were open, he drew his sword and was about to kill himself, supposing that the prisoners had escaped. ²⁸But Paul cried with a loud voice, "Do not harm yourself, for we are all here." ²⁹And he called for lights and rushed in, and trembling with fear he fell down before Paul and Silas, ³⁰and

---

Paulus et Silas orantes laudabant Deum, et audiebant eos, qui in custodia erant; ²⁶subito vero terraemotus factus est magnus, ita ut moverentur fundamenta carceris, et aperta sunt statim ostia omnia, et universorum vincula soluta sunt. ²⁷Expergefactus autem custos carceris et videns apertas ianuas carceris, eviginato gladio volebat se interficere, aestimans fugisse vinctos. ²⁸Clamavit autem Paulus magna voce dicens: "Nihil feceris tibi mali; universi enim hic sumus." ²⁹Petitoque lumine intro cucurrit et tremefactus procidit Paulo et Silae ³⁰et producens eos foras ait: "Domini, quid me oportet facere, ut salvus fiam?"

---

25. Paul and Silas spend the night praying and singing hymns. Commenting on this passage St John Chrysostom exhorts Christians to do the same and to sanctify night-time rest: "Show by your example that the night-time is not just for recovering the strength of your body: it is also a help in sanctifying your soul. [. . .]   You do not have to say long prayers; one prayer, said well, is enough. [. . .] Offer God this sacrifice of a moment of prayer and he will reward you" (*Hom. on Acts*, 36).

St Bede notes the example Paul and Silas give Christians who are experiencing trials or temptations: "The piety and energy which fires the heart of the apostles expresses itself in prayer and brings them to sing hymns even in prison. Their praise causes the earth to move, the foundations to quake, the doors to open and even their fetters to break. Similarly, that Christian who rejoices when he is happy, let him rejoice also in his weakness, when he is tempted, so that Christ's strength come to his aid. And then let him praise the Lord with hymns, as Paul and Silas did in the darkness of their prison, and sing with the psalmist, 'Thou does encompass me with deliverance' (Ps 32:7)" (St Bede, *Super Act expositio, ad loc.*).

30-34. This incident so affects the jailer with religious awe that he comes to be converted. He has been helped to react in this way as a result of listening to the prayers and hymns of the apostles: "Notice how the jailer reveres the apostles. He opens his heart to them, when he sees the doors of the prison open.

brought them out and said, "Men, what must I do to be saved?" ³¹And they said, "Believe in the Lord Jesus, and you will be saved, you and your household." ³²And they spoke the word of the Lord to him and to all that were in his house. ³³And he took them the same hour of the night, and washed their wounds, and he was baptized at once with all his family. ³⁴Then he brought them up into his house, and set food before them; and he rejoiced with all his household that he had believed in God.

Acts 8:38

Acts 8:39

Release and departure from Philippi

³⁵But when it was day, the magistrates sent the police, saying, "Let those men go." ³⁶And the jailer reported the words to Paul, saying, "The magistrates have sent to let you

---

³¹At illi dixerunt: "Crede in Domino Iesu et salvus eris tu et domus tua." ³²Et locuti sunt ei verbum Domini cum omnibus, qui erant in domo eius. ³³Et tollens eos in illa hora noctis lavit eos a plagis, et baptizatus est ipse et omnes eius continuo; ³⁴cumque perduxisset eos in domum, apposuit mensam et laetatus est cum omni domo sua credens Deo. ³⁵Et cum dies factus esset, miserunt magistratus lictores dicentes: "Dimitte homines illos!" ³⁶Nuntiavit autem custos carceris verba haec Paulo: "Miserunt magistratus, ut dimittamini; nunc igitur

---

He lights the way further with his torch, but it is another kind of torch that lights up his soul. [. . .] Then he cleans their wounds, and his soul is cleansed from the filth of sin. On offering them material food, he receives in return a heavenly one. [. . .] His docility shows that he sincerely believed that all his sins had been forgiven" (Chrysostom, *Hom. on Acts*, 36).

A person can meet up with God in all kinds of unexpected situations—in which case he or she needs to have the same kind of docility as the jailer in order to receive the grace of God through the channels which God has established, normally the sacraments.

33. As happened with Lydia and her family, the jailer's household is baptized along with him. Noting that these families probably included children and infants, the Magisterium of the Church finds support here for its teaching that baptism of children is a practice which goes right back to apostolic times and is, as St Augustine says, "a tradition received from the Apostles" (cf. *Instruction on Infant Baptism*, 20 October 1980, 4).

35. "Magistrates": in the Roman empire a *praetor* was a magistrate with jurisdiction either in Rome or in the provinces. The "police" (*lictores*) were officials who walked in front of higher magistrates bearing the insignia of Roman justice.

Acts 22:35 go; now therefore come out and go in peace." [37]But Paul said to them, "They have beaten us publicly, uncondemned, men who are Roman citizens, and have thrown us into prison; and do they now cast us out secretly? No! let them come Acts 22:29 themselves and take us out." [38]The police reported these words to the magistrates, and they were afraid when they heard that they were Roman citizens; [39]so they came and apologized to them. And they took them out and asked them

---

exeuntes ite in pace." [37]Paulus autem dixit eis: "Caesos nos publice indemnatos, cum homines Romani essemus, miserunt in carcerem; et nunc occulte nos eiciunt? Non ita, sed veniant et ipsi nos educant." [38]Nuntiaverunt autem magistratibus lictores verba haec. Timueruntque audito quod Romani essent, [39]et venientes deprecati sunt eos et educentes rogabant, ut egrederentur urbem.

37-39. St Paul decides to let it be known that he is a Roman citizen. He probably said nothing about this earlier to avoid giving his fellow Jews the impression that he was not proud to be a Jew or gave more importance to his Roman citizenship.

Ancient Roman law forbade beating of Roman citizens; from the beginning of the Empire it was allowed—once a person had been tried and found guilty.

The magistrates' fear was very much in line with attitudes at the time: very few people had the privilege of Roman citizenship, and the provincial authorities were responsible for the protection of the rights of Romans.

St Paul chooses what he considers to be the appropriate time to claim his rights as a citizen, doing so to protect the cause of the Gospel. Some might consider his action haughty or self-assertive; but in fact he is only doing what duty dictates, uncomfortable though it makes him. In this particular situation the dignity of the Word of God requires that he claim his rights. Paul sets an example to every Christian by showing him or her the line that should be taken in the interest of the common good. Sometimes charity requires that we do not exercise our rights; but at other times that would mean one was being irresponsible and unjust.

"That false humility is laziness. Such humbleness is a handy way of giving up rights that are really duties" (J. Escrivá, *The Way*, 603).

In the ecclesial sphere every Christian has a right— which he or she may not renounce—to receive the help necessary for salvation, particularly Christian doctrine and the sacraments. He has a right to follow the spirituality of his choice and to do apostolate, that is, to make the Gospel known without let or hindrance. He is free to associate with others, in keeping with whatever Church law lays down; and others have a duty to respect his right to freely choose his state, his right to his good name and his right to follow his own liturgical rite (Latin, Maronite, etc.).

to leave the city. ⁴⁰So they went out of the prison, and visited Lydia; and when they had seen the brethren, they exhorted them and departed.

⁴⁰Exeuntes autem de carcere introierunt ad Lydiam et, visis fratribus, consolati sunt eos et profecti sunt.

In the civil sphere citizens have rights which the State should recognize: for example, a right not to be discriminated against on religious grounds, a right to education in line with their legitimate beliefs and to be protected in their married and family life. They also have a right to engage in public affairs, that is, to vote, to occupy public office and to have some influence on legislation. These political rights can easily become serious obligations.

"Lay people", Vatican II teaches, "ought to take on themselves as their distinctive task this renewal of the temporal order. Guided by the light of the Gospel and the mind of the Church, prompted by Christian love, they should act in this domain in a direct way and in their own specific manner. As citizens among citizens they must bring to their cooperation with others their own special competence, and act on their own responsibility; everywhere and always they have to seek the justice of the Kingdom of God. The temporal order is to be renewed in such a way that, while its own principles are fully respected, it is harmonized with the principles of the Christian life and adapted to the various conditions of times, places and peoples" (*Apostolicam actuositatem*, 7).

"It is their duty to cultivate a properly informed conscience and to impress the divine law on the affairs of the earthly city" (*Gaudium et spes*, 43).

40. The last verb seems to imply that St Luke stayed behind in Philippi. Before leaving, Paul and Silas go to Lydia's house to encourage the Christians of Philippi: the treatment they have received and now the fact that they are to leave the city have not weakened their hope in God. When things go wrong, either for himself or others, and a Christian feels disconcerted, he should try to see the situation in a supernatural light and should realize that God's strength more than makes up for human weakness.

"The experience of our weakness and of our failings, the painful realization of the smallness and meanness of some who call themselves Christians, the apparent failure or aimlessness of some works of apostolate, all these things, which bring home to us the reality of sin and human limitations, can still be a trial of our faith. Temptation and doubt can lead us to ask: Where are the strength and power of God? When that happens we have to react by practising the virtue of hope with greater purity and forcefulness, and by striving to be more faithful" (J. Escrivá, *Christ is passing by*, 128).

179

17

Difficulties with Jews in Thessalonica

1 Thess 2:2

Lk 4:16
Acts 16:13

¹Now when they had passed through Amphipolis and Apollonia, they came to Thessalonica, where there was a synagogue of the Jews. ²And Paul went in, as was his custom, and for three weeks[p] he argued with them from the scriptures,

---

¹Cum autem perambulassent Amphipolim et Apolloniam, venerunt Thessalonicam, ubi erat synagoga Iudaeorum. ²Secundum consuetudinem autem suam Paulus introivit ad eos et per sabbata tria disserebat eis de Scripturis ³adaperiens

---

1. Thessalonica was the seat of the Roman governor of the province of Macedonia; it was about 150 kilometres (90 miles) from Philippi. It had been founded in the fourth century B.C. and declared a "free city" by Augustus in 42 B.C. It had a Jewish community, as can be seen from the fact that there was a synagogue.

In all, Paul must have stayed many weeks in this city, in the course of which he received donations from the Christians of Philippi (cf. Phil 4:16) and had to work to keep himself (cf. 1 Thess 2:9). It was a period of difficulties and joys, as he recalled later: "You yourselves know how you ought to imitate us; we were not idle when we were with you, we did not eat any one's bread without paying, but with toil and labour we worked night and day, that we might not burden any of you" (2 Thess 3:7-8).

Paul seems to have stayed with a prominent citizen called Jason (v. 5). It is not known whether Jason was a Jew or a Gentile; he probably had been converted to Christianity by Paul's teaching.

2. St John Chrysostom draws our attention to the ordinary everyday work of the preacher who, trusting in the power of God's Word, engages in a peaceful war of words in which he patiently strives to persuade others of the truth: "His preaching was based on the Scriptures. That was the way Christ preached: wherever he went he explained the Scriptures. When people oppose Paul and call him an imposter, he speaks to them about the Scriptures. For a person who tries to convince others by miracles quite rightly becomes the object of suspicion, whereas he who uses the Scriptures to win people over is not treated with suspicion. St Paul often converted people simply through his preaching. [. . .] God did not allow them to work too many miracles, for to win without miracles is more wonderful than all possible miracles. God rules without resorting to miracles: that is his usual policy. And so the Apostles did not devote much energy to working miracles, and Paul himself says, 'We preach Christ crucified [rather than provide wisdom or signs]' (1 Cor 1:23)" (*Hom. on Acts*, 37).

[p]Or *sabbaths*.

³explaining and proving that it was necessary for the Christ Lk 24:25-27; 46-47
to suffer and to rise from the dead, and saying, "This Jesus, Acts 18:5
whom I proclaim to you, is the Christ." ⁴And some of them Acts 17:12
were persuaded, and joined Paul and Silas; as did a great
many of the devout Greeks and not a few of the leading
women. ⁵But the Jews were jealous, and taking some wicked 1 Thess 2:14
fellows of the rabble, they gathered a crowd, set the city in
an uproar, and attacked the house of Jason, seeking to bring
them out to the people. ⁶And when they could not find them, Acts 24:5
they dragged Jason and some of the brethren before the city
authorities, crying, "These men who have turned the world Lk 23:2
upside down have come here also, ⁷and Jason has received Jn 19:12-15

---

et comprobans quia Christum oportebat pati et resurgere a mortuis, et: "Hic est Christus, Iesus, quem ego annuntio vobis." ⁴Et quidam ex eis crediderunt et adiuncti sunt Paulo et Silae et de colentibus Graecis multitudo magna et mulieres nobiles non paucae. ⁵Zelantes autem Iudaei assumentesque de foro viros quosdam malos et turba facta concitaverunt civitatem, et assistentes domui Iasonis quaerebant eos producere in populum. ⁶Et cum non invenissent eos, trahebant Iasonem et quosdam fratres ad politarchas clamantes: "Qui orbem concitaverunt, isti et huc venerunt, ⁷quos suscepit Iason; et hi omnes

---

3. St Luke, who has already reported at length one discourse of Paul to Jews (cf. 13:16ff), limits himself here to giving a very short summary of his preaching in the synagogue of Thessalonica. Paul develops his argument by using quotations from Scripture (probably Ps 2; 16; 110; Is 53) whose meaning he reveals to his listeners: Jesus must be the Messiah expected by Israel; the Messiah had to suffer and then rise from the dead.

What Paul proclaims here is essentially the same as what he says in 1 Corinthians 15:3-5, which is a passage based on very ancient traditions: it is very reasonable to suppose that the Apostle is reiterating accepted Christian teaching that Jesus was the Messiah and the Redeemer of man.

5-9. Once again Paul's preaching provokes the Jews to jealousy. They see many Gentiles following him who otherwise might have become converts to Judaism. However, the main motive for their opposition is not religious zeal. There is an element of malice here; their sense of guilt over resisting the grace of the Gospel plays a part in their behaviour. "God opens the lips of those who utter divine words," Origen writes, "and I fear that it is the devil who opens other people's" (*In Ex hom.*, III, 2).

St Luke calls the city magistrates "politarchs". This was unknown as a term for civic officials in non-Roman cities of Macedonia; but recently discovered inscriptions have shown it to be correct. As a "free city", Thessalonica had a popular assembly empowered to investigate charges.

them; and they are all acting against the decrees of Caesar, saying that there is another king, Jesus." [8]And the people and the city authorities were disturbed when they heard this. [9]And when they had taken security from Jason and the rest, they let them go.

Reception in Beroea

Jn 5:39 [10]The brethren immediately sent Paul and Silas away by night to Beroea; and when they arrived they went into the Jewish synagogue. [11]Now these Jews were more noble than

---

contra decreta Caesaris faciunt, regem alium dicentes esse, Iesum." [8]Concitaverunt autem plebem et politarchas audientes haec; [9]et accepto satis ab Iasone et a ceteris, dimiserunt eos. [10]Fratres vero confestim per noctem dimiserunt Paulum et Silam in Beroeam; qui cum advenissent, in synagogam Iudaeorum introierunt. [11]Hi autem erant nobiliores eorum, qui sunt Thessalonicae, qui susceperunt verbum cum omni aviditate, cotidie scrutantes

---

The Jews bring a religious charge against Paul, but they disguise it in the form of two secular charges. They accuse him of causing a civil disturbance and, by saying that he is proposing "another king", they accuse him also of high treason. These are exactly the same crimes as were alleged against our Lord (cf. Lk 23:2; Jn 19:12).

His accusers have already twisted Paul's teaching: he would certainly have spoken of Jesus as Lord, but not in the sense of predicting the establishment of an earthly religion.

The magistrates listen to the charges but they accept Jason's security and the charges fail to lead to a conviction.

11. The Jews of Beroea were the only ones not to reject Paul's teaching. They immediately began a search of the Scriptures, which led them to discover the truth of the Gospel. They were clearly very upright people who practised both the letter and the spirit of the law of God. "In order to study and understand the Scriptures," St Athanasius says, "one needs to be live a clean life and have a pure soul" (*De Incarnatione contra arianos*, 57).

The same preaching has different effects on different people. "It is a fact that the teaching of the truth is differently received depending on the listeners' dispositions. The Word shows everyone what is good and what is bad; if a person is predisposed to do what is proclaimed to him, his soul is in the light; if he is not and he has not decided to fix his soul's gaze on the light of truth, then he will remain in the darkness of ignorance" St Gregory of Nyssa, *On the life of Moses*, II, 65).

As St John of the Cross says, "to seek God one needs to have a heart which is naked and strong, free from all good and evil things that are not simply God" (*Spiritual Canticle*, stanza 3).

those in Thessalonica, for they received the word with all eagerness, examining the scriptures daily to see if these things were so. ¹²Many of them therefore believed, with not a few Greek women of high standing as well as men. ¹³But when the Jews of Thessalonica learned that the word of God was proclaimed by Paul at Beroea also, they came there too, stirring up and inciting the crowds. ¹⁴Then the brethren immediately sent Paul off on his way to the sea, but Silas and Timothy remained there. ¹⁵Those who conducted Paul brought him as far as Athens; and receiving a command for Silas and Timothy to come to him as soon as possible, they departed.

Scripturas si haec ita se haberent. ¹²Et multi quidem crediderunt ex eis et Graecarum mulierum honestarum et virorum non pauci. ¹³Cum autem cognovissent in Thessalonica Iudaei quia et Beroeae annuntiatum est a Paulo verbum Dei, venerunt et illuc commoventes et turbantes multitudinem. ¹⁴Statimque tunc Paulum dimiserunt fratres, ut iret usque ad mare; Silas autem et Timotheus remanserunt ibi. ¹⁵Qui autem deducebant Paulum, perduxerunt

16-21. St Paul's missionary activity in Athens shows us the Gospel's first encounter with Hellenist paganism, both popular and intellectual. This is an important episode in the spread of the Christian message because it shows us the capacity of Gospel preaching to adapt itself to different outlooks, different cultures, while still remaining completely faithful to itself.

The Athens visited by St Paul was no longer the brilliant intellectual capital it had been in the time of Plato and Aristotle. It was in decline, culturally and politically, but it still retained traces of its former glory. Here the philosophical currents of the day still had their spokesmen, and intellectual debate was always welcomed.

St Paul presents the Gospel to these pagan philosophers as "true philosophy" without in any sense taking from its transcendental, supernatural character. The point at which they coincide is this: philosophy is the science of life; it is a legitimate search for the answer to profound questions about human existence. Paul tries to lead them beyond mere intellectual curiosity, in a genuine search for perennial truth, which is religious in character. He supports the philosophers in their criticism of superstition, but points out that they have to go farther than just censuring aberrations of that kind.

Paul is well aware that preaching Christ crucified is "a stumbling block to Jews and folly to Gentiles" (1 Cor 1:23). However, this conviction does not prevent his feeling and expressing respect for pagan thought and religion, which he sees as providing a groundwork for the Gospel. In Paul's address we can see the first signs of the Church's and Christians' ongoing recognition of the value, albeit limited, of secular culture. "There are in profane culture", St Gregory of

St Paul in Athens

Acts 14:7-17

16Now while Paul was waiting for them at Athens, his spirit was provoked within him as he saw that the city was full of idols. 17So he argued in the synagogue with the Jews and the devout persons, and in the market place every day

---

usque Athenas, et accepto mandato ad Silam et Timotheum, ut quam celerrime venirent ad illum, profecti sunt. 16Paulus autem cum Athenis eos exspectaret, irritabatur spiritus eius in ipso videns idololatriae deditam civitatem. 17Disputabat igitur in synagoga cum Iudaeis et colentibus et in foro per omnes dies ad eos, qui aderant. 18Quidam autem ex Epicureis et Stoicis philosophi

---

Nyssa writes, "aspects which should not be rejected when the time comes to grow in virtue. Natural moral philosophy can, in fact, be the companion of one who wants to lead a higher life [. . .], provided that its fruit does not carry any alien contamination" (*On the life of Moses*, II, 37).

Two centuries before Gregory, St Justin Martyr wrote about the merits and defects of pagan philosphy and the relative truth it contains: "I declare that I prayed and strove with all my might to be known as a Christian, not because the teachings of Plato are completely different from those of Christ, but because they are not in all respects the same; neither are those of other writers, Stoics, the poets and the historians. For each discoursed rightly, seeing through his participation in the seminal divine Word what related to it. But they that have uttered contrary opinions clearly do not have sound knowledge and irrefutable wisdom. Whatever has been uttered aright by any man in any place belongs to Christians; for, next to God, we worship and love the Word which is from the unbegotten and ineffable God. [. . .] All the profane authors were able to see the truth clearly, through the seed of reason [*logos*, word], implanted in them" (*Second Apology*, 13, 2-3).

16. Paul's religious zeal makes him indignant at the failure to recognize the truth, the depraved forms of religious worship and the wretched spiritual situation of people who do not know God.

His devout, serene reaction brings him immediately to tell them about the true God and enlighten their darkened minds.

17. As usual Paul preaches in the synagogue, but he also addresses anyone in the market place who is ready to listen to what he has to say. The verb St Luke uses really means "preach", not "argue" (cf. 20:7, 9).

"Market place": *Agora* was the Greek name for the main city square. The people used to foregather in the Agora to debate the political questions of the day; it was also used for other activities, including trading. The Agora in Athens was particularly famous from very early on: it was the centre of Athenian democracy, but it was also used for informal, everyday affairs.

with those who chanced to be there. [18]Some also of the Epicurean and Stoic philosophers met him. And some said, "What would this babbler say?" Others said, "He seems to be a preacher of foreign divinities"—because he preached Jesus and the resurrection. [19]And they took hold of him and brought him to the Areopagus, saying, "May we know what this new teaching is which you present? [20]For you bring some strange things to our ears; we wish to know therefore what these things mean." [21]Now all the Athenians and the foreigners who lived there spent their time in nothing except telling or hearing something new.

---

disserebant cum eo. Et quidam dicebant: "Quid vult seminiverbius hic dicere?"; alii vero: "Novorum daemoniorum videtur annuntiator esse", quia Iesum et resurrectionem evangelizabat. [19]Et apprehensum eum ad Areopagum duxerunt dicentes: "Possumus scire quae est haec nova, quae a te dicitur doctrina? [20]Mira enim quaedam infers auribus nostris; volumus ergo scire quidnam velint haec esse." [21]Athenienses autem omnes et advenae hospites ad nihil aliud vacabant

---

18. Epicurean philosophers followed the teachings of Epicurus (341-270 B.C.), which tended to be rather materialistic. They spoke of there being no gods or at least they regarded the gods as taking no interest in the doings of men. Epicurean ethics stressed the importance of pleasure and a life of ease and tranquility.

The Stoics, who followed Zeno of Citium (340-265 B.C.), saw the *logos* as the cause which shapes, orders and directs the entire universe and the lives of those who inhabit it. The *logos* is the Reason for everything that exists, the ultimate principle, immanent in things; this is a pantheistic concept of the world. Stoic ethics stress individual responsibility and self-sufficiency; but although this philosophy speaks a great deal about freedom it sees Fate as playing a decisive role.

"Babbler": the Greek word does have a rather derogatory meaning and is used mainly to refer to people who never open their mouths without uttering clichés.

These people seem to take "Resurrection" as a proper name of some god accompanying Jesus.

19. The word "areopagus" can refer to a hill where the Athenians used to meet and also to a session of a tribunal or city council gathered together to listen to Paul's teaching. It is not clear from the text which meaning applies.

22-33. Of all Paul's addresses reported in Acts, this address in the Areopagus is his longest to a pagan audience (cf. 14:15ff). It is a highly significant one, paralleling in importance his address to the Jews of Pisidian

185

Paul's speech in the Areopagus

²²So Paul, standing in the middle of the Areopagus, said: "Men of Athens, I perceive that in every way you are very religious. ²³For as I passed along, and observed the objects

---

nisi aut dicere aut audire aliquid novi. ²²Stans autem Paulus in medio Areopagi ait: "Viri Athenienses, per omnia quasi superstitiosiores vos video; ²³praeteriens enim et videns simulacra vestra inveni et aram in qua scriptum

---

Antioch (cf. 13:16ff). It is the first model we have of Christian apologetic method, which tends to stress the reasonableness of Christianity and the fact that it has no difficulty in holding its own with the best in human thought.

The speaker is clearly the same person as wrote the first three chapters of the Epistle to the Romans, someone with a lot of experience of preaching the Gospel; his method consists in first talking about the one, true, living God and then proclaiming Jesus Christ, the divine Saviour of all men (cf. 2 Thess 1:9-10).

After an introduction designed to catch the attention of listeners and highlight the central theme (vv. 22ff), the address can be divided into three parts: 1) God is the Lord of the world; he does not need to live in temples built by men (vv. 24f); 2) man has been created by God and is dependent on him for everything (vv. 26f); 3) there is a special relationship between God and man; therefore, idolatry is a grave sin (vv. 28f). Then, in his conclusion, Paul exhorts his listeners to accept the truth about God, and to repent, bearing in mind the Last Judgment (vv. 30f).

The terminology Paul uses comes mainly from the Greek translation of the Old Testament—the Septuagint. Biblical beliefs are expressed in the language of the Hellenistic culture of the people.

22-24. "To an unknown God": St Paul praises the religious feelings of the Athenians, which lead them to offer worship to God. But he goes on to point out that their form of religion is very imperfect because they do not know enough about God and about the right way to worship him; nor does their religion free them from their sins or help them live in a way worthy of human dignity. Religious Athenians, he seems to say somewhat ironically, are in fact superstitious, and they do not know the one true God and his ways of salvation.

Paul criticizes pagan religion and points out its limitations, but he does not totally condemn it. He regards it as a basis to work on: at least it means that his listeners accept the possibility of the existence of a true God as yet unknown to them. They are predisposed to receive and accept the supernatural revelation of God in Christ. Revelation does not destroy natural religion: rather, it purifies it, completes it and raises it up, enabling a naturally religious person to know the mystery of God, One and Triune, to change his life with the help of the grace of Christ and to attain the salvation he needs and yearns for.

23. "Those who acted in accordance with what is universally, naturally and

186

of your worship, I found also an altar with this inscription,
'To an unknown god.' What therefore you worship as
unknown, this I proclaim to you. [24]The God who made the
world and everything in it, being Lord of heaven and earth,

Is 42:5
Acts 14:15

---

erat: 'Ignoto deo.' Quod ergo ignorantes colitis, hoc ego annuntio vobis. [24]Deus,
qui fecit mundum et omnia, quae in eo sunt, hic, caeli et terrae cum sit Dominus,
non in manufactis templis inhabitat, [25]nec manibus humanis colitur indigens

---

eternally good were pleasing to God and will be saved by Christ [. . .], just like
the righteous who preceded them" (St Justin, *Dialogue with Tryphon*, 45). The
Church's esteem for the positive elements in pagan religions leads her to preach
to all men the fulness of truth and salvation which is to be found only in Jesus
Christ. "The Catholic Church rejects nothing of what is true and holy in these
religions. She has a high regard for the manner of life and conduct, the precepts
and doctrines which, although differing in many ways from her own teaching,
nevertheless often reflect a ray of that truth which enlightens all men. Yet she
proclaims, and is in duty bound to proclaim without fail, Christ who is the way,
and the truth, and the life (Jn 14:6). In him, in whom God reconciled all things
to himself, men find the fulness of their religious life" (Vatican II, *Nostra aetate*,
2).

24. Paul's language is in line with the way God is described in the Old
Testament as being Lord of heaven and earth (cf. Is 42:5; Ex 20:21). The
Apostle speaks of God's infinite majesty: God is greater than the universe, of
which he is the creator. However, Paul does not mean to imply that it is not
desirable for God to be worshipped in sacred places designed for that purpose.

His words seem to echo those of Solomon at the dedication of the first
Temple: "Behold, heaven and the highest heaven cannot contain thee; how
much less this house which I have built!" (1 Kings 8:27).

Any worship rendered to God should be "in spirit and truth" (Jn 4:24). But
the Lord has desired to dwell in a special way and to receive homage in temples
built by men. "The worship of God", St Thomas Aquinas writes, "regards both
God who is worshipped and men who perform the worship. God is not confined
to any place, and therefore it is not on his account that a tabernacle or temple
has to be made. Worshippers, as corporeal beings, need a special tabernacle or
temple set up for the worship of God; and this for two reasons. First, that the
thought of its being appointed to the worship of God might instil a greater sense
of reverence; second, that the way it is arranged and furnished might signify in
various respects the excellence of Christ's divine or human nature. [. . .] From
this it is clear that the house of the sanctuary was not set up to receive God as
if dwelling there, but that his name might dwell there, that is, in order that the
knowledge of God might be exhibited there" (*Summa theologiae*, I-II, q. 102,
a. 4, ad 1).

Ps 50:10-12

Deut 32:8
2 Mac 7:23

does not live in shrines made by man, [25]nor is he served by human hands, as though he needed anything, since he himself gives to all men life and breath and everything. [26]And he made from one every nation of men to live on all the face

---

aliquo, cum ipse det omnibus vitam et inspirationem et omnia; [26]fecitque ex uno omne genus hominum inhabitare super universam faciem terrae, definiens

---

25. The idea that God does not need man's service and does not depend on man for his well-being and happiness is to be often found in the prophetical books. "Now in Babylon you will see", Jeremiah proclaims, "gods made of silver and gold and wood, which are carried on men's shoulders and inspire fear in the heathen. [. . .] Their tongues are smoothed by the craftsmen, and they themselves are overlaid with gold and silver; but they are false and cannot speak. [. . .] When they have been dressed in purple robes, their faces are wiped because of the dust from the temple, which is thick upon them. Like a local ruler the god holds a sceptre, though unable to destroy any one who offends it. [. . .] Having no feet, they are carried on men's shoulders, revealing to mankind their worthlessness. And those who serve them are ashamed because through them these gods are made to stand, lest they fall to the ground" (Bar 6:4, 8, 12-13, 26-27).

This does not mean that the Lord does not want men to respond to the love-offering which he makes them. "Hear, O heavens," Isaiah prophesies, "and give ear, O earth; for the Lord has spoken: Sons have I reared and brought up, but they have rebelled against me. The ox knows its owner, and the ass its master's crib; but Israel does not know, my people does not understand" (1:2-3).

In addition to being offensive and senseless, sin implies indifference and ingratitude towards God, who, in an excess of love, is tireless in seeking man's friendship. "When Israel was a child, I loved him, and out of Egypt I called my son," we read in the prophet Hosea. "The more I called them, the more they went from me. [. . .] Yet it was I who taught Ephraim to walk, I took them up in my arms; but they did not know that I healed them. I led them with cords of compassion, with the bands of love" (11:1-4).

By far the greatest sign of God's love for men is the Redemption, and the sacraments of the Church, through which the fruits of the Redemption reach us. His love is expressed in a special way in the Blessed Eucharist, which provides the Christian with nourishment and is where Jesus wishes us to adore him and keep him company.

26. "From one": St Paul is referring to the text of Genesis 2:7: "then the Lord God formed man of dust from the ground, and breathed into his nostrils the breath of life"; in other words, he is speaking of the first progenitor of the human race. The expression "from one" should not be interpreted as meaning from *one principle* but from *one man*.

188

of the earth, having determined allotted periods and the
boundaries of their habitation, ²⁷that they should seek God,
in the hope that they might feel after him and find him. Yet
he is not far from each one of us, ²⁸for

'In him we live and move and have our being';
as even some of your poets have said,
'For we are indeed his offspring.'

Deut 4:29
Is 55:6
Rom 1:19

---

statuta tempora et terminos habitationis eorum, ²⁷quaerere Deum si forte
attrectent eum et inveniant, quamvis non longe sit ab unoquoque nostrum. ²⁸In
ipso enim vivimus et movemur et sumus, sicut et quidam vestrum poetarum

---

27-28. St Paul is speaking about the absolute nearness of God and his
mysterious but real presence in every man and woman. St Augustine echoes
this teaching when he exclaims, "Yet all the time you were within me, more
inward than the most inward place of my heart, and loftier than the highest"
(*Confessions*, III, 6, 11).

Merely to exist, man needs God, his Creator. He also needs him if he is to
continue in existence, to live and act. He needs him if he is to think and love.
And in particular he needs him in order to love goodness and be good. It is
correct to say that God is in us. This intimate union of God and man does not
in any way take from the fact that there is a perfect distinction and radical
difference between God, who is infinite, and man, who is finite and limited.

"Men, who are incapable of existing of themselves," St Athanasius writes,
"are to be found confined by place and dependent on the Word of God. But
God exists of himself, he contains all things and is contained by none. He is to
be found within everything as far as his goodness and power is concerned, and
he is outside of everything as far as his own divine nature is concerned" (*De
decretis nicaenae synodi*, 11).

Christian spirituality has traditionally seen in these ideas an invitation to seek
God in the depth of one's soul and to always feel dependent upon him.

"Consider God", says St John of Avila, "who is the existence of everything
that exists, and without whom there is nothing: and who is the life of all that
lives, and without whom there is death; and who is the strength of all that has
capacity to act, and without whom there is weakness; and who is the entire good
of everything that is good, without whom nothing can have the least little bit
of good in it" (*Audi, filia*, chap. 64).

St Francis de Sales writes: "Not only is God in the place where you are, but
he is in a very special manner in your heart and in the depth of your soul, which
he quickens and animates with his divine presence, since he is there as the heart
of your heart, and the spirit of your soul; for, as the soul, being spread
throughout the body, is present in every part of it, and yet resides in a special
manner in the heart, so God, being present in all things, is present nevertheless
in a special manner in our spirit and therefore David called God 'the God of

Acts 19:26
Rom 1:22-23

Rom 3:25-26
²⁹Being then God's offspring, we ought not to think that the Deity is like gold, or silver, or stone, a representation by the art and imagination of man. ³⁰The times of ignorance God

dixerunt: 'Ipsius enim et genus sumus.' ²⁹Genus ergo cum simus Dei, non debemus aestimare auro aut argento aut lapidi, sculpturae artis et cognitationis hominis, divinum esse simile. ³⁰Et tempora quidem ignorantiae despiciens

his heart' (Ps 73:26); and Paul said that 'we live and move and have our being in God' (Acts 17:28). By reflecting on this truth, you will stir up in your heart a great reverence for God, who is so intimately present there" (*Introduction to the Devout Life*, II, chap. 2).

This quotation—in the singular—is from the Stoic poet Aratus (3rd century B.C.). The plural in the quotation may refer to a similar verse in the hymn to Zeus written by Cleanthes (also 3rd century).

"The devil spoke words of Scripture but our Saviour reduced him to silence", St Athanasius comments. "Paul cites secular authors, but, saint that he is, he gives them a spiritual meaning" (*De synodis*, 39). "We are rightly called 'God's offspring', not the offspring of his divinity but created freely by his spirit and re-created through adoption as sons" (St Bede, *Super Act expositio, ad loc.*).

29. If men are God's offspring, and are in some way like him, clearly an inanimate representation cannot contain the living God. Men have God's spirit and therefore they should recognize that God is spiritual. However, material representations of God do serve a useful purpose, due to the fact that human knowledge begins from sense experience. Visual images help us to realize that God is present and they help us to adore him. Veneration of images— as encouraged by the Church—is, therefore, quite different from idolatry: an idolator thinks that God dwells in the idol, that he acts only through the idol, and in some cases he actually thinks that the idol is God.

30. St Paul now moves on from speaking about natural knowledge of God to explaining the knowledge of God that comes from faith.

Although man can know God by using his reason, the Lord has chosen to make known the mysteries of his divine life in a supernatural way, in order to make it easier for man to attain salvation. "The Church maintains and teaches that God, the beginning and end of all things, can be known with certainty, by the natural light of human reason, from created things. [. . .] However, it pleased him in his wisdom and goodness to reveal himself to mankind and to make known the eternal decrees of his will in another, supernatural way" (Vatican I, *Dei Filius*, chap. 2).

"It was also necessary for man to be instructed by divine Revelation concerning those truths concerning God, which human reason is able to discover, for these truths, attained by human reason, would reach man through the work of a few, after much effort and mixed in with many errors; yet the

overlooked, but now he commands all men everywhere to repent, ³¹because he has fixed a day on which he will judge

---

Deus, nunc annuntiat hominibus, ut omnes ubique paenitentiam agant, ³¹eo quod statuit diem, in qua iudicaturus est orbem in iustitia in viro, quem constituit, fidem praebens omnibus suscitans eum a mortuis." ³²Cum audissent

---

entire salvation of man, which lies in God, depends on knowledge of these truths. So, for salvation to reach men more rapidly and more surely, it was necessary for them to be instructed by divine Revelation concerning the things of God" (St Thomas Aquinas, *Summa theologiae*, I, q. 1, a. 1).

Supernatural Revelation assures man of easily attained, certain knowledge of divine mysteries; it also includes some truths—such as the existence of God—which unaided human reason can discover (cf. Rom 1:20).

"It pleased God, in his goodness and wisdom", Vatican II teaches, "to reveal himself and to make known the mystery of his will (cf. Eph 1:9). His will was that men should have access to the Father, through Christ, the Word made flesh, in the Holy Spirit, and thus become sharers in the divine nature (cf. Eph 2:18; 2 Pet 1:4). By this revelation, then, the invisible God (cf. Col 1:15; 1 Tim 1:17), from the fulness of his love, addresses men as his friends (cf. Ex 33:11; Jn 15:14-15), and moves among them in order to invite and receive them into his own company" (*Dei Verbum*, 2).

The knowledge of the triune God and his saving will which supernatural revelation offers men is not just theoretical or intellectual knowledge: it has the aim of converting man and leading him to repent and to change his life. It is, therefore, a calling from God; and God expects man to make a personal response to that call. "The obedience of faith" (Rom 16:26; cf. Rom 1:5; 2 Cor 10:5-6) must be given to God as he reveals himself. By faith man freely commits his entire self to God, making 'the full submission of his intellect and will to God who reveals' (Vatican I, *Dei Filius*, chap. 3), and willingly assenting to the Revelation given by him. Before this faith can be exercised, man must have the grace of God to move and assist him; he must have the interior helps of the Holy Spirit, who moves the heart and converts it to God" (Vatican II, *Dei Verbum*, 5).

This practical knowledge of the living and true God revealed in Christ is in fact the only way for man to know himself, despise his faults and sins, and find hope in divine mercy. It is a self-knowledge—given by God—which enables the repentant sinner to begin a new life and work freely with God at his own sanctification: "As I see it, we shall never succeed in knowing ourselves unless we seek to know God," St Teresa writes. "Let us think of his greatness and then come back to our own baseness; by looking at his purity we shall see our foulness; by meditating on his humility, we shall see how far we are from being humble" (*Interior Castle*, I, 2, 9).

31. On Jesus Christ as Judge of all, see the note on Acts 10:42.

the world in righteousness by a man whom he has appointed, and of this he has given asssurance to all men by raising him from the dead.

³²Now when they heard of the resurrection of the dead, some mocked; but others said, "We will hear you again about this." ³³So Paul went out from among them. ³⁴But some men

---

autem resurrectionem mortuorum, quidam quidem irridebant, quidem vero dixerunt: "Audiemus te de hoc iterum." ³³Sic Paulus exivit de medio eorum.

---

32. When St Paul begins to tell the Athenians about Jesus' resurrection from the dead, they actually begin to jeer. For pagans, the notion of resurrection from the dead was absurd, something they were not prepared to believe. If the Apostle speaks in this way, the reason is that the truths of the Christian faith all lead into the mystery of the Resurrection; even though he may have anticipated his listeners' reaction, he does not avoid telling them about this truth, which forms the bedrock of our faith. "See how he leads them," Chrysostom points out,"to the God who takes care of the world, who is kind, merciful, powerful and wise: all these attributes of the Creator are confirmed in the Resurrection" (*Hom. on Acts*, 38).

The Apostle fails to overcome the rationalist prejudices of most of his audience. Here we have, as it were, an application of what he wrote later to the Corinthians: "The Greeks seek wisdom, but we preach Christ crucified . . . , folly to the Gentiles" (1 Cor 1:22), the reason being that if people do not have an attitude and disposition of faith, then reason goes out of control and haughtily rejects mysteries. If the human mind is made the measure of all things, it will despise and reject anything it does not understand—including things which are beyond human understanding. The mysteries God has revealed to man cannot be grasped by unaided human reason; they have to be accepted on faith. What moves the mind to accept these mysteries is not the evidence they contain but the authority of God, who is infallible truth and cannot deceive or be deceived. The act of faith, although strictly speaking an act of the assenting mind, is influenced by the will; the desire to believe presupposes that one loves him who is proposing the truth to be believed.

34. "Those careful to live an upright life do not take long to understand the word; but the same does not go for others" (Chrysostom, *Hom. on Acts*, 39).

Among the few converts in Athens St Luke mentions Damaris. She is one of the many women who appear in Acts—which clearly shows that the preaching of the Gospel was addressed to everyone without distinction. In all that they did the Apostles followed their Master's example, who in spite of the prejudices of his age proclaimed the Kingdom to women as well as men.

St Luke told us about the first convert in Europe being a woman (cf. 16:14ff).

joined him and believed, among them Dionysius the Areopagite and a woman named Damaris and others with them.

³⁴Quidam vero viri adhaerentes ei crediderunt, in quibus et Dionysius Areopagita et mulier nomine Damaris et alii cum eis.

Something similar happened in the case of the Samaritans: it was a woman who first spoke to them about the Saviour (cf. Jn 4). In the Gospels we see how attentive women are to our Lord—standing at the foot of the Cross or being the first to visit the tomb on Easter Sunday. And there is no record of women being hypocritical or hating Christ or abandoning him out of cowardice.

St Paul has a deep appreciation of the role of the Christian woman—as mother, wife and sister—in the spreading of Christianity, as can be seen from his letters and preaching. Lydia in Philippi, Priscilla and Chloe in Corinth, Phoebe in Cenchrae, the mother of Rufus—who was also a mother to him —, and the daughters of Philip (Acts 21:9): these are some of the women to whom Paul was ever-grateful for their help and prayers.

"Women are called to bring to the family, to society and to the Church, characteristics which are their own and which they alone can give—their gentle warmth and untiring generosity, their love for detail, their quick- wittedness and intuition, their simple and deep piety, their constancy . . ." (J. Escrivá, *Conversations*, 87). The Church looks to women to commit themselves and bear witness to human values and to where human happiness lies: "Women have received from God", John Paul II says, "a natural charism of their own, which features great sensitivity, a fine sense of balance, a gift for detail and a providential love for life-in-the-making, life in need of loving attention. These are qualities which make for human maturity" (*Address*, 7 December 1979).

When these qualities, with which God has endowed feminine personality, are developed and brought into play, woman's "life and work will be really constructive, fruitful and full of meaning, whether she spends the day dedicated to her husband and children or whether, having given up the idea of marriage for a noble reason, she has given herself fully to other tasks.

"Each woman in her own sphere of life, if she is faithful to her divine and human vocation, can and, in fact, does achieve the fulness of her feminine personality. Let us remember that Mary, Mother of God and Mother of men, is not only a model but also a proof of the transcendental value of an apparently unimportant life" (J. Escrivá, *Conversations*, 87).

Paul in Corinth, with Aquila and Priscilla

Rom 16:3
1 Cor 16:19
2 Tim 4:19

¹After this he left Athens and went to Corinth. ²And he found a Jew named Aquila, a native of Pontus, lately come from Italy with his wife Priscilla because Claudius had commanded all the Jews to leave Rome. And he went to see them;

---

¹Post haec discedens ab Athenis venit Corinthum. ²Et inveniens quendam Iudaeum nomine Aquilam, Ponticum genere, qui nuper venerat ab Italia, et Priscillam uxorem eius, eo quod praecepisset Claudius discedere omnes

---

1-11. St Paul must have arrived in Corinth very discouraged by what happened in Athens, and very short of money. Some time later he wrote: "And I was with you in weakness and in much fear and trembling; and my speech and my message were not in plausible words of wisdom, but in demonstration of the Spirit and power, that your faith might not rest in the wisdom of men but in the power of God . . ." (1 Cor 2:3-4). He would never forget his experience in the Areopagus before the Athenians, who "were friends of new speeches, yet who paid no heed to them or what they said; all they wanted was to have something new to talk about" (Chrysostom, *Hom. on Acts*, 39).

Corinth was a very commercial, cosmopolitan city located on an isthmus between two gulfs (which are now joined). Ships came to Corinth from all over the world. Low moral standards, concentration on money-making and voluptuous worship of Aphrodite meant that Corinth did not seem the best ground for sowing the word of God; but the Lord can change people's hearts, especially if he has people as obedient and zealous as Paul, Silvanus, Timothy and the early Christians in general. The Athenians' intellectual pride proved to be a more formidable obstacle than the Corinthians' libertarian lifestyle.

Christians should not soft-pedal if they find themselves in situations where paganism and loose living seem to be the order of the day: indeed this should only spur them on. When addressing his Father at the Last Supper Jesus prayed: "I do not pray that thou shouldst take them out of the world, but that thou shouldst keep them from the evil one" (Jn 17:15).

2. This married couple were probably already Christians when they arrived in Corinth. Since they came from Rome, the indications are that there was a community of Christians in the capital from very early on. Aquila and Priscilla (the diminutive of Prisca) proved to be of great help to Paul from the very beginning of his work in Corinth.

Later on they both must have returned to Rome (cf. Rom 16:3); and it may well be that apostolic considerations dictated their movements, as would be the case with countless Christians after them. "The Christian family's faith and

³and because he was of the same trade he stayed with them, Acts 20:34
1 Cor 4:12
and they worked, for by trade they were tentmakers. ⁴And

Iudaeos a Roma, accessit ad eos ³et, quia eiusdem erat artis, manebat apud eos

---

evangelizing mission also possesses this Catholic missionary inspiration. The sacrament of marriage takes up and re-proposes the task of defending and spreading the faith, a task which has its roots in Baptism and Confirmation and makes Christian married couples and parents witnesses of Christ 'to the ends of the earth' (Acts 1:8) [. . .].

"Just as at the dawn of Christianity Aquila and Priscilla were presented as a missionary couple (cf. Acts 18; Rom 16:3f), so today the Church shows forth her perennial newness and fruitfulness by the presence of Christian couples who [. . .] work in missionary territories, proclaiming the Gospel and doing service to their fellowman for the love of Jesus Christ" (John Paul II, *Familiaris consortio*, 54).

The edict of Claudius (41-54 A.D.) expelling the Jews from Rome was issued before the year 50. It is referred to by Suetonius, the Roman historian, but the details of the decree are not known. We do know that Claudius had protected the Jews on a number of occasions. He gave them the right to appoint the high priest and to have charge of the temple. Apparently, conflict between Jews and Christians in Rome led him to expel some Jews from the city, on a temporary basis, or at least to advise them to leave.

3. St Paul earns his living and manages to combine this with all his preaching of the Gospel. "This teaching of Christ on work," John Paul II writes, "based on the example of his life during his years in Nazareth, finds a particularly lively echo in the teaching of the Apostle Paul. Paul boasts of working at his trade (he was probably a tent-maker: cf. Acts 18:3), and thanks to that work he was able even as an Apostle to earn his own bread" (*Laborem exercens*, 26).

During this stay of a year and a half in Corinth St Paul wrote some rather severe letters to the Thessalonians, pointing out to them the need to work: "If any one will not work, let him not eat. [. . .] We command and exhort [idlers] in the Lord Jesus Christ to do their work in quietness and to earn their own living" (2 Thess 3:10, 12). St John Chrysostom, commenting on this passage of Acts, says that "Work is man's natural state. Idleness is *against his nature*. God has placed man in this world to work, and the natural thing for the soul is to be active and not passive" (*Hom. on Acts*, 35).

Taking Christ's own example, Monsignor Escrivá points out that "Work is one of the highest human values and a way in which men contribute to the progress of society. But even more, it is a way to holiness" (*Conversations*, 24). In Jesus' hands, "a professional occupation, similar to that carried out by millions of people in the world, was turned into a divine task. It became a part of our redemption, a way to salvation" (*ibid.*, 55).

he argued in the synagogue every sabbath, and persuaded Jews and Greeks.

Preaching to Jews and Gentiles

Acts 17:14-15   ⁵When Silas and Timothy arrived from Macedonia, Paul was occupied with preaching, testifying to the Jews that the

---

et operabatur; erant autem scenofactoriae artis. ⁴Disputabat autem in synagoga per omne sabbatum suadebatque Iudaeis et Graecis. ⁵Cum venissent autem de Macedonia Silas et Timotheus, instabat verbo Paulus testificans Iudaeis esse Christum Iesum. ⁶Contradicentibus autem eis et blasphemantibus, excutiens

---

In fact, it is in work, in the middle of ordinary activity, that most people can and should find Christ. God "is calling you to serve him in and from the ordinary, material and secular activities of human life. He waits for us everyday [. . .] in all the immense panorama of work" (*ibid.*, 114). Man thereby finds God in the most visible, material things, and Christians can avoid the danger of what might be called "a double life: on one side, an interior life, a life of relation with God; and on the other, a separate and distinct professional, social and family life, full of small earthly realities" (*ibid.*).

Like most people Paul spent part of his day working to earn his living. When engaged in work he was still the Apostle of the Gentiles chosen by God, and his very work spoke to his companions and friends. We should not think that there was any split between his on-going personal relationship with God, and his apostolic activity or his work—or that he did not work in a concentrated or exemplary manner.

4. It is easy to imagine the hope and eagerness Paul felt when preaching the Gospel to his fellow Jews. He knew from experience the difficulties they had about recognizing Jesus as the Messiah and accepting the Good News. Paul feels both joy and sorrow: he is happy because the moment has arrived for the sons of Abraham to receive the Gospel as is their right by inheritance; but he also realizes that although it brings salvation to some, it spells rejection for those who refuse to accept it.

Origen spoke in similar terms: "I experience anxiety to speak and anxiety not to speak. I wish to speak for the benefit of those who are worthy, so that I may not be taken to task for refusing the word of truth to those who have the ability to grasp it. But I am afraid to speak in case I address those who are unworthy, because it means I am giving holy things to dogs and casting pearls before swine. Only Jesus was capable of distinguishing, among his listeners, those who were without from those who were within: he spoke in parables to the outsiders and explained the parables to those who entered with him into the house" (*Dialogue with Heraclides*, 15).

Christ was Jesus. ⁶And when they opposed and reviled him, he shook out his garments and said to them, "Your blood be upon your heads! I am innocent. From now on I will go to the Gentiles." ⁷And he left there and went to the house of a man named Titius^q Justus, a worshipper of God; his house was next door to the synagogue. ⁸Crispus, the ruler of the synagogue, believed in the Lord, together with all his household; and many of the Corinthians hearing Paul believed and were baptized. ⁹And the Lord said to Paul one night in a

Acts 13:46-51; 20:26; 28:28

1 Cor 1:14

1 Cor 2:3

---

vestimenta dixit ad eos: "Sanguis vester super caput vestrum! Mundus ego. Ex hoc nunc ad gentes vadam." ⁷Et migrans inde intravit in domum cuiusdam nomine Titi Iusti, colentis Deum, cuius domus erat coniuncta synagogae. ⁸Crispus autem archisynagogus credidit Domino cum omni domo sua, et multi Corinthiorum audientes credebant et baptizabantur. ⁹Dixit autem Dominus

6. The blindness of the Jews once again causes Paul great sadness; here is further evidence of the mysterious resistance to faith of so many of the chosen people. As he did in Pisidian Antioch (cf. 13:51), the Apostle shakes the dust from his clothes to show his break from the Jews of Corinth: their apparent fidelity to the religion of their forefathers disguises their proud rejection of God's promises.

He finds himself confronted by the great enigma of salvation history, in which God dialogues with human freedom. As St Justin writes, "The Jews, in truth, who had the prophecies and always looked for the coming of Christ, not only did not recognize him, but, far beyond that, even mistreated him. But the Gentiles, who had never even heard anything of Christ until his Apostles went from Jerusalem and preached about him and gave them the prophecies, were filled with joy and faith, and turned away from their idols, and dedicated themselves to the Unbegotten God through Christ" (*First Apology*, 49, 5).

Paul's words on this occasion are addressed to the Jews of Corinth, not to Jews elsewhere. For a long time past he has directed his preaching to Gentiles as well as Jews. The phrase "From now on I will go to the Gentiles" does not mean that he will no longer address Jews, for in the course of his apostolic work he continues to evangelize Jews as well as Gentiles (cf. Acts 18:19; 28:17).

7. Titus Justus had a Roman name and was a Gentile, but the fact that he lived next door to the synagogue and, in particular, the Greek term used to identify him as a "worshipper" of God, indicates that he was a convert to Judaism. Cf. note on Acts 2:5-11.

9. In this vision, given him to strengthen his resolve, Paul sees the Lord, that is, Jesus. The brief message he receives is reminiscent of the language God uses

^qOther early authorities read *Titus*.

Is 41:10; 43:5
Jer 1:8
Jn 10:16

vision, "Do not be afraid, but speak and do not be silent; [10]for I am with you, and no man shall attack you to harm you; for I have many people in this city." [11]And he stayed a year and six months, teaching the word of God among them.

---

nocte per visionem Paulo: "Noli timere, sed loquere et ne taceas, [10]quia ego sum tecum, et nemo apponetur tibi, ut noceat te, quoniam populus est mihi multus in hac civitate." [11]Sedit autem annum et sex menses docens apud eos

---

when he addresses the prophets and just men of the Old Testament (cf. Ex 3:12; Josh 1:5; Is 41:10). The words "Do not be afraid" occur often in divine visions and are designed to allay the impact of God's overpowering presence (cf. Lk 1:30).

In this case, the words are meant to allay Paul's premonitions about the severe treatment his opponents will hand out to him in Corinth. The vision once again indicates the graces which the Lord is bestowing on him to support his intense contemplative life, which is also a life of action in the service of Jesus and the Gospel.

"I tell you," St Teresa of Avila writes, "those of you whom God is not leading by this road [of contemplation], that, as I know from what I have seen and been told by those who are following this road, they are not bearing a lighter cross than you; you would be amazed at all the ways and manners in which God sends them crosses. I know about both types of life and I am well aware that the trials given by God to contemplatives are intolerable; and they of such a kind that, were he not to feed them with consolations, they could not be borne. It is clear that, since God leads those whom he most loves by the way of trials, the more he loves them, the greater will be their trials; and there is no reason to suppose that he hates contemplatives, since with his own mouth he praises them and calls them his friends.

"To suppose that he would admit to his close friendship people who are free from all trials is ridiculous. [. . .] I think, when those who lead an active life occasionally see contemplatives receiving consolations, they suppose that they never experience anything else. But I can assure you that you might not be able to endure their sufferings for as long as a day" (*Way of Perfection*, chap. 18).

10. God has foreseen the people who are going to follow the call of grace. From this it follows that the Christian has a serious obligation to preach the Gospel to as many people as he can. This preaching has a guaranteed effectiveness, as can be seen from its capacity to convert men and women of every race, age, social condition etc. The Gospel is for all. God offers it, through Christians, to rich and poor, to the educated and the uneducated. Any person can accept this invitation to grace: "Not only philosophers and scholars believed in Christ [. . .], but also workmen and people wholly uneducated, who all scorned glory, and fear, and death" (St Justin, *Second Apology*, 10, 8).

Paul before Gallio

¹²But when Gallio was proconsul of Achaia, the Jews made a united attack upon Paul and brought him before the tribunal, ¹³saying, "This man is persuading men to worship God contrary to the law." ¹⁴But when Paul was about to open his mouth, Gallio said to the Jews, "If it were a matter of wrongdoing or vicious crime, I should have reason to bear with you, O Jews; ¹⁵but since it is a matter of questions about words and names and your own law, see to it yourselves; I refuse to be a judge of these things." ¹⁶And he drove them from the tribunal. ¹⁷And they all seized Sosthenes, the ruler of the synagogue, and beat him in front of the tribunal. But Gallio paid no attention to this.

Acts 25:18-19

Jn 18:31
Acts 23:29

Return to Antioch via Ephesus

¹⁸After this Paul stayed many days longer and then took

Acts 21:24

---

verbum Dei. ¹²Gallione autem proconsule Archaiae, insurrexerunt uno animo Iudaei in Paulum et adduxerunt eum ad tribunal ¹³dicentes: "Contra legem hic persuadet hominibus colere Deum." ¹⁴Incipiente autem Paulo aperire os, dixit Gallio ad Iudaeos: "Si quidem esset iniquum aliquid aut facinus pessimum, o Iudaei, merito vos sustinerem; ¹⁵si vero quaestiones sunt de verbo et nominibus et lege vestra, vos ipsi videritis; iudex ego horum nolo esse." ¹⁶Et minavit eos a tribunali. ¹⁷Apprehendentes autem omnes Sosthenen, principem synagogae, percutiebant ante tribunal; et nihil horum Gallioni curae erat. ¹⁸Paulus vero,

---

12. Gallio was a brother of the Stoic philosopher Seneca. He had been adopted in Rome by Lucius Iunius Gallio, whose name he took. From an inscription at Delphi (reported in 1905) we learn that Gallio began his proconsulship of Achaia, of which Corinth was the capital, in July 51. Paul must have appeared before Gallio around the end of 52. This is one of the best-established dates we have for the Apostle.

17. It is not quite clear what happened. Sosthenes may have been assaulted by the citizens of Corinth who were using the incident to vent their anti-Jewish feelings. But it is more likely that Sosthenes was in sympathy with the Christians and that the Jews were venting their frustration on him. In 1 Corinthians 1:1 a Christian called Sosthenes appears as co-author (amanuensis) of the letter; some commentators identify him with the ruler of the synagogue in this episode.

18. The vow taken by a "Nazarite" (one "consecrated to God") is described in the sixth chapter of the Book of Numbers. Among other things it involved not cutting one's hair (to symbolize that one was allowing God to act in one)

leave of the brethren and sailed for Syria, and with him Priscilla and Aquila. At Cenchreae he cut his hair, for he had a vow. [19]And they came to Ephesus, and he left them there; but he himself went into the synagogue and argued with the Jews. [20]When they asked him to stay for a longer period, he declined; [21]but on taking leave of them he said, "I will return to you if God wills," and he set sail from Ephesus.

[22]When he had landed at Caesarea, he went up and greeted the church, and then went down to Antioch.

---

cum adhuc sustinuisset dies multos, fratribus valefaciens navigabat Syriam, et cum eo Priscilla et Aquila, qui sibi totonderat in Cenchreis caput; habebat enim votum. [19]Deveneruntque Ephesum, et illos ibi reliquit, ipse vero ingressus synagogam disputabat cum Iudaeis. [20]Rogantibus autem eis, ut ampliore tempore maneret, non consensit, [21]sed valefaciens et dicens: "Iterum revertar ad vos Deo volente", navigavit ab Epheso; [22]et descendens Caesaream ascendit

---

and not drinking fermented drinks (meaning a resolution to practise self-denial). It is not clear whether it was Paul or Aquila who had taken the vow; apparently the vow ended at Cenchreae, for the votee's hair was cut there. For more information, see the note on Acts 21:23-24.

19. Ephesus was the capital of proconsular Asia and one of the most flourishing cities of the Empire. Its most famous building, the *Artemision*, or temple of Diana Artemis, was one of the wonders of the ancient world. The city's huge theatre had a capacity for 23,000 spectators. On this journey St Paul did not stay long in Ephesus—perhaps only long enough for the ship to unload and load. However, Ephesus will be the centre of his next missionary journey.

18:23 - 21:26. Paul's third apostolic journey starts, like the earlier ones, from Antioch, but it ends with his imprisonment in Jerusalem (Acts 21:27ff). It was a long journey, but Luke devotes most attention to events in Ephesus.

To begin with Paul tours the cities he already evangelized in Galatia and Phrygia: this would have taken him from the last months of 53 to early 54. Then he goes to Ephesus, where he stays for almost three years and meets up with all kinds of contradictions (cf. 2 Cor 1:8), as he describes it in his letter to the Corinthians in spring 57: "To the present hour we hunger and thirst, we are ill-clad and buffeted and homeless. . . . We have become, and are now, as the refuse of the world, the offscourings of all things" (1 Cor 4:11, 13). Despite this, or perhaps because of it, his apostolate was very fruitful and the Christian message spread through all proconsular Asia, to important cities like Colossae, Laodicae, Hierapolis etc and to countless towns; as he put it in a letter to the Corinthians (1 Cor 16:9), 'a wide door for effective work has opened to me".

The Apostle had to leave Ephesus on account of the revolt of the silversmiths,

ST PAUL'S THIRD APOSTOLIC JOURNEY

Galatia and Phrygia

²³After spending some time there he departed and went from place to place through the region of Galatia and Phrygia, strengthening all the disciples.

Apollos in Ephesus and Corinth

²⁴Now a Jew named Apollos, a native of Alexandria, came

1 Cor 3:6
Tit 3:13

---

et salutavit ecclesiam et descendit Antiochiam. ²³Et facto ibi aliquanto tempore, profectus est perambulans ex ordine Galaticam regionem et Phrygiam, confirmans omnes discipulos. ²⁴Iudaeus autem quidam Apollo nomine, Alexandrinus natione, vir eloquens, devenit Ephesum, potens in Scripturis.

---

moving on towards Macedonia and Achaia to visit the churches he founded on his second journey—Philippi, Thessalonica and Corinth. He stayed there the three months of the winter of 57/58. On his return journey (to Jerusalem, to bring money collected) he went via Macedonia to avoid a Jewish plot. He embarked at Neapolis (the port near Philippi), stopping off at Troas, Miletus (where he met with the elders from Ephesus whom he had called to come to him), Tyre and Caesarea, and managing to reach Jerusalem in time for the Passover.

24. Priscilla and Aquila knew how valuable a man with Apollos' qualities would be if he could be got to dedicate himself to the Lord's service; so they took the initiative and spoke to him. Monsignor Escrivá sees this episode as a good lesson about boldness in speaking about God, as "an event that demonstrates the wonderful apostolic zeal of the early Christians. Scarcely a quarter of a century had passed since Jesus had gone up to heaven and already his fame had spread to many towns and villages. In the city of Ephesus a man arrived, Apollos by name, 'an eloquent man, well versed in the scriptures'. . . . A glimmer of Christ's light had already filtered into the mind of this man. He had heard about our Lord and he passed the news on to others. But he still had some way to go. He needed to know more if he was to acquire the fulness of the faith and so come to love our Lord truly. A Christian couple, Aquila and Priscilla, hear him speaking; they are not inactive or indifferent. They do not think: 'This man already knows enough; it's not our business to teach him.' They were souls who were really eager to do apostolate and so they approached Apollos and 'took him and expounded to him the way of God more accurately'" (*Friends of God*, 269).

This was the kind of zeal the first Christians had; a little later on St Justin wrote: "We do our very best to warn them [Jews and heretics], as we do you, not to be deluded, for we know full well that whoever can speak out the truth and fails to do so shall be condemned by God" (*Dialogue with Tryphon*, 82, 3).

Acts 19:3

2 Cor 3:1
Col 4:10

Acts 9:22

to Ephesus. He was an eloquent man, well versed in the scriptures. [25]He had been instructed in the way of the Lord; and being fervent in spirit, he spoke and taught accurately the things concerning Jesus, though he knew only the baptism of John. [26]He began to speak boldly in the synagogue; but when Priscilla and Aquila heard him, they took him and expounded to him the way of God more accurately. [27]And when he wished to cross to Achaia, the brethren encouraged him, and wrote to the disciples to receive him. When he arrived, he greatly helped those who through grace had believed, [28]for he powerfully confuted the Jews in public, showing by the scriptures that the Christ was Jesus.

---

[25]Hic erat catechizatus viam Domini et fervens spiritu loquebatur et docebat diligenter ea, quae sunt de Iesu, sciens tantum baptisma Ioannis. [26]Hic ergo coepit fiducialiter agere in synagoga; quem cum audissent Priscilla et Aquila, assumpserunt eum et diligentius exposuerunt ei viam Dei. [27]Cum autem vellet transire in Achaiam, exhortati fratres scripserunt discipulis, ut susciperent eum; qui cum venisset, contulit multum his, qui crediderant per gratiam; [28]vehementer enim Iudaeos revincebat publice ostendens per Scripturas esse Christum Iesum.

---

27. God uses people, in this case Apollos, to channel his grace to the faithful. They are instruments of his; they preach his word and reap an apostolic harvest, but it is God himself who makes the harvest grow, by providing his grace. "It depends not upon man's will or exertion, but upon God's mercy" (Rom 9:16). "It is not we who save souls and move them to do good. We are quite simply instruments, some more, some less worthy, for fulfilling God's plans for salvation. If at any time we were to think that we ourselves were the authors of the good we do, then our pride would return, more twisted than ever. The salt would lose its flavour, the leaven would rot and the light would turn to darkness" (J. Escrivá, *Friends of God*, 250).

Hence the importance of supernatural resources in apostolic activity: building is in vain if God does not support it (cf. Ps 127:1). "All that exterior effort is a waste of time, if you lack Love. It's like sewing with a needle and no thread" (J. Escrivá, *The Way*, 967).

19

¹While Apollos was at Corinth, Paul passed through the upper country and came to Ephesus. There he found some disciples. ²And he said to them, "Did you receive the Holy Spirit when you believed?" And they said, "No, we have never even heard that there is a Holy Spirit." ³And he said, "Into what then were you baptized?" They said, "Into John's baptism." ⁴And Paul said, "John baptized with the baptism of repentance, telling the people to believe in the one who

Jn 7:39
Acts 8:15-17

Mt 3:6-11
Acts 13:24

---

¹Factum est autem cum Apollo esset Corinthi, ut Paulus, peragratis superioribus partibus, veniret Ephesum et inveniret quosdam discipulos, ²dixitque ad eos: "Si Spiritum Sanctum accepistis credentes?" At illi ad eum: "Sed neque si Spiritus Sanctus est audivimus." ³Ille vero ait: "In quo ergo baptizati estis?" Qui dixerunt: "In Ioannis baptismate." ⁴Dixit autem Paulus: "Ioannes baptizavit baptisma paenitentiae, populo dicens in eum, qui venturus esset post ipsum ut

---

1-7. This presence in Ephesus of a group of disciples who had received only John's baptism is open to various interpretations. The text seems to imply that they were not, properly speaking, Christians but people who followed the Baptist's teaching and whom Paul regarded as incipient Christians, to the point of calling them disciples. We say this because in the New Testament being a Christian is always connected with receiving Baptism and having the Holy Spirit (cf. Jn 3:5; Rom 8:9; 1 Cor 12:3; Gal 3:2; Acts 11:17; etc.).

2. Leaving aside questions as to the origin and composition of this group of disciples, their simple statement about knowing nothing about the Holy Spirit and his part in fulfilling the messianic promises points to the need to preach Christian doctrine in a systematic, gradual and complete way.

Christian catechesis, John Paul II reminds us, "must be systematic, not improvised but programmed to reach a precise goal; it must deal with essentials, without any claim to tackle all disputed questions or to transform itself into theological research or scientific exegesis; it must nevertheless be sufficiently complete, not stopping short at the initial proclamation of the Christian mystery such as we have in the *kerygma*; it must be an integral Christian initiation, open to all the other factors of Christian life" (*Catechesi tradendae*, 21).

3-4. "The whole teaching and work of John," St Thomas Aquinas writes, "was in preparation for Christ, as the helper and under-craftsman are responsible for preparing the materials for the form which the head-craftsman produces. Grace was to be conferred on men through Christ: 'Grace and truth have come through Jesus Christ' (Jn 1:17). And therefore, the baptism of John

was to come after him, that is, Jesus." [5]On hearing this, they

were baptized in the name of the Lord Jesus. [6]And when Paul
had laid his hands upon them, the Holy Spirit came on them;

---

crederent, hoc est in Iesum." [5]His auditis, baptizati sunt in nomine Domini Iesu;
[6]et cum impossuisset illis manus Paulus, venit Spiritus Sanctus super eos, et

---

did not confer grace, but only prepared the way for grace in a threefold way—in one way, by John's teaching, which led men to faith in Christ; in another way, by accustoming men to the rite of Christ's Baptism; and in a third way, through penance, which prepared men to receive the effect of Christ's Baptism" (*Summa theologiae*, III, q. 38, a. 3).

5. "They were baptized in the name of the Lord Jesus": the view of most commentators is that this does not mean that the Trinitarian formula which appears in Mt 28:19 (cf. note on Acts 2:38) ("in the name of the Father and of the Son and of the Holy Spirit") was not used. The reference here may simply be a way of distinguishing Christian Baptism from other baptismal rites which were features of Judaism in apostolic times—particularly John the Baptist's rite. Besides, Christian Baptism was administered on Jesus Christ's instructions (cf. Mt 28:19), in union with him and using his power: Jesus' redemptive action is initiated by the Father and expresses itself in the full outpouring of the Holy Spirit.

6. This passage speaks of the laying on of hands, something distinct from Baptism, as seen already in Acts 8:14-17, whereby the Holy Spirit is received. This is the sacrament which will come to be called Confirmation and which has been conferred, from the beginnings of the Church, as one of the sacraments of Christian initiation.

Referring to Confirmation, John Paul II has said: "Christ's gift of the Holy Spirit is going to be poured out upon you in a particular way. You will hear the words of the Church spoken over you, calling upon the Holy Spirit to confirm your faith, to seal you in his love, to strengthen you for his service. You will then take your place among fellow-Christians throughout the world, full citizens now of the People of God. You will witness to the truth of the Gospel in the name of Jesus Christ. You will live your lives in such a way as to make holy all human life. Together with all the confirmed, you will become living stones in the cathedral of peace. Indeed you are called by God to be instruments of his peace [. . .].

"You, too, are strengthened inwardly today by the gift of the Holy Spirit, so that each of you in your own way can carry the Good News to your companions and friends. [. . .] The same Holy Spirit comes to you today in the sacrament of Confirmation, to involve you more completely in the Church's fight against sin and in her mission of fostering holiness. He comes to dwell more fully in your hearts and to strengthen you for the struggle with evil. [. . .] The world of

204

and they spoke with tongues and prophesied. ⁷There were
about twelve of them in all.

Paul's preaching and miracles at Ephesus

⁸And he entered the synagogue and for three months spoke
boldly, arguing and pleading about the kingdom of God; ⁹but
when some were stubborn and disbelieved, speaking evil of
the Way before the congregation, he withdrew from them,

---

loquebantur linguis et prophetabant. ⁷Erant autem omnes viri fere duodecim.
⁸Introgressus autem synagogam cum fiducia loquebatur per tres menses
disputans et suadens de regno Dei. ⁹Cum autem quidam indurarentur et non
crederent maledicentes viam coram multitudine, discedens ab eis segregavit

---

today needs you, for it needs men and women who are filled with the Holy
Spirit. It needs your courage and hopefulness, your faith and your perseverance.
The world of tomorrow will be built by you. Today you receive the gift of the
Holy Spirit so that you may work with deep faith and with abiding charity, so
that you may help to bring to the world the fruits of reconciliation and peace.
Strengthened by the Holy Spirit and his manifold gifts [. . .], strive to be
unselfish; try not to be obsessed with material things" (*Homily at Coventry
Airport*, 30 May 1982).

As is the case with Baptism and Holy Orders, Confirmation imprints an
indelible mark or character on the soul.

8-10. This summarized account of Paul's activity in Ephesus is filled out by
the account we are given of the Apostle's farewell to the elders of that city (cf.
20:18-35) and by information contained in his letters to the Corinthians. Paul
made Ephesus the base for his missionary work in the surrounding region, for
which he counted on help from Timothy, Erastus, Gaius, Titus and Epaphras
of Colossae.

During his stay in Ephesus he wrote 1 Corinthians and the Letter to the
Galatians.

8. Paul returns to the synagogue where he taught previously (cf. 18:19-21);
the Jews' resistance and lack of understanding do not lessen his zeal.

9. The obstinacy of some of the Jews eventually obliges Paul to leave the
synagogue. He now moves to the school of Tyrannus—who must have been a
Christian or at least someone sympathetic to the Gospel. Paul may well have
presented himself to the inhabitants of the city as a teacher of "philosophy," in
the meaning of that word then current—the science of living.

The text also shows that Christians already had developed the practice of
meeting in private houses to hear the Word of God, thus avoiding any need to
go to the synagogue.

taking the disciples with him, and argued daily in the hall of Tyrannus.[r] [10]This continued for two years, so that all the residents of Asia heard the word of the Lord, both Jews and Greeks.

Acts 14:3
Mk 6:56
Lk 8:44-47

[11]And God did extraordinary miracles by the hands of Paul, [12]so that handkerchiefs or aprons were carried away

---

discipulos, cotidie disputans in schola Tyranni. [10]Hoc autem factum est per biennium, ita ut omnes, qui habitabant in Asia, audirent verbum Domini, Iudaei atque Graeci. [11]Virtutesque non quaslibet Deus faciebat per manus Pauli, [12]ita ut etiam super languidos deferrentur a corpore eius sudaria vel semicintia, et

---

10. To these "two years" should be added the three months Paul spent preaching in the synagogue (cf. v. 8), which means that he spent about two and a quarter years in Ephesus altogether. This ties in with what he says in his farewell remarks (20:31): "For three years . . .": at that time parts of years were regarded as full years.

The region evangelized by Paul and his helpers was not the whole province of proconsular Asia but the cities of Smyrna, Pergamon, Thyatira, Sardis, Philadelphia, Laodicea, Colossae and Hierapolis, all of which looked to Ephesus as their centre.

11-16. Here we have another reference to miracles worked by Paul (cf. 13:11; 14:10)—the signs which he himself tells us accompanied his preaching (cf. 2 Cor 12:12; Rom 15:19).

St Luke here contrasts the spiritual vitality and the divine character of Paul's message with the falsity and uselessness of magic. Genuine Christian preaching is on a completely different plane from that of opponents or imitators of the Gospel. The author of Acts seems to be anticipating the objections of people who will argue that there was a certain amount of magic in the Apostles' miracles. Origen dealt with similar objections in his reply to the pagan Celsus: "Did the disciples of Jesus learn to do miracles and thereby convince their hearers, or did they not do any? It is quite absurd to say that they did not do any miracles of any kind, and that, in blind faith . . . they went off everywhere to propagate a new teaching; for what would have kept their spirits up when they had to teach something which was so completely new? But if they did also work miracles, how on earth could these magicians have faced so many dangers to spread a teaching which explicitly forbade the use of magic?" (*Against Celsus*, I, 38).

In religions of ancient times there were lots of exorcists like the sons of Sceva. This man, probably a member of an important priestly family, gave himself the title of high priest to help promote and gain credence for the magic-making his family went in for. Many magicians, fortune-tellers and exorcists were ready to invoke any and every God. For example, there were pagans who used the

[r]Other ancient authorities add *from the fifth hour to the tenth*

from his body to the sick, and diseases left them and the evil
spirits came out of them. ¹³Then some of the itinerant Jewish Acts 5:15
exorcists undertook to pronounce the name of the Lord
Jesus over those who had evil spirits, saying, "I adjure you
by the Jesus whom Paul preaches." ¹⁴Seven sons of a Jewish
high priest named Sceva were doing this. ¹⁵But the evil spirit Mk 9:38
answered them, "Jesus I know, and Paul I know; but who Lk 4:41
are you?" ¹⁶And the man in whom the evil spirit was leaped
on them, mastered all of them, and overpowered them, so
that they fled out of that house naked and wounded.

---

recederent ab eis languores, et spiritus nequam egrederentur. ¹³Tentaverunt
autem quidam et de circumeuntibus Iudaeis exorcistis invocare super eos, qui
habebant spiritus malos, nomen Domini Iesu dicentes: "Adiuro vos per Iesum,
quem Paulus praedicat." ¹⁴Erant autem cuiusdam Scevae Iudaei principis
sacerdotum septem filii, qui hoc faciebant. ¹⁵Respondens autem spiritus
nequam dixit eis: "Iesum novi et Paulum scio, vos autem qui estis?" ¹⁶Et
insiliens homo in eos, in quo erat spiritus malus, dominatus amborum invaluit
contra eos, ita ut nudi et vulnerati effugerent de domo illa. ¹⁷Hoc autem notum

---

different names of Yahweh, and we have evidence in the form of a magician's
papyrus which reads, "I abjure you by Jesus, the God of the Jews."

In this instance the evil spirit turns on the seven brothers, showing that "the
Name does nothing unless it be spoken with faith" (Chrysostom, *Hom. on Acts*,
41).

"For the preacher's instruction to exercise its full force", writes St John of
the Cross, "there must be two kinds of preparation—that of the preacher and
that of the hearer; for, as a rule, the benefit derived from instruction depends
on the preparation of the teacher. For this reason it is said, Like master, like
pupil. For, when in the Acts of the Apostles those seven sons of that chief priest
of the Jews used to cast out devils in the same way as St Paul did, the devil rose
up against them [. . .] and then, attacking them, stripped and wounded them.
This was only because they had not the proper preparation" (*Ascent of Mount
Carmel*, III, chap. 45).

Paul's actions and their good effects, in contrast with the signs the agents of
superstition try to perform, fills many of the Ephesians with holy fear and brings
about their conversion. 'The sight of events like this can indeed cause
conviction and faith in those who love the truth, who are not swayed by opinions
and who do not let their evil passions gain the upper hand" (St Justin, *First
Apology*, 53, 12).

12. From the very beginning Christians had great respect for and devotion
to relics—not only the mortal remains of the saints but also their clothes or
things they had used or things which had touched their tombs.

Books of magic burned

Acts 16:17
Lk 5:26 [17]And this became known to all residents of Ephesus, both Jews and Greeks; and fear fell upon them all; and the name of the Lord Jesus was extolled. [18]Many also of those who were now believers came, confessing and divulging their practices. [19]And a number of those who practised magic arts brought their books together and burned them in the sight of all; and they counted the value of them and found it came to Acts 3:10 fifty thousand pieces of silver. [20]So the word of the Lord grew and prevailed mightily.

Paul's plans for further journeys

Acts 6:7
Acts 23:11 [21]Now after these events Paul resolved in the Spirit to pass

---

factum est omnibus Iudaeis atque Graecis, qui habitabant Ephesi, et cecidit timor super omnes illos, et magnificabatur nomen Domini Iesu. [18]Multique credentium veniebant confitentes et annuntiantes actus suos. [19]Multi autem ex his, qui fuerant curiosa sectati, conferentes libros combusserunt coram omnibus; et computaverunt pretia illorum et invenerunt argenti quinquaginta milia. [20]Ita fortiter verbum Domini crescebat et convalescebat. [21]Hic autem expletis, proposuit Paulus in Spiritu, transita Macedonia et Achaia, ire Hierosolymam, dicens: "Postquam fuero ibi, oportet me et Roman videre."

17-19. This fear which overtook the believers marked the start of their spiritual recovery. Fear of the Lord is a gift of the Holy Spirit, which inspires reverence towards God and fear of offending him, and helps us avoid evil and do good. It inspires the respect, admiration, obedience and love of one who wishes to please his Father.

Fear of offending God leads the people of Ephesus to have done with anything that distances them from him, in particular magical arts. Books on magic—each often only a few pages of manuscript—were common in ancient times; they were also worth a lot of money: firstly because of the much sought-after magical formulae they contained, and secondly because they were often very ornately produced.

The attitude of these Christians—inspired by the Holy Spirit—towards things which might lead them to offend God is to avoid them completely. "We Christians have a commitment of love to the call of divine grace, which we have freely accepted, an obligation which urges us to fight tenaciously. We know that we are as weak as other people, but we cannot forget that if we use the resources available to us, we will become salt and light and leaven of the world; we will be the consolation of God" (J. Escrivá, *Christ is passing by*, 74).

21-22. Paul's decision to go back to Macedonia and Achaia is another example of the way God encourages the Apostle to build up the churches he

through Macedonia and Achaia and go to Jerusalem, saying,
"After I have been there, I must also see Rome." ^{22}And Rom 15:22-23
having sent into Macedonia two of his helpers, Timothy and
Erastus, he himself stayed in Asia for a while.

The silversmiths' riot in Ephesus

^{23}About that time there arose no little stir concerning the
Way. ^{24}For a man named Demetrius, a silversmith, who 1 Cor 4:17
made silver shrines of Artemis, brought no little business to
the craftsmen. ^{25}These he gathered together, with the workmen of like occupation, and said, "Men, you know that from

---

^{22}Mittens autem in Macedoniam duos ex ministrantibus sibi, Timotheum et
Erastum, ipse remansit ad tempus in Asia. ^{23}Facta est autem in illo tempore
turbatio non minima de via. ^{24}Demetrius enim quidam nomine, argentarius,
faciens aedes argenteas Dianae praestabat artificibus non modicum quaestum;
^{25}quos congregans et eos, qui eiusmodi erant opifices, dixit: "Viri, scitis quia
de hoc artificio acquisitio est nobis ^{26}et videtis et auditis quia non solum Ephesi,

---

earlier established in these regions. Paul will also use this visit to collect the
donations set aside for the Jerusalem community.

His planned visit to Rome should not be seen in terms of a vague desire to
go there sometime, but as something he feels he really needs to do, something
God wants him to do.

23. St Luke describes Christianity and the Church as the "Way" (cf. Acts
9:2; 22:4; 24:14, 22). This term was probably fairly widely used, with this
meaning, by Christians of the period. It has Jewish roots and refers to a moral
and religious lifestyle and even a set of moral criteria. In the Book of Acts (and
among the first Christians) the word "way", then, often implies that "following
Christ", embracing his religion, is not just one way of Salvation among many,
but the only way that God offers man: in certain passages of Acts it is referred
to as *the* way (cf. 9:2). Sometimes "the" Way is equivalent to "the" Church of
Christ, outside of which there is no redemption.

"The preaching of the Gospel is rightly called "way", for it is the route that
truly leads to the Kingdom of heaven" (Chrysostom, *Hom. on Acts*, 41).

24. Artemis was the Greek name of the goddess the Romans called Diana,
but through syncretism it was identified with an oriental goddess of fertility. A
statue of Diana was worshipped in the *Artemision*. Feast-days of Artemis were
celebrated with disgraceful orgies, for which people flocked into Ephesus from
the surrounding region. Demetrius and his fellow-craftsmen did good business
selling little statuettes of Diana which many visitors took home as souvenirs
and cult objects.

^{Acts 16:16} this business we have our wealth. ²⁶And you see and hear that not only at Ephesus but almost throughout all Asia this Paul has persuaded and turned away a considerable company of people, saying that gods made with hands are not gods. ²⁷And there is danger not only that this trade of ours may come into disrepute but also that the temple of the great goddess Artemis may count for nothing, and that she may even be deposed from her magnificence, she whom all Asia and the world worship."

²⁸When they heard this they were enraged, and cried out, ^{Acts 17:29} "Great is Artemis of the Ephesians!" ²⁹So the city was filled with the confusion; and they rushed together into the theatre, dragging with them Gaius and Aristarchus, Macedonians who were Paul's companions in travel. ³⁰Paul wished to go in among the crowd, but the disciples would not let him;

---

sed paene totius Asiae Paulus hic suadens avertit multam turbam dicens quoniam non sunt dii, qui manibus fiunt. ²⁷Non solum autem haec periclitatur nobis pars in redargutionem venire, sed et magnae deae Dianae templum in nihilum reputari, et destrui incipiet maiestas eius, quam tota Asia et orbis colit." ²⁸His auditis, repleti sunt ira et clamabant dicentes: "Magna Diana Ephesiorum!" ²⁹et impleta est civitas confusione, et impetum fecerunt uno animo in theatrum, rapto Gaio et Aristarcho Macedonibus, comitibus Pauli. ³⁰Paulo autem volente intrare in populum, non permiserunt discipuli; ³¹quidam

---

26. Demetrius fairly accurately gives the gist of a central point of Paul's preaching against idolatry (cf. 17:29). Christians spoke out against the false gods of paganism, using arguments and passages from the Old Testament in the same way as Jewish apologists did (cf. Is 44:9-20; 46:1-7; Wis 13:10-19).

29. What started off as a meeting of craftsmen to discuss a threat to their business has become a huge popular gathering. The Ephesians flock into the city's theatre, which was where all huge meetings usually took place. They do not really seem to know very much about what is going on; but we can detect a certain amount of anti-Jewish feeling. They were more familiar with Judaism than with the new Christian religion, and this may have led them to blame the Jews for the threat to their pagan practices and beliefs.

Aristarchus was from Thessalonica (cf. Acts 20:4). He accompanied St Paul on his journey to Rome and during his imprisonment there (cf. Acts 27:2 and Col 4:10). Gaius may have been the same Christian as is referred to in Acts 20:4.

30-31. As in other similar situations, Paul wants to use the opportunity to justify his actions and speak to the people about the faith he preaches and is

³¹some of the Asiarchs also, who were friends of his, sent to him and begged him not to venture into the theatre. ³²Now some cried one thing, some another; for the assembly was in confusion, and most of them did not know why they had come together. ³³Some of the crowd prompted Alexander, whom the Jews had put forward. And Alexander motioned with his hand, wishing to make a defence to the people. ³⁴But when they recognized that he was a Jew, for about two hours Acts 18:12 they all with one voice cried out, "Great is Artemis of the Ephesians!" ³⁵And when the town clerk had quieted the crowd, he said, "Men of Ephesus, what man is there who does not know that the city of the Ephesians is temple keeper of the great Artemis, and of the sacred stone that fell from the sky?ˢ ³⁶Seeing then that these things cannot be contradicted, you ought to be quiet and do nothing rash. ³⁷For you have brought these men here who are neither sacrilegious nor blasphemers of our goddess. ³⁸If therefore Acts 20:4; 27:2

---

autem de Asiarchis, qui erant amici eius, miserunt ad eum rogantes, ne se daret in theatrum. ³²Alii autem aliud clamabant; erat enim ecclesia confusa, et plures nesciebant qua ex causa convenissent. ³³De turba autem instruxerunt Alexandrum, propellentibus eum Iudaeis; Alexander ergo, manu silentio postulato, volebat rationem reddere populo. ³⁴Quem ut cognoverunt Iudaeum esse, vox facta est una omnium quasi per horas duas clamantium: "Magna Diana Ephesiorum!" ³⁵Et cum sedasset scriba turbam dixit: "Viri Ephesii, quis enim est hominum, qui nesciat Ephesiorum civitatem cultricem esse magnae Dianae et simulacri a Iove delapsi? ³⁶Cum ergo his contradici non possit, oportet vos sedatos esse et nihil temere agere. ³⁷Adduxistis enim homines istos neque sacrilegos neque blasphemantes deam nostram. ³⁸Quod si Demetrius et, qui

---

proud to acknowledge. However, he goes along with the disciples' advice and decides that it would be imprudent to enter the theatre. Given the hysteria of the crowd he probably realizes that it would be counterproductive to appear before them.

The Asiarchs, as the magistrates of Ephesus were called, presided over meetings of the provincial assembly of Asia. Paul was apparently on friendly terms with them.

33-34. Alexander, a Jew, feels called to explain to those present that the Jews and their religion were not responsible for the events which led the people to assemble; but in fact this only causes further provocation.

35-40. The town clerk's sober remarks, especially his reference to legal

ˢThe meaning of the Greek is uncertain

Demetrius and the craftsmen with him have a complaint against any one, the courts are open, and there are pro-consuls; let them bring charges against one another. ³⁹But if you seek anything further,¹ it shall be settled in the regular assembly. ⁴⁰For we are in danger of being charged with rioting today, there being no cause that we can give to justify this commotion." ⁴¹And when he had said this, he dismissed the assembly.

20

Paul goes into Macedonia and begins his return journey

Acts 14:22;
16:40 ¹After the uproar ceased, Paul sent for the disciples and having exhorted them took leave of them and departed for Macedonia. ²When he had gone through these parts and had 1 Cor 16:5-6 given them much encouragement, he came to Greece. ³There

---

cum eo sunt, artifices habent adversus aliquem causam, conventus forenses aguntur, et proconsules sunt: accusent invicem. ³⁹Si quid autem ulterius quaeritis, in legitima ecclesia poterit absolvi. ⁴⁰Nam et periclitamur argui seditionis hodiernae, cum nullus obnoxius sit, de quo non possimus reddere rationem concursus istius." Et cum haec dixisset, dimisit ecclesiam.
¹Postquam autem cessavit tumultus, accersitis Paulus discipulis et exhortatus eos, valedixit et profectus est, ut iret in Macedoniam. ²Cum autem perambulasset partes illas et exhortatus eos fuisset multo sermone, venit ad Graeciam; ³cumque fecisset menses tres, factae sunt illi insidiae a Iudaeis

---

channels, show him to be admirably impartial. He probably has some impression of the merits of the Christian message; anyone, indeed, who looks at Christianity calmly and closely cannot fail to be impressed by it.

1. This verse connects up with 19:22, at which point the narrative branched off to deal with the riot of the silversmiths. Paul's exhortations to the disciples of Ephesus must have been on the same lines as his address in vv. 18-35.

This journey to Macedonia is probably the same one as mentioned in 2 Cor 2:12-13: "When I came to Troas to preach the gospel of Christ, a door was opened for me in the Lord; but my mind could not rest because I did not find my brother Titus there. So I took leave of them and went on to Macedonia."

2. From Macedonia Paul wrote 2 Corinthians, which was delivered by Titus.

3. During his stay in Corinth Paul wrote and despatched his letter to the Romans.

¹Other ancient authorities read *about other matters*

he spent three months, and when a plot was made against him by the Jews as he was about to set sail for Syria, he determined to return through Macedonia. ⁴Sopater of Beroea, the son of Pyrrhus, accompanied him; and of the Thessalonians, Aristarchus and Secundus; and Gaius of Derbe, and Timothy; and the Asians, Tychicus and Trophimus. ⁵These went on and were waiting for us at Troas, ⁶but we sailed away from Philippi after the days of Unleavened Bread, and in five days we came to them at Troas, where we stayed for seven days.

The celebration of the Eucharist. Eutychus' fall and recovery

⁷On the first day of the week, when we were gathered   Acts 2:42

---

navigaturo in Syriam, habuitque consilium, ut reverteretur per Macedoniam. ⁴Comitabatur autem eum Sopater Pyrrhi Beroensis, Thessalonicensium vero Aristarchus et Secundus et Gaius Derbeus et Timotheus, Asiani vero Tychicus et Trophimus. ⁵Hi cum praecessissent, sustinebant nos Troade; ⁶nos vero navigavimus post dies Azymorum a Philippis, et venimus ad eos Troadem in diebus quinque, ubi demorati sumus diebus septem. ⁷In una autem sabbatorum

---

We know nothing else about this Jewish plot which caused Paul to change his plans. Possibly some Jews, pilgrims to Jerusalem on the same boat as Paul, were planning to deal with him during the sea journey.

4. Paul has now set out on his last journey to Jerusalem. The seven brethren who travelled with him were presumably delegates of the churches appointed to help him bring the monies collected for the support of the Christians in Jerusalem.

5. The narrative changes again into the first person plural. Luke joined Paul at Philippi and will stay with him from now on. "We" means "Paul and I"; we have no reason to think that it includes other people.

6. The Azymes or days of the Unleavened Bread are the week when the Passover is celebrated. The Christian Easter and the Jewish Passover fell on the same days. See also the notes on Mt 26:2 and 26:17.

7. This is the first reference in Acts to the Christian custom of meeting on the first day of the week to celebrate the Eucharist (cf. 2:42; 1 Cor 10:16). "In una autem sabbatorum: that is," St Bede comments, "on the Lord's Day, the first day after the sabbath, when we gather to celebrate our mysteries" (*Super Act expositio, ad loc.*).

"We call this food," St Justin explains, "the Eucharist, of which only he can

213

together to break bread, Paul talked with them, intending to depart on the morrow; and he prolonged his speech until midnight. ⁸There were many lights in the upper chamber where we were gathered. ⁹And a young man named Eutychus was sitting in the window. He sank into a deep sleep as Paul talked still longer; and being overcome by sleep, he fell down from the third storey and was taken up dead. ¹⁰But Paul went down and bent over him, and embracing him said, "Do not be alarmed, for his life is in him." ¹¹And when Paul had gone up and had broken bread and eaten, he conversed with them a long time, until daybreak, and so departed. ¹²And when they took the lad away alive, and were not a little comforted.

1 Kings
17:17-24

cum convenissemus ad frangendum panem, Paulus disputabat eis, profecturus in crastinum, protraxitque sermonem usque in mediam noctem. ⁸Erant autem lampades copiosae in cenaculo, ubi eramus congregati; ⁹sedens autem quidam adulescens nomine Eutychus super fenestram, cum mergeretur somno gravi disputante diutius Paulo, eductus somno cecidit de tertio cenaculo deorsum et sublatus est mortuus. ¹⁰Cum discendisset autem Paulus incubuit super eum et complexus dixit: "Nolite turbari, anima enim ipsius in eo est!" ¹¹Ascendens autem frangensque panem et gustans satisque allocutus usque in lucem, sic profectus est. ¹²Adduxerunt autem puerum viventem et consolati sunt non

partake who has acknowledged the truth of our teachings, who has been cleansed by baptism for the remission of his sins and for his regeneration, and who regulates his life upon the principles laid down by Christ" (*First Apology*, 66, 1).

Christian writers have pointed to the profound connexion between the Eucharist and that true brotherhood which God lays as a duty on, and grants as a gift to, Christ's disciples. St Francis de Sales writes: "How the greatness of God has lowered itself on behalf of each and every one of us—and how high he desires to raise us! He desires us to be so perfectly united to him as to make us one with him. He has desired this in order to teach us that, since we have been loved with an equal love whereby he embraces us all in the most blessed Sacrament, he desires that we love one another with that love which tends towards union, and to the greatest and most perfect form of union. We are all nourished by the same bread, that heavenly bread of the divine Eucharist, the reception of which is called communion, and which symbolizes that unity that we should have one with another, without which we could not be called children of God" (*Sermon on the third Sunday of Lent*).

8-12. This is the only miracle recounted in Acts where Paul raises someone from the dead. St Bede sees in it a certain spiritual symbolism: "The restoring of this young man to life is brought about in the course of preaching. Thereby

From Troas to Miletus

¹³But going ahead to the ship, we set sail for Assos, intending to take Paul aboard there; for so he had arranged, intending himself to go by land. ¹⁴And when he met us at Assos, we took him on board and came to Mitylene. ¹⁵And sailing from there we came the following day opposite Chios; the next day we touched at Samos; andᵘ the day after that we came to Miletus. ¹⁶For Paul had decided to sail past Ephesus, so that he might not have to spend time in Asia; for he was hastening to be at Jerusalem, if possible, on the day of Pentecost.

Acts 18:21

Speech of farewell to the elders of Ephesus

¹⁷And from Miletus he sent to Ephesus and called to him the elders of the church. ¹⁸And when they came to him he said to them:

1 Thess 1:5

---

minime. ¹³Nos autem praecedentes navi enavigavimus in Asson, inde suscepturi Paulum, sic enim disposuerat volens ipse per terram iter facere. ¹⁴Cum autem convenisset nos in Asson, assumpto eo, venimus Mitylenen ¹⁵et inde navigantes sequenti die pervenimus contra Chium et alia applicuimus Samum et sequenti venimus Miletum. ¹⁶Proposuerat enim Paulus transnavigare Ephesum, ne qua mora illi fieret in Asia; festinabat enim, si possibile sibi esset, ut diem Pentecosten faceret Hierosolymis. ¹⁷A Mileto autem mittens Ephesum convocavit presbyteros ecclesiae. ¹⁸Qui cum venissent ad eum, dixit eis: "Vos scitis a prima die, qua ingressus sum in Asiam, qualiter vobiscum per omne

---

Paul's preaching is confirmed by the kindness of the miracle and the teaching; the effort involved in the long vigil is repaid with interest; and all those present are reminded vividly of their departed Master" (*Super Act expositio, ad loc.*).

13-16. The various little details given by Luke suggest that he very likely kept a diary which he later used when writing his book.

16. The Law laid down that all Jews should go up to Jerusalem three times a year, for the feasts of the Passover, Pentecost and Tabernacles (cf. Deut 16:16). St Paul's desire is to press on to Jerusalem to hand over the collection and to establish contact with the many Jews who would gather in the city for the festival.

18-35. Paul's address to the elders of Ephesus is his third great discourse related in Acts (the others being his address to Jews in Pisidian Antioch— 13:16ff—and to pagans at Athens—17:22ff). It is, as it were, an emotional farewell to the churches which he had founded.

ᵘOther ancient authorities add *after remaining at Trogyllium*

"You yourselves know how I lived among you all the time
2 Cor 11:23-31
Phil 2:3
from the first day that I set foot in Asia, [19]serving the Lord
with all humility and with tears and with trials which befell
2 Tim 4:2
me through the plots of the Jews; [20]how I did not shrink from
declaring to you anything that was profitable, and teaching

---

tempus fuerim, [19]serviens Domino cum omni humilitate et lacrimis et
tentationibus, quae mihi acciderunt in insidiis Iudaeorum; [20]quomodo nihil
subtraxerim utilium, quominus annuntiarem vobis et docerem vos publice et

---

The address divides into two parts. The first (vv. 18-27) is a brief resume of
Paul's life of dedication to the church of Ephesus, which he founded and
directed, with hints of the difficulties which he expects to meet in the immediate
future. Two parallel sections (vv. 18-21 and 26-27) frame the central passages
of this section (vv. 22-25).

In the second section the Apostle speaks movingly about the mission and
role of elders. Two series of recommendations (vv. 28-31 and 33-35) hinge on
the central verse (v. 32).

The pathos, vigour and spiritual depth of the discourse clearly show that it
is Paul who is speaking. Here we have the Paul of the letters addressing a
community which has already been evangelized, and inviting them to get to
know their faith better and practise it better.

18-20. Paul is not embarrassed to set himself as an example of how to serve
God and the disciples in the cause of the Gospel (cf. 1 Cor 11:1). He has worked
diligently, steadily, out of love for Jesus Christ and the brethren, doing his duty,
conscious that this kind of patient, persevering work is the way of perfection
and holiness that God expects him to follow.

The Apostle has learned to imitate Christ both in his public life and in the
long years of his hidden life, ever deepening in his love. In this connexion, St
Francis de Sales writes: "Those are spiritually greedy who never have enough
of exercises of devotion, so keen are they, they say, to attain perfection; as if
perfection consisted in the amount of things we do and not in the perfection
with which we do them. [. . .] God has not made perfection to lie in the number
of acts we do to please him, but in the way in which we do them: that way is to
do the little we have to do according to our calling, that is, to do it in love,
through love and for love" (*Sermon on the first Sunday of Lent*).

St Catherine of Siena understood our Lord to say to her something along the
same lines: "I reward every good which is done, great or small, according to
the measure of the love of him who receives the reward" (*Dialogue*, chap. 68).

As in his letters, Paul associates the idea of service with humility (cf. 2 Cor
10:1; 1 Thess 2:6), tears (cf. Rom 9:2; Phil 3:18) and fortitude to keep on
working despite persecution (cf. 2 Cor 11:24; 1 Thess 2:14-16). The Apostle's
true treasure is humility, for it allows him to discover his shortcomings and at

you in public and from house to house, [21]testifying both to Jews and to Greeks of repentance to God and of faith in our Lord Jesus Christ. [22]And now, behold, I am going to Jerusalem, bound in the Spirit, not knowing what shall befall me there; [23]except that the Holy Spirit testifies to me

Acts 21:4-11

per domos, [21]testificans Iudaeis atque Graecis in Deum paenitentiam et fidem in Dominum nostrum Iesum. [22]Et nunc ecce aligatus ego Spiritu vado in Ierusalem, quae in ea eventura sint mihi ignorans, [23]nisi quod Spiritus Sanctus

the same time teaches him to rely on God's strength. As St Teresa says, "The truly humble person will have a genuine desire to be thought little of, and condemned unjustly, even in serious matters. For, if she desires to imitate the Lord, how can she do so better than in this? And no bodily strength is necessary here, nor the aid of anyone but God" (*Way of Perfection*, 15, 2).

21. This very brief summary of Paul's preaching to Jews and pagans mentions repentance and faith as inseparable elements in the new life Jesus confers on Christians. "It is good to know", Origen writes, "that we will be judged at the divine judgment seat not on our faith alone, as if we had not to answer for our conduct; nor on our conduct alone, as if our faith were not to be scrutinized. What justifies is our uprightness on both scores, and if we are short on either we shall deserve punishment" (*Dialogue with Heraclides*, 8).

The presence of grace and faith in the soul equips it to fight the Christian fight, which ultimately leads to rooting out sins and defects. "From the very day faith enters your soul," Origen also says, "battle must be joined between virtues and vices. Prior to the onslaught of the Word, vices were at peace within you, but from the moment the Word begins to judge them one by one, a great turmoil arises and a merciless war begins. 'For what partnership have righteousness and iniquity?' (2 Cor 6:14)" (*In Ex hom.*, III, 3).

22. The Apostle is convinced that God is guiding his steps and watching over him like a father; but he is also unsure about what lies ahead: this uncertainty about the future is part of the human condition. "Grace does not work on its own. It respects men in the actions they take, it influences them, it awakens and does not entirely dispel their restlessness" (Chrysostom, *Hom. on Acts*, 37).

"The true minister of Christ is concious of his own weakness and labours in humility. He searches to see what is well-pleasing to God (cf. Eph 5:10) and, bound as it were in the Spirit (cf. Acts 20:22), he is guided in all things by the will of him who wishes all men to be saved. He is able to discover and carry out that will in the course of his daily routine" (Vatican II, *Presbyterorum ordinis*, 15).

23. "No man, whether he be a Christian or not, has an easy life. To be sure, at certain times it seems as though everything goes as we planned. But this

Acts 26:16-18
2 Tim 4:7

Acts 18:6

in every city that imprisonment and inflictions await me. [24]But I do not account my life of any value nor as precious to myself, if only I may accomplish my course and the ministry which I received from the Lord Jesus, to testify to the gospel of the grace of God. [25]And now, behold, I know that all you among whom I have gone about preaching the kingdom will see my face no more. [26]Therefore I testify to

---

per omnes civitates protestatur mihi dicens quoniam vincula et tribulationes me manent. [24]Sed nihil facio animam meam pretiosam mihi, dummodo consummem cursum meum et ministerium, quod accepi a Domino Iesu, testificari evangelium gratiae Dei. [25]Et nunc ecce ego scio quia amplius non videbitis faciem meam vos omnes, per quos transivi praedicans regnum; [26]quapropter contestor vos hodierna die quia mundus sum a sanguine omnium, [27]non enim

---

generally lasts for only a short time. Life is a matter of facing up to difficulties and of experiencing in our hearts both joy and sorrow. It is in this forge that a person can acquire fortitude, patience, magnanimity and composure [. . .].

"Naturally, the difficulties we meet in our daily lives will not be as great or as numerous as St Paul encountered. We will, however, discover our own meanness and selfishness, the sting of sensuality, the useless, ridiculous smack of pride, and many other failings besides: so very many weaknesses. But are we to give in to discouragement? Not at all. Together with St Paul, let us tell our Lord, 'For the sake of Christ, I am content with weakness, insults, hardships, persecutions and calamities; for when I am weak, then I am strong' (2 Cor 12:10)" (J. Escrivá, *Friends of God*, 17, 212).

24. Paul has come to love Jesus Christ so much that he gives himself no importance: he sees his life as having no meaning other than that of doing what God wants him to do (cf. 2 Cor 4:7; Phil 1:19-26; Col 1:24). He sees holiness as a constant, uninterrupted striving towards his encounter with the Lord; and all the great Fathers of the Church have followed him in this: "On the subject of virtue," St Gregory of Nyssa, for example, writes, "we have learned from the Apostle himself that the only limit to perfection of virtue is that there is no limit. This fine, noble man, this divine apostle, never ceases, when running on the course of virtue, to 'strain forward to what lies ahead' (Phil 3:13). He realizes it is dangerous to stop. Why? Because all good, by its very nature, is unlimited: its only limit is where it meets its opposite: thus, the limit of life is death, of light darkness, and in general of every good its opposite. Just as the end of life is the beginning of death, so too if one ceases to follow the path of virtue one is beginning to follow the path of vice" (*On the life of Moses*, I, 5).

26. "He considers himself innocent of the blood of the disciples because he has not neglected to point out to them their defects" (St Bede, *Super Act expositio, ad loc.*) Paul not only preached the Gospel to them and educated them

you this day that I am innocent of the blood of all of you,
²⁷for I did not shrink from declaring to you the whole counsel
of God. ²⁸Take heed to yourselves and to all the flock, in
which the Holy Spirit has made you guardians, to feed the
church of the Lord^v which he obtained with his own blood.^w
²⁹I know that after my departure fierce wolves will come in
among you, not sparing the flock; ³⁰and from among your

1 Tim 4:16
1 Pet 2:9; 5:2

Mt 7:15
Jn 10:12
2 Pet 2:1-2
1 Jn 2:19

subterfugi, quominus annuntiarem omne consilium Dei vobis. ²⁸Attendite vobis
et universo gregi, in quo vos Spiritus Sanctus posuit episcopos, pascere
ecclesiam Dei, quam acquisivit sanguine suo. ²⁹Ego scio quoniam intrabunt
post discessionem meam lupi graves in vos non parcentes gregi, ³⁰et ex vobis
ipsis exsurgent viri loquentes perversa, ut abstrahant discipulos post se.

in the faith: he also corrected their faults, putting into practice the advice he
gave to the Galatians: "if any man trespass, you who are spiritual should restore
him in a spirit of gentleness. Look to yourself, lest you too be tempted" (Gal
6:1). "A disciple of Christ will never treat anyone badly. Error he will call error,
but the person in error he will correct with kindness. Otherwise he will not be
able to help him, to sanctify him" (J. Escrivá, *Friends of God*, 9).

28. Using a metaphor often found in the New Testament to describe the
people of God (Ps 100:3; Is 40:11; Jer 13:17), Paul describes the Church as a
flock and its guardians or bishops (*epíscopos*) as shepherds. "The Church is a
sheepfold, the sole and necessary gateway to which is Christ (Jn 10:1-10). It is
also a flock, of which God foretold that he would himself be the shepherd (cf.
Is 40:11; Ex 34:11f), and whose sheep, although watched over by human
shepherds, are nevertheless at all times led and brought to pasture by Christ
himself, the Good Shepherd and prince of shepherds (cf. Jn 10:11; 1 Pet 5:4),
who gave his life for his sheep (cf. Jn 10:11-16)" (Vatican II, *Lumen gentium*,
6).

In the early days of the Church the terms "priest" and "bishop" had not yet
become defined: they both refer to sacred ministers who have received the
sacrament of priestly Order.

The last part of the verse refers to Christ's sacrifice: through his redeeming
action, the Church has become God's special property. The price of
Redemption was the blood of Christ. Paul VI says that Christ, the Lamb of God,
took to "himself the sins of the world, and he died for us, nailed to the Cross,
saving us by his redeeming blood" (*Creed of the People of God*, 12).

The Council of Trent speaks of this when it presents the Redemption as an
act of "his beloved Only-begotten, our Lord Jesus Christ, who . . . merited
justification for us by his most holy Passion on the wood of the Cross and made
satisfaction for us to God the Father" (*De iustificatione*, 7).

30. Errors derive not only from outsiders: they are also the product of

^vOther ancient authorities read *of God*   ^wOr *with the blood of his Own*

1 Thess 2:11
1 Pet 5:8-9

Deut 33:3
Eph 2:20-22

Mt 10:8
Acts 18:3
1 Cor 4:12
1 Thess 2:9

own selves will arise men speaking perverse things, to draw away the disciples after them. ³¹Therefore be alert, remembering that for three years I did not cease night or day to admonish every one with tears. ³²And now I commend you to God and to the word of his grace, which is able to build you up and to give you the inheritance among all those who are sanctified. ³³I coveted no one's silver or gold or apparel. ³⁴You yourselves know that these hands ministered to my necessities, and to those who were with me. ³⁵In all things I

---

³¹Propter quod vigilate memoria retinentes quoniam per triennium nocte et die non cessavi cum lacrimis monens unumquemque vestrum. ³²Et nunc commendo vos Deo et verbo ipsius, qui potens est aedificare et dare hereditatem in sanctificatis omnibus. ³³Argentum aut aurum aut vestem nullius concupivi; ³⁴ipsi scitis quoniam ad ea, quae mihi opus erant et his, qui mecum sunt, ministraverunt manus istae. ³⁵Omnia ostendi vobis quoniam sic laborantes oportet suscipere infirmos, ac meminisse verborum Domini Iesu, quoniam ipse

---

members of the Church who abuse their position as brethren and even as pastors, leading the people astray by taking advantage of their good will. "It is of this that John writes, 'They went out from us, but they were not of us' [1 Jn 2:19]" (St Bede, *Super Act expositio, ad loc.*).

31. "Here he shows that he actually taught them and did not proclaim the teaching once only, just to ease his conscience" (Chrysostom, *Hom. on Acts*, 44). Paul did not avoid the pastoral work which fell to him; he set an example of what a bishop should be. "Those who rule the community must perform worthily the tasks of government. [. . .] There is a danger that some who concern themselves with others and guide them towards eternal life may ruin themselves without realizing it. Those who are in charge must work harder than others, must be humbler than those under them, must in their own lives give an example of service, and must regard their subjects as a deposit which God has given them in trust" (St Gregory of Nyssa, *De instituto christiano*).

32. "It is not right for Christians to give such importance to human action that they think all the laurels depend on their efforts: their expectation of reward should be subject to the will of God" (*ibid.*).

33-35. "The teachings of the Apostle of the Gentiles [. . .] have key importance for the morality and spirituality of human work. They are an important complement to the great though discreet gospel of work that we find in the life and parables of Christ, in what Jesus 'did and taught' " (John Paul II, *Laborem exercens*, 26).

This saying of our Lord (v. 35) is not recorded in the Gospels.

have shown you that by so toiling one must help the weak, remembering the words of the Lord Jesus, how he said, 'It is more blessed to give than to receive.'"

[36]And when he had spoken thus, he knelt down and prayed with them all. [37]And they all wept and embraced Paul and kissed him, [38]sorrowing most of all because of the word he had spoken, that they should see his face no more. And they brought him to the ship.

Acts 21:5
Rom 16:16
1 Pet 5:14
Acts 20:25

PART FOUR

ST PAUL, IN IMPRISONMENT, BEARS WITNESS TO CHRIST

21

From Miletus to Caesarea

[1]And when we had parted from them and set sail, we came by a straight course to Cos, and the next day to Rhodes, and from there to Patara.ˣ [2]And having found a ship crossing to Phoenica, we went aboard, and set sail. [3]When we had come in sight of Cyprus, leaving it on the left we sailed to Syria,

---

dixit: 'Beatius est magis dare quam accipere!'" [36]Et cum haec dixisset, positis genibus suis, cum omnibus illis oravit. [37]Magnus autem fletus factus est omnium, et procumbentes super collum Pauli osculabantur eum [38]dolentes maxime in verbo, quod dixerat, quoniam amplius faciem eius non essent visuri. Et deducebant eum ad navem.
[1]Cum autem factum esset ut navigaremus abstracti ab eis, recto cursu venimus Co et sequenti die Rhodum et inde Patara; [2]et cum invenissemus navem transfretantem in Phoenicen, ascendentes navigavimus. [3]Cum paruissemus autem Cypro, et relinquentes eam ad sinistram navigabamus in Syriam et

---

36. For Christians every situation is suitable for prayer: "The Christian prays everywhere", Clement of Alexandria writes, "and in every situation, whether it be when taking a walk or in the company of friends, or while he is resting, or at the start of some spiritual work. And when he reflects in the interior of his soul and invokes the Father with unspeakable groanings" (*Stromata*, VII, 7).

37. They kiss Paul to show their affection for him and how moved they are. This is not the liturgical "kiss of peace". In the East kisses are a common expression of friendship and good manners—like handshaking in the West.

ˣOther ancient authorities add *and Myra*

Acts 20:23; 21:11

Acts 20:36

Acts 6:5; 8:40

and landed at Tyre; for there the ship was to unload its cargo. ⁴And having sought out the disciples, we stayed there for seven days. Through the Spirit they told Paul not to go on to Jerusalem. ⁵And when our days there were ended, we departed and went on our journey; and they all, with wives and children, brought us on our way till we were outside the city; and kneeling down on the beach we prayed and bade one another farewell. ⁶Then we went on board the ship, and they returned home.

⁷When we had finished the voyage from Tyre, we arrived at Ptolemais; and we greeted the brethren and stayed with them for one day. ⁸On the morrow we departed and came to Caesarea; and we entered the house of Philip the evangelist,

---

venimus Tyrum, ibi enim navis erat expositura onus. ⁴Inventis autem discipulis, mansimus ibi diebus septem; qui Paulo dicebant per Spiritum, ne ascenderet Hierosolymam. ⁵Et explicitis diebus, profecti ibamus, deducentibus nos omnibus cum uxoribus et filiis foras civitatem; et positis genibus in litore orantes, ⁶valeficimus invicem et ascendimus in navem, illi autem redierunt in sua. ⁷Nos vero navigatione explicita, a Tyro devenimus Ptolemaida et salutatis fratribus mansimus die una apud illos. ⁸Alia autem die profecti venimus Caesaream et intrantes in domum Philippi evangelistae, qui erat de septem,

---

4. These Christians of Tyre were the fruit of earlier evangelization (cf. 11:19). The Spirit gave them foreknowledge of the "imprisonment and afflictions" (20:23) awaiting Paul in Jerusalem. It was only natural for them to try to dissuade him from going—a sign of Christian fraternity and mutual affection. Without losing our serenity we too should be concerned about our brothers' and sisters' physical and spiritual health: "I am glad that you feel concern for your brothers: there is no better proof of your mutual charity. Take care, however, that your concern does not degenerate into anxiety" (J. Escrivá, *The Way*, 465).

5. "Kneeling down on the beach we prayed": every place is suitable for raising one's heart to God and speaking to him. "Each day without fail we should devote some time especially to God, raising our minds to him, without any need for the words to come to our lips, for they are being sung in our heart. Let us give enough time to this devout practice; at a fixed hour, if possible. Before the Tabernacle, close to him who has remained there out of Love. If this is not possible, we can pray anywhere because our God is ineffably present in the heart of every soul in grace" (J. Escrivá, *Friends of God*, 249).

8. Philip was one of the seven Christians ordained deacons to serve the needy, as described in 6:5. He played an important part in the evangelization

who was one of the seven, and stayed with him. ⁹And he had   Acts 2:17
four unmarried daughters, who prophesied.   .

The prophet Agabus

¹⁰While we were staying for some days, a prophet named   Acts 11:27-28
Agabus came down from Judea. ¹¹And coming to us he took   Acts 21:31-33
Paul's girdle and bound his own feet and hands, and said,
"Thus says the Holy Spirit, 'So shall the Jews at Jerusalem
bind the man who owns this girdle and deliver him into the

---

mansimus apud eum. ⁹Huic autem erant filiae quattuor virgines prophetantes.
¹⁰Et cum moraremur plures dies, supervenit quidam a Iudaea propheta nomine
Agabus; ¹¹is cum venisset ad nos et tulisset zonam Pauli, alligans sibi pedes et
manus dixit: "Haec dicit Spiritus Sanctus: Virum, cuius est zona haec, sic

---

of Samaria (cf. 8:5ff), opposed Simon the magician (cf. 8:9ff) and baptized the
Ethiopian courtier (cf. 8:26ff).

9. Virginity is a gift of God which Paul discusses in his letters (cf. 1 Cor
7:25-40). In his apostolic exhortation on the family, John Paul II devotes a
section to this form of self-dedication to God: "Virginity or celibacy for the
sake of the Kingdom of God not only does not contradict the dignity of marriage
but presupposes it and confirms it. Marriage and virginity or celibacy are two
ways of expressing and living the one mystery of the covenant of God with his
people [. . .].

"Virginity or celibacy, by liberating the human heart in a unique way (1 Cor
7:32-35), bears witness that the Kingdom of God and his justice is that pearl of
great price which is preferred to every other value no matter how great, and
hence must be sought as the only definitive value. It is for this reason that the
Church, throughout her history, has always defended the superiority of this
charism to that of marriage, by reason of the wholly singular link which it has
with the Kingdom of God (cf. *Sacra virginitas*, 2).

"In spite of having renounced physical fecundity, the celibate person
becomes spiritually fruitful, the father and mother of many, cooperating in the
realization of the family according to God's plan" (*Familiaris consortio*, 16).

10-11. Agabus was the Christian prophet who, years earlier, warned of
forthcoming famine and privation (cf. 11:27-28). In his present prophecy he
uses symbolic gestures—like Old Testament prophets, particularly Jeremiah
(cf. Jer 18:3ff; 19:1ff; 27:2ff). His action is somewhat reminiscent of our Lord's
prophecy about St Peter in John 21:18: "Truly, truly, I say to you, when you
were young, you girded yourself and walked where you would; but when you
are old, you will stretch out your hands, and another will gird you and carry
you where you do not wish to go."

hands of the Gentiles.' " [12]When we heard this, we and the people there begged him not to go up to Jerusalem. [13]Then Paul answered, "What are you doing, weeping and breaking my heart? For I am ready not only to be imprisoned but even to die at Jerusalem for the name of the Lord Jesus." [14]And when he would not be persuaded, we ceased and said, "The will of the Lord be done."

Mt 6:10; 26:42

Paul arrives in Jerusalem and meets the Christians

[15]After these days we made ready and went up to Jerusalem. [16]And some of the disciples from Caesarea went with us, bringing us to the house of Mnason of Cyprus, an early disciple, with whom we should lodge.

[17]When we had come to Jerusalem, the brethren received us gladly. [18]On the following day Paul went in with us to

Acts 12:17

---

alligabunt in Ierusalem Iudaei et tradent in manus gentium." [12]Quod cum audissemus, rogabamus nos et, qui loci illius erant, ne ipse ascenderet Ierusalem. [13]Tunc respondit Paulus: "Quid facitis flentes et affligentes cor meum? Ego enim non solum alligari sed et mori in Ierusalem paratus sum propter nomen Domini Iesu." [14]Et cum ei suadere non possemus, quievimus dicentes: "Domini voluntas fiat!" [15]Post dies autem istos praeparati ascendebamus Hierosolymam; [16]venerunt autem et ex discipulis a Caesarea nobiscum adducentes apud, quem hospitaremur, Mnasonem quendam Cyprium, antiquum discipulum. [17]Et cum venissemus Hierosolymam, libenter exceperunt nos fratres. [18]Sequenti autem die introibat Paulus nobiscum ad

---

12-14. The Holy Spirit's words and warnings (cf. 20:23; 21:4) confirm Paul's readiness to accept the will of God and bear the trials which they foretell (cf. 20:25, 27ff). His serenity contrasts with the concern felt by those around him, which stems from their affection for him. His long life of self-surrender and self-forgetfulness explains why he takes things so calmly at this time: "This consists mainly or entirely in our ceasing to care about ourselves and our own pleasures, for the least that anyone who is beginning to serve the Lord can truly offer him is his life. Once he has surrendered his will to him, what has he to fear?" (St Teresa, *Way of Perfection*, 12).

"Accepting the will of God wholeheartedly is a sure way of finding joy and peace: happiness in the Cross. Then we realize that Christ's yoke is sweet and that his burden is not heavy" (J. Escrivá, *The Way*, 758).

Paul's example impresses the disciples and moves them to accept what God has disposed, in words reminiscent of Jesus' in the garden of Gethsemane (cf. Lk 22:42).

18. Paul and his companions are received by James the Less, who was

224

James; and all the elders were present. [19]After greeting them, Acts 15:4
he related one by one the things that God had done among
the Gentiles through his ministry. [20]And when they heard it, Acts 15:1
they glorified God. And they said to him, "You see, brother,
how many thousands there are among the Jews of those who
have believed; they are all zealous for the law, [21]and they Rom 2:25-29
1 Cor 7:17-20

Iacobum, omnesque collecti sunt presbyteri. [19]Quos cum salutasset narrabat per singula, quae fecisset Deus in gentibus per ministerium ipsius. [20]At illi cum audissent, glorificabant Deum dixeruntque ei: "Vides, frater, quot milia sint in Iudaeis, qui crediderunt, et omnes aemulatores sunt legis; [21]audierunt autem de

probably the head of the church of Jerusalem during these years (cf. 12:17; 15:13; Gal 1:19; 1 Cor 15:7), and by the elders who aided him in the government and spiritual care of the community. St Luke usually distinguishes elders from Apostles. Apparently the Apostles, including Peter, were no longer resident in the city.

The narrative here ceases to use the first person plural and does not use it again until the account of the journey to Rome (cf. Acts 27:1). This indicates that Luke accompanied Paul as far as Jerusalem, and then was with him from Caesarea to Rome.

19. Paul's apostolic ministry among the Gentiles is readily accepted by the Christians of the mother church of Jerusalem because God has demonstrated its legitimacy by blessing it with great fruitfulness: God guides and plans the mission to the Gentiles.

Paul in fact attributes all his success to the Lord: "Neither he who plants nor he who waters is anything, but only God who gives the growth" (1 Cor 3:7). This conviction has guided every step he has taken. "Everyone who prudently and intelligently looks at the history of the Apostles of Jesus will clearly see", Origen writes, "that they preached Christianity with God-given strength and thereby were able to attract men to the Word of God" (*Against Celsus*, I, 62).

20. The "zealous" Jews referred to by St James should not be confused with "Zealots". Ardent attachment to the traditions of the fathers and hatred of the Romans had led to the development of a sect of "Zealots", men of violence who played a key role in the rebellion of 66. This anti-Roman revolt, described in detail by Flavius Josephus in his book *The Jewish War* (written between 75 and 79) ended with the total destruction of the temple and of Jerusalem by the armies of Vespasian and Titus.

21. The rumours which observant Jews had heard about Paul's preaching were not without foundation, because the Apostle regarded the Mosaic Law as something secondary as far as salvation was concerned: he did not accept circumcision as absolutely necessary (cf. Gal 4:9; 5:11; Rom 2:25-30). But the accusation was unjust. Paul never exhorted Christians of Jewish background

have been told about you that you teach all the Jews who are among the Gentiles to forsake Moses, telling them not to circumcise their children or observe the customs. ²²What then is to be done? They will certainly hear that you have

Acts 18:18

come. ²³Do therefore what we tell you. We have four men who are under a vow; ²⁴take these men and purify yourself along with them and pay their expenses, so that they may shave their heads. Thus all will know that there is nothing in what they have been told about you but that you yourself live in observance of the law. ²⁵But as for the Gentiles who have

Acts 15:28-29

---

te quia discessionem doceas a Moyse omnes, qui per gentes sunt, Iudaeos, dicens non debere circumcidere eos filios suos, neque secundum consuetudines ambulare. ²²Quid ergo est? Utique audient te supervenisse. ²³Hoc ergo fac, quod tibi dicimus: sunt nobis viri quattuor votum habentes super se. ²⁴His assumptis, sanctifica te cum illis et impende pro illis, ut radant capita, et scient omnes quia, quae de te audierunt, nihil sunt, sed ambulas et ipse custodiens legem. ²⁵De his autem, qui crediderunt, gentibus nos scripsimus iudicantes, ut abstineant ab

---

not to circumcise their sons, and he himself ensured that Timothy was circumcised (cf. 16:3). In Corinth he came out in support of women following the Jewish custom of wearing the veil at liturgical ceremonies (cf. 1 Cor 11:2-16); and he himself had no difficulty about taking a Nazarite vow (cf. 18:18).

"Paul was calumniated by those who did not understand the Spirit with which these customs should be kept by Jewish Christians, that is, in a spirit of homage to the divine authority and prophetic holiness of these signs—and not in order to attain salvation, which had been revealed with Christ and applied through the sacrament of Baptism. Those who calumniated were people who wanted to observe these customs as if believers in the Gospel could not attain salvation without them" (St Bede, *Super Act expositio, ad loc.*).

23-24. This was a Nazarite vow (cf. Num 6). A Nazarite committed himself to abstaining from certain kinds of food and drink and not cutting his hair during the period of the vow (cf. note on Acts 18:18). To end the vow the person arranged a sacrificial offering in the temple. St James suggests that Paul bear the expenses of this sacrifice—a common type of pious act. This will show to all who know him his respect for the Law and the temple. Paul is putting into practice here the advice he gave to Christians in Corinth: "To the Jews I became as a Jew, in order to win Jews; to those under the law I became as one under the law—though not being myself under the law—that I might win those under the law" (1 Cor 9:20).

25. St James quotes the decisions of the Council of Jerusalem, with which Paul was very familiar. Presumably he does this for the benefit of the Apostle's companions, who were not required, naturally, to go with Paul to the Temple.

believed, we have sent a letter with our judgment that they should abstain from what has been sacrificed to idols and from blood and from what is strangled[y] and from unchastity." ²⁶Then Paul took the men, and the next day he purified himself with them and went into the temple, to give notice when the days of purification would be fulfilled and the offering presented for every one of them.

Num 6:1-20
1 Cor 9:20

Paul is arrested in the temple

²⁷When the seven days were almost completed, the Jews from Asia, who had seen him in the temple, stirred up all the crowd, and laid hands on him, ²⁸crying out, "Men of Israel, help! This is the man who is teaching men everywhere against the people and the law and this place; moreover he also brought Greeks into the temple, and he has defiled this holy place." ²⁹For they had previously seen Trophimus the Ephesian with him in the city, and they supposed that Paul

Ezek 44:9
Acts 6:13

Acts 20:4

---

idolothyto et sanguine et suffocato et fornicatione." ²⁶Tunc Paulus, assumptis viris, postera die purificatus cum illis intravit in templum annuntians expletionem dierum purificationis, donec offerretur pro unoquoque eorum oblatio. ²⁷Dum autem septem dies consummarentur, hi, qui de Asia erant, Iudaei cum vidissent eum in templo, concitaverunt omnem turbam et iniecerunt ei manus ²⁸clamantes: "Viri Israelitae, adiuvate! Hic est homo, qui adversus populum et legem et locum hunc omnes ubique docens, insuper et Graecos induxit in templum et polluit sanctum locum istum." ²⁹Viderant enim

---

27-29. Paul's action, which should have reassured these Jews, has in fact the contrary effect and leads to the kind of violent reaction typical of the fanatic. Jews come as pilgrims to Jerusalem for the Jewish feast of Pentecost attack Paul as a loathsome man: everywhere he goes, they say, he speaks against the Jewish people, the Law and the temple, and now he has the effrontery to profane the sacred precincts.

These accusations are similar to those laid against our Lord in his time (cf. Mt 26:61; 27:40) and against Stephen (cf. Acts 6:11-14). They start shouting and soon bring everyone along with them—the crowd only too ready to indulge their prejudices by believing anything said against Paul. The (groundless) accusation that he has brought Gentiles into the inner courtyards of the temple was a very serious charge, because that type of offence was punishable by death under Jewish law, and usually the Roman authorities did execute those found guilty of it. Archaeologists have unearthed one of the temple's stone plaques warning Gentiles, under pain of death, not to cross over the low wall marking off the courtyard of the Gentiles; the notice is in Greek and Latin.

^yOther early authorities omit *and from what is strangled*

had brought him into the temple. ³⁰Then all the city was aroused, and the people ran together; they seized Paul and dragged him out of the temple, and at once the gates were shut. ³¹And as they were trying to kill him, word came to the tribune of the cohort that all Jerusalem was in confusion. ³²He at once took soldiers and centurions, and ran down to them; and when they saw the tribune and the soldiers, they stopped beating Paul. ³³Then the tribune came up and arrested him, and ordered him to be bound with two chains. He inquired who he was and what he had done. ³⁴Some in the crowd shouted one thing, some another; and as he could not learn the facts because of the uproar, he ordered him to be brought into the barracks. ³⁵And when he came to the steps, he was actually carried by the soldiers because of the violence of the crowd; ³⁶for the mob of the people followed, crying, "Away with him!"

Acts 21:11

Lk 23:28
Acts 22:22

Trophimum Ephesium in civitate cum ipso, quem aestimabant quoniam in templum induxisset Paulus. ³⁰Commotaque est civitas tota, et facta est concursio populi, et apprendentes Paulum trahebant eum extra templum, et statim clausae sunt ianuae. ³¹Quaerentibus autem eum occidere, nuntiatum est tribuno cohortis quia tota confunditur Ierusalem, ³²qui statim, assumptis militibus et centurionibus, decucurrit ad illos; qui cum vidissent tribunum et milites, cessaverunt percutere Paulum. ³³Tunc accedens tribunus apprehendit eum et iussit alligari catenis duabus et interrogabat quis esset et quid fecisset. ³⁴Alii autem aliud clamabant in turba; et cum non posset certum cognoscere prae tumultu, iussit duci eum in castra. ³⁵Et cum venisset ad gradus, contigit ut

---

30. It was probably not the main gates that were closed, but those between the court of the Gentiles and the other courtyards.

31-36. Paul would certainly have been killed if the Roman soldiers had not intervened. They were able to arrive on the scene so quickly because the Antonia Tower, where the Jerusalem garrison was based, was located at one corner of the temple, only two flights of steps from the court of the Gentiles.

Having arrested Paul, whom the Romans take to be the cause of the uproar, the tribune prudently decides to transfer him to the fortress. A new section of the book now begins, in which St Luke will describe in detail the Apostle's imprisonment (cf. Acts 21:33 - 22:29), his trial at Jerusalem and Caesarea (cf. chaps. 23-26) and his journey to Rome (cf. Acts 27:1 - 28:16) to appear before an imperial tribunal. From this point onwards Paul is not so much a tireless missionary and founder of churches as an imprisoned witness to the Gospel: even in these new circumstances he will manage to proclaim Christ.

³⁷As Paul was about to be brought into the barracks, he said to the tribune, "May I say something to you?" And he said, "Do you know Greek? ³⁸Are you not the Egyptian, then, who recently stirred up a revolt and led the four thousand men of the Assassins out into the wilderness?" ³⁹Paul replied, "I am a Jew, from Tarsus in Cilicia, a citizen of no mean city; I beg you, let me speak to my people." ⁴⁰And when he had

---

portaretur a militibus propter vim turbae; ³⁶sequebatur enim multitudo populi clamantes: "Tolle eum!" ³⁷Et cum coepisset induci in castra, Paulus dicit tribuno: "Si licet mihi loqui aliquid ad te?" Qui dixit: "Graece nosti? ³⁸Nonne tu es Aegyptius, qui ante hos dies tumultum concitasti et eduxisti in desertum quattuor milia virorum sicariorum?" ³⁹Et dixit Paulus: "Ego homo sum quidem Iudaeus, a Tarso Ciliciae, non ignotae civitatis municeps; rogo autem te, permitte mihi loqui ad populum." ⁴⁰Et cum ille permisisset, Paulus stans in

---

38. This Egyptian outlaw is also mentioned by Flavius Josephus as a leader of a group of bandits who tried to capture Jerusalem and were put to flight by Felix, the governor (cf. *The Jewish War*, II, 261-263).

The "Assassins" referred to were *sicarii*, so named because they always carried a dagger (Latin: *sica*). Together with the Zealots, they played a prominent and inglorious part in the Jewish rebellion against Rome.

39. Paul continues to say nothing about his Roman citizenship. He simply states that he comes from Tarsus, a city which enjoyed self-government and to which he was proud to belong. It would seem that from the time of Claudius onwards it was possible to hold dual citizenship—to be a Roman citizen and the citizen of a particular city.

In keeping with his courage and sense of mission, the Apostle decides to address the threatening crowd. He is more interested in winning over his adversaries than in escaping from them; in taking them on he is supported by the Gospel's inner strength and his own firm dedication to the service of Christ. "There is nothing weaker in fact", comments Chrysostom, "than many sinners —and nothing stronger than a man who keeps the law of God" (*Hom on Acts*, 26). "The soldiers of Christ, that is, those who pray," St Teresa writes, "do not think of the time when they will have to fight, they never fear public enemies; for they already know them and they realize that nothing can withstand the strength the Lord has given them, and that they will always be victors and heaped with gain" (*Way of Perfection*, 38, 2).

Once again, Paul relies on God giving him the right things to say; he does not settle for simply reproaching them for their behaviour: he knows that "truth is not preached with swords and lances, or the aid of soldiers, but rather by means of persuasion and counsel" (St Athanasius, *Historia arianorum*, 33).

40. "In the Hebrew language": this must mean Aramaic—the language

given him leave, Paul, standing on the steps, motioned with his hand to the people; and when there was a great hush, he spoke to them in the Hebrew language, saying:

22

Paul defends himself before the crowd

Acts 7:2

[1]"Brethren and fathers, hear the defence which I now make before you."

[2]And when they heard that he addressed them in the Hebrew language, they were the more quiet. And he said:

Acts 26:4-5
2 Cor 11:22
Gal 1:14
Phil 3:5-6

[3]"I am a Jew, born at Tarsus in Cilicia, but brought up in this city at the feet of Gamaliel, educated according to the strict manner of the law of our fathers, being zealous for God

---

gradibus annuit manu ad plebem et, magno silentio facto, allocutus est Hebraea lingua dicens.
[1]"Viri fratres et patres, audite a me, quam ad vos nunc reddo, rationem." [2]Cum audissent autem quia Hebraea lingua loquebatur ad illos, magis praestiterunt silentium. Et dixit: [3]"Ego sum vir Iudaeus, natus Tarso Ciliciae, enutritus autem in ista civitate, secus pedes Gamaliel eruditus iuxta veritatem paternae legis,

---

which, after the return of the Jews from the Babylonian captivity, gradually came into general use, due to the influence of the Persian empire.

1-21. St Luke gives us Paul's address to the Jews of Jerusalem, the first of three speeches in his own defence (cf. 24:10 - 21; 26:1-23) in which he tries to show that there is no reason why Christianity should be opposed by Jew or by Roman. Here he presents himself as a pious Jew, full of respect for his people and their sacred traditions. He earnestly desires his brethren to realize that there are compelling reasons for his commitment to Jesus. He is convinced that they can experience in their souls the same kind of spiritual change as he did. However, this speech is not a closely-argued apologia. His main intention is not so much to answer the accusations levelled against him as to use this opportunity to bear witness to Jesus Christ, whose commandments validate Paul's actions. What he is really trying to do is to get his hearers to obey the voice of the Lord.

1. "Brethren and fathers": the "fathers" may refer to members of the Sanhedrin present in the crowd.

3. Gamaliel (cf. 5:34) belonged to the school of the rabbi Hillel, which was noted for a less rigorous interpretation of the Law than that of Shammai and his disciples.

as you all are this day. ⁴I persecuted this Way to the death, Acts 8:3
binding and delivering to prison both men and women, ⁵as Acts 9:1-18;
26:9-18
the high priest and the whole council of elders bear me
witness. From them I received letters to the brethren, and I
journeyed to Damascus to take those also who were there
and bring them in bonds to Jerusalem to be punished.

⁶"As I made my journey and drew near to Damascus,
about noon a great light from heaven suddenly shone about
me. ⁷And I fell to the ground and heard a voice saying to me,
'Saul, Saul, why do you persecute me?' ⁸And I answered, Mt 2:23
'Who are you, Lord?' And he said to me, 'I am Jesus of
Nazareth whom you are persecuting.' ⁹Now those who were Wis 18:1
with me saw the light but did not hear the voice of the one

---

aemulator Dei sicut et vos omnes estis hodie. ⁴Qui hanc viam persecutus sum
usque ad mortem, alligans et tradens in custodias viros ac mulieres, ⁵sicut et
princeps sacerdotum testimonium mihi reddit et omne concilium; a quibus et
epistulas accipiens ad fratres, Damascum pergebam ut adducerem et eos, qui
ibi essent, vinctos in Ierusalem, uti punirentur. ⁶Factum est autem eunte me et
appropinquante Damasco, circa mediam diem subito de caelo circumfulsit me
lux copiosa, ⁷et decidit in terram et audivi vocem dicentem mihi: 'Saul Saul,
quid me persequeris?' ⁸Ego autem respondi: 'Quis es Domine?' Dixitque ad
me: 'Ego sum Iesus Nazarenus, quem tu persequeris.' ⁹Et qui mecum erant,
lumen quidem viderunt, vocem autem non audierunt eius, qui loquebatur

---

4. The situation described by Paul is confirmed by 1 Cor 15:9: "I am the
least of the apostles, unfit to be called an apostle, because I persecuted the
church of God"; Gal 1:13: "You have heard of my former life in Judaism, how
I persecuted the church of God violently and tried to destroy it"; Phil 3:6: "as
to the law a Pharisee, as to zeal a persecutor of the church"; and 1 Tim 1:13: "I
formerly blasphemed and persecuted and insulted him [Christ]".

6-11. Paul describes in his own words what happened on the way to
Damascus (cf. 9:3-9; 26:6-16). This account differs in some ways from—but
does not contradict—the two other versions of the episode, especially that of
chapter 9, which is told in St Luke's words.

Paul adds that the whole thing happened at midday (cf. 26:13), and he says
that Jesus referred to himself as "Jesus of Nazareth". He also includes the
question "What shall I do, Lord?", which is not given in chapter 9.

As far as Paul's companions were concerned, we know that they saw the
light (Acts 22:9) but did not see anyone (Acts 9:7): they did not see the glorified
Jesus; they heard a voice (Acts 9:7) but did not hear the voice of the one who
was speaking to Paul (Acts 22:9), that is, did not understand what the voice
said.

who was speaking to me. [10]And I said, 'What shall I do, Lord?' And the Lord said to me, 'Rise, and go into Damascus, and there you will be told all that is appointed for you to do.' [11]And when I could not see because of the brightness of that light, I was led by the hand by those who were with me, and came into Damascus.

[12]"And one Ananias, a devout man according to the law, well spoken of by all the Jews who lived there, [13]came to me, and standing by me said to me, 'Brother Saul, receive your sight.' And in that very hour I received my sight and saw him. [14]And he said, 'The God of our fathers appointed you to know his will, to see the Just One and to hear a voice from

Acts 3:14

---

mecum. [10]Et dixi: 'Quid faciam, Domine?' Dominus autem dixit ad me: 'Surgens vade Damascum, et ibi tibi dicetur de omnibus, quae staturum est tibi, ut faceres.' [11]Et cum non viderem prae claritae luminis illius, ad manum deductus a comitibus veni Damascum. [12]Ananias autem quidam vir religiosus secundum legem testimonium habens ab omnibus habitantibus Iudaeis, [13]veniens ad me et astans dixit mihi: 'Saul frater, respice!' Et ego eadem hora respexi in eum. [14]At ille dixit: 'Deus patrum nostrorum praeordinavit te, ut cognosceres voluntatem eius et videres Iustum et audires vocem ex ore eius,

---

10. Paul addresses Jesus as "Lord", which shows that this vision has revealed to him the divinity of him whom he was persecuting.

The divine voice orders him to get up from the ground and the future Apostle of the Gentiles obeys immediately. The physical movement of getting up is a kind of symbol of the spiritual uplift his soul is given by God's call. "This was the first grace, that was given to the first Adam; but more powerful than it is the grace in the second Adam. The effect of the first grace was that a man might have justice, if he willed; the second grace, therefore, is more powerful, because it affects the will itself; it makes for a strong will, a burning charity, so that by a contrary will the spirit overcomes the conflicting will of the flesh" (St Augustine, *De correptione et gratia*, XI, 31).

"Many have come to Christianity", Origen says, "as if against their will, for a certain spirit, appearing to them, in sleep or when they are awake, suddenly silences their mind, and they change from hating the Word to dying for him" (*Against Celsus*, I, 46).

Paul's conversion is an outstanding example of what divine grace and divine assistance in general can effect in a person's heart.

12-16. This account of Ananias and his role in Paul's conversion is much shorter than that given in chapter 9 (cf. vv. 10-19). St Paul adapts it here to suit his audience (who are all Jews). He presents Jesus as the one in whom the Old Testament prophecies are fulfilled. Like Peter (cf. 3:13ff) and Stephen (cf. 7:52)

232

his mouth; [15]for you will be a witness for him to all men of what you have seen and heard.[16]And now why do you wait? Rise and be baptized, and wash away your sins, calling on his name.'

[17]"When I had returned to Jerusalem and was praying in the temple, I fell into a trance [18]and saw him saying to me, 'Make haste and get quickly out of Jerusalem, because they will not accept your testimony about me.' [19]And I said, 'Lord, they themselves know that in every synagogue I imprisoned and beat those who believed in thee. [20]And when the blood of Stephen thy witness was shed, I also was standing by and approving, and keeping the garments of those who killed him.' [21]And he said to me, 'Depart; for I will send you far away to the Gentiles.'"

1 Jn 1:1-3

Acts 9:26
Gal 1:18

Acts 13:46-48;
18:6; 28:25-28

Acts 7:58; 8:1

Acts 9:15

---

[15]quia eris testis illi ad omnes homines eorum, quae vidisti et audisti. [16]Et nunc quid moraris? Exsurgens baptizare et ablue peccata tua, invocato nomine ipsius.' [17]Factum est autem revertenti mihi in Ierusalem et oranti in templo fieri me in stupore mentis [18]et videre illum dicentem mihi: 'Festina et exi velociter ex Ierusalem, quoniam non recipient testimonium tuum de me.' [19]Et ego dixi: 'Domine, ipsi sciunt quia ego eram concludens in carcerem et caedens per synagogas eos, qui credebant in te; [20]et cum funderetur sanguis Stephani testis tui, et ipse astabam et consentiebam vestimenta interficientium illum.' [21]Et dixit ad me: 'Vade, quoniam ego in nationes longe mittam te.'" [22]Audiebant autem

---

he speaks of the "God of our fathers" and the "Just One" when referring to God and to Jesus respectively.

17-18. Paul's return to Jerusalem took place three years after his conversion. Paul deliberately mentions his custom of going to pray in the temple, which at that time was a normal place of prayer for Christians. He refers to an ecstasy not mentioned anywhere else, and to a vision of Jesus Christ reminiscent of that described in Rev 1:10.

19. Synagogues were also used for non-liturgical purposes; they usually had additional rooms for meetings (cf. Mt 10:17; 23:34; Mk 13:9).

20. The word "witness" is beginning to acquire the meaning of "martyr" as now used in the Church: martyrdom is the supreme form of bearing witness to the Christian faith.

St Paul refers to his presence at the martyrdom of St Stephen to emphasize the miraculous nature of his own conversion.

21. By promising that he will "send" him to the Gentiles, our Lord makes him an "Apostle", on a par with the Twelve.

Paul the Roman citizen

Acts 25:24 ²²Up to this word they listened to him; then they lifted up their voices and said, "Away with such a fellow from the earth! For he ought not to live." ²³And as they cried out and waved their garments and threw dust into the air, ²⁴the tribune commanded him to be brought into the barracks, and ordered him to be examined by scourging, to find out why Acts 16:22-37 they shouted thus against him. ²⁵But when they had tied him up with the thongs, Paul said to the centurion who was standing by, "Is it lawful for you to scourge a man who is a Roman citizen, and uncondemned?" ²⁶When the centurion heard that, he went to the tribune and said to him, "What are you about to do? For this man is a Roman citizen." ²⁷So the tribune came and said to him, "Tell me, are you a Roman citizen?" And he said, "Yes." ²⁸The tribune answered, "I bought this citizenship for a large sum." Paul said, "But I Acts 16:38-39 was born a citizen." ²⁹So those who were about to examine him withdrew from him instantly; and the tribune also was afraid, for he realized that Paul was a Roman citizen and that he had bound him.

---

eum usque ad hoc verbum et levaverunt vocem suam dicentes: "Tolle de terra eiusmodi, non enim fas est eum vivere!" ²³Vociferentibus autem eis et proicientibus vestimenta sua et pulverem iactantibus in aerem, ²⁴iussit tribunus induci eum in castra dicens flagellis eum interrogari, ut sciret propter quam causam sic acclamarent ei. ²⁵Et cum astrinxissent eum loris, dixit astanti centurioni Paulus: "Si hominem Romanum et indemnatum licet vobis flagellare?" ²⁶Quo audito, centurio accedens ad tribunum nuntiavit dicens: "Quid acturus es? Hic enim homo Romanus est." ²⁷Accedens autem tribunus dixit illi: "Dic mihi, tu Romanus es?" At ille dixit: "Etiam." ²⁸Et respondit tribunus: "Ego multa summa civitatem hanc consecutus sum." Et Paulus ait: "Ego autem et natus enim sum." ²⁹Protinus ergo discesserunt ab illo, qui eum interrogaturi erant; tribunus quoque timuit, postquam rescivit quia Romanus

---

22. The mere mention of preaching to the Gentiles leads to interruption: his listeners are so bigoted, their fear is so irrational, that they cannot listen calmly to what Paul has to say, never mind take it all in.

24. Roman law allowed suspects and slaves to be put under the lash in order to extract confessions.

25. As at Philippi (cf. 16:37), Paul stands on his rights as a Roman citizen; but this time he does so at an earlier stage and avoids being scourged.

Speech before the Sanhedrin

³⁰But on the morrow, desiring to know the real reason why the Jews accused him, he unbound him, and commanded the chief priests and all the council to meet, and he brought Paul down and set him before them.

23

¹And Paul, looking intently at the council, said, "Brethren, I have lived before God in all good conscience up to this day." ²And the high priest Ananias commanded those who stood by him to strike him on the mouth. ³Then Paul said to him, "God shall strike you, you whitewashed wall! Are you sitting

Acts 24:16
Heb 13:18

Jn 18:22

Ezek 13:10-15
Mt 23:27

---

esset et quia alligasset eum. ³⁰Postera autem die volens scire diligenter qua ex causa accusaretur a Iudaeis, solvit eum et iussit principes sacerdotum convenire et omne concilium et producens Paulum statuit coram illis.
¹Intendens autem concilium Paulus ait: "Viri fratres, ego omni conscientia bono conversatus sum ante Deum usque in hodiernum diem." ²Princeps autem sacerdotum Ananias praecipit astantibus sibi percutere os eius. ³Tunc Paulus ad eum dixit: "Percutiet te Deus, paries dealbate! Et tu sedes iudicans me

---

30. This does not seem to have been a regular session of the Sanhedrin; it is an informal one arranged by Lysias (Acts 23:26) to enable documentation to be prepared, now that "evidence" cannot be extracted from Paul by torture.

1. In response to the Jews' accusations, which St Luke here takes as read, Paul sums up his defence with this key statement. Having an upright conscience is a central point in Pauline spirituality. It comes up all the time in his letters (cf. 1 Cor 4:4; 2 Cor 1:12; 1 Tim 1:5, 19; 2 Tim 1:3) and is borne out by his own conduct: even when he was a persecutor of the Church he was always trying to do his best to serve God; his sincerity was never in question, even if his zeal was misdirected. In this terse remark he rejects any suggestion that he was disrespectful to the Law.

2. This Ananias should not be confused with Annas (cf. 4:6). He was appointed high priest in 47 and deposed around the year 58. In 66 he was assassinated by Jews in revolt against Rome. He orders that Paul be struck, undoubtedly because he cannot answer what Paul says or because he feels personally offended. Josephus tells us that Ananias was an arrogant and hot-tempered man (cf. *Jewish Antiquities*, XX, 199).

3. Paul's harsh words are not due to his annoyance at being unjustly treated. We might have expected him, in imitation of Jesus (cf. Mt 27:12), to remain

235

to judge me according to the law, and yet contrary to the law you order me to be struck?" ⁴Those who stood by said,

Ezek 22:27

"Would you revile God's high priest?" ⁵And Paul said, "I did not know, brethren, that he was the high priest; for it is written, 'You shall not speak evil of a ruler of your people.'"

Acts 26:5

⁶But when Paul perceived that one part were Sadducees and the other Pharisees, he cried out in the council, "Brethren, I am a Pharisee, a son of Pharisees; with respect to the hope and the resurrection of the dead I am on trial." ⁷And when he had said this, a dissension arose between the Pharisees and the Sadducees; and the assembly was divided.

Mt 22:23

⁸For the Sadducees say that there is no resurrection, nor

---

secundum legem et contra legem iubes me percuti?" ⁴Et qui astabant, dixerunt: "Summum sacerdotem Dei maledicis?" ⁵Dixit autem Paulus: "Nesciebam, fratres, quia princeps est sacerdotum; scriptum est enim: 'Principem populi tui non maledices'." ⁶Sciens autem Paulus quia una pars esset sadducaeorum et altera pharisaeorum, exclamabat in concilio: "Viri fratres, ego pharisaeus sum, filius pharisaeorum; de spe et resurrectione mortuorum ego iudicor." ⁷Et cum haec diceret, facta est dissensio inter pharisaeos et sadducaeos, et divisa est multitudo. ⁸Sadducaei enim dicunt non esse resurrectionem neque angelum

---

silent. However, Paul thinks that the right thing to do here is to speak out. His words are a deliberate prophecy of the fate that awaits Ananias.

5. Many commentators think that Paul is being sarcastic here, as if to say, "I would never have thought that anyone who gave an order against the Law like that could be the high priest". Others think that the Apostle realizes that his words may have scandalized some of those present and therefore he wants to make it clear that he respects Jewish institutions and the commandments of the Law.

6-9. From St Luke's Gospel (cf. 20:27) we know that the Sadducees, unlike the Pharisees, did not believe in a future resurrection of the dead. This is the only place in the New Testament where it says that they also denied the existence of angels and spirits; however, this is confirmed by Jewish and secular sources.

In the course of his trial, Paul brings up a subject which sets his judges at each other. Personal advantage is not his main reason for doing this. He is obviously very shrewd, but he really does not expect to get an impartial hearing from the Sanhedrin. Therefore he tries to stir their consciences and awaken their love for the truth and thereby elicit some sympathy for Christians. Although Christian belief in the Resurrection was not the same thing as the Pharisees' belief, the two had this in common: they believed in the resurrection of the dead.

angel, nor spirit; but the Pharisees acknowledge them all. ⁹Then a great clamour arose; and some of the scribes of the Pharisees' party stood up and contended, "We find nothing wrong in this man. What if a spirit or an angel spoke to him?" ¹⁰And when the dissension became violent, the tribune, afraid that Paul would be torn in pieces by them, commanded the soldiers to go down and take him by force from among them and bring him into the barracks.

¹¹The following night the Lord stood by him and said, "Take courage, for as you have testified about me at Jerusalem, so you must bear witness also at Rome." Acts 18:9-10; 27:24

A Jewish plot against Paul

¹²When it was day, the Jews made a plot and bound Acts 9:23; 20:3

---

neque spiritum; pharisaei autem utrumque confitentur. ⁹Factus est autem clamor magnus, et surgentes scribae quidam partis pharisaeorum pugnabant dicentes: "Nihil mali invenimus in homine isto: quod si spiritus locutus est ei aut angelus"; ¹⁰et cum magna dissensio facta esset, timens tribunus ne discerperetur Paulus ab ipsis, iussit milites descendere, ut raperent eum de medio eorum ac deducerent in castra. ¹¹Sequenti autem nocte assistens ei Dominus ait: "Constans esto! Sicut enim testificatus es, quae sunt de me in Ierusalem, sic te oportet et Romae testificari." ¹²Facta autem die, faciebant

---

9. They are referring to his vision on the road to Damascus. They are not going as far as to say that it was Jesus who spoke to Paul, but they do not rule out the possibility that he had a genuine spiritual experience.

11. The Lord is Jesus. These words of consolation to Paul show him that God will guide him all along, right up to his court appearance in Rome. From this point onwards the prisoner is seeking primarily to bear witness to the Gospel and not just to defend himself. In imprisonment he will continue to do the same work as he did when free. "Keep alert with all perseverance," he tells the Ephesians, "making supplication for all the saints, and also for me, that utterance may be given me in opening my mouth boldly to proclaim the mystery of the gospel, for which I am an ambassador in chains; that I may declare it boldly, as I ought to speak" (6:18-20).

12-22. Blinded by fanaticism, a small group of Jews take an oath to do away with Paul. Their promise not to eat or drink until they fulfil their intention is in line with similar vows taken in the service of better causes (cf. 1 Sam 14:24). Hatred has misdirected their piety and what was originally religious conviction has changed into resistance to the Holy Spirit. "The Lord says, 'Blessed are those who hunger and thirst after justice'. These Jews, on the contrary, hunger

237

themselves by an oath neither to eat nor drink till they had killed Paul. [13]There were more than forty who made this conspiracy. [14]And they went to the chief priests and elders, and said, "We have strictly bound ourselves by an oath to taste no food till we have killed Paul. [15]You therefore, along with the council, give notice now to the tribune to bring him down to you, as though you were going to determine his case more exactly. And we are ready to kill him before he comes near."

[16]Now the son of Paul's sister heard of their ambush; so he went and entered the barracks and told Paul. [17]And Paul called one of the centurions and said, "Bring this young man to the tribune; for he has something to tell him." [18]So he took him and brought him to the tribune and said, "Paul the prisoner called me and asked me to bring this young man to you, as he has something to say to you." [19]The tribune took him by the hand, and going aside asked him privately, "What is it that you have to tell me?" [20]And he said, "The Jews have

---

concursum Iudaeo et devoverunt se dicentes neque manducaturos neque bibituros, donec occiderent Paulum. [13]Erant autem plus quem quadraginta, qui hanc coniurationem fecerant; [14]qui accedentes ad principes sacerdotum et seniores dixerunt: "Devotione devovimus nos nihil gustaturos, donec occidamus Paulum. [15]Nunc ergo vos notum facite tribuno cum concilio, ut producat illum ad vos, tamquam aliquid certius cognituri de eo; nos vero priusquam appropiet, parati sumus interficere illum." [16]Quod cum audisset filius sororis Pauli insidias, venit et intravit in castra nuntiavitque Paulo. [17]Vocans autem Paulus ad se unum ex centurionibus ait: "Adulescentem hunc perduc ad tribunum, habet enim aliquid indicare illi." [18]Et ille quidem assumens eum duxit ad tribunum et ait: "Vinctus Paulus vocans rogavit me hunc adulescentem perducere ad te, habentem aliquid loqui tibi." [19]Apprehendens autem tribunus manum illius, secessit cum eo seorsum et interrogabat: "Quid est quod habes indicare mihi?" [20]Ille autem dixit: "Iudaei constituerunt rogare

---

after iniquity and thirst after blood. [. . .] But there is no wisdom or prudence or counsel that can prevent God's will. For, although Paul, a Jew with the Jews, offered sacrifices, shaving his head and going barefoot, he did not escape the chains which had been foretold. And although these men make plans and swear an oath and prepare an ambush, the Apostle will receive protection to enable him, as he had already been told, to bear witness to Christ in Rome" (St Bede, *Super Act expositio, ad loc.*).

16. This is the only reference in this book or the letters (with the exception of Rom 16:7-11) to Paul's relatives.

agreed to ask you to bring Paul down to the council tomorrow, as though they were going to inquire somewhat more closely about him. [21]But do not yield to them; for more than forty of their men lie in ambush for him, having bound themselves by an oath neither to eat nor drink till they have killed him; and now they are ready, waiting for the promise from you."

Paul is transferred to Caesarea

[22]So the tribune dismissed the young man, charging him, "Tell no one that you have informed me of this."

[23]Then he called two of the centurions and said, "At the third hour of the night get ready two hundred soldiers with seventy horsemen and two hundred spearmen to go as far as Caesarea. [24]Also provide mounts for Paul to ride, and bring him safely to Felix the governor." [25]And he wrote a letter to this effect:

[26]"Claudius Lysias to his Excellency the governor Felix, greeting. [27]This man was seized by the Jews, and was about

Acts 22:25-29

---

te, ut crastina die Paulum producas in concilium, quasi aliquid certius inquisiturum sit de illo. [21]Tu ergo ne credideris illis; insidiantur enim ei ex eis viri amplius quadraginta, qui se devoverunt non manducare neque bibere, donec interficiant eum, et nunc parati sunt exspectantes promissum tuum." [22]Tribunus igitur dimisit adulescentem praecipiens, ne cui eloqueretur quoniam "haec nota mihi fecisti." [23]Et vocatis duobus centurionibus, dixit: "Parate milites ducentos, ut eant usque Caesaream, et equites septuaginta et lancearios ducentos, a tertia hora noctis, [24]et iumenta praeparate," ut imponentes Paulum salvum perducerent ad Felicem praesidem, [25]scribens epistulam habentem formam hanc: [26]Claudius Lysias optimo praesidi Felici salutem. [27]Virum hunc comprehensum a Iudaeis et incipientem interfici ab eis, superveniens cum

---

23-24. The information brought by Paul's nephew must have led Lysias to advance his plans for the transfer of the prisoner to the governor; besides, the Sanhedrin had only limited powers to detain a prisoner pending trial.

Felix had been governor or procurator of Judea since the year 52. He was a freedman who had risen remarkably high, but according to Tacitus he "exerted royal power with the mind of a slave". Felix was successful in repressing various riots which heralded the great Jewish uprising in the year 66, but he was recalled in 60 on account of his harsh and cruel rule (cf. 24:27).

25-30. This letter from Claudius Lysias is the only secular letter recorded in the New Testament. Lysias gives the governor a brief report on the detainee.

239

Acts 25:18-19;
26:31

to be killed by them, when I came upon them with the soldiers and rescued him, having learned that he was a Roman citizen. [28]And desiring to know the charge on which they accused him, I brought him down to their council. [29]I found that he was accused about questions of their law, but charged with nothing deserving death or imprisonment. [30]And when it was disclosed to me that there would be a plot against the man, I sent him to you at once, ordering his accusers also to state before you what they have against him."

[31]So the soldiers, according to their instructions, took Paul and brought him by night to Antipatris. [32]And on the morrow they returned to the barracks, leaving the horsemen to go on with him. [33]When they came to Caesarea and delivered the letter to the governor, they presented Paul also before him. [34]On reading the letter, he asked to what province he belonged. When he learned that he was from Cilicia [35]he said,

---

exercitu eripui, cognito quia Romanus est. [28]Volensque scire cuasam, propter quam accusabant illum, deduxi in concilium eorum; [29]quem inveni accusari de quaestionibus legis ipsorum, nihil vero dignum morte aut vinculis habentem crimen. [30]Et cum mihi perlatum esset de insidiis, quae in virum pararentur confestim misi ad te denuntians et accusatoribus, ut dicant adversum eum apud te." [31]Milites ergo, secundum praeceptum sibi assumentes Paulum, duxerunt per noctem in Antipatridem; [32]et postera die dimissis equitibus, ut abirent cum eo, reversi sunt ad castra. [33]Qui cum venissent Caesaream et tradidissent epistulam praesidi, statuerunt ante illum et Paulum. [34]Cum legisset autem et interrogasset de qua provincia esset et cognoscens quia de Cilicia: [35]"Audiam

---

He bends the facts a little in that he does not mention that at an early stage he planned to have Paul scourged: significantly the letter only mentions the Jews' religious accusation to the effect that Paul was speaking against the Law (cf. 21:28) and does not give weight to the charge that he brought Gentiles into the temple (cf. 21:28b).

31. Antipatris was 60 kilometres (40 miles) from Jerusalem and 40 from Caesarea. It had been founded by Herod the Great in honour of his father, Antipater.

33-35. Felix acts in line with what the law lays down. He acquaints himself firsthand with Paul's case and decides to try him as soon as his accusers arrive. The governor could have remitted the case to the legate of the province of Syria, which at that time included Cilicia. But he prefers to deal with the matter himself.

"I will hear you when your accusers arrive." And he commanded him to be guarded in Herod's praetorium.

24

The trial before Felix

[1]And after five days the high priest Ananias came down with some elders and a spokesman, one Tertullus. They laid

---

te, inquit, cum et accusatores tui venerint"; iussitque in praetorio Herodis custodiri eum.
[1]Post quinque autem dies descendit princeps sacerdotum Ananias cum senioribus quibusdam et Tertullo quodam oratore, qui adierunt praesidem adversus Paulum. [2]Et citato eo coepit accusare Tertullus dicens: "Cum in multa pace agamus per te, et multa corrigantur genti huic per tuam providentiam,

---

Herod's praetorium was a palace built by Herod the Great which later became the residence of the Roman governor.

1-21. By being sent to Caesarea by the tribune, Paul has entered the jurisdiction of Roman law. The Jews fail to change things so that he can be tried by the Sanhedrin. The judicial hearing now begins. Here we have an instance of the Roman judicial process known as *cognitio extra ordinem* or extraordinary procedure, to distinguish it from the *cognitio ordinaria*—the normal kind of trial, and which was marked by more flexible procedures. In the *cognitio ordinaria* the magistrate allowed charges to be brought against the accused according to established legal procedures which did not allow much flexibility in the way the trial was conducted or in the type of sentence that could be passed. The *cognitio extra ordinem* allowed a judge more initiative; it had five stages: 1) private accusation; 2) a formal *pro tribunali* hearing; 3) use by the judge of expert legal advice; 4) hearing of evidence from the parties concerned; and 5) assessment of this evidence by the judge.

Chapters 24 and 25 of Acts are in fact an important source of information about the use of extraordinary procedures in criminal cases. The narrative tells us about Paul's being accused privately by Jews (cf. 23:35; 24:1). It uses the correct legal terminology when referring to hearings by the judge (cf. 25:6, 17). It mentions the committee of experts who assist the judge (cf. 25:9, 12). It describes the charges in some detail and shows the kind of discretion the magistrates (Felix and Festus) had in the way they handled the case and approached the evidence.

1. The charge had to be presented by a professional lawyer. Tertullus may have been a Jew skilled in Hebrew and Roman law. His language, at any rate, shows that he shares his clients' point of view.

before the governor their case against Paul; ²and when he was called, Tertullus began to accuse him, saying:

"Since through you we enjoy much peace, and since by your provision, most excellent Felix, reforms are introduced on behalf of this nation, ³in every way and everywhere we accept this with all gratitude. ⁴But, to detain you no further, I beg you in your kindness to hear us briefly. ⁵For we have found this man a pestilent fellow, an agitator among all the Jews throughout the world, and a ringleader of the sect of the Nazarenes. ⁶He even tried to profane the temple, but we seized him.ᶻ ⁸By examining him yourself you will be able to learn from him about everything of which we accuse him."

⁹The Jews also joined in the charge, affirming that all this was so.

¹⁰And when the governor had motioned to him to speak, Paul replied:

Acts 17:6

Acts 21:28

---

³semper et ubique suscipimus, optime Felix, cum omni gratiarum actione. ⁴Ne diutius autem te protraham, oro breviter audias nos pro tua clementia. ⁵Invenimus enim hunc hominem pestiferum et concitantem seditiones omnibus Iudaeis, qui sunt in universo orbe, et auctorem seditionis sectae Nazarenorum, ⁶qui etiam templum violare conatus est, quem et apprehendimus, ⁽⁷⁾ ⁸a quo poteris ipse diiudicans de omnibus istis cognoscere, de quibus nos accusamus eum." ⁹Adiecerunt autem et Iudaei dicentes haec ita se habere. ¹⁰Respondit

2-4. Tertullus' opening words are sheer flattery. Felix's administration was in fact notoriously inefficient and had disastrous effects.

5-9. The Jews make a timid effort to have Paul transferred back into their own jurisdiction. They see him as a kind of Jewish heretic, and Christianity as just a Jewish sect. They level four charges against the Apostle: Paul is a social undesirable, an agitator and a leader of a dangerous sect. These three vague charges frame a fourth charge, which is much more specific: he has tried to profane the temple, the symbol of the Jewish nation. Even though the charge is basically religious in character, Tertullus tries to present Paul as a politically dangerous type.

10-21. In his defence Paul points out that the Jews, by failing to recognize Jesus, have failed to understand the true religious tradition of Israel, and also that their charges about creating a disturbance and profaning the temple are groundless and they have no proof for them.

The tone of the address is serious and sober, as befits the authority by which

---

ᶻOther ancient authorities add *and we would have judged him according to our law.* ⁷*But the chief captain Lysias came and with great violence took him out of our hands,* ⁸*commanding his accusers to come before you*

"Realizing that for many years you have been judge over this nation, I cheerfully make my defence. ¹¹As you may ascertain, it is not more than twelve days since I went up to worship at Jerusalem; ¹²and they did not find me disputing with any one or stirring up a crowd, either in the temple or in the synagogues, or in the city. ¹³Neither can they prove to you what they now bring up against me. ¹⁴But this I admit to

Acts 20:16

Mt 5:17
Rom 3:31;
16:26

---

autem Paulus, annuente sibi praeside dicere: "Ex multis annis esse te iudicem genti huic sciens bono animo de causa mea rationem reddem, ¹¹cum possis cognoscere quia non plus sunt dies mihi quam duodecim, ex quo ascendi adorare in Ierusalem, ¹²et neque in templo invenerunt me cum aliquo disputantem aut concursum facientem turbae neque in synagogis neque in civitate, ¹³neque probare possunt tibi, de quibus nunc accusant me. ¹⁴Confiteor autem hoc tibi quod secundum viam, quam dicunt haeresim, sic deservio Patri

---

he is being judged. This is in keeping with what the Gospel teaches us about the respect due to civil authorities: they should be obeyed by all citizens because they are designed to protect the common good. "A Christian", Tertullian will write, "is an enemy of no one, least of all the emperor. Since he knows him to be appointed by his own God, he must love, reverence, honour, and wish him well, together with the whole Roman Empire, as long as the world shall last. [. . .] In this way, then, do we honour the emperor, as is both lawful for us and expedient for him, as a man next to God: who has received whatever he is from God; who is inferior to God alone" (*To Scapula*, 2).

"The political community and public authority", Vatican II teaches, "are based on human nature, and therefore they belong to an order established by God; nevertheless, the choice of political regime and the appointment of rulers are left to the free decision of the citizens (cf. Rom 13:1-5).

"It follows that political authority, either within the political community as such or through organizations representing the State, must be exercised within the limits of the moral order and directed toward the common good (understood in the dynamic sense of the term) according to the juridical order legitimately established or due to be established. Citizens, then, are bound in conscience to obey (cf. Rom 13:5). Accordingly, the responsibilty, the dignity, and the importance of State rulers is clear" (*Gaudium et spes*, 74).

11-12. Paul did not go up to Jerusalem to preach but rather to worship God in the Temple.

14-16. The Apostle rejects the charge that Christianity is a Jewish sect. It is something much more than that. For St Paul the Old Testament finds its fulfilment in the Gospel, and without the Gospel Judaism is incomplete. The central beliefs of the Jewish religion can be summed up as belief in God and in

you, that according to the Way, which they call a sect, I worship the God of our fathers, believing everything laid down by the law or written in the prophets, ¹⁵having a hope in God which these themselves accept, that there will be a resurrection of both the just and the unjust. ¹⁶So I always take pains to have a clear conscience toward God and toward men. ¹⁷Now after some years I came to bring to my nation alms and offerings. ¹⁸As I was doing this, they found me purified in the temple, without any crowd or tumult. But some Jews from Asia—¹⁹they ought to be here before you to make an

Jn 15:29

Acts 23:1

Rom 15:25

Acts 21:27

---

et Deo meo credens omnibus, quae secundum Legem sunt et in Prophetis scripta, ¹⁵spem habens in Deum, quam et hi ipsi exspectant, resurrectionem futuram iustorum et iniquorum. ¹⁶In hoc et ipse studeo sine offendiculo conscientiam habere ad Deum et ad homines semper. ¹⁷Post annos autem plures eleemosynas facturus in gentem meam veni et oblationes, ¹⁸in quibus invenerunt me purificatum in templo, non cum turba neque cum tumultu; ¹⁹quidam autem ex Asia Iudaei, quos oportebat apud te praesto esse et accusare

---

a future life and also upright conduct in line with the dictates of conscience; all this, Paul says, is also at the centre of Christian preaching.

The Apostle establishes a direct connexion between hope in the resurrection and good deeds in this present life. The *St Pius V Catechism* will say, many centuries later, that the thought of a future resurrection "must also prove a powerful incentive to the faithful to use every exertion to lead lives of rectitude and integrity, unsullied by the defilement of sin. For if they reflect that those boundless riches which will follow after the resurrection are now offered to them as rewards, they will be easily attracted to the pursuit of virtue and piety.

"On the other hand, nothing will have greater effect in subduing the passions and withdrawing souls from sin, than frequently to remind the sinner of the miseries and torments with which the reprobate will be visited, who on the last day will come forth unto the resurrection of judgment.

"An ardent desire of the promised rewards of eternal life will always be one of the most effective encouragements in our Christian life. However sorely fidelity to our faith as Christians may be tried in certain circumstances, hope of this reward will lighten our burden and revive our spirit, and God will always find us prompt and cheerful in his divine service" (I, 12, 14; 13, 1).

St Paul says that both the just and the unjust will experience the resurrection of the body.

17. This is the only reference in Acts to the collection in aid of the Jerusalem community (cf. Rom 15:25).

19. Paul's objection carries great legal weight because Roman law laid down that those who brought charges had to appear before the tribunal.

accusation, if they have anything against me. [20]Or else let these men themselves say what wrongdoing they found when I stood before the council, [21]except this one thing which I cried out while standing among them, 'With respect to the resurrection of the dead I am on trial before you this day.' "

[22]But Felix, having a rather accurate knowledge of the Way, put them off, saying, "When Lysias the tribune comes down, I will decide your case." [23]Then he gave orders to the centurion that he should be kept in custody but should have some liberty, and that none of his friends should be prevented from attending to his needs.

A further appearance before Felix

[24]After some days Felix came with his wife Drusilla, who was a Jewess; and he sent for Paul and heard him speak upon faith in Christ Jesus. [25]And as he argued about justice and self-control and future judgment, Felix was alarmed and said, "Go away for the present; when I have an opportunity

Mk 6:17-20
Jn 16:8

---

si quid haberent adversum me [20]aut hi ipsi dicant quid invenerint iniquitatis, cum starem in concilio, [21]nisi de una hac voce, qua clamavi inter eos stans: De resurrectione mortuorum ego iudicor hodie apud vos!" [22]Distulit autem illos Felix certissime sciens ea, quae de hac via sunt, dicens: "Cum tribunus Lysias descenderit, cognoscam causam vestram," [23]iubens centurioni custodiri eum et habere mitigationem, nec quemquam prohibere de suis ministrare ei. [24]Post aliquot autem dies adveniens Felix cum Drusilla uxore sua, quae erat Iudaea, vocavit Paulum et audivit ab eo de fide, quae est in Christum Iesum. [25]Disputante autem illo de iustitia et continentia et de iudicio futuro, timefactus Felix respondit: "Quod nunc attinet, vade; tempore autem opportuno accersiam te," [26]simul et sperans quia pecunia daretur sibi a Paulo; propter quod et

---

24. Drusilla was a daughter of Herod Agrippa (cf. 12:1ff). She had left her lawful husband to marry the Roman governor.

25. It is very daring of Paul to speak about chastity to this couple living in concubinage. "Observe", says Chrysostom, "that, when he has the opportunity to converse with the governor, Paul does not say anything which might influence his decision or flatter him: he says things which shock him and disturb his conscience" (*Hom. on Acts*, 51).

Felix's fear of future judgment has little to do with true fear of God, which is the beginning of wisdom and therefore of conversion. The governor's attitude shows that he does have remorse of conscience—but it does not make him change his lifestyle.

I will summon you." [26]At the same time he hoped that money would be given him by Paul. So he sent for him often and conversed with him. [27]But when two years had elapsed, Felix was succeeded by Porcius Festus; and desiring to do the Jews a favour, Felix left Paul in prison.

25

Festus resumes the trial. Paul appeals to Caesar

[1]Now when Festus had come into his province, after three days he went up to Jerusalem from Caesarea. [2]And the chief priests and the principal men of the Jews informed him against Paul; and they urged him, [3]asking as a favour to have the man sent to Jerusalem, planning an ambush to kill him

---

frequenter accersiens eum loquebatur cum eo. [27]Biennio autem expleto, accepit successorem Felix Porcium Festum; volensque gratiam praestare Iudaeis, Felix reliquit Paulum vinctum.
[1]Festus ergo cum venisset in provinciam, post triduum ascendit Hierosolymam a Caesarea; [2]adieruntque eum principes sacerdotum et primi Iudaeorum adversus Paulum, et rogabant eum [3]postulantes gratiam adversum eum, ut iuberet perduci eum in Ierusalem, insidias tendentes, ut eum interficerent in via.

---

26. Felix may well have wanted to get some of the money Paul brought to Jerusalem, funds which Paul in fact has referred to (v. 17). Venal officials were common enough during this period.

27. "Two years": a *biennium*, a technical word used in Roman law for the maximum length a person could be detained without trial (cf. 28:30).

It was normal practice for an outgoing governor to leave to his successor the resolution of important cases pending.

1-12. Paul's case is now re-heard before Festus, following the same procedure as described in the previous chapter. The new governor wants to examine the matter for himself before making a definitive judgment. He probably realizes or suspects that Paul is innocent, but he will soon be as perplexed as Felix his predecessor and as subject to the same pressures from the Jews.

Porcius Festus seems to have been a good governor. He held this position for two or three years, until the year 62, when he died.

1-2. Festus' courtesy visit to Jerusalem would enable him to be briefed on all matters awaiting decision, including Paul's case.

on the way. ⁴Festus replied that Paul was being kept at Caesarea, and that he himself intended to go there shortly. ⁵"So," said he, "let the men of authority among you go down with me, and if there is anything wrong about the man, let them accuse him."

⁶When he had stayed among them not more than eight or ten days, he went down to Caesarea; and the next day he took his seat on the tribunal and ordered Paul to be brought. ⁷And when he had come, the Jews who had gone down from Jerusalem stood about him, bringing against him many serious charges which they could not prove. ⁸Paul said in his defence, "Neither against the law of the Jews, nor against the temple, nor against Caesar have I offended at all." ⁹But Festus, wishing to do the Jews a favour, said to Paul, "Do you wish to go up to Jerusalem, and there be tried on these charges before me?" ¹⁰But Paul said, "I am standing before

Mt 26:59-60
Lk 23:14-15

Acts 24:14

Acts 24:27

---

⁴Festus igitur respondit servari Paulum in Caesarea, se autem maturius profecturum: ⁵"Qui ergo in vobis, ait, potentes sunt, descendentes simul, si quod est in viro crimen, accusent eum." ⁶Demoratus autem inter eos dies non amplius quam octo aut decem, descendit Caesaream, et altera die sedit pro tribunali et iussit Paulum adduci. ⁷Qui cum perductus esset, circumsteterunt eum, qui ab Hierosolyma descenderant, Iudaei, multas et graves causas obicientes, quas non poterant probare, ⁸Paulo rationem reddente: "Neque in legem Iudaeorum neque in templum neque in Caesarem quidquam peccavi." ⁹Festus autem volens Iudaeis gratiam praestare, respondens Paulo dixit: "Vis Hierosolymam ascendere et ibi de his iudicare apud me?" ¹⁰Dixit autem Paulus: "Ad tribunal Caesaris sto, ubi me oportet iudicari. Iudaeis nihil nocui, sicut et tu melius nosti.

---

9. The governor is not thinking of handing the prisoner over to the Jewish courts. But his political prudence leads him to take Paul's accusers' requests partly into account and give the Sanhedrin a say in the trial. Festus can also use the Sanhedrin as a *consilium*, a source of expert advice. It is in this sense that he invites Paul to agree to be tried in Jerusalem. The Governor's question is in fact a rhetorical one: he is simply notifying Paul of a decision he has already made.

10-11. Paul realizes what Festus intends to do, and he appeals to Caesar in order to avoid being tried in unfavourable circumstances. From a strictly judicial point of view, Paul's action is not an "appeal" but what is termed in Roman law a *provocatio*. An appeal only operated once a lower court had passed sentence. A *provocatio* meant insisting that the case be brought to a higher court, for that court to decide whether the accused was guilty or not.

Caesar's tribunal, where I ought to be tried; to the Jews I have done no wrong, as you know very well. ¹¹If then I am a wrongdoer, and have committed anything for which I deserve to die, I do not seek to escape death; but if there is nothing in their charges against me, no one can give me up to them. I appeal to Caesar." ¹²Then Festus, when he had conferred with his council, answered, "You have appealed to Caesar; to Caesar you shall go."

Festus briefs Agrippa

¹³Now when some days had passed, Agrippa the king and

---

¹¹Si ergo iniuste egi et dignum morte aliquid feci, non recuso mori; si vero nihil est eorum, quae hi accusant me, nemo potest me illis donare. Caesarem appello!" ¹²Tunc Festus cum consilio locutus respondit: "Caesarem appellasti; ad Caesarem ibis." ¹³Et cum dies aliquot transacti essent, Agrippa rex et

---

Only Roman citizens could ask for their cases to be examined by the imperial tribunal in Rome.

These various legal proceedings, ordained and used by Providence, help ensure that Paul fulfil the task God has marked out for him and foretold (cf. Acts 23:11). "He appeals to Caesar and hastens to Rome to persist still longer in preaching, and thereby go to Christ crowned with the many who thereby will come to believe, as well as those who already believe [through him]" (St Bede, *Super Act expositio, ad loc.*).

Paul's characteristic generosity once again brings him to contemplate and accept the prospect of having to die. For him death would in the last analysis be God's will for him and not just the decision of a human court. But his sense of justice obliges him to ask that his actions be judged on the basis of his merits and demerits in the eyes of the law. "These are not the words of a man who condemns himself to death, but of a man who firmly believes in his own innocence" (Chrysostom, *Hom. on Acts*, 51).

12. Possibly Paul's appeal did not take automatic effect: the governor may not necessarily have been obliged by law to send the detainee to Rome. But once the latter invoked his right of appeal, Festus would be able to escape the dilemma he faced, by sending Paul to Rome. If he did not transfer the case to Rome, this might have been taken as an insult to Caesar—involving political risk (cf. 26:32)—and if he set Paul free he would be needlessly offending the Jews.

13. Herod Agrippa II was a son of Herod Agrippa I. He was born in the year 27. Like his father he had won favour with Rome and had been given various territories in northern Palestine, which he was allowed to rule with the title of king. Bernice was his sister.

Bernice arrived at Caesarea to welcome Festus. [14]And as they stayed there many days, Festus laid Paul's case before the king, saying, "There is a man left prisoner by Felix; [15]and when I was at Jerusalem, the chief priests and the elders of the Jews gave information about him, asking for sentence against him. [16]I answered them that it was not the custom of the Romans to give up any one before the accused met the accusers face to face, and had opportunity to make his defence concerning the charge laid against him. [17]When therefore they came together here, I made no delay, but on the next day took my seat on the tribunal and ordered the man to be brought in. [18]When the accusers stood up, they brought no charge in his case of such evils as I supposed; [19]but they had certain points of dispute with him about their

Acts 24:1; 25:2

Acts 18:5; 23:29
1 Cor 15:14

Berenice descenderunt Caesaream et salutaverunt Festum. [14]Et cum dies plures ibi demorarentur, Festus regi indicavit de Paulo dicens: "Vir quidam est derelictus a Felice vinctus, [15]de quo cum essem Hierosolymis, adierunt me principes sacerdotum et seniores Iudaeorum postulantes adversus illum damnationem; [16]ad quos respondi quia non est consuetudo Romanis donare aliquem hominem, priusquam is, qui accusatur, praesentes habeat accusatores locumque defendendi se ab accusatione accipiat. [17]Cum ergo huc convenissent, sine ulla dilatione sequenti die sedens pro tribunali iussi adduci virum; [18]de quo cum stetissent accusatores, nullam causam deferebant, de quibus ego suspicabar malis, [19]quaestiones vero quasdam de sua superstitione habebant adversus eum et de quodam Iesu defuncto, quem affirmabat Paulus vivere.

---

19. Festus' words show his indifference towards Paul's beliefs and his religious controversy with the Jews. The conversation between the two politicians reveals a typical attitude of worldly men to matters which they consider far-fetched and irrelevant as far as everyday affairs are concerned. This passage also shows us that in the course of his trial Paul must have had an opportunity to speak about Jesus and confess his faith in the Resurrection.

Jesus Christ is alive; he is the centre of history and the centre of each and every person's existence. "The Church believes that Christ, who died and was raised for the sake of all (cf. 2 Cor 5:15) can show man the way and strengthen him through the Spirit in order to be worthy of his destiny: nor is there any other name under heaven given among men by which they can be saved (cf. Acts 4:12). The Church likewise maintains that the key, the centre and the purpose of the whole of man's history is to be found in its Lord and Master. She also maintains that beneath all that changes there is much that is unchanging, much that has its ultimate foundation in Christ, who is the same yesterday, and today, and forever (cf. Heb 13:8)" (Vatican II, *Gaudium et spes*, 10).

own superstition and about one Jesus, who was dead, but whom Paul asserted to be alive. [20]Being at a loss how to investigate these questions, I asked whether he wished to go to Jerusalem and be tried there regarding them. [21]But when Paul had appealed to be kept in custody for the decision of the emperor, I commanded him to be held until I send him to Caesar." [22]And Agrippa said to Festus, "I should like to hear the man myself." "Tomorrow," said he, "you shall hear him."

Lk 23:8

Paul before Agrippa

[23]So on the morrow Agrippa and Bernice came with great pomp, and they entered the audience hall with the military tribunes and the prominent men of the city. Then by command of Festus Paul was brought in. [24]And Festus said, "King Agrippa and all who are present with us, you see this man about whom the whole Jewish people petitioned me, both at Jerusalem and here, shouting that he ought not to live

---

[20]Haesitans autem ego de huiusmodi quaestione, dicebam si vellet ire Hierosolymam et ibi iudicari de istis. [21]Paulo autem appellante, ut servaretur ad Augusti cognitionem, iussi servari eum, donec mittam eum ad Caesarem." [22]Agrippa autem ad Festum: "Volebam et ipse hominem audire! "Cras, inquit, audies eum." [23]Altera autem die, cum venisset Agrippa et Berenice cum multa ambitione, et introissent in auditorium cum tribunis et viris principalibus civitatis, et iubente Festo, adductus est Paulus. [24]Et dicit Festus: "Agrippa rex et omnes, qui simul adestis nobiscum viri, videtis hunc, de quo omnis multitudo

---

"Stir up that fire of faith. Christ is not a figure that has passed. He is not a memory that is lost in history.

"He lives! '*Jesus Christus heri et hodie, ipse et in saecula*', says Saint Paul,—'Jesus Christ is the same today as he was yesterday and as he will be for ever'" (J. Escrivá, *The Way*, 584).

21. "Caesar" and "Augustus" were titles of the Roman emperor. At this time the emperor was Nero (54-68).

22. Agrippa's reply is reminiscent of a similar scene when his grand-uncle Herod Antipas expressed a desire to see Jesus (cf. Lk 9:9; 23:8). "His conversation with the governor awakens in Agrippa a strong desire to hear Paul. Festus meets his wish, and thereby Paul's glory is further enhanced. This is the outcome of the machinations against him: without them no judge would have deigned to listen to such things, nor would anyone have heard them with such rapt attention" (Chrysostom, *Hom. on Acts*, 51).

250

any longer. [25]But I found that he had done nothing deserving death; and as he himself appealed to the emperor, I decided to send him. [26]But I have nothing definite to write to my lord about him. Therefore I have brought him before you, and, especially before you, King Agrippa, that, after we have examined him, I may have something to write. [27]For it seems to me unreasonable, in sending a prisoner, not to indicate the charges against him."

26

Paul's speech in the presence of Agrippa

[1]Agrippa said to Paul, "You have permission to speak for yourself." Then Paul stretched out his hand and made his defence:

[2]"I think myself fortunate that it is before you, King Agrippa, I am to make my defence today against all the accusations of the Jews, [3]because you are especially familiar

---

Iudaeorum interpellavit me Hierosolymis et hic, clamantes non oportere eum vivere amplius. [25]Ego vero comperi nihil dignum eum morte fecisse, ipso autem hoc appellante Augustum, iudicavi mittere. [26]De quo quid certum scribam domino, non habeo; propter quod produxi eum ad vos et maxime ad te, rex Agrippa, ut interrogatione facta, habeam quid scribam: [27]sine ratione enim mihi videtur mittere vinctum et causas eius non significare."

[1]Agrippa vero ad Paulum ait: "Permittitur tibi loqui pro temetipso." Tunc Paulus, extenta manu, coepit rationem reddere. [2]"De omnibus, quibus accusor a Iudaeis, rex Agrippa, aestimo me beatum apud te, cum sim defensurus me hodie, [3]maxime te sciente omnia, quae apud Iudaeos sunt consuetudines et

---

1-30. Paul has already defended himself before Festus, and his words (cf. 25:8ff) make it clear that he is innocent of any offence against Roman law. Now he will speak before Agrippa, in an address aimed mainly at Jews rather than Romans. He bears witness to the Gospel before a king—fulfilling the prophecy of Acts 9:15 and Lk 21:12.

2-3. "Observe", comments St John Chrysostom, "how Paul begins this exposition of his teaching not only about faith in the forgiveness of sin but also about the rules of human conduct. If his conscience had been heavy with any fault he would have been concerned about the idea of being judged by one who was in a position to know all the facts; but it is proper to a clear conscience not only not to reject as judge one who knows the facts but actually to rejoice at being judged by him" (*Hom. on Acts*, 52).

Acts 22:3

with all customs and controversies of the Jews; therefore I beg you to listen to me patiently.

⁴"My manner of life from my youth, spent from the beginning among my own nation and at Jerusalem, is known Gal 1:14
Phil 3:5 by all the Jews. ⁵They have known for a long time, if they are willing to testify, that according to the strictest party of Acts 23:6 our religion I have lived as a Pharisee. ⁶And now I stand here on trial for hope in the promise made by God to our fathers, Dan 12:1-3
2 Mac 7 ⁷to which our twelve tribes hope to attain, as they earnestly worship night and day. And for this hope I am accused by Jews, O king! ⁸Why is it thought incredible by any of you that God raises the dead?

⁹"I myself was convinced that I ought to do many things

---

quaestiones; propter quod obsecro patienter me audias. ⁴Et quidem vitam meam a iuventute, quae ab initio fuit in gente mea et in Hierosolymis, noverunt omnes Iudaei, ⁵praescientes me ab initio, si velint testimonium perhibere, quoniam secundum diligentissimam sectam nostrae religionis vixi pharisaeus. ⁶Et nunc propter spem eius, quae ad patres nostros repromissionis facta est a Deo, sto iudicio subiectus, ⁷in quam duodecim tribus nostrae cum perseverantia nocte ac die deservientes sperant devenire; de qua spe accusor a Iudaeis, rex! ⁸Quid incredibile iudicatur apud vos, si Deus mortuos suscitat? ⁹Et ego quidem existimaveram me adversus nomen Iesu Nazareni debere multa contraria agere;

Paul wants to convince Agrippa, whom he regards as well versed in Jewish beliefs, that the Gospel is simply the fulfilment of the Sacred Scriptures.

5. Paul uses the word "Pharisee" here to indicate his strict observance of the Law prior to becoming a Christian (cf. Phil 3:5).

6-8. In his addresses Paul frequently defends himself by referring to the fulfilment of the Old Testament prophecies and promises (cf. 23:6; 24:25; 28:20). In addition to revealing his own attitudes and convictions, he is saying that the fundamental question at issue is whether the Jews really believe in these prophecies or not.

Although he is speaking about resurrection in general terms, Paul's words obviously refer to the resurrection of Jesus, which legitimates him as the Messiah. "Paul offers two proofs of resurrection. One is taken from the prophets. He does not quote any particular prophet; he simply says that this is what Jews believe. His second proof the Apostle takes from the facts themselves. And what is it? That Christ, after rising from the dead, conversed with him" (Chrysostom, *Hom. on Acts*, 52).

9-18. Paul once more gives an account of the circumstances of his conversion (cf. 9:3-9 and 22:6-11).

in opposing the name of Jesus of Nazareth. [10]And I did so in Jerusalem; I not only shut up many of the saints in prison, by authority from the chief priests, but when they were put to death I cast my vote against them. [11]And I punished them often in all the synagogues and tried to make them blaspheme; and in raging fury against them, I persecuted them even to foreign cities.

[12]"Thus I journeyed to Damascus with the authority and commission of the chief priests. [13]At midday, O king, I saw on the way a light from heaven, brighter than the sun, shining round me and those who journeyed with me. [14]And when we had all fallen to the ground, I heard a voice saying to me in the Hebrew language, 'Saul, Saul, why do you persecute me? It hurts you to kick against the goads.' [15]And I said, 'Who are you, Lord?' And the Lord said, 'I am Jesus whom you are persecuting. [16]But rise and stand upon your feet; for I have appeared to you for this purpose, to appoint you to serve

Jn 16:2
Acts 9:13;
22:20

Ezek 2:1

Jer 1:7

---

[10]quod et feci Hierosolymis, et multos sanctorum ego in carceribus inclusi, a principibus sacerdotum potestate accepta, et cum occiderentur, detuli sententiam, [11]et per omnes synagogas frequenter puniens eos compellebam blasphemare, et abundantius insaniens in eos persequebar usque in exteras civitates. [12]In quibus dum irem Damascum cum potestate et permissu principum sacerdotum, [13]die media in via vidi, rex, de caelo supra splendorem solis circumfulgens me lumen et eos, qui mecum simul ibant; [14]omnesque nos cum decidissemus in terram, audivi vocem loquentem mihi Hebraica lingua: 'Saul Saul, quid me persequeris? Durum est tibi contra stimulum calcitrare.' [15]Ego autem dixi: 'Quis es, Domine?' Dominus autem dixit: 'Ego sum Iesus, quem tu persequeris.[16]Sed exsurge et sta super pedes tuos; ad hoc enim apparui tibi, ut constituam te ministrum et testem eorum, quae vidisti, et eorum, quibus

---

10. It is possible that Paul was involved in some way in Sanhedrin decisions to persecute the Church; or he may be referring to the part he played in the martyrdom of Stephen (cf. 8:1).

14. The final sentence in this verse is not given in Paul's two previous accounts of his conversion on the road to Damascus (cf. 9:4; 22:7). It is a Greek turn of phrase to describe useless resistance, but it was also known and used by Jews as a proverb (cf. *The Psalms of Solomon*, 16, 4).

16-18. Paul's calling and mission are described in terms similar to that of the calling of the prophets of Israel (cf. Ezek 2:1; Is 42:6f). God makes known his design in an imperious command which radically changes the whole life of

and bear witness to the things in which you have seen me and to those in which I will appear to you, [17]delivering you from the people and from the Gentiles—to whom I send you [18]to open their eyes, that they may turn from darkness to light and from the power of Satan to God, that they may receive forgiveness of sins and a place among those who are sanctified by faith in me.'

Is 42:7, 16
Jn 8:12
Acts 9:17-18
Col 1:12-14

[19]"Wherefore, O King Agrippa, I was not disobedient to the heavenly vision, [20]but declared first to those at Damascus, then at Jerusalem and throughout all the country of Judea, and also to the Gentiles, that they should repent and turn to God and perform deeds worthy of their repentance. [21]For this

Mt 3:8
Gal 1:16

Acts 21:30-31

---

apparebo tibi, [17]eripiens te de populo et de gentibus, in quas ego mitto te [18]aperire oculos eorum, ut convertantur a tenebris ad lucem et de potestate Satanae ad Deum, ut accipiant remissionem peccatorum et sortem inter sanctificatos per fidem, quae est in me.' [19]Unde, rex Agrippa, non fui incredulus caelestis visionis, [20]sed his, qui sunt Damasci primum et Hierosolymis, et in omnem regionem Iudaeae et gentibus annuntiabam, ut paenitentiam agerent et converterentur ad Deum digna paenitentiae opera facientes. [21]Hac ex causa me

---

his chosen one. He addresses the man's free will to get him to do what God wills simply because God wills it. But he also enlightens his mind to show him what his vocation means, so that he accept it in the conviction of being the recipient of a special grace to perform an important task.

19-23. This section is a summary of Paul's preaching, presenting Christianity as the fulfilment of the ancient prophecies.

19. The Apostle asserts that he has not embraced Christianity blindly: he is totally convinced of its truth. He explains his change of heart in terms of docility and obedience to the divine voice he heard. Paul's experience is repeated in different (usually less dramatic) ways in the lives of every man and woman. At particular moments in life the Lord calls us and invites us to a new conversion which draws us out of sin or lukewarmness. What we have to do is to listen carefully to that calling and obey it. "We should let our Lord get involved in our lives, admitting him trustingly, removing from his way any obstacles or excuses. We tend to be on the defensive, to be attached to our selfishness. We always want to be in charge, even if it's only to be in charge of our wretchedness. That is why we must go to Jesus, so to have him make us truly free. Only then will we be able to serve God and all men" (J. Escrivá, *Christ is passing by*, 17).

Response to God's grace is a necessary pre-condition for being helped by God in the future. Accepting one grace is important for equipping us to accept the following one, a process which continues right through our life. "In this true

reason the Jews seized me in the temple and tried to kill me. [22]To this day I have had the help that comes from God, and so I stand here testifying both to small and great, saying nothing but what the prophets and Moses said would come to pass: [23]that the Christ must suffer, and that, by being the first to rise from the dead, he would proclaim light both to the people and to the Gentiles."

Acts 13:47;
17:3
1 Cor 15:20-23
Col 1:18

His hearers' reactions

[24]And as he thus made his defence, Festus said with a loud voice, "Paul, you are mad; your great learning is turning you mad." [25]But Paul said, "I am not mad, most excellent Festus,

Jn 10:20

Jn 18:37

Iudaei, cum essem in templo comprehensum, tentabant interficere. [22]Auxilium igitur assecutus a Deo usque in hodiernum diem sto testificans minori atque maiori, nihil extra dicens quam ea, quae prophetae sunt locuti futura esse et Moyses, [23]si passibilis Christus, si primus ex resurrectione mortuorum lumen annuntiaturus est populo et gentibus." [24]Sic autem eo rationem reddente, Festus magna voce dixit: "Insanis, Paule; multae te litterae ad insaniam convertunt!" [25]At Paulus: "Non insanio, inquit, optime Feste, sed veritatis et sobrietatis verba

---

perfection lies," St Gregory of Nyssa writes, "never stopping on the path towards the best and never putting limits on perfection" (*De perfecta christiani forma*).

"The grace of the Holy Spirit," Gregory says elsewhere, "is granted to every man with the idea that he ought to increase what he receives" (*De instituto christiano*). The same idea is expressed by St Teresa of Avila when she writes that "we must seek new strength with which to serve him, and endeavour not to be ungrateful, for that is the condition on which the Lord bestows his jewels. Unless we made good use of his treasures, and of the high estate to which he brings us, he will take those treasures back from us, and we shall be poorer than before, and His Majesty will give the jewels to some other person who can display them to advantage and to his own profit and that of others" (*Life*, 10, 6).

23. Paul identifies the Messiah with the suffering Servant of Yahweh (cf. Is 42:1ff; 49:1ff), and asserts that Jesus is the fulfilment of both these prophecies.

24. Festus cannot understand what Paul is saying; he thinks his mind is gone. He seems to have a certain sympathy for the Apostle, but he cannot make him out. The fact is that divine wisdom does seem to make no sense humanly speaking. "He regarded it as madness for a man in chains not to deal with the calumnies that threatened him but, instead, to be speaking about the convictions which enlightened him from within" (St Bede, *Super Act expositio, in loc.*).

Jn 18:20

but I am speaking the sober truth. ²⁶For the king knows about these things, and to him I speak freely; for I am persuaded that none of these things has escaped his notice, for this was not done in a corner. ²⁷King Agrippa, do you believe the prophets? I know that you believe." ²⁸And Agrippa said to

Acts 11:26
1 Pet 4:16

---

eloquor. ²⁶Scit enim de his rex, ad quem et audenter loquor; latere enim eum nihil horum arbitror, neque enim in angulo hoc gestum est. ²⁷Credis, rex Agrippa, prophetis? Scio quia credis." ²⁸Agrippa autem ad Paulum: "In modico

---

27. Paul's only interest is in upholding the Gospel and bringing salvation to his hearers. He is trying to get Agrippa, who is presiding over this session and is Paul's main questioner, to react interiorly and allow grace move his heart. "How admirably he behaves! Imprisoned for spreading the teachings of Christ, he misses no opportunity to preach the Gospel. Brought before Festus and Agrippa, he declares unflinchingly: 'To this day I have had the help that comes from God and so I stand here testifying to small and great. . .' (Acts 26:22).

"The Apostle does not silence or hide his faith, or his apostolic preaching that had brought down on him the hatred of his persecutors. He continues preaching salvation to everyone he meets. And, with marvellous daring, he boldly faces Agrippa [. . .].

"Where did St Paul get all his strength from? *Omnia possum in eo qui me confortat!* (Phil 14:13). I can do all things in him who strengthens me. I can do all things, because God alone gives me this faith, this hope, this charity" (J. Escrivá, *Friends of God*, 270f).

Apostolate is a responsibility and a duty with which Christ charges every Christian at all times."Nothing is more useless than a Christian who is not dedicated to saving his brethren. Do not appeal to your poverty: he whose alms amounted to only two little coins would rise up to accuse you, if you did; and so would Peter, who says, Silver and gold I have none; and Paul, who was so poor that he often went hungry. Do not appeal to your humble circumstances, because they too were humble people, of modest condition. Do not appeal to your lack of knowledge, for they too were unlettered. Are you a slave or a runaway? Onesimus was one also. [. . .] Are you unwell? So was Timothy" (St John Chrysostom, *Hom. on Acts*, 20).

28. The king's remark, which is angry yet serious, shows that Paul's words have touched him. He feels he cannot respond to the Apostle's call, but his conscience and his position as a Jewish prince prevent him from denying that he has any faith in the prophecies God has given his people.

However, he resists the divine grace extended to him by what Paul has been saying and now by Paul's question. He lacks the inner dispositions which faith calls for—that is, the moral predisposition and attitude which allows someone to accept God's word and decide to give his life a new direction. He is not genuinely interested in seeking God. "If any man's will is to do his will, he

Paul, "In a short time you think to make me a Christian!"
²⁹And Paul said, "Whether short or long, I would to God that
not only you but also all who hear me this day might become
such as I am—except for these chains."

³⁰Then the king rose, and the governor and Bernice and
those who were sitting with them; ³¹and when they had
withdrawn, they said to one another, "This man is doing
nothing to deserve death or imprisonment." ³²And Agrippa
said to Festus, "This man could have been set free if he had
not appealed to Caesar."

---

suades me Christianum fieri!" ²⁹Et Paulus: "Optarem apud Deum et in modico
et in magno non tantum te sed et omnes hos, qui audiunt me hodie, fieri tales,
qualis et ego sum, exceptis vinculis his!" ³⁰Et exsurrexit rex et praeses et
Berenice et, qui assidebant eis, ³¹et cum secessissent, loquebantur ad invicem
dicentes: "Nihil morte aut vinculis dignum quid facit homo iste." ³²Agrippa
autem Festo dixit: "Dimitti poterat homo hic si non appellasset Caesarem."

---

shall know whether the teaching is from God or whether I am speaking on my
own authority" (Jn 7:17).

29. Once again Paul shows his practical zeal for all souls; he is not overawed
by the circumstances in which he finds himself.

"Charity with everyone means . . . apostolate with everyone. It means we,
for our part, must really translate into deeds the great desire of God 'who desires
all men to be saved and to come to the knowledge of the truth' (1 Tim
2:4). [. . .] For Christians, loving means 'wanting to want', 'wanting to love',
making up one's mind in Christ to work for the good of souls, without
discrimination of any kind; trying to obtain for them, before any other good,
the greatest good of all, that of knowing Christ and falling in love with him"
(J. Escrivá, *Friends of God*, 230f).

32. To declare Paul innocent and set him free in spite of his appeal to Rome
would have caused offence both to the emperor and to the Jews.

27:1 - 28:15. This account of St Paul's sea journey is so exact in its
terminology that it is regarded as an important source of information on
seafaring in ancient times. It gives a great deal of detail and describes things so
vividly that it obviously is what it is—an account of an eyewitness, St Luke,
who may even have made notes during the journey.

The narrative also shows how St Paul maintains supernatural outlook despite
new difficulties; and how he keeps up his apostolic work and entrusts himself
entirely to God's loving providence.

The departure for Rome. The voyage to Crete

Acts 19:29

Acts 24:23;
28:16

¹And when it was decided that we should sail to Italy, they delivered Paul and some other prisoners to a centurion of the Augustan Cohort, named Julius. ²And embarking in a ship of Adramyttium, which was about to sail to the ports along the coast of Asia, we put to sea, accompanied by Aristarchus, a Macedonian from Thessalonica. ³The next day we put in at Sidon; and Julius treated Paul kindly, and gave him leave to go to his friends and be cared for. ⁴And putting to sea from there we sailed under the lee of Cyprus, because the winds were against us. ⁵And when we had sailed across the sea which is off Cilicia and Pamphylia, we came to Myra in Lycia. ⁶There the centurion found a ship of Alexandria

---

¹Ut autem iudicatum est navigare nos in Italiam, tradiderunt et Paulum et quosdam alios vinctos centurioni nomine Iulion, cohortis Augustae. ²Ascendentes autem navem Hadramyttenam, incipentem navigare circa Asiae loca, sustulimus, perseverante nobiscum Aristarcho Macedone Thessalonicensi; ³sequenti autem die devenimus Sidonem, et humane tractans Iulius Paulum permisit ad amicos ire et curam sui agere. ⁴Et inde cum sustulissemus, subnavigavimus Cypro, propterea quod essent venti contrariii, ⁵et pelagus Ciliciae et Pamphyliae navigantes venimus Myram, quae est Lyciae. ⁶Et ibi inveniens

---

2. Prisoners were not sent on a special ship; instead, places were negotiated for them on merchant ships. The centurion finds places for these prisoners on a ship which has to call into various ports on the coast of Asia Minor, in the hope of eventually finding a ship bound for Italy.

3. The centurion Julius sees the Christians of Sidon as "friends" of Paul. St Luke uses the word "friend" here, but it was not the normal thing for Christians to call each other "friend"; however, they are friends of God—"you are my friends" (Jn 15:14)—and from this friendship is born the loving friendship which binds them together. So it is quite understandable that pagans should see Christians as good friends of one another.

6. The ship of Alexandria on which they embark must have been a grain ship, one of many used to transport grain from Egypt to Rome. These broad, heavy boats had one mast amidship and another forward; the hull was covered by a deck which had openings or movable timbers which gave access to the hold, where the cargo was stored and where passengers took shelter in bad weather.

sailing for Italy, and put us on board. [7]We sailed slowly for a number of days, and arrived with difficulty off Cnidus, and as the wind did not allow us to go on, we sailed under the lee of Crete off Salmone. [8]Coasting along it with difficulty, we came to a place called Fair Heavens, near which was the city of Lasaea.

The journey is resumed against Paul's advice

[9]As much time had been lost, and the voyage was already dangerous because the fast had already gone by, Paul advised them, [10]saying, "Sirs, I perceive that the voyage will be with injury and much loss, not only of the cargo and the ship, but also of our lives." [11]But the centurion paid more attention to the captain and to the owner of the ship than to what Paul said. [12]And because the harbour was not suitable to winter in, the majority advised to put to sea from there, on the chance that somehow they could reach Phoenix, a harbour of Crete, looking northeast and southeast,[a] and winter there.

Lev 16:29-31

---

centurio navem Alexandrinam navigantem in Italiam transposuit nos in eam. [7]Et cum multis diebus tarde navigaremus et vix devenissemus contra Cnidum, prohibente nos vento, subnavigavimus Cretae secundum Salmonem, [8]et vix iuxta eam navigantes venimus in locum quendam, qui vocatur Boni Portus, cui iuxta erat civitas Lasaea. [9]Multo autem tempore peracto, et cum iam non esset tuta navigatio, eo quod et ieiunium iam praeterisset, monebat Paulus [10]dicens eis: "Viri, video quoniam cum iniuria et multo damno non solum oneris et navis sed etiam animarum nostrarum incipit esse navigatio." [11]Centurio autem gubernatori et nauclero magis credebat quam his, quae a Paulo dicebantur. [12]Et cum aptus portus non esset ad hiemandum, plurimi statuerunt concilium enavigare

---

9. By the time they reach Fair Havens Paul and his companions have been travelling for almost forty days. At that time travel on the high seas was considered unsafe from the middle of September onwards, and out of the question from early November until March. The fast was that prescribed for all Jews on the day of Atonement (cf. Lev 16:29-31). In the year 60 it fell at the end of October.

10-13. Prior to this St Paul had suffered shipwreck three times (cf. 2 Cor 11:25), and he knew very well how risky the voyage would be, but most of the people on board were hoping to reach Sicily or at least some port more suitable for wintering in. As soon as they got a suitable wind they weighed anchor and went along the coast in an easterly direction, using a skiff (which doubled as a sort of lifeboat) to take the ship out of harbour.

[a]Or *southwest and northwest*

259

¹³And when the south wind blew gently, supposing that they had obtained their purpose, they weighed anchor and sailed along Crete, close inshore. ¹⁴But soon a tempestuous wind, called the northeaster, struck down from the land; ¹⁵and when the ship was caught and could not face the wind, we gave way to it and were driven. ¹⁶And running under the lee of a small island called Cauda,^b we managed with difficulty to secure the boat; ¹⁷after hoisting it up, they took measures^c to undergird the ship; then, fearing that they should run on the Syrtis, they lowered the gear, and so were driven. ¹⁸As we were violently storm-tossed, they began next day to throw the cargo overboard; ¹⁹and the third day they cast out with their own hands the tackle of the ship. ²⁰And

Jn 1:5

---

inde, si quo modo possent devenientes Phoenicen hiemare, portum Cretae respicientem ad africum et ad caurum. ¹³Aspirante autem austro, aestimantes propositum se tenere, cum sustulissent, proprius legebant Cretam. ¹⁴Non post multum autem misit se contra ipsam ventus typhonicus, qui vocatur euroaquilo; ¹⁵cumque arrepta esset navis et non posset conari in ventum, data nave flatibus, ferebamur. ¹⁶Insulam autem quandam decurrentes, quae vocatur Cauda, potuimus vix obtinere scapham, ¹⁷qua sublata, adiutoriis utebantur accingentes navem; et timentes, ne in Syrtim inciderunt, submisso vase, sic ferebantur. ¹⁸Valide autem nobis tempestate iactatis, sequenti die iactum fecerunt ¹⁹et tertia die suis manibus armamenta navis proiecerunt. ²⁰Neque sole autem neque

---

St John Chrysostom draws this lesson from the passage: "Let us stay firm in the faith, which is the safe port. Let us listen to it rather than to the pilot we have within, that is, our reason. Let us pay attention to Paul rather than to the pilot or the captain. If we do listen to experience we will not be injured or disdained" (*Hom. on Acts*, 53).

17-18. They managed to haul up the skiff, but due to the dark they were afraid of going on to the dangerous Syrtis sandbanks off the north coast of Africa. To prevent this they put out a sea anchor to brake the progress of the ship. They also go to drastic lengths to lighten the vessel.

19-20. These perils at sea remind us of the difficulties a person can come up against in the course of his life as he makes his way towards eternity. If we are in danger of being shipwrecked, of losing supernatural life, we need to throw out everything which is in the way, even things which up to then were necessary, such as the tackle and the cargo, in order to save our life.

In moments of disorientation and darkness, which the Lord permits souls to experience, when we cannot see the stars to work out which way to go, we need to use the resources God gives us for solving problems: "Christ has given his

^bOther ancient authorities read *Clauda*   ^cGreek *helps*

when neither sun nor stars appeared for many a day, and no small tempest lay on us, all hope of our being saved was at last abandoned.

Paul's vision. He rallies his companions

²¹As they had been long without food, Paul then came forward among them and said, "Men, you should have listened to me, and should not have set sail from Crete and incurred this injury and loss. ²²I now bid you to take heart; for there will be no loss of life among you, but only of the ship. ²³For this very night there stood by me an angel of the God to whom I belong and whom I worship, ²⁴and he said, 'Do not be afraid, Paul; you must stand before Caesar; and lo, God has granted you all those who sail with you.' ²⁵So take heart, men, for I have faith in God that it will be exactly as I have been told. ²⁶But we shall have to run on some island."

²⁷When the fourteenth night had come, as we were drifting

Acts 27:33

Acts 23:11

---

siferibus apparentibus per plures dies, et tempestate non exigua imminente, iam auferebatur spes omnis salutis nostrae. ²¹Et cum multa ieiunatio fuisset, tunc stans Paulus in medio eorum dixit: "Oportebat quidem, o viri, audito me, non tollere a Creta lucrique facere iniuriam hanc et iacturam. ²²Et nunc suadeo vobis bono animo esse, nulla enim amissi animae erit ex vobis praterquam navis; ²³astitit enim mihi hac nocte angelus Dei, cuius sum ego, cui et deservio, ²⁴dicens: 'Ne timeas, Paule; Caesari te oportet assistere, et ecce donavit tibi Deus omnes, qui navigant tecum.' ²⁵Propter quod bono animo estote, viri; credo enim Deo quia sic erit, quemadmodum dictum est mihi. ²⁶In insulam autem quandam oportet nos incidere." ²⁷Sed posteaquam quarta decima nox supervenit, cum ferremur in Hadria, circa mediam noctem suspicabantur nautae

---

Church sureness in doctrine and a flow of grace in the sacraments. He has arranged things so that there will always be people to guide and lead us, to remind us constantly of our way" (J. Escrivá *Christ is passing by*, 34). In particular, we have Mary, the Star of the Sea and the Morning Star, who has protected and will continue to protect and guide seafarers to their destination.

24. Paul prays to God for his own safety and that of his companions, and is made to understand that this prayer will definitely be granted. St John Chrysostom is very conscious of how apostolic Paul would have been in these circumstances and, referring to his predictions about the fate of the ship, he says that "the Apostle does not make them out of boasting; he wants to bring the seafarers to the faith and make them more receptive to what he has to teach" (*Hom. on Acts*, 53).

across the sea of Adria, about midnight the sailors suspected that they were nearing land. ²⁸So they sounded and found twenty fathoms; a little farther on they sounded again and found fifteen fathoms. ²⁹And fearing that we might run on the rocks, they let out four anchors from the stern, and prayed for day to come. ³⁰And as the sailors were seeking to escape from the ship, and had lowered the boat into the sea, under pretence of laying out anchors from the bow, ³¹Paul said to the centurion and the soldiers, "Unless these men stay in the ship, you cannot be saved." ³²Then the soldiers cut away the ropes of the boat, and let it go.

³³As day was about to dawn, Paul urged them all to take some food, saying, "Today is the fourteenth day that you have continued in suspense and without food, having taken nothing. ³⁴Therefore I urge you to take some food; it will give you strength, since not a hair is to perish from the head of

Mt 10:30

---

apparere sibi aliquam regionem. ²⁸Qui submittentes bolidem invenerunt passus viginti et pusillum inde separati et rursum submittentes invenerunt passus quidecim; ²⁹timentes autem, ne in aspera loca incideremus, de puppi mittentes anchoras quattuor optabant diem fieri. ³⁰Nautis vero quaerentibus fugere de navi, cum demisissent scapham in mare sub obtentu, quasi a prora inciperent anchoras extendere, ³¹dixit Paulus centurioni et militibus: "Nisi hi in navi manserint, vos salvi fieri non potestis." ³²Tunc absciderunt milites funes scaphae et passi sunt eam excidere. ³³Donec autem lux inciperet fieri, rogabat Paulus omnes sumere cibum dicens: "Quarta decima hodie die exspectantes ieiuni permanetis nihil accipientes; ³⁴propter quod rogo vos accipere cibum,

---

30-32. The sailors were trying to escape, but their skill was needed if everyone was to be saved. By letting the boat go, the centurion sees to it that all will contribute to ensuring that everyone on board reaches safety. This solidarity produces the desired result. In this we can see a symbol of what should happen in the ship of the Church: no one should leave the ship in an effort just to save himself, abandoning the others to their fate.

33. St John Chrysostom explains that "this long fast was not a miracle; it was that fear and danger took away their appetite completely. The miracle was that they escaped from the shipwreck. Despite all the misfortunes of the voyage, it provided Paul with the opportunity to instruct the soldiers and crew, and how happy he would have been if all had embraced the faith" (*Hom. on Acts*, 53).

St Paul inspires the other seafarers with his own confidence; his serenity and initiative are in contrast with the despair felt by the others, who have no supernatural outlook of any kind.

any of you." ³⁵And when he had said this, he took bread, and giving thanks to God in the presence of all he broke it

and began to eat. ³⁶Then they all were encouraged and ate some food themselves. ³⁷(We were in all two hundred and seventy-six^d persons in the ship.) ³⁸And when they had eaten enough, they lightened the ship, throwing out the wheat into the sea.

Shipwreck and rescue

³⁹Now when it was day, they did not recognize the land, but they noticed a bay with a beach, on which they planned if possible to bring the ship ashore. ⁴⁰So they cast off the anchors and left them in the sea, at the same time loosening the ropes that tied the rudders; then hoisting the foresail to the wind they made for the beach. ⁴¹But striking a shoal^e

---

hoc enim pro salute vestra est, quia nullius vestrum capillus de capite peribit." ³⁵Et cum haec dixisset et sumpsisset panem, gratias egit Deo in conspectu omnium et, cum fregisset, coepit manducare. ³⁶Animaequiores autem facti omnes et ipsi assumpserunt cibum. ³⁷Eramus vero universae animae in navi ducentae septuaginta sex. ³⁸Et satiati cibo alleviabant navem iactantes triticum in mare. ³⁹Cum autem dies factus esset, terram non agnoscebant, sinum vero quendam considerabant habentem litus, in quem cogitabant si possent eicere navem. ⁴⁰Et cum anchoras abstulissent, committebant mari simul laxantes iuncturas gubernaculorum et, levato artemone, secundum flatum aurae tendebant ad litus. ⁴¹Et cum incidissent in locum dithalassum, impegerunt navem; et

---

35. This food which they eat is ordinary food, not the Eucharist or Christian *agape*; before the meal he gives thanks in accordance with Jewish custom. Commenting on this, St Bede draws a lesson about our need of the bread of life to save us from the dangers of this world: "Paul encourages those whom he has promised will come safe out of the shipwreck, to take some food. If four anchors had kept them afloat during the night, when the sun came up they were going to reach terra firma. But only he who eats the bread of life can avoid the storms of this world" (*Super Act expositio, ad loc.*).

41. The present-day 'St Paul's Bay' on the island of Malta exactly fits the description St Luke gives here. The sailors tried to steer the ship into the small inlet, but it ran aground on a sandbank before they could get there. Athough they were within striking distance of the beach, the sea was so rough that it broke up the ship, whose prow was trapped. "This is what happens to souls given to this world who do not strive to despise worldly things: the prow of their intentions is completely locked into the earth and the force of the waves

^dOther ancient authorities read *seventy-six* or *about seventy-six*   ^eGreek *place of two seas*

they ran the vessel aground; the bow struck and remained immovable, and the stern was broken up by the surf. [42]The soldiers' plan was to kill the prisoners, lest any should swim away and escape; [43]but the centurion, wishing to save Paul, kept them from carrying out their purpose. He ordered those who could swim to throw themselves overboard first and make for the land, [44]and the rest on planks or on pieces of the ship. And so it was that all escaped to land.

28

Waiting in Malta

[1]After we had escaped, we then learned that the island was called Malta. [2]And the natives showed us unusual kindness,

---

prora quidem fixa manebat immobilis, puppis vero solvebatur a vi fluctuum. [42]Militum autem consilium fuit, ut custodias occiderent, ne quis, cum enatasset, effugeret; [43]centurio autem volens servare Paulum prohibuit eos a consilio, iussitque eos, qui possent natare, mittere se primos et ad terram exire [44]et ceteros, quosdam in tabulis, quosdam vero super ea, quae de navi essent; et sic factum est ut omnes evaderent ad terram.

[1]Et cum evasissemus, tunc cognovimus quia Melita insula vocatur. [2]Barbari

---

completely demolishes all the work they have accomplished" (St Bede, *Super Act expositio, ad loc.*).

"Why did God not save the boat from shipwreck? So that the travellers would realize the scale of the danger and that they were saved from it not by any human help but by God, who saved their lives after the boat broke up. In like manner the just are well off even in storms and tempests, on the high seas or in a rough bay, because they are protected from everything and even come to the rescue of others.

"Aboard a ship in danger of being engulfed by the waves, the enchained prisoners and the whole crew owe their safety to the presence of Paul. See how useful it is to live in the company of a devout and saintly person. Frequent and terrible storms buffet our souls. God can free us from them if we are as sensible as those sailors and pay attention to the saints' advice. [. . .] Not only were they saved from shipwreck but they embraced the faith.

"Let us believe St Paul. Even if we be in the midst of storms we shall be set free from dangers; even if we be fasting for forty days, we shall stay alive; even if we fall into darkness and obscurity, if we believe in him we shall be freed" (St John Chrysostom, *Hom. on Acts*, 53).

2. "Natives": literally "barbarians". The Maltese were Phoenicians by race and did not speak Greek—which is why Luke describes them in this way.

for they kindled a fire and welcomed us all, because it had begun to rain and was cold. ³Paul had gathered a bundle of sticks and put them on the fire, when a viper came out because of the heat and fastened on his hand. ⁴When the natives saw the creature hanging from his hand, they said to one another, "No doubt this man is a murderer. Though he has escaped from the sea, justice has not allowed him to live." ⁵He, however, shook off the creature into the fire and suffered no harm. ⁶They waited, expecting him to swell up or suddenly fall down dead; but when they had waited a long time and saw no misfortune come to him, they changed their minds and said that he was a god.

Mk 16:18
Lk 10:19
Acts 14:11

⁷Now in the neighbourhood of that place were lands belonging to the chief man of the island, named Publius, who received us and entertained us hospitably for three days. ⁸It happened that the father of Publius lay sick with fever and dysentery; and Paul visited him and prayed, and putting his hands on him healed him. ⁹And when this had taken place, the rest of the people on the island who had diseases also

Lk 4:38-40;
10:9

vero praestabant non modicam humanitatem nobis; accensa enim pyra suscipiebant nos omnes propter imbrem, qui imminebat et frigus. ³Cum congregasset autem Paulus sarmentorum aliquantam multitudinem et imposuisset super ignem, vipera, a calore cum processisset, invasit manum eius. ⁴Ut vero viderunt barbari pendentem bestiam de manu eius, ad invicem dicebant: "Utique homicida est homo hic, qui cum evaserit de mari, Ultio non permisit vivere." ⁵Et ille quidem excutiens bestiam in ignem, nihil mali passus est; ⁶at illi exspectabant eum in tumorem convertendum aut subito casurum et mori. Diu autem illis exspectantibus et videntibus nihil mali in eo fieri, convertentes se dicebant eum esse deum. ⁷In locis autem illis erant praedia principis insulae nomine Publii, qui nos suscipiens triduo benigne hospitio recepti. ⁸Contigit autem patrem Publii febribus et dysenteria vexatum iacere, ad quem Paulus intravit et, cum orasset et imposuisset ei manus, sanavit eum. ⁹Quo facto et ceteri, qui in insula habebant infirmitates, accedebant et curabantur; ¹⁰qui autem multis honoribus nos honoraverunt et navigantibus imposuerunt, quae

4. "Justice", here, is a proper name. The notion of justice was personified in a goddess of vengeance or vindictive justice.

5. This is a fulfilment of a promise made by our Lord: "These signs will accompany those who believe: in my name they will cast out demons; they will speak in new tongues; they will pick up serpents, and if they drink any deadly thing, it will not hurt them" (Mk 16:17-18).

came and were cured. [10]They presented many gifts to us;[f] and when we sailed, they put on board whatever we needed.

Arrival in Rome

[11]After three months we set sail in a ship which had wintered in the island, a ship of Alexandria, with the Twin Brothers as figureheads. [12]Putting in at Syracuse, we stayed there for three days. [13]And from there we made a circuit and arrived at Rhegium; and after one day a south wind sprang up, and on the second day we came to Puteoli. [14]There we found brethren, and were invited to stay with them for seven days. And so we came to Rome. [15]And the brethren there,

---

necessaria erant. [11]Post menses autem tres navigavimus in nave Alexandrina, quae in insula hiemaverat, cui erat insigne Castorum. [12]Et cum venissemus Syracusam, mansimus ibi triduo; [13]inde solventes devenimus Rhegium. Et post unum diem, superveniente austro, secundo die venimus Puteolos, [14]ubi inventis fratribus rogati sumus manere apud eos dies septem; et sic venimus Romam. [15]Et inde cum audissent de nobis fratres, occurrerunt nobis usque ad Appii

---

12-14. Syracuse was then the main city of Sicily. From there they went along the eastern coast of the island and crossed the straits of Messina to reach Rhegium, where they stopped for a day. Finally, they disembarked at Pozzuoli, which was the principal port in the gulf of Naples. There Paul found a Christian community and stayed with them for a week, and they would have sent word on to the Christians at Rome to tell them that Paul would soon be with them.

14. The text conveys the atmosphere of human and supernatural brotherhood that obtained among the Christians. Paul would have been extremely happy to be received so affectionately by the brethren. Now at least he would have a chance to rest after his long journey.

"How well the early Christians practised this ardent charity which went beyond the limits of mere human solidarity or natural kindness. They love one another, through the heart of Christ, with a love both tender and strong. . . .

"The principal apostolate we Christians must carry out in the world, and the best witness we can give of our faith, is to help bring about a climate of genuine charity within the Church. For who indeed could feel attracted to the Gospel if those who say they preach the Good News do not really love one another, but spend their time attacking one another, spreading slander and rancour" (J. Escrivá, *Friends of God*, 225f).

15. The Forum of Appius and Three Taverns were 69 kilometres (about 40 miles) and 53 kilometres from Rome, respectively, on the Via Appia, which ran south from Rome to the port of Puteoli (modern Pozzuoli). We do not know

[f]Or *honoured us with many honours*

when they heard of us, came as far as the Forum of Appius and Three Taverns to meet us. On seeing them Paul thanked God and took courage. [16]And when we came into Rome, Paul was allowed to stay by himself, with the soldier that guarded him.

Paul and the Roman Jews

[17]After three days he called together the local leaders of the Jews; and when they had gathered, he said to them, "Brethren, though I had done nothing against the people or the customs of our fathers, yet I was delivered prisoner from Jerusalem into the hands of the Romans. [18]When they had examined me, they wished to set me at liberty, because there was no reason for the death penalty in my case. [19]But when

Acts 23:29

Acts 25:11;
26:32

Forum et Tres Tabernas; quos cum vidisset Paulus, gratias agens Deo, accepit fiduciam. [16]Cum introissemus autem Romam, permissum est Paulo manere sibimet cum custodiente se milite. [17]Factum est autem ut post tertium diem convocaret primos Iudaeorum; cumque convenissent dicebat eis: "Ego, viri fratres, nihil adversus plebem faciens aut mores paternos, vinctus ab Hierosolymis traditus sum in manus Romanorum, [18]qui cum interrogationem de me habuissent, volebant dimittere eo quod nulla causa esset mortis in me; [19]contradicentibus autem Iudaeis, coactus sum appellare Caesarem, non quasi

---

anything about the Christian community in Rome at this time or how it came to be founded. The tradition is that it was founded by St Peter, which does not necessarily mean that no other Christians arrived there before him, or that there had not been conversions there of pagans or of Jewish residents. In fact, St Augustine (cf. *Letter 102*, 8) quotes the philosopher Porphyry as saying that there were Jews in Rome shortly after the reign of Caligula (March 37 to January 41 A.D.).

16. Paul must have arrived in Rome around the year 61. He was allowed to stay in a private house; in other words he was under *custodia militaris*, which meant that the only restriction was that he was guarded by a soldier at all times.

This is the last verse where St Luke uses the first person plural.

17. In keeping with his missionary custom, Paul immediately addresses the Jews of Rome; in fact there is no further mention of his contact with the Christians in the city. The Apostle wants to give his fellow Jews a kind of last opportunity to hear and understand the Gospel. He presents himself as a member of the Jewish community who wants to take a normal part in the life of that community and feels he has to explain his own position.

19. The use of Roman privileges by a Jew might have been regarded by Jews

267

the Jews objected, I was compelled to appeal to Caesar —
though I had no charge to bring against my nation. 20For this
reason therefore I have asked to see you and speak with you
since it is because of the hope of Israel that I am bound with
this chain." 21And they said to him, "We have received no
letters from Judea about you, and none of the brethren

Acts 17:19 coming here has reported or spoken any evil about you. 22But
we desire to hear from you what your views are; for with
regard to this sect we know that everywhere it is spoken
against."

Acts 13:15-41 23When they had appointed a day for him, they came to
him at his lodging in great numbers. And he expounded the
matter to them from morning till evening, testifying to the
kingdom of God and trying to convince them about Jesus

Acts 13:46-47 both from the law of Moses and from the prophets. 24And
some were convinced by what he said, while others disbelieved. 25So, as they disagreed among themselves, they
departed, after Paul had made one statement: "The Holy
Spirit was right in saying to your fathers through Isaiah the
prophet:

---

gentem meam habens aliquid accusare. 20Propter hanc igitur causam rogavi vos
videre et alloqui; propter spem enim Israel catena hac circumdatus sum." 21At
illi dixerunt ad eum: "Nos neque litteras accepimus de te a Iudaea, neque
adveniens aliquis fratrum nuntiavit aut locutus est quid de te malum. 22Rogamus
autem a te audire quae sentis, nam de secta hac notum est nobis quia ubique ei
contradicitur." 23Cum constituissent autem illi diem, venerunt ad eum in
hospitium plures, quibus exponebat testificans regnum Dei, suadensque eos de
Iesu ex Lege Moysis et Prophetis a mane usque ad vesperam. 24Et quidam
credebant his quae dicebantur, quidam vero non credebant; 25cumque invicem

---

as a sign of disrespect towards their own beliefs and customs. Therefore, Paul
tries to explain why he took the exceptional step of invoking his Roman
citizenship and appealing to Caesar.

23. Paul speaks now not about his own salvation but about the Gospel, and,
as he usually did in synagogues, he proclaims to his Jewish listeners that Jesus
is the Messiah foretold by the prophets and promised to the people of Israel.

25-28. Since now, in Rome also, many Jews have rejected the Gospel, Paul
announces that he is free of his self-imposed obligation to proclaim the Gospel
first to the Jews. His words suggest that it is the Christians who have understood
the meaning of the promises made by God to the chosen people, and that it is

26'Go to this people, and say,
You shall indeed hear but never understand,
and you shall indeed see but never perceive.
27For this people's heart has grown dull,
and their ears are heavy of hearing,
and their eyes they have closed;
lest they should perceive with their eyes,
and hear with their ears,
and understand with their heart,
and turn for me to heal them.'
28Let it be known to you then that this salvation of God has
been sent to the Gentiles; they will listen."g

Is 6:9-10
Mt 13:14

Jn 12:39
2 Cor 3:14

Paul's ministry in Rome

30And he lived there two whole years at his own expense,h

---

non essent consentientes, discedebant, dicente Paulo unum verbum: "Bene
Spiritus Sanctus locutus est per Isaiam prophetam ad patres vestros 26dicens:
'Vade ad populum istum et dic: Auditu audietis et non intellegetis, et videntes
videbitis et non perspicietis. 27Incrassatum est enim cor populi huius, et auribus
graviter audierunt, et oculos suos compresserunt, ne forte videant oculis et
auribus audiant et corde intellegant et convertantur, et sanabo illos.' 28Notum
ergo sit vobis quoniam gentibus missum est hoc salutare Dei; ipsi et audient!"
(29) 30Mansit autem biennio toto in suo conducto; et suscipiebat omnes qui

---

they who are really the true Israel. Christ's disciples have not abandoned the
Law. It is, rather, the Jews who have renounced their position as the chosen
people. "We are the true, spiritual people of Israel," St Justin writes, "the race
of Judah, and of Jacob, and of Isaac and of Abraham, he who was testified to
by God even while he was still uncircumcised, he who was blessed and named
the father of many nations" (*Dialogue with Tryphon*, 11, 5).

30-31. "Not only was he not forbidden to preach in Rome", St Bede writes,
"but despite the enormous power of Nero and all his crimes which history
reports, he remained free to proclaim the Gospel of Christ to the furthest parts
of the West, as he himself writes to the Romans: 'At present, however, I am
going to Jerusalem with aid for the saints' (Rom 15:25); and a little later: 'When
therefore I have completed this, and have delivered to them what has been
raised, I shall go on by way of you to Spain' (v. 28). Finally he was crowned
with martyrdom in the last years of Nero" (*Super Act expositio, ad loc.*).
    We do not know exactly what happened at the end of the two years. It may

gOther ancient authorities add verse 29, *And when he had said these words, the Jews departed, holding much dispute among themselves*
hOr *in his own hired dwelling*

Phil 1:14
2 Tim 2:9

and welcomed all who came to him, ³¹preaching the kingdom of God and teaching about the Lord Jesus Christ quite openly and unhindered.

---

ingrediebantur ad eum, ³¹praedicans regnum Dei et docens quae sunt de Domino Iesu Christo cum omni fiducia sine prohibitione.

---

be that Paul's Jewish accusers did not appear, or they may have argued their case before the imperial tribunal and Paul was found not guilty. At any event, he was set free and Luke considers his task done—the work God gave him to do when he inspired him to write his book.

"If you ask me", St John Chrysostom observes, "why St Luke, who stayed with the Apostle up to his martyrdom, did not bring his narrative up to that point, I will reply that the Book of the Acts, in the form that has come down to us, perfectly fulfils its author's purpose. For the evangelists' only aim was to write down the most essential things" (*Hom. on Acts*, 1).

The kind of conventional way the book concludes has led many commentators (from early times up to the present day) to think that it had already been finished before Paul's first imprisonment in Rome came to an end. Christian tradition has nothing very concrete to say about exactly when the Acts of the Apostles was written.

Index

HEADINGS ADDED TO THE TEXT OF ACTS FOR THIS EDITION

Index

HEADINGS ADDED TO THE TEXT OF ACTS FOR THIS EDITION